THE GIRL FROM GOMORRAH

THE COMPLETE BAILEY SPADE SERIES

DIMA ZALES

♠ MOZAIKA PUBLICATIONS ♠

DREAM WALKER

BOOK 1

CHAPTER ONE

I SWALLOW a droplet of diluted vampire blood.

"Alarm and surveillance disabled," Felix whispers in my earpiece. "Breaking and entering may commence."

Before I can reply, the blood kicks in, lifting the weight off my eyelids as my sleep deprivation retreats. Except the droplet must've been too big, or I drank it too soon after the last dose. I feel an unwelcome side effect—orgasmic pleasure—coming on.

Tightening my grip on the lockpick until it hurts, I stab myself in the forearm.

"What the hell?" Felix exclaims. "What'd you do *that* for?"

The camera on my lapel didn't catch my stealthy sip, so I can see why this looks odd on his end. "Never mind that."

The pain quickly annuls my euphoria, and I thank my lucky stars I took the time to sterilize my equipment, or else this would end with gangrene. When I pull the lockpick out of my arm, the wound heals instantly—and best of all, no sign of the orgasmic pleasure remains.

There we go. I didn't enjoy that vampire blood one bit, other than the boost of alertness that was my goal—and my libido skyrocketing to the levels of a teenage boy in a strip club.

"I thought your weirdness was limited to cleansing rituals." Felix sounds bizarrely sexy in the vamp blood afterglow.

I don't reply. Instead, I take a quick internal scan to make sure no part of me is still feeling the pull of the highly addictive substance. With all my current problems, becoming a vampire blood addict would be like jumping off a cliff after drowning myself in cyanide.

All good so far. I grasp the doorknob. "I'm going in."

"What you're about to do is illegal on this world," Felix reminds me, as if I didn't already know.

"What about hacking all those banks?" I whisper back. "You wouldn't like it if I lectured you about that."

A Cognizant like me, albeit one permanently residing on Earth, Felix calls himself a technomancer. He can make silicon-based technology do his bidding, a power he wastes on feats that any human with in-depth computer knowledge could pull off.

"Dreamwalking won't help you escape human prison," he replies. "Or survive it, for that matter."

"That's arguable." I decide against telling him about the time I gleaned one of his wet dreams, specifically the one where he fancied himself a guard getting attacked by suspiciously attractive female convicts. "But if you've done your job properly, I won't end up in prison."

"I can only take care of the smart alarm. If this Bernard guy is paranoid enough, he might have the older, dumb alarm set up as well, and it'll blare as soon as you get inside. Or he might have a dog. Or he might even be awake."

I sneak a guilty peek at my wrist, where most people would see a furry bracelet. But he's actually a creature called a *looft*. Normally, his kind live on cow-like *moofts*, but Pom, as he calls himself, has adopted me as his host. Right now, he's sleeping, as usual, but the pitch-black shade of his fur reflects my inner turmoil. If I die, Pomsie dies with me; that's how our relationship works.

So I'll have to not die. Simple.

Turning my attention back to the heavy wooden door, I stroke Pom to calm myself down. When my hands have steadied and his fur has turned a more neutral shade of blue, I pick the lock.

"Seriously, Bailey," Felix says as I touch the doorknob, "there've got to be better ways to make money. With your—"

I mute the earpiece. Obviously, there are more legit ways to earn what I need, but those ways don't pay nearly as well as my current employer. I'm already a month behind on Mom's medical bills, and if I don't come up with two million cc—Gomorran cryptocash—in the next two weeks, they'll turn off her life support. No honest jobs would let me make that kind of cash in the little time I have left. As is, I've had to forgo sleep in order to make ends meet. In fact, I haven't slept more than a couple of hours at a stretch since Mom's accident four months ago, staying up naturally at first, then using pharmacological stimulants, and eventually resorting to vampire blood.

I reach into my pocket for one of my last two sleep grenades and twist the doorknob.

No alarm blares.

No dog barks.

No one shoots me dead with a gun.

I press the button on the grenade and toss it into the apartment.

Sleeping gas hisses as it spreads throughout the place.

"That gas goes inert in two minutes," I whisper for Felix's benefit. "If there's a dog in there, or if Bernard was awake, they're asleep *now*."

I unmute in time to hear Felix grumbling something about a *decent plan*. What he doesn't realize is that the most dangerous part of this job is coming up.

I tiptoe inside the penthouse. Valerian, the guy who hired me to do this, must pay Bernard well. This place is spacious, especially for New York, where real estate is nearly as pricey as on my home world of Gomorrah.

I locate the bedroom and squint through the darkness at the bed. Whew—Bernard is curled up in a fetal position, covered by a heavy blanket.

I creep toward the bed.

"Doesn't he look like Mario?" Felix whispers.

Comparing a man to a digital plumber isn't as crazy as it sounds. When I first met Felix, we bonded over our love of video games.

I examine the pudgy man's mustachioed face. "More like Wario, Mario's archrival."

"Neither of them has a scar like that."

He's right. The scar on Bernard's forehead belongs on the face of an interdimensional warrior, not an engineering executive at a VR company on Earth.

"So what now?" Felix asks.

"I have to touch him."

Felix chuckles.

I roll my eyes. "Not in a dirty way."

I peer at my victim's eyelids for rapid eye movement. Nothing. Crap. I pull off my gloves and do my best to prepare for the unpleasantness that is to come—specifically, the least risky but most disgusting aspect of what I'm about to attempt.

Skin-to-skin contact.

The bead of sweat wobbling along the edge of the scar on Bernard's forehead doesn't help, nor does his mooft-dung breath.

"What are you waiting for?" Felix asks. "Is it your OCD again?"

"Caring about hygiene doesn't mean I have OCD." I touch the bottle of hand sanitizer in my pocket, my lifesaver here on Earth. "Besides, he's not in REM sleep."

"Which means you'll have to do that dangerous subdream battle thing when you enter him?"

"You make it sound way too rapey. I'm not going to 'enter him.' I'm just visiting his dreams. But yes, if the subdream battle thing kills dream-me, real-me will go insane."

Actually, that's an understatement. Not long before her accident, as a way of discouraging me from using my powers, Mom showed me footage of what happened to a dreamwalker who'd died in the dream world. He went on a killing rampage like a rabid puck and cannibalized his victims. I checked on this, and even years later, he's still being kept in restraints in a padded cell.

"So you're going to wait until he goes into REM sleep?" Felix asks.

"Ideally."

"How long's that going to take?"

I sigh and consult my Earth phone. "Ninety minutes, if it was my gas that knocked him out."

I hear Felix clicking away on his keyboard. Then he says, "I see that he takes Ambien. I doubt it was your gas that put him under."

"Dammit." I resist the urge to kick the leg of the bed. "That drug suppresses REM sleep. I might have to come back later or—"

"Bailey." His tone sharpens. "You're about to have company."

I spin around to the door, my heart rate spiking as Pom's fur darkens on my wrist.

"Vampires," Felix rattles out. "Enforcers. They have every exit covered. Running would be pointless."

Pucking puck. Why couldn't it be any other type of Cognizant? Vampires only sleep if they want to, so my remaining grenade won't knock them out—and I don't have anything else at my disposal.

My gaze falls on the walk-in closet in the corner of the bedroom. "Can I hide?"

"They probably have your DNA. How else could they have zeroed in on you with such precision?"

He's right. Even *I* didn't know I'd be here until I'd read my encrypted email an hour ago. This is bad. Armed with my DNA, a vampire could find me anywhere in the Cogniverse.

I stroke Pom, trying not to panic. "What do they want?"

"No idea," Felix says, "but I doubt they care about your breaking and entering."

"Arguable." I whirl back toward Bernard. "Sounds like I have no choice. If I want to keep Mom's life support running, I have to go in, REM sleep or not."

"And I'll do my best to stall the Enforcers. I think I can make the elevator run slower, maybe even—"

"Thanks." Ignoring the shaking of my hands, I pull out the hand sanitizer and slather it on Bernard's hairy forearm. "Here goes nothing." I reach for the (hopefully) decontaminated patch of skin.

In a way, there are silver linings to this clusterpuck. If the subdream kills me and I go homicidally crazy in the real world, at least the vampires will put me down before I can cannibalize anyone. Plus, all this adrenaline is short-circuiting my usual fears of picking up *Staphylococcus aureus* and other cooties from my target.

My fingers touch the man's skin, and my muscles stiffen for a moment as I catch a faint whiff of ozone and experience the sensation of falling. Then the room darkens around me, and the world of wakefulness goes away.

CHAPTER TWO

I'M STANDING on top of black water, with a sky like magma above. Barreling toward me are a dozen creatures, each more hideous than the next.

The first looks as if twenty sets of ant mandibles had mushroomed to the size of a truck and had sprouted antennae and legs. Another resembles a massive spiral worm, or maybe a syphilis bacterium, with centipede-like legs ending in knife-sharp talons. The least horrific of the creatures reminds me of a tardigrade, a microscopic animal that lives in water and has no discernable eyes or nose, a hole for a mouth, and eight limbs that end in claws attached to the body of a sea cow—except there's nothing microscopic about this tardigrade. It's ten feet tall.

The mandible creature is in the lead, leaping toward me as it shrieks through each of its mandibles. If I decided to chew up some diamonds, that's probably what it would sound like. Magnified a thousandfold. I get the creepy feeling that the thing is trying to say something, but on a frequency more likely to make my ears bleed than to pass on any information.

A furry appendage snakes from my wrist and elongates into a whip as the shrieking beast leaps at me, mandibles clacking in unison.

I crack the whip. A sonic boom ripples the black water around me. My whip slices the mandible creature into even halves that plop at my feet, spraying me with sticky green goop. I'm paralyzed with disgust—which is when the syphilis creature's talon pierces my left shoulder.

The pain is nauseating and sharp, and I feel lucky that my whip is attached to my body, else I would've dropped it. Disgust now a distant memory, I crack my weapon again. With a second sonic boom, I cleave the syphilis thing in half and dodge the bloody stream that spurts out.

Seeing what happened to their brethren, the remaining monsters attack with a lot less enthusiasm, which is good because I'm losing blood from my shoulder by the bucketful. Before they realize that I'm weakening, I go on the offensive, cracking the whip.

Boom. Boom. Boom.

Only the tardigrade is left standing, and it turns to flee with a speed one wouldn't expect from such humongous bulk.

I leap after it, whip ready. "Oh, no, you're not going anywhere." A sonic boom later, the tardigrade rains down in pieces.

As soon as it does, the world around me changes.

CHAPTER THREE

MY SHOULDER THROBS as I whip my head around to take in forty-foot squared-dome ceilings, yellowish blue marble floors, reddish green walls, and a floating collection of glowing geometrical shapes that are impossible in the waking world, such as the overlapping-on-itself Penrose triangle. I inhale deeply, dragging in the sweet-savory aroma of *manna*, my favorite Gomorran food.

Of course. I'm in the main lobby of my palace. Meaning this is the dream world, and the monsters I just defeated were part of what I call the subdream. Puck. Once again, I didn't realize what was happening, despite such unrealistic bits as walking on water and Pom's turning into a whip.

A stab of pain brings me back to the moment. This shoulder injury is behaving all too realistically, which means I'm just a few liters of blood loss short of dying in the dream world and thus going insane.

Oh, well. Now that I know where I am, I can change things as I see fit.

I float out of my dream body as if I were having a near-death experience. The pain instantly disappears. I study the body beneath me and mentally cringe. That shoulder is *bad*. The rest of me, though, looks pretty boring for a dream.

With barely any effort, I heal my shoulder. Then, because I can, I make my body taller and thinner and exchange my utilitarian cargo pants and camo shirt for a cool leather jacket, tight black jeans, and knee-high boots. A good start. I replace my frizzy black curls with the look I prefer

—fierce flames of fire that make my head look as though a firebird has made a nest on it. Since I'm in a rush, this will have to suffice.

I jump back into my body. As soon as I do, Pom appears in front of me —something he does whenever I'm dreamwalking and he's in REM sleep, which is almost always.

Here in the dream world, he's not a fluffy wristband. Like me, he takes on a dream form.

The size of a large owl, with ginormous lavender eyes, highly mobile triangular ears, and fluffy fur that changes colors to match his emotions, Pom is pure weaponized cuteness. Allegedly cute beings like otters, pandas, and koalas are downright fugly in comparison.

"You left your face the same," he says in his singsong falsetto. "How come?"

"You don't like my face?" I muss his fur until he turns blue, and head toward my tower of sleepers.

He floats up and flies behind me like a selfie drone. "Your face is tolerable. At least Earth humans seem to like it."

"If you're referring to the staring, I think they're just trying to figure out my race and ethnicity."

He zooms in front of me. "What's that?"

"It's like when we're trying to figure out what type of Cognizant someone is on Gomorrah. Earth humans use those labels in similar ways, with some groups not liking other groups—like necromancers and vampires."

"Oh, but that's an easy guessing game." His ears waggle in excitement. "Orcs are green, elves are thin and willowy, dwarves have beards, giants are—"

"Right." I speed up as I get to the staircase. Though time moves faster in the dream world, or feels like it does, there's still good reason to make haste. What the heck—I take flight instead of bothering with each step. "But it's not always that simple," I continue as Pom catches up to me. "Werewolves look no different from me, unless they turn."

His furry face takes on a sage look. "So what do most humans guess for your lace and felicity?"

"It's *race* and *ethnicity*. And their guesses are all over the place: Latin America, Africa, the Middle East… Some think I'm just a tanned person of European descent with a perm—I guess it's the tiny nose and gray eyes."

"I like your eyes." Pom flits in front of me again, his gaze unblinking.

This lack of common-sense social skills is why I usually ask him to be invisible when I work with my clients.

He must pick up on my thought because the tips of his ears turn red.

"Thanks for the compliment," I say to appease him. On a whim, I change my eyes to flame red to match my hair.

Pom's ears go back to blue. "Humans are stupid. You're obviously not from any of those places."

"Right." I take a shortcut by making a portion of the wall evaporate in front of me. "The good news is that my looks give me an advantage. We Cognizant tend to settle in those parts of human-occupied worlds where we most resemble the native population—which means if I ever decide to permanently move to Earth, I could have my pick of much of the planet."

Pom's fur darkens. "Why would we ever want to live in such a backward place?"

He has a point. The sanitation system on Earth is still water-based, the VR technology is in its infancy, and the cars don't yet drive themselves.

"Gomorrah is better in every way." He's clearly picking up on my thoughts again.

"I need to be around humans to keep my powers," I remind him for the umpteenth time. "Plus, thanks to my amazing reputation among Earth Cognizant, I can get high-paying jobs here."

"As in illegal, high-risk jobs," he grumbles.

I suppress a surge of worry about the Enforcers in the waking world. Why stress Pom about something he can't help with? Instead, I put on a burst of speed and reach the tower of sleepers.

The tower is a cylindrical glass structure made up of several levels of glass-walled nooks, each with a single piece of furniture: a bed. Once I've successfully created a dream connection with someone, when they dream, they show up in one of those beds. Thanks to this tower, I only have to go through the unpleasantness of touching people in the real world once.

Bernard, the newest sleeper in my collection, has taken the place that freed up when I cured my most recent legit patient of his bedwetting problem and severed our link.

As we get closer to Bernard's nook, the rest of Pom turns black, and I curse under my breath.

Miniature dark clouds are flying above Bernard's head.

"That figures," I mumble. "Why'd I think I'd finally get a break?"

Those clouds indicate a trauma loop—a type of dream that's based on traumatic events in Bernard's life. Trauma loops plague sleepers on a regular basis, and they're so powerful that I find it easier to just witness them without changing anything. The good news for the sleeper in question is that my mere presence during these special dreams usually breaks their repeat cycle, which helps the sleeper feel better in the waking world.

This might be Bernard's lucky day. Not so much mine, though. I'm in a rush.

Pom flies up to the clouds and gives them a sniff, which is when a miniature lightning bolt hits his nose. "Ouch! That's a bad one."

I erase his pain and encase the clouds in a protective glass bubble. "Probably deep trauma."

"I won't join you, then." Pom's fur looks like coal. "The last time we worked with someone like this, it disturbed my sleep."

To highlight his point, he zooms behind me, as if Bernard might reach out and snatch him from the air, forcing him to see the nightmare.

"Something disturbed *your* sleep?" I turn to grin at him. "Did you sleep twenty-three hours and forty-four minutes, instead of the full twenty-three hours and forty-*five* minutes?"

He sniffs. "At least I'm not on vampire blood, like some."

"Well, technically, given our symbiotic relationship, you are on it. It just doesn't work on you, but—"

"Whatever. I'm not going in, no matter how much you beg." Pom lifts his chin and disappears like a Cheshire cat. Instead of his smile, it's his furry chin that hovers in the air until he's completely gone.

"I don't need you there, anyway," I say to the empty air. "I'm in a rush, and this will go faster without your yammering."

He doesn't take the bait.

I'm almost to Bernard when I smack myself on the forehead. Almost forgot to make myself invisible again.

Pointedly turning myself undetectable by sight, sound, or smell, I touch Bernard on the forearm the way I did in the waking world—except without any worry of contamination.

And then, unlike in reality, where I'm standing in a sleep-like trance, in the dream world I disappear from the palace and reappear inside Bernard's trauma loop.

CHAPTER FOUR

I FIND MYSELF ON A PLAYGROUND, one of Earth's most primitive anachronisms where children physically play. On Gomorrah, fully immersive virtual spaces replaced these long ago, which means no dirt, no germs, and a lot more entertainment options for the little ones.

This particular playground is creepy. Spiders and maggots crawl inside the sandbox, and the empty swing sways as though ridden by ghosts. Even the monkey bars look warped, and the trees remind me of an evil forest from a dark fairy tale.

I bet the original playground wasn't like this. Bernard's emotions are twisting the surroundings.

The man himself is strolling toward a see-saw, the hands of two cute children in his grip—a little girl who's a toddler and a slightly older boy.

Hmm. There'd been no sign of a family when I broke into his apartment.

"Daddy, I need to wee-wee." The girl is dancing from foot to foot.

"Me too," the boy says. "And I go first."

"No, me first." She gives her brother an imperious look. "Princesses first."

They bicker about it as Bernard herds them toward a park bathroom. *A public bathroom.* Gross. Private water-based plumbing is horrific enough.

I float a few feet behind them. Though this dream could easily be fiction—driven by, say, Bernard's subconscious regret over never starting a family—my powers allow me to know the truth without a shadow of a doubt: This dream is based on a memory. All trauma loops I've encountered have been memories—though, in theory, one day I might come across a dream that twists the memory too much. Should that happen, I'd use my powers to pull out the truth and, hopefully, break the loop that way.

So it's a memory—but from when? The scar on Bernard's forehead is missing, so it's safe to say this must've been a while ago.

"I can't hold it anymore," the boy says when they reach the bathroom.

The girl starts crying.

"You're such a baby," the boy says.

The girl stomps her foot and cries louder.

"Let's go." Bernard drags them into the men's room.

Oh, the smell… the sights… the *germs*. Pom was right to disappear; this could traumatize someone for life.

The walls begin to close in.

Puck, I'm changing the dream without meaning to. That's not good. If Bernard notices my influence, he could wake up.

I close my eyes. This is just a dream, and one colored by Bernard's emotions at that. No germs can get me here. I should think of this as exposure therapy for myself—a bit like what I do with my clients who have phobias.

Yeah, that's it.

The bathroom walls get back to normal, but just in case, I disable my sense of smell.

The siblings are still fighting. Visibly frustrated, Bernard helps the boy start his business at a low urinal and then drags the crying toddler into a stall. My nebulous presence follows them in, as this is Bernard's dream/memory and I can only experience what he does.

Through the crying, I hear someone new enter the bathroom.

The boy yelps.

Bernard freezes for a moment, then kicks open the stall door—just in time to see the back of a man rushing out of the bathroom.

The boy is gone.

This time, the walls are closing in because of Bernard. He grabs the hysterical toddler like a sack and rushes out of the bathroom, looking frantically around the playground. He spots the man at the park entrance.

"Stop," he yells. "Give him back!"

The kidnapper dives for a car parked by a hydrant, tosses the boy into the back seat, and jumps behind the wheel.

Bernard sprints after him, but the tires are already burning rubber. "What was that license plate?" Bernard shouts at the toddler in his grip.

The girl cries hysterically.

The agony on Bernard's sheet-white face is painful to look at.

"Bailey," a familiar voice says in my ear. "They're there."

Puck, I'm not done yet. There's more to this, I can tell. But there's a pressure on my arm that has nothing to do with the dream, and my cheek stings as if someone has slapped it.

Like a balloon popping, my dreamwalking trance breaks, and I open my eyes in the waking world.

A pale, weaselly man slaps my other cheek so hard that I stagger back, nearly falling on the slumbering Bernard.

Hearing the commotion—or more likely, waking from his nightmare—Bernard opens his eyes and sees the same thing I'm looking at.

A room full of vampires.

CHAPTER FIVE

THE EYES of the vampire who slapped me turn into mirrors as he catches Bernard's gaze.

"You will go into the kitchen and sit for ten minutes," he says in a honey-laced voice with a slight Scottish accent. "Afterward, you'll forget we were ever here. Understood?"

"Yes," Bernard says in the robotic tone people tend to take on under glamour. "I'll go."

"And forget," the vamp says.

"And forget." Shamelessly flashing us his hairy body, Bernard lumbers to his destination.

I do my best to get my racing pulse under control. "What's this about?" Taking out my hand sanitizer, I apply a generous amount to my slapped cheeks and touched arm. Who knows where that vampire's hands have been? "I was in the middle of something."

"We're here on behalf of the Council," says the tallest of the bunch, an unusually unattractive specimen of his kind. His hooked nose sits above a thin, downturned mouth, and his brown hair is limp and greasy-looking. However, his pale eyes hold an intense sort of intelligence.

"It's probably true," Felix whispers. "That's Kain, the new leader of the Enforcers. I remember him because of the *Legacy of Kain*. He even looks a little like the guy in that game series."

I'd tell Felix to shut it, but I don't want to give away his presence. No reason for him to go down as my accomplice.

"Why does the Council wish to see me?" I ask in a tone so calm it surprises even me.

"You will only speak when spoken to," growls the vampire who slapped me earlier.

"No need to be rude, Firth," Kain says to his lackey. He shifts his pale gaze to me. "I'm afraid you'll have to appear in front of the Council to learn more."

I count at least a dozen vampires around me. Not good. "Do I have to?"

"If you want to live," Kain says without emotion.

"Okay, then. I guess I'm dying to go."

He tips his head. "Put the contents of your pockets on the bed."

For a fleeting moment, I consider fighting my way out. Why else did I learn all those martial arts in the dreams of renowned masters? The problem is that vampires are much stronger and faster, not to mention I'm completely outnumbered.

Not looking at Pom, lest they realize he's contraband from another world, I take out the sleeping grenade, my Earth smartphone, my Gomorran comms, and the vial of diluted vampire blood. I gingerly place it all on the wrinkled sheets, which are still warm from Bernard.

"I should check her," Firth says—overeagerly, in my opinion.

"Don't," Kain says imperiously. He strides over to poke in my stuff. Right away, he homes in on my Gomorran comms. "This is Otherland technology. It's forbidden to bring it to Earth."

"Oops." I grimace. "I didn't show it to any locals, I swear."

Kain nods at Firth, and the thin vamp crushes the device in his fist and pockets the broken pieces. What an ass. I'm glad I didn't bring my pricey hygieia wand from home. Earth hand sanitizers are infinitely worse at germ-killing, but at least they shouldn't be confiscated.

I'm about to snap at Kain for destroying my property—comms aren't exactly cheap, either—but Felix whispers into my earpiece, "He just did you a huge favor. If the Council caught you with that, you'd be in major trouble—well, more trouble than whatever you've gotten yourself into already."

Fine. Maybe he's right. Being an Earth native, Felix knows all the dumb rules here much better than I do.

Kain examines my phone before homing in on the grenade.

"That's to help with my work," I say quickly. "It puts people to sleep."

He puts down the grenade and picks up the vial. Uncorking it, he takes a sniff and looks at me with a raised eyebrow.

I feel my blood rush to my face. "It's not what you think it's for."

His eyebrow lifts higher.

"I only use that to suppress the need to sleep."

His eyebrow goes back down. "I thought even dreamwalkers needed sleep to survive."

I shrug, resisting the urge to point out the irony of a vampire lecturing me about blood consumption.

"You can have those back." Kain gestures at the bed.

I sanitize the phone, the vial, and the grenade before stuffing them back into my pockets. At this rate, I might need another bottle of sanitizer, unless they kill me soon and render that point moot. And since I'm already on this morbid train of thought, I hope they sterilize the sword or ax they plan to behead me with, a bit like humans do with needles for their lethal injections. One thing's for sure: There's no way these vampires are going to be willing to stop by a pharmacy for more hand sanitizer, even if it's on the way.

Firth catches my gaze with his beady eyes and mouths something that looks suspiciously like *blood whore*—a derogatory term for a vampire addict, which I'm not. Hopefully.

Either way, it's official: From here on out, Firth is Filth, though perhaps I'll only call him that behind his back, for safety reasons.

"What was in that vial?" Felix whispers.

Glad the diluted solution looks more like water than blood, I ignore his question. It's not like I'm in a position to answer him, anyway.

The vampires escort me out to a limo, and we drive down the night streets of Manhattan at race car speeds.

"I hacked into the limo's GPS," Felix informs me. "They're going to the Council castle, just as they claimed."

Good to know. Now if only I knew whether that's good news or bad news.

Since Felix doesn't say more, I stare out the car window to stay sane. We're passing Times Square, one of the busiest parts of this city. It can't compare to even the quietest street back on Gomorrah, but the hustle and bustle makes me feel at home. Except there are no humans on Gomorrah —which is what all these people are.

It's mind-boggling. The Cognizant make up less than one percent of Earth's population, but from what I know about this world's homo sapiens, if they learned of beings with powers like ours, they'd see us as a threat and act accordingly. I don't know if they'd catch us for vivisection or simply wipe us out, but I'm sure the outcome wouldn't be fun. This is why we keep our existence under strict secrecy, going as far as enforcing the silence with a barbaric practice called the Mandate, which decrees death to anyone dumb enough to blab about the Cognizant on advanced human-dominated worlds like Earth.

Maybe that's what the vamps want. Have I been on this world long enough to need the stupid Mandate Rite? I thought you were supposed to request it—and plan to settle on Earth, to boot. I doubt you'd get escorted to the ceremony like a VIP.

Felix yawns into my earpiece. I could strangle him right now. The last thing I need is for my sleep deprivation symptoms to resurface.

He yawns again.

That does it. I sneak my hand into my pocket, pull out my phone, and stealthily text, *Take a nap.*

"What?" Felix says. "I'm not going to—"

Please, I text. I hide my phone before Filth sees me and breaks it like he did with the Gomorran comms.

"You sure?" my friend mumbles.

Turning so the vampires can't see, I show my lapel camera a thumbs-up and clasp my hands as if in prayer.

"Okay, fine," he whispers. "If they're really taking you to see the Council, there's not much I can do for you, anyway."

Great. I'm so much calmer now.

When we get outside the city, I decide Bernard has had enough time to go back to bed. That means I can return to his dreams, finish my job, and email Valerian with the account number of Mom's hospital on Gomorrah. Hopefully he'll still pay if I'm dead. I'm hoping I'll live, though. The money from this gig will only cover the outstanding bills, not her future stay.

But that's enough worrying.

It's dreamwalking time.

There are many ways to get into dreams. The classic method is to fall asleep myself, which could be tough thanks to the vampire blood I've ingested and all this existential dread. The strategy I've used more often lately is to touch a dreamer—like my legit therapy clients, illegal job targets à la Bernard, and most often, Pom, the looft on my wrist.

I stealthily slide one hand toward Pom. The last thing I want is to draw attention to his existence. As a looft, Pom spends ninety-nine percent of his life in REM sleep, providing me with a gateway into the dream world that's always at my fingertips. Well, almost always—he is, on a super-rare occasion, awake. Though you wouldn't be able to tell by looking at him in the waking world. Here, he's a fur bracelet regardless.

Stroking him to soothe myself, I concentrate on my intent to go into his dream.

Just like when I touch any other sleeper, my muscles tense and relax, I smell ozone, and I experience the sensation of falling as the limo around me darkens and the world of wakefulness goes bye-bye.

CHAPTER SIX

I FIND myself in my dream palace once more. Awesome. The vamps will be none the wiser—there's a reason I put up with what's essentially a parasite living on my wrist.

"What?" Pom appears in front of me in the angriest shade of red I've seen. "I can't believe you used the P-word."

I make my hair and eyes extra fiery. "How many times do I have to ask you not to snoop on my thoughts? You're only allowed to be upset when I say something mean with my mouth."

"But a *parasite?*" The tips of his ears go from red to blue. "I'm a symbiont."

"Sure." I fly up and head for the tower of sleepers. "Whatever you say."

"You have to mean that." He zooms in front of me, his ears going back to red.

"If you insist on having this discussion, let me ask you something: Am I or am I not your food source?"

"In a manner of speaking. I get my nutrients from your bloodstream."

"And where do your metabolic byproducts go?" Even as I ask the question, I shudder at the images it generates.

Pom turns a shade paler. "You mean like farts and poop? I don't think I do those things, but if I did, I guess it would go into your bloodstream. But your liver—"

"Is not there to save me from looft poo, I'm sure. In any case, what do you call a creature that lives off someone like this?"

He zips around me. "If it was useless, like a tick, you'd rightfully call it a parasite. But if the noble being provides the host with benefits, it's a symbiont."

"Benefits?" I fly over the staircase. "What are they? Besides blasting my eyeballs with extreme cuteness and helping me get into the dream world —both things I could hypothetically use a koala bear for. Did you know koalas sleep up to twenty-two hours a day? That's only an hour and fifty-five minutes less than you."

He huffs. "You can't bring a koala from world to world. And I do more for you than you think. I help you stay thin when you consume too many calories and—"

"Wait." I slow down to look into his big, guileless eyes. "Are you saying I pig out?"

"Well… I also help you regulate your appetite."

Huh. That may explain why I haven't been as hungry lately. "I didn't know that."

He puffs up. "There's a lot you don't know about loofts."

"You win," I say, mostly because we've reached the tower and I need to focus on Bernard. "You're a symbiont." Under my breath, I add, "Like gut bacteria."

"I heard that," Pom grumbles as I float over to Bernard's nook. "But guess what? All you Cognizant are parasites when it comes to humans. You wouldn't have powers if it weren't for their belief in you. You wouldn't—" He stops, seeing my crestfallen expression. "I'm sorry. That was mean."

I wave dismissively. "No, you can call me a parasite if you want. I was just hoping to finish the job." I eye Bernard's empty bed in disappointment.

"Oh, yeah, he's no longer sleeping," Pom says. "Check back in a few hours. I'm sure he'll be back later."

I do my best to suppress a thought along the lines of *assuming I have a later*. No need to worry the little guy.

Pom cocks his head at me. Did he catch that worry, after all?

Before he can question me and because I need to soothe myself, I take to the air, heading to an adjacent part of the palace.

Pom's fur brightens to golden as he realizes where I'm going. "Which memory will you relive this time?" he eagerly asks, flitting around me.

"Not sure yet."

My memory gallery serves a purpose similar to photo albums on Earth and VR videos on Gomorrah, making it easier to put myself into a dream that's based on a treasured recollection. Each plasma-framed painting hanging in the cavernous, museum-like space depicts an important snapshot of my life.

I float along the walls, scanning the various images until I settle on one.

"This?" Pom asks when I stop next to my choice.

"It's my earliest memory."

The tips of his ears turn light orange. "How old were you when that happened?"

"Seven, I think."

"And that's your earliest memory?" His ears are now a hodgepodge of colors. "Don't most people recall events before that age?"

I try not to show how much his innocent question bothers me. "I think it varies for everyone. I've always felt like there were parts of my childhood I couldn't recall—and Mom wasn't helpful when I asked her to fill in the blanks."

An understatement. Most fights between us over the years boiled down to her snapping at me for asking something about the past, like "who was my father?" or "where is he?"

Pom clasps his little paws together. "Well, then, do what you came here to do."

"Be back soon," I say and jump into the painting.

CHAPTER SEVEN

I'M SHORTER THAN USUAL. My body is that of my seven-year-old self, as are my emotions—unless I stop the replay and reflect as my adult self, which I rarely do.

Mommy's in the bathroom, and I'm bored. Spying an interesting object on Mommy's dresser, I climb onto a chair and rise on tiptoes to reach it.

It's coarse to the touch, unlike any other material I've ever handled. Is it clay? I don't know where I know that word from, but I'm pretty sure the object—a vase—is made of that.

Even more interesting are the handprints on it. There are four of them, and they belong to two smaller children. Or one child who put their prints onto the vase twice.

I strain my memory to figure out if they're mine.

Nothing.

"What are you doing?"

Mommy's voice startles me, and I drop the vase.

It hits the floor and shatters, clay bits flying everywhere as her eyes widen in horror.

I climb off the chair, head hanging low.

Mommy drops to her knees, pawing through the pieces as her face turns red and blotchy and her eyes fill with moisture.

I don't want her to cry. "Mommy, I'm so sorry. It was an accident."

Blinking rapidly, she envelops me in a hug. "It's okay, darling—it was just a material object. We can get another." But her voice is strained, and a wet drop falls on my forehead.

I begin to sob.

"No, no, darling, hush." She rocks me back and forth. "We can always make another vase."

I pull back, my mood lifting. "Can I put my handprints on it?"

She smiles, though her eyes continue to glisten wetly. "Of course."

The memory-dream ends, and I'm back outside the painting, my emotions in turmoil.

Maybe I shouldn't have chosen that specific memory. When I relived it before, prior to Mom's accident, it'd made me feel comforted, soothed, like Mom's arms were still around me. But today, it only intensified the hollow ache in my chest. I miss Mom so much it hurts. For all our fights, she's my only family, the only person in the world who loves me unconditionally. I'd give anything to turn back the clock and—

"Did you end up making another vase?" Pom bops around me, the happy purple of his fur proving that he's staying out of my head, as promised.

I shove away the gloomy thoughts, just in case, and paste on a smile. Now's not the time to dwell on my family or lack thereof. "Sort of," I reply as I take flight, heading back to the tower of sleepers. "The next day, Mom got me a VR headset so I could make hundreds of vases—and those never broke."

Pom speeds up to hover in front of me. "Whose handprints were those on the vase?"

I raise my hands and picture them tiny. "Mine, maybe. Could also be Mom's when she was small. She said she didn't remember." That was her response to most of my questions, in fact—a response I hated because it made no sense.

Why get so upset over a broken vase if you don't remember anything about it?

Pom must've gleaned that last thought. "She didn't yell at you for breaking it," he points out helpfully.

"No, she didn't." I sigh as the hollow ache returns. "She never yelled at me—unless I asked about the past."

Thinking about all this generates an overwhelming desire to check on Mom at the hospital. If I get lucky, there might be a way—but I need to deal with Bernard first.

Only Bernard is still not in his bed when Pom and I reach the tower.

Sounds like I have time to check on Mom, after all.

I fly over to another nook. *Score*. The dreamer I need is there. I'm lucky today—being taken to my possible death aside.

"Who's that?" Pom lands on the bed and examines the gargoyle female from wingtip to pointy tail.

"She's a nurse I found sleeping on the job when Mom was first admitted to the hospital. I made a sneaky connection to her, in case I wanted to check on Mom via dreams."

"Ah." Pom leaps onto my shoulder. "I want to go with you."

I scratch behind his ear, make both of us invisible, and enter the nurse's dreams.

———

THE GARGOYLE IS DREAMING of the hospital—another bit of luck. She's doing data entry at the nursing station, her head down.

Catching a moment when her attention is on the screen, I change the surroundings to match Mom's room.

It's a room I've grown to loathe. There, machines do everything Mom's brain refuses to, from breathing to nourishment.

Pom's feet reassuringly squeeze my shoulder.

When the nurse looks up from the screen, her subconscious mind fills in the details of the dream—using her memories, which is a boon for me.

"Hi, Lidia," the nurse says, approaching Mom's bed.

Mom doesn't reply. With her lack of brain activity, it's a philosophical question whether she actually heard what the nurse said.

The nurse lifts Mom's leg. "How about we do a little exercise?" She proceeds to move Mom like a doll.

Of course. Being in bed for so long, Mom's muscles are atrophying, or would if it weren't for what the nurse is doing. My chest squeezes tight. This is why I need the money, why I need to survive.

This is also why I should, at the very least, finish Valerian's job.

Exiting the nurse's dream, I check on Bernard.

He's still not back.

I return to the gallery and play a memory to banish the hospital room from my mind's eye. It's a memory of me blowing out the candles on a cake for my ninth birthday, and unlike the vase incident, it doesn't make me feel worse when it's done.

When I return to check on Bernard, he's still missing.

Pom's visibility returns in that Cheshire cat manner. "Isn't that Felix?"

I glance at a nearby nook. So it is. My friend fell asleep, after all.

Though I told Felix to do this very thing, a part of me thought he'd have trouble snoozing while I was in danger. Then again, it must be four in the morning, and unlike me, he hasn't imbibed vampire blood.

I float over to the nook where he's audibly snoring, his dark hair in even greater disarray than usual. Like me, Felix must stump anyone on Earth who tries to pinpoint his ethnicity—though unlike me, he comes from a long line of Earth Cognizant and does, in fact, resemble the humans from his home country of Uzbekistan. If I had to describe him to a fellow Gomorran, I'd say he looks like a tanned, skinny elf, only extra hairy and without the pointy ears.

"You might want to sit this one out," I tell Pom. "He's been through some ordeals."

Pom promptly goes away to do whatever he does when he's not pestering me. Good. I actually want him out of the picture so Felix and I can talk freely about the danger I'm about to face.

Making sure I'm still invisible, I reach out with one finger to touch Felix right above his unibrow. Connection established, I leap into his dream.

CHAPTER EIGHT

I'M in an abandoned warehouse with windows facing the Empire State Building. Huh. Do they even have warehouses in this part of NYC? Somewhere off to my right, a girl is screaming so loudly I'm glad my eardrums aren't real.

I turn to see what's going on. A foaming-at-the-mouth puck is clutching Felix's petite girlfriend in his furry paws as a dozen or so other pucks try to rip her out of his clutches. Poor girl. With hairy bodies, horns, and hoofed feet, pucks look a lot like the depictions of satyrs and demons on this world—only with shark-like teeth. On Gomorrah, pucks have the worst reputation of any creature, in part due to negative portrayal in the media, but mostly because they like to rape, kill, and eat their victims—and not always in that order.

Put another way, Felix's girlfriend is pucked.

"Help me, Neo Golem!" she cries out in a voice that's surprisingly intact, given all that screaming. "You're my only hope."

Seriously?

As if in reply to her plea, the warehouse door bursts into tiny pieces and a huge figure lumbers in.

Ah, right. When Felix got embroiled in saving the world, he and our gnome friend created a robotic power suit for him. Having obviously read too many Earth comic books, particularly *Iron Man*, Felix made this design—and even chose a superhero name for himself: Neo Golem.

The robot lunges at the nearest puck with a speed something this big shouldn't be capable of. Grabbing the puck by the left horn, he tosses him out the window, where the creature smashes into the Empire State Building.

The pucks let the girl go and circle Felix.

He slams a robotic arm into the stomach of the puck who'd held his girlfriend, causing the creature to fly at the wall and slide down in a broken heap.

A bigger puck gores Felix's shoulder with a diamond-hard horn, shredding metal like tinfoil. But when he rips the horn out, there's no blood. He must've missed Felix's flesh. That's good. From what I recall, my friend faints at the sight of blood, especially his own.

As I watch, Felix retaliates with a kick, hurling the attacking puck at his brethren. They tumble like bowling pins.

"Yeah!" Felix shouts. "You don't mess with Neo Golem."

The robot's chest opens up. In the place where Felix's nipples would be, two giant guns show up—and fire at the remaining pucks.

One spectacular explosion later, Felix is left alone with his sobbing girlfriend.

Wow. I can tell that the last part of the attack was based on a real memory of some fight Felix was in. I'm tempted to check it out, but I'm here for a different reason.

Felix sheds his robot suit and strides over to the girl.

Now this part is clearly pure fiction; his naked body looks way more muscular than his figure would imply in the waking world.

They kiss. Oh, boy. If I don't interfere now, I'm pretty sure I'll find out the X-rated way this damsel intends to reward her knight in shining armor.

Making myself visible, I clear my throat.

Felix's head snaps toward me. As he takes in my face and fiery hair, his eyes grow to the size of saucers, literally so—which is only possible in a dream.

I hastily return my hair to normal and clothe Felix in jeans and a T-shirt with a wave of my hand. "It's me, Bailey. I asked you to take a nap so we can speak, remember?"

Felix looks between me and his girlfriend. To make sure she doesn't distract him, I make her disappear.

Felix rubs his eyes. "What the hell is going on?"

"This is a dream," I say patiently.

He doesn't look like he believes me, so I change our environment to the place where I usually perform talking therapy—a pillowy cloud floating above a soothing ocean.

"A dream?" Felix plops onto the plush white couch my patients like to sit on.

"An unrealistic one, at that." I perch on a cushy, fleece-covered chair that appears conveniently under my butt. "Think about it. The warehouse was in Manhattan, as in Earth, but there are no pucks on Earth. Also, the pucks could've—and would've—killed the girl first, then attacked you. And that *You're my only hope* bit… Would anyone really say that, outside of *Star Wars*?"

I can see the dawning comprehension in his eyes.

"Don't feel bad. Dreams are my thing, after all."

He swivels his head from side to side, taking in our surroundings. "Unreal. I was totally clueless."

"It's hard to question dream reality." I let my hair go fiery again.

He looks awed. "It's like being in *The Matrix*."

Oh, crap, his favorite. If I don't change the subject, I'll get an earful. "I wanted to ask you about this Council that kidnapped me. I have a vague idea of how they work, but I could use more details."

"Hold on." He sits straighter. "How'd you get into my dreams? You're in that limo with the vampires."

I'd hoped he wouldn't question this part. "I had a connection with you already."

"Since when?"

I sigh. "Remember how you fell asleep during that video game design course we took together?"

"Nooo…"

"Well, you did." I change the environment around us to match that classroom, so he can see what I saw that day: his head on the desk, some drool in the corner of his mouth. "See how your eyes are twitching? That's REM sleep. Too good an opportunity to pass up." I pantomime touching his forehead. Of course, when I'd really done it, there was hand sanitizer involved.

"So you snuck into my dream without my permission?" His voice rises, and I worry he might try to wrestle control of his dream world from me—something I can fight but prefer not to, especially with a friend.

"This was right after you hacked my laptop and made fun of my project," I remind him.

"That's different. This is a much bigger invasion of privacy."

"You started it."

He pinches the bridge of his nose. "Fine. What was it that you wanted to know about the Council?"

"Anything you can tell me. Pretend I know nothing."

"Right," he says in a professorial tone. "In that case, the Councils are a form of government. Their main objective is to make sure the Cognizant remain hidden from humans."

"Okay, maybe not so basic." I stand up to pace along our cloud.

"Then I don't know what to tell you."

"How about something that can help me?"

He considers it for a moment. "Councils are made up of the most powerful Cognizant in the region they cover. The New York Council is among the most powerful Councils on Earth."

I roll my eyes. This is going nowhere fast. "So?"

"So don't piss them off."

"That's a huge help, thanks. Any other pearls of wisdom you wish to impart?"

His unibrow furrows. "Well, yeah. Think about it: The very fact that the Enforcers took you to see the Council is good news."

"Oh?"

"Without the Mandate, your standing in our community is shaky at best. They could've just killed you on the spot, and no one would've said boo."

I halt my pacing. "Some government."

"Before going to sleep, I tried using my powers to figure out what they want. Unfortunately, their computers aren't connected to the human internet."

He tried to hack them? Is he nuts? "Don't do anything that'll make them come for you next."

"Nothing I *can* do, anyway." He studies me. "Do you seriously have no idea what they might want?"

"No clue. I only know a couple of people from this Council, and the most powerful of them isn't even on Earth at the moment." I run my fingers through my fiery hair, sending embers flying. "There's Kit—you know, the shapeshifter? We met at the rehab where I work. I think she likes me, and she's on the Council. Maybe she can help? I doubt she's behind whatever this is."

Felix nods. "Kit's good people."

I strain my memory for anyone else on the Council. "Hey, maybe it's—"

Before I can finish my sentence, Pom appears next to me, his fur light orange.

Felix's eyes widen improbably yet again. "What is *that*?"

"I told you about Pom." At Felix's blank stare, I clarify, "My looft."

"The fuzzy bracelet?" Felix eyes my currently naked wrist.

I grin. "In here, Pom looks like this."

Pom bends his short, chubby legs in a curtsy. "Nice to meet you, Felix. This dream isn't as bad as Bailey made it out to be."

Felix studies him warily. "Thanks… I think."

"I think it's best you wake up now," I tell him.

"But—"

"No reason to bore Pom with our problems," I say pointedly.

An actual lightbulb appears over Felix's head; I'm not sure he realizes he's inadvertently summoned it. "Got it. But before I go, can you show me some cool dream stuff?"

I smile and snap my fingers to take us to my palace.

Felix looks around, agog. "Cool… Reminds me of Peach's castle from *Mario*, but with Escher and Salvador Dalí influences."

I snatch a Penrose-triangle clock from the air and let it melt into my hand. "You're not far off. I changed this place a bit after we took that course. Video game design made me a much better dreamwalker."

Felix looks up at the ceiling, a part of the palace so old I don't even recall making it. Consisting of multicolored glass, it's a mosaic depicting a mandala shaped like an archery target. He then stares at the walls and the floor. "What's with the crazy color scheme?"

I grin. "They're known as 'forbidden colors' because their light frequencies automatically cancel each other in our eyes. But we're not really seeing through our eyes here, hence red-green and blue-yellow, as I imagine those shades to be. I'm thinking of adding ultraviolet and infrared accents as well."

Eager to show off further, I take us to the memory gallery and explain how I use it.

Felix looks enviously at a painting of a surprise birthday party Mom threw for me when I turned twelve. "I'd pay a million dollars to revisit some of my childhood memories."

"I could make it happen for you," I say. "Just not today."

"Of course." He grins. "Thanks for showing me this."

"You should take him to the tower of sleepers," Pom suggests. "It's *my* favorite spot."

I grab Felix by the shoulder and fly him to the tower.

"Trippy," he breathes when he sees the nook with another version of him sleeping and another version of me standing over him with my finger on his forehead.

"That's you and me in Pom's dream, my gateway to the dream world in this case," I explain. "We're now in the same location, of sorts, but in your dream. Hence the extra bodies. When I exit your dream, I'll be in that body—and I'll get back to my *real* body in that limo after I'm done in Pom's dream."

"Like I said, trippy." He looks up and squints at a nook a floor up. "Wait, hold on... Is that Ariel?"

Crap. I forgot they're roommates. In hindsight, I shouldn't have taken him here. What if Ariel doesn't want him to know she's a patient of mine?

"You seriously need to wake up," I forcefully tell him. "Now."

He intuits my concern. "Oh, don't worry. She told me you're helping her."

I give him my best poker face. "I can neither confirm nor deny."

"Well, I want to thank you anyway. Ariel's been through a lot, and ever since she went to rehab and started your treatments, I noticed real progress with all her issues."

I wince internally. "Please, let's not talk about my hypothetical therapy sessions."

"Understood. Just keep doing what you do. I don't need to know what it is."

I sigh. "Anything else?"

"Sure." He looks around again. "How do I wake up?"

"Just wish to do so."

He closes his eyes, which I didn't tell him to do, and gets a constipated expression on his face—but clearly doesn't wake up. After a few seconds, I grow bored and push him from the dream world with a small jolt of my powers.

Both Felixes shimmer into nothingness. On my end, the version of me from Felix's dream disappears, and I find myself in the body next to the empty bed where Felix was a moment ago.

Pom flies up and lands on the pillow. "So. Are you going to help Ariel now?"

"Might as well." I head over to her nook.

"Good," Pom states. "I like Ariel."

Of course he likes Ariel. Pom's male, after all. Sort of. Maybe.

On Gomorrah, we call Ariel's kind of Cognizant *ubers*. That's not because they chauffeur everyone around—our cars drive themselves—but because they're uber strong and uber attractive. The term among Earth

Cognizant is *strongmen*, which is dumb because female ubers are just as strong as males, and because the label doesn't begin to cover their extraordinary looks.

Reaching Ariel's bed, I look her over. With her glossy dark hair and lightly bronzed skin, she's striking even for an uber. Her face, with its strong nose and finely defined jaw, is so symmetrical you'd think a video game designer had toiled for years to craft such perfection, and her body is what humans on Earth label "an impossible standard of beauty."

I'm actually glad Felix noticed her here. This might be my last chance to provide therapy for anyone, and Ariel isn't just a patient anymore. She's become a friend.

"Stay invisible," I tell Pom.

He nods disappointedly.

I touch Ariel's melted-candy-smooth forehead and sink into her dreams.

CHAPTER NINE

DRESSED IN AN ARMY UNIFORM, Ariel is running effortlessly with a hundred-pound pack on her back. She looks stunning, as usual, despite being sweaty, barefaced, and covered in grime.

I've been in a version of this dream before. This is an echo of Ariel's Army training.

"Ariel," I call gently.

She stops short and pulls out her gun, panic in her dark brown eyes.

Just in case, I turn the bullets into cotton. "I'm Bailey. You know me."

"I do," she says, still obviously disoriented. "What are you doing here?"

"You're dreaming," I tell her.

She looks confused for another moment, then a grin slowly spreads across her face. "I'm at the rehab facility?"

"Not sure. I'm doing remote therapy right now, so I have no idea where your body is."

I take us to my therapy space in the clouds above the ocean, and before she asks me to do so, I change her clothes into her favorite little black dress.

Instead of sitting down on the couch, she shifts from foot to foot. "So… what did you want to do today?"

I give her a soothing smile. "That's a question for you. Did you want to experiment with memory or—"

"No!" She tenses like a cobra ready to strike. Then she deliberately relaxes and, in a calmer tone, asks, "Can we do some more of that exposure therapy? I feel like I'm almost ready to be around vampires without freaking out."

As I thought—Ariel has deep trauma she's not ready to deal with. A terrible thing happened to her during her service, an event I witnessed in a trauma loop when I first started working with her. She's blocked her waking memories of it. I've been coaxing her to go there again, but she's clearly not ready. At least she's up for *some* forms of dream therapy. Not like some other patients of mine... and definitely not like Mom.

I've always suspected that Mom has been through something traumatic, but I have no idea what it is, as she's never let me treat her in any capacity. Quite the opposite: The mere idea of my dreamwalking in her sends her into a fit. When I was a kid, she made me swear never to enter her dreams, and I've kept my oath to this day. I sometimes wonder if she came to Gomorrah—a place without humans and their power-boosting beliefs—to lose her dreamwalking abilities completely. Maybe our powers are somehow tied to whatever traumatized her.

Familiar guilt floods me at the thought. The morning of Mom's accident, we argued about this very topic. I said things I regret and wish—

Ariel clears her throat.

"Sorry," I say, "what kind of exposure should we start with?"

"Blood," she says, her gaze downcast. "I feel brave today."

She doesn't need to say more. Vampire blood addiction is the reason she checked herself into rehab. She got hooked after she was healed by the substance and then started using it recreationally, probably as a form of self-medicating.

"Blood it is." I take us to a room I've used a few times, one modeled on a club in Gomorrah frequented by vampire blood aficionados. There are so many toys and instruments of sexy torture you'd think a BDSM dungeon threw up in here. Chained to a cross in the middle of it all is a vampire, who I make look like Filth—a small token of spite.

Ariel picks up a big knife and approaches Filth. I get out of her way and observe.

"You know you want it," Filth says in a tone much friendlier than I think the real version of him is capable of. "Drink from me."

With small, careful steps, Ariel draws near enough to cut a deep gash on his forearm. I try to make sure the blood pours slowly and, for lack of a better word, temptingly.

Ariel stares at it, hypnotized. I do as well. I sometimes worry I'll become addicted myself, thanks to my use of vampire blood to banish sleep, but so far, I seem to be okay. Then again, even if I were a blood addict, I doubt I'd be tempted by Filth's blood.

Ariel's face shows her mental turmoil. I hold my breath. She's either going to lean in and greedily gulp from the wound, as she's done during most of our sessions, or she's going to turn away, as she's managed to do only a couple of times.

Sweat beading on her forehead, she turns away from the blood and walks toward me.

"Great job." I pat her shoulder and usher us back to the clouds.

Ariel still looks doubtful. "This is all well and good, but I don't know if I'd be able to resist such temptation in the real world."

She doesn't give herself enough credit. "I think you'd be able to. You're—"

The whole world quakes.

"Open your eyes, bitch," booms a voice that sounds like Filth's.

Ugh, not now.

A slap wrenches me from the dream world, and I find myself back in the limo, Filth looming over me.

"What?" I snap.

"You're not supposed to dream," he hisses.

"I wasn't. That was a meditative trance."

"Don't do that, either."

I slather hand sanitizer on my stinging cheek and glare at Kain accusingly.

The head of the Enforcers shrugs. "We know you can communicate with people in your sleep."

"So what? Even the police allow an arrested person a phone call."

"We don't." Filth settles back into his seat with a sneer. "Close your eyes again, and I'll cut your lids off."

"Don't talk back," Felix urges in my ear. He sounds on the verge of fainting. "He looks like he means that."

It's true. Filth looks eager to mutilate me.

What a puckwad.

"Firth," Kain says, "she's not to be harmed." He turns his glare on me. "Do stay awake until we arrive at our destination."

"Fine." I stare at Filth for a few miles straight, doing my best not to blink. The bastard doesn't seem to care, though. He just sits there with a smirk on his weaselly face.

Deciding that the stare-off hurts me more than him, I look out the window instead. A full moon illuminates picturesque forests and distant mountain peaks as we drive into a fenced area past a sign that forbids trespassing. As we approach one large mountain, the dirt road turns into a nicely paved one, and a few minutes later, we reach a blockade manned by vampires who salute us—or rather, who salute Kain.

My hopes of escape evaporate.

Enforcer vampires are everywhere.

The limo crosses a moat and heads toward skyscraper-sized doors on the side of the mountain, thrown wide to reveal a medieval castle that puts even my dream palace to shame. The craziest part is that the entire castle is inside the mountain—a Cognizant with stone control must've helped with this project, because it's truly impressive.

The limo pulls into the mountain, where very unmedieval lighting illuminates gorgeous bastions and crenellated towers. I mentally file away the images in case I want to plagiarize them for my own dream architecture.

The limo comes to a stop.

"We're inside the bailey," Filth says libidinously.

I force out the most maniacal false laugh I can muster. "You're *so* clever."

He grabs my upper arm and drags me out of the car.

"Let go of her," Kain orders with a frown.

Filth releases me, and I massage my smarting arm as I apply more sanitizer to it. Pretty sure I'm going to have finger-shaped bruises there.

Inside the castle, we pass through cold stone corridors filled with hooded figures of monks. One of them hands a folded bundle to Kain without saying a word.

"Is that the Brotherhood?" I ask no one in particular.

"Speak only when spoken to," Filth barks.

"Yes, they are," Kain replies almost at the same time. "Don't you have them on Gomorrah?"

"I think so," I say, "but I've never met them myself."

The Brotherhood is a group of Cognizant without any powers, or at least any powers I'm aware of. They follow some strange religion, the details of which I don't know.

Eventually, we reach a large set of doors opening into a miniature indoor coliseum lit by candles floating in the air—a nice touch.

Filth points at the circular platform in the middle. "Stand there. Don't go to sleep."

"That will be all," Kain says to his minions.

As all the Enforcers leave, Filth included, Kain unfolds the bundle of fabric given to him by the monk. It turns out to be a black robe with a hood.

He puts it on. "Now we wait for the Council meeting. It's going to happen first thing in the morning."

"That's a long time away," I say. "Any chance you can tell me what this is about?"

"No. But what I can do is make the time pass faster while you wait."

"Sure, but how—"

As his eyes turn into mirrors, I realize my mistake.

He's about to glamour me.

I'm resistant to vampire glamour, at least from the run-of-the-mill vamps, but Kain is clearly powerful, and drinking vampire blood does make one more susceptible to their—

"You won't remember the next five hours," Kain says in a voice made of melted caramel.

The next thing I'm aware of is how stiff I feel standing in the same spot.

Only now I'm surrounded by the Council.

CHAPTER TEN

DRESSED in multicolored hooded robes similar to the one Kain put on, the New York Councilors look as though they took their fashion advice from some creepy secret society.

"Good morning," I say politely, and even contemplate curtsying. "I'm ready to learn why I've been detained."

"Finally," Felix says in my ear. "I thought you'd never snap out of it."

Kain stands up. "Please state your name for the record."

"Bailey Spade." I scan the room for allies, but it's hard to recognize anyone in these hooded getups.

"Thank you," Kain says. "I'll be the designated neutral party in these proceedings."

"I think that's good," Felix whispers. "He let your Gomorran tech slide. Maybe he's more than neutral."

In the third row, a slender figure in a magenta robe stands up and pulls her hood back.

I know her. This is Kit, the shapeshifter I met through my rehab job. She's currently in her favorite guise, that of a round-cheeked blonde straight out of a Japanese role-playing game or anime.

"I'm serving as the Defense for today's proceedings," she says in a high-pitched voice that matches her video game appearance.

Another woman in teal robes stands up and pushes back her hood, revealing high cheekbones in a familiar oval face. "And I'm Gertrude, the Plaintiff in today's proceedings."

Puck. I know her as well. I just hadn't realized she was on this Council.

Gertrude came to see me on Gomorrah, complaining of symptoms that sounded like REM Sleep Behavior Disorder. People with that condition physically act out their dreams, sometimes by speaking and sometimes by moving their arms and legs. I told Gertrude I couldn't help with that, or anything else physical, because my powers only work inside the dreams. Instead, I advised her about obvious safeguards she could take, like installing a padded floor, removing dangerous objects from reach, and sleeping alone. Something—probably the sleeping alone bit—really upset her, and now it seems like she's been holding a grudge this entire time. At least enough of a grudge to want to speak against me today.

Has she never heard of the whole "shooting the messenger" thing?

"Be careful. This Gertrude has a scary power," Felix whispers in my ear. "Her skin mortifies any tissue it comes into contact with."

That's just great. A gangrene-giver has a grievance with me. Can things get any worse?

"Why don't I explain the charge?" Gertrude offers. When no one argues, she says, "The Defendant has revealed her powers to humans."

I did *what*? When?

There are hushed whispers in the audience.

"Crap, that's like breaking the Mandate," Felix says in the earpiece. "Not good."

I wish he'd stop with the pessimistic commentary. I'd silence the earpiece, but if the Council realizes I have it, I could get Felix into trouble.

"I'm sure whatever happened was an honest mistake." Kit turns herself into a version of me, with an unnaturally innocent expression.

"What *did* you do?" Felix whispers.

I still have no clue. I certainly never revealed anything to any humans. Why would I?

"Why don't we all decide for ourselves?" Gertrude fiddles with a phone.

A moment later, Filth comes into the room rolling a cart holding a 75-inch TV.

"Thank you." Gertrude's smile shows too many teeth, and Filth bows to her before leaving.

Gertrude descends from her seat with feline strides. At the first row, she pauses next to a hooded figure. "Hekima, do you mind helping with this?"

The hooded figure stands up and reveals his face. His frizzy gray hair and kind, deeply weathered features make him look how I've always pictured my grandfather—not that I know anything about my grandparents. Mom always refused to speak about them.

"That's Dr. Hekima," Felix says. "He's a good guy. I had him for Orientation—a sort of school for the young Cognizant here on Earth."

That makes sense. His grandfatherly looks fit a wise teacher to a T.

Hekima joins Gertrude next to the TV and addresses the crowd in a deep, melodic voice. "Please speak up if you don't want the illusion of immersion."

"Oh," Felix says, "forgot to mention. He's an illusionist."

Another illusionist? Valerian, the guy who hired me for the Bernard job, said he was this type of Cognizant. Illusionists can make you see what they want you to see, creating a sort of virtual reality without the need for any hardware.

A few Councilors raise their hands to indicate that they don't want their minds messed with, but most are okay with it. I keep mine at my side as that will let me see the evidence better—plus I'm not sure if I'm allowed to refuse.

As Gertrude turns the screen toward the people who won't be subjected to Hekima's power, Hekima dramatically raises his arms, as if planning to conduct an orchestra.

Before I can blink, pulsing red energy streams from Hekima's fingers into everyone's heads.

As if switching from one dream environment to another, the meeting hall vanishes, replaced by an art gallery. Only three people are there to enjoy the countless paintings: Kain, Gertrude, and a very familiar human —a painter from my past.

Puck. I'm beginning to have an inkling as to my crime.

Kain's eyes go into glamour mode, and he directs them at the human painter. "You will answer all questions honestly."

"I will," the painter says robotically.

Gertrude points at the wall opposite them. "Why did you paint that?"

"Crap," Felix says.

Crap, indeed. The painting is of me—the way I look in the dream world, with fiery hair.

"This is my dream muse," the painter says. "She appeared in my dream on the night I got the idea to explore a completely new medium. Ever since then—"

Hekima must do his thing, because the gallery is whisked away, replaced by a bedroom I recognize as belonging to the painter. The

Enforcers scour the room like crime scene investigators until Filth snatches a single curly brown hair from the carpet and gives it a disgusting sniff.

"That's it for now," Gertrude says as the coliseum reappears around us. "To clarify, the Enforcers used that to find the dreamwalker."

"Vampires can do that, use DNA to locate someone," Felix explains needlessly in my ear.

"Furthermore," Gertrude continues, "Kain and his team followed her for several weeks. They witnessed her breaking into the homes and apartments of various humans, no doubt revealing her powers to them as well. The Enforcers finally caught her red-handed and brought her here." She looks at Kain. "Isn't that correct?"

He shakes his head. "We have no evidence that she showed herself in the dreams of anyone but the painter. And some of the apartments she broke into belong to fellow Cognizant."

Kit loudly clears her throat. "How is any of this news? We've all heard Bailey's nickname of Freda Krueger." She morphs into the burn victim and horror movie villain that inspired the nickname I dislike. "And we all know of Bailey's reputation as a Cognizant private detective of sorts."

Kain gets an unreadable expression on his face.

"When we need secrets stolen," Kit continues, "we go to her. Obviously, she does her thing by dreamwalking. It's like accusing me of shape-shifting." She demonstrates by morphing into several random people and animals.

Gertrude gives Kit a nasty smile. "If anyone hired the accused to expose herself to humans, we should hold similar hearings for them."

Expose myself? She makes it sound like I was hired to work in a strip club.

I'm unsure of the proper protocol here, but this has gone on long enough. "Maybe I could explain?" Before anyone can say no, I rattle out, "Nobody hired me to show my dream form to that painter or anyone else. I was hired to encourage him to work for a VR company—that's all. Dreamwalking is usually performed while invisible, but I forgot to conceal myself that time. It was an honest mistake. It hasn't happened since, and it won't happen again."

Actually, it almost happened today with Bernard, but they don't need to know that. Everything else I said is absolutely true. Valerian, the illusionist who hired me for Bernard's job, wanted me to "inspire" the painter to create masterpieces in VR. I think Valerian owns a VR company, likely the one where Bernard works.

"We can verify this claim and question the other victims," Kain says.

Gertrude frowns. "It doesn't matter. There's physical evidence of her crime. If she were under the Mandate, it would've activated when she 'forgot' to hide herself in that human's dream—assuming she's telling the truth about that, which I doubt."

"I think we should vote," Kit says. "I'm sure Bailey will be exonerated."

"I agree," Kain says, "and there's something unrelated to this case I want everyone to bear in mind."

Gertrude's frown deepens, but the other Councilors regard Kain with curiosity.

"As you know, we have a very puzzling investigation on our hands," he says, causing hushed murmurs to start again. "And Bailey is a sleuth."

I'm as much a sleuth as I am a ballerina, but I see no need to counter what he's saying if it could help me.

"I don't think anyone should worry about matters unrelated to her crime," Gertrude snaps. "It's time to put this to a vote. If you think the dreamwalker should die, as consistent with our laws regarding the exposure of our powers to humans, please stand up."

Die? Is she kidding me?

My heartbeat skyrockets as the hooded figures rise to their feet one by one.

I'm so pucked.

CHAPTER ELEVEN

EXCEPT THEY DON'T **all stand up.**

Kit and Kain sit down, and as I scan the room, I realize only a minority of this Council wants me dead.

Whew.

"That settles the matter," Kain says. "Now I move that we vote to task Bailey with our investigation."

"You know," Felix whispers, "I'm getting a feeling that the whole exposure thing was a ruse to get you to comply with the next bit."

He might be right. After dodging execution, I do feel quite ready to do whatever they want. Besides, this might be an opportunity I can't pass up, for Mom's sake. The Council has resources that—

"All for, stand up," Kain says.

Most of the Councilors rise to their feet, including the ones who wanted me dead a second ago. Flip-flop much? Either way, it sounds like I just got some kind of a job thrust at me.

As people begin to leave their seats, I speak up. "Isn't there something you're forgetting?"

"What are you doing?" Felix shouts in my ear.

Everyone looks at me as if my hair has caught fire—something I can't do safely in the waking world.

I fold my arms across my chest and stare them down. "My payment. I don't work for free."

Kain gives a rare smile. "You don't know what we want you to do."

"Whatever it is, I need to get paid for it," I say. "My mother was in an accident. Machines keep her alive, and my jobs barely cover her life support bills. So as payment for this job, I want you to heal her. Not with vampire blood—that didn't work—with an actual healer. Do that, and I'll do whatever it is you want."

Kain doesn't look surprised in the least. He glances at a woman two rows from him, who pulls her hood back to reveal fine features surrounded by glossy black hair.

"That's Isis," Felix says. "She's a healer who recently got a Council seat."

"Solve the case, and I'll help your mother." Isis levels an arrogant look at me. "I hope you realize what such a payment is worth."

Oh, I realize, all right. It would take all the money I've seen in my life multiplied a thousandfold to hire a healer on Gomorrah.

"Let's talk details," Kain says and strides out of the coliseum.

I follow his silent form through the castle and up a narrow staircase into what must be a tower. The rusty iron hinges screech as he pushes open the massive door, and we enter a circular room with stone walls.

"Hey, your camera just cut out," Felix says worriedly. "Did you—"

"So," I say to Kain, ignoring Felix's technical problems. "What is it you want me to figure out?"

"Before I explain, you should know that this is a delicate matter." Kain leans against the wall and folds his arms across his chest.

Great. Delicate matter, powerful people. What could go wrong? "I keep all my work confidential," I say, eyeing him warily.

"Good. But I still want to highlight how sensitive this situation is." He flashes his fangs, turning his already unattractive face practically ghoulish. "If news of this gets out, I will personally kill you. Slowly."

The threat is delivered in the casual tone I'd use when asking a coworker what time it is. Wow. I thought Kain was on my side, but it seems he only protected me from Filth because he needed me intact for this job.

I raise my chin. "If news of whatever this is gets out, it won't be because I blabbed."

"Fine." His fangs disappear. "Here's the deal. Four members of the Council have died under strange circumstances. At this point, everyone thinks it's murder and that a member of the Council must be responsible."

Felix whistles in my earpiece, reminding me that the secret is already out.

I swallow hard. Someone killed four of the most powerful Cognizant on this world? How the hell am I supposed to solve something like that? I can't even figure out which of my coworkers at the rehab facility keeps eating my leftovers—at least not without invading their dreams.

Oh. He can't mean *that*.

"I'll convince everyone to give you access to their dreams," Kain says, way ahead of me already. "You'll be able to see their memories and figure out the culprit, right?"

"Maybe." I try to keep my voice even. "It's not as straightforward as that. Sometimes I have to work on—"

"Don't worry about the details. Whatever it takes, you'll do it."

"Yes, of course I will," I say, more to hype myself up than to reassure him. "My mom's life depends on it."

"Indeed." His fangs show up again. "And in case that's not motivation enough, your own life depends on it, too." Leaning in, he whispers into my ear, the one without the earbud, "I didn't inform the Council about the full extent of your crimes. Bringing Gomorran technology to this world is forbidden, and as you can imagine, if forced to vote again, especially after your failure, the Council would not let you off so easily."

I back away, my heart rate uneven. Around my wrist, Pom has turned pitch black. "You don't need to threaten me," I say, amazed by how steady my voice is under the circumstances. "I'll do anything to heal my mother."

"All the better," he says. "I just wanted us to be on the same page."

I straighten my spine. "I need the details of the murders and access to everyone's dreams, as well as the authority to interview people and review any records I wish."

"You'll get all that. I'll make the arrangements. Wait here." He disappears from the room with vampiric speed.

Felix clears his throat. "An unsolved murder case must look bad for him, what with being the new head of the Enforcers and all."

I hadn't thought of that. Still, he didn't need to be so—

"Hello, Bailey," comes a smooth, deep male voice from my right. "Given the circumstances, I decided we need to talk."

CHAPTER TWELVE

"WHO'S THAT?" Felix asks in the earpiece.

Great question. I peer intently at the location the voice came from but see no one there.

Then a man materializes in front of me.

And what a man. Tall and broad-shouldered, he's wearing a bespoke suit that hugs his muscled body in all the right places. His face, framed by thick, silky-looking dark hair, is even more impressive. Ocean-blue eyes glint at me from beneath straight black slashes of eyebrows, and his high cheekbones appear to have been carved by a sculptor, along with his chiseled jaw and dimpled chin. Oh, and there's a hint of stubble on that gorgeous face, as if he hadn't shaved this morning.

It's official. He's hotter than Adonis, the most popular uber singer on Gomorrah. Wait—maybe he *is* a celeb. Something about his face does look familiar...

As I study each feature, I catch myself wanting to kiss those firm yet plush lips. Which is beyond insane. We've just met, and I have huge problems with touching in general, let alone touching that leads to the exchange of bacteria-laden bodily fluids.

Puck. I'm still staring at him. How long is it socially acceptable to stare at someone? Worse yet, my furry wristband has just turned an embarrassing coral pink—the color of sexual arousal.

At least this guy doesn't know that my looft displays my emotions this way, or what each color means.

Hold on. All this time, he's been staring at me just as intently. I've got to say something. Anything.

What comes out is a lame "Hi."

A sensual smile touches those kissable lips. "Hi, Bailey." He extends his hand. "I'm Valerian."

On autopilot, I clasp his palm, noting with some small corner of my mind just how big and warm it is. He squeezes my hand gently, then releases it, his smile widening at my continued dumbstruck silence.

For four straight seconds, I don't reach for the sanitizer—a record of some kind.

Then my common sense kicks in, and I get the bottle out and sterilize my hand, finally processing his introduction.

Valerian. That's the guy who hired me for all those VR-related jobs.

This is what he looks like? Until now, we'd been communicating via encrypted email. If I'd known all the facts, our meetings would've been in person. Maybe even in some romantic, scenic locations, like the shore of that beautiful lake on—

With effort, I tamp down on the inappropriate fantasy forming in my mind and say in as even of a tone as I can manage, "Nice to meet you in person, Valerian. Are you on this Council?"

"I'm not." The way he says it, though, makes it sound like he omitted the word *yet*.

I blink up at him. "Then how did you manage to get into the castle? For that matter, how were you invisible?"

"He was invisible?" Felix asks. "How—"

"Same answer to both." Valerian's sensual lips curve again. "As you know, I'm an illusionist. While you talked to Kain, I gave both of you the illusion of being alone in the room. Same when I came to the castle. I made it so nobody could see me. Oh, and I carry a device that turns off any cameras around me."

My earpiece fills with grumbling. "So that's why I can't see anything. Let's hope the camera comes back on when he leaves."

Ignoring Felix, I process what Valerian has said. When Hekima did his illusionist thing, he shot those energy arcs at everyone's heads. Apparently, that's not the only way that power is used. The reality is much scarier: You may have no idea when an illusionist is working his mojo.

Then something very disappointing occurs to me. Given Valerian's powers, he might not actually look like a sex god. I bet no one looks like this, and certainly not this Valerian guy.

How sad.

The weird part is that he seems equally fascinated with me, his eyes scanning my face as if he plans to draw me later. "I know this will sound like a pickup line," he murmurs, stepping closer, "but I can't shake the feeling that you look familiar. Have we met?"

I catch a pleasant whiff of warm male skin and pine, and my mind fills with images of sunlit forest meadows and long, lazy kisses on a picnic blanket. I swallow to combat the sudden dryness in my throat. "I don't think so, but you look familiar to me, too. Have you ever visited Tranquility? The rehab facility on Gomorrah?" *Or did you make yourself look like a celebrity?* is what I don't ask.

His hypnotic eyes gleam with amusement. "Afraid not. I keep my vices under control."

I'm suddenly dying to know all about those vices, but I force myself to focus. "Based on the jobs you've given me, you're into VR. Maybe you took some video game design classes here on Earth? Or on Gomorrah?"

"I'm self-taught." He looks at his watch, then at the door. "We don't have much time, so I'd like to get to the point."

"Sure." I conceal my irrational disappointment. "What point is that?"

All hints of amusement disappear from his face. "The last job I gave you is very important."

Job, right. That's why he's talking to me. "You're paying a lot for it, so I figured as much," I say, matching his businesslike tone. "Unfortunately, as you can see, I'm in a bit of a predicament right now."

He nods, his gaze somber. "If said predicament interferes with your ability to complete my job, I'd be happy to use my powers to lead you out of this castle."

"Wow," Felix whispers. "He can actually save you."

"I can't leave," I say to them both. "The Council gave me an opportunity I can't pass up."

Valerian cocks his head. "What if I match whatever they offered you?"

"I doubt you can. Besides, they have my DNA, which means they can track me anywhere you take me. I don't really want to spend the rest of my life looking over my shoulder for vampires."

"I see." He frowns, and even that expression looks good on his chiseled face. "So you're saying you're giving up on Bernard?"

"No, I already did the heavy lifting with Bernard. I established a dream link. When night falls, I'll find time to slip inside his dream and finish what I started."

The frown is instantly gone, and I decide I like his face much more without it. "Thank you," he says. "Are you sure you don't want to escape? I'm going to Gomorrah for a couple of days, so I won't be reachable if you change your mind."

"I'm sure. Oh, and there is a way I can reach you, even on another world." I try to make my next question sound as casual as possible. "How do you feel about taking a nap right now?"

He grins, flashing even white teeth. "Nice try, but I don't think I'm ready to let you loose inside my subconscious. We've only just met."

I do my best to ignore the butterflies filling my stomach. "Your call. It could've been fun to be in a dream together." Especially for me. I almost lick my lips at the thought.

"Are you coming on to this guy?" Felix hisses.

Crap, I totally forgot we have a third wheel.

Valerian's grin turns wicked. "We don't need your powers to have fun," he says in a voice like heated molasses as the room around us shimmers and becomes a lush bedroom with an enormous bed swathed in silk sheets and scattered with rose petals.

My pulse spikes as the butterflies start a gunfight in my belly. Is this really happening? Am I about to—

"Alas, we can't today," Valerian says, and to my huge disappointment, both the bed and his gorgeous self disappear.

"Wait!" I look around the empty room. "Why do you even need me? For the Bernard job, I mean? As you just demonstrated, your powers are very similar to mine."

His disembodied voice comes from near the doorframe. "I'm under the Mandate. That heavily limits what I can and can't do with humans. Besides, your way is going to be much better. Dream inspiration is a classic, after all."

"Uh-huh. Are you sure you don't just want someone else to take the risk?"

He doesn't reply. Must've already left.

I sigh, feeling strangely deflated. The idea of "having fun" with Valerian was more than a little appealing, and not just because we'd be able to do it via his powers of illusion or my ability to dreamwalk—and therefore without any exchange of bodily fluids. No, it's him. Something about the guy almost makes me forget the dangers of viruses and bacteria.

Speaking of which—I slather my hands again with sanitizer. What's wrong with me? I talk to a hot guy for two minutes, and I'm ready to risk syphilis? He might not even look the way he appeared to me.

Must be my lack of a sex life catching up with me. I have a complex relationship with my libido. In other people's dreams, I've experienced thousands of orgasmic encounters, both from their memories and their fantasies. In my own dreams, too, I've done whatever I wanted with anyone who took my fancy. Sometimes with many of them at once. In the waking world, however, I've never actually been intimate with anyone.

Despite an entire harem of partners in the dream world, I'm a twenty-six-year-old virgin who's never even kissed a guy.

Hey, that gives me a crazy idea. What if the Brotherhood monks were behind my being snatched by the Enforcers? Maybe whatever deity they worship needs a virgin sacrifice.

Nah. Too convoluted a plan for something like that.

Felix crackles in my ear. "The camera just started working again."

Before I can so much as reply with a thumbs-up, Kain strides back into the room with a thick folder in his hand. "Let's go to your quarters so we can review all this." He waves the folder and turns on his heel.

I have quarters?

I follow, panting to keep up—though for a vampire, he's practically crawling.

We hustle across half the castle to what at one point must've been the dungeon where prisoners were kept before being tortured or worse.

"How dreary," Felix mutters.

That's putting it mildly.

Kain leads me down a corridor that even the rats must find too depressing to frequent. The place smells faintly like fermented sewage, and I have to fight my gag reflex. With a determined expression on his face, Kain makes a sharp right and stops next to a large cell with an iron ring welded to the wall—always a nice little touch. He makes a gentlemanly gesture, ushering me inside.

"You've got to be kidding me," I mutter as I step in.

These are my quarters? Instead of a solid door, there are iron bars, exactly like in a prison cell, and there isn't even a modern toilet. There's just a hole in the floor with murky muck a few feet down, which looks suspiciously like the liquid that was slushing in the moat around the castle. Major eww.

The only thing that makes this place feel like anything other than a prison cell is a new bed, table, and chair. And the fact that the door isn't locked with the rusty padlock that's hanging on the outside. Instead, it actually has a bolt on the inside.

Hekima appears in the corridor behind Kain and peers through the bars disapprovingly. "Are these the best accommodations we can provide? Bailey is our guest, after all."

Kain sets the folder on the table. "You may have a point. This is where we were going to put her if she was found guilty, but she wasn't. I'll see if we can scrounge up something better."

"Please do," Hekima says. "Meanwhile, do you mind if I change the scenery?"

Kain and I shrug.

Hekima shoots his showy arc of energy at our heads, and the cell becomes a fresh-smelling, sunlit meeting room. Only the furniture looks the same.

"Right, then." Kain opens the folder. "Let's get to the murders."

CHAPTER THIRTEEN

INSIDE THE FOLDER, on the top, is a photo of a striking woman.

"She looks like Lara Croft," Felix whispers. "Or looked. Past tense."

"That's Tatum," Kain says somberly. "The first victim."

He flips the page, and I see Tatum's body lying on the roof of one of the castle's towers, an arrow in her heart.

"Why don't I show you what we think happened?" Hekima offers.

More illusions. Why not?

I agree, and an arc of illusionist energy hits my head.

I find myself at the scene of the crime, standing in front of a living Tatum. She smells amazing, which gives me an inkling of her Cognizant type. She takes a joint from her pocket and is beginning to light up when —with a sharp *whoosh*—an arrow pierces her chest.

"Let me slow that last part down," Hekima says after she collapses.

This time, I can see the arrow's flight path. It seems to come from the ground below—an impossible shot.

"When was this?" I ask as the arrow crawls toward the chest of the poor woman.

"Six days ago," comes Kain's disembodied voice. "At four p.m."

"And what can you tell me about her?"

"She was a succubus. The most powerful I'd ever met."

Just as I thought. That yummy smell is unmistakable. "Do you have any idea who would want her dead?"

The arrow begins to penetrate Tatum's breast.

"No one," Hekima says. "Everyone loved her."

"A bit too literally," Kain says. "As you can imagine, she had many lovers."

Right. When one of her kind wants someone, they use their power to make themselves sexually irresistible. This is why I stay as far away from succubi and incubi as possible; they no doubt have countless germs from all those partners, plus they can drain energy from their lovers during intimacy—something that can even lead to death, if they wish it.

No, thanks. I'll take my dream lovers any day of the week.

I turn away before I can get splattered with illusory blood. "Could a lover have killed her? Murders are often committed by people close to the victim. Maybe someone got jealous."

The room becomes normal again—that is, it goes back to its guise as a meeting room.

"As I said, she had many lovers," Kain says. "The pool of suspects is too large."

I examine the photo of her corpse again. "That arrow. Are you sure your recreation of her death is accurate?"

"We consulted experts," Hekima says. "I'm sure."

"But who could make such a shot? There are no elves on this world, so—"

I stop as Kain and Hekima exchange a glance.

"Some elves get plastic surgery to make themselves look more human in order to settle here," Hekima says.

Huh. I didn't know that. "Is there such an elf on the Council?" I ask.

"There is, for sure," Felix whispers excitedly in my ear. "He helped us in a recent conflict."

I'm about to ask some questions, but Kain flips a few pages in his folder and shows me a picture of a thin man.

"Yeah, that's who I meant," Felix says. "Doesn't he look like Tingle from *Zelda*?"

Kain flips the page again to a photo of a broken body sprawled over some rocks—a body that had to be the same individual as in the previous image.

"Oh, crap," Felix whispers. "He's another victim."

"We found Ryan dead just a few hours after we found Tatum," Kain says. "And before you ask, he was the only elf on the Council, and he wasn't merely Tatum's lover. He was her husband."

I rub my temples. I'm only on the second murder victim, and my head already hurts. To focus on something this brain-intensive, I'd need a full night's worth of sleep, something I haven't had in four months. "Is it possible the elf killed the succubus out of jealousy and then killed himself in grief?" I ask. "Humans commit this sort of murder-suicide all the time, don't they?"

"That's what we thought," Kain says, "until the next murder."

"Right," I say, remembering that there were four. I picture the broken body on the rocks. "So you think someone pushed the elf?"

"It seems so," Hekima says.

"Except that makes no sense," Kain says. "Ryan was extremely paranoid. I don't think he'd let an enemy ambush him like that."

"So maybe it was a friend," I say. "Did he have many?"

"One," Kain replies with a scowl.

"Leal?" Hekima asks. "But he—"

"It's feasible he could've done the deed before," Kain says.

Hekima raises his arms. "Do you want me to play out that theory?"

"Please," I say, and Kain nods.

Hekima shoots us with his mojo again, and we find ourselves on top of a cliff with the elf's back to us. A man with wild gray hair dressed in a white lab coat approaches the elf from behind. The elf spins around and aims a drawn bow at the newcomer.

"Leal," he says with a hint of a smile. "You startled me, old friend." He lowers the bow and turns his back to the newcomer. "I come here when I feel unsettled. It's almost—"

The gray-haired dude pushes him over the cliff, and we're back in the meeting room before the elf strikes the rocks.

Kain looks thoughtful. "I don't know about this. Why would Leal kill his closest ally?"

Why indeed? "Maybe I could go into his dream to find out?"

Kain sighs and turns a few pages in his folder. There's a picture of a balding man in a white coat, a dove sitting on his shoulder as if he were a pirate and there were a parrot shortage.

"I don't mean to disrespect the dead," Felix says, "but he totally looks like Dr. Wily from the *Mega Man* games."

Or any mad scientist, for that matter.

"The next image is disturbing," Kain says. "Take a deep breath."

I do as he suggests, and he turns the page.

Puck. The slab of meat in the photo is barely recognizable as a man.

Felix makes a strange wheezing sound. Did he just faint?

I drag my gaze away from the horrible image. "What could do that?" I ask Kain.

"The doves," he says.

I blink at him uncomprehendingly.

"I think he means like in the Alfred Hitchcock movie," Felix says in a thin voice. I guess he didn't faint, after all. "You know, *The Birds*?"

Kain turns to Hekima. "Can you show her a simulation?"

Before I can say *thanks but no thanks*, I see an intact Leal standing in a lab filled with cages of white birds. Without warning, the doves become agitated. One manages to break through the cage, followed by another and another.

Leal looks at the freed birds with no fear. "What spooked you, dears?" he asks in a raspy voice.

This is when a dove dives and pecks him in the eye.

He screams, clutching his eye, but another bird is already diving for his face again. More doves leave their cages and join the attacking horde (or dule, as a group of doves is called). Some of them hurt themselves in the process, but that doesn't seem to stop them.

"Enough!" I snap. "I get it."

Instantly, the blood and gore are replaced by the meeting room.

"Sorry," Hekima says, "I didn't—"

"It's fine." I force a smile, ignoring the nausea twisting my stomach. "I did need to know what happened."

Kain and Hekima wait as I even out my breathing. And hey, a benefit of not having eaten in a day is that I can't puke—one of my least favorite activities.

"Is there someone on the Council who can control animals?" I ask when my voice is steady enough. "On Gomorrah, we call people who can do that—"

"Gemma." Kain flips a page in the folder.

A long-haired beauty stares at me from the photo. She's dressed in all leather and stands on high heels.

"This one looks like Bayonetta," Felix says, his voice back to normal. "She's this kickass video game witch who—"

Kain flips to the next page, and Felix makes a gagging sound. My stomach roils too. Though arguably not as bad as the prior image, it's still pretty gruesome.

Someone or something literally ripped this woman in half.

"I don't want to see a recreation of this," I tell Hekima before he can do his thing. "It's self-explanatory. Someone very strong pulled her in two different directions."

"Indeed," Kain says. "Gemma's kind are fragile, so unfortunately, we have many Cognizant on the Council with enough strength to do that."

Well, this is going to be fun. "Do you have any idea how any of this ties together?" I ask. Maybe if they—

Kain slams the folder shut. "That's what you're here to find out."

Right, okay. Lucky me. "Did the bird guy—"

"Leal," Kain corrects.

"Right. Did Leal have a grievance with the last lady—"

"Gemma," Kain provides.

"Yes, Gemma. Did Leal—"

"Leal only had one friend—Ryan, the elf," Hekima says, his grandfatherly features wreathed in pity. "Nobody on the Council liked him much, except maybe Kain and the other vampires."

"Oh?"

"I'd go as far as to say I considered Leal a friend," Kain says. "Or at least an ally."

"But why does everyone else not like the guy?" I resist the temptation to open the folder and look at the man in question.

"His powers," Kain says. With a sharp-edged smile, he adds, "He was a dreamwalker."

Another dreamwalker? I glare at Kain. "Why are you only telling me about that now?"

The vampire shrugs. "When was I supposed to tell you? Rumor has it, he had blackmail material on all the other members of the Council. They thought he'd gathered it in their dreams."

The ache in my temples intensifies. "So you're telling me he might've been killed for snooping around people's dreams?"

"It's feasible," Hekima says gently.

I take a deep breath and try not to look at Pom, who's rapidly turning black on my wrist. "But that's exactly what you're asking me to do. What's to stop them from wanting to kill *me*?"

Kain waves dismissively. "You should worry about the murderer. That's who'll really want to kill you—if you're any good."

"Thanks. That makes me feel so much better."

Kain smirks. "If I were you, I'd do my best *not* to find any compromising information inside the Councilors' heads."

I cup my hands over my eyes, the enormity of the task hitting me like a punch to the face.

"Why don't you do your thing with those Council members who have more reason to be under suspicion?" Hekima suggests. "Anyone strong."

I lower my hands. "Sure, I'll start with the ones who can rip me in half. I feel safer already."

"It's not a bad idea," Kain says. "Still, I want you to set up a dream link to everyone on the Council. Even me."

I take another breath, trying to think like the detective I'm not. "This Leal, did he leave any notes? As you said, he knew secrets about the Council. Maybe he wrote them down somewhere."

And maybe, just maybe, he also wrote something about the art of dreamwalking itself. I've never met any dreamwalkers besides Mom—we're pretty scarce on Gomorrah—and between her diligently avoiding the topic of our abilities and the fact that I never received any formal training in how to use my powers, there's a lot I don't know about my own kind.

"I'll take you to his lab," Kain says, his expression unreadable.

Hekima withdraws his illusion, and the dreary cell room comes back —as does the stench.

"Let me know if I can help any further," Hekima tells Kain. "And Bailey, if you need to know anything about the history of the Council or anything else, I'm here for you."

Felix chuckles. "Good old Hekima. He'll look for any excuse to run an Orientation."

I smile at the elderly illusionist. "Thank you. I'll find you if I need that."

Hekima's dark eyes twinkle. "I guess I'll see you tonight in my dreams."

"Not if I'm just setting up a connection," I say.

Hekima leaves, and Kain picks up the folder and strides out.

I sprint to keep up with him.

A few winding corridors later, we arrive at the lab I saw in Hekima's recreation of the grisly bird attack. Though someone has cleaned up, I can picture the bloody corpse all too easily. What's worse is that the doves are here now, roosting in the same cages they broke out of to murder their caretaker. And the smell emanating from those cages...

"Creepy," Felix remarks just as Kain says, "I'm going to leave you to it. Be back in an hour."

Hundreds of saffron-colored eyes stare at me hungrily from the cages. Before I can beg Kain not to leave me alone with the stinky killer birds, he disappears, closing the door behind him.

As if that's what they had been waiting for all along, the dule of murderous feathered beasts begins to coo menacingly.

CHAPTER FOURTEEN

THE COOING SWELLS to fill the room, mimicking the growing knot in my throat. But the birds don't attack me. They don't even try to escape from their cages. They just coo and eat grain from their feeders, and on occasion, I hear a wet splatter as one of them poops.

Serious eww.

Despite the stench choking my nostrils, the death-by-birds-inspired adrenaline begins to leave my system. And as it does, my eyes get gritty, my lids grow heavy, and a yawn escapes my mouth. Oh yeah, I'm starting to feel like someone who hasn't slept for four months.

I'd give a lot of money to take a nap right now. Then again, needing money is how I ended up so sleep deprived in the first place.

There's no time to sleep, though, no matter how I feel, and it's too soon to take another dose of my "medicine." So I do the next best thing, an exercise called *bellows breath*. I inhale deeply and rapidly for a short while, as if hyperventilating. Bellows breath can give a little burst of energy in a pinch, and I'm certainly in a pinch.

It helps a little. Instead of a ten out of ten on the horribleness scale, I only feel like a good, solid nine.

"You okay?" Felix asks softly.

I take out my phone and furtively text, *Never been better. Time to get back to my investigation.*

"You can just talk out loud," he says. "I doubt Leal's lab has any listening devices."

You sure? I text.

"Positive."

"All right," I say out loud. Even if someone *is* listening, they'll probably just think I'm crazy.

I look around, taking in the surreal paintings on the walls around me.

Stinky birds aside, this lab clearly belonged to a dreamwalker.

"Very cool," Felix says as I walk over to stand before a famous painting by Salvador Dalí—*Dream Caused by the Flight of a Bee around a Pomegranate a Second before Awakening*. "Makes me wonder what it would've been like to walk in the artist's dreams."

"Maybe Leal did just that," I say as I turn to see a painting depicting a staircase that loops in a circle instead of going up or down. Such structures can't exist in the real world, but they can exist in art and dreams. In fact, I have stairs similar to these in my own dream palace.

"That's M.C. Escher," Felix says needlessly. "That piece is called *Ascending and Descending*."

I force myself to ignore the cool art and search for anything relevant to the case. But there are no notes on the desk, no diary on the bookshelf, nothing else I can use. If the doves were parrots, I could ask them to repeat something, but as is, this is leading nowhere.

I study the way the art is laid out, using my dreamwalker's eye for detail.

Aha. Every painting is hung flush with the wall, except one. *Ascending and Descending* is not. I pull the heavy frame away from the wall and peer at the back. Score. There's a pocket here, and something inside it.

Fishing out the small device, I examine it carefully.

"Gomorran comms," Felix says, confirming my guess.

"Must be generations old." I turn the clunky little thing in my hands. "My unit was ancient, and it was way sleeker."

"Even an old comms device probably has a petabyte of data and more processing power than any supercomputer on this world," Felix says reverently. "Be careful with that."

"Otherland tech is totally forbidden," I say in my best imitation of Kain. In my normal voice, I add, "Unless you're on the Council, that is."

"They're hypocrites," Felix says. "At least the dreamwalker hid the device. Some of the other Councilors break their own rules a lot more openly."

Feeling a yawn coming on, I shake my head. "Back to the investigation. Let's get into this thing." I bring the comms device closer to the camera. "This is your chance to show off your powers, in case that's not obvious."

He sighs. "I can't."

"What?" I tap the earpiece as if that's going to change his answer.

"I mean, I could, but it would have to be in person. The device is not connected to the internet and—"

"You can't be here in person." I twirl around to remind him where I am. "Maybe I can ask them to take me to you? But no, then they'd know about you."

"Yeah, I'd rather not be pulled into this. But there *is* a way I can get into the castle in person without much fuss. Ariel's cousin's best friend's daughter is having her Mandate ceremony there in a couple of days."

"Oh? What does that have to do with you?"

"Mandate ceremonies are a big deal. Everyone attends to show support, so it won't be suspicious if I tag along with Ariel."

"I hope I'm alive by then," I say dubiously.

"Well… maybe I can get some of the data from the cache right now. But we risk damaging the device."

"Do it then—but carefully." I don't think I have a couple of days to dick around.

"I'll do my best. Put the comms on top of your phone."

I set my Earth phone on the desk and place the comms device on top.

"Now be quiet," he says.

I watch the device for any sign of *something*. Just as I'm about to ask Felix what gives, a strange magenta energy snakes from the phone into the comms unit.

"Got something," he crows. "A few excerpts from some kind of diary. Emailing them to you now."

I pocket the device and open the first email from Felix on my phone.

Roger came back with the newest batch of the medicine today. The bird I tested it on fell asleep instantly, and stayed asleep for six hours, three hours longer than with the prior formulation. But just like before, it died instead of waking up. Still, at only $10 per dove, this provides unlimited access to the dream world. Next time, I'll have him—

The passage ends there.

"That's it?" I ask Felix. "Any chance to see what came before or after this excerpt?"

"No, but there's another piece when you're ready."

"In a second," I say and start searching the room again.

But no matter how hard I try, I find no sign of the strange drug described in the email.

"Why would he kill birds by making them dream?" Felix asks as I finish looking through a nearby desk.

"To enter the dream world without falling asleep." I look behind yet another painting—to no avail. "I use Pom for that. I guess this Leal guy found his own method."

"By killing the poor doves," Felix says disapprovingly.

"Right." I cast an uneasy glance at the cooing creatures. "They got their revenge in the end, didn't they?"

"I guess. Sending you the other bit of text I found in the cache."

I check behind the last painting. Nothing. Oh, well.

I open my email.

Another werewolf, another failure. The inner wolf and the man attacked me together yet again, and I found them too hard to fight off. Lost my powers for the day as a result. Werewolves are proving to be the most difficult of all Cognizant to dreamwalk in. Eduardo isn't making it easy, either. He forbade his pack from allowing me to continue this research. The son of a bitch likes me powerless against him. I'll have to master the multibody technique if I'm to succeed. That way, one of my consciousnesses can attack the wolf while the other deals with the man. Alas, I fail at this too. Maybe if—

Crap, cut short again. I tap the earpiece. "Hey, I want to read the rest of that."

"Sorry, there's only one more tidbit left, and it's from a different part of the diary."

"Send it to me."

"One sec. I want to understand what he meant by what you just read."

"Isn't it obvious? Werewolves are a problem when it comes to dreamwalking. I've heard of this sort of thing with some other types of Cognizant. They say you can never sneak into the dreams of gnomes, for instance, not unless they let you in."

"Right, that part was more or less clear," Felix says. "But I don't get the part about losing his powers and the multibody thing."

I reread the message. "I think he meant that he had to use his dreamwalking power so much inside the werewolf's dream that he ran out of juice. There's a limit to how much dreamwalking one can do in a day. He must've reached that limit."

"And the multibody bit?"

I read the text once more. "Sounds like he's talking about having two bodies in the dream world that can simultaneously think and feel. If so, that's very intriguing and not something I've ever tried to do. I can sort of leave my body and reenter it, but that's not the same. I'm going to have to give this a shot one day."

"How trippy," Felix says. "I can't imagine what it would be like to be in two places at once, even in a dream."

"Logic takes a vacation in the dream world, that's for sure. Now stop stalling and send me the next piece of this diary or whatever."

He types something so loudly I can hear it. "Done."

I pull up the email.

Any dream can be hidden behind the black window—my own, a dream of another subject, or the dream of the subject herself. The remarkable thing is that when a dream is a memory of the subject, the memory itself becomes deeply suppressed. She has no recollection of the events at all. More fascinating still is that the subject doesn't recover her memory when I reenter the black window. The breaking of the black window is the only way the subject gets to experience the events locked behind it. If it's her memory, she recovers them, but if it's an implanted dream, she dismisses it as a figment of her—

It cuts off.

Disappointed, I reread what is there. "You sure there was nothing more about this?"

"No, why?" Felix asks. "Does it make sense to you?"

"Vaguely." I greedily scan every sentence for clues. "Whatever this black window is, it seems to let you erase people's painful memories. I've never heard of that."

"That's *Eternal Sunshine of the Spotless Mind* kind of shit." Felix's voice is full of awe. "Makes sense, though—you do deal with the subconscious. Still, scary."

"Yeah." I pocket my phone. "And the bit about hiding his own or other people's dreams inside someone else's dreamscape—that's just as crazy. It would give dreamwalkers a way to hide information so that only another dreamwalker could find it."

"Not the best method," Felix says. "What if the person who has information hidden inside their dreams dies?"

We both fall silent. It's obvious he's thinking what I'm thinking: Could Leal have hidden something inside the dreams of the other victims, something that someone killed them to hide? But if so, who?

I head for the door. "I think I'd better get more information to work with." Another yawn threatens as I walk, and I instinctively pat the vial of vampire blood in my pocket.

Wait a second. It's too soon for another hit, so why am I even thinking about this? Is this a craving? The start of an addiction?

I'd better keep a close eye on this.

Performing the bellows breath technique to wake myself a little, I reach for the door knob.

What the hell? It's locked.

Did Kain do that?

That's just great. Now I need to do the opposite of bellows breath to fight my panic.

"He said he'd be back in an hour," Felix chimes in, as if reading my mind. "You don't have to wait long."

"Still." I eye the cooing doves. "These cannibals have a taste for dreamwalker flesh. We're probably delicious."

"Cannibal doves would eat other doves, not people."

"Thanks, Felix, that really puts my mind at ease." Before he can reply, I say, "In any case, the good thing about having Pom on my wrist is that I'm always ready to go into the dream world. Since I'm stuck here, I'm going to test out some of the things the dead dreamwalker was talking about."

Raising my hand so that Felix can see, I touch Pom's fur and slip into a trance.

CHAPTER FIFTEEN

THE YUMMY SCENT of manna fills my nostrils as I appear in the lobby of my dream palace.

Pom pops up next to me. "I've missed you."

I grin at him. "We're attached, you know. But yes, I've missed you too."

Pom turns purple, and his ears flap in a sort of happy dance.

I tell him an edited version of the events that have transpired so far, which boils down to getting "hired" to solve a case for the New York Council.

When I get to the part about Valerian, he says, "I can tell if he really looks the way you think. I can see through any illusion."

I look my furry friend up and down, which doesn't take long, given his small stature. "How?"

He floats up to my eye level. "I see through your eyes when I'm awake. Pretty sure the illusionist would have to target *me* with his powers to make us both see the same thing."

"See through my eyes, right. Perfectly normal behavior for a symbiont. Not something a parasite would do at all."

"Indeed," he says, oblivious to my sarcasm. "And it can be useful."

I snort. "Not really. You said you have to be awake. You're almost never awake."

His ears turn the color of carrots. "But you can wake me up."

"I can? How?"

"By mentally shouting for me." A lightbulb appears above his head. "Why don't you wake up and try it right now?"

Intrigued, I exit the dream world and open my eyes back at the lab.

Pom, I mentally shout. *Pom, wake up!*

Then I look at my wrist.

The way to tell if he's awake is that his fur will start to express his emotions instead of mine. Oh, and on a rare occasion, he'll deign to speak as a voice in my head.

The fur is light orange, which could be his curiosity or mine. There's not a peep from him in my mind.

Pom! Pom, wake up.

No reaction.

I touch his fur and draw myself back into the dream world.

"What happened?" he asks when I reappear in the palace. "You didn't do it."

"I shouted from the top of my brain like a lunatic." I shake my head. "I don't know, Pom. I don't think you can be roused."

He huffs. "With all that lack of sleep, your mind is just too muddy."

"Sure, blame it on me."

He gives me a furry frown. "It's a wonder you can function at all."

I just barely hold back an eye roll. "You know what? Let me tell you the rest of it." I proceed to explain about the bits of dreamwalker diary—my reason for coming here in the first place.

"Do you have a link to a werewolf to see this inner wolf business?" he asks when I'm done.

"Afraid not. I've never worked with their kind. I guess I'll find out what they're like when I have to deal with the werewolf on this Council."

The tips of his ears darken. "Remind me not to join you when you do. Sounds scary."

"Deal." I scratch the top of his furry head until his ears turn purple. "Now I'm going to attempt the whole 'double consciousness' thing."

"I'll watch." Flying up a few feet, he stares down at me intently—an act that makes him look borderline freakish, thanks to his tea-saucer-sized eyes.

I exit my body, becoming a dream ghost, and create an exact duplicate of that body. So far, so good. Next, I attempt to return to both bodies at the same time. I end up in only one—the original. The second body just stands there like a mannequin.

I exit my body again, give the two Baileys fiery hair, and will myself to enter both.

Nope. Still end up in just one.

Pom zooms down and pokes the second body with a toe. "Maybe you need to turn this into one of those dream characters you like to have sex with?"

"Pom!" I give him a menacing glare. "How many times do I have to tell you that's private?"

He turns beet red. "You didn't ask me not to spy on you every time. I assumed it was okay."

Great. First, I'd forgotten to make myself invisible when dreamwalking in humans, and now it turns out I'd also forgotten to ask Pom for privacy during my R & R. Must be the sleep deprivation.

"Let me try your idea," I say and replace the body in front of us with a dream character of me, something I've never tried before.

"Hello," the new me says sensually. "How can I be of service?"

Pom looks between me and my creation. "Do they all want to have sex?"

I shrug. "They're just like any person you meet in a dream."

"What we dream characters say and do is driven by the dreamer's subconscious," my other self says. "That's how I know she's often wondered about *this*." Leaping at me, she plants a wet kiss on my lips.

"Hey!" I push her away. "Not in front of Pom."

She smirks. "I'll stop if you admit it."

"Fine. Guilty as charged. I *have* thought about it. You. Doing things with myself. But I've never done it because it seems a bit narcissistic."

She strikes a centerfold pose. "Anyone you have sex with in this dream world is essentially me. I may pretend to be them, but we both know it's really you, or a part of you, pulling the strings."

This is not going as I'd anticipated. "Just stay still," I command her.

She freezes in a comical pose. I focus to see if my consciousness is in both of us.

Nope.

I float out of my body and attempt to land back in both bodies.

Another fail.

I dismiss the second me. "Looks like I'm not powerful enough to pull off the double consciousness."

"Or you might be too sleep deprived to use your power properly," Pom suggests helpfully, flitting over to sit on my shoulder. "It's like I told you. It's been more than four months since—"

"You're like a nagging husband." I grab his furry body and hold him in front of my face. "I can't raise enough money for Mom's bills if I waste time sleeping. Now I also need to solve this case ASAP."

His lavender eyes are unblinking. "So you're not avoiding sleep because you're afraid of bad dreams?"

Ugh. Who died and made Pom my therapist? "Remember that privacy thing we talked about a minute ago?"

His shoulders slump.

"Yeah, you guessed it." I set him down. "Can I please get some for the next few minutes?"

"If you insist," he says glumly.

"I insist. And you must promise not to spy. I mean it."

"I pinky swear." He extends a three-fingered paw.

Since every digit is the same, I guess the rightmost to be the pinky and solemnly shake it to seal the deal. "Now scram."

He performs the slowest Cheshire Cat disappearance ever.

When I'm sure he's gone, I change my surroundings to my favorite bedroom in the palace and let my mind drift to Valerian. Even if his looks were to impress me, they *were* impressive. Visualizing him is easy; I guess his mouthwateringly hot face is burned into my imagination.

Without further ado, I make a dream version of Valerian appear in front of me, dressed in the same suit as in the real world.

"Hi, gorgeous," Dream Valerian drawls. "Miss me already?"

"Shut up." I try to keep my voice steady. "You know what I want."

He grins wickedly, and unbuttoning the top button of his shirt, he comes toward me. Even though I'm in the dream world and he's a simulation of what was likely an illusion, my body's response feels quite realistic—down to every detail.

This will be fun.

Even if the real Valerian doesn't look this way, I owe him for inspiring this dream design.

Moving with predatory grace, Dream Valerian closes the distance between us and kisses me. His sensual lips are as soft as I imagined. I melt in his arms, feeling his—

"Bailey," Felix's voice booms from all over. "The door."

Seriously? I had no idea Felix was such a cockblocker.

"The investigation, remember?" Felix shouts from the outside world. "Someone's here."

"Fine," I growl, and leaving a disappointed Dream Valerian, I return to the waking world.

The cooing of the cannibal birds is back, as is the stomach-turning smell of their cages.

I open my eyes. The door is already open, and Kit is standing much too close to me, a look of curiosity on her face.

I step back awkwardly. "Hi."

"I'm here to take over for Kain for a bit," she says, turning into him. "Did I come at a bad time?"

I plaster a smile on my face. "It's fine. I was waiting to get out of here."

"To do what?" she asks in Kain's voice.

"I want to interview the strongest members of the Council. Anyone able to rip a person in half."

"I see." Kit morphs back into her anime character self. "Who would you like to start with?"

I prepare to watch her reaction. "You."

Her face reveals nothing.

"With your power, you could turn into an orc and have its strength, right?"

She morphs into a giant green orc—a muscle-bound creature that Earthlings might confuse for the Hulk with tusks. "I'm a suspect?" she booms.

Being next to something this big activates primal fear in my amygdala, so all I can do is bob my head.

"Okay then," Orc Kit growls and smashes a fist into the door. The heavy wood shatters into tiny pieces, answering my question about her strength. The birds stop cooing and blink at the orc with panic in their cannibalistic eyes.

I know what they're thinking: *We're about to die.*

Then again, they might be thinking how delicious my remains will be.

"Now," Kit growls, taking a menacing step toward me. "Let's talk."

CHAPTER SIXTEEN

MY BREATHING SPEEDS UP.

Am I a victim of my own success? The first person I formally question turns out to be the culprit?

It could be. Kit could've turned into Leal, the dreamwalker, to get close enough to push Ryan, the elf, off the cliff. She could've turned into a bird, pecked Leal to death, and opened the cages to blame it on the doves. And she's just proven that she could've turned into an orc to rip Gemma, the animal controller, in half. The only part I'm not clear about is how she could've shot Tatum, the succubus, with an arrow from so far away—but perhaps she'd turned into an elf and got their perfect marksmanship?

But if Kit is the killer, why did she root for me at the trial? Reverse psychology, maybe?

One thing's for sure: If she kills me now, it will prove I'm right.

I back away. As much as I love to be right, this is too high a price. Maybe I can still run? She's blocking the door, but—

Instead of lunging forward and ripping me to shreds, Kit transforms back into her tiny round-cheeked self. "I only get the physical qualities of whatever I turn into, not the powers."

Does this mean she isn't going to kill me? That's good. Now if only my racing heart would chillax.

"Is elven marksmanship a power?" I ask warily. "Or is that like orc strength, something you develop by having the right body?"

"That's a great question." She turns herself into a female elf. "Do you have a bow and arrow?"

I pantomime patting my pockets. "Let me just pull out the bow and arrow I carry on me at all times. It's right next to my sword and ax."

"Don't be mean." Elf Kit walks past me and sits on a chair, seductively crossing her legs. "As flattered as I am to be a suspect, why would I want to kill those four? Especially Tatum."

I take a seat across from her. "Why especially Tatum?"

"She was the best lover I'd ever had," Kit says wistfully and turns into Tatum, but without the signature succubus scent.

"Kit's a sex addict," Felix chimes in. "No surprise there."

I know that; it's the reason she was in rehab when we met. How does Felix know, though?

Hmm, maybe I don't want to know the details.

Kit shifts back into herself, and her expression turns unusually fierce. "Killing Tatum was an atrocity akin to destroying an irreplaceable work of art. When I find out who did it, I won't just kill them—I'll turn into a drekavac to do it."

I suppress an instinctive shudder. Drekavacs are horrifying creatures that are said to kill victims through unspeakable pain. They're even scarier than pucks.

"I don't think she's bluffing," Felix whispers. "She's killed someone that way before. Someone who deserved it, but still."

So Kit *can* torture-kill if she feels like it. She's looking more innocent by the second. *Not.*

"Can you please tell me where you were and what you were doing at the time of the murders?" I ask in as steady of a voice as I can manage. "Kain said Tatum died six days ago, at—"

"I know when every one of the victims died." Kit's face darkens further. "We all do. When Tatum died, I was having sex."

I blink.

"Not with Tatum, obviously." She turns into a blond bombshell. "I got embroiled with Lola two weeks ago and only wrenched myself away from her the other day."

"Lola's a nymph who's an enabler for her," Felix whispers.

I debate muting him again; he keeps telling me things I already know.

Refocusing on Kit, I ask, "What were you doing when the elf—"

"Lola. In every case." She flashes back to her normal self. "As you well know, when Lola and I get together, things can spiral a bit out of control."

A bit out of control? Sure, we'll call it that. I saw some of Kit's dreams featuring Lola when she was in rehab. To me, it seemed like Kit wasn't the one with the addiction—Lola was. That, or being insatiable is part of Lola's nature. The word *nymph* is the root of *nymphomaniac*, after all.

"Can you give me some details?" I ask as Felix uncomfortably clears his throat. "Was there anything memorable about those lovemaking sessions? What did the room look like?"

When Kit smiles at me in an overly friendly way, I also clear my throat, adding, "It's for dreamwalking."

She tells me about the rooms they used; then, with relish, she details the positions she and Lola got into, which toys went into which orifices, how many orgasms each of them had, and how often she changed shape into something or someone Lola felt like having sex with—as well as how many phalluses each of those forms had. Though Felix usually only faints at the sight of blood, he's so deathly silent in my earpiece that I wonder if Kit's details have knocked him clean out.

Pulling out my phone, I make a few notes to avoid forgetting anything, as unlikely as that seems. "I'll have to check all this in your dreams," I tell Kit when I'm done. "But if you were with Lola the way you say, you're not guilty."

"Great." She stands up. "Now who do you want to interview next?"

"Who else is strong enough?"

She turns into Kain, hooked nose and all. "An old vampire?"

"You suspect him?" I glance furtively at the door.

She turns back into herself. "I'm just telling you who's strong."

"But still, would Kain be working so hard to solve this case if he's the culprit?"

"Cute." She turns into me—a well-rested version, without bags under my eyes. "You're assuming that hiring you is the same as 'working hard to solve this case.'"

I narrow my eyes at her.

"Don't be mad." She turns back into her usual self. "You're an amazing therapist, don't get me wrong, and you can surely steal secrets when you try. But since when are you a detective?"

Up yours, lady. "You yourself called me a detective at the trial."

She shrugs. "I was trying to save your life. If Kain really wanted a detective, he could glamour a human one or find someone on—"

"But I can tell when people lie to me. I can go into dreams and compare stories with memories."

"There are more direct ways to figure out if someone is lying," Kit says. "I'd say hiring you isn't that."

She's probably talking about the man I playfully call Bowser, a member of the Council who's currently on vacation. He simply *knows*, without a doubt, if someone is telling him the truth. If he were here, the case would be as simple as having him ask everyone, "Was it you?"

I wonder if that's why the killer chose to strike now, with Bowser away indefinitely. It's his or her only chance to get away with it.

"Let's see if Kain lets me dreamwalk in him," I say. "As a vampire, he doesn't need to sleep, so it would have to be voluntary."

"Good thinking." Kit turns into a giant, albeit a small one, and says in a voice deep enough to sing death metal, "Another strong person is obviously Colton."

"Who totally looks like the giants from the *Skyrim* game," Felix says conspiratorially.

"Who else?" I ask.

"There's Eduardo." Kit turns into a shaggy-haired man not much smaller than the giant, who then morphs into a huge wolf.

"I think Eduardo looks like Donkey Kong," Felix chimes in. "But never mention this to him, or I'm dead."

Sure, I was totally about to walk up to a werewolf and tell him he looks like a video game gorilla. I'm *that* suicidal. "Okay, who else?"

Kit transforms back into herself. "Does it have to be physical strength?"

"What do you mean?"

She turns into a striking black-haired woman with thick dark eyebrows, a small hoop in her right nostril, and silver studs in the upper and lower lips. "Nina isn't physically strong, per se," she says in a melodic voice that I assume belongs to Nina. "But her telekinesis is so strong she could use that to rip someone in half."

Oh, a telekinetic too. Fun. "I'd like to speak to her as well. Who else could rip someone apart?"

"No one I can think of," Kit says.

I stand up. "Then let's start with Kain, Colton, Eduardo, and Nina."

"Sure." Kit assumes her big-eyed, overly cute anime guise and dashes for the door.

I follow her through a couple of corridors. When we reach a massive door, her phone rings.

She pulls it out. "Hello?" She listens for a few seconds, but I can't hear the other side. "Sure, I'll get the usual. If they have sashimi-grade salmon, five pounds."

"Someone's hungry," Felix mutters. "Or, like me, has a cat with exquisite taste."

Kit listens for another second. "Yep, she's with me." She covers the phone. "Kain sent Firth shopping. Do you need anything?"

I ask for a case of bananas, six gallons of distilled water, a dozen bottles of hand sanitizer, and—just to mess with Filth—every feminine hygiene product I can think of, plus laxatives and adult diapers.

Kit doesn't blink an eye as she repeats my list to Filth. Sadly, I can't hear if he complains.

I sneak out my phone and text Felix:

See if you can hack into the store camera to record Firth buying all that stuff. Bonus points if the adult diapers don't scan, so the clerk has to look up the price manually.

He chokes with laughter. "I'll try."

Kit hangs up. "I think I know why you requested everything except the bananas." She turns into a monkey and scratches her head with her foot before transforming back into herself.

Felix groans. "I can't believe she just walked into *that* lecture. I'm going to put you on mute."

"If you must know," I tell Kit, "it's one of the very few things I feel safe eating on this world. You can carefully peel bananas without touching the inside. Even if the outside is crawling with salmonella, you can be safe."

Kit's eyes widen. "Really?"

I'm unable to resist the opening. "The food industry here on Earth is an abomination. Did you know there's human DNA in hotdogs? Or that the United States FDA allows maggots, rodent hair, cigarette butts, and mold in food? Did you realize that milk is allowed to have pus and blood in it, or that every meat you can think of has fecal—"

"Stop, please." Kit makes her ears disappear and reappear. "I don't want to end up eating bananas for the rest of my life."

"Sorry. Do you want to know what the sanitizer's for?"

She rolls her eyes. "That's pretty clear. I assume the other stuff is a prank on Firth?"

"That obvious?"

She assumes Filth's weaselly visage. "You know how many jokes feature a vampire and a tampon?"

I grin. "You should tell me some. But only after I solve this case."

"Right." She becomes herself and knocks on the huge wooden door in front of us.

The giant—Colton—opens up. Unsurprisingly, he looks just like Kit's impersonation of him, except he's wearing an apron.

"I have a brisket in the oven," he booms. "Is this going to take long?"

Felix snorts. "Cue the banana rant."

I surreptitiously flick the earbud to hopefully deafen Felix. "Not long. But we can do this later."

"No, come in." The giant opens the door wider.

I step in but stay vigilant about touching anything that he could've contaminated during food prep. The aroma of fried animal flesh is unmistakable.

"Sit," he urges as we enter a surprisingly modern kitchen—well, modern for Earth. Given the medieval ambiance of the castle, I was half expecting to see some unfortunate pig's head on a spittle over a fire. Instead, there are white quartz countertops, stainless steel appliances, and a sleek table with backless chairs that appear to be sized for a giant. And, I guess, a brisket in the oven.

I clutch the sanitizer in my pocket for comfort. "I'll stand, thanks."

"Suit yourself." He plunks down in one of the chairs, making it creak under his weight. "What did you want to know?"

"It all boils down to one question," I say, eager to escape the unsanitary environment as quickly as possible. "What were you doing at the time Gemma was ripped apart?"

He frowns deeply. "You think I'd—"

"She has to ask everyone," Kit says. "Even me."

He lets out a resigned sigh. "I was herding the goats."

I shift my gaze from him to Kit, who turns into one of the puckish creatures and bleats.

Colton gives her a chiding look. "Goats keep the shrubs around the mountain at bay, give the monks a source of milk and cheese, and provide everyone with occasional mutton."

"Milk, cheese, mutton—another chance for the banana rant," Felix murmurs.

If I deigned to acknowledge his existence, I'd tell him that free-roaming goat products feel way safer to me than germ-infested industrial farm food, at least as far as *Salmonella* and *E. coli* go.

"What I really need are some details," I tell Colton. "Like what the sky was like or in what formation the goats stood—anything that made that afternoon memorable."

"Sure." He tells me that the day was foggy, and that a bunch of mushrooms had sprouted on the nearby hill. As he keeps going, I take notes on my phone.

"Thank you," I say when he's done. "That's all we needed."

"You sure you don't want to taste—"

"We shouldn't keep Nina waiting. Maybe some other time."

Kit looks at the oven longingly. I carefully elbow her. She turns into a monkey—no doubt a dig at my banana eating—and scampers out of the giant's lair with me literally on her tail. She leads me through more corridors to a door as big as the one that led to Colton's abode. Becoming herself again, she presses the doorbell.

A bloodcurdling wolf howl emanates from behind the door.

CHAPTER SEVENTEEN

"I KNOW," Kit says when she sees how white I've turned. "Eduardo's door chime takes getting used to."

"That was a chime?" Felix whispers. "It sounded like someone getting murdered."

The door opens on a tall, shaggy-haired man with intent lupine eyes. He also looks like Kit's impersonation of him—and like Donkey Kong, as Felix mentioned, only dressed in a bespoke suit.

"I was just on my way out," he growls. "What's this about?"

The guy is so intense I can't help but take a step back. "Do you have a minute? I'm interviewing everyone for the investigation."

He looks at his Jaeger-LeCoultre watch. "You have two minutes."

"Where were you when Gemma died?" I blurt. "Tell me in as much detail as you can."

His eyes narrow. "I was hunting with my pack. It was foggy. We took down a buck with a broken antler. Is that detailed enough?"

"It is, thank—"

"Then get out of my way." He moves forward.

"Just one second," Kit says, staying put. "Where are you going in such a hurry?"

He stares at Kit the way The Big Bad Wolf must've looked at Little Red Riding Hood. I gulp. Werewolves on Gomorrah are notorious for their bad temper, and Eduardo doesn't strike me as a particularly zen member of his kind.

Without blinking an eye, Kit shifts into an orc.

"Pack business," he growls. "Now move."

"He's the alpha of said pack," Felix whispers more quietly than usual. "I'd obey."

I pointedly pull on Kit's sleeve. "Again, thanks. Kit, we have more people to interview."

"Have fun." Orc Kit turns back into herself and steps leisurely out of his way.

The next door Kit leads me to is no more than a large slab of rock. I see no handle or hinges. To the side on the wall is a doorbell with a camera, which Kit presses.

"Yes?" calls the melodic voice Kit simulated earlier. "What do you want?"

"Bailey is here to interview you," Kit says. "It's to help with the investigation. I'm sure you don't mind."

In reply, the giant stone slides up.

Nina looks just as Kit showed me earlier, only dressed in a black leather jacket and jeans. She's gesturing at the stone slab with her hand, a look of concentration on her striking face.

Of course—she opened the door using telekinesis.

"Come in." She waves us in with her free hand.

Kit waltzes in, but I hesitate as Pom turns black on my wrist. If Nina stops holding up that rock with her power, whoever is under it at the time will turn into a pancake.

Nina frowns. "Come on. I won't harm you."

Puck. If she didn't want to squish me before, she might after this perceived slight. "I didn't mean to imply you'd do it on purpose. It's just such a big stone, and—"

"If I wanted to kill you, I could make it fly *at* you." The stone rises another foot off the floor, then starts hovering in my direction.

"Fine." I hurry through the doorway. "Thanks for not dropping it."

Not dignifying that with a reply, Nina lowers the slab into place and leads us into her living room, where she gestures for us to sit on what looks like an IKEA futon. In general, her décor appears to be of minimalist persuasion, with a sort of New Age vibe.

"A drink?" A bottle of wine rises from the bar on its own and uncorks itself.

I shake my head. "Not on duty."

"Don't mind if I do," Kit says.

A glass flies up from the nearby table, the bottle pours wine into it in the air, and the glass glides into Kit's outstretched hand.

"Not just raw power but fine control," Felix mutters. "Impressive."

"How can I help?" Nina asks.

"Can you tell us what you were doing when Gemma was killed?" I ask. "It happened—"

"I know when," she says, her expression darkening. "Does this mean I'm a suspect?"

"Don't piss her off," Felix whispers. "She could go Darth Vader on your ass and choke you with her power."

"Everyone on the Council is a suspect," I say carefully, not loving the picture Felix paints. "I'm merely starting with whoever had the ability to easily commit the last crime, but—"

"She asked me the same thing." Kit's form flows into Colton, then Eduardo. "Others as well, and that's just so far."

Nina's face clears, and she peers at me curiously. "You're a dreamwalker, right? Just like Leal?"

"We have the same power, yes, though I'm not sure how I measure up to his abilities."

She pours herself a glass of wine in the air and sips it thoughtfully.

Could she be the culprit, after all? She's not answering my question, and overall looks like she's hiding something.

"So," I prompt cautiously, "when Gemma—"

"I was doing yoga," she says abruptly.

Huh. I suppose that goes with the New Age vibe. "Anything specific you recall about that session?"

"This is so you can verify in my dreams if I'm telling the truth, right?"

"Exactly. The more details, the easier my job."

"I was in this room." She makes a gesture that causes all the furniture to float up several feet, clearing the floor—as she presumably would do for yoga practice. "I started with child's pose, then flowed into downward-facing dog." She throws more yoga poses at me, and I note each one in my phone. "At the end, I always do a relaxing corpse pose. I'd never reflected on how macabre that sounds until saying it just now—as a murder suspect," she adds, fiddling with the hoop in her nostril.

"You won't be a suspect for long," I promise. "Now that I know what you were up to, I can easily clear you."

"Right. In my dreams." Her dark eyebrows pull together. "Talk to me once you have no doubt of my guilt." She glances at Kit. "Privately."

Okay, what is *that* about?

I throw out a wild guess. "If you know who the real killer is, I can ask Kit to leave so we can—"

"I don't." She lowers the furniture back to the floor. "But we should talk. Afterward. Now if that's all, you'd better go talk to the rest of your suspects."

Kit stands up and sets her glass on the nearby table. "Thanks for the drink."

Our exit beneath the giant rock comes with a lot less fear.

"Kain's next," Kit says over her shoulder. "Hopefully he's back."

Before I can ask her where he'd gone, I spot a familiar figure coming down the corridor.

It's Filth, and he's giving me the evil eye.

"If it isn't the blood whore," he sneers when I'm within earshot. "Do let me know when you're ready for an undiluted fix."

I give him a placid stare. "Did you have any trouble getting the tampons, errand boy?"

Felix chuckles. "I forgot to tell you, I did make the checkout process harder for him—and there *is* a video."

Filth's fangs emerge. "I'll rip your—"

"No, you won't." Kit has turned into Kain.

"Speaking of ripping…" I look over Filth's sickly body. "Are you strong enough to rip someone in half?"

Kain Kit gives me a glare. "Don't antagonize him further."

"I'm asking as part of my investigation," I say, stretching the truth only a little. "It's a compliment, in a way. You said only the oldest vampires can accomplish such a feat."

"I've never tried to rip something in half. I suspect I'd greatly enjoy it, though." Filth gives me a deliberate once-over.

"That's nice," I say. "So what were you doing when Gemma was killed?"

"I was on a job with Kain." His fangs go away. "Someone without a Mandate stepped out of line, so we put him down like a rabid dog—the way we should've done with you."

"Thank you," I say calmly. "Sounds like you and Kain are each other's alibis. I hope you don't take it personally when I verify your story with Kain and in the dream world."

"You keep doing your pretend work. I'll wait until you fail." He brushes past us.

Kit turns back into her usual self and heads down the corridor to a black metal door. She knocks on it, and just as I catch up, Kain opens the door.

"She's yours again," Kit says. She turns to me. "I have some business to attend to, but I guess I'll see you in my dreams?"

I smile. "Thanks for your help."

"How goes the investigation?" Kain asks, gesturing for me to come inside.

He leads me into a sleek kitchen that reminds me of Colton's, just with a normal-sized table and chairs, and sits me down on a stylish black bar stool as I bring him up to speed on everything except the alibi Filth provided a minute ago. It's unlikely their stories won't match, but if so, that would be a major breakthrough. And I can't dismiss what Kit said about Kain's potential culpability.

The vampire opens a bottle of distilled water and puts it in front of me like a bartender. "Tonight, you'll establish a dream link with everyone on the Council. You'll dreamwalk in everyone you've spoken with thus far, plus a few people I personally suspect."

I greedily gulp the water. "Actually, I might have to do one or the other. There's a limit to how much I can use my power in a day, and setting up links is draining. Why don't I just set up links and dreamwalk in the people I've spoken with so far?"

"I want everyone on the Council to feel as though their dreams can be invaded at any moment." He perches on a stool next to me. "Then, if you have enough power, we can dive deeper into the suspects."

"You don't think it was Eduardo, Colton, Kit, or Nina who killed Gemma?"

"Doesn't matter what I think. Just do as I say."

I swallow a less-than-polite retort. "Sure. By the way—and this is mere formality—can you tell me what *you* were doing when Gemma was killed?"

He doesn't blink. "No problem. Use your power to clear me of suspicion right away, so you can speak to me more openly about the case."

"I will—though it could mean I won't be able to set up links with everyone on the Council today."

"Fine, fine. Can always leave people with strong alibis for later." He gets up, takes a blood bag from the fridge, and tosses it into the microwave. "It'd been quite a day. An insane werewolf from one of the Otherlands arrived at the local airport and attacked the humans there. We had to kill him and glamour hundreds of victims to forget the incident."

"Wow," Felix whispers.

Indeed. I wouldn't want to be an Enforcer, that's for sure.

"JFK airport?" I ask as the microwave beeps.

"That's the one." He takes out his snack and returns to his seat next to me. Ripping open a corner of the bag, he takes a big gulp from it.

I suppress my instinctive disgust at the sight of him consuming someone's bodily fluids. "Can you tell me something about the event that makes it memorable?"

"How often do you think insane Cognizant show up on this world?"

"No idea. Not often?"

"This was the first incident I'd been involved with. Newcomers such as yourself usually keep their heads down. They know that without the Mandate, they can be killed without due process just for being here."

He downs the rest of the blood bag, no doubt to illustrate what would happen to someone with yummy blood in such circumstances. If it's a threat, it works well.

I force my voice to stay steady. "That's enough detail."

"Good." He slides down from his stool and extends his hand. "Come with me."

I look at his hand, the very one that only a second ago held a bag containing someone's blood. He gives me a look that seems to suggest the handholding isn't optional. Inwardly cringing and making plans to use a whole bottle of sanitizer later, I limply take his hand and let him lead me deeper into the apartment.

Oh, puck.

The last room we enter is his bedroom.

A vampire's bedroom, or what passes for one, given that they don't need to sleep.

My heart rate skyrockets. This place looks too much like the dream room where I do Ariel's exposure therapy. Instruments for erotic and not-so-erotic torture glitter and gleam everywhere. The bed itself has iron rings built into the headboard and the base, clearly to make it easier to chain people for nefarious purposes.

On Gomorrah, everyone thinks vampires are kinky, and this one is playing right into that stereotype.

Kain lets go of my hand and looks between me and the bed with a strange expression.

I loudly swallow.

Is he hungry… or worse?

CHAPTER EIGHTEEN

CAN'T BE HUNGRY. He just drank that whole bag, and why ruin his appetite before dinner, right? Which means—

Before I can complete this thought, Kain climbs onto the bed.

Does he think I'll follow him? Not in a million years.

He sprawls on his back, his pale eyes intent on my face. "I know it sounds crazy, but I'm a little uneasy about what's to come."

Uneasy about what? Inviting me for an exchange of bodily fluids?

He swipes at his forehead, brushing back a string of limp brown hair. "I haven't slept for decades. I can't remember the last time I dreamed at all, and now I'm about to do it with a witness."

I blink as everything clicks into place. He wants me to clear him of wrongdoing *right now*. Whew—that makes more sense. Damn sleep deprivation is making me paranoid.

"I'll be invisible as you dream," I say as soothingly as I can with all that adrenaline in my system. "There's also a good chance you'll forget the dream when you wake up."

He nods and closes his eyes. "Give me a few seconds."

I've seen this before. Vampires don't need to sleep, but when they want to, they drift right off, no mooft counting required. Before long, Kain's breathing changes, and a few minutes later, I see his eyes moving rapidly behind his eyelids in the telltale sign of REM sleep.

"Wow," I mutter, "if only it were that easy with everyone else."

Felix doesn't reply. In fact, now that I'm paying attention, I hear faint snoring on the other end of our connection. Of course, he *has* been awake all this time. Oh, well. I guess he'll miss this.

Reaching out with the hand Kain contaminated earlier, I touch his forehead and fall into his dream world.

———

I FIND myself in Kain's kitchen.

He's talking animatedly on the phone—I think it's about taxes—so I make myself invisible before he can spot me. Decades without sleep and his subconscious concocts a dream this boring? How disappointing. In any case, I can breathe a sigh of relief. He was indeed already in REM sleep, so I've skipped over the dangerous subdreams. And unlike Bernard, Kain seems to have no deep-seated nightmares to worry about—nightmares I would be in right now if they existed. Unless he *really* dislikes talking on the phone to his accountant? It wouldn't be that crazy. When it comes to death and taxes, vampires don't have to worry too much about the former.

I grope for my empty wrist. Because I'm in Kain's dream and not Pom's, Pom doesn't instantly show up here. That's probably for the best, as I think he'd prefer to miss the bit with the werewolf.

Dream manipulation time.

I manifest the date and time I want and morph the environment to an international airport at midday. I always do this as smoothly as I can manage. In this case, the kitchen already has barstools, so it becomes an airport bar. Kain doesn't question this new reality, so I slowly add noises of talking people and clanking glasses.

Still good. Kain keeps chatting on the phone.

I end the call.

He shrugs and leaves the bar as if it were the most natural thing in the world. I get bolder, adding details from his story: screams of bloody murder from the werewolf's victims, panicked humans, fellow Enforcers rushing into action. It's more art than science, giving the dreamer enough details that they can run with the dream from there, their subconscious adding in whatever is needed. As Kain begins to do this, I relax and watch the events unfold.

Foaming at the mouth, the wolf rips an old lady into pieces. Kain shoots it with a tranquilizer dart, and it lets go of the human and dashes for Terminal 8. Filth and a few other Enforcers are already waiting there, holding stun guns.

Uninterested in the bloody outcome, I ask myself a single question: Is this dream a memory? My power confirms it, just as it did in Bernard's dream. Good. If Kain were the killer, I'd be in a vulnerable real-world position, being in his dungeon bedroom and all.

Job done, I yank myself from the dream and into the waking world.

————

BEFORE KAIN WAKES UP, I use what's left of the sanitizer to finally clean my hand.

After I'm done, I softly call, "Kain. Wake up."

Fangs out, he leaps off the bed as if to battle for his life. Spotting me, he halts, recognition appearing in his eyes.

"You're officially not guilty of killing Gemma," I tell him. "This clears Firth and a bunch of other Enforcers, too."

He massages the bridge of his nose. "I was in my kitchen and the airport. That makes no sense, but at the time it was so logical and real. I somehow knew the date and time without looking at any clocks. Felt it, almost."

I nod. "Dreamers almost never ask themselves, 'How did I get here?' Those who do sometimes realize they're in a dream. It's called lucid dreaming, and it can cause problems for me, so I'm glad it's rare."

"I think I could go for centuries without dreaming again." He strides out of the bedroom, and I gladly follow.

Without stopping, he heads out of the apartment and down a spindly corridor teeming with monks. When we reach a dilapidated wooden door, he opens it. "This is your new quarters."

The place looks spartan, with just a small bed and a wooden table inside a small windowless room, but it's luxurious compared to the dungeon cell. It even has a washroom with a shower and a proper toilet.

"The stuff you wanted is there." He gestures at a pile of plastic bags behind the bed. "You have a little time while I make the arrangements for the Councilors to go to sleep."

When he leaves, I rummage through the shopping bags. Yep, everything I asked for is here, adult diapers and laxatives included. I fish out the bananas, water, and sanitizer and set it all on the table.

Vampire blood has many side effects, one of them being the suppression of hunger along with sleep. While on it, I eat based on common sense—a few hundred calories every few hours. I'm actually way behind on my quota, so I sanitize seven bananas and force myself to eat them one after another—which takes twenty minutes that feel like five hours.

Feeling like a stuffed ape, I chase the fruit with plenty of water and use the toilet while I have it handy. A side effect of eating so rarely and being constantly dehydrated is that I don't have to do this often.

The drowsiness of a food coma hits me so hard I have to slap my face to wake myself up. But I can't sleep now. Kain will be back any second. I sanitize my hands until my skin feels raw, then pull out the vial with the diluted vampire blood. Keeping it out of sight of Felix's camera, I take the tiniest sip I can manage.

Instantly, I'm wide awake. A wave of orgasmic pleasure sweeps over me, double the intensity of the last time.

Puck.

Imagining the wall is Filth's face, I slam my fist into it as hard as I can. There's no pain at all, only pressure, and the pleasure continues unabated.

Double puck.

I smash my fist into the same spot again and again, leaving bloody prints on the stone. When the skin splits on my knuckles, it mends instantly—the healing properties of vampire blood. If I break any bones, they will mend also, all without a hint of pain.

Eventually, the pleasure subsides, leaving only the equally unwelcome sexual arousal.

Wow, this time was bad. Even diluted, it's affecting me almost beyond my control. I've got to solve this case and save Mom so I can get off the vile substance, else I might end up following in Ariel's footsteps. For now, I dilute the half-empty vial with water until it's full again. Maybe an even more diluted version will work more like it used to?

Now I wish Kain would come back so I could do something useful.

Actually, there *is* something I can do. If Kit has gone to bed, which would be reasonable, I could check if she's behind all the crimes. Despite what she said about Tatum, she's still one of my main suspects.

Touching Pom, I go into a trance and meet Pom's dream form in my palace. He floats contentedly in the air, waving a furry paw at me in greeting.

"I'm going into Kit's dreams." I give myself my fiery hair. "I'd like some privacy."

If Kit didn't lie, her dreams will be X-rated, and that's not an experience I want to share with a fuzzy creature with no visible genitals.

"I'll go play Jenga," he says. A tower of wooden blocks appears on the floor. "Go do what you do."

I pat his head and hasten to the tower of sleepers.

I'm lucky for a change. Kit is here sleeping, and so is Felix—my earlier guess was right.

I touch Kit's forehead and end up smack in the middle of an orgy featuring every type of Cognizant I can think of, plus some I've never seen. Alrighty, then. It should be easy to morph this dream into the situation Kit described earlier.

I begin by giving Kit a sense that this is all happening on the date and time when Gemma was ripped apart. Then I remove a dozen or so participants and turn one of the remaining ones into Lola.

Almost there. The problem is that this Lola isn't doing what Kit described. Feeling like a total perv, I take control of Dream Lola and have her ask Kit to turn into whatever she described to me earlier, making sure to request the right number of phalluses while I'm at it.

The scene starts to look like what Kit described—and as soon as it does, I know it's a memory.

Whew. As much as I want this investigation to be over, Kit is my friend, so I'm really glad she's not the culprit.

On the way out of Kit's dream world, I contemplate talking to Felix but decide against it. Between the vampire blood and Kit's dreams, I'm too sexed up to face him.

But there's something I *can* do to take the edge off.

With a deep, delicious inhalation, I think back to the luxurious bedroom Valerian created around us using his illusionist powers. I begin the recreation with the big bed swathed in silk sheets and covered in rose petals before creating the man himself, in all his (probably fake) glory.

"Hi, beautiful," Dream Valerian murmurs. "Finally found time for me?"

"Come closer." I make my clothes disappear with a flick of my powers.

Ripping the buttons off his shirt, he strides toward me.

My overclocked libido goes into overdrive.

Dream Valerian kisses me deeper than last time, his right hand stroking my lower back as his left slides—

"What is the meaning of this?" Kain's voice sounds like thunder.

With a sigh, I pull myself away from the dream world and open my eyes to Kain's fury.

"You said your power has limits," he growls with a lisp, due to his extended fangs. "How dare you waste it on pleasuring yourself?"

What the hell? How does he know? Can he smell it on me?

Yuck. I need to bathe my brain in sanitizer.

Seeing his eyes turn into mirrors, I blurt, "I was doing my job."

His eyes fade to normal, giving me hope that I'll never learn what he intended to glamour me into doing.

"Explain," he hisses.

"Kit. I verified her alibi, and it checks out."

"I see." His fangs retreat. "I spoke to Lola the day after the murder, but it's good to confirm Kit's story. That nymph would say anything to protect her insatiable girlfriend."

He knew? Then again, Kit has never been shy about her adventures. Oh, well. I grab a water bottle and pocket my hand sanitizer. "I'm ready to connect with others and check alibis."

"Let's go to my quarters."

His quarters again? Why?

Given the earlier threat of glamour, I don't ask.

When we reach our destination, he leads me toward his dungeon/bedroom—which makes all my earlier concerns resurface.

Just before entering the dreaded room, he wheels around, so quickly I nearly smash into him.

"This is going to stay between us," he says harshly. "Understood?"

CHAPTER NINETEEN

I STARE AT HIM, my heart rate doubling.

"It's a delicate situation," he continues. "The woman hates dreamwalkers with a passion."

I blink at him, even more confused.

"Just go inside," he snaps. "Go, or I'll make you."

With Pom turning pitch black on my wrist, I enter the cursed room and freeze, unable to believe what I'm seeing.

It's Gertrude.

She's lying on Kain's bed, staring emptily at the ceiling.

"She's my primary suspect," Kain says as though she's not there. "She envied Tatum and Ryan's marriage—don't ask me why—and she fiercely and openly despised Gemma. You already know how she feels about dreamwalkers."

"But no one died by rotting to death," I say.

"Of course not. She's not stupid enough to kill that way—she'd be the only suspect."

I peer at her unmoving body. "What's wrong with her?"

"I had to glamour her," Kain says. "She has a huge problem sleeping in front of others, to put it mildly."

"She's got good reason." I step to the side and back, putting him between me and Gertrude. "Between her REM Sleep Disorder and the gangrene-giving, it would be dangerous for any witnesses."

"And yet I'll make her sleep, and you'll check to make sure she's not behind the murders." He turns to the empty-eyed woman and instructs in a honey-laced voice, "Gertrude, cuff your right ankle to the right bottom corner of the bed."

She sits up and does as ordered. Another command, and she locks her left ankle and right hand, leaving herself mostly spread-eagled. I expect Kain to do something about her left hand, but he doesn't.

"With that arm free, she can still grab one of us and make whatever she touches rot," I tell him. "You've got to lock it up."

"Do *you* want to lock it up?" he asks with a sneer. "I'm not getting anywhere near her skin."

So vampires can rot. What a gross discovery.

I look Gertrude over. With her short skirt and sleeveless top, she's showing way too much skin to approach without a hazmat suit.

"Gertrude, sleep," Kain croons.

She closes her eyes right away, her breathing evening out.

Wow, I'd give a lot for that particular power.

"Now do your thing," Kain orders.

I gingerly step closer to observe her eyelids.

"What's the holdup?" he asks.

I turn back toward him. "I have to wait until she's in REM sleep."

"Isn't REM sleep when that free arm becomes a problem?"

I sigh. "If I go in now, I'll have to deal with the subdream, which carries its own danger."

He raises an eyebrow.

"I could die in the dream world."

The eyebrow goes almost comically high.

"If I die there, I'll become homicidally insane."

The eyebrow comes back down and meets its neighbor in a frown. "Is that how things work for all dreamwalkers?"

"As far as I know."

Kain's gaze sharpens. "Could that have happened to Leal? As in, he died during dreamwalking and became—"

"Didn't Gemma get killed *after* he was already dead? Besides, are you suggesting he killed himself using those birds?"

"We do have to consider the possibility that there might've been more than one killer," he says with less enthusiasm.

"If it was Leal, the murders would've been a lot more brutal," I say. "All of you would've known he'd gone crazy. He'd have acted like a puck."

"I see," Kain says. "Still, I say it's a good thing you've been focusing most of your attention on Gemma's murder."

"Right." I go back to watching Gertrude's eyelids.

"So what are you waiting for?"

"I just told you. The subdream—"

"Go in," he snaps. "And don't die. Waiting is riskier, trust me."

I back away from the bed as his eyes turn to mirrors. "I'll do it—"

His eyes fade to normal.

"—but there're a few more problems. If I survive the subdream section, my power will force Gertrude to snap into REM sleep. That means her loose hand will become an issue."

"I'll pull you away from her as soon as I see signs of REM sleep," he says. "You can then come back into her dreams from a distance, as I know you can do."

He knows? I was trying to keep that under wraps.

"That might work," I say grudgingly. "But there's another, bigger problem. For me to use my power, I have to touch her—and if I touch her, I'll lose my finger." I glance warily at Gertrude's exposed skin.

"Can you enter someone's dream by touching their hair?" he asks. "I've seen Gertrude zone out while one of the monks was giving her a trim, which tells me the hair should be safe to touch."

"'Should be' doesn't sound reassuring."

His eyes turn into slits. "Can you or can you not use hair to do your job?"

"No idea. In theory, I don't see why not. The body has hair all over, so I've probably done it inadvertently. But I've never tried it with the hair on someone's head, because that's a cesspool of dandruff, oil, mites, germs—"

Inside their slits, his eyes turn into mirrors again. "Bailey," he says in that special voice, "you'll touch the tips of Gertrude's hair, far from her skin. Now."

I attempt to fight the compulsion, but it overtakes me even faster than when he glamoured me before the Council meeting. My body moves forward on its own, my arm extends, and my finger lands on the strand of hair farthest away from Gertrude's face.

If my face were under my control, it would be cringing.

To my relief, my finger doesn't rot. Then again, maybe that's still to come.

"Bailey, I release you from glamour," Kain says ceremoniously. "Enter her dream now."

The only reason I don't explode into obscenities is that I'd wake Gertrude, and she'd rot me first, ask questions later.

"Stop it with the hesitation," Kain growls. "I told you I'll pull you away as soon as I see her eyelids move. Now do your job."

Fine. I hope this works, else I'm fairly sure he'll make me touch her where my finger would be in even more trouble.

Gritting my teeth so hard my jaw hurts, I will myself to enter Gertrude's dreams.

The hair is a go. I catch a whiff of ozone and experience the sensation of falling as the room darkens around me, propelling me into the familiar trance.

Now I just hope the subdream doesn't drive me insane.

CHAPTER TWENTY

I'M STANDING on a calm black ocean with magma skies above. In the distance, two creatures ride toward me astride some other kind of creatures, hooting out horrific battle cries as they come.

Something snakes from my wrist to the ground and grows into a furry unicorn.

"We'd better get out of here," I tell my new steed. "Whatever those things are, they don't sound friendly."

The unicorn snorts, and as soon as I clasp his neck, he gallops away so fast his hooves barely touch the water.

The battle cries, if that's what they are, draw closer behind us. They're terrifying. I imagine that's how pucks' teeth must sound scraping the bones of their victims. Still, for some reason, I can't shake the feeling that there's a message embedded in those ugly shrieks, just in a language I don't know.

Casting a glance over my shoulder, I take in the monstrosities. The mounts look like warthogs crossed with spiders, and their riders remind me of naked mole rats—only huge and with tentacles.

I speed up, but one of the pairs gains on us anyway. As it pulls up next to us, the second pair shrieks directly behind me.

A tentacle lassoes my neck. Before it gets the chance to rip me away, my mount veers sideways and spears the rider with his horn.

As the thing dies, the tentacle loosens its grip on my neck.

The riderless beast roars. With an angry flutter of nostrils, my unicorn rears, and I hold on to his furry mane for dear life as he smashes a hoof into its temple, killing it instantly before kicking the head of the warthog behind us. The beast staggers, mortally wounded, but its tentacled naked mole rat rider lands on its hind legs and bares its saber-like tusks at us.

My unicorn charges.

The mole rat dodges the horn and catches my wrist with a tentacle. Like a bungee cord, the tentacle contracts, pulling the vile creature toward me. I jerk my hand, but it's useless. The thing is already on me, its tusk piercing my neck.

Blood gushes out of the wound, and I start to feel woozy.

Ignoring the pain, I headbutt my opponent in its maw, launching it back. Since it's still attached to me by its tentacle, it doesn't fly far—but it's far enough.

With a twist of his neck, my unicorn shish-kebabs the creature, dealing it a deadly blow.

PANTING AND BLEEDING PROFUSELY, I look around at the reddish green walls and floating impossible objects.

Of course. This is my palace, and that bloody mess was another subdream.

Yet again, I didn't have any clue that I was dreaming. Why does this happen? What will it take for me to get a clue—Unicorn Pom farting rainbows?

I zoom out of my body and heal the neck and forehead wounds.

It's official: This is the closest I've ever gotten to dream death and the subsequent insanity.

Speaking of death, I've completely forgotten about Gertrude. Since I've just put her into REM sleep, she could touch me with her free hand at any moment.

I jump back into my body and wake myself up.

CHAPTER TWENTY-ONE

MY EYES open to the sight of Gertrude's unbound hand swinging erratically.

Puck, it's now flying my way.

Before I can even think the word *dodge*, someone forcefully jerks me back. Gertrude's hand zooms right by my nose.

I sway slightly in my new location, stunned. Did that touch my nose? If so, I'll lose it—in the best case.

Kain examines my face like a plastic surgeon prepping for a rhinoplasty. "You're fine. She didn't touch you."

"Fine?" I look at my finger that touched Gertrude's hair. Though unrotted, it's still unsanitized.

"Come." Kain leads me to the kitchen sink, takes the finger I touched her hair with, and pours dish detergent on it.

"Pucker," I hiss under my breath.

I scrub my hands for several minutes to stop myself from antagonizing a vampire, which is what I *really* want to do.

Kain hands me a roll of paper towels. I dry my hands and top it off with half a bottle of sanitizer.

"I assume you didn't get a chance to clear Gertrude," he says.

I shake my head, still too angry for words.

"Do so now. I don't want to keep her here any longer than necessary."

"There's a problem." I plop onto a barstool. "To make it fast and easy, I need to know what she did at the time of the murder. Otherwise, this might be a huge project."

"Oh, she told me that." He grabs another water bottle from the fridge and hands it to me. "She was watching a movie in her room."

"Alone?" I grudgingly take a sip of the water—no point in being dehydrated just because I'm mad at the vampire in front of me.

"Right, no witnesses." He leans against the counter. "Yet another reason I suspect her."

"Can you describe her room for me? And what movie was she watching?"

He describes her living room, then says, "The movie was *Catwoman*. I didn't realize we had that crap in our library."

"I've never seen it. What's it about?"

He waves a hand impatiently. "I haven't seen it either. It has a horrible reputation, to the point that I found it suspicious that Gertrude would watch it, of all things."

I pinch the bridge of my nose. "Well... just knowing that Catwoman's in it might be enough."

"Okay, good."

"Can you go watch Gertrude?" I say. "Let me know if she wakes up."

If he realizes I don't want him to see how I do my magic from a distance, he doesn't show it.

As soon as he's gone, I stroke Pom's fur a few times to calm myself and slide into the trance.

———

POM IS pitch black when I reappear in my dream palace. "That was some subdream, wasn't it?"

I take flight. "Let's talk on the way to the tower of sleepers. I assume you also had no idea it was a dream?"

He catches up to me in the air, his fur now a dark beet hue. "Yep, no clue."

"Even though you were a unicorn?" I make a miniature replica of the unicorn fly next to us.

"You didn't know it was a dream either." He zips forward to float in front of my face. "And you're the one with dream powers."

"But all you do is sleep and dream. Out of the two of us, you have more chances to realize that a subdream is just a dream—and once you do, you could tell me that."

"Well, I didn't know." The tips of his ears look like carrots. "Maybe next time?"

"I don't want there to be a next time." I enter the tower. "That was too close for me."

We fly in sullen silence as I locate Gertrude. As we approach, I spot the telltale miniature dark clouds flying above her head.

"Not this again," I mutter. As with Bernard, I'll have to deal with her trauma loop before I can verify her innocence.

Fine. Given the complication, I'll do a little more prep.

I locate the sleeping Felix and enter his dreams.

———

FELIX IS PLAYING a violent video game with his second roommate, a girl I jokingly call Princess Peach. They each have a pet on their laps—a cat for him and a chinchilla for her.

Felix unleashes a flurry of onscreen kicks and punches, ripping the head off Peach's character.

Interesting. With so much blood and gore, I'd expect him to faint, but he's grinning instead. Either game violence doesn't feel real to him, or it's because this is a dream. Probably the latter. In the real world, his opponent would anticipate his every move with her seer powers.

I clear my throat.

They both look at me, but only Felix's eyes have real intelligence in them.

"This is a dream," I say. "In case that wasn't obvious."

Felix jumps to his feet. "I fell asleep?"

I transport the two of us to my cloud environment. "You did."

He adjusts his "there is no spoon" t-shirt. "I'm sorry. I drank two Red Bulls and—"

"Don't worry about it." I sink into my cloud chair. "I need your help. Have you seen the movie *Catwoman*?"

He plops onto the therapy couch. "It's crap."

Pom appears next to me, and I idly fluff his fur. "I don't need your skills as a movie critic. I'm going into the dream of someone who saw this movie, and I need details."

"I think it had like a three point three out of ten on IMDb," he says, looking askance at Pom. "Halle Berry, the star of the film, was dishonored with a Razzie award for her performance."

"Okay, so it sounds like you at least know the actress who was in it." I lean forward. "What does she look like?"

He regards me thoughtfully. "A bit like you, actually."

Pom turns a curious light orange as I place him on my lap and tell Felix, "How about you picture her in your mind, so I can see for myself?"

I give him a moment before shooting him with a burst of power.

An attractive woman appears next to Pom. She's wearing the kind of leather suit that vampire addicts often wear back on Gomorrah. Must be the infamous catsuit.

Pom wrinkles his furry nose. "She doesn't look at all like Bailey."

I wistfully file away those perfect cheekbones into memory. "Yeah, she's way prettier."

"If you really need the plot, ask Ariel," Felix says, oblivious. "She loves anything to do with Batman and wouldn't have missed that movie no matter how bad it was."

"Good idea," I say. "Stay here and talk to Pom. I'll be back."

Before either of them can say anything, I return to the tower to see if Ariel is sleeping.

I'm in luck—she's here.

I touch her forehead and enter her dream.

———

AN ORC IS THROWING a giant fist at Ariel's jaw. She dodges it, pulls a huge knife from somewhere, and spears his fist in a swift motion. The orc roars and tries to kick her—but she dodges that too.

Wow. Ariel is very good at this, even adjusting for the embellishment so common in dreams. I might visit her dreams later to learn some of her fighting tricks. For now, I need to pick her brain, so I gently help her defeat the orc, and when he falls down, I step in front of her.

"Bailey." Ariel sheathes her knife. "What are you doing here?"

I smile. "And where is *here*?"

Ariel strains to answer but doesn't come up with anything.

"It's common not to question the location of a dream," I say.

She examines the dead orc. "This is a dream?"

"Orcs don't come to Earth." I make the dead body disappear. "Also, why would one attack you?"

"Right, it *is* a dream." Her perfectly smooth forehead creases. "Is it time for my therapy?"

"No, I need you for something." I guide her to my cloud office, where Felix and Pom are floating in the air over a game of checkers.

"Oh, hey, Felix. And Pomsie!" Ariel snatches my furry symbiont from the air, grinning like a five-year-old opening a present. "I missed you."

Pom turns the deep purple of happiness in her arms.

Whew. At least it's not coral pink. It would be a bit awkward, though understandable, if he got turned on by Ariel. I guess their love is platonic, at least on Pom's side. They met after I'd decided Ariel might benefit from something akin to pet therapy, and they got along so well that I eventually had to ask Pom to avoid her sessions, lest she do nothing but pet him nonstop.

"Did Ariel tell you?" Felix's unibrow dances a jig on his forehead.

"Tell her what?" Ariel clutches Pom tighter.

"*Catwoman.*" Felix looks from me to her. "Bailey wanted to know the plot of that atrocity."

"I didn't get a chance to explain." I plop into my chair. "Have you seen that movie?"

She squeezes Pom again. If he weren't a dream creature, her enthusiastic smooshing might've broken his back by now. "Felix knows I have."

"Told you." Felix grins at me. "Probably liked it, too."

"I did not." Done with squeezing, she gently scratches Pom's belly, which promptly turns blue.

"You liked *Batman and Robin.*" Felix sprawls on the therapy couch. "That isn't much better."

"*Liked* is a strong word." She gives Pom the under-the-chin scratch that cats like so much. "In my defense, it had Batman in it. And George Clooney. And—"

"Guys, I need the plot of *Catwoman* for an important job," I say. "Please."

Ariel casts a warning glare at Felix and launches into a summary of the movie.

"Thanks," I say when she's done. "Now I can leave you all to hang out here as I take care of my business, or I can let you wake up. Whichever you prefer."

"I'll stay," Felix says.

"Me too." Ariel rubs her cheek against Pom's fur.

"And me," Pom purrs.

Felix motions to the cloud and the ocean below. "How will this work?".

"When I'm done with my business, I'll wake myself up," I say. "And because I pulled you in, you'll disappear from here at that point, which means waking up."

Felix nods. "Got it. And we'll see you in person soon. Remember I told you about Ariel's cousin's best friend's daughter's Mandate ceremony? I'm definitely joining so I can look at that dreamwalker's comms for you."

"Sounds great," I say. "See you both then."

I take myself into the tower of sleepers, muttering under my breath, "Assuming I'm not dead."

Making my way to Gertrude's bed, I shimmer into invisibility and touch her forehead.

Trauma loop, here I come.

CHAPTER TWENTY-TWO

THE GERTRUDE in this dream looks younger. She's sitting on a couch with a handsome blond guy, who's sipping from a bottle of beer as she gazes longingly at his lips.

He offers her the bottle. "Want some?"

She recoils as if it were poison. "I need to be in absolute control of my faculties to suppress my power."

His grin is cocky. "All so I can touch you, right?"

She takes the bottle from his hand, puts it on the table, and kisses him. As they proceed to make out, I realize two things: this is a memory, as most trauma loops are, and the guy isn't rotting despite his contact with her. I guess gangrene-givers can turn off their powers. It makes sense. If they couldn't, how would they reproduce?

Speaking of reproduction, the guy fishes out a condom from his pocket, and they take things all the way.

I yawn, watching them. They're not very creative—definitely nothing like some of the dreams I've seen. If I ever get around to doing this with Dream Valerian, there will be a lot more acrobatics.

"You have to leave now," Gertrude says sleepily when they're done.

He gives her puppy eyes. "Can't we spoon for a few minutes?"

"Two minutes. Put a blanket between us, just in case."

He does as she says, and they cuddle through the blanket until her breathing changes. When he notices she's asleep, he carefully climbs off the couch and starts picking up his clothing. Before he can put on his pants, she sinks into REM sleep. He's none the wiser.

At this point, the dream isn't a memory but Gertrude's extrapolation of what must have happened.

Her arm swings wildly, the way it did when she nearly took out my nose. By pure chance, her hand connects with his ankle and, as if it has a mind of its own, wraps around it.

The rot is instant. In mere moments, his leg looks as if it's been infected for weeks.

He clutches his leg, screaming.

She stirs as if she's waking up, but her grip doesn't release, and the gangrene spreads and spreads until his screaming ceases and he collapses in a rotten heap.

The dream is a memory again.

Gertrude opens her eyes—and jumps off the couch, emitting a scream of such horror and agony that my chest aches with genuine sympathy.

However awful she was to me at the trial, she doesn't deserve this.

But this is my chance to do what I came here for, so I make the guy's corpse disappear, put her back on the couch, and make her fall back asleep. I then change the room to look as Kain described, moving the couch, adjusting the clock's date and time to that of Gemma's murder, and putting *Catwoman* on pause on the TV.

Then I use my power to "wake" Gertrude here in the dream world.

Remote control in hand, she rubs her eyes in confusion, her anguish gone for now. As I hoped, she thinks she's snoozed before starting her movie. Later, when she really wakes up, she'll process the horrific incident I just witnessed, as much as such a thing can be processed.

To my relief, Gertrude falls into the new dream perfectly. She unpauses the movie and watches it, everything else forgotten. It doesn't take long before I see that watching this movie is indeed a memory.

Kain was wrong to suspect her. Her alibi checks out.

A part of me is disappointed. Given how much she seems to hate me for little reason, it would've made life easier if she were the culprit. Still, after seeing that trauma loop, I understand why she's so angry with anyone who can't help her sleep condition.

Oh, well.

Time to wake up.

I OPEN my eyes in Kain's sleek kitchen and head over to his bedroom, where he's supposed to be keeping an eye on Gertrude. I find him diligently engaged in that duty, standing over the bed like a sentinel.

"Hey," Felix says in my earpiece. "I just woke up."

Ignoring him, I tell Kain, "Gertrude isn't guilty. She really *was* watching a movie, like she said."

Kain curses under his breath. He looks ready to kill someone.

"What now?" I ask cautiously.

"I'll take you to deal with the next sleeper, then come back to clean up this mess." He strides out of the room.

I speed after him. "How?"

"I'll use glamour on Gertrude to make her forget what just happened," he throws over his shoulder as we exit his quarters.

"Won't she get suspicious if she's the only person not to have to undergo a dreamwalk?"

"I'll tell her she'll be the last one." He covers the corridor with long strides. "And we'll find the real killer before that."

"Assuming you do," Felix says as I strive to keep up without breaking into a jog. Thankfully, Kain slows a bit as we make the next turn.

"Where are we going?" I ask breathlessly.

"Colton's," he replies and speeds up again. "He's the only one of your suspects available tonight."

Puck it. I launch into a full-out run to catch up with him. "What do you mean?"

"Eduardo left on pack business, and Nina said she's going on some important trip to the Otherlands."

Panting, I pull up next to him. "You don't find that suspicious?"

"A little." He slows down a bit to look at me. "They know they'll have to undergo a dreamwalk tomorrow night."

"But what if they don't come back?"

He stops next to the massive wooden door. "In that case, I'll consider the case closed and the problem solved. Our main priority is stopping the murders. Justice is a distant second."

He pushes open the door and leads me to the giant's bedroom.

"Wow," Felix says. "I think that's two California king beds."

Yep, I can see where one bed ends and the other begins. I guess no one on this world makes beds for people Colton's size.

"He's not in REM sleep," I whisper to Kain. "You go deal with Gertrude, and I'll wait for my moment."

He leaves as I perch on the edge of the bed to watch Colton's closed eyes—a boring enough activity that a yawn tugs at my jaw despite the vampire blood I recently consumed.

"That dream session with Ariel and Pom was so cool," Felix says—a welcome distraction for once. He proceeds to tell me what they did while I was dealing with Gertrude: mostly goofing around.

After a few long minutes, Kain comes back and eyes me impatiently. I point at Colton's eyelids and shrug. If I weren't afraid to wake up the giant, I'd explain that REM sleep typically happens around ninety minutes after someone first falls sleep.

Kain makes his way over to a corner and becomes very still, like an alabaster statue. Must be some weird vampire meditation.

I turn my attention back to Colton. After what feels like an hour, his eyelids finally indicate REM sleep—though if I had my way, I'd be using equipment to know for sure. If I get this wrong, I'll have to deal with the subdream again. Still, I'm pretty sure he's dreaming. His eyes, like the rest of him, are ginormous. The movement is hard to miss.

Carefully, I touch the back of the giant's hand and plummet into the dream world.

———

"ARIEL AND FELIX ARE SO FUN," Pom pants excitedly as I appear in my dream palace lobby. "You've got to bring them back some day."

"I will," I tell him as I head to the tower of sleepers. "Tell me what you guys did."

I barely listen as he repeats some of the stuff Felix told me. I'm contemplating a theory that's been brewing in my head since we left Gertrude's room.

There's a way Kain could still be behind the murders despite his alibi. What if he used glamour to get others to do his dirty work and forget it ever happened? After all, he was able to glamour Gertrude, a fellow Council member. Then again, there's no way he's powerful enough to do it to anyone he wants. He was only able to glamour *me* thanks to my vampire blood consumption.

Hmm. Could Gertrude also be on the blood? If I suffered from her condition, I might go that route to avoid sleep as much as possible.

Either way, I'm proceeding with my current plan of action. If Kain has planted a fake alibi in someone's head, it won't check out in the dream world. In fact, I should see if I can retrieve a memory of being glamoured. I've never tried that, but it could work.

Thus determined, I locate sleeping Colton in the tower.

"Huh," Pom says. "The bed grew to fit him."

I'm not surprised. "The nook, too. That's the beauty of the dream world for you."

The good news is that no trauma loop clouds gather above Colton, so this will be a get-in, get-out situation.

I turn invisible and enter his dream.

Around us is a world lacking any technological advancements, even modest ones like the tech on Earth. Instead, I spot mud huts the size of high-rise buildings, dirt roads the width of a large speedway, enormous windmills, and plainly dressed giants walking to and fro.

Colton is trudging down the street, looking very small next to his kin. I guess it makes sense for him to be tiny. In order to live on Earth, he has to pass for a human. If he were actually human, though, he'd probably have serious pituitary gland issues.

Beginning my work, I draw in a deep fog to obscure the huts and the people. I thin the crowds on the streets and remove the huts completely, replacing them with a hilly landscape dotted with mushrooms. Finally, I set the date and time and add in the goats.

As if it were the goal all along, Colton begins serenely herding the beasts.

Yep, this is memory. Another person with an alibi.

Disappointed, I wake up.

———

WAVING FOR KAIN TO FOLLOW, I tiptoe out of Colton's bedroom and head directly for the exit.

Once we're outside the giant's quarters, I sanitize my finger. "He's not guilty. This doesn't look good for Eduardo and Nina."

Kain looks grim. "Just connect with as many Councilors as you can. Albina is nearby, so you can start with her."

I don't object, and he leads me to a regular-sized steel door, which we enter.

Albina isn't in her bed. Instead, there's a note on the pillow:

Kain, I'm very sorry, but something came up. I'll have to participate in the dream investigation tomorrow night.

Regards, Albina

"Sketchy," I say. "Is she strong enough to rip someone apart?"

"No." Kain heads out of Albina's place. "She can break matter into nothing. If she'd used her power, we would've thought the victim had disappeared without a trace. It would've been dumb of her to leave bodies behind."

We head to another subject's quarters as I ask, "Isn't it always a bad idea to leave bodies behind?"

"Unless you're Albina, it might be hard to get rid of a body in this castle. But you have a point. It's possible that the murderer is making a statement by leaving the bodies like this—in which case, it could be Albina. Somehow."

We stop next to a new wooden door, and he holds it open for me.

"Is Gertrude on vampire blood?" I ask as casually as I can.

"Indeed." He frowns. "Firth is the supplier—and the only reason I allow it is that it gives me power over her."

"Is anyone else on the Council on vampire blood?" I ask, still striving for casualness.

"Not that I know of." His fangs extend. "And Gertrude is the only person on the Council I can glamour the way I did earlier. I couldn't, for example, make Colton rip Gemma apart."

"Of course he'd say that," Felix whispers. "If I were you, I wouldn't dismiss that theory so quickly."

Ignoring Felix, I scowl at Kain. "Don't get touchy. Isn't it my job to think of all possibilities?"

"I'd rather you focus on the part of your job that's in there." He nods at the apartment.

As I step past him to enter, his fangs go away.

The sleeper in this bedroom is Isis, the Councilor who committed to healing Mom when I successfully accomplish my job.

Better be on my best behavior.

Silently, I wait until Isis goes into REM sleep before I enter the dream world. Once there, I check to make sure she shows up in the tower of sleepers and get back out, moving carefully in order not to wake her. I'll only snoop on Isis's dreams if explicitly ordered. Her power is too valuable for me to upset her. In fact, if she turns out to be the killer, I might blackmail her to save Mom instead of telling the Council about her guilt. Not that I think a healer is likely to be behind it.

The sleeper Kain takes me to next isn't familiar to me. Again, we wait for REM sleep, then I make the link and get out of the dream world.

The next Councilor I recognize. It's Hekima, the grandfatherly illusionist. He reaches another phase of REM sleep in minutes, and I pop into his dream and right back out again, as I did with the other Councilors.

The following person I kind of know as well. Though we've never spoken personally, I've seen him in Ariel's dreams. His puckish—or more accurately, satyric—face is distinctive. It's Chester, and he's a probability manipulator—or trickster, as his kind are locally nicknamed. A probability manipulator isn't someone I'd want as an enemy, so I carefully make a connection and tiptoe out of his bedroom.

The next Councilor is a beautiful woman who takes over an hour to get to REM sleep.

The person after her only takes five minutes.

I keep making connections over and over, until we walk into the bedroom of a thin man who opens his eyes and glares at us.

"It's morning," Kain says as we scurry out of the thin guy's abode. "You'll have to continue tonight."

Yay, me. I get a little reprieve.

We head back toward my quarters.

"Was that most of them?" I ask when we get there.

"Ninety percent of the Council." He opens the door for me. "You thought you wouldn't have enough power, but what we actually ran out of is time."

I stop in the doorway. "I'm game to see if anyone is sleeping in."

He shakes his head. "I promised everyone you won't be an inconvenience. Besides, actually making a connection is less important than making them *think* you did so."

"What do you mean?" I enter the place and plop down on a chair.

He remains by the door. "My hope is that the killer thinks you're a threat. They'll move to eliminate the threat, and that's when they'll reveal themselves to me."

I scowl at him. "So I'm bait? You're hoping they'll try to kill me so you'll know who it is?"

"Me or one of the Enforcers will protect you," he says dismissively. "And you'll get your reward."

"If I live."

He gives me a level look. "I swear your mother will be healed even if you're dead."

"Well, that's morbidly reassuring," Felix whispers.

Some of my anger dissipates. "Thank you. That means a lot."

Not bothering with a "you're welcome," Kain leaves, and I hear the lock turn in the door.

I guess I'm a prisoner. Oh, well.

The first thing I do is grab some bananas and start munching, consuming one after another while ignoring Felix's jibes.

"When you're done with that monkey business, it would be a good time for a nap," he says when I get to banana number six. "I sure could use one."

I finish the banana, clean my hands, and take out my phone to text: *You go ahead.*

"I will," he says with a yawn. "Wait, why are you texting? Do you think there're listening devices in the room?"

Can't dismiss the possibility, I text. *If Kain doesn't trust me, I wouldn't put it past him.*

"Good point. Enjoy your nap." He yawns again. "Feel free to visit me in the dream world if you feel like it."

I make a thumbs-up gesture in front of my lapel camera.

"Talk later." I hear rustling as he puts down his headset.

I down some water and try to decide what to do next. Napping is out of the question; the vampire blood I imbibed won't let that happen. Since I haven't run out of power, I decide to finish Valerian's gig—then maybe reward myself with a visit to the dream version of my employer.

Petting Pom's fur, I enter the prerequisite trance. On the way to the tower of sleepers, I update Pom on the investigation and tell him what I'm about to do.

"You're lucky," he says when we reach Bernard's nook. "He's sleeping in today."

"I don't feel very lucky." I eye the clouds around Bernard's head. "His trauma loop consists of more than one dream, it seems."

"This one is less severe than the last," Pom says, sniffing at the clouds. "Still, I'm not going in there with you. Sorry."

I shrug and reach out to touch Bernard.

CHAPTER TWENTY-THREE

A WOMAN—BERNARD'S wife—is angrily packing a suitcase.

"Don't go." Bernard tugs on his messy beard, his hair disheveled around his tired face. "Please don't."

"I can't live this way," she says without looking at him. "That killer is more important to you than either me or your living daughter."

A killer? What a pity. Sounds like the kidnapping I witnessed ended in the worst possible way.

Bernard's hands tighten into fists, but instead of yelling at his wife—or worse—he turns on his heel and slams the door behind him so hard it nearly flies off the hinges.

He storms into his office, where I can see the scope of his obsession. The place is completely covered with newspaper clippings. On the wall is a map with pushpins, and there's even a collection of milk cartons with pictures of kids on them.

The good news for me is that this section of the trauma loop looks to be over. The bad news is that there's at least one more coming. I can feel it approaching.

A familiar pressure appears on my arm that has nothing to do with the dream. Confirming my suspicion, my cheek stings from a slap.

Just like it happened the last time, my dreamwalking trance breaks, and I open my eyes back in the waking world.

Filth stands over me with a satisfied expression on his pale, weasely face.

"Kain said you need to save your powers for the investigation," he snarls. "And here I come and catch you entertaining yourself."

I debate lying that I was doing my job but decide not to risk it. Resisting the urge to sanitize the skin he touched, I say in the nicest tone I can manage, "I'm glad you're here."

He looks at me as if I've sprouted an elephant trunk. Then a nasty smile splits his face. "Do you need something from me?" he asks in what he probably thinks is a seductive tone. It's repugnant. "Some precious liquid, perhaps?"

I fight my gag reflex. "Actually, I need information. It's related to what you're talking about."

"Oh?" He cocks an arrogant eyebrow.

I remind myself that I'm talking to a killing machine and that it wouldn't be wise to punch him in that weaselly mug. "Keep in mind I'm asking for the investigation, okay?" I take a breath. "Is it true you supply Gertrude with said precious liquid?"

His fangs show up, making his face truly frightening—less weasel and more wolverine.

I surreptitiously back away. "I ask because Kain told me as much. I just want to double-check, so—"

"Kain is the only reason you're not a blood bag. Push me again, and I'll risk his wrath." His gaze drops to the vein pulsing in my neck. "I'd love to show you your place in the food chain."

I figure I can safely take this reaction as a yes. Time for some reconciliation. "I didn't mean to upset you."

He stares at me the way I plan to look at a proper Gomorran meal after all these Earth bananas.

I decide to throw him another olive branch. "Your alibi checked out, by the way. I don't know if Kain told you that."

His expression doesn't change.

Clearing my very dry throat, I say, "Is there a place where the Council keeps records of things like voting, the Mandate ceremonies, or when each member joined the Council?"

Might as well dig through some files, like a real detective.

Filth glares at me for another second, then turns on his heel and strides to the door.

I grab a bunch of bananas and follow him through the maze of corridors, keeping a few feet between us at all times, just in case.

He stops when we reach a set of doors with a fancy design carved into them. Without a word, he opens them for me.

As soon as I step inside, he slams them shut behind me.

CHAPTER TWENTY-FOUR

RELIEVED TO BE out of his sight, I sanitize all the places where he touched me and look around, whistling appreciatively. This is the largest library of paper books I've ever seen. How many trees died to make this happen? On Gomorrah, a tree costs as much as a week of Mom's medical bills, so most people read electronically. Only the obscenely wealthy enjoy printed books.

"Anything interesting happening?" Felix asks in a gravelly voice. "I couldn't fall asleep after all."

Not much, I text him. *About to look through some records.*

The faint sound of typing emanates from the earpiece. When he's not hacking Earth banks and such, Felix makes his living working for humans as a software engineer and, ironically, as a cybersecurity consultant.

I advance deeper into the library. In the back, I spot a person sitting in a lounge chair. He's holding a bagel in one hand and a paper book in the other.

I know him. It's Chester, the probability manipulator whose dream I entered a few hours ago—and he's not alone.

Felix stops typing. "Wow."

You can say that again. Next to Chester lies an enormous white lion ravaging something that looks suspiciously like a chunk of goat. At least I hope it's a goat and not, say, an unlucky monk.

I stop several yards away and warily eye the tableau. Neither man nor lion are paying attention to me, so I speak up. "Excuse me. I hope I'm not interrupting your breakfast."

The lion's ear twitches, but he keeps eating his grisly meal.

Chester puts down his book, revealing a satyric grin. "If it isn't the detective extraordinaire. Do you have questions for me as part of your investigation?"

I nervously peel one of the bananas. "I'm just here to review some records."

Chester's grin widens. "A coincidence, huh?"

"Doesn't he look just like the Joker from the Arkham video game franchise?" Felix whispers. "It's Ariel's favorite."

I smile at Chester and say politely, "You're a probability manipulator, right?"

"You looked into me?" He scratches the lion behind the ear as one would a cat. The beast doesn't seem to mind, perhaps because it's too busy with the meal, or perhaps because Chester's luck prevents him from getting mauled.

I swallow a piece of banana without chewing. "I created a dream link with you while you slept last night. It's only prudent for me to know more about you."

This is a lie, of course. I can't say what powers many of the Councilors I connected with have. Kain didn't bother telling me that.

"Did you hear that, Bertie?" Chester looks down at the lion. "I didn't banish you from my bed just for shits and giggles." He gives me a crooked grin. "Bert is still surly with me over that."

"He sleeps with that lion?" Felix exclaims, echoing my thoughts. "How does he still have all his limbs attached?"

"I appreciate your asking Bert not to be there." I dry-swallow another piece of banana. "I have a feeling he wouldn't like someone touching his master in the middle of the night."

Chester's grin turns sinister. "Oh, he'd love it if someone tried. If you don't count napping, killing things is Bertie's favorite pastime."

How lovely. I picture the lion engaged in said pastime and suppress a shudder. "Well, it's nice to have met you both. Research awaits."

"One second." Chester's grin evaporates. "Don't you want to know what I was doing when Gemma died?"

"You're not really a suspect." I squeeze the remains of my banana a little too hard, and it plops onto the floor, where Bert the lion gives it a disgusted glare. "Why bug you until I have to?"

"It's no trouble. I was walking Bert at the time."

The lion's ears perk up. He must recognize the word *walk* the way dogs seem to.

"Don't you think the lady doth protest too much?" Felix whispers. "If he wasn't already on your suspect list, I'd add him."

Felix might be right, but I have to tread carefully, and not just because of the lion a few feet away.

"Thanks for that," I say with a hopefully enthusiastic smile. "Now I won't need to bother you or your friend here ever again."

"Let's hope you don't," Felix whispers.

"Start your search over there." Chester points at a stack of books to his left.

"Thanks." I obligingly head where he suggests. The first book I touch happens to be about probability manipulators and the feats they can perform.

"Do you think that was an intimidation tactic?" Felix asks as I drag my finger over a section in the text that talks about a trickster's ability to increase the probability that their enemies will get cancer or suffer accidental death.

Or a way to clear himself, I text back. *Why leave bodies around when he can use more subtle means?*

"To make a statement?" Felix says, echoing Kain's earlier suggestion. "Not to mention that by the second or third accident, everyone would suspect him anyway."

True, I text. *Still, I'd need a motive before I get on his bad side.*

"Smart. Just keep in mind that if it's some kind of vendetta, it wouldn't be Chester's first. He—"

"Let's go, Bertie," I hear Chester say. "If you're a good boy, I'll take you to Africa tomorrow."

"Did he just provide himself with an excuse to run?" Felix asks.

Maybe, I text back.

I watch Chester leave the library, hand draped casually over the lion's white mane, and decide that the "trickster" label fits this particular probability manipulator extremely well.

Okay. Time to look for something useful.

I walk all around to see if the dust patterns can tell me whether anything was recently updated, or if the book jackets can give me a hint on where to start.

Nope. The room looks to have been meticulously dusted, no doubt by the monks, and the bindings on most books are identical, forcing me to have to open each tome to figure out what's inside.

I sigh and peel another banana as I look for anything resembling records.

Nothing.

I eat banana after banana and keep looking, finding nothing but useless minutiae. Is it possible they keep the day-to-day records on higher shelves? There's a ladder here, but I'd need months to go through them all.

A few hours and bananas later, when I've made almost a full circle back to the place where Chester pointed me earlier, I spot something useful on an easy-to-reach shelf.

Voting records—score.

You seeing this? I text Felix.

His typing ceases in my earpiece. "Interesting. Can't help but notice that by starting where Chester pointed, you took the longest possible time to come across that book."

You're right, I write back. *Was he hoping I'd give up? Or is this a coincidence?*

"There are no coincidences when probability manipulators are involved. He'd be the first to tell you that."

He's probably right. Flipping to the back of the book, I eagerly check the last entry. Yep, the vote over my fate is already part of this record. I examine the names of everyone who wanted me dead.

Gertrude. No surprise there.

Eduardo the werewolf. Interesting.

Albina, the Councilor with the matter-dissolving power who dodged getting a dream link with me last night. Also interesting.

And surprise, surprise: Chester also voted to kill me.

I don't recognize a few of the other names, so I note them in my phone so I can check if they have an alibi—in part out of spite but more out of solid logic. Before the vote, the idea of using my skills for sleuthing had been mentioned. If the guilty party believed in my skill, they'd have voted to kill me to prevent me from figuring out their identity.

I text Felix my thoughts.

"I think I agree with you. But just to play devil's advocate, if the killer is cautious, they might not have voted against you."

Good point, I text back. *Still worth examining the voting records closely.*

Felix yawns. "You do that. Meanwhile, I'll give napping another shot."

I open the book to a random spot and read about a case that sounds very similar to my own. Like me, the young woman, Siti, didn't have a Mandate at the time of her crimes. Though it doesn't say what her powers were, she apparently used them to make human hospice patients feel better in their final days. According to the Council, she risked "exposing the existence of the Cognizant to the human population at large." Unfortunately for her, the outcome of her case was unlike mine: The vote did not go in her favor, and she was executed.

I recognize a lot of the names on the list of people who voted against this girl. Interestingly, Chester isn't among them. I flip pages until I find a similar type of case.

Yep, the same people voted to kill this guy as the Siti girl, but Chester did not.

I keep looking.

The voting pattern remains eerily consistent, which I guess makes sense. If one is dead set against any exposure to humans, they would be likely to remain so.

I skim the pages faster until I come across a case where the voting record is slightly different. Very interesting indeed. The defendant in this case was Princess Peach, Ariel and Felix's roommate. In her case, Chester voted for the ultimate penalty.

An even more interesting case waits on the next page. This time, Chester himself is on trial. Not much detail is given apart from "spoke about Cognizant secrets to the uninitiated." Unlike all the prior cases, where the vote was to decide execution, Chester risked nothing more than being expelled from the Council. The vote didn't go in Chester's favor; they removed him. Huh. He must've earned his way back since then. But not surprisingly, the same people who typically voted for execution in similar cases voted to expel Chester as well.

Could that be his motive? All the dead Councilors came from the list of people who voted for execution in these cases. Could Chester be getting revenge for what he perceived as an indignity? It would explain his out-of-character vote to kill me, a person who could potentially expose him.

If this is true, the next person to die will be one of the Councilors who voted to execute or expel in cases of exposure to humans.

Hey, are you napping? I text Felix.

He doesn't reply.

I go into the dream world, tell Pom he has a chance to see Felix again, and enter Felix's dream.

He's sitting on the couch, playing a video game in which creatures that look a bit like Pom fight each other with cool superpowers.

"Hey," I say. "I figured you might be asleep."

Felix looks at his video game controller, at the creatures on his screen, at me, and finally at Pom. His unibrow seesaws on his forehead. "Every single time, it's so freaking hard to believe I'm dreaming." He looks back at the screen again. "Also, why am I not doing something more interesting in my dream, like flying?"

"I'm sure you do that sometimes." I join him on the couch, and Pom flits over to sit between us. "Sorry to interrupt, but I need to talk to you about Chester."

"And I need to play the game." Pom is all but bouncing with eagerness. "What are those creatures?"

"Pokémon." Grinning, Felix hands Pom the video game controller. "Try playing as Pikachu or Jigglypuff."

A happily purple Pom starts mashing the buttons.

Felix turns to me. "So. Chester."

I tell him what I've discovered and ask, "Do you think he could be the killer?"

"Thinking about probability manipulation gives me a headache." Felix theatrically rubs his temples. "I think he could be."

"Oh?"

"Let's start with the arrow. If there was a chance Tatum could be hit with it, Chester's power would've made it a certainty. And when it comes to sneaking up on the elf, he could've used his power so the elf wouldn't have noticed his arrival until too late, or he could've made the elf fall off the cliff by accident."

I was thinking along the same lines, but it's good to hear another person confirm it.

"He could've also been behind the bird attack," Felix continues. "If there was a chance the birds would go crazy one day and peck the dreamwalker to death, Chester could've increased that probability."

"Right, but what about Gemma?" I ask. "She was ripped in half. There's no chance he could've done that, is there?"

"Maybe his lion?"

"Maybe. That thing did look like pure muscle. It has to be incredibly strong."

Felix scoots away from Pom, who's going at the game with ever-greater enthusiasm. "You should talk to Kain about this as soon as you can. But do it carefully. Part of Chester's power is being in the right place at the right time, so he might overhear."

"Then how am I—"

"Am I interrupting you again?" Kain's voice booms from the sky.

Speak of the devil. He's caught me in my trance again.

"Thanks, Felix. I've got to go." I wake myself up.

As expected, Kain is standing next to me in the library, his thin mouth more downturned than usual.

I put my hand over my rapidly beating heart. "I was working on the case, I swear."

"And?"

"We need to talk, but not here." I look around the book stacks furtively. "Can we go outside where we can't be overheard?"

Kain raises an eyebrow. "Sure."

He leads me through the stone corridors until we reach the castle entrance and emerge from the mountain to the woodsy smell of wet vegetation and the light drizzle of rain.

"Let's go talk by the moat," I say, ignoring the water droplets striking my face. Hopefully they're not too contaminated. On Earth, one never knows.

Kain nods, and we walk in silence until we almost reach our destination—at which point I realize a couple of problems with my plan.

The moat smells like a sewer, and Hekima is already standing in the middle of the bridge that goes over it.

The elderly illusionist is holding an umbrella and puffing on a pipe. I guess with all those carcinogens flowing into his lungs, he can't smell the stench wafting off the water. When he spots the two of us, he exhales a cloud of smoke and waves with his pipe.

So much for a private chat.

Kain's expression suddenly changes. "Watch out," he yells, pointing at something behind Hekima. "Run!"

Hekima spins on his heel and screams in horror.

I follow the path of Kain's finger and bite back a scream of my own.

A huge head is rising from the moat on a long slender neck. It looks like a dinosaur, although I have no idea what kind.

Hekima starts backing away, only to slip on the wet stones, falling to his hands and knees. Mouth open for another scream, he lifts his arm defensively—just as the creature opens its tooth-filled maw and strikes, chopping off Hekima's upper torso in a single bite.

CHAPTER TWENTY-FIVE

WHAT REMAINS of Hekima spouts a fountain of blood.

I shriek.

Fangs busting out, Kain flashes toward the edge of the bridge. The beast must fear vampires, because it seizes the rest of Hekima in its jaws and disappears into the murky waters.

"What the hell?" Shaking uncontrollably, I lurch after Kain. "What was that?"

The vampire curses and glares at the water as though he's contemplating diving in.

"Are you insane?" I grab his shoulder. "Hekima is dead. Do you want to join him?"

He twists around to face me. "You're not going to tell anyone about this," he says through gritted teeth. "The rain will wash away the blood and…"

I don't know what he says next. Moving purely on adrenaline-filled autopilot, I pull out the hand sanitizer and clean my hands, as though the blood Kain speaks of is on them.

"Don't worry," I say numbly when he gives me a shake. "I won't tell anyone."

"And you realize that was another murder, right?" He stares into my eyes as though he's about to glamour me.

"It was?" I reflexively sanitize my hands again.

"Come inside." He grabs my fresh, clean hand and drags me behind him like a rag doll.

I'm not sure if he glamours me or not, but I somehow find myself back in his quarters.

"What did you want to talk to me about?" he growls. "Speak."

Shaking off the residual shock, I look around for listening devices. I don't see any, but that doesn't mean much. "Can you go to sleep again? No one can overhear us if we speak in the dream world."

He rolls his eyes but obediently stalks into his bedroom and puts himself to sleep. I slip into the dream world, ask Pom not to show himself, and find Kain. He's already deep within a dream of drinking blood from a woman I've never seen.

I make the woman disappear, convince him he's dreaming, and place us in my cloud office—in this case, to soothe my own raw nerves. Kain can fend for himself.

"Sit there." I point to where I usually sit and take the therapy couch myself. "Now, what was that thing?" I replicate the creature that ate Hekima a few feet away. "Do things like that live on Earth?"

He gives my recreation a baleful glare. "It was Nessie. She was a gift from the Council in Scotland."

I goggle at him. "As in the Loch Ness monster?"

He nods. "Humans got wind of the poor creature, so she had to be relocated."

Oh, crap—he's serious. I make Nessie disappear and create a stuffed replica of Pom's usual dream shape so I can hug him to my chest. "Why would you put something so dangerous in your moat?"

Kain shrugs wearily. "It happened before my time, back when the Council kept prisoners in the dungeon. Anyone escaping through the sewers became Nessie's lunch."

Disgusting. The cell they initially gave me as a room—if I'd used that hole-in-the-floor excuse of a toilet, I'd literally have been putting my butt on the line. I take in a deep breath and reassure myself that I never would've come near that hole to the sewer anyway, monster or no monster. Way too unsanitary.

Shoving the unpleasant image away, I ask, "Was this the first time Nessie's attacked people outside her domain?"

Kain dips his chin in a single nod. "I didn't know it was possible. Now that I think about it, I guess someone with Gemma's power could make Nessie act like that, but—"

"Is there someone else with Gemma's powers on the Council? They could be behind Leal's death *and* this murder."

Kain sighs. "She was the only one."

"What about probability powers?" I create a replica of Chester in front of us. "I imagine there's always been some small chance Nessie would attack someone by the moat. A trickster could've boosted those odds."

"Maybe. In theory. But why?"

I tell him my suspicions about Chester.

"That doesn't track," he says. "Hekima wasn't yet on the Council when they kicked Chester out."

Puck, that's right. Hekima wasn't on the list of people who voted against Chester—or anyone else, for that matter. There goes that theory.

I hug my Pom replica harder. "So maybe it was an actual accident. Maybe Nessie got hungry after all this time without prisoners to munch on."

Kain scoffs. "The monks feed her a goat per day. I think we need to treat this as a murder, which is why I told you to keep quiet."

I don't have a good feeling about this. "What do you mean?"

"As I said, if there's another murder, your fate becomes uncertain. To put it mildly."

My heart rate triples. Since this is the dream world, I zoom out of my body to calm it the puck down.

"I bet the real reason is his reputation as the head of the Enforcers," Pom—who must've gone invisible to listen to the whole thing—whispers in my ear as soon as I'm back.

He's right. This murder happened under Kain's nose. He's bound to look bad if anyone learns about it.

Making Dream Chester disappear, I ask, "What if Hekima upset him in some way?"

"Could be," Kain says. "Why don't you check his alibi?"

"I will. Do you happen to know where he was when Tatum was shot with that arrow, by any chance? He volunteered information about his whereabouts during Gemma's murder, but—"

"Vegas. I think he was in Las Vegas." Kain stands and starts to pace the cloud. "His lion has a girlfriend among the lions at The Mirage hotel, but that's just the excuse. Chester likes to walk into casinos and use his power to win at slot machines. Usually an unsuspicious amount."

I make a mental note to check on what The Mirage's casino looks like. "As soon as Chester goes to sleep, I'll check those alibis."

"Until then, you're to stay in my quarters so I can keep an eye on you,"

Kain says. "We're not going to discuss any of this, in case your paranoia is right. You're also not going to eat or drink anything. We want to avoid any unfortunate accidents."

I solemnly nod and wake us up.

Opening his eyes, Kain jackknifes from the bed and heads toward his dining area without a second glance.

Fighting the urge to lie down on the fuzzy coverlet, I follow him and plop onto a barstool by the kitchen counter. He's already on his laptop and ignores me completely.

I take out my phone and look up the casino to note a few key details. Then I put my phone away and just sit there, too tired to do anything else. After a while, the last remnants of adrenaline trickle out of my system, and the strongest drowsiness I've ever experienced hits me.

I jump up and begin to pace—but I still feel on the verge of falling asleep.

This is why humans on this world use sleep deprivation as torture. It is. I'd do anything to get some shut-eye. Well, evening is only a few hours away. Maybe I could nap? If I'm lucky, it'll be dreamless. But even if it isn't, at this point I'm willing to face my worst nightmares just to make this feeling stop.

"Can I use your bed?" I ask, stifling a yawn.

Kain looks up from his laptop. "To sleep? What about your vice?"

I drop my gaze. "It's been some time since I drank. There's a chance I might be able to fall asleep—a small one, but—"

"Be my guest." He returns his attention to the screen. "I'll wake you when I need you."

What a relief. I go into the bedroom, and ignoring the BDSM paraphernalia all around me, I hurl myself into the bed.

Of course, now that I'm horizontal, sleep doesn't come—typical of how this works on vampire blood.

I give it a good attempt anyway by counting moofts.

At 5,407, Kain walks into the room. "It's time."

I wearily roll to my feet. "You think Chester is sleeping?"

"I know it. Do what you must," Kain says and heads out of the room.

Without further deliberation, I touch Pom and enter the dream world.

The looft appears in front of me, turns purple, and squeals as if he's not seen me in forever. Then again, since he's in the dream world so much, his sense of time might be warped.

"Hey, bud," I say as I head to the tower of sleepers. "How are things going?"

"I'm happy to see you." He flies circles around me. "I was worried."

My adrenaline spike must've affected him. As a parasite—I mean, symbiont—he gets all my hormones.

His ears turn red. "You thought that P-word again."

"And you read my thoughts again. If you'd read them carefully, you'd know I mentally corrected myself."

"Still," he says grumpily. "You wouldn't like it if I thought of you as a meanie-poo and then reminded myself that you're just having PMS and it's your hormones to blame."

"I don't even know where to start with that." Reaching the tower, I skim the nooks for Chester. "You realize that thanks to your symbiont nature, when I have PMS, you do as well?"

Pom's enormous eyes grow wider. "I do?"

"You're flooded with the same hormones—and get just as cranky."

He wiggles his ears. "I think you're just so irritable you *perceive* me as cranky."

Ignoring him, I fly over to Chester's bed, where a cloud gathers above his head. "Puck."

Pom sniffs the cloud. "It's bad. Like rotten eggs."

I reach for Chester's forehead. "I'm going in anyway."

CHAPTER TWENTY-SIX

"SWEETHEART?" Chester shouts from his office. "Sweetheart, the baby is crying."

No response.

He frowns and goes to the infant. Stopping next to the crib, he smiles at her, and the little girl stops wailing immediately. Either she's missed her dad, or he's using his power to increase the chances of her feeling soothed.

"I'm going to look for Mommy," he croons. "It's strange she didn't hear you. Her earsies are as sensitive as the Big Bad Wolf's."

The baby gives him a toothless grin. He reluctantly exits the nursery and starts searching the house room by room.

"Matilda?" he calls out by the master bathroom door. "You in there?"

No reply.

He tries the handle. It's locked. "Sweetheart, everything okay in there?"

Silence.

Frown returning, he tugs on the door handle. A strange click sounds, and the door unlocks—no doubt the probability of its doing so just got boosted.

He peers inside.

There's a razor blade on the tile floor and water spilling over the sides of a bathtub. Reddish water.

Pom was right. This is a bad one.

Face losing all color, Chester rushes in.

In the tub lies a gorgeous woman with flawless skin that resembles white chocolate melted over silk. Flawless skin that's marred by the no-longer-bleeding cuts on her wrists.

Frantically, he checks her pulse. "No!" He grabs her naked body and pulls it out of the tub. "No. Please no."

He points at the body with his hand and strains, using his power to its fullest potential.

It doesn't work. There must be zero chance for this woman to come back to life.

"How could this happen?" he wails.

I wish Pom were here now so I could squeeze him. A mother gone forever—it hits too close to home. Would it be so bad to run back to my dream palace to recover and come back to deal with Chester later?

I steel myself. The investigation awaits—and it's a means to save my mother, who, unlike Chester's wife, still *can* be saved.

I force my attention back to the dream at hand. The trauma loop is now over, but some intuition forces me to let the next set of dreams play out anyway.

Chester is sitting in his living room, the baby in his arms. "I'm going to find out what happened to Mommy." He readjusts his grip on the warm milk bottle. His voice turns grim. "When I do, whoever's responsible will pay."

The rest of the dream doesn't seem to have any answers, and neither does the one after that.

Then I hit the jackpot.

Around us is the lab with cannibal doves, and Chester is there, speaking with Leal the dreamwalker.

"Our dear seer colleague, Darian, prophesied that if my wife didn't die, our child would," Chester says in a low, furious voice. "But of course you already knew that."

Leal stands up. "I didn't. I mean, we all know how much you hate Darian, but—"

Chester rises as well. "She learned that foul prophecy from a dreamwalker. How many of you scum can there be?"

"It wasn't me." Leal backs away in the direction of the bird cages. "I have no reason to lie."

"You have all the reasons." Chester's jaw flexes menacingly.

"I don't." Stopping his retreat, Leal straightens his spine. "I uncovered some interesting things in your dreams. If something were to happen to me—even by accident—everyone would learn what you did."

"You threaten me?" In his fury, Chester's face looks eerily like that of a puck.

"I'm just reminding you of the consequences of rash action," Leal says. "And driving home a simple point: I have no reason to lie to you. If your wife had asked for something I thought you'd disapprove of, I'd have come to you first. You're my fellow Councilor. She wasn't."

The dream cuts off here, and the next one isn't a memory. I let it play out in the background as I process what I've learned.

Chester had a dispute with Leal. He also had to be careful about antagonizing him. Leal had something on him, something that would've come out in case of his death. Could it be that Chester went ahead and killed him anyway? Or is my earlier theory correct, and Chester has been killing those who voted him off the Council? But then why didn't Leal make good on his threat? Why didn't his secrets about Chester get out?

Also, why did Chester kill Hekima?

In any case, this explains Chester's vote against me. It sounds as though his wife's suicide drove him to dislike seers and dreamwalkers, and I'm one of the latter.

Well, he'll hate me even more once I reveal him as the killer.

I observe his dreams flickering by until I see his lion viciously killing a man. I shift that dream into the lion walking outside the castle in a fog, Chester close behind him. I set the date and time to match Gemma's murder and wait for Chester to fill in the details.

They amble peaceably down the trail.

What the hell? This dream is a memory. Neither Chester nor his lion ripped Gemma in half.

What about shooting Tatum with the arrow?

I set the date and time to match that murder and replace the castle grounds with a casino. Chester fills in the details again, and I see him winning a small jackpot—again, a memory. If he was in Las Vegas, he couldn't have shot Tatum with an arrow in New York, probability powers or not.

"Are you satisfied now?" Chester says, looking right at me.

I stare at him openmouthed.

"You forgot to make yourself invisible." He grins. "As luck would have it, so to speak."

He's right. I indeed forgot.

"I just proved you're not guilty," I say quickly, before he decides to give me cancer or worse.

He puts a coin into a nearby slot machine and wins again. "Which is why I made sure I was in REM sleep when you needed me to be."

I use my powers to make myself look smaller and frailer. "I didn't learn anything… overly personal."

He chuckles humorlessly. "Let's cut to the chase. I know that you know that I voted to kill you." He feeds a coin into yet another slot machine and gets a river of them back. "I did that because I dislike dreamwalkers on general principle—and now you have an idea why."

I nod warily.

He grins as he pokes through a handful of coins for the one he wants. "When my power brought us together in the library, I realized you might actually be useful. I was right, of course—you just cleared me of any wrongdoing. I think Kain suspected me somewhat, so make sure to set him straight."

"I will. Are we cool now?" *Do I have to worry about DNA mutations and things like that?* is what I want to add, but I don't in case that gives him the idea.

"If you stay out of my dreams from this moment forward, you won't need to worry about me," he says magnanimously. "Now wake up."

I do.

Locating Kain, I tell him Chester isn't guilty.

"Because of Hekima, I didn't think so either," Kain says. "So, what's next?"

"I think I should make dream connections with Eduardo and Nina to verify their alibis. After that, I can link up with the rest of the Council."

Kain nods and leads me to Nina's quarters.

The stone slab isn't blocking the way—she's expecting us.

I sweep my gaze over the area where she'd indicated she does yoga, memorizing a few key details, and follow Kain into the bedroom.

I'm in luck.

Nina's in REM sleep, so I quickly enter her dream world.

———

POM GREETS me as I speed to the tower of sleepers. "Who are you working on now?"

"Nina. And I fear she'll have a trauma loop."

"Oh?" He turns a light orange color.

I shrug. "Something about her."

When I locate Dream Nina, I breathe a sigh of relief.

"No cloud," Pom says. "I guess she's not as troubled as you thought."

"Yeah." I make sure to turn invisible. "It's your call if you want to join me or not."

"I will," he says conspiratorially and turns invisible also. "Can we talk telepathically?"

Fine, I think pointedly. *But don't get used to reading my thoughts.*

I won't, Pom says as a voice in my head. *Thank you.*

I touch the space between Nina's sharply defined dark eyebrows.

————

THE TENNIS BALL machine shoots balls at Nina at a machine-gun clip. She catches each ball using her telepathy and throws it into a basket. Another ball gun starts shooting at her from a different angle, and she diverts those projectiles just as easily.

What's she doing? Pom asks.

Training her power, I think back. *Please let me concentrate.*

I look around the tennis court for a way to turn it into Nina's apartment.

Something odd catches my attention: The windows of this building are solid black. Shrugging it off, I settle in to wait until Nina tires of practice.

She finally gathers up her things and heads for the locker room. I set the date and time to Gemma's murder and shift the location. Instead of a bathroom, Nina walks off the court into her own apartment—and as so often happens with dreamers, she doesn't blink an eye at the switcheroo.

The windows here are black as well, an odd detail I can't recall adding.

It doesn't matter, though.

Nina levitates the furniture, unrolls a mat, and flows into her first yoga pose.

Puck, I think for Pom's benefit. *This is a memory.*

So she's not guilty?

Appears that way. I'm going to wake up now. See you soon.

Before Pom can protest, I come out of the trance.

————

AFTER I UPDATE Kain on my finding, we set off to Eduardo's quarters. When we get there, the bed is empty.

Kain's fangs emerge. "He said he'd be here tonight."

"Maybe he goes to bed later?" I look around the spartan bedroom for any hints.

"We'll give him a few hours," Kain growls.

For a while after that, we walk around the castle, and I enter people's bedrooms and make connections—going down the remaining list of Councilors who voted to kill me. When we get to the last on that list, I recognize the living room we enter.

This is the dwelling of Albina, the Councilor who'd left a note apologizing for missing her dream link the last time.

I perk up. Avoiding me that time was shady. Maybe she should be higher on my list of suspects.

Kain sniffs the air, his face darkening. Fangs out in full force, he rushes into Albina's bedroom.

I sprint into the room after him, only to halt abruptly.

On my wrist, Pom turns black.

On the bed lies Albina, or so I assume. Her naked body is vampire pale, with hideous bruises on her neck. Given her disheveled appearance, it's not difficult to work out a case of erotic asphyxiation gone wrong—or worse.

Kain checks the pulse on her wrist, and I hold my breath, preparing for what he's about to say.

"Nothing." He releases her wrist. "She's dead."

CHAPTER TWENTY-SEVEN

A SURGE of adrenaline wipes away all traces of my earlier sleepiness. Kain said if more people die, I would follow—and now two have died on my watch.

Moving so fast he almost blurs, Kain rips open his wrist with his teeth and forces blood into Albina's mouth.

Nothing happens.

Actually, that's not true. Something happens, but not to Albina—to me. I stare hypnotically at the blood as Kain checks Albina's pulse again, curses, and blurs out of the room.

Stumbling out of the bedroom, I locate the kitchen and heave half-digested bananas into the sink.

Where did Kain go? What should I do? Questions swirl through my mind, but not a single answer. I grope for a glass, pour some probably contaminated tap water into it, and gulp it down.

With yet another dead body on my watch, I'm unlikely to live long enough to get sick.

On every level possible, I feel horrible. I'm shaking, my mouth and throat are on fire, and I crave sleep the way a man craves water in a desert.

The walls around me close in.

I'm having trouble breathing.

Did I just discover another dead body? Did I really witness Hekima being eaten?

Could the sleep deprivation be giving me hallucinations?

I reach for the vial of diluted vampire blood. Am I craving this? Seeing Kain's blood pour out of his body didn't gross me out as it should have. It fascinated me. Is that the first stage of addiction? Some later stage?

Then again, if I don't want to collapse and fall asleep this very second, I need to do *something*.

I can try severely limiting my dose. I pour a droplet of the watered blood into my glass and fill it again with water. Pocketing the vial, I dip my finger into the glass and flick off most of the moisture. It doesn't get more diluted than this.

I lick the finger.

The pleasure is as intense as the last time, maybe even more so. I moan and smash my forehead into the refrigerator.

I can barely feel the pain.

Pucking puck, something's trickling down my forehead.

I swipe at it and stare at the red liquid staining my fingers. Blood. Unlike before, my wounds aren't healing. I guess my medicine was too diluted for that particular effect.

Worse still, I feel almost as sleep deprived as before.

Kain barges into the apartment with a disheveled Isis in tow.

Of course—when his blood didn't work, he went to get a healer.

Isis narrows her sleepy eyes at me and points a finger at my forehead, shooting it with golden energy.

The healing warmth feels good, but not as intensely as vampire blood.

I touch my forehead.

The wound is closed.

"Don't bother with her," Kain growls. "Your patient's in there." He drags her into the bedroom.

I follow them in just as Isis hits Albina with a beam of golden energy, which she maintains as she checks the dead woman's vitals.

The beam stops.

"I'm sorry," she says in a sleep-raspy voice. "She was beyond healing."

Kain slams a fist into the wall, burying his arm to the elbow.

Isis pulls a blanket over the body. "We should have Roger—or better yet, a human forensic expert—take a look."

Roger. That name sounds familiar. Wasn't he the one who'd made a sleeping drug for Leal?

Isis catches my gaze. "I take it you don't know who did this?"

I shake my head, and Kain gives me such a murderous glare I fully expect him to drain my blood—or worse—right here and now.

"The werewolf. Eduardo." I try to keep my voice even. "Did he have a relationship with her?" I glance at the corpse.

Jaw tight, Kain shakes his head.

"He wasn't in his room earlier," I remind him. "Maybe this is where he was."

"Take care of this," Kain barks at Isis and strides out so quickly I have to run to keep up.

By the time we get back to the werewolf's apartment, I'm wheezing for breath.

"He'd better be there," Kain growls.

We barge into the bedroom and find the large man in his bed, snoring like a geriatric dog.

Kain nods at the bed. "Do your job," he tells me in a low, hard voice.

"He's not in REM sleep," I whisper. "We've got to wait."

His voice rises in volume. "I'm running out of patience. Two more Councilors dead. If I were you, I'd make myself useful forthwith."

Puck. I guess this isn't a good time to tell him about the dreamwalker's notes where he talked about the difficulty of entering werewolf dreams.

Wait a second. How could I forget? The black windows in Nina's dream. They're—

"There," Kain says, quieter this time. "Look at his eyelids."

He's right. The werewolf has entered REM sleep—a record, considering he wasn't in bed only a few minutes ago.

Faking confidence, I sidle up to the prone figure and touch his muscled neck.

CHAPTER TWENTY-EIGHT

POM SHOWS up as soon as I enter the dream world, and I pet him to relax a little before attempting the multibody technique from Leal's diary.

Just as before, I create a second body for myself far away from where I stand, in case that helps. Next, I exit my current body and will myself to come back into both.

Nope. I end up in the original body.

I do it again, straining my willpower.

I end up in the farther body instead of the original, but not in both.

"I guess that's still something," Pom says dubiously. "You've learned a type of teleportation."

"Right, but that's not what I need."

Still, Pom has a point. This *is* a way to teleport around the dream world. Then again, isn't going to a different dream already teleportation? Or is that building reality around myself?

Leaving the metaphysics for later, I exit my body, create one in the tower of sleepers, and dismiss the original one. Reentering myself, I end up in the tower—functional teleportation.

Hey, it's something.

For good measure, I test out the multibody technique once more and fail. I guess there's no helping it. I'll need to deal with the werewolf the usual way, in one body.

I teleport to his nook, turn invisible, and touch him the same way I did in the waking world.

———

AS SOON AS I materialize inside Eduardo's dream world, I see what the problem is—and it's a big one.

Somehow, the werewolf is having two dreams at the same time, something I've never experienced and didn't think possible. The two dreams are juxtaposed on top of each other, at least from my point of view, like two movie projectors playing different movies aimed at the same screen.

In one dream—a violent nature show—Eduardo is in wolf form, ripping a gazelle to shreds and relishing the feeling of warm blood in his maw. In the other dream, Eduardo the man is doing it doggy style—or is it wolfy style?—with a woman I don't recognize.

Could she be Albina?

It's hard to tell, especially with the sex and violence crossing over into each other.

The wolf abruptly stops eating, raises his bloodied muzzle, and sniffs the air. Looking right at me with animal eyes, he howls and bounds forward. At the same moment, the naked man stops thrusting and twists to look at me.

I want to run, but the two environments make it difficult to orient myself, and pain explodes in my neck as the wolf's teeth bite down.

Before he can shut those jaws and kill me, I wake myself up.

———

BACK IN MY REAL BODY, my heart is hammering so hard I'm afraid it'll punch a hole through my ribcage. If the wolf had dug his teeth any deeper, I'd have died in the dream and would be homicidal right about now.

Speaking of homicidal, the way Kain is looking at me isn't good.

"I'm sorry." I back away. "I couldn't check his alibi."

"You what?" His fangs slide out.

"I knew this might happen. Werewolves are difficult to dreamwalk in."

Kain's eyes turn into mirrors. "Tell me the truth," he orders in a tense version of his usual honey-laced voice.

I speak robotically without meaning to. "He was dreaming two dreams at once, one for the wolf side and one for the man side. Before I could manipulate anything, he lunged at my—"

Kit bursts in. "What's going on here?"

"I release you," Kain spits at me. He turns to Kit. "I used glamour to finally get some truth out of this useless blood bag."

She frowns at me. "You're susceptible to glamour?" Glancing back at Kain, she says, "If you knew you could get her to tell the truth that way, why didn't you clear her of guilt at the hearing?"

Great question. I bet the answer is he needed me as bait to unmask the killer. Or maybe he'd hoped I'd actually solve the stupid case.

"Why are you here?" he asks Kit harshly.

"Isis woke me." Her anime-like form ripples and becomes the healer's. "She told me what happened to Albina, said Bailey mentioned a werewolf."

My attention drifts back to Eduardo. Despite seeing me in his dream, despite my waking up, and despite everyone's raised voices, the werewolf is not only still sleeping, he's dreaming like a baby.

"We should take this conversation elsewhere," I whisper, figuring that if they force me to go back into his dream—something I'd like to avoid at all costs—it's better if he stays in REM sleep.

They both glance at the sleeping werewolf and head out, with Kit assuming her usual guise on the way.

As we exit the apartment, a soul-wrenching noise blasts through the castle. It sounds as if someone's trying to replicate a bomb explosion with some infernal string instrument.

"What was that?" I exclaim when the noise stops.

My ears are still ringing.

Kit turns into a woman I've never seen. "Emergency meeting call for the Council."

"That sound could wake the dead." I sneak a glance at the werewolf's quarters.

"It's what happens when you let a siren onto the Council." Kain grabs my wrist. "Let's go."

I blink at that. "Your siren is a siren?"

"Hey, the monks used trumpets before that," Kit says, turning back into herself. "This is much better."

Without comment, Kain herds me through the corridors until I see Filth standing next to a familiar door.

"If she leaves her quarters, kill her," Kain tells him.

Filth gives me a look that seems to say, *Please leave. Pretty please with a blood cherry on top.*

"See you soon," Kit says as Kain pushes me in and slams the door behind me.

Great. The Council is going to meet, and I'm not going to be there to speak for myself.

I'm so screwed.

Washing my hands in the sink soothes me a little; sanitizing them after calms me even more. Grabbing a banana, I pace the room as I chew. When I tire of pacing, I sit on the chair and eat four more bananas in a row.

It's been at least an hour. How long does a stupid Council meeting take? I'll go crazy if I keep waiting here.

I grab hold of Pom's fur and enter the dream world.

———

"DOESN'T this make the wait even worse?" Pom asks when I apprise him of my situation. "Time feels like it passes much slower here."

"But here, I have you." I fluff the fur on top of his head. "Besides, I can also do something useful here."

I teleport to the tower and float around a bit, looking at the sleepers available to dreamwalk in. There's Felix, but I leave him alone. He deserves some sleep after that sleep deprivation marathon I put him through. I look for Nina but don't find her, which is too bad. I want to discuss something important with her. It makes sense she's not here, though; she's at the Council meeting.

Interestingly, though, some other Councilors *are* sleeping—skipping the meeting to do so. This includes Eduardo the werewolf, the deep sleeper himself.

"Is that good for you or bad for you?" Pom asks when I point this out.

"Good, I guess. Most of the sleepers voted to kill me, so if there's another vote taking place right now, their absence will help my cause."

Pom gives the sleeping werewolf a pouty glare. "Do you plan to enter his dreams again?"

"No pucking way." I fly past the werewolf's room without a second thought. "I'll just work on Bernard again."

I approach the Mario/Wario doppelgänger.

Yep. He's still got clouds indicative of a trauma loop—and I already saw his child get kidnapped and his wife leaving. How much worse can it get?

Bracing myself, I touch his forehead.

———

BERNARD IS SITTING on the edge of his seat in a courtroom. His wife and daughter are in a separate section, and he gives them a longing look they don't return. He turns to glare at the defendant, a wiry, balding middle-aged man with shifty eyes. As if he feels Bernard's death stare, the man turns around and winks at him nastily, then looks back at the judge, who's holding a paper in her hands.

"The bastard did it," Bernard mutters under his breath. "He did it, and he's mocking me."

The judge begins to speak, commanding Bernard's full attention. He looks like he's holding his breath.

"...find the defendant not guilty," the judge states.

Bernard leaps to his feet. "That's bullshit! The—"

The dream cuts off before he can be held in contempt of court.

Wow. I feel another trauma loop coming on. This is probably a record number. Most people have one, maybe two. Did Valerian know how tough this job would be? Is that why he paid me extra? Or maybe he simply needs the final results that badly—results I've yet to produce.

Speaking of Valerian, I feel a sudden urge to take a break from Bernard's doom and gloom and revisit my uber-attractive employer in my dream bedroom. I can think of many ways his simulacra could make the time pass. He could feed me plump, juicy grapes, massage my feet with his strong, warm hands, use that sensual mouth for—

"Bailey," Kit's voice booms. "Wake up."

There goes *that* idea.

I come out of my trance, the taste of sweet grapes fading from my tongue.

CHAPTER TWENTY-NINE

"YOU'RE ONE COOL CUCUMBER," Kit says when I open my eyes. "I don't know if I'd be able to sleep under such circumstances."

"I wasn't sleeping, per se." I sit up. "How screwed am I?"

She perches on the edge of the bed and puts down the stack of papers she's holding. "The good news is they won't kill you outright. I had to use all my oratory skills to pull that off, but Kain helped."

"He did?" I move from the bed into a chair opposite her. That doesn't sound like the vampire I know.

She turns into Kain. "He's not as bad as he seems. He's just in a shitty position. Since he's the head of the Enforcers, everyone blames him for not preventing the murders. Clearly, he's decided to shift some of that pressure onto you."

As I thought. "Makes me feel so much better. What a saint."

Kit shifts back into herself. "The head of the Enforcers before Kain left very big shoes to fill."

I take in a deep breath. "What's the bad news?"

"You've got three more days to find the killer," Kit says. "And, if anyone else dies, that's it for you."

"Pucking great." I leap out of the chair and start pacing the room. I'm failing. Failing badly. If I don't get my act together, Mom stands no chance.

"I swear I did my best," Kit says. "But when Kain told everyone about

Hekima and Albina's death, Gertrude made it sound like they voted to spare you in the hope that you could solve this thing. She said we needed to revote. Then Kain chimed in to give you another chance. I told them you can't prevent someone as powerful as one of us from murdering, but they didn't care." She shimmers, transforming herself into Eduardo. "You're lucky a few negative ninnies like their beauty sleep so much. As unbelievable as it sounds, the vote could've gone worse. One of the options was to kill you now."

I grimace, stopping in front of her. "Why don't I feel lucky?"

"If you want, I can help you escape." She turns into me. "There's going to be a Mandate ceremony soon, and we can disguise you to sneak out along with the guests. I can pretend to be you for a while, give you a head start."

Tempting. Very tempting—and very nice of her to offer.

Regretfully, I shake my head. "I need Isis to heal my mom. Besides, Kain has my DNA. I don't want to have to look over my shoulder for the rest of my days." It's the same reasons I had to turn down Valerian's offer in the beginning.

Like it or not, I have to see this through.

Kit turns into Isis. "You're also lucky no one's killed *her* yet."

She's right. That wouldn't be good at all. "Speaking of luck," I say, pushing away the upsetting possibility, "did Chester vote for or against me just now? He had an alibi, but I still wonder if he could be behind it all."

"He voted to give you another chance," she replies in Chester's voice while still wearing Isis's face. "Chester can be a pain, but I don't think he's the culprit."

"Fine," I say tiredly. With the adrenaline leaving my system, the sleep deprivation is hitting me again, hard. I sink back into the chair. "Now what?"

Kit assumes her preferred anime blonde guise and hands me the stack of papers. "Kain made everyone write down what they were doing during the murders. They all swore to go to sleep in a bit, and Kain will check everyone's compliance shortly. The idea is that you'll dreamwalk in the rest of the Council as soon as possible."

"Not a bad idea." I glance at the papers. "I haven't finished connecting with everyone, though."

"That's where I come in. I'll walk you into the right people's bedrooms." She waggles her eyebrows lasciviously.

Ugh. Leave it to Kit to make the necessities of my power feel dirty.

"There's another problem," I say. "Some of the people I suspect didn't attend your meeting."

"Kain thought of that also. All but Eduardo"—she points at a highlighted section on the top paper—"were in the company of fellow Council members at the time of the murders, so you can clear multiple people for the price of one alibi."

"I already know what Eduardo was doing, or at least what he said he was doing."

"Kain mentioned your difficulties with his werewolf nature." Her forehead creases in a concerned frown. "What will you do?"

"I figure I'll start with the others and leave him for last. The more people I clear, the worse he looks, right?"

"Makes sense. Well, if you're ready, how about we—"

There's a knock on the door.

"Yes?" Kit asks in my voice.

"It's Nina," says a familiar voice.

"Come in," Kit says, fully transforming into me.

Nina walks in. Her gaze flits between Kit and me. "With all this waking up in the middle of the night, I guess I should be grateful I'm not seeing triple."

"Thank you for your vote," Kit says, still as me. "You're one of the good ones."

Nina heaves an exasperated sigh. "Can whichever one of you is Kit give us privacy?"

I look at Kit, and Kit looks at me.

"I can do this all day," I say.

Kit pouts.

"What I have to say wouldn't interest you that much, anyway," Nina says reassuringly.

Kit's pout gets poutier.

Nina raises her hand. "I solemnly swear we're not going to Netflix and chill without you."

"Fine." Kit trudges toward the door. "Be like that."

"If you leave looking like me, Firth might try to kill you," I say to Kit's back.

Her nails grow to the size of talons. "In that case, I'm definitely not changing. Might be fun to see him try."

Outside the door, I hear Filth say something nasty. Before I can figure out if he's calling me a B- or a C-word, a thud stops his rant in its tracks. In the silence come heavy footsteps.

Nina rolls her eyes. "I wonder if she turned into Colton or some orc."

"Anything's possible with her." I tilt my head, studying Nina. "I think I know why you came."

She sits on the edge of the bed. "Kain said you cleared me already, which means you've been into my dreams."

"I did and I have." I draw in a breath. "And I saw the black windows."

"So you did. Do you mind?" She points at one of my water bottles.

"Not at all."

Before I can get up and give her a bottle, she uses telekinesis to make it fly into her hand. Swiftly, she drains it and then sits, chewing on her pierced lip.

"You came to me," I remind her as the silence wears on.

She floats the water bottle back. "Sorry. This isn't easy."

I smile reassuringly. "Just start somewhere, see how it goes."

She fiddles with her nose ring. "I'm Leal's dead man's switch."

"You're what?"

She takes a deep breath. "I allowed Leal to make it so that if he dies, I'd know damaging information about his killer."

I gape at her. "You know who killed him?"

"That's just the thing." She plays with a stud above her lip before touching the one above her chin. "Until I know for sure who did it, the information won't reveal itself to me."

"I don't understand."

"I thought you knew about black windows," she says. "You're a dreamwalker like him."

"I kind of do," I say cautiously. At least I do now, having read his notes. "They're a way to hide a dream."

She nods. "A dream that can be someone's memory. Or my own."

"So the black windows I saw in your—"

"One contains something I desperately wanted to forget. Whatever it was, forgetting it was the payment for letting Leal use my subconscious as a safe." She wraps her arms around her slim frame.

"And the other windows?"

"Each will be about something someone on the Council didn't want anyone else to know," she says. "Those windows are programmed to show me a dream about someone that I believe caused Leal harm."

I sit up straighter. "What if *you* had killed him?"

"My own memory would come back to me." She visibly shudders.

"A memory of what?" I ask, frowning.

"I don't know," she says softly. "That's the whole point. After Leal did his thing, I forgot what it was. All I remember is that I don't want to remember whatever it was."

Huh. So I was right when I thought she might have a trauma loop. After Leal created her black window, she forgot whatever it was—not the healthiest way to deal with problems. Then again, if the memory was truly impossible to live with, repressing it might've been her only good option.

Nina extends her hand, and I feel myself levitate. Before I can blink, my back is brushing the ceiling.

"Hey!" I flail my arms and legs—to no avail. "What are you doing?"

She stares at me unblinkingly. "I want to make sure you really hear what I say next."

I stop flailing and give her my full attention.

"If you go into my dream and make me recall whatever Leal locked away, I will kill you when I wake up," she says evenly.

Whew. I was worried she'd demand something impossible. Relieved, I bob my head. "Got it. That really got through, I swear. For good measure, I'll stay out of your dreams, period."

She lowers me to my feet, and I sink into the chair, knees shaking.

"You may want to enter my dreams," she says as if nothing has happened. "It's worth taking a look at the other windows. They might contain clues as to who the killer is."

I lay my palm over Pom's black fur to calm my racing heartbeat. "Do you know which window is which? I wouldn't want to accidentally—"

"I know the one to avoid."

Pom's fur goes from black to light orange.

"How would I even—"

"Leal would fly into the windows from time to time," she says. "I remember seeing dreams when he'd do it, but I would forget them when I woke up."

Interesting. I'm learning something about dreamwalker craft after all. "He'd just fly into them?"

"That's what it looked like to me, but it might be more involved than that. He said he risked losing his power for the day each time. A few times it even happened, and we'd have to resume our dream collaboration the next day."

Oh, puck. That could be seriously problematic. "In my current position, losing my power for a day would be tantamount to suicide. You were there for that vote. You know that."

She shrugs. "Perhaps consider the black windows your last resort?"

I nod slowly. She's right; I don't have to try some crazy, unproven technique. Yet. "Let's see if I can find the killer without them. Speaking of, I should probably start soon."

She stands up. "I'll get Kit for you."

"Thanks." I give her what I hope is a warm smile. "And if you could go to sleep afterward, so I have the option to check out those windows, I'd appreciate it."

"Remember what I said about my own black window." She glances at the spot on the ceiling where she'd pinned me, then at the table I would've crashed into if she'd dropped me.

I gulp. "Don't worry. I remember."

"Great."

She leaves, and I resume pacing.

When Kit doesn't immediately return, I decide to go into the dream world to see if some of the sleepers I haven't cleared are ready for me.

I ignore Felix and the still-sleeping werewolf and locate one of the Councilors from the list of those who voted to kill me. According to the papers Kit brought, this guy was having cocktails with a few other Council members. Since I've already seen the room, I go into his dream to check if he was really there.

He was indeed. In one fell swoop, I clear him and everyone else sharing cocktails.

When I wake up, it's to the sight of a large male orangutan eating a banana.

"Kit?" I say to the ape. "Please tell me that's you."

The orangutan morphs into Kit and tosses the half-eaten banana into the trash. "I wanted to see if it would taste better when I'm in that form." She grimaces. "It didn't."

She leads me to the bedroom of an older guy. I wait an hour for him to reach REM sleep before swiftly ascertaining he's not the murderer. I clear the next Councilor the same way, and the next five as well.

With each not guilty verdict, I grow more and more worried. What will the Council do when I tell them I couldn't figure out who the murderer is?

Nothing good.

"What time is it?" I ask Kit. "How many people are left?"

She looks at her watch. "It's eight in the morning. Vickie, the siren, is our last suspect."

The last suspect. What will I do if she's not guilty? I guess that will be the time to risk either my sanity with the werewolf or my power for the day with Nina.

Vickie is in REM sleep when we arrive, as expected. REM periods become more prolonged toward morning. I touch the siren's forehead and end up in the dream world. Most of the Councilors are gone from the tower of sleepers, but Nina, my possible plan B, is still sleeping. So is the werewolf, who's plan C, where *c* stands for crazy.

I check the siren. She really had been playing the piano, as she told Kain.

I exit the dream world, and Kit and I leave the siren's apartment—only to bump straight into Kain.

"Update," he demands.

Kit keeps moving. "I'll be in my room, getting my beauty sleep."

"Can you give me five minutes?" I ask Kain.

He grudgingly agrees. I turn away from him and use Pom to go back into the dream world.

Pom greets me, and I tell him what happened on the way to the tower of sleepers.

"So by process of elimination," he says, "it's the werewolf."

I nod mournfully. "Which blows. They'll make me go into his dream to check, and he'll make me go insane."

"It's all moot now." Pom points behind me, and I whirl around. "He woke up."

He's right. The werewolf isn't in his nook anymore.

I exhale the breath I was holding. "It's just a stay of execution. They can ask him to go to sleep again."

Pom's fur darkens. "Maybe whatever you find inside Nina's black windows will be so damning you won't need to dreamwalk in him in the first place."

"Maybe," I say and seek out Nina.

She's still asleep.

Oh, well.

Here goes plan B.

CHAPTER THIRTY

THIS TIME, Nina's dreaming about eating sushi. She doesn't use chopsticks like the customers nearby. Instead, pieces of raw fish dip themselves into soy sauce and fly into her mouth.

The windows in the restaurant are black, just like the windows from her other dreams.

"Remember me?" I slide into the booth across from her, pick up a piece of raw salmon, and plop it onto my tongue. If someone were to put a gun to my head in the waking world to make me repeat that action, I'd probably refuse. Death by gun is certain but less painful than having your brain eaten by the parasites that live in raw fish on Earth.

Nina looks around. "This is a dream?"

"I imagine the Mandate would prevent you from using your powers in a human restaurant," I say.

"You're right." She looks at the windows. "I think I remember what you've come here to do."

"Yep." I follow her gaze. "Now which is the one to avoid?"

"That one." She points at the black window nearest the restaurant entrance.

"Got it." I eat a piece of fatty tuna. "So I just fly in?"

"That's what Leal did."

I stand up, already bobbing a few inches off the ground. "Before I go, I was wondering... Why didn't you tell me about the black windows earlier?"

"I needed you to know I wasn't guilty. After all, my black window is a motive for me to kill Leal."

I lift my eyebrows.

"I would've killed him if he'd tried to use whatever I forgot against me," she explains with the calmness of someone discussing the weather. "Same if he'd tried to make me remember whatever I forgot."

Note to self: Definitely don't piss off Nina.

"Makes sense," I say. "But why do you think Leal set up a dead man's switch in the first place? Why use your dreams?"

A piece of squid sails into her mouth, and she looks thoughtful as she chews. "For all we know, he might have another fail-safe besides me. Or many. When I asked the same question, he said computers could be hacked and that lots of hackers would be eager for that job. But dreamwalkers are rare, and dreamwalkers who know about black windows are rarer still."

She's got me there. I nod wisely.

"You know what? Try that window." She points at the black glass to my left.

"Why?" I float higher.

"I don't know." She studies the window intently. "I'm hoping that on some level I know which ones have something to do with the murders."

That's good enough for me. "Let's go for that one, then." I confidently torpedo into the black window she just chose.

———

I HALF EXPECT the onyx glass to shatter around me, slicing my skin, but instead I end up plunging into a freezing black lake. Struggling to swim, I will myself to become lighter than water.

It doesn't work.

I will the water to become saltier and thus heavier, but that doesn't work either—nor does willing myself a life vest.

My ragged breathing speeds up. What the hell? I try exiting my body so I can strategize, but I'm stuck inside myself as much as I'm stuck in this lake.

Fine. I'll just swim.

Stroke after stroke, I edge closer to the nearest shore, testing my powers as I go. Changing water to clouds doesn't work. Teleportation doesn't, either. I call out to Pom but get no answer. So odd.

Unlike the times I'm in a subdream, I know that I'm in the dream world now. It's just that my powers don't work. I guess I'll have to do the obvious—just keep swimming.

I focus on swimming, only swimming. And swimming. And swimming. My breathing grows labored, yet the shore is still far away. After what feels like an hour, every muscle is aching, even some I didn't know I had.

The shore is still a mile away, and I feel like giving up.

But I can't sink. Sinking will either kill me—and make me go insane—or it might be the way one "fails to enter" a black window, which carries the penalty of losing power for the day.

Gasping for air, I let the motions of my arms and legs become my whole world. With every excruciating stroke, I tell myself that my muscles aren't really burning, that it's not real air I'm greedily gulping. Everything around me is as real as a mirage.

The moment my hand touches the dirt of the shore, the lake—and my exhaustion—disappears.

———

I FIND myself in a dream where Gemma is alive and standing in a well-lit gym. One of the windows is black. Perhaps my way back?

In front of her, a donkey-sized wolf is running on a treadmill nearby. Must be a werewolf. He or she is going cheetah fast, working the machine so hard it creaks under the strain.

"Don't stop," Gemma orders. "I want to see what your kind's really capable of."

Foaming at the mouth, the werewolf keeps running until the machine starts to smoke and stops on its own.

"Good boy," Gemma says. "Now let's see if you can use the elliptical."

Moving as if under glamour, the werewolf attempts to mount a machine clearly not designed for an animal with paws. Gemma watches his struggles with amusement.

This is weird. Why did Leal store this dream as blackmail? Also, is this an actual memory he stole from Gemma or just a figment of his imagination? My usual sense of "memory or not" isn't working, but that could be because the dream is stored in Nina's dream space, not Gemma's.

The wolf looks to be in pain as he futilely tries to climb onto the elliptical, over and over.

Then it hits me.

Gemma's power was controlling animals, regular animals, yet here in this dream she's able to control werewolves in animal form, too. This must be something only the most powerful of her kind are able to do; I had no idea it was even possible.

Maybe Eduardo, as alpha of the pack, found out and disapproved. Having been subjected to glamour, I can say without a shadow of doubt that if I were a werewolf, I'd very much disapprove. Puck, maybe this is his friend she's putting through hell, or even Eduardo himself.

In other words, this could be a motive for Eduardo to kill Gemma—a solid motive, at that.

I watch Gemma put the poor wolf through a half-dozen more cruel ordeals before I end up back in the sushi place.

Nina blinks at me with an amazed expression.

"You saw that?" I ask.

"I think I saw through your eyes. It's so strange to know that I'll forget it as soon as I wake up. It's so clear in my mind now."

I steal another piece of salmon from her plate. "Do you think Eduardo would've killed Gemma over what I just saw?"

She traces circles on her napkin with a fingernail. "If someone on the Council had that sort of power over *me*, I'm not sure I'd let them live."

That note not to mess with this woman? I mentally underline it as well.

"I'm going to check another black window," I say. "Which one do you want me to try next?"

"How about that one?" She gestures across the bar. "I have a feeling that will also be about Eduardo, though no idea how I know."

I gulp down a glass of water and launch myself into the window she chose. This time, I pay closer attention to what happens during the process.

As soon as the tip of my head touches the glass, I'm plunging into the cold water, only this lake is much larger, so I have to swim at least a mile farther. Only curiosity and iron will prevent me from drowning.

When my hand touches the shore, a new dream starts.

———

I FIND myself in a bedroom with a black window. Tatum is in this dream, making the room smell yummy in the disturbingly sexual way typical of her kind. And she is very much alive. Entwined with Eduardo in his human form, she's going at it with the enthusiasm of a teenage male bunny, but all the skills of a courtesan.

It's a shame someone this good at something is no longer alive. I bet she could've written a book that would make the Kama Sutra seem dry.

When they're done with all the gymnastics, Eduardo wraps himself around her sweat-covered body. Licking her delicate earlobe, he murmurs, "I love you. Leave the wimp… please."

Tatum stretches in his arms like a cat. "You don't *really* love me, my pet. You're just under my spell."

He lets her go, his eyes turning wolfish. "I'm not under anyone's spell. I just want you—and I get what I want."

"Of course," she purrs. "Big bad alpha is *always* in control."

The room smells yummier than ever, and Eduardo's pupils dilate. Soon, other parts of his anatomy fill up with new vigor.

Wow.

The next session is more impressive than the last, and more such sessions follow. After Tatum uses her powers to make him go crazy with lust five more times, the dream stops.

―――――

NINA IS BLUSHING when I get back to the sushi place, and I can't really blame her.

"Well, that just happened," I say lightly.

"I know." She sips her plum wine. "Tatum was also controlling Eduardo with her powers—a grave offense."

"When he said she should leave the wimp, he meant her husband, Ryan the elf, right?"

"Without a doubt," she says. "Eduardo sometimes called him that when they disagreed."

Finally, a promising lead. "So what happened? Did Ryan find out about the affair, get pissed, and plant an arrow in Tatum? Or did the werewolf learn how to use a bow like an elf?"

"I imagine the latter," she says. "He could easily have pushed Ryan off the cliff. In his wolf form, he could've gotten close enough before Ryan realized what was happening."

"But I don't understand why he'd kill them both. I mean, I can see why he'd kill the husband of the woman he desired, but—"

"He probably killed her to regain control. There was pressure within the pack for him to take a mate, and that has to be another werewolf. He could've killed the elf to cover his tracks. Or he could just as easily have done it in a jealous rage—and that kind of thing doesn't follow logic," she adds with a shrug.

"I don't know," I say. "It feels too premeditated for a jealous rage. But let's say Eduardo's the killer. Why would he kill Leal too?"

Nina floats a piece of shrimp into her mouth. "That's hard to say. Maybe because he knew Leal would know his motives for killing the others. Or maybe Leal knew something else."

I consider that. "You know, Leal *was* going out of his way to get into the dreams of werewolves."

Her gaze sharpens. "There you go. Maybe he succeeded, and one of the windows is going to hold Eduardo's secret."

I look at said windows. "Which one do you think it is?"

"No idea," she says. "My intuition isn't making any more suggestions."

"Puck. I guess I can try one at random."

"Let's just hope you don't learn a secret that someone will later want to kill you over."

"Great, thanks," I mutter. Taking a breath, I eeny-meeny-miny-moe myself a window. "Here goes nothing."

I fly at the black surface before I can change my mind.

———

THIS TIME, it would be more accurate to call the lake a sea. It's so big I can't even see the shore. Having no other choice, I swim.

And swim.

And swim.

When my muscles tire to the point of failure, I finally glimpse the shore in the far distance. The sight gives me a boost of strength to swim some more. But an hour later, I can swim no longer. The shore is five hundred yards away, but it might as well be across an ocean.

I grit my teeth and keep moving my leaden limbs.

A muscle in my leg cramps, and I begin to sink.

Puck. I've got to at least hold my breath.

Nope. That's an impossibility with breathing this ragged.

Burning like acid, water flows into my sinuses, and pain explodes in my lungs.

A few agonizing seconds later, I drown.

CHAPTER THIRTY-ONE

I'M IN THE HALLWAY, my back to Kain and my heart drumming with terror.

I just died in my dream. Does that mean I'm homicidally insane?

Examining myself for murderous desires, I don't find any—no more than usual, at least.

Whew. I must've merely lost my powers.

Touching Pom, I attempt to enter the dream world.

Nothing happens.

So that's that. No more dreamwalking until tomorrow. With a sinking feeling, I face Kain.

"Who's the killer?" he barks.

I brace myself. "I checked almost everyone. They're all clear."

His fangs pop out. "I didn't ask you who *isn't* the killer. I asked who *is*."

"I think it's Eduardo." I wish I sounded more certain.

"You figured out how to enter his dreams?"

I shake my head. "He woke up before I could."

Kain's eyebrows snap together. "Then…?"

"I have reason to believe he was having an affair with Tatum. He was jealous of Ryan and didn't like Leal for stealing some secret."

Kain's upper lip curls, exposing more of the fangs. "You could say that about most of the Council. How did you arrive at *him*?"

"By process of elimination."

"That's not much of a proof." But the fangs slowly retreat.

Emboldened, I suggest, "Why don't we go talk to him anyway? The least he can do is not fight me when I enter his dreams again."

"Fine." He grabs my shoulder and drags me to the werewolf's apartment.

At the doorway, he sniffs the air and rushes in, leaving the door ajar. In the bedroom, Eduardo is still sleeping—or looks like he's sleeping. Kain must've sniffed out something else, because he checks Eduardo's pulse.

"Dead." He spins around, his face a mask of fury. "Your alleged murderer was murdered."

I back away.

His eyes turn into mirrors. "Do not move."

The glamour roots me in place, despite every instinct screaming for me to run.

Kain rips open his own wrist and forces blood into Eduardo's mouth. Just as with Albina, nothing happens, apart from my mouth watering in a disturbing way.

Kain curses and flashes out of the room, leaving me alone with the corpse.

I still can't move. My nose starts to itch and I can't even scratch it, which feels like a creative form of torture.

Soon, Kain comes back with Isis. As before, she shoots the victim with her power, but he doesn't stir. They bustle out, paying no attention to me.

A while passes.

My legs cramp, and the itch on my nose gives birth to a daughter itch under my left boob. On some level, I'm grateful for the discomfort, because it keeps my mind off the fact that I'm standing next to a dead guy. And the fact that I'm going to be dead myself soon for so spectacularly failing at my job.

Kain comes back with a new group of people. Gertrude is with him, and the siren as well, plus a person I've never seen: a pale, ginger-haired dude with glasses so thick they make his eyes look tiny. He's carrying a suitcase.

"Roger," Kain says to the new guy. "Tell us why he died."

Roger hovers over Eduardo's body with a magnifying glass. Zooming in on the crook of his elbow, he says, "There's a puncture wound. Strange. I didn't think he was a drug user."

"I don't think he was," Gertrude says.

"He used steroids to get even bigger than he already was," Kain says disapprovingly. "Maybe that went wrong?"

Roger shrugs and sets about systematically searching the room. Kneeling to peer under the bed, he grunts approvingly and stands, clutching a syringe. When he holds it up to the light, there are a few ounces of liquid inside.

"Let's have a look-see." He opens his suitcase and takes out some high-tech gizmo that looks as though it came from Gomorrah. Placing a droplet of the liquid into the instrument, he waits.

Beep.

He pushes his glasses farther up his nose and squints at a tiny screen on the side of the device. "Interesting. I know this formula. I made this substance myself for Leal, your dearly departed dreamwalker. He was using it to try to put his birds into REM sleep for a few hours, at which point they would die. I'd been trying to improve the formula before he stopped needing it anymore. You know, on account of being dead."

Right. Leal's notes did mention someone named Roger working on the sleep drug—the one I couldn't locate in his lab. And now I know why: because the killer took it and used it for one of the murders.

No wonder Eduardo had been in REM sleep and wouldn't wake up.

Gertrude points at me accusingly. "It was her. She murdered poor Eduardo."

If the glamour weren't stopping me from speaking, I'd ask her why I would want to kill the werewolf—especially since he was my only suspect.

As if she heard my question, she continues. "I bet she found this drug in Leal's lab and used it on Eduardo because she had trouble entering his dreams without it."

I know I didn't do it, but I guess it's vaguely feasible. Keeping him in REM sleep for so long would give me the most opportunity to dreamwalk in him. But why would I be so dumb as to give a lethal drug to a member of the Council?

"It doesn't matter if she did it." Kain's fangs are so prominent his speech slurs. "Besides, she couldn't have killed the others."

Gertrude puts her hands on her hips. "Still, if she—"

"What do you want?" Kain barks. "If she killed Eduardo, she'd be executed—but we're going to execute her anyway, for allowing another murder. Do you want to kill her twice?"

Gertrude scowls. "I just don't want her to weasel out of her rightful punishment like she did before."

"Oh, she won't," Kain says coldly. He points his finger millimeters from my itching nose. "She's done."

CHAPTER THIRTY-TWO

I AM? If it weren't for the damn glamour, I'd have lots to say on this matter.

What's truly insane is that the glamour is even preventing my body from freaking out. My breathing is normal and my heartbeat is steady. The only sign of my turmoil is Pom's fur. It's darker than a black hole.

"Should I call the Council meeting?" the siren asks in a heavenly voice.

"Give me a second." Kain's eyes turn into mirrors as he glances my way. "Walk behind me."

I zombie-walk after him across half the castle to a familiar dungeon.

Of course. I should've guessed I'd end up here to await my execution.

The place still smells like fermented sewage, but thanks to the glamour, my gag reflex isn't bothering me right now.

Kain makes a sharp right into the cell that was my original quarters. With the bed, table, and chair now gone, it looks even drearier—an impressive feat.

He catches my gaze. "I release you."

Instantly, my heart begins hammering against my ribcage like a starved woodpecker.

"You will wait here." He moves toward the door.

"Morning," Felix says in my ear, drowsy but loud. "Did I miss anything?"

Puck. What horrible timing. I turn my back, fish out my phone as quickly as I can, and type out: *Hush. Let's talk in a sec—*

A steely hand grabs my shoulder, spinning me around. "None of that." Kain grabs the phone and crushes it in his grip.

"Bailey?" Felix squawks. "What's going on?"

Kain makes pincers with his fingers and snatches the earpiece from my ear with a strike worthy of a cobra.

It's as I feared. With his vampire hearing, he detected Felix's voice. I wonder if he's been hearing it all along but just didn't bother to do something about it. I hope he at least doesn't know who's on the other end of the conversation—I don't want Felix to get in trouble.

"Consider her dead," Kain growls into the earpiece. "And if I learn who you are, you will be as well."

Okay, so he doesn't know. One piece of good news in this avalanche of manure.

Tossing the device on the floor, Kain grinds it into powder with his foot. Then he rips the camera Felix was seeing through from my shirt and gives it the same treatment.

"You should've solved the case," he tells me grimly and strides toward the cell entrance.

My gaze falls on the sliding bolt on my side of the door. As soon as he's outside, I lunge and snap it into place.

"That's not going to help," Kain sneers from the other side of the bars. "I can rip that door off the hinges. Or I could just let you sit in this cell until you starve."

On that cheerful note, he padlocks the door on his side and leaves.

My breathing is so fast I'm inhaling too much of the foul dungeon air. Bile rising, I frantically locate the horrific hole in the floor meant to be a toilet and lose the bananas from my stomach into it.

Perfect. Now I'll starve that much sooner.

Muttering obscenities under my breath, I stand up and begin to pace. I feel like a caged animal. The seconds tick by, each one longer than the next. It feels like an hour passes as I pace back and forth, trying to avoid the sewage hole. After the third time I nearly fall into it, I plop down on the floor and hug my knees to my body.

Puck. Puck. Puck. How could I have screwed up so badly? The goal was to save Mom. Now I'll be executed, and without me, she's as good as dead too. If I'd finished Valerian's job, I could beg him to pay her bills, extending her life a while longer, but I don't have my phone or my powers so I can't even do that much.

My throat constricts, my eyes burning as a sob bubbles up in my chest. Another sob quickly follows—those bastards travel in packs—and no matter how hard I try, I can't stop the tears from sliding down my cheeks. I cry for myself and for my mom, for all the dreams I'll never walk in and the conversations the two of us will never get to have. *For the apologies I'll never get to make.* I've never wished I could turn back the clock so intensely, have never wanted to rewrite history this much. But I only have that power in the dream world; out here, I'm as useless as a human, utterly at the mercy of the Council and their whims.

Eventually, my tears dry up and I just sit, beyond miserable. If I had my powers, I could at least escape into the dream world. But no such luck, at least not until tomorrow—assuming there is a tomorrow.

Of course, there *is* another form of escape, a way I could make myself feel better. The vial of vampire blood is still in my pocket. Even as diluted as it is, it would make me feel good. Very good.

But no. I'm showing signs of addiction—there's no doubt about that anymore. Then again, I'm awaiting my execution, so does it matter?

I take out the vial. It's so tempting. It would make me forget everything, if only for a little while. And when I'm dead, I won't have to deal with the consequences of addiction.

No, screw that. I'm not dying an addict. Besides, using this stuff might've contributed to how I ended up in this hellhole. I can't help the feeling that if I'd just let myself get a good night of sleep, with my mind fresh, I would've figured out who the murderer is.

Grimly resolved, I push up to my feet and step over to the hole in the floor. Unscrewing the vial, I make sure Nessie isn't staring at me from the murky water and ceremoniously pour out the liquid.

"Never again," I vow out loud.

To my surprise, I feel a little better—enough to resume pacing for a while instead of crying. Eventually, I tire and sit again, my eyes dry and gritty as I count the bars on the cell door.

A yawn tugs at my mouth. The effects of the vampire blood are wearing off. And for the first time in four months, I have no reason to fight the exhaustion, to hold off on the sleep I've been craving for so, so long.

Well, I guess there's one reason.

Something tells me I'll face my own trauma loop.

I yawn again. The weight of the world presses on my eyelids with a titanic foot. Without the vampire blood, fighting a four-month sleep debt is like holding my breath beyond a couple of minutes. Failure is guaranteed.

Fine. So be it.

I get as comfortable as I can on the stone floor, close my eyes, and instantly fall asleep.

CHAPTER THIRTY-THREE

I'M in the apartment I've been sharing with Mom on Gomorrah. She's looking at me, her pretty brown eyes sad as always. I know for a fact she's had at least a week of poor sleep, yet she's as beautiful as ever. Whatever pleasant facial features I have, I undoubtedly inherited from her. In fact, out of the two of us, she's the one who looks like Halle Berry.

"Not this again," she says, sounding tired.

"Your symptoms are worsening." My voice rises an octave; I can't help it. "I heard you screaming at night."

Her face turns ashen. "Did you walk into my bedroom?"

I glare at her. "No. More importantly, I didn't break my promise. I didn't invade your precious dreams."

She exhales in relief. "I just had a nightmare, that's all."

"About what?" I cross my arms in front of my chest.

"Can't remember. Can we talk about something else now?"

"Was it something to do with my father?" I watch for her reaction.

Some emotion flashes in Mom's eyes, but so fleetingly I can't be sure I really saw it, let alone figure out what it was. "How many times do I have to tell you?" she snaps. "I don't remember him, nor is it a topic I like to talk about."

"If you don't remember, how do you know you don't want to talk about it?"

She shrugs and looks away.

"Fine. You haven't been eating much, either. And haven't left the house in forever. In fact, this is the first time this week I've seen you in real life." I pointedly glance at the last-generation VR goggles on the end table.

Her jaw juts out mulishly. "Maybe it's because no one pesters me in VR. I'm the parent and you're the child, remember?"

I reach deep for my patience. "Look, Mom. I see your symptoms all the time. If you would just let me into—"

"No!" She beelines for the door, throwing over her shoulder, "Don't ever suggest that again."

"If your symptoms keep worsening, I might not have a choice," I yell at her back. "If your life's on the line, I'll break my stupid oath!"

She freezes and turns to look at me, her expression so full of betrayal I regret my words instantly.

"You wouldn't," she says hollowly, backing up toward the door. "Please say you wouldn't."

"Fine." She's been making me swear not to dreamwalk in her since I was a kid—and I've kept my promise, despite the overwhelming temptation. "But you have to see *someone*. A conventional shrink, perhaps? Maybe make a friend and talk to them? Or—"

"You don't understand! I've tried everything."

"Not *everything*."

With a growl, she turns on her heel and storms out, slamming the door behind her.

"Well, good!" I shout to the closed door. "At least you'll get some fresh air."

———

I'M in the emergency room. Mom's unconscious body is hooked up to an array of machines that do everything for her, from breathing to eating. Her brain activity is completely flat.

"She got hit by a car," the elf social worker says, as if from a distance. "We're figuring out what to do…"

I tune out the rest of it, my guilt and grief so overwhelming I can barely stand straight, let alone think. *She went out because of my nagging. She went out angry and didn't see that pucking car coming at her.*

"…don't have a lot of experience with this," the elf's voice reaches me again. "Self-driving car algorithms prevent pretty much all accidents. The last time—"

"Who gives a puck?" I bite out. "You think it makes me feel better that my mom is a one-in-a-million victim?"

The social worker backs away from me, mumbling platitudes—and I realize why she was telling me this.

Money.

Gomorrah has free universal healthcare, but on occasion, the free hospitals can't handle something, so they defer to paid establishments, ones usually patronized only by the rich. *Like this place.* And given the extreme rarity of what happened to Mom, there's no insurance that would cover it, just like there's no insurance for getting hit by a meteorite.

"I'll pay whatever's necessary to continue her care," I say to the elf. "Let me know what I need to sign."

She looks relieved. "I'll have a doctor speak with you shortly."

The wait for the doctor is the longest twenty minutes of my life.

When he finally arrives, I feel a slight sense of relief. He's a gnome, a rarity in the medical profession. Gnomes have a reputation of being the best in any scientific field, but they rarely choose medicine. Here, apparently, is the rare gnome who did—although it figures that the best of the best would be working in this *paid* facility.

"I'm Dr. Xipil," the round-cheeked gnome says in a voice distorted by his breathing mask. "When your mother first got here, I thought we'd lose her. After five nanosurgeries and a vampire blood transfusion, we were able to heal most of the bodily trauma. Her brain, however, is a different story."

He peppers me with a torrent of medical jargon that boils down to this: Mom is in a coma, and her brain isn't running her body's functions as it should.

"There isn't much more we can do," he says. "It's possible that a healer might help, but given the expense of—"

I hold up a hand. "Assume money isn't an obstacle."

"Then you should try hiring a healer. In the meantime, you need to keep her on the machines." He frowns. "Bear in mind, most hospitals would unplug her at this point, but here we can keep her hooked up until—"

I WAKE up drenched in cold sweat. Blinking my tear-swollen eyes open, I realize I'm still in the stinky cell.

I was right to fear falling asleep. Without being in control in the dream world, I can't avoid the memories I've been trying to suppress—my own trauma loop. Though I've been telling myself that I've been taking vampire blood to have more waking moments in which to make money, avoiding these dreams was a big part of my motivation.

Well, I've faced them now.

If I were one of my clients, I would feel less intensely about what happened. But I don't. Maybe I need another dreamwalker's assistance in order to enjoy the healing effects of dreaming.

Still, at the very least, I'm no longer terrified of going to sleep. In fact, I can't wait to sleep more. The drowsiness is like a heavy blanket cocooning me, dulling the impact of the painful memories.

I yawn, struggling to keep my eyes open. I don't want to fall asleep again before I do what I recommend to my clients: examine my emotions with an open mind.

Guilt, of course, is the main one. I know Mom's accident wasn't *really* my fault. It was good advice to tell her to leave the apartment. Living as a shut-in, staying in VR for days on end, wasn't healthy. But I *was* the reason she'd stormed out onto the street. It wasn't just the driving algorithm that had failed; Mom must not have seen that car, either. That part's my fault—and I'll always carry that knowledge with me.

Underneath the guilt is anger. At her, at myself, at the pucking algorithm that didn't stop the car in time. At the Council, for interfering with the Bernard job and tasking me with this impossible mystery, then punishing me for failing to solve it. And deeper still is the hollow ache that I've carried with me for as long as I can remember... a longing for a father, for some family other than my moody, taciturn mom. A part of me has always hoped that one day, she'll relent and tell me about our family, about where we came from and why she's been unwilling to talk about them all these years. Now that hope is gone, extinguished as surely as my life is about to be. I'll never learn about my past—or kiss a guy in real life.

I'm going to die a virgin.

I picture Valerian and his sensual lips, his ocean-blue eyes, the way his body looks in that bespoke suit... Puck, we should've done it at least in the dream world.

Speaking of—how much time has passed? Based on how sore my body is from lying on the stone floor, I must've snoozed for at least a few hours. Could my powers be back?

I touch Pom and try to go into the dream world that way.

Nope.

Despite the disappointment banding my chest, I yawn so loudly it fills the small room. Maybe the introspection can wait until I get more sleep—or better yet, until I'm in the afterlife.

Even the thought of the pending execution doesn't suppress my next yawn.

Fine. Why fight it?

I close my eyes again and instantly fall asleep.

CHAPTER THIRTY-FOUR

ISIS and I are riding in a limo, and I'm giddy with excitement.

"Again, props to you," Isis says. "I can't believe Eduardo was behind it all—and you're the only one who figured it out."

Something about what she says feels wrong, but I let it go because what really matters is that we're on the way to finally heal Mom. I look out at the city as Isis showers me with compliments. If Manhattan could pass for a small outskirt of Gomorrah, that's not the case for Brooklyn.

We get stuck in traffic twice, but eventually, the limo reaches JFK airport and drops us off among the hordes of people rushing to their flights. We navigate our way to a secret door guarded by wards; no human could ever go this way. Opening it, we slip into an underground labyrinth of corridors leading to the hub—an enormous circular room with reflective floors, a fairly typical setup as far as these things go. The circumference of the hub is peppered with gates, each colorful plasma warp point leading to a different Otherland. Hubs like this give the Cognizant access to countless universes, each as different from each other as Earth is from Gomorrah.

"My world is this way." I point at the turquoise gate opposite us.

"I've been to Gomorrah," Isis says. "Who hasn't?"

"Let me guess." I head for the gate. "Earth Club?"

"Hey, everyone goes there," she says defensively.

Sure, everybody from *this* backward place. There are much better clubs for us natives.

Catching up with me, Isis sashays into the gate first. I follow, as usual finding it fascinating how the front of me disappears into the shimmer of the gate as I walk into it.

We cross the gate's threshold, and we're not underground anymore, nor are we on Earth.

We're on top of a proper-sized skyscraper on Gomorrah.

I inhale the familiar ozone-scented air and smile. Isis looks at me like I'm crazy. I shrug and head for the elevator. As usual, the time here doesn't match New York on Earth. It was daytime there, yet here it's night, a time when the differences between the two worlds are the most telling.

I look up. There's no moon on Gomorrah, and I'm glad. That thing always looks ready to crash into Earth in some horrible cataclysm. Instead, we have a majestic nebula. The yellows and reds of its interstellar dust and gases form long trails that look like fire falling from the sky.

"I wonder if ancient Cognizant blabbed to humans about this sky," Isis says, falling into step next to me. "It looks exactly like fire and brimstone about to rain down on us."

"Who knows," I say, glancing down at the city sprawled below us.

The world of Gomorrah has only one city, a mega-metropolis that shares its name. It's larger than the entirety of the North American continent. The tallest building on Earth would look like a one-story suburban house here. The scale is staggering, even for those of us who grew up here. On a cloudy day, there's no skyline at all, as the tops of most buildings disappear into the clouds.

We take the elevator down to ground level and exit through the lobby onto the street. Immediately, I spot an orc, an elf, and a dwarf staggering drunkenly from some bar.

"Ahhh." I exhale. "Home sweet home."

Isis grins. "No place like it."

"I still haven't gotten acclimated to the homogenous human crowds in New York," I say.

She nods at a life-sized hologram of a supermodel beamed toward us by the nearest storefront. "Do you miss that also?"

"That's propaganda I could do without," I say and lead the way to a parking lot on the corner.

"Finally, normal-looking cars," I say as we approach. "The cars on Earth remind me of horse-drawn buggies."

"Yeah, these look like sleek spaceships." Isis looks around. "Hey, I smell food."

She's right. And this isn't just food—it's safe food. There's no such thing as foodborne illness here. I sniff the air, salivating at the thought of eating something that's not a banana, and the mouthwatering aroma of manna fills my nostrils.

I point at a vehicle Earth humans would probably describe as a flying saucer. "It's the Gomorrah version of a food truck. You've got to try it."

I get us each two packets of manna and rip into mine on the spot, moaning in pleasure as the flavor explodes over my starved taste buds.

After the first bite, Isis digs in with equal gusto. "If it were possible to have an orgasm from eating, this would do it," she says with her mouth full. "How many calories are in this thing?"

I hand her the second packet. "Don't worry. You can't gain weight from manna."

After I've had my fill, I remember our very important mission and get us a car. As we ride to the hospital, Isis gapes at our surroundings like the tourist she is.

"Everything looks like a set from *Ghost in the Shell*," she says, "or *Blade Runner*."

I grin. "Don't you think the orcs and elves break the cyberpunk vibe?"

She laughs, and we chatter the rest of the way about Felix's favorite topic, the cross-Otherland "borrowing" of creative ideas, including movies, video games, and books. Isis finds it as amusing as I do that there's Pac-Man and Mary Poppins on both Gomorrah and Earth—only in the Gomorran version, Mary Poppins is a vampire.

When the car stops at the hospital, we hurry into the intensive care unit.

"Miss Spade," calls a voice so high it borders on ultrasonic. "I need to talk to you."

I will myself to slow down and smile at the billing administrator—or Horseshoe Bat as I call her, in part because she seems batty and in part because her face reminds me of the Earth creature.

"I'll pay whatever I owe," I tell her preemptively.

"Good." She looks disappointed not to have to give me a lecture. "If you could step into my office—"

"Look, lady, my time is valuable," Isis says. "Get out of our way or I'll heal all your patients, and there go your profits."

"You're a healer?" Horseshoe Bat bats her eyelashes at Isis. "Maybe we—"

"Out of the way," Isis growls.

Horseshoe Bat retreats.

I locate Dr. Xipil in the unit and apprise him of what Isis is here to do. He grabs a few colleagues, and we meet in Mom's room.

Mom looks the same. Machines maintain all her basic bodily functions, and her brain activity is flat.

Dr. Xipil shifts his weight uneasily. "Do you want us to unplug her first?"

"Too risky," Isis says. "Let me do my thing first."

He glances at her hands and shuffles back a step or two. "Go ahead."

Isis shoots Mom with an arc of golden energy.

I hold my breath.

Mom's brain activity goes from flat to frantic.

My breath whooshes out. It's all I can do to not rush over to her as she gasps and flails, clearly bothered by the breathing apparatus.

Maintaining her focus, Isis speaks over her shoulder. "Now you take your crap out. Quick."

The medical staff scurry to comply as Isis keeps a steady stream of healing energy directed at Mom.

When the last machine is disconnected, Mom's eyes blink open, and she gives me a tender smile.

"Mom," I say, my voice choked. "How are you doing?"

"I feel great," she says, looking around. "Where am I?"

"You're at the hospital," I say, wiping a tear with my sleeve. I tug more fabric discreetly into my palm so I can make another pass at my nose. "There's been an accident and—"

That's when I notice it.

Pom.

Or, more precisely, the lack of Pom on my wrist.

Hold on. Pom is never missing from my wrist. Not unless I'm dreaming.

The world around me freezes.

Of course. This isn't actually happening. It's a fantasy. It's what might've happened if Eduardo had turned out to be the killer, as I thought.

Unable to stand the disappointment, I shut out Mom's beatific face and will myself to my dream palace.

CHAPTER THIRTY-FIVE

POM APPEARS AT MY ELBOW. "Hey! How're things going?"

Usually I wouldn't worry the little guy, but since his fate is tied to mine, I give him the bad news—and as I speak, he turns ever-darker shades of black.

"It's so unfair," he says when I finish. "You did your best for them."

My hair goes fiery without my conscious direction. "Don't get me started."

Pom's huge, lavender eyes turn overly bright, his fur lightening to gray —a rare color signifying deep sadness. "I don't want them to hurt you. Can you take me to their dreams? Maybe if I beg, they'll change their minds."

My chest tightens. My looft is clearly more worried about me than himself. I fluff his fur. "I don't think that would work, but you just gave me an idea. Before they execute me, I'll tell them about you, mention that you're a protected species on Gomorrah. Maybe they can attach you to someone or something else. They've got goats, for example, or maybe they could—"

"I've been meaning to tell you something." His ears turn a deep beet color. "I was still early in my development when I attached to you at the zoo. Once I got to know you, I let myself grow something like your circulatory and nervous systems—and now they're irreversibly interlinked with yours."

He can't mean—

"I can't be removed without killing us both," he confirms, reading my face. "I didn't tell you because I didn't want you to call me a parasite again. Or a tumor."

"A tumor? Come on, what kind of a monster do you think I am?" I give him a hug, my eyes watering. "Sweetie, I never would've wanted to take you off my wrist in either case. We're symbionts for life. I'm just sorry I screwed up so badly, because now that life is going to be very short."

"It's not your fault," he says. His ears fade to gray again. "It's the stupid Council."

I sigh in silent agreement and take to the air, floating among the impossible shapes decorating my palace's lobby.

Pom loops around me. "I wonder who the killer actually is. That's ultimately who's to blame."

I flick the tip of one of his ears. "That's a great question. Everyone on the Council seems to be *not* guilty."

His ears turn light orange. "Could it be someone not on the Council?"

I stare at him. It's unlikely, but... "Maybe, Pom, maybe. Access to the castle is restricted, but people do get in. For instance, Felix and Ariel will be at a Mandate ceremony."

The rest of Pom turns light orange. "Could someone have hidden in the castle after such an event? Maybe that's who's killing the victims."

Huh. It's possible. I sink both hands into his fur as my mind flips through the alternatives. "What about the monks? One of them could've done it. They're the closest to something like a butler—and in Earth mysteries, it's always the butler who's done it."

Pom wriggles out of my hold and circles around me. "I thought the monks didn't have any powers."

"They don't. That's why no one suspects them. Killing the most powerful Cognizant isn't easy."

"Then who else could it have been?"

I have no idea. I rub my forehead. "Someone good at sneaking?"

With no answers to give him, I can't face the hope and trust in his eyes. Floating over to a prism mirror, I stare blankly at my iridescent reflection. It has to be someone from outside the castle, someone from outside the Council's domain entirely. As busy as they've kept me, I've had no time to notice who might be—

The mirror reflects a dream manifestation of a lightbulb above my head as the idea hits me.

There *is* someone who's able to get in and out of the castle on a whim. He did it the very first day I was there.

"Valerian!" I exclaim, whirling around. "Valerian uses his illusionist powers to make himself invisible."

Pom's lavender eyes widen, his pupils transforming into red hearts. "But don't you want him?"

I'm not going to dignify that with a response. "Think about it. His power is uniquely useful against powerful Cognizant."

"How so?"

"An illusionist can make you see anything." I change our surroundings to illustrate my point, creating a room where the ceiling is the floor and the floor is the ceiling, with pucks scampering across the walls. "An illusionist can use his powers to make others do the dirty work for him, so Valerian could've made Ryan see an enemy where his wife stood, causing him to shoot her with his own arrow." I change our surroundings to the scene of Tatum's death, the arrow protruding cruelly from her chest before conjuring up a translucent Valerian, who sends an arc of his mojo at the elf.

Then I show Pom what happens from Ryan's point of view: Tatum becomes Eduardo and begins screaming at the elf, telling Ryan what he's done with his wife, calling him a cuckold and worse. Eventually, Ryan snaps and, raising his bow, shoots the "werewolf" in the chest.

Except, of course, it wasn't the werewolf. It was Tatum.

"Huh," Pom says. "Go on."

I dispel the crime scene and make a cliff appear. "Valerian could also have made it so that Ryan walked off the cliff on his own—no push needed. Or he could've made himself invisible and simply pushed." I make that scenario play out in front of Pom. "Or maybe both. Maybe Ryan realized he'd shot his own wife instead of an illusion, so he committed suicide."

"It tracks." Pom's ears wiggle. "But what about the others?"

I recreate the bird attack crime scene. "Valerian could've made Gemma think Leal was her enemy, and then had her summon the birds to kill him. For that matter, he could've made the birds see something tasty where Leal was standing, thus causing that attack." I create Leal and turn him into a bowl of grain.

Pom turns black. "Illusionists have too much power."

"Yeah. Yeah, they do." I recreate Gemma's torn body. "Here again, Valerian could've made someone strong—probably Eduardo—see an enemy attacking, so Eduardo ripped the 'enemy' in half. Or he could've shown Eduardo the illusion of Gemma provoking him, until he snapped and killed her. He could've even used his powers to drive that werewolf insane at JFK, to make sure the Enforcers were away."

Pom bobs his head, his eyes bigger than usual.

I'm on a roll now. It's coming together so clearly. "Finally, Valerian could've shown Eduardo something that drove him to choke Albina to death." I create a bedroom with Albina lying in bed, then swap her for Ryan the elf. "Alternatively, the choking might've been part of sex play, but Valerian could've made Eduardo think that Albina was asking him to squeeze harder. He could've used illusion to hide any sign she was choking."

Pom's ears droop. He looks sick. "What about Eduardo? Could you make someone give themselves an injection using illusions?"

"Sure," I say. "Valerian could've made himself invisible, then waltzed in and swapped the syringe with steroids for the one with the REM drug." I recreate the scene. A translucent Valerian watches as Eduardo accidentally kills himself. "For all we know, Valerian was still there, invisible to us when we found the body."

Pom's fur trembles.

I turn the translucent Valerian more opaque and study his perfect features. Can someone with such a gorgeous face be a killer?

What am I thinking? Of course he can. Besides, who says Valerian even looks this way? He might look like a leper with missing teeth and—

"You think they'll stay the execution when you tell them all this?" Pom asks.

I make Valerian disappear. "Well… this theory has a major flaw: I have no clue *why* he would kill all these Councilors. Motive is a pretty important part of crime investigations. Without that, plus some kind of proof, the Council won't listen to me. At the end of the day, this is just a wild theory."

"I still think you should talk to someone," Pom says. "Maybe Kit will think of a motive. How about we go into the tower and see if someone from the Council is sleeping?"

I shake my head glumly. "I'd need my powers to enter other people's dreams."

"You haven't recovered yet? I thought that's how you create stuff like this." He waves a paw around us.

"Just changing my surroundings doesn't mean I have my powers back. Even humans can learn to do something like this, à la lucid dreaming. To really know if I've recovered, I need to try to enter someone's dream."

"Let's do that, then." He torpedoes toward the tower of sleepers, and I hurry to catch up.

"Felix and Ariel aren't here," he says when we get to the nooks.

I take a quick glance at where a few of the Councilors would be if they were sleeping, but they aren't there. "Maybe it's daytime in New York."

"Then why is Bernard sleeping?" Pom points at the mustachioed man's room.

"He's been keeping odd hours." I make my way over to the clouds representing more dreams in the poor guy's trauma loop. "I guess I could use him to see if my powers are back. That'll give us a clue as to how long it's been in the waking world."

Pom gives me a baffled look. "You're going to finish Valerian's job? Even though we think he's the killer?"

"I don't have to finish the job. I could guide Bernard through the rest of his trauma loop but not do what Valerian actually hired me for. Then again, I think I *should* finish it."

Pom's ears twitch quizzically.

"If I finish, when Felix goes to sleep, I could ask him to send word to Valerian that the job is complete, so he remits the funds as promised. Killer or not, Valerian's got lots of money."

Pom turns an indeterminate mix of colors. "I guess."

I approach the sleeping Bernard. "I'll deal with his remaining dreams in the trauma loop first, then decide."

"Good luck," Pom says, bouncing up and down.

I give him a wave, make myself invisible, and touch Bernard's scarred forehead.

CHAPTER THIRTY-SIX

I'M IN. My powers are back—and I almost wish they weren't.

A dirty, beaten-up man is chained to a radiator in an abandoned warehouse.

I recognize him instantly. It's the wiry, balding middle-aged defendant from Bernard's courtroom dream, the one pronounced not guilty of murdering Bernard's boy. When his smell reaches me, I gag. What the hell? He stinks so bad my only option is to disable my olfactory sense. He also looks much thinner than at the trial, his shifty eyes filled with insanity and desperation.

His face stony, Bernard approaches, wood saw in hand.

"I'm sorry," the chained guy croaks. "Please let me out. I didn't mean to kill him. Things got out of control. I was abused when I was—"

"You want out? Here." Bernard drops the saw and kicks it within the prisoner's reach.

The guy frantically saws at the chain but only destroys the tool in the process. He hurls the toothless saw back at Bernard with a guttural cry—and misses.

"You can't cut metal with a wood saw," Bernard says coldly. "You know what you really need to do. You're just not ready yet."

Oh, no. I kind of knew where this was going, but still. Mega yuck.

A few days pass in a blink, and Bernard returns with a new saw identical to the last. This time, the insanity in the prisoner's eyes is even clearer. He doesn't even plead with Bernard, just sits there, gaze glued to the saw in his tormentor's hands. Without a word, Bernard drops the saw to the floor and kicks it over. The guy grabs it and reluctantly places the sharp edge above his wrist.

I shift my gaze to Bernard's face, and when the nauseating sounds begin, I disable my hearing. From Bernard's expression, you'd think it was *his* wrist being sawed in half. He's muttering something, and though I'm not great at reading lips, I think he's saying, "I'm a monster. I've become worse than the very evil I was trying to—"

Suddenly, his eyes widen to the size of plates.

I follow his gaze.

His right arm a gory mess, the prisoner leaps at Bernard with an animalistic snarl, shouting something.

I reenable my hearing.

The guttural roar is something I'd expect from a wounded bear, not a man.

Clutching the saw in his remaining hand, the man slices at Bernard's face. The teeth of the saw bite into his forehead, and Bernard screams in pain.

I shudder. So this is how he got that scar.

Bernard shoves his attacker away. The malnourished man tips backward but instantly begins crawling back toward Bernard, growling like a demon.

Hand trembling, Bernard reaches into his pocket and pulls out a gun.

Bang.

The growling stops, but the guy still crawls forward.

Bang.

The crawling stops as well.

Bernard keeps shooting until his gun is empty. Then he falls onto his hands and knees and vomits.

The dream shifts at this point. Bernard is staring at the empty walls of his apartment.

I swallow down the bitter tang of the previous dream. Okay, so his trauma loop is over. That's a good thing. Now that it's handled, I could in theory perform my job.

This dream is a memory, though, and I'm curious to let it play out.

The phone rings, and he lets voicemail pick up.

It's the ex-wife. "Your daughter's birthday is today. She misses you. Call her."

A shiver ripples through Bernard. "Why?" he whispers raggedly. "Why would she want to talk to a monster?"

The next dream is also a memory but takes place years later. Bernard watches his daughter from afar, his eyes filled with regret.

The next dream is later still. Bernard is sitting in a large conference hall surrounded by other humans. I recognize the keynote speaker.

It's Valerian.

In this memory, Valerian looks exactly as he appeared to me. Does that mean this is what he really looks like?

"By the end of next year, Bale Inc. will take virtual reality to the next level," the gorgeous illusionist says passionately, channeling Tony Robbins. "Further down the line, the world you see around you"—he clicks his remote control, and a space view of Earth appears on the screen behind him—"will be one of the many possible places people can inhabit. My hope is that most will thrive in these limitless illusory worlds that we will create for them, worlds undistinguishable from vanilla reality. It will be the biggest…"

I stop listening because something dawns on me.

What Valerian is trying to do. And why.

He wants to bring illusory worlds to billions of Earth humans. More than that, he wants his name—his and his company's—to be the name everyone associates with these worlds. He wants his name to be synonymous with illusions.

It's a mind-boggling ambition.

There's a relationship between Cognizant powers and the human belief in said powers. That's how Lilith, a vampire who declared herself a goddess of blood on a world she subjugated, became nearly unstoppable. By making his company synonymous with illusions, Valerian might become the most powerful illusionist on Earth, if not throughout the Cogniverse, all without declaring himself a god—something that would get him executed by the local Cognizant.

This must be why he hires me for shady jobs such as what I might be about to do: He needs to keep his nose clean as far as the Earth Councils are concerned.

Bernard's dream shifts to a time some nine months later. He's sitting in a meeting room with a bunch of people. Valerian is there too, looking at Bernard expectantly with those hypnotic blue eyes.

"The VR motion sickness is the most urgent issue to resolve before we go live," Valerian says. "Has your team made any progress on that?"

Bernard glances at his notepad. "We've been slaving at it for months, but we don't have much. We don't even know if the problem is caused by sensory conflict or postural instability. You're against removing body visualization…"

I ignore the rest of Bernard's speech. It's time to decide if I want to finish the job Valerian hired me for. Given this dream, it would take almost no effort to do so, as the dream happens to be about the very issue in question. Valerian is working on producing VR products that don't make people nauseated, a major hurdle facing the industry at the moment, so he's hired me to secretly provide Bernard with an inspiration —a solution to come "in a dream." The task is trivial, of course, since Gomorrah is light years ahead of Earth when it comes to all technology, but especially anything to do with virtual reality.

Fine. Given how easy this is, I'm just going to do it.

I leave my body and jump into Valerian's, then stride up to the drawing board. "What if we tried this?" I proceed to present a comprehensive solution, from hardware to software tricks.

Bernard's eyes light up greedily as I draw an algorithm that's particularly ahead of its time. I can't help but grin; the most difficult part of this job was actually memorizing all this.

When I'm done, I exit Valerian's body and wake Bernard with a jolt of my power. If I allow him to dream more, he could forget what he's just learned.

Pom is waiting eagerly in Bernard's nook in the tower of sleepers.

"That's it," I tell him when I reappear. "I've gone *Inception* on his ass."

Pom claps his tiny paws together. "So he'll make a technological discovery when he wakes up?"

"And he'll be positive he came up with it on his own. Valerian, of course, will profit." I leave the nook behind me to fly alongside Pom. "I wonder how often my kind has been responsible for big discoveries that are really just information from another world? Maybe this is how Earth's Dmitri Mendeleev came up with the periodic table in his dream. Niels Bohr is also said to have come up with the structure of the atom in his dream, and even Albert Einstein—"

I stop short because I notice something that can't be.

A sleeper who shouldn't be sleeping, yet is.

I look at Pom. "You see him too, right?" I point at the nook in question.

Pom turns a hodgepodge of colors. "I see. But isn't that—"

"Exactly." I whoosh toward the room.

"But how?" He flies after me.

"I think he was doing his best to stay awake until I'm executed, but he must've accidentally fallen asleep." I loom over the sleeper, still having trouble believing my eyes.

"Do you think it means—"

"Oh yeah." My voice crackles with excitement. "This must be the murderer."

CHAPTER THIRTY-SEVEN

WE BOTH EXAMINE the deceptively kind, grandfatherly face in front of us —a face belonging to someone who's supposedly dead.

A face belonging to Dr. Hekima.

"But he died," Pom says, bewildered. "Nessie ate him."

I shake my head. "Hekima's an illusionist. He made me and Kain believe we'd seen his death in a way that conveniently left no body to be examined."

Pom's pupils morph into red hearts again. "So Valerian isn't the killer after all?"

I grin at him. "No, but the way Hekima pulled off the crimes is probably the way I said Valerian would've. I almost figured it out—I just suspected the wrong illusionist."

Pom's ears flap back and forth. "But why did he kill all those people?"

That's what I have to go in and find out. I point at the clouds swirling over Hekima's head. "I bet his trauma loop has something to do with it."

Dragging in a steadying breath, I touch the illusionist's wrinkled forehead with unsteady fingers and jump into his dream.

———————

"PLEASE, SITI," a younger version of Hekima says. "What you're doing isn't safe."

He's talking to a teen who looks just like him, frizzy hair, kind face, and all. Her name sounds vaguely familiar to me.

"I'm easing people's pain, Daddy," Siti says. "If you weren't under the stupid Mandate, you'd do the same thing. You know you would."

Hekima sighs. "I'm not saying what you're doing isn't kind. It is. It's just that using your powers that way is forbidden by—"

Puck, now I recall where I heard her name. It was when I was researching the voting patterns. The case about the young woman who eased the pain of human hospice patients in their final days—her name was Siti.

"I make them think they're somewhere beautiful," Siti says, confirming my suspicions, "and sometimes I surround them with their loved ones. Is that so wrong?"

It all clicks into place. Siti was caught. There was a Council trial, and Eduardo, Tatum, Ryan, Gemma, Leal, Albina, and a bunch of others voted for the ultimate penalty—and the Council executed the poor girl.

When Hekima learned what had happened, he gained prominence in the Cognizant community by running the Orientation program Felix mentioned—all so that one day he'd be chosen to serve on the Council and be positioned to take his revenge.

And he's not done yet. There are still people on the Council who voted to execute his daughter. With me out of the picture and everyone else thinking him dead, he's free to finish what he started, one Councilor at a time.

Realizing I missed a shift from one dream to another, I start paying closer attention.

Hekima is standing over an unmarked grave, tears streaming down his face.

"I'm sorry, Siti," he says thickly. "I should've forced you to stop. I should've dragged you to another world before you got caught. I should've—"

He stops talking and looks right at me.

Puck. What's wrong with me? I forgot to make myself invisible again —and at the worst time ever.

I belatedly disappear, but it's too late. Hekima saw me, I can tell by his expression. Looking at the spot where I stood, he smashes his fist into his own nose—and that must cause him to wake up.

I end up back in the tower of sleepers, Hekima gone from the bed.

"He knows that I know," I tell Pom grimly.

He turns black and grabs my wrist with his little paws. "Wake up and do something."

So I wake myself—and end up back on the dirty floor of my stinky dungeon cell.

CHAPTER THIRTY-EIGHT

THEN AGAIN, all is not the same as when I first got locked in here. Having slept, I feel amazing. I must've gotten at least a few additional hours of rest. Leaping to my feet, I whip out my sanitizer and wipe down every part of me that touched the floor.

Wow, my mind is sharp as a diamond. No wonder I couldn't solve the case earlier. After months of sleep deprivation, I was a shadow of myself. I resist the urge to smack my forehead. Why did it take me so long to kick vampire blood? Given my work with insomniacs, I know better than anyone that lack of sleep can lead to impaired thinking, memory problems, and eventually even death.

Here's how bad my memory had become: I'd forgotten about my lockpicks. I still have them in my pocket from when I broke into Bernard's apartment. My hand slaps my pocket—yep, still there. I dash over to the rusty padlock on the door of my cell.

Oh yeah, I can handle this. Hopefully.

The lock puts up a small fight but eventually yields. I slide open the bolt on my side and open the cell door. Now what?

If I'd done this before I realized Hekima was the murderer, I would've had to escape from a heavily guarded castle and elude Enforcer vampires for the rest of my life—a venture with almost zero chance of success. But now, armed with my new discovery, I only need to locate someone from the Council and tell them what I know.

Assuming Hekima doesn't stop me.

And assuming they believe me.

Still, better chance now than before.

I take a dozen hurried steps down the corridor before Filth rounds the corner, beady eyes locking onto me.

Puck. The last thing I need.

"I figured out who's been killing the Councilors," I say quickly. "It's Hekima. He—"

"Don't care." Filth smiles nastily, and his eyes turn into mirrors as his voice shifts to glamour mode. "Freeze, stupid blood bag."

CHAPTER THIRTY-NINE

I WRIGGLE my toes inside my shoes. I was right—they're wriggling away. His glamour didn't work. The vampire blood has left my system and my resistance to glamour is back—or Filth simply isn't as powerful as Kain when it comes to penetrating my defenses.

I pretend like I *am* frozen, though, and frantically ponder my next move.

Filth takes a syringe out of his pocket. "I've been designated as your executioner. The Council wants me to provide you with a choice between euthanasia"—he waves the syringe in the air—"or starvation." He nods at the room behind me.

Inside my chest, my heart is jackrabbiting, but I do my best to keep my face placid, as if frozen by glamour.

"I'll simplify it for you, though." He turns the syringe needle downward and presses the plunger until all the poison is on the floor. "I'll drink you dry, then toss your body out for Nessie to munch on. As far as the Council is concerned, you opted for starvation and then proved dumb enough to try to escape via the sewers."

He's thought this through. Anyone who doesn't know me well might even believe him—never mind that I'd sooner starve a hundred times before I'd jump into that excuse for a toilet... even if there weren't a monster lurking in the sewers.

Filth stalks toward me.

I furtively position the lockpicks to stick out of my fist and wait for my moment. This is a vampire, and no martial arts training can overcome the fact that even a skinny, weaselly specimen like him is ten times stronger than I am, and impossibly fast. The element of surprise is my only hope—and a faint one, if I'm honest with myself.

"I *could* command you not to feel anything," he says when he's within striking distance, "but I won't. This will hurt."

He's right. It will hurt.

Him.

Without warning, I smash my fist into his face. With a disgustingly squishy sound, the lockpicks enter his right eye.

He staggers back, roaring in pain. I fight the urge to heave, and kick him in the groin. He roars again and strikes me with the back of his hand. My head jerks sideways, and stars explode in my vision.

He throws a punch at my jaw. I somehow dodge it, moving purely on autopilot. By now, I've recovered enough to hit him, only he moves preternaturally fast and I miss. Before I can block, his elbow crashes into my midsection. My solar plexus explodes in pain, and I bend over, wheezing.

He grabs me by my shirt and effortlessly tosses me into the air. As I fly through the hallway, I spot a ray of hope down the corridor.

Thud. I crash into the iron bars with my back, and the two molecules of oxygen left in my lungs escape with a *whoosh*. The pain tries to drag me into unconsciousness, but I fight it with my whole being. I need to stall in case that ray of hope wasn't a hallucination of my rattled brain.

Gulping in greedy breaths, I look up at Filth pleadingly and raise my hand as if I need to say something.

He doesn't look like he wants to talk. His eye hasn't healed. Some vamps have better recuperation abilities than others, and his is clearly on the lower end of the spectrum.

Fangs sliding out, he hisses, "I'll make this slow."

CHAPTER FORTY

I SPIT out blood and croak, "I told Kit. She knows—she knows about Hekima. About seeing him in the dream world. You won't get away with this."

There's a flash of movement at the end of the corridor.

Yep. There's no doubt now.

I sneak a peek through Filth's legs.

Creeping toward us are Ariel and Felix. He's dressed in a tux, and she's wearing a dress that shows off every curve. In her hand is a butterfly knife. I don't even want to think about where she hid it when they went through castle security.

They must be here for the Mandate ceremony Felix mentioned.

I can't get my hopes up, though. Without his robot suit or some powerful weapon, Felix is basically human. Ariel is another matter. She's an uber and they're strong—but not quite vampire strong. And Ariel has issues with vampires.

Filth grips my throat and lifts me off the ground with one hand. "I believe your Kit bullshit as much as I believe in Hekima's miraculous resurrection." With a swift chomp, he sinks his fangs into my neck, startling a pained cry from me.

It hurts even more because it's the grossest thing to ever happen to me.

He begins to suck—and that's when Ariel rips him away by the shoulder while stabbing him in the torso.

My tailbone hits the floor, hard. Gritting my teeth against a wave of nauseating pain, I scoot away from the combatants, clasping my bleeding neck. Vampire saliva is known to act as a coagulant, but I've never been bitten and have no idea how long it'll take for my neck to stop bleeding. Also, gross.

Ignoring the stab wound, Filth throws a punch at Ariel's face. She dodges, rips the knife out, and stabs him an inch lower.

Felix kneels next to me. "Are you okay?"

"Help me up," I rasp, extending my free hand toward him. My throat's in agony, and not just from the wound on the side. Filth all but crushed my trachea while lifting me off the ground.

Felix grips my hand and helps me to my feet while Ariel and Filth fight, moving so fast it's hard to follow them.

Swaying in place, I pull my hand away from the wound in my neck. The bleeding seems to have stopped. Seeing that I'm not in imminent danger of dying, Felix jumps in to help Ariel, but Filth knocks him out with a punch to the temple. As Felix collapses, Ariel uses the distraction to slice a bone-deep gash in Filth's bicep. The vampire grunts in pain as blood sprays them both.

If Felix weren't already knocked out, he'd faint from the gore. I'm less sensitive to these things, and even I feel woozy. Or maybe I'm just woozy from the blood loss. Either way, it's my turn to help Ariel—and I want it to count. Ignoring the pain in my bruised throat, I sprint back to my jail cell, grab the heavy padlock I defeated earlier, and rush back.

Filth smashes an elbow into Ariel's solar plexus, same as he did with me. But Ariel must've done an obscene number of crunches and built abs of steel, because she keeps fighting as if nothing's happened.

I wait for a moment when Filth's back is to me, then lunge forward and slam the padlock into the back of his head.

What would've stunned or knocked out a human only seems to distract the vampire. He throws a punch at my face. I duck. He still manages to block Ariel's next hit.

I jump back and hurl the padlock at his head with all my might. He twists out of the way—and that's what puts his throat within reach of Ariel's blade.

Whoosh.

Blood gushes from the gaping neck wound.

Puck, I might've underestimated Ariel's strength. She's nearly beheaded Filth with one slice.

Some sort of gurgling sound escapes Filth's mouth, but Ariel takes no chances. She chops at his throat again and again, until the head and body separate completely—a wound no vampire in history has been able to heal.

Filth's torso collapses to the ground, and his head rolls over to Felix. At that moment, Felix's eyes flutter open. As soon as he sees the bloody mess next to him, he faints again.

Ariel stares at her bloody knife with eerie fascination. She looks—oh crap, she looks on the verge of licking the blade.

This is it. Her vampire blood addiction is being put to a real test.

I hold my breath. It's better if she does this on her own. She's at the stage where what she needs most is to believe in her ability to resist temptation.

I, too, was recently on my way to addiction, but I feel zero urge to imbibe any of the crimson liquid around us. Then again, I should find the situation a lot more gross than I actually do. Is that a bad sign? Still, I've got a feeling that if I avoid vamp blood for a while, it will eventually seem as yucky as other bodily fluids.

Ariel's jaw firms. I guess she's made her choice.

She lifts the knife.

My fingernails bite into the palms of my hands. *Don't lick it!*

She tosses the knife into the jail cell. It clanks on the floor as she ceremoniously spits on Filth's body and turns away.

Grinning, I clap her on the shoulder. "See? You *can* resist the temptation in the real world."

She grins back, then kicks Filth's head back toward his body and walks over to kneel next to Felix. Her lips quirk in a rueful smile as she lifts his limp arm and lets it drop. "Out cold. I guess a severed head is where he draws the line."

Something flickers in my peripheral vision, but when I look down the hall, I see nothing. When Ariel follows my gaze, however, she stiffens, her smile disappearing.

"Leave now!" she yells at the empty hallway. "If you don't, you'll join your underling here." She jerks her chin toward Filth's remains.

Underling? Is she talking to Kain? Then I realize what's happening—and my remaining blood turns to ice.

"That's not Kain!" I shout. "It's Hekima. He's using illusions on you."

She doesn't seem to hear me. Leaping to her feet, she rushes an invisible foe, throws a punch at nothing, and dodges an invisible strike. Jaw clenched tight, she follows her illusory enemy until she's a few feet from where I'm still standing, gaping at her.

She looks at my feet and screams. "No!"

Puck. I can guess what Hekima is showing her: Kain is here, and he's just killed me. I'll bet Hekima's making me look like Kain, a trick he used to commit those other murders as well.

As if to prove my theory correct, Ariel balls her hands and advances on me, her beautiful face twisted with hate. "You're dead."

CHAPTER FORTY-ONE

PUCK, puck, puck. I don't think I can bring myself to hit Ariel or hurt her in any way—not that my qualms are anything but academic. After seeing what she did to Filth, I know I don't stand a chance of hurting her. She'll be the one doing the hurting, and it won't even take that long.

My heart gallops at two hundred miles per hour. This is called a fight or flight response for a reason—and the time to fight is over.

Turning on my heel, I bolt for the jail cell.

Ariel's footsteps echo behind me. Panting like a dog after a day in a desert, I leap inside the cell and slam the door in her face, sliding the bolt into the locked position.

"You think this will stop me?" She slams her palms against the bars.

I jump back. "I certainly hope so."

She grabs a bar in each hand and strains to pull them apart, her lean muscles flexing beneath her skimpy dress.

No way. She can't—

But the heavy-duty bars are bending. She's stronger than any uber I've heard of.

I'm so dead.

Or not. I scoop her knife from the floor and frantically squirt a bunch of hand sanitizer onto the hilt. *No blood, can't have all this blood.* Once it's clean, I turn to face the door, where she's diligently working on the bars.

Would she give up if I stabbed her? Maybe I could do it in the arm or some other nonlethal place?

The bars are almost wide enough for her to fit her head through. I look around frantically for some alternate solution. Looking down, I finally see it—a horrible, horrible option, something I'd normally say is a fate worse than death. Except here, faced head on with my mortality, I realize this fate may be just a little bit better. I guess my will to live overrides my squeamishness.

Maybe.

I dash to the hole leading to the sewer.

My first mistake is looking down. When I see the murky, foul-smelling liquid down there, I decide maybe Ariel can kill me after all. If I have to be killed, it might be nicer for a friend to do it.

Except it's not just my life that's on the line. Pom will die as well—and so will Mom, if I don't convince the Council that Hekima's the murderer.

Shaking all over, I sanitize the blade of the butterfly knife, fold it, and slip it into my pocket. And yes, I realize how crazy I am to do this, given what I'm about to dive into. Gulping in a breath of fetid air, I plug my ears with my index fingers and my nose with my pinkies, like a kid learning to dive for the first time, and sneak one last peek at the cell bars to see if maybe Hekima has given up.

Nope. Ariel is sticking her head into the opening she's just made. It's now or never.

Squeezing my eyes shut, I jump feet first into the sewer abyss.

CHAPTER FORTY-TWO

AS I FALL, obscenities in all the languages I speak repeat on a loop in my head.

Sploosh.

The gooey substance closes over my head, and I don't feel anything resembling a floor under my feet. The sewer must be really deep. *Don't think about flesh-eating bacteria and the open wound in my neck. Or brain-eating amoebas. Or the people-eating monster that's made these sewers a home. Or where the monster goes to the bathroom. Or—*

Survival instinct wrenches my hands away from my face, and I begin to flail. My head emerges, and I suck in a breath. The stench is unbearable, as if someone had formulated the worst odor that could exist in nature. What the hell is this stuff?

I'd rather not know. That way lies insanity.

Everything around me is dark, but there's a faint light in the far distance. I swim toward it. No one jumps into the sewer behind me. That's good. I guess Hekima can't maintain the illusion without joining Ariel, and he isn't willing to follow me here. He doesn't want his earlier lie of being eaten by Nessie to become reality.

Speaking of the monster, I haven't been eaten by her either. Not yet, anyway.

I keep on swimming.

The horrific liquid is thick and viscous, and I'd rather not think about why that is. At least that makes floating here easier than in the lakes from the black windows in Nina's dreams. Now that I'm out of immediate mortal danger, the grossness of what I'm doing is overwhelming. Is it possible to die from disgust? Desperate, I remind myself that even when I'm clean, there are more microbes in and on me than cells with my own DNA.

Nope, that doesn't help at all. Better not think, period.

I focus on the movement of my arms. Upstroke. Downstroke. Upstroke. Downstroke. The light is nearer. It's daylight outside the castle's mountain.

My foot bumps against something mushy, and I'm able to stand and rest. *Best not to think about what I'm standing on.*

In the direction I came from, the muck ripples. Has Ariel finally jumped in? Hekima? I pull out the knife, unfolding it frantically—not that it'll help much. Defending myself with this knife will be like trying to put out a forest fire with a water gun.

The ripples intensify, and a head emerges from the mucky water.

My stomach drops to my feet.

There's no mistaking the long neck and the maw full of dagger-like teeth.

It's Nessie, and she's here to eat me.

CHAPTER FORTY-THREE

I SQUEEZE the knife so hard my knuckles whiten.

"Go away!" I shout at the creature.

She doesn't even blink. Her head rises from the muck atop a neck like an anaconda.

"I'm not a pucking goat," I shout, waving the knife. "Last warning."

Nessie strikes. Her maw opens as her head flashes toward me. It takes all my martial arts training to stay still and wait for my moment. When the teeth are ready to close around me, I strike.

My blade sinks into her squishy tongue. Yes!

Nessie jerks her head back, ripping the knife from my hand. I dive for the sewer exit and swim for all I'm worth.

Behind me, Nessie roars.

My arms windmill with insane speed, and the light draws nearer. I might be beating a world record of some kind—assuming some sadist keeps track of sewer swim times.

The beast roars again. She's gaining on me. I impossibly speed up, the proximity of the exit urging me on.

When I finally burst into the light, my eyes take a second to adjust. I'm in the moat in front of the castle, just outside the mountain. The shore is nearby, filled with monks carrying a goat.

Just my luck—Nessie has come across me at lunch time. The good news is that if I hurry, she might eat the goat instead of me.

Fresh air gives my muscles a much-needed boost, and I close the distance in seconds. The stunned monks help me stumble out of the water.

"Nessie," I pant. "I think she—"

Before I can finish, two monks seize the poor goat and heave it into the moat.

A familiar head appears above the water. Nessie opens her maw again. There's no sign of the knife I left there, or a wound of any kind. I guess it makes sense that she has some super-healing ability. She's an incredibly long-lived creature; the legends about her go way back.

A blink later, the goat is gone. So is Nessie.

Whew.

I fish my hand sanitizer out of my soaked pocket and use it all up on my face and hands. "I need to see someone on the Council."

The tallest of the monks eyes me like I'm crazy. "You can't. They're in a meeting and—"

"Does this sound like a normal request?" I growl. "They're going to want to know what just happened, why I just emerged from the sewer with Nessie on my tail, trying to tell them the truth about who's kill—"

He holds up a hand. "I'll take you there."

With a wary glance at me, he heads for the castle. I follow, doing my best to shake off the worst of the slime clinging to me before we reach the familiar door into the coliseum where the Council meets.

"They'll be upset if you just barge in," the monk says, wrinkling his nose. "And not just because of your smell."

I shrug, and trying not to breathe too deeply, I step into the Council chambers.

CHAPTER FORTY-FOUR

KAIN IS STANDING in the center of the amphitheater, the place usually reserved for whoever's in trouble.

"I suggest we vote," Nina is saying. "Those in—"

"I know who the murderer is," I announce loudly.

All heads turn toward me.

Kain sniffs the air and looks half perplexed, half horrified. I open my mouth to say more when someone pushes me out of the way. I stagger and look around.

No one's visible.

My pulse spikes into the stratosphere.

Hekima. He's here.

CHAPTER FORTY-FIVE

INSTANTLY, my surroundings change.

I'm still in an amphitheater, only one a thousand times larger than where the Council meets. It looks like the Colosseum in Rome, only brand new. Confirming the Rome connection, screaming people appear in the seats. They look like extras in a movie about gladiators.

The emperor rises. It's Hekima, dressed in a purple toga, with a gold laurel wreath perched on top of his frizzy gray curls.

He's looking down at me, his dark eyes filled with genuine sadness. "You remind me of Siti," he says in a warm, grandfatherly tone. "I wish I could let you live, but you know too much. It's me or you—basically self-defense."

My upper lip curls. "Whatever you need to tell yourself. If Siti were alive, she'd be ashamed of you."

He looks as if I've punched him. Stiffening, he sinks onto his imperial seat, and an expression of concentration appears on his face. He must be showing illusions to the members of the Council.

The crowd cheers as though a rock star just walked onstage. I look down. My filthy clothing is gone, replaced with a hybrid of armor and a bikini—apparently Hekima's dirty fantasy of what a gladiatrix would wear.

I scowl up at him. "I know this costume is an illusion, but it makes no sense as battle gear." I slide my hand over my exposed cleavage. "It's basically daring someone to stab me in the heart."

As if in reply, the doors leading to the stage burst open and a puck saunters out.

It's an illusion. I know that. There can be no pucks on Earth. Hekima is making me see that hairy body, the horns and the hoofed feet. In the real world, this is someone from the Council, or maybe no one at all. Yet the sights, sounds, and even smells are exactly as if I were at the real Colosseum facing a goat-reeking puck. Not that I have much room to talk —though now that I'm in Hekima's illusion, I can't smell my own funk.

The monster opens its mouth, flashing a grill a shark would envy and bathing me in the stench of decomposing meat.

The crowd goes wild.

Is pain one of the senses illusionists can control? Will it feel real when those teeth tear at my flesh?

The puck lunges at me and tries to punch me in the mouth. I dodge and strike at his sternum. I miss—yet I don't see how I could have. Either I'm fighting someone smaller than a puck, or there's no one around me at all.

The puck smashes a fist into my face.

Ouch.

That hurt, and my lip feels genuinely split. Either there's a real person fighting me, or Hekima's powers are megastrong.

I dodge another swing, then another. My face stings, but not proportionally to how much it would hurt if a real puck hit me—they're incredibly powerful. Since I see no reason Hekima would hold back on illusory pain, I conclude that my opponent is real and isn't super-strong. I guess that's good. Still, I need to finish this battle before my opponent inevitably uses his or her Council-level powers.

The puck sweeps my feet. I jump over his hoof and throw a punch at his throat. My hand connects with flesh that feels more like a jawbone than neck. The puck staggers and falls down.

Yeah, right. No way a puck would be bested by such a hit.

The crowd goes wild.

The doors fly open again, and a monster more terrifying than a puck ambles out.

It's a drekavac, a creature that kills by causing unspeakable pain.

I stagger back. Just looking at the thing is painful. It's a nightmarish, insectoid wraith with too many tentacles and teeth.

Then something dawns on me.

If Hekima wants this encounter to seem realistic, he'll use someone with the power to kill with a single touch.

Blood drains from my face.

There's a Councilor perfectly suited for this, one whose touch causes gangrene.

Gertrude.

CHAPTER FORTY-SIX

"I CAN'T FIGHT GERTRUDE!" I scream, in case Hekima cares.

He doesn't.

I back away and do my best to strategize. Even if I land a punch, I'll lose.

The drekavac charges and whips at me with a tentacle.

I dodge.

Shrieking, the monster sends another tentacle my way.

I leap to the side but barely miss getting touched.

There has to be something more effective I can do, some way to penetrate this illusion.

Another tentacle strike, another dodge.

A chat with Pom suddenly pops into my mind. He once claimed that if he were awake, he could show me what Valerian really looks like, based on the assumption that an illusionist wouldn't think to target my symbiont.

Two tentacles go for me at once, and I perform a backflip to get away. The crowd cheers.

The problem is that Pom must be awake to see through my eyes, and he sleeps all the time. Unless—

Pom, I mentally shout as I dodge yet another tentacle strike. *Pom, wake up!*

Nothing happens. A tentacle lashes at my legs, and I jump over it.

Pom! Pom! Pom!

"What's with the shouting?" Pom says groggily in my head.

I'm inside an illusion, I mentally shout. *Need you to see through it, or we both die!*

"Should've led with that." He sounds much more awake. "How's this?"

The world flashes with every color of the rainbow, and I barely dodge the next tentacle strike. When the swirl settles, I do my best to make sense of the visual confusion. The Colosseum isn't gone, but it looks a bit ghostly.

Then I realize it's actually overlaid with reality, a reality that looks odd. The edges of objects are fuzzy, and something strange is going on with colors. For instance, I see an orc fighting Colton the giant, but instead of the orc being green, both fighters are monochrome.

Puck, that's not an orc. It's Kit. Hekima is having her fight for her life, and Pom doesn't like it. Neither do I. I bet all that black is Pom's feelings seeping into my perception.

Whoosh. A ghostly tentacle flies at my face, only now I see that the tentacle isn't a tentacle at all. It is, as I suspected, Gertrude's arm. Fingers outstretched, she's trying to touch my cheek in the real world.

I sidestep and grab her arm near the elbow, where her sleeve protects my hand from her skin. I'm not sure what she's seeing in her own version of Hekima's illusion, but it must be something terrible because her face contorts with fear.

This won't help matters.

I twist her arm behind her back and pull hard. She drops to her knees, crying out in pain. I grab hold of one of my slimy shoes and club Gertrude with the makeshift weapon. There's no way I'm risking a touch again, even if it's only her hair.

She claws at me with her free hand, so I smack her again and again. My arm muscles burn, but I accomplish my goal.

Gertrude collapses.

This is when I notice who else is lying unconscious nearby.

Felix.

He must've recovered from his blood-induced fainting spell, only to fall under Hekima's influence. He must've been the "puck" I fought. No wonder his punches didn't hurt much—and no wonder I was able to win. He's a little sensitive about it, but Felix's powers aren't useful in hand-to-hand combat.

I rush over and check his vitals. He'll probably have a headache, but he'll be fine—and his headache isn't going to be half as bad as Gertrude's. I glance back to see how Kit is doing and see her morph from an orc into a giant much bigger than Colton. She raises a massive fist in an arc so wide, she knocks a couple of nearby Councilors off their feet. *Pow!* She smashes that fist into Colton's temple.

He roars in pain. Poor dude. I bet his headache's going to be even worse than Gertrude's.

Someone needs to stop this madness. The real Hekima is on the other side of the room with a wall of Councilors between him and anyone wishing to cause him harm. Everyone in his line of defense shows grim determination; they must each be experiencing illusions in which they're protecting someone or something they care about. There goes my hope of knocking *him* out.

I recognize some of the defenders—Isis and Chester—and note that not a single one of them is among those Hekima still wants to get revenge on.

I soon see why.

Nina, standing a stone's throw from me, raises her hands with a look of concentration. The stone benches where the Councilors usually sit rip out of the ground, break apart, and begin zooming all over the room.

I dodge one, then another—but not all the Councilors are so fortunate. Unlike me, they can't see what's real. At least four get hit in the head. I can't help but notice they're all on Hekima's kill list.

Two benches fly in Hekima's direction, giving me hope that his revenge may backfire. But no. A bench that seemed to be flying at Chester lands an inch away from him. How lucky for Chester—and Hekima, by extension. The other bench lands in front of the wall of Councilors, hitting Vickie on the head.

Isis shoots an arc of golden energy at the siren, healing her instantly.

Is Hekima being nice to the siren because she's not on his list? Nah, that's giving him too much credit. The real reason becomes apparent a moment later. Gulping in a large breath of air, Vickie shrieks at a nearby Councilor on the list, and two seconds later, only the man's skeleton remains.

Puck. What do I do? I can't get to Hekima, and if Nina keeps flinging those benches around, I might get knocked out too.

I sweep my gaze over the room for ideas and spot Ariel fighting Kain. There's too much hatred on their faces for two people who don't know each other—Hekima's illusions in action again.

Ariel smashes a fist into Kain's ear. He strikes back. She blocks with her forearm, but the force of his hit is so powerful that the back of her hand recoils and splits her lip.

Crap. Fighting Kain isn't as easy as taking down Filth—and I don't know if Ariel even realizes she's battling a vampire.

Another bench piece crashes down next to my feet, courtesy of Nina. Now *that* could work. I scan the floor for the biggest chunk of stone I can lift and find one that weighs about thirty pounds. Straining, I raise the rock above my head and charge at Kain.

Oblivious to my existence, Kain lands a punch in Ariel's midsection. Ariel crumples in pain.

Before Kain can go for the kill, I slam the stone into his head.

The vampire sways, a stunned look on his face. Ariel recovers enough to stumble toward him, and I shove the stone into her hands. With a startled expression, she grabs on. I can't guess what it must feel like to have a bloody rock materialize in your grasp, but Ariel's a trooper. She doesn't waste time pondering her good fortune.

Easily lifting the stone, she smashes it into Kain's face.

Kain staggers back.

Ariel hits him again.

Kain stumbles to the floor.

Ariel jumps on his chest and slams the rock down on his forehead, again and again.

"Enough!" I yell at her, but she doesn't seem to hear me. She bashes and bashes what remains of Kain's head, way past the point of his demise. Clearly, whatever illusion Hekima is giving her has generated a murderous rage.

I feel a surge of pity for the vampire—for all our differences, he was just trying to do his job—but I remind myself that Kain's death is on Hekima's conscience. Same goes for the Councilors Hekima wanted revenge on.

They're dead now too.

But Hekima himself? He's staring at me.

Puck.

I frantically look for a smaller rock, but he points his hand at Nina.

"Wait!" I yell.

Too late.

An invisible telekinetic force hurls me into the air.

CHAPTER FORTY-SEVEN

I FLAIL as I sail through the air.

This isn't the dream world. This flight will end in a painful crash at best, a bashed-in head à la Kain at worst. Heart pounding, I rummage through my pockets for something to throw at Hekima.

Nina boomerangs me a new direction, breaking my concentration. Does she think I'm a drone or something?

My patting hands discover an object in the last pocket I check. Is that what I think it is? Clearly, sleep deprivation made my memory worse than I thought. Here's yet another tool from the Bernard job I've completely forgotten about.

I pull out the sleep grenade as Nina makes me circle the room even faster.

If I use the grenade, everyone here will fall asleep. That includes Nina, which means I'll crash-land. If I don't use the grenade, she's bound to tire of playing with her drone and crash me into something. Not a big difference. At least this way, I stand a chance.

So be it.

Holding my breath, I activate the grenade and toss it.

Gas fills the room, and I feel myself plummet. I keep holding my breath until I land atop Chester's sleeping body.

Ouch. That hurt, but I'll definitely live. But there's one problem: I can't hold my breath any longer.

Lungs screaming for air, I inhale—and join everyone in sleep.

CHAPTER FORTY-EIGHT

I'M STANDING under a shower that sprays tomato juice instead of water, soaking the pink tutu I'm wearing. A purple llama stands just outside the stream, chewing the shower curtain.

"Can you pass me the body wash?" the llama says in a Scottish accent, after the curtain is kaput.

I obligingly reach for the bottle, only to notice something missing from my wrist.

Pom isn't where he should be.

Of course. I'm dreaming. For the millionth time, I wonder why such absurdities as the tutu and the llama don't clue me in.

Recalling what happened right before I fell asleep, I change my outfit and head for my dream palace.

I'm lucky Chester fell where he did. Was that his luck or mine? It's possible that his probability power guided my fall so as to save him from Hekima's trap. Hopefully that means I can figure out how to do exactly that.

Pom materializes in front of me. "Did it help when I let you see what I see?"

I pull him close and fluff his fur. "Yep, but no time to talk. I think I have a plan."

"Good luck." His ears turn black. "If you don't mind, I'll stay out of it— I have a feeling it's going to be scary."

"Suit yourself."

I teleport to the tower of sleepers. A few Councilors are already here, but not Hekima. He must not have reached REM sleep yet.

Since Kit *is* here, I enter her dream. Surprise, surprise, she's dreaming of an orgy.

I interrupt the proceedings. "Hey, Kit, this is a wet dream. We need to talk."

When she looks at me, I remove the naked people and the bedroom from around us and replace them with a recreation of the Council meeting chamber—or at least the way the place looked before Hekima's massacre.

"Have a seat," I tell her, and fill her in on everything that's happened.

By the time I finish, her eyes are almost as wide as Pom's. "I can't believe it was Hekima. But that does explain what happened to me. I saw Colton admit that *he* was the murderer, and then he attacked me."

"I bet Colton thought you admitted the same thing."

"So many dead." She shakes her head mournfully.

"About that. Filth and Kain's deaths—"

"—are Hekima's fault." She turns into Hekima and imitates cutting a throat. "I'll make sure the rest of the Council understand that you, Felix, and Ariel aren't guilty of anything, nor is anyone who killed a colleague due to Hekima's trickery. Don't worry."

Great. And it's almost true. No one needs to know the particulars of Filth's demise. He had it coming, but Ariel could still get into trouble unless Hekima takes the blame.

"Thank you," I say.

Kit reverts to her usual guise. "What now?"

"I'm going to bring more Councilors here and ask you to bring them up to speed."

Leaving her, I go back to the tower of sleepers and enter Nina's dream. She's flying over a field of daisies. I take to the air and loft up next to her.

Her eyes boggle.

"You're in a dream," I say.

She floats down to earth and bends to literally smell the flowers. "Seems so real."

"I know."

She rubs her forehead. "Did I really—"

"Let's hold off on the explanation for a moment." I take us to the dream version of the Council meeting room. "Kit, please tell Nina what happened. I'll get the others."

Without waiting for a reply, I return to the tower of sleepers and get Chester, followed by Colton, Isis, the siren, and a few other Councilors.

Eventually, I spot Hekima in one of the nooks.

My sleep grenade has finally worked on him.

I return to the Council meeting place.

"Do you have a plan?" Isis asks when I appear.

"I do. But before we go into that, I want to make sure we're all good." I look at each Councilor one by one. "Is my execution canceled?"

Isis raises her chin. "The majority of the Council is here, and we've voted for amnesty in your case. Furthermore, I'm still going to heal your mother."

My heart leaps. "Today?"

"If we survive Hekima," she says with an eye roll. "Are you ready to talk about your plan in regard to that little problem?"

I take a deep breath and face the Councilors. "The plan is simple. You all try to wake up. Meanwhile, I'll go into Hekima's dream to make sure he keeps dreaming and therefore can't thwart you. Once you're in the waking world, knock him out."

"I'll do it," Kit says eagerly.

"I'm closer to him," Chester says.

"Doesn't matter who," I say. "Just wake up."

"How?" Nina asks.

"Will yourself to wake up. If that doesn't work, use a little bit of pain."

Chester disappears right away, but most others stand there with expressions of concentration. Then Kit punches herself, and that wakes her up. Colton does the same and also disappears. Nina looks like she's having trouble, so I give her a jolt to assist her.

When the last Councilor is gone, I take myself to Hekima's room in the tower of sleepers. It would be extremely unfortunate if he happened to wake up before someone could knock him out.

Making it a point to turn myself invisible, I touch him on the forehead.

———

HEKIMA IS SITTING on a couch reading a book. A confused expression appears on his face. He lowers the book to his lap and raises it again, and even I see the text is different on the second go. His confusion deepens.

Crap. What he's just done is one of the many techniques lucid dreamers use to determine whether they're in a dream or not, a bit like what I do with Pom on my wrist. Text often becomes blurry and changeable in dreams. If Hekima ascertains this isn't real, he could wake himself up.

I gently shoot him with my power to keep him in the dream state. It's not a surefire method; if he punches himself the way he did in the graveyard, he could still wake up.

As if hearing my thoughts, Hekima stands up and raises his fist to do exactly what I don't want him to do.

I make his couch grow two plush arms like a giant teddy bear, and the arms grab him by the wrists, preventing him from hurting himself.

He looks right at me. "Ah, Bailey. I'm definitely dreaming."

To my shock, I become visible.

What the hell? Is this what had happened the last time I'd been in his dream? Maybe I hadn't forgotten to make myself invisible after all. Maybe he'd done the same thing to me then.

Hekima gives me a level look. "I'm an experienced lucid dreamer. I may not be able to enter other people's dreams, but I'm not so easy to fool."

He looks at the teddy bear bindings, and they turn to dust.

Puck.

Before he can punch himself, I teleport to him and grasp his wrists myself. No matter how good he is at lucid dreaming, he can't wish *me* away.

"You can't wake up even if you hit yourself," I say, hoping he can't read the lie on my face. "I have you sedated."

His lips curve in his grandfatherly smile. "I grew up side by side with your kind on Soma. I know all the tricks."

"Soma?" I ask, partly to stall for time but also because I'm genuinely intrigued. I've never heard of this place before, and it sounds like I should have, if it's where a bunch of "my kind" live.

Hekima cocks his head. "You're not from Soma? Then perhaps this will work."

An arc of pulsing red energy streams from his fingers into my head.

Pucking puck.

He's trying to use his illusion powers inside a dream—and it does work.

Well, sort of.

I'm back in the gladiatorial arena, but I'm also still holding his wrists. This odd state of being isn't like Pom letting me see through his eyes, but more like the werewolf's dream, where I'm being torn between two places at the same time.

The biggest orc I've ever seen ambles into the arena, and the crowd goes wild.

Hekima tries to twist out of my hold.

Puck. To fight the orc, I'll need to let go of Hekima's wrists. But what would happen if I didn't fight the orc? I'm dealing with an illusion, but inside a dream. For all intents and purposes, there's no difference between those two, so if the orc kills me in a dream, I might die, and the consequence would be murderous insanity. If this is similar to the werewolf situation, though, maybe the solution is the same as it was there.

Leal's so-called multibody technique.

The orc is almost upon me. I don't have time to dwell on the fact that the multibody thing failed the last time I tried it. I'm just going to have to trust in the mind-boosting power of sleep.

I zoom out of my body and create a second Bailey in the path of the orc, this one with fiery hair. Straining my bodiless self to the point of fainting, I will myself to enter both bodies.

Bam. The orc smashes his fist into my stomach—the stomach of the me with fiery hair.

It worked!

Fiery Me crumples in pain, but the me still holding Hekima's wrists feels nothing but the illusionist's struggles. Fiery Me hits the orc with everything I have, and the orc flies through the arena and crash-lands in a crater.

The crowd pees their pants in excitement.

Hekima tries to headbutt me. I make my head the consistency of a plush pillow to make sure he doesn't feel any pain.

At the same time, Fiery Me teleports to the weakened orc and waits for the crowd to quiet. As soon as it does, the flaming hair rises from my head and torches my opponent to a crisp.

Some in the crowd have heart attacks.

Hekima bares his teeth. "You're powerful. Even some of the dreamwalkers on Soma couldn't do the multibody technique."

Soma again—and the place sounds more interesting by the moment. Both of me reply in unison, "Tell me more. What is Soma? Where is it?" At Hekima's incredulous stare, both of me add quickly, "I'll do my best to get the Council to go easy on you if you tell me the truth."

Kit or Chester must be about to knock him out by now, but I almost wish they weren't. My question isn't a stalling tactic. If Soma is where dreamwalkers live, I want to learn all about it. With Mom refusing to speak about our roots, I've always wondered if—

Hekima's face twists. "We never should've left Soma. Siti would still be alive. On Soma, we—"

A shriek of unspeakable pain erupts from him as his dream bursts like a soap bubble, and I find myself back in the tower of sleepers.

Puck. Just when he was getting to the good part, someone knocked him out. Oh, well. Hopefully I'll be able to question him when he recovers. They didn't execute *me* right away, so there should be time.

I give myself a jolt and wake up.

CHAPTER FORTY-NINE

I FEEL AMAZING—AND not just because of more sleep. My pain and injuries are gone without a trace. I open my eyes and see why. Isis is moving calmly around the Council meeting room, healing everyone with her powers.

Rising to my feet, I look for Hekima—and instantly avert my gaze, wishing I could rub sanitizer on my eyeballs.

So much for my plan to question him.

Hekima is no more. At least I assume those are *his* remains in a pile approximately where he last stood. Someone has done something unspeakable to the grandfatherly illusionist.

His skin—all of it—is missing.

Kit grins at me. "He won't be bothering anyone ever again."

I swallow down a surge of nausea. "What happened? You were supposed to knock him out."

Kit shimmers briefly, and I catch the outline of a drekavac. "A promise is a promise."

Oh, right. She'd said she would kill Tatum's killer as a drekavac. This raw meat is the result. I don't know what it says about Kit that she was able to do this—or me, that I'm more upset about losing out on a chance to learn about Soma than the unspeakable torment Hekima must've experienced in his final moments. Then again, he did murder all those Councilors and was going to kill me and my friends, not to mention some members of the Council who had nothing to do with his daughter's unfortunate fate.

"Speaking of promises," I say, pushing aside all thoughts of Hekima and Soma for the moment. "I need to talk to Isis."

It's time the Council gave me my reward and healed my mom.

Kit follows me, and we wind our way through the confusion of Councilors, catching up with Isis as she heals her last patient.

"Can we go to Gomorrah now, as agreed?" I ask.

She wrinkles her nose. "One condition: You need to take a serious shower. Or maybe ten."

Kit sniffs the air. "Oh, yeah. I'm on board with ten. And I should have some clothes in your size."

"Deal," I say, doing my best not to inhale my own stench. As much as I want to get Mom out of the coma right away, I doubt she'd want to wake up to the perfume of the sewers.

The three of us go to Kit's quarters, where she grabs a box of garbage bags, an entire rack of clothes, and two big bottles of soap and shampoo. We take it all back to my quarters.

"I'll be back in an hour." Isis looks me over. "Or do you think you need two?"

"Two should do it."

They leave, and I bustle into the bathroom with the soap, shampoo, and garbage bags.

The first thing I do is take out Leal's comms from my pocket. I hope it's a waterproof model—or if not, that Felix can get the info from it anyway. Cleaning the thing, I put it into a bag.

My stinky clothes go into another bag. That bag goes into another bag and so on until I run out of bags. Then I turn on scorching water and begin lathering and rinsing. Even after I run out of products, I stay under the spray, hoping to wash off any remaining cooties. Eventually, I get pruney enough to improve the stools of an army of cannibals. Reluctantly turning off the shower, I dry off, use my last remaining hand sanitizer on my body, and dress in Kit's clothes.

Pocketing the bag with the comms gizmo, I inhale the air.

No stench.

But hmm... Now that I'm paying attention, I do detect a faint pine scent.

Wait a minute—

Someone clears his throat.

"Valerian?" I look around the empty room with wild eyes. "I just smelled you."

"You did?" He materializes two feet away, as gorgeous as the last time I saw him. "I'm losing my touch."

Pom, I mentally shout. *Pom, wake up!*

What is it? Pom's voice is groggy. *Can I not get uninterrupted sleep anymore?*

Quickly, what does this guy look like?

Pom sounds thoroughly bored. *Tall and muscular. Wide in the shoulders. Dark hair, blue eyes. Chin dimple, well-defined cheekbones.*

Don't describe him—show him to me, I mentally growl.

Why? You're seeing what I'm seeing.

I feel the tension leave my forehead. *I am? There's no illusion? He really looks like a pucking sex god?*

A beat of silence, then: *I don't know what a pucking sex god looks like.*

A silly grin threatens to stretch my lips. *Right. You can go back to sleep now. Thank you.*

How about you only wake me up in emergencies going forward? Pom grumbles.

Whatever, I reply as Valerian arches a black eyebrow in amusement.

Puck, I've again been staring at him in silence, like an idiot.

Pulling myself together, I scowl up at him. "How long have you been hiding there?"

His sexy lips quirk. "Are you asking if I saw you like this?" He casts an illusion, conjuring up a more attractive version of me—who looks exceptionally naked thanks to the sanitizer glistening like oil on her perfect skin.

"Or this?" he continues as I stare at him openmouthed. This time, the modelesque Bailey is engaged in what looks like the *Playboy* version of showering. I doubt my movements were remotely that sensuous, and I doubt even more that I paid that much attention to my boobs.

Still, my cheeks—and other places—feel hotter than the surface of the sun. "You watched me in the shower?"

A mischievous grin appears on his face, reinforcing the feeling that I've met him before. Except I haven't. He's the kind of man I'd remember forever. "I came here to thank you." He dispels the shower illusion. "Bernard made the breakthrough I needed. The money has been transferred to your account on Gomorrah."

Right. The money. He's got me so off balance I almost forgot about that.

"Good," I manage to say. "But that doesn't excuse your invading my personal space."

His grin turns wicked. "You're right. It's rude of me. You showed me yours; the least I can do is show you mine."

Another Valerian appears to the side of us, gloriously naked and covered in some liquid.

Oh. My. Estrogen.

Sex god doesn't even begin to cover it. My blood rushes to all sorts of private places, and I feel a bizarrely unsanitary urge to lick every one of those toned muscles.

The fully clothed Valerian winks as his naked doppelgänger steps into the shower and lathers himself with soap.

Can you faint from arousal? Or have a heart attack?

He makes his showering self disappear. "Are we even now?"

I just stand there, doing my best not to fan myself.

He steps closer, ocean-blue eyes gleaming. "You know, I still feel like we know each other from somewhere."

I dampen my suddenly dry lips. "Same."

"I wonder if there's a way to jog our memories?" He leans toward me, and the room around us transforms into a familiar lush bedroom with a king-sized bed covered in silk sheets and rose petals.

My lungs cease functioning, and my body feels like I'm in the middle of a heat wave. For some reason, the thought of those sensual lips on mine doesn't—

The door to the room bangs open, making my heart spring into my throat.

"Ready?" Isis asks as if Valerian isn't here—and I bet for her, he isn't.

"Yeah," I reply breathlessly. "Let's go."

"Rain check," Valerian whispers in his heated molasses voice. When I look back, he's gone.

I blow out a shaky breath. Mom better appreciate the sacrifices I'm making to heal her.

Isis leads me to the parking lot, where a limo is already waiting for us. I spot Ariel and Felix walking to another car and call out to them.

"Can you give me a second?" I ask Isis.

"Sure."

She climbs into the limo and closes the door as I hurry over to my friends. Their nice clothes are ruined, but their bodies seem fine—at least Ariel's. Felix is more covered up, so it's harder to tell.

"How are you guys?"

Ariel makes a check mark in the air. "Killed not one but two vampires, yet didn't drink any blood."

I beam at her. "I think you're officially cured."

Felix shuffles from foot to foot. "Kit said Hekima made me fight you. I'm so sorry I hit you."

"Well, I knocked you out." I grin and pantomime a punch. "I think that makes us even."

The limo with Isis honks.

"I've got to go." I take out the bag with the comms device and hand it to Felix. "This is the gizmo we spoke about. I'd be grateful if you could pull anything you can from it, especially if it has to do with a place called Soma."

Felix's unibrow comes to life. "Is that a whole Otherland or a town?"

"No idea. I just know it has something to do with dreamwalkers. I'd like to learn more."

He pockets the bag. "I'll work on this ASAP."

"Thanks. I'll see you guys later." Suppressing all thoughts of germs, I give each of them a hug.

It's amazing what a little swim in the sewers does to one's squeamishness.

THE RIDE to JFK happens almost as it did in my dream, but when we get to Gomorrah, I don't waste time on snacks. I get us a car right away, so anxious to get to the hospital I almost forget to breathe.

No one brings up the billing as I locate Dr. Xipil and introduce Isis. As he did in my dream, the gnome doctor gathers a few colleagues in Mom's room. My heart squeezes as I look at her. Her brain activity is flat, and the pucking machines make her look so frail.

"Do we unplug the patient?" Dr. Xipil asks Isis.

"No," she says, "not until I'm done."

"Makes sense." He stares intently at her hands.

Again—or rather, for the first time in real life—Isis shoots my mom with an arc of golden energy as I watch with bated breath.

With an eerie sensation of déjà vu, Mom's brain activity goes from flat to frantic, and my heartbeat spikes alongside it. I can already picture all the things I'm going to say to her, how I'm going to apologize for the fight we had, for all the times that—

"Remove the machines," Isis orders. "Now."

The medical staff does as she says, while Isis keeps the healing energy pouring into my mom. If someone were monitoring my heartbeat, the needle would be jumping up and down like a seismograph during an earthquake.

The machines get disconnected, but unlike in my dream, Mom's eyelids stay shut. Isis stops the flow of healing energy and touches Mom's forehead.

"There's nothing more to heal," she says, "but something seems to be wrong. Is she sleeping?"

I try not to panic as Dr. Xipil looks at the brain scan. "It doesn't look like regular coma activity," he says. "It *is* reminiscent of sleep, but something seems off. I've never seen anything like this."

Oh, that doesn't sound good at all. I clench my hands, the nails digging into my palms as Isis says, "How about we wake her up?"

The doctor gently shakes my mom's shoulder.

Nothing happens.

He shakes her less gently—still nothing.

Isis rolls her eyes and slaps my mom on the cheek. The others gasp, and one man moves to stop her. Dr. Xipil shakes his head in warning.

Mom doesn't wake up.

I feel like I'm on the verge of a meltdown.

Isis grabs a cup of water from a nearby doctor's assistant and splashes Mom in the face.

Still nothing.

"Maybe we wait for her to wake up naturally?" Dr. Xipil suggests.

Isis shrugs, so we all wait.

And wait.

And wait.

Each second that passes increases my anxiety. Unable to stand still, I pace around the room, nearly tripping over the doctor's feet twice. "I'll be back in a few," he says after it happens for the third time, and disappears for the next hour.

When he finally reappears, Isis grips me by the shoulder. "I need to go. There's not much more I can do. Sleeping is more your area of expertise."

I inhale sharply. "But—"

She turns on her heel and exits.

Dr. Xipil regards me speculatively. "What did she mean about your expertise?"

I push back a frizzy curl with an unsteady hand. "I'm a dreamwalker. If Mom is really sleeping, theoretically I can go into her dreams."

His eyes narrow. "So do it. Maybe you can wake her up from within."

"I…" I cast a glance at Mom's prone figure. Worry for her is like a worm eating me on the inside, but I can't ignore the heavy weight of my promise. "I can't," I say bleakly. "She doesn't want me in her dreams. Let's just give her a chance to wake up."

Dr. Xipil looks exasperated. "You stay here and wait then. Get me when she awakens."

I can tell he wanted to say *if* she awakens.

He and the rest of the staff disappear to go about their business, and I take a seat on a low-slung couch near the bed, silently begging Mom to wake up. But she just keeps sleeping. An hour goes by, then another and another. Eventually, exhaustion overcomes me—my four-month sleep debt is still weighing on me—so I ask a nurse to keep an eye on Mom in my stead and close my eyes for a few minutes. I doubt I'll actually fall asleep; I just need to rest for a little bit…

I wake up to Dr. Xipil's voice and jackknife to my feet.

"Any progress?" I ask, frantically rubbing the sleep from my eyes. "How long have I—"

"Thirty-six hours asleep—ten for you—and not a single REM cycle," he says. "I tried giving her stimulants, but it didn't help. This might be a type of coma I've never heard of, one that can only happen when a healer is involved. Your powers may be the thing to try next."

My breath catches in my throat. They're going to make me do it. "Dr. Xipil, I don't know if… I mean—"

"I'm sure your mother didn't anticipate this situation when she said she doesn't want you dreamwalking in her."

My hands begin to tremble. Why is this so hard? I look at Mom's serene face. "I don't know. I just don't know."

"If you don't wake her up now, we'll have to put the feeding tube back in."

I swallow, staring at Mom, already seeing her with all those tubes poking out of her. Would she rather have that, really? If it were me, I'd want my daughter to do everything in her power to wake me. Maybe Dr. Xipil is right. There's no way Mom could've anticipated this dilemma. It's one thing to keep me out of her dreams when she's dealing with depressive episodes; it's another matter entirely when her life—or at least, her consciousness—is on the line.

I square my shoulders. Screw my promises. I'll beg Mom's forgiveness when she wakes. "I'll do it," I tell the doctor. "But since she's not in REM sleep, you need to prepare to subdue me if I start acting weird. You remember that case about a dreamwalker killing people?"

Nodding solemnly, he leaves and comes back a few minutes later with a syringe and several burly security guys. They form a semicircle around me, hard faces reflecting equal parts curiosity and concern. I ignore them, mentally steeling myself to survive yet another subdream.

There's never been a worthier reason to risk my sanity.

Stepping over to Mom's bed, I place my hand on her cool, still forehead.

"See you soon," I say softly, and taking a deep breath, I jump into her dreams.

DREAM HUNTER

BOOK 2

CHAPTER ONE

I STAND on the surface of a calm black ocean, with fiery, angry-looking skies above my head. Six humanoid figures are sprinting toward me, their strange feet making them look like they're tiptoeing on the water. Their right index fingers sport sword-like claws, and they lack noses and eyes. In general, their heads are pretty lacking—no hair, no ears, just baby-smooth skin and a huge mouth in the middle of where the face would be. And if that weren't creepy enough, the horror nearest me starts screeching like a cat in heat.

To my shock, I realize it's saying something.

"You!" the creature is shrieking. "You're not dead?"

I gape at it. "Why would I be? What are you? How do you know me?"

The creature slices at me with its sword-claw, and I duck to avoid losing my head.

"Stay still!" the monstrosity screeches. "If I slay you now, Master will be pleased."

Yeah, right. An appendage-like growth extends from my wrist, turning into a furry sword in time to parry the next sword-claw strike. "What master?" I demand as I lunge and slash.

My opponent's cleaved in half before it can answer.

A second creature reaches me, swinging its sword-claw. "Master hates you!" it screeches when I parry. "Your existence is a blight."

I counterattack with my furry blade, burying it in my opponent's chest. "Me, a blight?" I yank out the blade. "Talk about the pot calling the kettle black."

The time for talking about their master must be over. The next two attackers come at me with even greater violence. Their claws hack and slash without any strategy, making them easy prey for my furry blade.

The next two are more cautious. They circle me silently, looking for an opening.

I feint, then lop one's head right off. The next opponent ducks beneath my blade by crouching on the water. As I loom over it, it strikes out with its claw, stabbing me in the thigh.

I jump back, crying out in pain. The affected muscle burns agonizingly.

The monster goes for the kill, but I parry. With a screeching yell, it lunges again—and its claw pierces my shoulder.

Ignoring the dizzying wave of agony, I swing my blade and slice its head clean off.

I'M in a huge palatial lobby with reddish green walls and yellowish blue marble floors, the richly appetizing scent of manna filling my nostrils as impossibly shaped objects float in front of my eyes.

My dream palace. I made it.

Blood is still oozing from my thigh and shoulder. Pucking puck. That subdream was worse than others. If there'd been one more monster in there, I'd be foaming at the mouth and trying to kill everyone in the waking world. It's a good thing I asked Mom's doctor to prepare for that eventuality. If I'd emerged from my dreamwalking trance in a homicidal mood, he could've subdued me with the help of the burly security guys he brought in—or knocked me out with whatever's in his syringe.

Well, the good thing is, none of that is necessary now, since I'm safely in the dream world. I exit my body, heal it, give myself a fiery hair makeover, and jump back into myself.

Pom shows up next to one of the impossible shapes. He's a looft, a symbiotic creature permanently attached to my wrist who's also my companion here in the dream world. The size of a large bird, with gargantuan lavender-colored eyes, triangular pointy ears, and fluffy fur that changes colors to match his emotions, he usually belongs in the dictionary next to the word "cute."

Currently, though, he's solid black and his ears are droopy. "I accidentally read your mind again," he confesses guiltily. "You're here to wake up Lidia, aren't you?"

Reminded of my important mission, I take flight, heading for the tower of sleepers. "That's right. Mom was stuck in non-REM sleep—hence the subdream we just experienced."

He zooms around me, shuddering. "Scary."

"For sure. But hey, you were a sword this time." I demonstrate by recreating the weapon I just used. "Did you have any clue that was actually a dream?"

He turns an even darker black. "No. I was just living in the moment, not questioning being that sword—as weird as that sounds."

"Same here. No clue I was dreaming."

Pom circles around my head. "The creatures spoke this time."

So they did. How weird. I think back to all the other subdreams I've experienced and the bizarre, terrifying creatures I've met in them. "Maybe they've always tried to speak," I say. "But this time, they had mouths that let them be understood."

Pom's fur takes on a light orange hue. "Where do subdreams come from?"

I slow my flight. He's raised a question I've pondered a lot, without ever coming up with a satisfactory answer. "I don't know. I've nicknamed them subdreams because I think they tap deeper into the subconscious than regular dreams do."

"Whose subconscious, yours or the dreamer's?"

"Great question." I conjure up the creatures from the subdream I experienced when I invaded Bernard's non-REM sleep—the ones that look like oversized bacteria and viruses. "Theoretically, these could be my fears of contamination made flesh."

Pom peers at them as I recreate the creatures I encountered in Gertrude's subdream—tentacled giant naked mole rats riding warthog-spider hybrids. "Nothing about these riders fits that pattern," I say, studying them, "so they might be something Gertrude dreamed up."

Pom floats in front of my face. "So you think it was your mom who created the monsters we just defeated?"

"Could be. Though I don't like the implications."

He blinks at me.

"The monsters said their master hated me," I explain. "If Mom created them, she'd be their master, right?" Reaching the glass-walled tower of sleepers, I locate the nook where Mom's form resides now that I've forced her into REM sleep. "I know we had that fight before her accident," I continue as I fly toward it, "but I hope she doesn't *really* feel that my existence is a blight—whatever that means."

Pom flies next to me. "You feel bad about that fight, don't you?"

"Of course. I made Mom think I might invade her dreams, something she made me promise never to do. *That's* why she got so upset and stormed out. Her accident wouldn't have happened if it weren't for my big mouth."

Pom turns gray, a color rare for him. "You didn't know what would happen."

"True." I take a breath to suppress the heavy swell of emotions thinking about Mom's accident always generates. "In any case, it doesn't matter now. I *am* breaking my promise."

"To save her life."

"Yes." Outside, in the waking world, Mom is in a strange coma-like sleep, one that neither Isis, a powerful healer, nor Dr. Xipil, a rare gnome doctor, could get her out of. The only thing left to try was for me to go into her dreams and wake her from within.

Hopefully she'll understand and forgive me.

Entering her nook, I land next to the bed. To my surprise, there's no trauma loop cloud above her head—something I always suspected I'd find if I dreamwalked in her. Before the accident, she'd displayed all the symptoms I've seen in my most troubled clients.

"I'm sure she'll forgive you," Pom says sagely, landing behind me. "What's more important is that you forgive yourself. From my experience, that's harder."

I turn to see if he's kidding, but he's still that depressing gray color. "What experience are you talking about? What did you ever need to forgive yourself for?"

His cute face twists into a miserable expression, and his ears droop. "I permanently attached myself to you without asking your permission."

So he had. I certainly hadn't expected to end up with a symbiont when I petted a mooft—a cow-like creature loofts normally live on—at a Gomorran zoo. But now I can't imagine my life without him.

"Sweetie." I snatch him up, bringing him up to my eye level. "I already told you, I wouldn't want to take you off even if I could."

The tips of his ears turn a light shade of purple. "You told me that when you thought you'd be executed. Now that you know you'll live, do you still mean it?"

"We're symbionts for life," I say solemnly. "Don't you ever forget it."

The rest of Pom turns purple, and he grins. "We make a good pair of symbionts, don't we?"

"I don't know what I'd do without you." I kiss his furry forehead and set him down. "Now how about I do what I came here to do?"

We both look over at Mom. Her beautiful features appear so peaceful in her slumber.

"Do you want some privacy?" Pom asks.

"Please." It's been four months since Mom entered her coma. The chances that I'll cry when we finally speak are pretty high, and seeing that might upset Pom.

He obligingly disappears.

I place my hand on Mom's forehead. "I'm sorry," I whisper. "If I could save you without breaking my promise, I would."

Steeling myself, I dive into her dream.

CHAPTER TWO

MOM IS CHOPPING something in an unfamiliar kitchen, while a child version of me is opening a packet of manna.

My younger self looks to be about five and must be filtered through Mom's memories. I doubt I was *that* adorable, and I'm skeptical of that innocence in my eyes. Though I don't remember anything from when I was younger than seven, I couldn't have changed *this* much.

A part of me is disappointed. My dreamwalker powers allow me to tell if a dream is based on a memory, and that's not the case here. It would've been a chance to learn something of my early years—one of Mom's many taboo subjects.

Mom starts chopping with greater intensity.

Something prevents me from clearing my throat to inform her of my presence. As much as I yearn to speak with her, curiosity and a certain intuition lead me to observe for now. I turn invisible—and just in time.

Clutching the knife so hard her knuckles turn white, Mom lunges at the little me.

What the puck?

Mom's face is an unrecognizable mask of hatred as she stabs the little me in the heart. My child self screams in pain—which is the only thing that covers my shocked gasp.

I disable my sounds and breathe deeply to calm myself.

It's just a dream. Dreams can be chaotic and crazy. This doesn't mean Mom wants to kill me.

What I just saw doesn't have to be a manifestation of Mom's anger about our fight.

A new dream starts.

We're in our apartment on Gomorrah. Mom is watching as a teenage version of me stands in the middle of the room with a VR headset on her head. As I look around, I notice something curious—some of the windows around us are black.

I first came across the concept of a black window in the notes of Leal, the murdered dreamwalker from the New York Council, and I learned more about them in the dreams of Nina, the telekinetic who acted as a sort of memory storage for said dreamwalker. Nina herself had a troublesome memory that she'd had Leal lock away behind a black window.

Is that the case for Mom? Are these windows events that she, or someone else, erased from memory? It could explain why she didn't have a trauma loop. Whatever's troubling her could be hidden behind the black windows.

Before I can follow this chain of thought further, the same look of hatred appears on Mom's face, and she tackles the unaware teenage me like an NFL linebacker, shoving her with all her might.

My teenage self flies at one of the regular windows. Flailing, she crashes through the glass and plummets to the pavement far below.

What. The. Hell?

The dream changes again. This version of me looks to be ten or so, and is sleeping. Mom is looming over her with that same frightening expression on her face.

"Please tell me you just want to dreamwalk in her," I whisper, but she can't hear me. My voice is still disabled.

Grabbing a pillow, Mom places it over the face of the sleeping me, smothering her.

Puck.

I give myself the ability to make sounds again and become visible.

"Mom," I say tightly. "I think you're stuck in some hellish nightmare."

At least I hope that's what's happening. There's no way she's enjoying killing me over and over like that. I wasn't *that* annoying of a daughter.

Confusion replaces hatred on Mom's face.

"You're dreaming," I say quickly. "This—"

"You're dreamwalking in me!" Mom looks furious enough to kill the real version of me this time.

I instinctively back away. "You don't understand. I didn't have a choice."

She points her hand at me, and an arc of lightning shoots from her fingers into my head.

I feel like someone's turned me into a lemon, squeezed me dry, and blended the leftover meat and peel into a smoothie.

I open my mouth to scream, but it's too late.

I'm no longer in the dream world.

CHAPTER THREE

I'M BACK in the hospital room, with Dr. Xipil and the burly security guys watching me intently, ready to subdue me in case I became a psychotic killer.

I paste a smile on my lips, even though I'm freaking out. The last thing I need is for Dr. Xipil to stab me with that syringe he's holding.

"What happened?" he asks with a worried expression.

"It didn't work," I say and place my hand back on Mom's forehead. It's strangely clammy. "I'm going to try again."

"Wait—"

Tuning out the gnome doctor's objections, I will myself to return into Mom's dreams.

Nothing happens.

Huh.

I touch my furry wristband—Pom—trying to get into the dream world that way.

Nothing. There's no scent of ozone, no sensation of falling that comes along with the transition into a dreamwalking trance. I might as well be touching a rock.

I grip Mom's hand and strain harder. Still nothing. Eventually, I have to accept it: The violent dream world expulsion Mom performed on me robbed me of my powers for the day.

Unbelievable.

I didn't realize such a thing was possible—or that Mom could do it. In general, her dreamwalking powers seem to be much stronger than mine.

What's extra amazing is that Mom is this strong despite having lived here on Gomorrah for as long as I can remember. Us Cognizant slowly lose our powers unless we regularly travel to Otherlands that contain humans, like Earth.

Dr. Xipil exchanges a glance with the guard nearest me. "Are you sure you're okay?"

Puck. He's worried I *am* homicidal.

I force another smile to my lips. "I'm fine. I'm just disappointed I failed."

"As I was trying to tell you, you didn't *just* fail." The doctor nods at the screens monitoring Mom's heartbeat and brain activity. "Your dreamwalking drove her vitals through the roof."

"What?" I peer at the monitors, wishing I had medical training. I know a lot about sleep, but not much else. "How?"

"I don't know, but she had a dangerously fast heartbeat, shortness of breath, excessive sweating and trembling—all signs of a nocturnal panic attack, but without the awakening that typically follows."

My stomach sinks as I look Mom over. Her forehead is beaded with sweat, and her bronzed skin has a gray tinge. "So what do I do?"

Dr. Xipil adjusts his breathing mask, an apparatus all gnomes wear due to their anatomy. "Well... it's a unique case. Your powers may still be the best way to wake her, but you might want to let her body recover for a day or two before you try anything else."

I take a deep breath. "Actually, I don't know if it's worth trying again." I explain my theory that Mom may be much more powerful than I am.

He gestures for the security guys to leave. "Maybe you can reason with her next time?"

"I told you, she doesn't want me dreamwalking in her." I look at Mom, my chest squeezing with guilt at the ashen hue of her face. "Maybe I should've listened."

Dr. Xipil readjusts his mask. "I'll see what we can do on our end. Meanwhile, we have to reattach some life support."

On my wrist, Pom turns black—reflecting my emotions this time. I swallow against the bitter lump in my throat. "I understand."

"You might also want to talk to a sleep expert," the doctor says. "Or find another dreamwalker."

I blink at him. "I don't know another dreamwalker." We're not exactly thick on the ground.

He regards me speculatively. "In that case, have you ever heard of Dr. Cipactli?"

I shake my head.

"He's a sleep expert with a great reputation. He heads up the ZIZZ Sleep Clinic." Dr. Xipil's chin lifts. "Not surprising, really, as he's a fellow gnome."

I'm genuinely impressed. "Yet another gnome in a medical field?"

Dr. Xipil huffs through his mask. "I was as surprised as you. I know I'm an outlier. I became a doctor when I lost my parents to a rare genetic disease. Still, even I can't fathom why a fellow gnome would want to study sleep of all things."

He can say that again. Gnomes usually thrive in technology-heavy fields. My friend Itzel, for instance, is obsessed with space exploration and gadgets of all kinds, and her famous grandfather, Cadmael, invented the Vega reactors that run everything on Gomorrah.

"I'll talk to this Dr. Cipactli," I say.

"Great." Dr. Xipil makes some gestures in the air. "I just sent you his info."

"Thank you. Can you also give it to me verbally? My comms died, and I haven't replaced them." Actually, my comms were crushed by a vampire on Earth—but who's keeping track.

Dr. Xipil tells me where I need to go and adds, "I'll talk to Dr. Cipactli right after I leave, and send him all the information about your mother."

I thank him again, and he leaves the room. I clasp Mom's hand again. "Bye," I tell her softly. "I'll see you soon, okay?"

There's no reply. With a heavy heart, I head out.

––––––––

AS I WALK past the nurses in the hallway, I ponder why Mom kept killing me in her dream. The best answer I can come up with is that even though I was invisible, she'd detected my dreamwalking presence and it'd angered her. After all, my whole life I'd promised her I *wouldn't* enter her dreams.

But why was she killing me at different ages? Why not just push me out the way she did when I made my presence known?

More importantly, should I respect her wishes and not go back?

I try to imagine leaving her hooked up on those machines indefinitely, and everything inside me revolts at the thought. Even if I can come up with the money to keep her in the paid hospital long term, she'll eventually waste away, machines or not. If I don't wake her, she's as good as dead.

So that's that. Unless the sleep expert can come up with another solution, I'm going to have to figure out a way to gain more power, go back, and try waking her up again. I even have an idea when it comes to power gathering—

The hospital doors slide open, and I look around.

This is the Health District, named so due to the slew of paid hospitals, pharmaceutical companies, and research centers all around. It vaguely resembles Gardens by the Bay in Singapore, as the water-collecting trees here look a lot like the Supertrees there.

My destination is walkable, so I make my way through the busy crowds of fellow Cognizant. After Earth, seeing so many non-humanoid pedestrians is a little jarring, especially when I spot a couple of weres in their animal shapes.

The building where the sleep clinic resides is small and reminds me of the Freedom Tower in New York. I go inside and take the elevator to the sleep clinic floor. An elf secretary tells me the soonest I can see Dr. Cipactli is tomorrow afternoon, no matter how urgent my issue is.

Cursing under my breath at the delay, I leave the building and locate the nearest store where I can buy a replacement comms device; without it, I feel like a cavewoman.

"Would you like to check out the newest model?" the uber saleswoman asks me with a megawatt smile.

I look around. "Is there a place I can check my cc balance?"

She nods at a nearby mirror, and I realize it's a screen in disguise.

I walk up to the screen, authenticate myself, and have a look at my money.

Wait a second. The number here is much bigger than I expected.

It doesn't take long for me to figure out what happened. Valerian paid nearly double the amount we agreed upon. Wow. He's given me bonuses for a job well done before, but never this much.

Once I have my comms, I'll need to thank him. With this amount, I can pay Mom's outstanding bills and still have enough left over to consider the newest, most expensive model of comms.

"Show me," I say to the uber woman.

She takes out a sleek-looking comms device I've never seen before and opens it like a clam shell—another novelty.

Inside the comms are almost invisible earphones, two contact lenses, and ten clip-on nails.

I examine it all in awe. "I've heard these were in development, but didn't realize they were out."

My last set of comms interfaced via special glasses and gloves, so I couldn't openly use them on Earth. This is so much stealthier.

"Put them on," she says with a knowing grin.

I reach for the contact lenses, then yank my hand back. "Are these new?"

She cocks her head. "Are you from some Otherland?" Before I can tell her I'm local, she adds, "These comms have *hygieia* built in—a cleaning technology."

I know what she's talking about, of course. Hygieia is why things like salmonella are extinct on Gomorrah. Her answer also tells me the stuff *was* in other people's eyes before—which is a problem, even though I know my concern is not rational. It's like drinking out of a sterilized toilet on Earth—icky, at least to me.

She must read my mind because she smiles sagely and takes out a sealed unit.

"I don't promise to buy it," I say reluctantly.

"That's fine." She hands it to me.

Right. She knows the next customer won't have my qualms.

I unwrap the device as if it were a Christmas gift, put in the contacts, and whistle under my breath. They're extremely comfortable—as in, I don't feel them at all.

The saleswoman smiles wider. She knows I'm almost on the hook.

The earphones are amazing. Once in my ears, it's impossible to see them, and I can still hear external sounds.

I hold the nail things to my nails, and they latch on as if magnetized. The result isn't bad at all—a bit like if I got blue gel nails on Earth.

"Are the gestures the same as with the gloves?" I ask.

She nods, so I gesture for the comms to activate.

The usual spherical icons appear in the air in front of me. With glasses, these looked like *Star Wars* holograms, but the contacts make everything sharper, almost real.

I gesture at the login app, and once I'm in, the interface changes to the way I'd previously set it up, with icons that look like impossible shapes, such as the Penrose triangle. It gives me the feeling that I'm in the dream world.

I have a ton of messages waiting, but before I check them, I bring up the paying app and say, "I'll take this."

"Pleasure doing business with you." The saleswoman grins her widest smile yet.

As I walk out, I check some of my messages. Most are from the hospital, telling me I must pay the bills. I do that and then craft a message to Valerian. He's instrumental to my new idea on how to gather more power—at least that's what I tell myself.

This has nothing to do with what almost happened between us the other day.

Nothing at all.

To my disappointment, he doesn't instantly reply. Nor does he reply by the time I get into a car. Well, he does spend half his time on Earth and half on Gomorrah, so hopefully he's just away and not ignoring me.

The car drops me off by our building, a modest skyscraper with one hundred and fifty floors.

Stepping into the apartment is an odd experience after being away. The first thing that stands out, as usual, is how few personal touches Mom gave the place. The walls are bare, and the kitchen is immaculately clean. There are showrooms at furniture stores with more personality. If I were to enter Mom's bedroom, it would be even more bland—just walls and a bed. Sometimes I wonder if Mom thought that by decorating, she might accidentally reveal to me some secret from her past.

I enter my own room. Like inside my virtual reality interface—and dream world—I have a lot of art that features visual paradoxes and surreal scenarios. Works reminiscent of Earth's M. C. Escher and Salvador Dalí slideshow on screens that are my room's walls. On the ancient portable screen that I borrowed from Mom, I spot the cover of the textbook on video game design I was reading before my life turned upside down. My unmade bed is floating a couple of inches off the ground thanks to magnets and superconductivity, and it looks ridiculously inviting.

I guess those four months without sleep are still weighing on me.

Yawning, I check to see if Valerian has replied.

He hasn't.

I guess I might as well use the wait time to chip away at my sleep debt.

I program my comms to ring loudly if I get a message, and I set an alarm so I don't miss my appointment with Dr. Cipactli. I doubt I'll need the latter—it would mean I'd slept over twenty hours. Still, better safe than sorry.

Picking up a hygieia wand, I properly disinfect myself and plop onto the bed. Immediately, my tense muscles relax. Earth's best memory foam mattresses are a joke compared to smart beds on Gomorrah. I feel like

I've been enveloped in a cloud, with the floating sensation completing that illusion.

Not surprisingly, I go under faster than if I'd inhaled sleeping gas.

———

I WAKE to the blaring of an alarm.

Puck. I slept all the way into the next day, and now I need to rush to see Dr. Cipactli.

I gleefully use my highly sanitary, eco-friendly bathroom. My least favorite part of Earth is all that filthy water wasted as part of the plumbing. The only water we have on Gomorrah is the drinking kind coming out of the faucets, and I imbibe it with gusto. Next, I hygieia my body and teeth, put on a nondescript black shirt and dark cargo pants—one of my many outfits calibrated to fit both Earth and Gomorrah fashions—and rush out of the building. Once on the street, I get some manna and jump into a self-driving car.

Munching on the yumminess, I realize I didn't have a single dream in over twenty hours of sleep. In general, I feel great. Way better than before I slept—which tells me I needed the whole twenty hours, if not more.

The car stops, and I go up to Dr. Cipactli's office.

"I have an appointment," I tell the elf secretary.

With a polite smile, she presses some button only she can see in her VR. "One moment."

A few seconds later, the tallest gnome I've ever seen steps out of the nearby office. Gnomes grow tall in adolescence and then shrink as they grow older, so this specimen must be young—which can still mean up to a thousand years old given the typical gnome lifespan.

Like most other gnomes, this one needs to wear a special mask due to the respiratory problems they develop on worlds with air that's about twenty percent oxygen—like Earth and Gomorrah. According to Itzel, these breathing issues are what initially drove gnomes to explore technology.

Dr. Cipactli's mask is unusual in that you can't really see much of his face under its shiny black surface. If Felix were here, I bet he'd say this mask makes Dr. Cipactli look like Darth Vader.

"Bailey," he says in a deep voice distorted by the mask—strengthening the Vader comparison. "It's a pleasure to meet you." He extends his hand in an Earth-like greeting.

Ignoring the proffered appendage, I curtsy—which usually lets me avoid skin-to-skin contact.

It works. Dr. Cipactli inclines his head and says, "Step into my office."

I follow him in and do a double take.

His wall screens slideshow horror-movie-worthy images that remind me of the creatures I've met in subdreams.

"I study nightmares," he explains, noticing my shock. "Which is why I got excited when Dr. Xipil told me about your case."

I take a seat in a hovering chair and cross my legs. "Oh?"

He examines me as if I were a celebrity—or an exotic bug. "I've never met a dreamwalker before."

I smile uncomfortably. "We are pretty rare."

"Exceedingly." He sits behind his desk. "Which is why, in lieu of payment, I hope you'll demonstrate your powers."

Payment, right. This isn't a free hospital, either. I uncross my legs. "I'd be happy to. The only issue is that you're a gnome. You're not the first one to ask this of me, and I'll tell you the same thing I told them: It may or may not work."

Gnomes are renowned for being immune to many Cognizant powers. Vampire glamour doesn't work on them, tricksters can't influence their fate directly, illusionists fail to make them see their illusions, seers can't see them in their visions of the future—the list goes on and on.

Dr. Cipactli nods eagerly. "Gnome resistance to dreamwalking is why I want to try this. My grandmother told me it would work if a gnome gave consent—but didn't explain further. Once I grew up, I realized what she said doesn't make sense. If I'm sleeping—and therefore unconscious—how can I give my consent?"

Hmm. Interesting. "Maybe you agree I dreamwalk in you while you're awake?"

"Maybe." He rubs the chin part of his mask. "But wouldn't that give you unlimited dream access forever and ever? Or can I revoke my consent after I wake up? Or maybe even during the dreamwalking session itself?"

I smile. "Now I'm actually curious to do this."

"Excellent." He leaps to his feet. "How about we try it right now?"

"One second." I turn away from him and use Pom to go in and out of the dream world.

Good. My powers have recovered.

I turn back to him. "Now's fine. Do you have a place to sleep?"

"This is a sleep clinic," he says and strides to the door.

I follow him through a corridor and into a large hall brimming with floating beds. On each bed is a sleeper. Some have IV bags attached to them, some don't. Many are also strapped to their beds, like dangerous madmen.

What the puck?

Then I recognize one of them, and things become clearer.

It's Gertrude, the New York Councilor who hates my guts. She suffers from a condition that sounds like REM Sleep Behavior Disorder—which combines poorly with her ability to give gangrene to anyone she touches. That must be what's going on with the other tied-up patients as well: They have some dangerous sleep disorders.

In any case, I'm glad Gertrude found this clinic. I recently learned that she killed someone she cared about in her sleep, so it would be good if she got the help she needs. I just hope she doesn't wake up and see me; not only does she hate me for not being able to solve her problem with my dreamwalking, but I knocked her unconscious the other day, and she might hold a grudge.

"How about here?" Dr. Cipactli points at an empty bed.

I cast a wary glance at Gertrude. "I'd prefer to do it someplace more private."

Nodding in understanding, the gnome leads me to an empty room with a bed and medical equipment that reminds me of Mom's setup.

"Would this work?" he asks.

"Sure. Are you going to be able to sleep on demand, or do you have sleeping gas on hand?"

"Something even better." He takes out a small gizmo. "A drug developed for my research. Puts the subject right into REM sleep."

Huh. Sounds like the drug Leal, the dreamwalker from the New York Council, developed. Of course, Leal's drug had an itsy-bitsy side-effect: whoever took it never woke up again. I assume Dr. Cipactli's drug isn't like that; otherwise, I'm about to partake in the strangest form of assisted suicide in history.

"I'll need to remove my mask to use this," he says gravely. There's a strange look in his eyes—embarrassment, maybe? "Will you please put it back on my face?"

I nod vigorously.

The gnome lies down and slides off his mask.

Poor guy. I now see why he wears a mask that covers so much. He must've been in an accident or something; the right side of his face is twisted by scars that look like a chemical burn.

He points the gizmo at his face and activates it.

There's a distinct hiss.

The medicine is odorless and seems to take effect immediately. His eyes start to move rapidly behind their lids.

I hygieia his mask on both sides and put it back on him. Then I hygieia his exposed forearm and place my fingers on it.

Here we go. I'm about to dreamwalk in a gnome.

CHAPTER FOUR

EXCEPT NOTHING HAPPENS when I will myself to go in.

Wait, no. Something *is* happening. Something odd.

The more I strain my powers, the more I get the feeling that I have a small voice in my head. It reminds me of how Pom communicates with me when he's awake; only it doesn't sound like my furry friend.

The voice seems to be saying, *Who are you, and what do you want?*

Feeling silly, I do what I'd do if it were Pom. Mentally, I reply, *I'm Bailey. You asked me to visit your dreams.*

No mental reply comes; instead, something yields, and with a whiff of ozone, I plummet into the gnome's dream world.

———

AS SOON AS I show up in my dream palace, I teleport to the tower of sleepers.

"How did it go with Lidia?" Pom's voice inquires. Then he appears bit by bit, in a Cheshire cat fashion.

"Not great," I say and bring him up to speed on what happened.

He glances at a nook nearby. "And that's the gnome doctor?"

"That's him." I fly to my target, with Pom next to me.

As soon as he notices the scar on Dr. Cipactli's face, his ears turn black. "I'm going to stay out."

"Fair enough." I touch the gnome's forearm and will myself to go in.

This time, there's no voice in my head. I simply fall into the gnome's dream.

———

FOR A MOMENT, I think I accidentally woke up.

We're back in the exact same room where Dr. Cipactli went to sleep.

Of course, if it were the waking world, there wouldn't be two of me here. The second me is wearing a cruel expression and holding Dr. Cipactli's neck in a death grip.

"You leave me no choice," the gnome croaks out, forming a ball of lightning with his hands.

Boom.

Her chest a charred mess, the second me smashes into a wall and slides down, dead.

Hey now. Why is everyone dreaming about killing me?

The dream world changes again.

Maskless and without his scar, a younger Dr. Cipactli is standing next to a ginormous machine made up of steam engines, levers, and pistons indicative of technology even more primitive than that of Earth.

An older gnome shoots a section of the device with a lightning ball—powering devices is how gnomes usually use that ability of theirs.

"The number values will be represented by gear wheels," the elder says as the ball flies at its target. "Each digit of a number has its own—"

As the ball lands, something explodes.

"Oh, no!" the elder gnome shouts.

A hissing liquid splashes Dr. Cipactli in the face.

As he screams, I realize this nightmare is a memory. This is how he got hurt.

The dream changes yet again.

This time, Dr. Cipactli is his current age, but still without the mask and scar. Nightmarish creatures that look like the images in his office appear all around us. This isn't a memory, at all.

"This is enough." I turn the nightmare beings into fluffy kittens. "You wanted a demonstration of my power, so here it is."

Dr. Cipactli gapes at me, openmouthed.

"This is a dream." I turn the kittens into tiger cubs to illustrate my point.

He rubs his eyes. "I can't believe it."

"Don't you remember giving me consent to go into your dreams? I heard you ask me who I was and what I wanted."

"I asked what?" He shakes his head. "This is so much stranger than I thought."

"Yeah." I take us to my cloud office and gesture for him to sit where my clients usually would. "Now, about my mom."

"Right." He sits and assumes his usual professional demeanor. "I reviewed all the records and concur that she needs to be awakened from inside her dreams."

I plop into my own chair. "As in, by me?"

"Not necessarily." Probably without realizing it, he makes his scar reappear on his face, followed by the mask. "We can use the same medicine on her as I used on myself."

I sit up straighter. "The one that puts you into REM sleep?"

"Right. What I forgot to tell you is that it does more than that." He pauses. "As you noticed, I had nightmares. That's not a coincidence. The medication—Koshmar—is very consistent in eliciting that response."

"Your drug gives its users nightmares?" I make my hair fiery.

His eyes widen, but he quickly composes himself and nods. "Koshmar was specifically formulated for that purpose, so it's much more potent than a drug that merely has that as a side effect. It's invaluable to my research."

I frown. "You want to give my mom a potent nightmare?"

"Yes," he says eagerly. "Koshmar nightmares get progressively worse until the sleeper wakes up, which is what we want in this case. Furthermore, an interesting aspect of these specific nightmares is that the first one always features whatever the sleeper experienced last—in your mom's case, a bad car crash. I bet she'd wake up just from that."

I regard him thoughtfully. "So this is why your first nightmare was set in the room where you fell asleep. It was your last experience—and the starting point of a nightmare where the dream version of me was choking you."

"Exactly. I didn't even realize I was sleeping. It was as though my brain had erased the memory of spraying myself with the drug, and then my surroundings took a dark turn. That's how it works every time."

"And you're suggesting I give this horrible drug to my mother?"

He shrugs. "If she *can* be scared into waking up, this would do it."

"But what if she can't wake up? With the nightmares escalating, she'll end up in the worst hell imaginable, with no way out."

"Then you have to wake her using your power, after all." He doesn't bother hiding the disappointment in his voice. He must've wanted another subject to test the drug on. "Speaking of your power," he continues, "do you mind another experiment?"

I stare at him warily. "Like what?"

He stands up. "I'd like to see what happens if I withdraw my consent."

"Oh, that's fine."

He nods and scrunches his face, tensing—

———

I FIND myself back in the waking world, in the empty room where Dr. Cipactli is lying on the bed.

Looks like gnomes *can* take away their consent for dreamwalking—impressive.

Dr. Cipactli opens his eyes and sits up. "That was fascinating."

"Yeah," I say with a lot less enthusiasm.

"Can we do another experiment?"

I gesture to activate my comms and glance at my messages.

Valerian just replied, and I'm eager to know what he said.

"I'm sorry, maybe another time," I tell Dr. Cipactli. "I hope what we did thus far is payment enough for your time." *Especially considering how unhelpful you were*, is what I don't add.

"Fair enough," he says. "If you ever need a job, please keep us in mind. Someone with your powers could be invaluable when—"

"Thanks. I appreciate the offer. First, though, I need my mom safe and sound."

"Of course. If I can think of anything that might help her, I'll let you know."

We exchange contact details, and he leads me out.

As I walk out of the building, I finally read Valerian's terse response:

Let's talk. Can you meet me at Erato's at four?

Responding in the affirmative, I jump into a car and have it drop me at the hyperloop station. Erato's is on the other side of the city, so I need a speedier mode of transportation.

The hyperloop station in the Health District is typical for Gomorrah, in that it would put the poshest airport on Earth to shame, both in terms of the sleekness of its design and the comfort for the waiting passengers.

Not that we have to wait long. The train arrives every few seconds.

When I get on it, it's pretty empty. As usual, I can barely feel anything as it zooms forward and transports me the distance of ten Manhattans in an eyeblink.

Another car ride later, I step into Erato's building and ride the glass elevator to the top.

Erato is a powerful dryad who channeled her love of plants into vertical farming, making it something of an art form. The glass walls of the elevator allow me to ogle plants of every color and shape that cover every surface of the building. They're not just visually pleasing; the scents are divine as well, and the gorgeous nuts, fruits, and vegetables that peek out of the foliage make my mouth water.

I've got to hand it to Valerian. He picked a great place for our meeting—and a romantic one at that.

Maybe I'm not the only one affected by that crazy chemistry I've been feeling.

When I step out of the elevator into the restaurant, I feel like I'm in a magical forest. A green-skinned dryad dressed in a leaf bikini greets me with a smile that reveals her tree-root-like teeth. "Bailey?" she asks in a voice that sounds like autumn leaves falling.

I nod, looking into her chlorophyll-filled eyes.

"Come this way." She leads me through the thick greenery, her powers effortlessly commanding the branches to move out of our way.

The booth she leads me to looks like a miniature forest meadow with a large tree stump serving as the table, and smaller ones as chairs.

Valerian is already here, sitting on a stump and sipping a beaker of tea. Spotting me, he stands up and smiles.

I suddenly feel overly warm. Those sensual lips should be illegal, along with that chin dimple and the rest of that perfectly proportioned face. Not to mention that tall, muscled body… I remember the illusion he gave me the last time we met—that of him naked and covered by a glistening liquid—and it's all I can do to contain my drool. Thankfully, he's not naked right now, though the green tunic he's wearing might as well have been painted on. Not that he didn't look crazy hot in the bespoke suit he sported on Earth. He looks hot in everything—but especially in nothing.

That's actually a flaw in the idea that occurred to me earlier.

He's going to be a massive distraction.

He notices my staring, and his ocean-blue eyes gleam brighter, his grin turning wicked. "I'm glad you reached out," he murmurs as I plop gracelessly on the nearest stump. Even his voice brims with sex appeal. "I was afraid that after the clusterpuck that was the last job, I'd never hear from you again."

I swallow to moisten my dry throat. "Well… I appreciated the double payment." I'm still staring at him, I know, but I can't help it. Something about him looks familiar, always has. I have no idea where I could've met him, though. Initially, I'd thought that as an illusionist, he made himself look like a mix of celebrities, but then I learned that's not the case.

This is the true Valerian in all his mouth—and other body part—watering glory.

Finally tearing my gaze away from him, I activate my comms, so I can see the augmented reality menu through my new contacts. After a few seconds of deliberation, I select a mix of different teas and an appetizer fruit sample bowl—all species unique to this place.

"Hazard pay," he says dismissively when I'm done. "Did you already spend it and need more?"

"Not exactly." I disable the comms so nothing obscures my view of him. Immediately, my drooling resumes, so I hide it under a brisk, businesslike tone. "I'd like to run a theory by you."

His dark eyebrows arch.

"In Bernard's dream, I saw you speaking to your VR company and had an epiphany. You're planning to leverage giving VR to humans to grow your illusionist powers, right?"

His eyebrows rise higher. "An impressive deduction. No wonder you solved the case of the murdered Councilors."

I think I solved that case because I got lucky, but I'm not going to tell him that—the higher his opinion of me, the better. "So you don't deny it?"

A dryad arrives with a tray and puts a beaker of tea next to me, then sets down two identical fruit bowls.

Valerian grins. "We got the same thing. Great minds think alike."

I wait for the dryad to leave and for my heart to recover from the hormone-induced spike. Talk about a killer grin—if I were elderly and frail, I might've keeled over already. "So am I right about your plans?" I press when my voice is steady enough.

"More or less." He takes a round fruit that looks like Earth's guava and bites into it with gusto.

I fight an uncharacteristic urge to lick up the fruit juices from around his mouth. "In that case, I want in," I say and grab my own version of the same fruit before I can do something totally unprofessional, not to mention unsanitary.

Biting into the fruit, I taste its sweet, yet somehow savory goodness, and my heart resumes racing as I notice him eyeing the juices around *my* mouth with a hungry expression.

My licking-things-up idea must be contagious.

"What do you mean?" he murmurs, his attention still on my lips.

I pick up my tea beaker with unsteady hands. "I want to grow my powers with the help of your VR company." I take a deep breath as his gaze snaps to mine and sharpens. "Your plan is to become associated with the illusory worlds of VR so that you become, in a way, a lord of illusions in human minds. I want you to let me do the same. Virtual reality can be dreamlike, so with the right game or app, I can be seen as a mistress of dreams—and therefore, my powers should grow. In theory."

I half expect him to laugh in my face and walk away, but he looks thoughtful instead. "One of the games we're developing features an illusionist hero," he says slowly. "Given how similar our powers are, that means the nuts and bolts for a dreamwalker character already exist. If we added some dream-related levels and your likeness as an alternate character..."

Oh, puck. I almost jump up in excitement. "You'll do it?"

His eyes gleam like blue diamonds. "I could—but it is a big ask. As beautiful as you are, I'll need something in return."

CHAPTER FIVE

I BLINK AT HIM, shell-shocked. He, this gorgeous creature, thinks I'm beautiful? Me?

The glow from the compliment almost obscures the other part of his statement: that I'd have to pay for my request. Now that I'm thinking about it, though, is it wrong that I hope he asks for something inappropriate as payment—say, my body?

"The Senate asked me to look into a certain classified matter for them," he continues, "and I could use someone with your investigative skills to help me out."

My horny bubble bursts. The Senate is the main governmental body on Gomorrah—which, unlike the Councils elsewhere, is elected by a democratic process. Going by what I've heard in the media, a classified investigation for the Senate might be an extremely dangerous undertaking.

I take a sip of my tea to calm myself. "I've just barely survived one investigation. What do they want you to figure out? I can't help my mom if I'm dead."

He frowns. "What's wrong with your mom?"

I put down the beaker. "It's a long story."

"Tell me." He grabs a blue fruit reminiscent of an orange and peels it.

I hesitate for a second, then tell him everything: how Mom got into the accident and how the medical bills drove me to accept jobs of dubious legality, including his. I also explain that the healing Isis performed was incomplete and that I now need to get more power so I can wake Mom from inside her dreams.

As I speak, Valerian's chiseled features soften, and as I'm wrapping up my explanation, he covers my hand with his big, warm palm. "I'm sorry," he murmurs. "I'm glad those jobs I gave you helped out."

I resist the urge to pull my hand away—in part because I like his touch and in part because he's being nice and I don't want to insult him by implying he has cooties. Though he totally does. In his case, though, I weirdly don't mind it too much.

I bet even his cooties are hot.

I clear my throat. "This investigation, how long do you think it'll take?"

Before he can reply, the dryad comes back with two plates and what must be the second part of his order—a selection of vegetables in nut-based sauces.

Valerian deftly divides the food between our two plates and tastes a mushroom-like morsel. "Delicious," he breathes, his eyes closing in ecstasy.

The dryad beams at him. "Erato will be pleased with your praise."

I feel a sudden urge to choke an innocent server, for no reason at all. I mean, all she did was smile at Valerian. Would I rather women be depressed around him?

Hmm. Maybe.

The dryad leaves, and I try my own version of the mushroom.

The thing is so foodgasmic a moan escapes my lips.

When I blink open my eyes—I didn't realize I'd closed them—Valerian is watching me with a hunger that has nothing to do with produce.

My face turns hot, my heartbeat ramping up. "You never answered my question," I mumble around a mouthful. "How long is the investigation?"

He peers at the greenery all around us, as if seeing other patrons and servers through the foliage. Then he refocuses on me. "I've just given us privacy with my powers," he explains. "If the waitress comes back, she'll see us eating and exchanging trivialities about the weather. Meanwhile, we can do anything we want and no one will be the wiser."

Nearly choking at the thought of doing "anything I want" with Valerian, I locate a juicy, broccoli-like stalk and stuff it in my mouth.

He watches me chew with evident fascination before finally answering my earlier question. "I have no clue how long the investigation will take."

Ignoring my disappointed grimace, he locates his own version of the plant that I just ate and attacks it.

Watching his jaws move, I realize this process *can* be fascinating—I have an especially hard time keeping my eyes away from his mouth. With effort, I marshal my wayward thoughts. "How about you tell me what exactly we'll be investigating?"

He swallows his food with obvious pleasure. "That's classified. Without clearing it first with the Senate, there's not much I can tell you."

"Good thing we have privacy, though." I spear a giant bean with my fork. "Wouldn't want someone to overhear the nothing you just told me." I put the sauce-drenched bean in my mouth. Just like everything else so far, it's divine.

Peeling his eyes away from my mouth, Valerian says, "The mere fact that I'm investigating something is need-to-know information. I only told you because I trust you."

I narrow my eyes. "I wish that were mutual."

"You don't trust me?" He makes boyish puppy eyes—and it's unclear if he uses his powers to make me melt at the sight, or if his control over his face is that good.

A short fantasy plays in my head, one where he and I reproduce and have a boy child who makes those exact eyes at me to get a pony made out of chocolate frosting.

Wait, what? What am I thinking?

I grab the beaker and slurp the tea loudly to banish the insane thought. "What about the game development?" I ask. "How long do you think that would take?"

He smiles. "I'd need to talk to my team to find out for sure. I know this much: The Illusion Scope—the hardware for our games—is going live in a few days, along with a couple of games, so my team is stretched thin. The game in question is phase two, so lower priority." He makes short work of his own giant bean—as in, the legume, not the part of his body my mind keeps drifting to.

Tamping down on my unruly libido, I ask, "Would it be possible to make it higher priority? Maybe have your team start working on the changes to the game in parallel with your investigation?"

He raises an eyebrow. "As in, you want to get your payment before the job is even done?"

"Why not? You just said you trust me. Either way, you don't have to release the game until I finish the investigation. I just want to help Mom as soon as possible."

He gives me a dazzling grin. "You've got chutzpah, I'll give you that."

Forking something that looks like a bright orange asparagus into his mouth, he consumes it with that signature relish of his.

I cross my arms in front of my chest. "Is that a no?"

"If you take all the money I've ever paid you and put a few zeroes at the end, that's about how much it would cost to do what you ask." He devours another morsel.

I edge forward on my stump-chair. "What if I helped with the game development?"

Mouth busy with the largest veggie on his plate, he gives me an incredulous look.

"I took courses in video game design," I say defensively. "On top of that, dreamwalking and game design are quite similar—and I have lots of experience with the former."

He chews thoughtfully, clearly not convinced.

"A good friend of mine also took those same courses. What if I convince him to help as well?"

Valerian swallows his food, his expression unreadable.

Possessed by some inner demon, I blurt, "He and I are *not* romantically involved."

Now he looks amused. "You should've led with that. He suddenly seems perfect for the job."

I tap my fingers on the stump-tabletop. "Felix is a wizard with computers. Literally so—he has power over silicon on top of his deep knowledge of computer science."

Valerian's gaze sharpens. "Is he that technomancer everyone hires to do their cyber security?"

"I think so. He certainly calls himself a technomancer." I give him a level look. "He owes me a favor, and I think I can get him to help."

That's a fib. If anything, I owe Felix a favor—or several. Still, I think I can convince him to lend a hand. In the worst case, I could pay his usual rates—assuming he'd accept payment in Gomorran cc instead of US dollars.

"Fine." Valerian extends his hand. "You've got a deal."

With almost no hesitation, I grasp his palm. Cooties or not, his handshake is strong and firm, his skin pleasantly warm and dry as his palm engulfs my fingers. A part of me never wants to let go, even though the knowledge of the germs we're sharing freaks me the puck out.

A few loud heartbeats later, I realize we're still holding hands—and that he's gently massaging my palm. Whoa. His thumb is rubbing in the exact spot where my palm feels tense, and it feels both soothing and—

Something chimes in Valerian's pocket.

Frowning, he lets me go and makes a gesture that looks like a VR command. "That was my alarm," he says apologetically. "I have an important meeting I have to get to."

Flabbergasted by the handholding, I just nod.

He rises to his feet. "Get Felix on board and meet me at my headquarters on Earth later today. I'll send you the time and the address."

I nod again, still mute.

He makes a few gestures that look like he's taking care of payment, then leans in and brushes his lips over my cheek.

My heartbeat goes supersonic. Openmouthed, I stare as he exits my personal space and strolls out of the restaurant as if he has no care in the world.

When he disappears from sight, I hygieia my hands and face and gulp down the rest of my tea before mindlessly devouring the rest of my food. Though everything is as delicious as before, the overactive state of my parasympathetic nervous system prevents me from enjoying it. Finishing the meal, I open up the app to pay and find that Valerian already paid for my portion.

That's nice of him. It's as if we were on a date. Wait a minute —were we?

Shoving aside the unsettling thought, I leave the restaurant and retrace my steps, taking the hyperloop and then a car to the hub building.

When I get into the elevator, I check my messages.

As promised, Valerian sent me the deets for our meeting.

I memorize the location in case my comms stop working when I get to Earth—though I doubt they will. Strictly speaking, I should leave all Gomorran tech here, but I'm feeling daring today. The New York Council owes me one, so even if I get caught, I'll probably get off scot-free.

Hopefully.

Exiting the elevator, I take in the view from the top of the skyscraper and bid civilization farewell. With a few decisive strides, I enter the pulsing energy of Earth's gate and arrive in the hidden section of the JFK airport. A few labyrinthian corridors later, I join the human travelers who have no idea this airport can take you to another world.

First things first: I find a place that sells hand sanitizer and get a few bottles. With no access to hygieia, this is the best I can do.

Ready to face this germ-infested world, I head for the taxi pickup location and text Felix on my Earth phone: *Need to talk to you in person.*

His answer comes back instantly: *Come to my apartment.*

I reply in the affirmative and use an app on my phone to summon a ride. Soon after, we hit traffic, my least favorite aspect of this place—besides the lack of proper sanitation, that is. On Gomorrah, we share the cars, which, combined with hyperloop and flying vehicles, has made traffic a thing of the past.

Eventually, we arrive in Manhattan.

Battery Park, the neighborhood where Felix lives, is nice—at least for Earth. There's lots of greenery all around, and the views of the toxic waters of the harbor are pleasing to the eye. When I get up to Felix's floor, it's bullet—and maybe even rocket—proof, something that's not the case with other apartments in the building.

I ring the doorbell.

CHAPTER SIX

THE DOOR OPENS, revealing Ariel's grinning face.

Ariel is an uber, an extremely good-looking and super-strong type of Cognizant. She and Felix are roommates, so seeing her here isn't a big shock.

"Bailey!" Before I can blink, she envelops me in a hug so tight a bear would be proud of it.

Since she doesn't touch any exposed skin, I find it easy to calm myself after the contact—especially once I catch my breath and ascertain that my ribs aren't broken.

"What are you doing here?" she asks excitedly, waving me in. "I didn't think you'd come back to Earth so soon after the last adventure."

"I'm surprising myself, trust me." I close the door behind myself.

Three furry creatures come out from the kitchen area and look up at me with varying levels of curiosity.

One is a chinchilla, an adorable rodent who isn't what he seems. From our last encounter, I know that this is a domovoi, a rare type of Cognizant that are extremely powerful in their limited domain. His name is Fluffster, probably on account of all that fluff.

Hi, Bailey, he says as a voice in my head. *Good to see you again.*

Smiling, I return the greeting and examine the second creature, a cat of the Persian variety. Though she's not a Cognizant of any kind, there's a royal air about her, and the kind of evil intelligence in her eyes that makes me want to avoid getting on her bad side.

The third animal is another chinchilla, which prompts me to ask, "You got another pet?"

Ariel rolls her eyes. "We didn't. That's Kit."

"Oh, hi, Kit." Kit is a shapeshifter, and a powerful one at that—so much so she's on the New York Council. She can obviously be any creature crazy humans keep as pets, be it a chinchilla, or a dog, or a hippo.

I'm not a pet, Fluffster says in my mind, managing to "sound" grumpy.

"Sorry." I do my best to keep a straight face. "I meant 'another pet besides the cat.'"

The cat gives me a look that seems to say, "In reality, they're all *my* pets."

The extra chinchilla shimmers and transforms into Kit's petite, anime-like blonde form. "I'm here to keep Fluffster company," she says with a wink.

"Don't ask," Ariel whispers. "They're friends with disturbing benefits."

I don't actually see a problem with such an arrangement—apart from this being potentially bad for Kit's sex addiction. Ariel is a product of a world where anyone enjoying intimacy always looks humanoid, so I can't blame her for the bias. We're more open-minded on Gomorrah. Besides shapeshifters—who are rare—we've got a plethora of weres, and other Cognizant regularly hook up with them in various forms.

"What brings you here?" Kit asks and turns herself into Felix. "If it's to see the technomancer, he's busy with someone else at the moment."

"His girlfriend," Ariel clarifies conspiratorially. "I'm still getting used to the idea of him having one."

Not liking the look Kit gives me, I say, "Felix and I are just friends." Her expression doesn't change, so I add, "Not the kind of friends you and Fluffster are."

"That's good to know," says an unfamiliar female voice.

A beet-red Felix and a tiny young woman step into the living room. She looks familiar—this is the girl I've seen him defend from pucks in his dream, I realize.

"Maya, this is Bailey," Felix says. "We go way back."

Maya extends her hand to me, and I have no choice but to shake it, making a mental note to sanitize soon.

She peers at me through her glasses. "Felix said you took video game courses together, but he never mentioned how pretty you are."

I grin at her. "Thanks. Video game development is why I'm here, actually. Felix, can you help me add levels and features to a VR game?"

"Why?" he asks.

"What are you up to?" Kit inquires.

More questions follow from everyone except the cat, and bit by bit, I bring them up to speed about my mom, Valerian, and the deal we made. To avoid talking about my plan to gain power, I just tell them that Valerian will help me in exchange for some services that include the game.

"Valerian is ambitious," Kit says when I finish. "Releasing his VR headset and applying to be on the Council at the same time? I have no idea how he's juggling it all."

I frown. "He applied to be on the Council?"

"Wants to replace Hekima," Kit says, her face turning into the late illusionist's grandfatherly visage. "Will likely succeed, too. His predecessor proved just how powerful their kind can be—a boon to the Council."

"I still can't believe I took classes taught by someone capable of all those murders," Maya mutters. "He seemed so nice."

She took classes with Hekima?

Oh yeah, that's right. He taught something called Orientation here on Earth—a sort of school for the young Cognizant.

This Maya must not just look like a teen—she *is* one. I hope Felix knows what he's doing.

Felix directs a guilty look at Ariel. "A chance to work on VR. Maybe I could—"

"No," she says sternly. "We need you."

I raise an eyebrow.

"Felix can't help you," Maya says with a little too much eagerness. "His other friend from Gomorrah has dibs."

Is she jealous of me? If so, why? Her boyfriend is roommates with Ariel and Princess Peach—both more attractive than I am.

Deciding to ignore her, I look at Felix skeptically. "You have *other* friends on Gomorrah?"

"Itzel," Kit explains and turns into the person in question: a round-cheeked young gnome with a goofy smile. In the real world, that smile would be hidden by a mask, since Itzel, like all of her kind, suffers from breathing issues.

"What's wrong with Itzel?" I ask, worried. She's a friend of mine as well.

"It's her famous grandfather," Ariel says.

Famous is an understatement. Cadmael singlehandedly boosted the quality of life on Gomorrah to the levels we currently enjoy. In his youth, he invented a reactor that provides energy that's almost free and therefore powers every aspect of our day-to-day life.

"What did he do this time?" I ask in exasperation.

For as long as I've known Itzel, her grandfather has been a pain in her butt. Recently, for example, he acquired a gambling debt so large that Itzel had to take a risky job to help Felix and his friends. She was so traumatized from their adventure that she asked me to treat her with dream therapy—which I intend to do at some point in the near future, since I now know how to enter gnome dreams.

"He disappeared off the face of Gomorrah," Felix says. "Itzel asked us to help, and we owe her."

"Of course," I say. "And I'd like to help too."

Everyone except Maya looks happy at the news—though it's hard to tell what Fluffster is thinking under all that fur, and the cat's flat face must always look a little bit grumpy.

What about your mother? Fluffster asks mentally.

Momentarily forgetting about cooties, I reach down and pick him up.

Wow. The risk of disease is worth it. Chinchilla fur is almost as heavenly as Pom's.

"My mom takes priority, of course," I reply, looking into his rodent eyes. "But I'm hoping the video game stuff and my payment to Valerian won't occupy all of my waking time."

I don't add that I'm beginning to miss vampire blood. With this much going on, sleep is a luxury. But I'd better resist these thoughts; it could be addiction rearing its ugly head. If my waking time isn't enough for people, they can bite me. Especially Valerian—that way, I might even enjoy it.

Felix grins. "Awesome. We'd love your help—and maybe I can still help you with the game when *I* have free time."

I put Fluffster back on the floor. "That would be great. Maybe you can do it in place of some of your paid gigs. I'll pay your usual rate."

At the mention of money, Fluffster puffs up. *Felix will gladly help you. Itzel's favor isn't going to pay rent or put groceries into the fridge.*

"But he can't do it *now*," Maya says. "We're going to Cadmael's apartment so I can use my powers to locate him." She puts her tiny hands on her hips. "I only have a short window of time when I'm free, so we need to go. Right now."

"Right," Felix says sheepishly. "We'd better leave."

Funny how this rush seemed to materialize only when I did. I decide against saying anything, though; Maya will be even more certain that I want her boyfriend, which I don't.

All my amorous thoughts are directed at Valerian as of late.

I look at Felix with a stony expression, lest Maya thinks I'm undressing him with my eyes. "Before you go, can you give me an update on Leal's comms?" I glance at Maya apologetically. "Leal was a dreamwalker whose murder the New York Council asked me to solve. His comms contain his notes and may provide useful information about my powers."

Felix perks up. "Oh, yeah, forgot to tell you. I was able to hack those. Got his whole journal. Checked on Soma, as you asked—no mention of it. He did seem obsessed about some secret society that's like the Illuminati but on steroids. At least that's as far as I got before I grew bored."

It's all I can do to conceal my disappointment. I was really hoping there'd be something about Soma in Leal's notes. Hekima had implied that it's a place where dreamwalkers live, but it's unclear if he meant a city or a whole Otherland.

Thanks to my mom's secretiveness, I know so little about my kind—or my family. She's never even talked about my early childhood years—which sucks, since I don't remember anything from before I was seven.

Ariel cocks her head. "A secret society?"

"Yeah," Felix says. "A group called Icelus."

Kit morphs into Leal and rolls his/her eyes. "That again? He brought that up in front of the Council a few times. A ridiculous notion." She turns back into her usual self. "According to him, Icelus are a cult of Cognizant worshipping some weird god."

Ariel looks intrigued. "Like the Brotherhood?"

"The monks are not secret about their faith." Kit turns herself into one of the hooded figures.

"Right," Felix chimes in. "Unlike the Brotherhood, Icelus hide their affiliation—and their deity isn't very nice. Leal says Icelus are behind some terrible things here on Earth."

Kit scoffs. "Delusions of an old man. He claimed they started wars and invented terrorist acts. His list went on and on. There's no way a group of Cognizant could've gotten away with all that under the noses of the Councils."

"Unless they'd infiltrated the Councils," Felix says. "Which is what Leal claimed. He even—"

"Can I get the notes so I can read them myself?" I glance at the door. "You're in a rush, remember?"

"Right." Felix disappears into his room and comes back with the dreamwalker's antiquated comms.

I take out my own shiny new model and my local phone. "Send them to one of these, please."

Felix snatches my new comms out of my hands and examines them with the excitement males usually save for the female form.

Maya scowls at me.

"Where are the glasses for this thing?" Felix asks. "And the gloves?"

I explain about the invisible headphones, the contacts, and the nails. Felix looks so enthralled I half expect him to have an orgasm, while Maya's scowl grows into a death glare.

"I think I'm going to get these once we find Itzel's grandfather," Felix whispers reverently.

I blow out an exasperated breath. "Do what you wish. But send me the files now, okay?"

"Oh, right." He shoots both devices with an arc of his technomancer energy. "Done."

I turn on my VR and see a new message with an attachment. I open it to find many pages of text.

Fine. I'll read this when I have more time.

Maya possessively grabs Felix's elbow. "We'd better go."

"Good idea," I say. "I'll get in touch with you through Itzel once I'm back on Gomorrah and have a free moment."

As Ariel and the others put on their shoes, I double-check when I need to meet Valerian and do the math on how long it'll take to get to his company's offices.

I have about an hour to kill.

"Can I hang out with Fluffster here?" I ask Felix and Ariel.

"Of course," Ariel says and hugs me without warning.

Before I can recover from her hug, Kit does it to me as well.

Maya coldly waves goodbye, and Felix cautiously shakes my hand.

I wait until they exit, then run to the bathroom to sterilize myself with soap and hand sanitizer. Feeling as clean as is possible without hygieia, I return to the living room and chat with Fluffster until it's time for me to leave.

One day you should come when I'm sleeping, the domovoi tells me as I head for the door. *I'm curious to experience your powers.*

"Deal." Unable to resist, I pet his heavenly fur. "See you later."

CHAPTER SEVEN

IN THE CAB, I sanitize the hand that touched Fluffster's fur and open Leal's journal.

Oh boy. There's a lot of boring stuff here—experiments on his poor birds and pages upon pages of stream of consciousness on mundane issues, including such gross bits as records of his bowel movements.

I search for Soma as a keyword and find nothing, just as Felix warned me.

Disappointed, I settle in and just read. Eventually, I come across what Felix mentioned—paranoid-sounding ramblings about a secret society.

They worship Phobetor, the lord of nightmares. They think him a god. Does he exist? If so, what is he? Could he be a creature that is to Cognizant what we are to humans?

I try to parse that paragraph:

There are worlds where we, the Cognizant, are worshipped as gods. In fact, this happened in the distant past of Earth too. For example, Loki, the god of mischief, was a famous probability manipulator. But what would it mean for some being to be a god to us Cognizant?

The cab stops next to a shiny building, interrupting my musings.

I ride to the top floor, where a large "Bale Inc" plaque proudly announces the name of the company, and approach the front desk.

"Mr. Bale, your guest is here to see you," the receptionist announces into her phone.

Valerian comes out wearing another bespoke suit. Puck, he looks good in it. Like, cover-of-fashion-magazine kind of good.

Oh, and he must be the Mr. Bale she was referring to. That's why the company is Bale Inc.

Huh. So if I married Valerian and followed the antiquated coverture custom of taking the husband's last name, I'd be Bailey Bale.

Not sure how I feel about that.

"Where's the technomancer?" Valerian looks around as if Felix could be hiding in a corner somewhere.

"Turns out he has another commitment." I put my hands in a praying position. "Please don't renege on the deal."

He sighs. "How about you join us in the meeting room?"

I follow him into a big, glass-encased space where two other men are waiting at a glass conference table. One I already know, I realize—a mustachioed guy who looks like the video game character Mario, but with a scar on his forehead.

It's Bernard, the human Valerian commissioned me to "inspire" in his dreams. It's the job Valerian paid me that nice bonus for—as he should have, now that I'm thinking about it. Not only was I busted by the New York Council while doing it, but the job itself was quite complex due to Bernard's endless trauma loops. The poor guy lost a child to a monster, then himself became monstrous in his revenge.

Looking at him now, you'd never be able to tell what happened. He's the very picture of a mild-mannered software engineer. I wonder if he's a psychopath on some level, or if what he did lives in every parent, ready to be triggered by a horrible-enough stimulus.

The other man I've never met before, and it's a shame.

Despite being waif thin, he's almost as attractive as Valerian, with similarly symmetrical masculine features and strong dark eyebrows. His hair is pure black, and his skin tone is similar to mine.

"Bailey Spade, please meet Bernard Anderson and Ratridevi Bhairava," Valerian says and sits down.

"Nice to meet you, Mr. Anderson," I say to Bernard. "And you, Mr. Bhairava."

"Please call me Bernie." Bernard smiles. "Because of the *Matrix* movies, I never go by Mr. Anderson."

Another fan of that franchise. He and Felix would get along—particularly if I never tell Felix about Bernie's gruesome past.

"I also don't go by my last name," Mr. Bhairava says with a slight Indian accent. "Please call me Rattie."

I blink at him.

"It's a play on Ratri, the short version of my first name," he explains. "People here find it easier to say it that way."

Well, okay then. If he doesn't mind that nickname, so be it. For what it's worth, he doesn't look at all ratty. If I had to compare him to a rodent, I'd say he looks more like a very handsome beaver. Or an otter, though that's no longer a rodent. Or even a *cheburashka*—a koala-like creature that lives in the preserved equatorial jungle on Gomorrah.

"Do I also have to come up with a nickname?" I ask, plopping into a sleek office chair.

Could I go by Bails? Or Beernuts?

Valerian sits down. "No need. We don't *all* go by nicknames."

I salute crisply. "Fair enough, *Mr. Bale, sir.*"

A sensuous smile tugs at the corner of his lips. "I do let those close to me call me Valerian." His voice deepens in a way that sends a tendril of excitement into my nether regions—an awkward situation, especially in front of Bernie and Rattie.

Taking a deep breath to settle my speeding pulse, I pull my sleeves down to cover Pom's fur—it's turned an embarrassing coral pink.

Valerian, meanwhile, is back to being all business. "Do you want your teams dialed in?" he asks Bernie and Rattie in a brisk tone.

"Not yet," Rattie says, and Bernie concurs.

"Fine." Valerian looks at me. "I've already explained the idea to them. You're going to be the model for a project we're calling *Lucid Dreamer.*"

Rattie grins at me. "I convinced them that instead of this being a new character in an existing game, a new standalone VR game experience makes a lot more sense."

"One that uses the foundational work of the other projects," Bernie chimes in. "To deeply cut on prerequisite resources."

I drum my fingers on the glass table. "A new game? Does that mean it'll take longer?"

"In a way, yes," Valerian says. "But there's also good news. Rattie thinks his team could have a working level in a matter of days—between their Trembling in the Dark project and everything else, they have almost everything they need. It's just a matter of stitching bits together."

Trembling in the Dark? I heard about it from Felix. He said, and I quote, "It's the scariest horror video game of all time."

"So *Lucid Dreamer* will be scary?" I ask Rattie.

He shrugs. "If the game is about the mistress of dreams, I figured why not have her fight nightmares? Especially since my team is so good at that sort of thing."

"Valerian recently purchased Rattie's whole studio," Bernie explains. "They've been helping out on everything, but they want to sink their teeth into a game of their own."

"Which means a thousand-plus people will be working on this," Valerian says meaningfully.

Oh, puck. No wonder he said this is a big ask; the budget must be in the millions.

Bernie opens his mouth to speak, but his phone rings. He surreptitiously glances at the screen, and a tender smile appears on his face as he takes the call.

"Hi, honey, thank you so much for calling me back." Muting his phone, he looks at us apologetically. "It's my daughter. We haven't spoken in years. I'll be right back."

Valerian nods and Bernie takes the phone out of the room.

So they reconnected? In his dreams, it was something that tormented Bernard—I mean, Bernie. Perhaps having gone through his trauma loops under my watch, he feels better and has reached out to his family?

"Let me answer this for Bernie," Rattie says. "We'll obviously need to figure out more of the story than simply 'fight nightmares,' but given my team's expertise and that Valerian wants the game bumped to phase one, this is the smart play."

"Right," I say, feeling a bit overwhelmed. "Whatever can speed this up sounds good to me."

Bernie comes back with an apology.

Ignoring him, Valerian gives me a knowing smile. "I never finished explaining why having a working level is good news. We have testers equipped with the Illusion Scope prototypes, waiting for something to play. There are twenty thousand of them, and growing." He looks at me pointedly.

I stare back at him blankly; other than being even more impressed with the budget he's throwing at this thing, I don't see what the special good news is.

Disembodied letters suddenly appear in the air in front of me. They look like LEGO pieces and form a paragraph of text—clearly the work of Valerian's illusion powers:

When thousands of humans play that demo, your powers will get a boost—I know this from personal experience. Not as big a boost as when the game goes live, obviously, but a noticeable one. If you're lucky, that boost might be what you need to best your mother.

Wow. I was settling in for a wait that would span months, but it turns out I might be able to save Mom in a matter of days.

I beam at him. "This is great news indeed. What can I do to speed this up?"

"I got that part," Valerian says to Rattie and Bernie. "Get in touch with your teams before Bailey and I leave."

We're leaving? Okay then.

Rattie presses a button on the side of the desk, and a bunch of giant screens slide from the ceiling and cover the walls. A video conference app chimes, and soon every screen displays the enthusiastic faces of hundreds of people—most likely developers, designers, animators, audio engineers, and so on.

Please introduce yourself and we'll go, Valerian tells me via the LEGO text.

"Hi, everyone," I say, looking into the cameras. "My name is Bailey, and I will be the model for the *Lucid Dreamer* project. I also happen to know something about game design, so I'd be happy to help in any way I can—just let me know what you need when you need it." I keep going in that vein, eventually starting to sound like an army general psyching his troops for an attack.

"Thank you," Valerian says when I finish my speech. "Why don't we go to the motion capture lab so we can get started?"

Everyone applauds and waves to me as we leave.

I feel pleasantly odd, as if I just took a tiny sip of diluted vampire blood for the first time.

Am I high on being involved in game development, or is it Valerian's proximity?

As we enter the elevator, I notice him watching me intently.

"I feel strange," I blurt. "In a good way."

Valerian presses the button for the fifteenth floor. "There's a chance your powers got boosted by merely having that many humans believe in you as the game model for a dreamwalker-related game," he says in a low voice. "When my own power got boosted, I felt very peculiar." He closes his eyes, as if in bliss, and I store that expression in my memory banks for use in the dream world.

I imagine that's what his O-face looks like.

The elevator opens, and we enter a room with green screens for walls and enough computer equipment to oversee a space launch.

Valerian picks up a small piece of cloth from a chair and hands it to me. "Put this on."

It's a onesie-like outfit made from a blue material with big gray dots. I look at it, then at him.

Nope, he's not kidding. He actually expects me to wear it.

I heave a sigh. "Where's the fitting room?"

An amused gleam appears in his ocean-blue eyes. "Why?"

I don't justify that with a reply.

"I'll just look away." Matching actions to words, he turns his broad back to me.

At least I think his back is to me. He can be using his powers to make me *think* he's looking away, while in actuality, he's standing there with a magnifying glass directed at my privates.

Then again, where do I draw the line when it comes to paranoia? He can just as easily use his power to make himself invisible and stand in any fitting room—like he did the other day in the bathroom while I showered.

It's a recollection that should enrage me, but it makes me feel warm and tingly instead.

Without further ado, I strip off my clothes and pull on the onesie. It's stretchy, so it fits.

I look at Valerian's back.

There's a tension in his shoulders that I choose to interpret as him suffering with the effort not to turn around and gawk at my awesomeness.

"Done," I announce.

He turns around and grins at me before going to a nearby table to pick up a bunch of objects that look like the dots attached to my outfit.

"I need to glue these to your face," he says, approaching me.

"You what?"

"They're sterile, I swear," he says, and before I can object, he attaches the first one to my forehead, the tips of his fingers brushing over the skin around the dot.

Holy digitization. I had no idea my forehead was an erogenous zone.

He attaches another dot to my forehead, then another.

My breathing turns shallow.

Valerian grins, his eyes gleaming wickedly, and starts gluing dots to my nose, cheeks, and near my lips. By the time he finally attaches a dot to my chin, I feel like I need a change of panties.

Leaving me utterly discombobulated, he goes to set up the primitive Earth equipment.

"Can you follow instructions?" he asks with a smirk.

I clear my dry throat. "What do you need me to do?"

He asks me to display different emotions with my face, and I do my best—sometimes doing such a good job that Pom changes color on my wrist to match the expression. He then asks me to move for him, directing me this way and that. The weird part is that I find all this bossing around kind of hot—and not just the parts where he asks me to sway my hips and things like that.

Hours of motion capture later, Valerian says, "That's enough. We should be good for the demo, but might need you back after that."

I hold my breath as he carefully removes the dots from my face and turns his back to me again.

I shake off my hormone-induced daze and slip out of the onesie. Before putting on my original outfit, I use up all of my remaining hand sanitizer on my face and body—because that's the rational thing to do.

However much it turns me on, I can't forget that Valerian's touch is full of Earth germs.

"I have some business on Gomorrah," he says when he turns around. "But you should stay and work with Rattie and the team for as long as you can. In fifteen hours, though, I'll need you for the first part of the Senate investigation, so meet me back at Erato's then."

Erato's? "We're eating there again?"

He shakes his head. "In fifteen Earth hours, it will be midnight on Gomorrah. Instead of dining, we'll be invading Erato's dreams."

"We?" Is he including himself in this dreamwalking adventure?

"We'll talk details after you make a dream link and get away from Erato's dwelling. I assume you can dreamwalk in a dryad?"

"I don't see why not, but—"

"Good. Let's go."

He leads me back to the elevator, and as he presses the button for the top floor, I recall something I've been meaning to ask him. "Does the word 'Soma' mean anything to you?"

He stiffens for a second, then his expression smooths out. "Can you give me some context?"

"It's something Hekima mentioned in his last moments," I say, puzzled by his reaction. "He made it sound like a place where dreamwalkers live. It also sounded like at least one illusionist family lived there too—Hekima's own."

Valerian's jaw tightens. "You can't trust anything that murderer said."

"So you don't know?" I ask—though it's obvious to me that he does.

"I'm sorry. I can't help you with this."

"But—"

"If you want me to keep helping you, drop it," he growls just as the elevator doors open.

Fine. If he's going to ask me nicely like that, I guess I won't pry anymore.

He strides back into the meeting room, and I follow. Bernie and Rattie are there, but instead of the teleconference, the screens feature drawings of bone-chilling monsters and mind-bending environments. Clearly, the work on the demo is proceeding at breakneck speed.

"My team is extremely excited," Rattie says to Valerian. "I already have some stuff I want to run past you."

Valerian holds up his hand. "I have a prior commitment, but Bailey can serve in my stead." He glances at me. "I trust her implicitly when it comes to the *Lucid Dreamer*."

As Valerian leaves us there, Bernie looks at me dubiously, but Rattie doesn't bat an eye. "So, Bailey," he says, "in your opinion, when in someone's dream, should the dreamwalker character actually walk? Some folks suggested she fly or teleport around."

"Let her walk," I say. "If dreamwalking were real, I imagine all of the above would be possible, but she might still walk by default as that's what's familiar and doesn't require extra effort and concentration."

"Logical," Rattie says. "And no flying cuts on dev time."

"We haven't done flying in VR before," Bernie adds.

"Flying also has a higher chance of giving the gamer VR sickness," I say, without sharing why I think so. There are flying games on Gomorrah that did that to me—and I'm an experienced flyer, at least in my dreams.

Rattie peppers me with more questions, and I answer as best I can, drawing on my game design knowledge when I need to, as well as on dreamwalker experience.

After a while, Rattie yawns in the most contagious manner. "I think it's time for a few hours in the pod," he says apologetically. "I'm still on Bangalore time."

Bernie stifles a yawn of his own. "It's not your jet lag. I could use some time in the pod myself."

Catching the bug, I can't help but yawn too. "What's this pod business?" I stretch to banish the sleepiness.

Rattie stands up. "Game development is a crazy business. We often work so much there isn't time to go home and sleep."

"Which is why we installed sleeping pods here at the New York offices," Bernie says, rising to his feet as well.

I look at each man in turn. "You sleep on the job?"

Rattie shrugs. "When it's needed. Usually during crunch times."

I nod, then yawn again.

"We have a pod not assigned to anyone," Bernie says. "It's yours if you want a power nap." Seeing me cringe in disgust, he adds, "It's brand new. You'd be the first person to use it."

Curiosity getting the better of me, I agree.

Rattie leads the way until we reach a room filled with the aforementioned pods—which look like a hybrid between a rocket and a coffin.

Rattie opens the clear plastic lid of one of them. With a wave, he lies down, shuts the lid, and closes his eyes.

"This is the pod I mentioned." Bernie points at one that does indeed look brand new.

"Thanks," I say. "I just might use it."

Bernie smiles and heads over to a pod that has a picture of a child glued on the inside. I recognize the image as that of his daughter—I've seen her in his dreams. Climbing in, he mumbles something about sweet dreams and closes the lid.

Huh. I never realized game development was such hectic work that you don't even get to go home to sleep. I think I might stick to dreamwalking as my primary career, after all—at least once I save Mom.

Setting my alarm on "vibrate" so I don't wake up others, I climb into my own pod and close my eyes.

CHAPTER EIGHT

THE VIBRATION of the alarm wakes me.

I feel groggy, like I could sleep for many more hours. Oh, well. Maybe I'll sleep after I help Valerian with the Erato business.

Climbing out of my pod, I notice Bernie and Rattie are still slumbering in theirs. I approach Rattie and check his eyelids. Yep. He's dreaming right now. That means I could establish a dream link with him if I wanted to.

It doesn't take me long to decide. I *do* want to. I could then inspire him when it comes to levels of my game, for starters.

Stealthily lifting the lid, I touch Rattie's forehead.

———

I APPEAR in my dream palace and come face to face with Pom.

"Bailey," he exclaims, turning a deep purple. "I've missed your face."

I fluff his fur. "Can't you just make yourself a dream version of my face and stare at it in a pinch?"

To demonstrate, I create a disembodied replica of my grinning mug and leave it floating in the air next to me.

He gives a small shudder. "That looks kind of disturbing."

I roll my eyes. "Good to know. I didn't realize my face has that effect on you."

"When not attached to the rest of you, it gets creepy," he says seriously. "I guess your arms and legs keep your face from being that way."

Shaking my head, I teleport to the tower of sleepers and look for Rattie.

He's indeed in a nook, not far from Bernie, who's also showed up in his bed.

"Trauma loop," Pom says, the tips of his ears darkening as he eyes the clouds above Rattie's head.

He's right. And not just any clouds, but turbulent ones. I rub the tip of my nose. "I don't get it. Does Valerian seek out software engineers with deep psychological trauma, or is it just bad luck on everyone's part?"

Pom's fur darkens further. "I'm not going in there with you."

"I don't think I'm going in either. I have to meet Valerian and do a job for him in the waking world. I've set up a link with this guy so I can inspire him in the future, not deal with that." I wave at the clouds.

"Inspire him?" Pom turns light orange. "Are you talking about the private things you do with Valerian that you asked me not to witness?"

I put my hands on my hips. "First of all, I never got further than first base with Dream Valerian. Secondly—"

"What's first base?"

"*Secondly*, that is not the kind of inspiration I'm talking about. Besides, Rattie might be pleasant to look at, but doing stuff like that with him would feel like cheating on Valerian, even in dreams."

Wait, what am I saying? How can you cheat on someone when you're not in a relationship?

Pom takes on the colors of root vegetables—first a carrot, then a beet. "Did I upset you?"

"It's fine." I sigh. "The private stuff you mention is a sensitive subject, that's all."

He waggles his ears. "Like the P word for me?"

The P-word stands for "parasite"—which Pom contends he's not, preferring "symbiont" instead. Of course, considering that he uses me as his food source, feels my emotions, possibly excretes his metabolic byproducts into my blood stream, and is attached to my wrist to the end of our days, the jury on parasite-versus-symbiont is still out.

He bristles. "I can't believe you just thought that."

"I was just testing if you're reading my thoughts. You said you wouldn't, but you did."

He turns a deeper shade of beet. "Sorry. I'll stay out of your thoughts going forward."

"Thanks." I fluff his fur. "And we're definitely symbionts."

His ears perk up. "Like a bee and a flower?"

"Definitely *not* like a bee and a flower," I say and jolt myself out of the dream world.

STRUGGLING NOT TO GIGGLE, I open my eyes next to Rattie's pod. Though it's unclear which of us Pom views as the flower, I know this much: If anyone's going to do any pollination of me, it better be Valerian.

Speaking of which, I need to get moving, else I won't make it to Gomorrah on time. I leave the building and buy more hand sanitizer before grabbing a taxi to JFK. Once we hit the inevitable traffic, I open up Leal's journal in my VR view to have another look.

Skimming over a lot of minutiae, I locate something that piques my interest:

Another day, another failure. I'm beginning to think touchless dreamwalking is impossible—or if it is possible, it may be something only those of us with more power can master.

Touchless dreamwalking? How does that work?

I search the journal for more mentions of this term and eventually puzzle out that it's basically a way to enter someone's dream from a short distance—in lieu of touching them skin-to-skin.

Puck, that would be amazing. My least favorite thing about my powers is all this exposure to cooties. Next time I meet a sleeper, I'll see if I can do this.

Arriving at JFK, I make my way to the secret hub and enter the gate that leads to Gomorrah. Once there, I stop by my place to use the bathroom, change my clothes, hygieia myself from head to foot, drink like a camel, and scarf down some manna. Then I head over to my destination —Erato's restaurant.

Valerian is already there, waiting for me by the building.

He's changed his suit for an outfit that would definitely look out of place on the parts of Earth I'm familiar with. It's a black, sporty bodysuit, a skintight contraption that shows off every muscle on his body as thoroughly as if he were naked and covered in tar.

Another flush heats my skin. This outfit will definitely make it hard to concentrate on the job, whatever it is.

Valerian's clearly not in the mood for flirting, though. "You're late." He puts on a breathing mask that blocks his features and makes him look like a gnome, then hands the same thing to me. "Put this on."

Before I can ask any pertinent questions—such as, "What the puck are we doing?"—he stalks into the building and summons the elevator.

I hurry after him, fitting the mask on the way. "Wha—"

He places a finger to where the lips would be under the mask, and the LEGO letters show up in the air: *My powers can't fool listening devices if they're there.*

I nod in comprehension, and we ride the elevator in silence. When we get to the hundred-and-fifth floor, Valerian steps out, and I follow, staring at our surroundings in awe.

The walls are covered from floor to ceiling with vertically growing plants, each one with a dedicated lamp and a mist machine nourishing it.

"I feel like we're in a greenhouse," I whisper.

Don't talk and stay in the middle of the corridor, he tells me via LEGO letters.

Demonstrating what he means, he keeps away from the walls as he creeps forward.

I mime his actions as closely as I can, though I doubt my movements achieve the predatory grace of his.

He stops next to a moss-covered door and waves an unfamiliar device over a lock. There's a click, and the door slides out of our way. He takes out another gizmo and tosses it inside.

That will disable all electronics for a while, he tells me via LEGO letters.

I nod.

He waves for me to follow and moves even stealthier, which is logical since we've now officially broken into someone's lodgings.

Bringing up my VR, I write him a message: *If we get caught, will the Senate pardon us?*

Stern-looking LEGO letters show up in the air immediately: *Never refer to this job in electronic messages again. And to answer your question: it would be easier for them to make us disappear, so let's not get caught.*

Great. Just great. *Now* he tells me that.

Sighing, I follow him deeper into the apartment, which reminds me of the restaurant—a veritable jungle of different plants of all shapes and sizes. Only unlike the restaurant, there's a sinister quality to some of the vegetation—like the acid seed okra, a flowering plant that can open its pods and spit out seeds up to two hundred feet. Those seeds, as the name implies, are covered with a powerful acid. And that's an unmodified plant. Others appear to have been engineered from their nasty natural brethren, like the one that looks like poison hogweed—a plant covered by deadly poison, only with thorns. There's also a cousin of the famous strangle vine, only bigger. The winner of the creep show, though, is sitting in a giant pot in the middle of the room. It's a distant brother of the bug trap flower, except it's big enough to eat a person instead of a bug.

Press here, Valerian's LEGO text informs me as he touches a button on the right cheek of his mask.

I do the same, and the scent of the air coming into the mask changes, becoming more sterile. It must be getting filtered.

Valerian takes out a sleep grenade.

Interesting.

Gliding through the plants like a jaguar, he stops next to a door and quietly opens it before tossing the grenade inside.

Touch her to make a connection, he orders a few seconds later. *If she wasn't asleep, she should be now.*

Doing my best not to make any sounds, I slink into the room and examine the sleeping dryad inside.

Based on her reputation, I figured Erato had to be older, but I didn't realize she was downright ancient. Her green hair is almost entirely gray, and the green skin of her face looks like weathered tree bark.

Watching her eyelids, I frown.

What are you waiting for? Valerian asks.

I point at her lids, then at the eyeholes of my mask as I rapidly move my eyes to explain what I need.

So we're just going to stand here until she starts dreaming?

Since I don't know how to pantomime "I don't want to risk going homicidally crazy," I pointedly shrug.

With a barely audible sigh, he crosses his arms over his broad chest and closes his eyes.

Ignoring his pouting, I switch my attention to Erato's eyelids.

Nothing.

I bring up my VR display and set a timer for the length of time it typically takes for the gas to leave a large person's system. If this small woman doesn't go into REM sleep by the time the alarm rings, I'll have to risk dealing with the subdream. Hopefully I won't have to, though. The last time, with my mom, was brutal.

Feeling like the worst cat burglar in the history of thievery, I open Leal's journal in my VR view and look for something interesting to read. I still haven't found anything by the time the VR alarm rings, so I close the journal.

And that's when I realize something odd is happening in the room.

All the plants around us seem to be coming alive and moving with an eerie purpose.

She's in REM sleep, Valerian informs me.

I glance at her eyelids. She is indeed, and she must be dreaming about something that makes her agitate the plants.

I carefully approach her bed and extend my hand. Before my fingers touch her leathery skin, I remember the power I recently learned about—touchless dreamwalking—and decide to try it.

Keeping my hand extended, I will myself to go into Erato's dream.

Nothing happens.

I strain so hard a vein pops in my forehead.

Still nada.

The way the plants move grows spookier.

What's the holdup? Valerian asks. *Make the connection, and let's get out. You'll do the actual dreamwalking once we're safely away.*

Fine. Maybe now isn't a good time for experimentation.

I touch the dryad's green forehead and go in the regular way, popping in and out of the dream palace before Pom has a chance to say hi.

Task accomplished, I nod at Valerian and pull my hand away. "Let's go," I say quietly—which is when the dryad's eyes open and the plants around us coil for a strike like an army of snakes.

CHAPTER NINE

PUCK. I cast a frantic glance at Valerian. Why isn't he conjuring up some illusions to save us?

I made us invisible to her senses, he says, reading the panic on my face. *But her plants are aware of us somehow, and I don't know how to fool them.*

Plants with senses? I guess that makes sense. How else are they able to lean toward light or grow roots downward into the soil instead of in some random direction?

"Is someone here?" The dryad sits up, and the plants move with greater purpose, tendrils and branches reaching out like arms.

Grasping my hand, Valerian begins to tiptoe out of the room.

The dryad leaps naked out of the bed, grabs a knife, and starts slicing at the air.

Valerian drags me out of the bedroom.

Midway through the living room, a strangle vine snakes from the ceiling and wraps around my neck. Gasping, I flail my limbs as it pulls me up. Valerian rips at the vine, but all this does is slightly loosen its grip so I suffocate slower.

"Whoever you are, you're not leaving here alive!" Erato shouts, running out of the bedroom. Her gaze is still blindly sweeping the room, not noticing us thanks to Valerian's powers.

Suddenly, she looks directly at me.

Puck.

Knife ready, she lunges at me. The blade slices an inch above my head, cleaving the vine holding me.

As I fall into Valerian's arms, I understand what happened. He made Erato see whatever she needed to see in order to strike where she did—and to accidentally free me from the vine.

He must still be showing her whatever it is because she growls in anger and leaps to the center of the room as Valerian lowers me to my feet.

We run for the door.

The poison hogweed swipes at me, its thorns missing my face by a hair's width.

Pucking puck. Remind me to never break into a dryad's home again.

I glance back and see Erato stumbling into the deadly embrace of the bug trap flower. The flower's giant trap closes, muffling the dryad's confused cry. Before I can celebrate our narrow escape, the pods of the acid seed okra turn toward me, moving as if in slow motion.

I don't even get the chance to think the word "duck" before an acid seed flies at my chest like a bullet.

CHAPTER TEN

ONLY IT DOESN'T SMASH into me. With the speed a Secret Service agent would be proud of, Valerian yanks me behind him, taking the projectile in the chest in my stead.

The material of his outfit begins to sizzle, and terror rips through me. Pucking idiot! What was he thinking? Who made him my bodyguard? I want to yell at him, but there's no time. Hands shaking, I grab my hand sanitizer and squirt the cleansing liquid at the spot where the acid is attacking Valerian's suit.

The sizzling seems to lessen.

Valerian tears at the front of his suit, ripping a chunk away.

There's a nasty burn on his chest, which I squirt with more hand sanitizer.

I'll live, he informs me via LEGO letters. *We have to go.*

Grimacing in pain, he grabs my hand and pulls me toward the door as Erato's knife slices open the side of the bug trap.

We sprint for the elevator. Erato is on our heels, and the plants in the hallway try to stop us—except these are regular, non-deadly plants, so they fail.

As he summons the elevator, Valerian must spare a second to make Erato see something that isn't there because she hurls her knife in the direction opposite us.

We leap into the elevator, and he punches the button for the roof.

The doors close, shutting out the dryad, but I don't exhale until we get all the way to the top, where a flying car is waiting for us. As soon as we jump inside, it lifts off the roof.

I rip the stupid mask off my face and squirt more sanitizer at the burn on Valerian's chest. He won't die, I know that now, but I'm still furious that he took that kind of risk.

"What were you thinking?" I say through gritted teeth. "You could've—"

"It's okay." Removing his own mask, he covers my hand with his. "It doesn't hurt anymore."

"But why did you even—" I stop short because he pulls out a small vial and takes a sip.

His eyes close in that blissful O-face expression, and the wound instantly heals.

I narrow my eyes at the vial. "Vampire blood?"

He puts it away. "I only use it in case of emergencies."

I take a deep breath, some of my fury abating. If he had that with him, then he wasn't in as much danger from the acid seed as I thought. Still, the idea that he took that deadly projectile for me…

"Don't do that again. Ever," I say grimly. "The risking your life for me part, I mean. And be careful with that blood."

He arches his eyebrows. "I'm always careful. Do you have a problem with it?"

"I almost did." I tell him about my recent troubles with that highly addictive substance, and when I finish, he takes out the vial and demonstratively pours it out the car's window.

"No need to have that sort of temptation around you," he explains. "I don't need it that much."

Before I can process that, the car descends onto a landing strip on a rooftop. Distracted, I peer at it. It looks like a private rooftop, in which case Valerian is even richer than I thought.

We land, and as we exit, he tells the car not to expect us for a while.

I blink up at him. "It's your personal car?"

Most citizens of Gomorrah share rides—both driving and flying ones —which is how we don't have traffic the way they do in New York and other Earth cities. Only one percent of the richest one percent bother with private rides.

He lovingly pats the shiny surface of the vehicle. "Sometimes you order a ride, and it takes time to arrive."

"Sure. It makes sense to spend a fortune to avoid wasting those valuable milliseconds."

He grins and leads me to the elevator.

Surprise surprise. We only descend one floor, to the penthouse of this skyscraper—the most expensive dwelling you can imagine. He waves his hand, and the shiny black door quietly slides open, revealing an expansive loft-like space with twenty-foot-high ceilings made almost entirely of glass.

Talk about skylights.

That's not what makes my breath catch in my chest, though.

Someone put a thirty-foot-wide water pond here, smack in the middle of the penthouse.

Is this real? I've never seen such a thing. Then again, I guess if you can have a pool, you can have a pond—if you're into throwing money away, that is. Unless this thing is an illusion, Valerian must own the floor below this one just to make room for the bottom of this body of water.

As I come closer, I see a few swamp flowers that have multicolored legu sitting on them—frog-like amphibians that squeak instead of croak.

It's a whole pucking ecosystem, and a nice one at that. The scent of the flowers, their colors, the sounds of the water splashing, and the little squeaks all seem to be carefully calculated to pleasantly stimulate the senses.

"This is not an illusion," Valerian says before I can ask. "There's also ri living in the water."

Sure enough, I spot the little fish-like creatures. They look like rubies with fins and tails.

Valerian takes off his shoes, sits on the edge of the pond, and dips his naked feet into the water with a contented sigh. Catching my gaze, he grins and pats the spot next to him.

I gingerly crouch there.

"You can put your feet in." He curls and uncurls his toes, clearly relishing the feel of the water. "It's nice."

I grimace. "No, thanks. I could live my whole life without soaking my feet in the same place those legu and ri go to the bathroom."

"Your loss." His expression turns serious. "Are you ready to go into Erato's dream?"

I get more comfortable by twisting my legs into a lotus pose I learned in a yoga class on Earth. "Sure. What am I looking for when I'm in there?"

"Right." His gaze is intent on my face. "I have to tell you what the Senate asked me to do."

Finally. "Go ahead."

"How much do you know about Icelus?" His voice tightens on the last word.

Icelus? Is he talking about the secret society cult from Leal's notes? The one Kit dismissed as the dreamwalker being delusional? "Well," I say slowly, "allegedly, they did some bad things on Earth and—"

"What the puck do you mean by 'allegedly?'"

I scoot back, startled by his vehement reaction. "I don't know. During my investigation for the Council, I got Leal's journal—you know, the dead dreamwalker?—and he'd made claims about Icelus that sound like conspiracy theories. Nobody on the Council took him seriously, so…"

Valerian's forearm muscles flex, like he's fighting not to clench his fists. "Whatever heinous crimes Leal accused them of, Icelus are guilty of far worse."

I give him an incredulous stare. "Worse than wars and terrorist acts?"

He nods grimly. "Their goal is to maximize the number and frequency of nightmares everywhere to serve their deity."

Huh, okay. Maybe Leal wasn't all that delusional. "That deity being Phobetor, the god of nightmares?"

"Do *not* utter that name," Valerian snaps. "Just like the nightmares, it gives him power."

Wait, what? Is Phobetor like Voldemort, He Who Must Not Be Named? Actually, I don't think Harry Potter's nemesis got more power when his name was said out loud. Either way, why does Valerian sound like he believes the same mumbo-jumbo as Icelus?

There's no way there's such a thing as Phobetor.

"I won't do it again," I say reassuringly, just in case. "How about I call him something safe, like Collywobbles? In English, that means stomach pain or queasiness."

"I know English well," Valerian says, his gaze softening slightly. "I've been on Earth more than you."

"Oh?"

"I immigrated there a while back."

I scooch back toward him, driven by curiosity. "What about your parents? Did they also immigrate?"

"No." His features darken. "Icelus took them from me before that."

The torment in his eyes makes my chest ache, and on my wrist, Pom turns darker than a black hole. Unbidden, my hand reaches out and rests reassuringly on Valerian's stiff shoulder.

"I'm so sorry," I murmur.

His shoulder minutely relaxes. "It was a long time ago." Eyes glinting, he adds, "The killer paid dearly for what he did."

No doubt. I don't even want to imagine what kind of horrific things Valerian can do with his powers to someone he hates.

He places his palm over mine, his gaze growing heavy-lidded.

Wow. His touch is like the heat of an exploding quasar. It spreads through my body and settles somewhere low in my core.

I snatch my hand away before I do something crazy, like lean over and plant a kiss on those sensuous lips. "Back to the Senate job."

"Right." His features grow taut again. "Since the government here knows of their existence, Icelus have been very careful when it comes to their operations on Gomorrah—until recently, that is. The Senate have reason to believe that Icelus *are* plotting something here, and they've asked many people, me included, to look into it."

"And that dryad—"

"Is the reason the Senate needed *me* for that part of the investigation. Because of some of the horrific genetically modified plants she recently patented, they think she's an agent or at least a lead to one, but they don't want to spook her. They want me to use my powers to extract the information from her without her realizing they're on to her, but I think your powers will work even better."

I massage the bridge of my nose. "You don't think our little visit spooked her?"

"Hopefully not. As we were flying, I got the Senate to replace the surveillance footage in her home and the rest of that building. When she checked it, she saw herself running around like a madwoman."

I whistle. "Isn't that illegal?"

He shrugs. "The Senate decides what's legal."

"Right. So much for the rule of law."

He splashes at the water with his foot. "Do you have what you need for the dreamwalking?"

"No. I could use an anchor."

He raises an eyebrow.

"Something that would help me get the right dream started," I explain. "Saves a ton of time."

"Use her patent filings." He gestures around, clearly activating his comms.

I check my inbox. Yep. A message from him is waiting there, full of attachments.

As I review the plant designs, a shiver goes down my spine.

These make the man-eating plants from her apartment seem like cuddly kittens.

The tamest one is a tree with blooms that remind me of corpse flowers native to Earth, but uglier. The pollen these trees produce would be toxic enough to fell even a vampire. With the right wind, a single tree could wipe out whole neighborhoods.

"She's insane," I mutter as I review more of the deadly flora.

"Icelus seek to create nightmare fuel whenever they can," Valerian says. "Even someone writing an article about these plants can be helpful to them."

"No kidding." I turn off the VR. "I myself might have a nightmare about a garden with these abominations. Do you think Icelus plan to unleash these plants on us?"

"That's what I want you to find out," he says. "Will those filings work as an anchor?"

"Only one way to find out." I rise to my feet. "Please don't disturb me as I go into my trance."

I don't know why, but I turn away from him before I touch Pom. I guess I still don't trust him with this information.

Hand resting on my looft's soothing fur, I dive into the dream world.

CHAPTER ELEVEN

I FIND Pom in the lobby of my dream palace, shooting a laser gun at targets that remind me of inter-Otherland gates, only with a shimmering bull's eye in the middle.

A pang of guilt bites at me. Before all my problems started, I'd regularly play competitive games with Pom, everything from tennis to fencing. They'd brought my little friend incalculable joy, and were fun for me also. Now I've ignored him for so long, he's been forced to play with himself.

But not in a dirty way.

Probably.

Hopefully.

"Bailey!" Pom makes his game accoutrements disappear and flies around my head with the enthusiasm of an overcaffeinated puppy. "What's going on?"

I take a slow route to the tower of sleepers so I can bring him up to speed.

"And that's her? The dryad?" He looks at the green newcomer in one of the nooks.

"Yep." I fly over to her bed. "Looks like she was able to fall back asleep."

He lands on my shoulder. "Can I join you in her dreams? Doesn't seem like it'll be very scary."

"Just don't give away our presence," I say and make us both invisible as I reach out to touch Erato's forehead.

———

ERATO IS LYING naked on her bed. A nearby shrub extends a cucumber-like fruit toward her groin.

Before Pom and I witness something we'll never be able to unsee, I change the plant into a giant VR screen.

Despite the incongruity, the dryad doesn't wake up. Good. I put the plant designs from her patents on the screen, and she focuses on them, as I hoped.

With her attention occupied, I change the room around us to be more generic, then clothe her and make sure she's standing upright.

This is it. If this is close enough to a memory—and intuition tells me it is—she'll take care of the rest. And she does. The room starts to look like her living room, except the front door is different.

Suddenly, the door in question breaks into tiny pieces, and a giant wolf leaps through what remains. With a flash, he turns into a naked male with Elvis-like sideburns and a Mohawk hairdo popular with gremlins.

Anger twists Erato's features. She recognizes him.

"Stupid bitch," he growls. "Which part of 'discreet job' was unclear to you?"

Three strangle vines snake from the ceiling. One wraps around the guy's throat, and two grab his wrists. "Now," Erato says menacingly, "what were you saying?"

The guy sneers. "If something happens to me, the people I work for will have your spleen."

Erato waves a hand, and a poison hogweed coils within a hair's width from his feet. "Given your lack of intellect, I doubt you're as indispensable as you think."

"Test it and see," he snarls.

She waves her hand again, and the acid seed okra pod zeroes in on the guy's torso. "I don't have to kill you, you know. Something tells me if I make you look even uglier, the people you work for will thank me."

Interesting. It doesn't sound like they're part of the same group. Does that mean she's not Icelus?

"The patents," he grits out. "How could—"

"I patent all of my creations," Erato says calmly. "I offered you exclusive rights, but it was outside your budget."

He shows his teeth. "I didn't realize that was what we were talking about."

"Didn't realize. Didn't think." She taps her temple. "Are you beginning to see a pattern here?"

In a flash, the werewolf turns back into his wolf form.

A wall of greenery rises between him and Erato.

"If something happens to me, a letter will go to the Senate," she says. "If you work for who I think you do, that's the last thing you want."

He growls and bounds back through the door, disappearing from sight.

The dream stops being a memory at this point as some of the plants turn into green creatures that don't exist, at least not on Gomorrah.

Figuring I have enough info to share with Valerian, I leave the dream world.

————

HE'S STANDING RIGHT NEXT to me as I emerge from the trance, close enough that his bacteria could easily jump on me if they wished. And he's staring at my face like a dermatologist looking for a scary mole.

I instinctively step back, flushing all over.

He cocks his head.

I dampen my lips. "Were you staring at me that whole time?"

"Not staring," he murmurs, his gaze briefly dipping to my mouth. "Admiring."

My flush deepens. Clearing my dry throat, I say, "Ready to hear about Erato's dream?"

His expression turns serious, and I tell him what I just saw.

"That makes sense," he says.

I blink at him. "It does?"

"The Senate had two theories for why Erato would file those patents. One was that she's with Icelus, and the filing was designed to give nightmares to the clerks at the patent office and others in the know."

I scratch my eyebrow. "Sounds like too much trouble for relatively few nightmares."

He nods. "This is why I think their second theory must be the right one. She took that job from Icelus but filed the patents to mitigate the damage her work would actually do."

"Oh?"

"If someone were to use those plants for a terrorist attack, the Senate would already have countermeasures in place," Valerian says. "And I bet

Erato knew that would be the case—which is why she filed in the first place. No wonder her employer was so pissed."

That does make sense. "So what now?"

"Give me a second." He makes some gestures, querying something in his comms. "I can't seem to find a werewolf matching your description in the Enforcer database," he says after a moment. "He was probably in disguise."

I think back to the sideburns and Mohawk. "That might explain why he looked so odd."

Valerian makes a few more VR gestures. "I'm going to use my powers on you in a second, if you don't mind."

Before I can actually say if I mind or not, the living room goes away, replaced with a giant stadium. All around me stand people with different faces but the same Elvis sideburns and Mohawks as the werewolf in the dream. Each wears a name tag, as though this were an orthodontist convention.

"I'm showing you every werewolf on Gomorrah who has a record." Valerian's disembodied voice seems to be coming from every direction. "I added the hair to make it easier for you to identify the one from the dream."

I nod, and the werewolves begin to parade in front of me, each giving me a good chance to have a look at his face.

After about an hour of this, I yawn.

"I'm sorry," Valerian says from everywhere. "I wish I knew a faster way to do this."

"I could show him to you in a dream," I say, looking at the sky.

"Just a few more suspects," he says. "Then you can go home and rest."

The werewolf parade continues in the same vein until I spot a guy who might be the one.

"Him," I say when he gets closer, and I know for sure. "Hans Stubbe."

"Are you certain?" Valerian asks.

"His sideburns were longer, but it's him. I'm positive."

The stadium and all the werewolves except Hans go away, leaving me back in Valerian's living room.

Valerian shifts his gaze from something in his VR display to me. "Based on his profile, he's probably a hired gun instead of an actual Icelus initiate."

I yawn. "Do you know where we can find him? Because if not, I know a guy."

"Yeah, leave it with me." Valerian makes Hans go away. "By tomorrow night, I'll have the location."

"In that case, I'd better go get my beauty rest," I say, suppressing yet another yawn. "I still owe myself hours and hours of sleep."

"You know," Valerian murmurs, eyes darkening, "you can sleep here."

My throat goes dry. "I'm not sure that's a good idea."

Wait. Why did I say that? It *is* a good idea. In general, why am I not all over him already? How long can I stay a virgin before it seems creepy? I may already be there, in fact. And if I were to lose it, I can't think of a better person to find it than—

He steps toward me. "I know you want to."

"You do?" I sneak a glance at my coral-pink Pom bracelet.

Is that what gave me away? Or is it something about the way I smell or look?

Instead of replying, he dips his head and presses his lips to mine.

Wow. Wow. Wow.

At first, I'm too shocked to do anything but process the sensations. His lips are soft and warm, their gentle, undemanding pressure making me crave more. But then unwelcome statistics flood my brain, the ones about the millions of bacteria we're already exchanging, even with our mouths closed.

If the kiss gets more intimate, our microbiomes will merge and stay that way forever and ever. And bacteria are just the tip of the frightening iceberg. Viruses such as herpes simplex or papilloma are also real possibilities—depending on who else Valerian has kissed before me.

I don't know if it's the idea that he's kissed others or my dread of germs, but I pull away from the kiss.

There's a hurt expression on his gorgeous face.

Puck. Did I pull away too sharply? And, germs aside, was pulling away what I really wanted?

Feeling like an idiot, I take a step back—and my foot plunges into the cold pond water. I squeal and flail my arms to regain my balance, but my other foot slips off the edge.

Valerian lunges forward and catches me, yanking me to safety.

As soon as I'm steady on my feet, he releases me, his face unreadable.

Mumbling a weak thanks, I beeline for the door, leaving wet footprints behind me.

———

MY EMOTIONS IN TURMOIL, I get into a car. Thank the stars it's self-driving. The last thing I want is to face a sentient being in my current state.

Once we set out, I exhale a frustrated breath. What the puck was that all about? I've wanted to kiss Valerian ever since I first laid eyes on him, yet when he finally made the move, I totally pucked everything up.

Now he knows I'm a freak, the only woman my age who's never kissed anyone. I can only have intimacy in my dreams—and even there, not with a real person but a figment of my own imagination.

This is why I haven't dated. I'd rather face Earth's dentists than explain all this to a guy I like.

Needing to get my mind off the clusterpuck that is my love life, I open Leal's diary. Now that I have reason to believe he wasn't just a paranoid curmudgeon, I read his thoughts on Icelus with a lot more interest.

According to him, someone had been killing Icelus agents on Earth—a mystery person Leal felt great gratitude toward.

I freeze for a second, recalling what Valerian just told me about his parents. Could that have been him? Is he capable of being so ruthless? I picture his expression when he was talking about Icelus and realize the answer is yes.

I can imagine him taking out Icelus agents in all sorts of gruesome ways.

My chest tightens with sympathy again as I think about him dealing with the loss of both of his parents. I can't picture losing my mom. Even now, with her in a hopefully reversible coma, I feel like an orphan. How much worse would it have been for Valerian at that age?

Ugh, I'm a horrible person. He opened up to me, telling me about this tragedy in his past, and I treated him like a leper because of my stupid germ issues.

Glumly, I return to the notes and skim through a bunch of boring stuff. But then I come across something interesting.

Leal claims that Icelus have a drug that puts people into REM sleep. He says it has a dire side effect but doesn't say what it is before going on about how invaluable to him such a drug would be.

Skimming further, I'm not surprised to find him talking about hiring someone to replicate said drug. I know he succeeded in that. Of course, his version also had a side effect, the worst possible kind. Whoever took his drug never woke up. That's what happened to Eduardo, the werewolf on the New York Council.

I continue to skim until a yawn overcomes me. Now that the

adrenaline from the kiss is fading, my sleepiness is returning full force, and Leal's boring notes aren't helping.

Closing the journal, I open my messages and find Itzel in my contacts.

I can help you guys look for your grandfather tomorrow, I tell her. *Let me know where I can meet everyone.*

I send the message just as the car stops next to my building. The ride on the elevator happens in a sleepy haze, as does undressing and treating myself to hygieia all over my body.

When I finally get into bed, I'm asleep before my head touches the pillow.

CHAPTER TWELVE

AS I EAT BREAKFAST, I activate the VR and check my messages. There's a reply from Itzel telling me where to meet her and the gang on Gomorrah, so as soon as I finish my meal, I head out to Nebulabucks.

Nebulabucks is a teashop chain, and the location Itzel chose must be new—the line of thirsty Cognizant is only ten minutes long. Felix, Ariel, Itzel, and Kit are sitting at the biggest table in the corner, hot drinks in everyone's hands.

Felix holds out a cup to me. "Nebula flower, the way you like it."

Thanking him, I take the cup and sniff it as I sit down next to Ariel. The fruity notes of the tea are divine.

"How did your game development thing go with Valerian?" Ariel asks with an eyebrow waggle.

I flush at the reminder of the kiss fiasco. "Long story." I look at Itzel's masked face. "Did you find your grandfather?"

"No," the gnome says, her nasal voice disguised by the breathing apparatus. "But we made some progress."

"Or Maya did," Felix says proudly.

I look around the table again, then peek under it. "Where's your little friend?"

"She's eighteen," Felix says defensively—and no wonder. I'm pretty sure he's at least in his mid-twenties.

Ariel grins. "Legal as of very recently."

"But do tell Bailey where she is." Kit turns herself into the petite girlfriend in question and gives Felix an evil smirk. "I'm sure it'll make it crystal clear how mature she is."

Felix glares at Ariel and Maya/Kit. "She's got a trigonometry exam."

Kit morphs into Felix. "*Advanced* trigonometry," she says in his voice. "Must not forget that."

Ariel's grin widens. "Still a high school subject. And no, it won't help matters if you tell Bailey about the advanced placement classes Maya takes."

"Come now," I say, my face exaggeratedly serious. "Maya sounds like a very bright young lady."

Felix slurps his tea very loudly, then says, "Anyway, this high school student was the only one who could help us make heads or tails of Cadmael's disappearance."

"Indeed," Itzel says sternly. "And if we could get back to said disappearance, that would be swell."

I turn my attention to her grumpy face. "What did you learn?"

"We found a vaping pen in Grandpa's apartment," Itzel says. "It didn't seem to be his, so we asked Maya to touch it."

"Her power is psychometry," Felix chimes in. "She can tell who an object belongs to when she—"

"We all know what psychometry is," Ariel says with an eye roll.

Itzel puts down her cup. "Do you want to see how it went?"

"Please." I take a big gulp of my tea.

Itzel puts on a set of VR glasses and gloves and makes a few gestures.

I hide my surprise at seeing that she has an older model of comms. Since she's a gnome, I expected her to have the latest gadgets. Then again, she might resent that stereotype, similar to how peaceful orcs dislike being perceived as violent brutes.

Opening my own VR interface, I click on the video she's just sent me.

———

THE VR PUTS me in a cluttered room, presumably in Cadmael's apartment. Maya is sitting on the floor next to dirty socks, holding the vape gizmo in her tiny hands.

A glowing, purple-tinted energy seeps from her skin into the object, and her expression turns trance-like. "He's punching an elf in the face," she chants under her breath. "Now he's punching a dwarf, then a—" Her eyes roll back. Then she exhales, and her eyes return to normal.

"His name is Vas Lube," she says, sounding tired. "He's an extremely aggressive orc."

So much for not stereotyping. Nobody around me looks surprised to hear of an orc's involvement either.

Itzel's voice rings out from where the VR camera must've stood. "Where can we find this orc?"

Maya shrugs. "I can only tell you who he is, not his location."

The VR recording terminates.

———

I DISMISS my VR and find myself back at the table in the teahouse.

"So it's safe to assume he took Cadmael," I say, looking at my friends. "An orc named Vas Lube."

Kit is grinning. "I hope Vas isn't short for Vaseline."

"Leave it to Kit to turn an orc's name into something sexual," Felix mutters under his breath.

I pick up my tea. "What did you guys do once you got the name?"

"Nothing," Itzel growls. "I don't know anyone who's ever heard that name. Nor do they." She sweeps her gaze around the table.

"It's a good thing you have me then," I say, "because I know a guy."

"Who?" Ariel asks, her eyebrows furrowing.

"I don't think you guys know him. I helped him out once, and now he helps me when I need something from the Gomorrah underworld." *Such as vampire blood* is what I don't add, since it might still be a sensitive topic for Ariel.

Itzel jackknifes to her feet. "Let's go see him now."

———

AS WE DRIVE to the bar where my guy—Napoleon—always hangs out, I ponder whether it wouldn't be wiser to ask Valerian for help with this instead. If he can locate the werewolf from Erato's dreams, he might also be able to find this orc.

Problem is, I'm not sure I can face Valerian after last night's debacle, let alone ask him for favors. In fact, I wouldn't be surprised if he were to find someone else to help him with the werewolf and disappear from my life for good. He's probably canceling the *Lucid Dreamer* project at this very moment, so even my mom will suffer due to my inability to kiss a guy I like.

"Bailey." Ariel touches my shoulder. "We're here."

And so we are. This is exactly the seedy bar we need.

Taking a few steadying breaths, I exit the car and lead everyone to our destination.

———

"THIS PLACE REMINDS me of the Mos Eisley Cantina from *Star Wars*," Felix whispers as we enter.

"All the bars and clubs on Gomorrah remind you of that," Ariel says. "You need to get out more."

Napoleon is sitting on an extra-tall barstool to the side, looking red, horned, and tiny, as usual.

I nod toward him. "That's my guy."

"Wait a second," Felix says. "I know him. He sold me a gun once."

I gape at him. Guns are extremely illegal here on Gomorrah, to the point that even the Enforcers—our law enforcement—are not allowed to carry them. Only the Senate Guard, a type of secret service for the government, and the Gomorrah equivalent of SWAT carry guns.

Then again, given what I know about Napoleon, it doesn't surprise me that he sells guns and other taboo items.

"What kind of Cognizant is he?" Ariel whispers loudly. "He looks like a little red devil."

I cast a worried glance at Napoleon. I hope his hearing can't pick up what we're saying. "He calls himself a nain rouge."

"That's just 'red dwarf' in French," Itzel whispers.

Of course she speaks French. Gnomes are very good at languages.

"I believe his kind are more commonly called the lutin," Kit says in a hushed tone and turns herself into a pretty and feminine little red devil. "They're forced to look like humans on Earth." She transforms into a petite human with the same features as the little devil. "The lutin are amazing lovers."

"Someone really needs to get laid," Felix mutters under his breath.

"You volunteering?" Kit shimmers into Maya and licks her lips in a disturbingly sexual manner.

Felix reddens to Napoleon's levels as Ariel chokes on laughter. At the bar, Napoleon's pointy ear twitches.

"Hey, Napoleon!" I call loudly and head toward him.

The nain rouge puts down his murky, ruby-colored drink and turns around to scan the bar. Spotting me, he bares his sharp, predatory teeth in a wide smile.

"Bailey." He pronounces my name with a district French accent. "Nice to see you outside my dreams for a change."

I smile and greet him in French before switching to English for the benefit of my American friends. "This is Kit, Itzel, and Ariel, and you already know Felix."

Napoleon looks Felix up and down. "*Oui*, the gun. I hope you only used it on your backwater world, as you assured me you would."

Felix bobs his head. "I'd never brandish it on Gomorrah."

"Good. Good." Napoleon picks up his drink and takes a sip. "I charge double the price I gave you if it's for local use."

Itzel huffs. "Worried if someone gets caught, it could come back to bite you?"

"Gnomes and their bluntness." Napoleon gulps the rest of his drink. "Even orcs have more finesse."

"Speaking of orcs," I say casually, hoping to keep the cost of the information we need as low as possible. "We're looking for one named Vas Lube. Where can we find him?"

Clicking his little red fingers, Napoleon summons the elf bartender and orders another drink—Chimera's Fire.

I inwardly cringe. He's about to get a concoction so hot and spicy, some say it's made by fermenting reaper peppers—abominations with a Scoville Heat Unit in the millions.

The bartender places the drink in front of Napoleon, and as a drop of it spills on the coaster, it sizzles.

The nain rouge takes a long sip and grins as contentedly as a child chasing a chocolate chip cookie with warm milk.

"So, about Vas," I say with exaggerated patience. "We need information."

Napoleon lowers his drink to study me. "I like you," he says, his breath smelling of pepper spray. "I don't want you to get yourself killed."

My friends and I exchange glances.

"He's dangerous?" Felix asks.

"As dangerous as they come." Napoleon looks around furtively. "He runs with the Filthy Bastards."

I glance at Itzel to see if she knows what he's talking about.

She looks just as blank as I do, and our off-world companions appear even more clueless.

Napoleon sighs deeply. "I'm talking about a gang that chose to name themselves Filthy Bastards. Do I really need to explain this further?"

Itzel's eyebrows snap together. "I don't care if they call themselves

Abominable Rascals or Repulsive Reprobates," she growls, leaning into Napoleon's personal space. "This Vas person knows something about my grandfather's disappearance, and I intend to speak with him."

"Remind me never to let Itzel name a gang," Felix whispers. "Rascals?"

If Napoleon minds being face to face with Itzel's breathing mask, he doesn't show it. "Who's your grandfather?" he asks, seemingly offhandedly.

"You wouldn't know him," I say quickly. If Itzel mentions that her gramps is a famous inventor, the price of the information we seek will get a number of zeroes tacked on to it, if it hasn't already.

"By telling you what I know, I'll be putting myself at risk," Napoleon says right into Itzel's face. "I hope you're ready to compensate me accordingly."

Itzel's eyes water—probably from Napoleon's spicy breath. Wiping at her face with her sleeve, she steps back.

"How much?" I ask.

Napoleon names an insane figure.

"Throw in guns for each and every one of us, and you've got yourself a deal," Itzel says before I can even start to bargain.

He picks up his hellish drink. "I only have one gun left. And you'd have to use it off-world."

"We plan to use the gun when we face Vas," I say evenly. "Take it or leave it."

There's no way this is actually the last gun he owns, but if I challenge him on it, it'll do more harm than good.

Napoleon grins, exposing his fangs. "I'll take it... *if* you visit my dreams one more time."

Itzel better appreciate this. "At a time of my choosing," I say reluctantly. "And not soon."

"*Oui.* Just bear in mind, that time will need to be before you need my help again." He downs the rest of his drink, probably getting an ulcer right then and there.

We all chip in to pay for Napoleon's services, with Itzel insisting on contributing the lion's share. When we tell him to check his balance, Napoleon gestures in his VR like an opera conductor. Upon seeing the money in his account, he gives us a predatory grin and gesticulates a few more times before saying, "Check your messages."

Sure enough, he's sent us the location of the gang's hangout.

"Pleasure doing business with you," he says when I confirm I got the directions.

"What about the gun?" Itzel asks.

Grunting, he reaches under the bar in front of him and pulls out a sleek, short-musket-like device. Before anyone can see the highly illegal weapon and report us, I snatch it and hide it in the back of my pants.

We quickly hustle out of the bar and summon a ride. Itzel instructs the car to go to her place. "Felix's suit is there," she explains. "If we're going to look for a gang member inside their own hideout, we need all the help we can get."

———

ITZEL'S APARTMENT looks like a mad rocket scientist's lair. There are countless screens with rocket designs on them, half-built drones, tangles of wires, and jars of exotic fuels.

In the walk-in closet by the living room stands the suit in question—which looks like a sci-fi B movie robot.

"Felix claims he was inspired by the very first clunker of a suit built by Iron Man," Ariel says. "While I think he ripped off the Mech Batsuit."

Felix puffs out his chest. "This is a Neo Golem original." He launches into an explanation behind the name, which boils down to this: If Felix were a superhero, that would be his code name.

"So we have a gun"—I pat the back of my pants—"and the Neo-Golem suit. Anyone else feel like it's not enough?"

"Depends on how many of the so-called Filthy Bastards will be there," Itzel says. "I don't care, though. It's the only lead we've got."

I stroke Pom's fur. She's beginning to scare me slightly. "How about we swing by my apartment?" I suggest. "I've got sleep grenades there, which might help us avoid violence altogether."

Felix steps into his suit and snaps the robot-like faceplate in place. "Sounds good." His voice comes out muffled.

As we exit onto the street, Felix receives a few curious glances, but not as many as he'd get on Earth, outside of theme parks.

We take a car to my apartment, where we grab a couple of sleep grenades and a bite to eat. While we're at it, I ask Felix to teach me how to use the gun, since he seems to have the experience.

"Right." He takes the gun from me and presses a button on the side. An antiquated-looking screen shows up above the gun—clearly, this isn't a new model. He points at a self-explanatory label on the screen. "This controls if the gun's ray is lethal or not." He sets the gun to stun mode and aims it at Ariel.

"Ha-ha," she says humorlessly. "Suit or not, I can still break you in half."

With a huff, Felix points the gun at my window. "It's really this simple. Point and shoot." He mimes squeezing the trigger.

I take the gun and practice summoning and hiding the screen. It's as easy as Felix said. I stick the gun into the back of my pants. "Got it. Let's go."

We summon another car and head straight for the location Napoleon provided, which turns out to be a seedy-looking cul-de-sac in one of the worst parts of Gomorrah.

"At least no one will mind Felix's suit," Ariel says, wrinkling her nose as we step out onto a urine-stained street decorated by piles of never-picked-up garbage. It's beyond gross, even with the cool breeze that's blowing away the worst of the stench. I hold my breath the best I can, but the putrid aroma seeps into my nostrils anyway.

Itzel really owes me one. The germs here must be almost as bad as on Earth.

Napoleon's directions lead us to what once was a storefront but is now boarded up and missing a sign.

"No way to see what's waiting for us inside," Ariel whispers as she tries to peek behind the plastic covering the windows.

Kit makes herself look like an orc. "I could pretend to be a newbie who wants to join the gang."

"No," Itzel whispers. "Let's stick to Bailey's sleep grenade plan."

Nodding, I check the door.

It's locked.

I take out my lockpicks, but Felix puts a hand on my shoulder before I can use them. He then shoots the door with an arc of magenta energy. "In case there's an alarm," he quietly explains.

Still in her orc form, Kit eyes the door dubiously. "I don't think this place has functional indoor plumbing, let alone alarms."

I shush them and get to work with the lockpicks. Everyone watches my hands in fascination. As soon as the lock gives in, I carefully open the door and toss in the grenade. Closing the door, I count the seconds in my head to make sure whoever's inside has fallen asleep and the gas has neutralized, letting us walk in safely.

"Hey!" a voice growls behind us. "What the puck are you doing?"

Startled, we spin around as one.

Scowling at us is a veritable army of Filthy Bastards.

CHAPTER THIRTEEN

"THEY MUST'VE SNUCK up on us as Bailey was dealing with the lock," Felix whispers, and everyone is too tense to chastise him for stating the blatantly obvious.

Ariel reacts first, her military training kicking in as she leaps forward and punches an orc twice her size in the chest. Her opponent flies back at his comrades, who stagger back before they catch him and shove him back at her.

Before I can see how Ariel fares, I spot a stone flying our way.

It smashes into Felix's metallic chest. His Neo Golem face shield goes up, and the robotic suit rips into the crowd of our attackers, making disturbing flesh-meets-metal smacking sounds along the way.

If it weren't for the breeze that would take the gas away too swiftly, I'd consider using my remaining sleeping grenade. As is, I yank out the gun, activate it, and aim it at the head of the nearest orc.

The gun beeps. Though nothing seems to come out of the barrel, the orc falls unconscious. The gun is still on the nonlethal setting—a good thing, as this orc may well be the one we seek.

"We just want to talk to Vas," Itzel shouts. "There's no need for anyone to get hurt!"

A Filthy Bastard with the perfect features of an uber spits at Itzel, and his saliva lands on her mask.

Puck. If that were me, I'd kill him for that unauthorized sharing of bodily fluids.

Itzel must feel the same. Eyes turning into slits, she forms a ball of lightning between her hands and hurls it at her assailant.

The guy flies back and crashes into his brethren, knocking them off their feet like bowling pins.

An orc takes his place.

Heart hammering, I render him unconscious with my gun and survey the rest of the battlefield.

Felix is battling a dwarf and an orc—and looks to be winning. Ariel is effortlessly beating up two elves. Still in her orc form, Kit is facing off with an elf who has an ugly scar on his face. A smash of Orc Kit's fist later, the elf slumps to the ground, but another Filthy Bastard—a vampire—takes his place.

I aim the gun at the vampire and squeeze the trigger, but nothing happens. I switch to lethal mode and shoot him again—still nothing.

Puck. What gives?

Before I can freak out properly, Kit transforms into a giant and kicks the vampire with all her might. The guy flies to the end of the cul-de-sac and doesn't get up. Exhaling in relief, I switch my gun back to stun mode and put down Felix's dwarf, as well as one of Ariel's elves.

Two vampires wielding wicked-looking knives attack Giant Kit, and a dwarf appears out of nowhere and yanks on my gun-holding wrist. The weapon clanks to the ground. Before I can grab for it, the dwarf throws a punch at my stomach.

I jump back, softening the impact of the blow. Still, my breath whooshes out of my lungs. Pucking puck. Dwarves are incredibly strong, and fierce fighters on top of that. Even with my martial arts training, I'm in big trouble without that gun.

Deciding to play dirty, I dodge the next punch, grab the dwarf by his bushy beard, and give it a vicious tug. My opponent's pained cry is my reward—well, that and the gross souvenir that looks like something a lion might cough up after giving the whole pride a tongue bath.

Hurling the disgusting clump of hair back at its owner, I smash my fist into his solar plexus.

It's like a rock, and there's no sign of pain from the dwarf.

A booted foot tries to sweep me. I jump over it, land like a cat, and kick my attacker in the crotch.

The dwarf barely blinks.

Double puck. This must be a female dwarf—no way would a male be able to keep fighting after that. Both male and female dwarves have beards, though some females opt to get rid of theirs with nano hair removal, probably so that other Cognizant don't make the same mistake I just did.

Yep. Now that I'm looking for it, I see a hint of breasts under her baggy clothes. Feeling better about ripping out that beard—it's often a source of male dwarves' pride—I hit her in the face.

The dwarf staggers back for a moment. Then, with a roar, she launches at me like a rabid honey badger.

CHAPTER FOURTEEN

USING a maneuver from a dream of an Aikido master on Earth, I use the dwarf's momentum to put her on the pavement. Then I break with Aikido philosophy and gracelessly kick my opponent in the head until she stays down.

I don't get to enjoy my victory for long. As I look up, I see a vampire whooshing my way.

This is it. I'm completely screwed now.

"That's enough," Felix's voice booms through the cul-de-sac, no doubt boosted by his suit.

Startled, the vampire halts, as does everyone else.

Neo Golem's chest opens up. In the place where Felix's nipples would be, two giant guns show up and fire at an empty spot nearby.

Boom. The explosion vibrates everyone's inner organs.

The robot points the guns at the still-standing Filthy Bastards. "Do I make myself clear?"

A few angry nods.

His faceplate turns from orc to orc. "Which one of you is Vas?"

"Inside," the vampire nearest me hisses.

"Stay here," I tell Felix. "I'll go look for him."

The metal head of the robot nods, and I slip inside the abandoned store.

The gang has transformed the place into a hybrid between a gym and a casino. There are weights everywhere and a boxing ring in the middle of the room, but also card tables and even a small track, likely for illegal races with small animals.

Sleeping bodies are everywhere. The problem is, there are five orcs.

I dig through the pockets of the first one for ID.

Not my guy.

I check the next one. Nope.

On the third orc, I hit pay dirt. Not only is this Vas, but he's in REM sleep to boot.

Reaching out, I make the connection and get back to the waking world. Then I make connections with a few more members of the gang— in case running around Vas's dreams doesn't yield gnome grandfather fruit.

Leaving the store, I nod at my friends as I sterilize my hands.

"You killed him?" the nearest orc booms.

"No. I just needed to see what he looks like," I lie. "Now that I have, we'll go."

"If we let you," the orc growls.

The guns in Felix's chest point in his direction, and the orc steps back.

A vampire blurs into the store, then comes out just as quickly.

"Vas is alive," he reports. "So is everyone else."

"And they will stay that way if you don't puck with us," I say.

The Bastards step out of our way.

I pick up my gun and stand shoulder to shoulder with my friends as we back out of the cul-de-sac. Once we're out of sight, we break into a run and grab a car a few blocks away.

"That was intense," Kit says, turning into several gang members in quick succession.

Ariel looks at Felix's chest. "I thought you only had one round in those boob guns of yours."

Felix raises the faceplate and grins. "The Filthy Bastards didn't know that."

Itzel turns to me, her eyes shining with hope. "Did you find out where my grandfather is?"

"About to." I touch Pom's fur.

APPEARING IN THE DREAM PALACE, I update Pom on the goings-on as I look for Vas in the tower of sleepers.

"Whew," I say when I find my green quarry. "The other gang members haven't woken him up yet."

Pom flies up to the orc and looks him over with distrust. "You should still hurry. If you don't mind, I'll join you."

I agree, and Pom perches on my shoulder. I can't resist taking on the visage of a pirate before I make both of us invisible and jump into the orc's dream.

———

THE ROOM where the dream is taking place is familiar. It's the Filthy Bastards' abandoned store hangout. Vas and another orc are wearing gloves and standing in the boxing ring.

The dream is a memory, I realize.

I let it play out until Vas goes to the locker room. While his attention is consumed by changing his outfit, I transform the locker room into Cadmael's cluttered room that I saw in VR.

Done changing, Vas looks up and fills out the rest of the information himself, starting with the vape gizmo, which shows up in his mouth.

A few of the gang members are here, looking scorched—probably by lightning balls. Itzel's famous grandfather is also here, lying on the floor in an unconscious heap.

"Call him," Vas says to a vampire nearby, one of the ones who attacked Kit in the cul-de-sac.

The vamp fiddles in his VR for a second, and a hologram appears in the middle of the room.

It's a tall, thin man whose face is obscured by a puck mask, a popular adornment worn at costume parties on Gomorrah, and therefore one that doesn't tell me much about the person hiding behind it.

"Do you have him?" the guy asks in a voice that sounds like creaking floorboards.

Vas gestures at the unconscious gnome.

The masked dude nods approvingly and points at the vampire who started the hologram. "I want *him* to bring the gnome to me."

Puck. It would've been better if he'd asked Vas—that way, I could bring up that meeting in the dream world.

Oh, well. Maybe Vas had met this guy at some point anyway?

As Vas's dreams start to stray away from memory territory, I find opportunities to put the puck-masked man into a variety of environments.

Unfortunately, nothing prompts the dream I seek. The mystery man must've never met Vas outside that hologram conversation.

Giving up, I go back to the waking world for a moment, then recall a few more gang members I'd made connections with and snoop around their dreams next.

No luck.

Outside the hologram conversation, no one seems to have met the masked stranger.

Exiting the last person's dream, I apprise the team on what I've just learned.

Itzel grunts. "We almost got killed for nothing."

"I'm not so sure." Kit transforms into a male vampire, bares fangs, and looks at me with glamour-ready eyes. "Is this the one who escorted the masked guy?"

I shake my head.

Kit turns into another vampire from the fight. Then another.

"This one," I say when she turns into the vamp from the dream.

"Ah, good." Kit turns back into herself. "One of the more handsome devils. This should be fun."

Everyone stares at her as she pauses dramatically, enjoying the attention. When Itzel appears ready to shoot her with a ball of lightning, Kit says, "My plan is simple. I'm going to take on a different guise and use my feminine wiles to extract the information from that vampire."

Ariel winces, probably thinking of her issues with vampires, and Itzel eyes Kit worriedly. "Are you sure? I love my grandfather, but I don't know if—"

"Don't worry about it." Kit turns herself into a beautiful woman, followed by an even more attractive one. "I plan to enjoy this mission— vampires make great lovers."

"What kind of Cognizant doesn't?" Felix mutters under his breath.

"Technomancers," Kit says without a second of hesitation. "At least so far. Care to prove that wrong?"

Felix reddens, and we all chuckle at his expense. He certainly walked right into that one.

"How long do you think it'll take?" Itzel asks Kit.

Kit turns back into her usual self. "A night, maybe two."

Itzel frowns.

"Fine. One night," Kit says soothingly. "If the carrot approach doesn't work, I'll tie him up under the pretext of more fun and torture the information out of him."

We ride in silence for a few blocks, digesting this even more disturbing part of Kit's plan. Then Ariel and I start to question her about the safety of this, and she reminds us she's on the New York Council and can take care of herself.

Shrugging in defeat, I go into VR and check my messages.

Nothing from Valerian. Did he really give up on me, or is he having trouble locating that werewolf?

For the sake of my mom, I can't accept the former.

I look at Felix. "What are your plans for the night or two while Kit is doing her thing?"

He blinks. "I haven't made any."

"Want to help me with a VR video game? I'll pay for your time."

He grins. "No need. I've always wanted to try it, but I've been typecast as a security expert."

I thank him and ask Kit where she wants to go. After the car drops her off there, we swing by Itzel's place to drop her off and stash Felix's suit before heading to the gate hub building to return to Earth.

———

WHEN WE COME out of JFK, Ariel takes her own cab, and Felix and I go straight to Valerian's office.

"There's a chance we'll get kicked out of the building," I tell Felix once we're in the elevator. "Valerian and I had a little fight, so it all depends on how much of an ass he decides to be about that."

When we approach the front desk, the lady there smiles at me as if I were a celebrity. "Ms. Spade. How can I help?"

"I'm here to see Rattie or Bernie," I say.

She blinks in incomprehension.

"Mr. Bhairava and Mr. Anderson," I clarify.

Felix's unibrow lifts at the second name, as I figured it might—*The Matrix* being his favorite movie and all.

"Mr. Anderson took some personal time to see his daughter," the woman says. "I'll let Mr. Bhairava know you're here. Please take a seat."

Spending time with his daughter? Good for Bernie. He's indeed making progress with resolving his issues.

Felix and I take a seat, but we don't end up waiting long. Rattie arrives in mere minutes and smiles at me in the same way as the front desk lady.

What's up with that?

"Hey, Rattie." I rise to my feet and gesture at my technomancer friend.

"This is Felix. He's a brilliant developer. I brought him to help on the *Lucid Dreamer* project."

Rattie shakes Felix's hand. "Mr. Bale mentioned you."

"That's Valerian," I whisper to Felix as Rattie insists Felix call him by his weird nickname and leads us through the floor.

Looking around, I begin to have an inkling about all the strange looks. The majority of the cubicles are covered by images of me, only with breast augmentations and wearing completely impractical outfits, like a bikini made out of chainmail.

Felix stares at one of the images in a way Maya would not approve. I clear my throat, and he blushes.

"Umm." He clears his throat as well. "Are you a warrior princess in this game?"

"Of course not. I'm a dreamwalker."

Felix cringes. Unlike me, he's under the Mandate, a tool Cognizant use on worlds like this in order to hide their nature from humans. As a result, he wouldn't be able to say he's a technomancer to Rattie without deadly consequences.

Rattie doesn't bat an eye, of course. "I hope you don't mind that," he says, eyeing the images with distaste. "The marketing team is behind these; they anticipate seventy-five percent of the game audience to be men. For what it's worth, when in VR, the player takes your point of view, so they don't really see you much. Not unless they look into a mirror."

"It's fine," I say magnanimously. What I don't add is that I'd let them depict me completely naked and rolling on gigantic breasts as a mode of locomotion if that meant I'd gain enough power to save Mom.

Looking relieved, Rattie herds us into a meeting room, where the screens are already down and his team from India looks at me with the same adoration. Sitting down, he folds his hands on the table like a boarding school student. "How about I give you an update?"

I take a seat opposite him. "That would be great."

"The team has worked almost without sleep since we last met," Rattie says, glancing approvingly at the faces on the screens. "Kind of ironic, given the subject matter of the game."

I nod sympathetically at him and the screens. "I know how crappy sleep deprivation feels. Let me know if Valerian doesn't properly compensate you guys for your hard work."

On the screen, one of the developers goes from happy to worried. "Our compensation is generous. It really is."

"It's true," Rattie says.

I immediately feel like an idiot. "Of course. I wasn't trying to say anyone's ungrateful or anything. Please go on with the update before I stuff more of my feet into my mouth."

Rattie smiles. "The good news is that we got lucky breaks every step of the way, and the level is almost ready." He pauses to give me a chance to beam happily at him. "But before we can let the testers play it, we need to solve a problem that isn't game development, per se. There's a security issue that—"

"Felix can help you," I blurt.

"With security?" Felix looks at me like a puppy whose squeaky toy was taken away. "I thought I'd get to work on the game."

"I'm sure once you prove yourself with security, the team will find some game-related tasks for you as well." I look at Rattie pointedly.

"Definitely." Rattie examines Felix intently. "If you're experienced with—"

"I am." Felix puffs up like a horny peacock. "Whatever it is, it won't be a problem."

Rattie looks at me dubiously.

"Felix is amazing at his job," I say. "Consider your security issue solved."

"In that case"—Rattie takes out a box, two pieces of paper, and two pens—"let's get to the fun part." He slides the papers in front of each of us. "Sorry about the NDAs. It's a standard precaution for unreleased intellectual property."

Waving his apology away, Felix and I sign the non-disclosure agreements while Rattie opens the box with a flourish and takes out the headset inside. "This is the Illusion Scope."

"Wow," Felix whispers. "So small."

Actually, it's bigger than any Gomorran headset, but for Earth's primitive technology, it's not bad.

"The room is already wired for hand tracking," Rattie says and gives me the gizmo. "It's only right you try it on first."

I walk over to the open part of the room and put on the headset. The dashboard here is basic and only has one icon, a small version of me in a skimpy outfit. When I gesture at the icon, the game starts to load, and as I wait, I read the text under the heading of "Backstory:"

Bailey's mother was kidnapped by an evil dreamwalker, the Rat King. Using her own dreamwalking powers, Bailey finds her way to the Rat King's twisted palace and is about to face him in a fight to—

The game starts, and I'm holding a giant sword.

With no mirrors around, there's really no way to tell if I look like me at this moment. The only parts of me visible are my hands—which, pixelation aside, look close enough to mine. It's a blessing no one bothered to give me those boobs as per the marketing department— they'd be blocking my downward view completely, not to mention smacking me in the face if I needed to run.

I wave the sword a few times and begin studying the dark cavern when a disturbing monster jumps down from the ceiling.

He/it has the body of a spider but the head of a clown. In case that wasn't terrifying enough, the lower portion of the clown's face is covered by a surgeon's mask and the front legs are holding scalpels.

Before I so much as blink, the thing leaps at me.

CHAPTER FIFTEEN

I SWIPE WITH MY SWORD, cutting off one of the scalpel-wielding legs. The clown's eyes shoot fire at me. I tilt to the side, dodging the projectile.

I've got to hand it to the cameras and the primitive headset: My real-world motions are copied pretty well in VR.

Just to see how well the physics work, I hurl my sword at the creature's head. It flies in a very realistic arc and slices at the mask. The mask falls, revealing a clown face that seems vaguely familiar underneath all that white makeup.

Did they model it on a celebrity?

The creature yelps in anger, and a little cloud appears above me. Above it, a text box proclaims, "DREAM POWER."

I activate the cloud, and a new sword grows inside my hand, but it's too late.

The monster's head rushes toward me, and its fangs rip into my chest.

The world around me grows red, but for one line of black text hovering gravely in the air.

GAME OVER.

"So cool." I take the headset off and hand it to Felix. "You've got to check it out."

Rattie beams at me. "I'm so glad you like it."

Felix puts on the headset. A minute later, he shouts obscenities and jerks it off his head. "I hope you don't let little kids play that," he says, his breathing uneven. "Or people with arachnophobia, coulrophobia, and whatever the phobia of medical staff is called."

Rattie nods. "The industry consensus is that little kids shouldn't play VR at all. As to adults with phobias, they can always stop playing when they see something they dislike."

As he speaks, I realize why the monster's face looked familiar.

It shares features with Rattie himself.

Then another thing dawns on me: The villain mentioned in that backstory was called the *Rat* King.

I catch Rattie's gaze. "Did your team use your likeness in the game?"

Everyone on his team chuckles, and he smiles shyly. "My team likes to put Easter eggs like that into all our games. That way, people on the street might think me a dreamwalker and see my face in their nightmares for years to come."

"If you're sick of your face being in all these games, you can use mine," Felix says hopefully.

I grin. "I don't think we want to scare the user base *that* much."

Felix groans. "Second time I walk into something today." He looks at Rattie. "Tell me about the security issue you need solved."

Rattie explains it to Felix and looks excited when it becomes clear that Felix understands what he's talking about.

I yawn. Cryptography and sleep debt don't mix well.

After what feels like days of mind-numbing tech talk, Rattie pulls out a laptop with proper access, and Felix begins typing away on it.

I suppress another yawn. "What can I do to help?"

Rattie glances at his team. "You can't do much for the demo at this point, but we could use your help with level design beyond that. Valerian said you'd be good at it."

I'm sure Valerian's praise predated the kiss fiasco. I doubt he'd say nice things about me *now*.

Banishing anything kiss-related from my mind, I describe some good dream-world-like levels for the team, relying in part on my game design background and much more on the actual dreamwalking experience. Rattie particularly likes it when I describe the ceiling in my dream palace —a mosaic depicting an archery target-like mandala made out of multicolored glass.

Just as I'm about to yawn out loud again, Rattie says, "That's more than enough to get us started."

"Good." I rub my eyes. "If you guys don't need me for the next few hours, I'd like to use a sleeping pod."

Rattie smiles wryly. "Of course. The one you last used can be officially yours."

I walk over to Felix to make sure he's okay with my slacking off, and he gestures his dismissal without looking up from the screen.

"Take the nappy nap. I should finish with this in a few hours."

Sweet.

I drag my sleep-heavy feet to the pod and pass out.

I WAKE up refreshed and with no clue how much time has passed.

Heading to the bathroom, I see that the floor is empty. When I come out, I hurry over to the front desk. The receptionist is gone too. Must not be regular business hours anymore.

Rattie meets me by the elevators. "Ah, good, you woke up. Felix left some time ago, said to reach out to your friend Itzel when you need him."

"Right." I smile. "Did Felix finish what he started?"

"He did," Rattie says admiringly. "Thanks to him, the demo is going to the testers in mere hours. The rest of the team are now taking a well-deserved break and will resume the development after."

"That's great." I press the button to summon the elevator. "You should rest too."

He sighs. "I will. First, I need to get confirmation that the demo is in the hands of the testers."

"Good luck," I say, entering the elevator. "See you later."

As I ride down, I allow myself to get excited. Even if Valerian plans to pull out of our arrangement, it sounds like the demo is still happening—unless he shows up last minute and cancels that, which I doubt. And since Valerian said I should get a power boost just from the testers, it's possible that'll be enough to save Mom.

THE RIDE to JFK and the trip from there to Gomorrah are uneventful. I take a car to my apartment, hygieia myself from head to foot, change into clean clothes, and eat.

Refreshed and revived, I check my messages.

Nothing from Valerian.

I look at the clock. He's had the rest of the previous night and almost a whole day after that to look for the werewolf. I bet he's located his quarry and has dealt with him without me.

It's time to accept the unpleasant reality.

Valerian is not talking to me anymore.

Just in case I'm wrong, I set my inbox to give an alert if he does message me. Then, trying not to give in to the strange malaise gripping me at the thought of never seeing him again, I scroll through the recent messages until I find one from Itzel.

She says we're all to gather at Nebulabucks at nine p.m.

I look at the dusk outside and check the clock.

If I hurry, I'll make the meeting.

———

WALKING into Nebulabucks is like déjà vu. Felix, Ariel, Itzel, and Kit are sitting at the same table, hot drinks in everyone's hands.

Just like the last time, Felix hands me my favorite nebula flower tea.

"Thank you for your help today," I tell him, enjoying the fruity notes as I take a sip. "The demo is going to be out any moment."

He swells with pride. "It was my pleasure. In fact, Rattie already let me work on the physics in one of the—"

"I think we should let Kit give an update," Itzel interrupts. "So far, all I know is that she's failed."

"It's not my fault." Kit turns into the vampire she left to question. "I don't think he knew anything. You can't fail to extract information that isn't there."

Ariel raises a perfect eyebrow. "Are you sure your wiles are as irresistible as you think?"

"And your torture methods," Felix adds, turning noticeably pale.

Kit turns back into herself. "I was *exceedingly* persuasive."

"How about *I* question him?" Itzel says, her hand tightening on her cup. "I'm more motivated than you are."

"There's a slight problem with that." Kit avoids everyone's gazes. "I might've... kind of killed him."

I narrow my eyes. "You what?"

She examines her fingernail. "He wouldn't tell me what I needed to know, so I might've escalated the questioning a bit. He must've been freshly turned—most vampires I usually deal with are made of sturdier stuff."

I shake my head and focus on my tea.

Itzel's shoulders droop. "What now?"

I scratch my chin. "Maybe Felix could hack the stores that sell those puck masks?"

Felix frowns. "Gomorran security is—"

An alarm blares in my comms.

"One sec," I tell everyone and activate the VR dashboard.

There's a message from Valerian in my inbox:

Come to my house as soon as you can.

Releasing a breath that I didn't realize I was holding, I grin like a loon.

"Valerian?" Ariel asks with a knowing smile.

"The one and only." I look at Itzel apologetically. "I have to run. He and I have a deal where—"

"It's fine." Itzel waves her small hand. "We'll give your hacking idea a go, with Felix or someone else at the helm."

"Right." I leap to my feet. "Keep me posted."

AS I RIDE to Valerian's place, variations of one thought loop in my mind, over and over.

He isn't ignoring me.

The question is whether he's dealing with me as a necessary evil to get the information he wants, or he's actually okay with that travesty of a kiss.

I ponder this the whole way to his penthouse, but when he actually opens the door, my mind goes completely blank.

It must be the "absence makes the heart grow fonder" effect in action because he looks more mouthwateringly hot than I remember—and I have memories I can masturbate to for a year.

"Please come in." He gestures in the direction of the pond.

I walk in on unsteady legs and plop into the lotus pose by the pond.

He crouches next to me, eyes level with mine. "First, I want to talk about the other day."

I swallow so loudly they probably hear it on the floor below us. Is he about to tell me he wants to pretend it never happened? Or—

"I'm sorry," he says softly. "I misread the situation. I thought you—"

"You didn't," I blurt.

"I didn't?" He tilts his head, perplexed. "I thought you wanted to kiss me, but when I tried, you didn't like it."

My face burns. "I *did* want you to kiss me. I still kind of do. And I didn't dislike—"

"You pulled away." His jaw flexes.

I bite my lip. "Wanting and liking wasn't enough, it seems. I guess I wasn't quite ready yet. I… have some issues when it comes to intimacy."

His face darkens, and his power makes the room around us thunderous and gloomy, like a storm is about to hit. "Did someone do something to you?" he asks with soft menace.

"No, no, it's not that." Recalling the blank spots when it comes to my childhood, I add, "At least not that I know of. I pulled away for a completely different reason."

The room goes back to normal as his expression changes to one of curiosity. "Oh?"

"If I tell you, you'll think I'm weird."

A hint of a smile touches the corners of his eyes. "That implies I don't already think you're weird."

"Forget it." I start to untangle my legs from the lotus pose.

"I never said weird was bad." The smile moves down to his lips. "Please, tell me."

My shoulders hunch. "I've… never done that before."

His eyes widen, the smile disappearing. "You've never kissed anyone?"

"Nor done anything else," I say, Pom turning beet red on my wrist. "Even if it weren't for my other issue, kissing—or doing anything for the first time—is kind of a big deal."

He rubs the dimple on his chin. "Other issue?"

I take in a deep breath. "I don't like germs."

"Germs?"

"Bacteria, viruses, yeasts. Just name a microscopic creature, and I'm going to be afraid to catch it."

"And you think I—"

"I'm not saying your germs are worse than those of any other person," I say quickly. "Or that my fears are one-hundred-percent rational. Though if you read about the microbiome, it *is* permanently altered with—"

He lifts his hand, stopping me mid-word. "You have the right to feel any way you choose. You also have the right to do or not do things with me." His face darkens again. "Or anyone else."

"If I *were* to do things with someone, it would be you." This time, Pom turns pink, and I hide the treacherous fur in case Valerian somehow guesses what it means.

He gives me a look of pure male satisfaction. "What if the risk of germs didn't exist at all?" As he speaks, the living room around us turns into a bedroom I've seen via his illusions before, one with a giant bed covered by silk sheets and rose petals.

A second Valerian is sitting on the edge of the bed—this one only wearing a fig leaf over his groin.

I blink rapidly as I take in the illusory Valerian.

Somewhere in the distance, I can hear the sound of my ovaries screaming in joy.

"Come to me," Illusion Valerian orders gruffly and stands up, giving me a better look at his rippling muscles.

I leap to my feet as he closes the distance between us.

"No germs," the real Valerian murmurs.

I reach out and touch the naked Illusion Valerian. His chest feels real—and good enough to lick. My gaze shifts between him and the real Valerian. What's the proper etiquette for this sort of situation?

"Before we do anything," I say hesitantly, "you should know I'm not a *typical* virgin."

Both Valerians arch their eyebrows.

"I've done things in the dream world. I've even kissed you—well, a version of you—there before. So I have some idea of what to expect."

"No, you don't." Illusion Valerian frames my face with his big hands and kisses me.

Holy hormones. He's right. This is infinitely better than when I kissed "him" in my dream—and this isn't even real either.

His tongue tentatively explores my mouth, sending waves of heat throughout my body as his hands stroke down my back. I feel like time stops, like there's nothing outside the physical sensations, and knowing that this is an illusion allows me to enjoy the pleasure without fear—and get the closest to orgasm I've ever been around another person.

Panting, I slide my hands down his muscled back to grab the firm globes of his ass, but before I can reach my destination, Illusion Valerian disappears.

"Hey!" I look at the still-crouching real version of him. "What gives?"

"I didn't want to overwhelm you." He pats the place where I was sitting before.

Well, puck.

Getting back on the ground, I take a few calming breaths as I stare at real Valerian's lips. Would they feel the same as the illusion's?

"Was that exposure therapy?" I ask, still breathless.

He frowns. "You mean my lack of clothes?"

"I mean you let me kiss you in a safe space in the hopes of making it easier for me to do it in the real world. I do something like that with my clients—when they have fears, that is."

He smiles. "And how effective is it?"

I dampen my lips. "Very."

"Good." His gaze falls to my mouth. "My illusions are one-way only, so I'm dying to taste you again."

I gulp. On my wrist, Pom's fur turns a shade of pink corals would be jealous of.

Am I ready to try it in the real world again?

I feel like I am. I really want to. But then again, I also wanted it last time—until the very last moment.

"How about now?" I say before I can talk myself out of it. "We could—"

"No." His smile holds a note of mischief. "This time, I'm going to wait until you're good and ready."

Does he mean "ready to beg for it?" Because I'm nearly there.

"Besides." His face turns serious. "We do have important Senate business to discuss."

"Oh, right." The mention of the dangerous Senate case works like the cold shower I sorely needed.

"I'm afraid I have some bad news on that front." He uses his power to make the werewolf he was seeking appear in the room with us. "None of my sources have any idea where to find him. You said you had a guy, so I was hoping you could ask *him*."

"Puck." I rub my eyebrow. "I just used him on behalf of Itzel, and I can't ask him for another favor until I've given him the dream—"

"Please." Valerian's ocean-blue eyes are so intense I feel like I might drown in them. "It's important."

How can I say no to that? Especially after that kiss?

I enable VR to check the time. Napoleon *could* be sleeping. At least he was at this time of night when I did this for him before.

"Give me a few minutes." Turning away, I touch Pom's fur and jump into the dream world.

———

AGAIN, I catch Pom playing sports. This time, he's bowling by himself.

"Bailey!" He turns purple from furry head to fluffy toes. "How are you?"

"About to do something you'll find interesting," I say, though for the life of me, I can't understand *why*. "I'm going into Napoleon's dreams so he can do his thing."

Pom takes flight and swirls around me excitedly. "We haven't done that in forever."

Because it's weird and creepy, and again, I have no idea why Pom actually likes it.

"Well, I'm doing it now," I say. "Ready?"

He nods, so I teleport us both to the tower of sleepers and look for Napoleon.

Yep. He's there, sleeping like a devil's baby.

Pom lands on my shoulder as I take the guise of a pirate and, without bothering to make myself invisible, enter Napoleon's dreams.

———

AS IT OFTEN HAPPENS IN his dreams, Napoleon is in his human guise— that of a short man with nice white teeth, a slightly curved nose, deep-set gray-blue eyes, and an air of power that's difficult to explain.

Also, as is usual, on his head is a bicorne, while his torso is dressed in a white jacket with a blue overcoat. Underneath the jacket is a red sash.

I look around.

We're on a beach on an island he called Elba the last time I was in his dreams. He must've spent a lot of time on a real island like this because I can tell this stroll on the beach is a memory.

"Hey," I call out when it becomes clear he's not noticing our presence.

Napoleon's head whips around, and he stares at me and Pom uncomprehendingly for a few moments. Then his eyes light up, and he grins predatorily. "This is a dream?" He looks around, the grin widening.

"It is." I make a pink unicorn appear next him, then exchange it for a five-headed cobra. "I need your help, so I figured I'd visit your dreams."

Napoleon's eyes light up with avarice. "Six battles. And obviously, money in the awake world."

"Three." I ignore Pom's excited grip on my shoulder—he wants all six. "And a reasonable sum in the waking world."

"Four." Napoleon crosses his arms over his chest.

"Fine." I make the island around us phase out and get ready to replace it with a terrain of his choosing. "Which ones?"

"Hastings, Bosworth, Gettysburg, and Somme," he rattles out excitedly.

I sigh. "You *know* my Earth military history is close to zero. We've done Hastings once before, but the others don't sound familiar. Except maybe Gettysburg—something to do with a famous address?"

Napoleon shakes his head disapprovingly. "How can you spend so much time on that world and not know these things?"

I shrug. "War is one of the worst things humans do to each other. Why should I learn about it?"

He turns back into his red devil form. "So ignorance is bliss? That's your excuse?"

"I don't need an excuse." I make our surroundings a serene hill where, according to Napoleon, the battle of Hastings took place. "You like battles, and I don't."

"I don't like battles. I win them."

"Sometimes I think you do this just to torment me," I mutter under my breath.

He grins. "I don't, but it's a nice bonus."

Straining my powers, I make thousands of soldiers appear. The uniforms and positions were all provided by Napoleon with nauseating attention to minute details.

Immediately, I feel tired. Aside from blood, gore, and losing faith in humanity, I don't like these war reenactments because they severely drain my power—too many little details to manifest at once.

Making us float above the soon-to-be battlefield, I add a few more details here and there and inform Napoleon that I'm finished.

He frowns. "This time, I want the cavalry to start off there." He points at a spot at the base of the hill.

I sigh and move the soldiers and horses where he wishes.

"This is going to be so cool," Pom exclaims.

I stroke his fur. I guess one redeeming thing about this unpleasant task is that it'll entertain my looft. Maybe I'll feel less guilty about not spending as much time with him as I should.

Turning light orange, Pom asks Napoleon, "Will you be William the Conqueror or King Harold II this time around?"

"King Harold." Napoleon glances at me as if to say, "See? Some people aren't as ignorant about these things as others."

"Doesn't that mean you'll lose and get shot with an arrow?" Pom flies over to perch on Napoleon's shoulder, and I resist the temptation to call him a traitor.

"Not if I win," Napoleon says with cocky confidence, then looks at me. "Ready?"

I nod, change him to look like Harold, and teleport him to the top of the hill so he can take command of his forces.

Then I strain my powers once more.

All the soldiers come to life, and war cries ring out as two armies face each other. Arrows fly. A shield wall goes up. Horses leap forward. Napoleon/Harold shouts orders at "his" men. Bucketloads of blood are spilled onto the green grass.

Not for the first time, I wonder how this works. Is a part of my subconscious controlling those thousands of soldiers on the battlefield, or is Napoleon helping as well?

Eventually, Harold's forces win.

I turn him back into Napoleon, who looks disturbingly happy—especially for someone whose army has sustained thousands of casualties.

The next three battles consume a lot more time and dream power. First, Napoleon has to describe all the details to me for what feels like days. Then I have to build it all out and animate the soldiers. By the end of it all, I feel like a squeezed lemon that got run over by a bus.

"Thank you." Napoleon squeezes my shoulder—something he knows he's only allowed to do in the dream world. "You kept your end of the bargain, so I'll keep mine."

"Good. Here." I make two copies of the werewolf appear in front of us, one with side burns, one without. "His name is Hans Stubbe. I need his location."

Napoleon rubs his chin. "I know this one. Nasty piece of work. Come see me in the bar—I'll wake up and head over there. I'll tell you where to find him and decide how much to charge you."

"You agreed to keep the cost reasonable."

He grins. "I agreed on four battles." With that, he poofs out of existence, and Pom and I find ourselves back in the tower of sleepers.

"That's what I get for teaching him how to wake himself up," I say to Pom and exit the dream world as well.

———

TURNING TO FACE VALERIAN, I explain that we need to make a trip to my guy's favorite hangout.

"Let's go," he says and ushers me to his private flying car, which gets us there so quickly that we end up sipping drinks until Napoleon arrives.

"Napoleon, this is Valerian," I say. "Valerian, this is Napoleon."

"Pleasure," Valerian says evenly, his expression unreadable.

"If you're who I think you are, the pleasure is all mine," Napoleon says, managing to look even more like a little devil.

I put down my empty mug. "Where's Hans?"

"First things first," Napoleon says and blurts out an enormous sum.

Before I can even start to haggle, Valerian says, "You'll have it."

Puck. I forgot to tell him to never agree to the first number Napoleon names. Hopefully the Senate will let him expense this.

"I'll send Bailey his home address," Napoleon says and gesticulates with his little red hands. "He's there now."

I check my inbox. "Got it."

"You're a useful person to know," Valerian says, extending his hand to Napoleon.

My little red friend shakes the offered hand enthusiastically. "I have a feeling this is the beginning of a beautiful friendship."

Sure, if we redefine "friendship" as "extortion."

"We'd better go," I say.

"Be careful," Napoleon says earnestly. "He's dangerous."

I give him a sharp-edged smile. "Don't worry. We'll live so you can shake us down another day."

ONCE WE'RE BACK in the car, I turn to Valerian. "There's something I've been meaning to tell you. Because of their dual nature, werewolves are difficult to dreamwalk in. When I attempted it during the New York Council investigation, I failed."

He cocks his head. "And you're just telling me this now because…?"

I shrug. "There's a technique I know that might help. In the dream, I'd split into two, one of me to tackle the wolf's dream, and the other to handle the man's. I did something like that when I fought Hekima, who, as an illusionist, was also difficult to deal with in the dream world."

His dark eyebrows knit together. "I have to think about this."

I fight the urge to kiss the frown off that face. "What's there to think about?"

"When I make a decision, I'll tell you." He hands me a familiar breathing mask. "For now, it's moot anyway. Like with Erato, we're just going to establish a connection and scram."

"Hopefully not just like with Erato," I mutter and put on the mask.

He covers his face with his mask as well—a pity.

"Remember, don't talk out loud when we're in the building," he says, the mask muffling his voice.

Going into VR, I message him one word: *affirmative.*

He chuckles.

Before I can say or write more, we land on the roof of the werewolf's building.

Our elevator ride is uneventful, and the hallway on the fortieth floor is empty—not that making us invisible would be a problem for Valerian's powers. When we reach the apartment door, I message Valerian to hold on for a few seconds.

I've just remembered the touchless dreamwalking I read about in the journal, and I want to try it again. Not only would it spare me contact with germy skin, but also the need for breaking and entering.

Assuming it works, of course.

I strain.

And strain.

The only thing I have to show for my efforts is a vague feeling. When I focus on it, I find the sensation strange. If I didn't know any better, I'd say a part of me thinks a person is sleeping nearby. Well, obviously people are sleeping nearby; it's night. But this feeling is not just common sense. It's… well, a kind of sense, but so faint that I have to conclude it's all in my head.

Probably just nerves.

I message Valerian that we're a go.

Nodding, he takes out the device he used the last time and waves it over the lock. There's a click, and the door slides out of our way. He takes out his electronics-disabling gizmo and tosses it inside.

Getting his sleep grenade ready, he steps in, and I follow—only to freeze when he does.

Five feet away from the door is a giant dog bed, where a shaggy werewolf in his animal form is sleeping. At least, I hope he's sleeping. I don't have that much experience when it comes to slumbering wolves.

Suddenly, the werewolf whimpers, and his giant paws swat at something that isn't there.

That settles that. He's sleeping.

Valerian looks at the wolf, then at the grenade in his hand.

I shake my head and quietly crouch next to the beast.

As I touch the fur on his muscular back, I pray canines—and especially werewolves—are in REM sleep when they whimper and flail like that.

With a whiff of ozone, the room darkens around me, and I fall in.

I APPEAR in my dream palace—and, thankfully, not in a subdream.

Good. Connection made. Now Valerian and I need to skedaddle.

With a quick wave at Pom, I hop out of the dream world and carefully rise to my feet.

But not carefully enough, it seems.

The werewolf's eyes pop open, staring directly at me.

My adrenaline spikes to toxic levels.

The wolf growls menacingly and tenses for a leap.

CHAPTER SIXTEEN

REACTING ON AUTOPILOT, I grab my gun, aim at the ferocious maw, and shoot.

The werewolf slumps onto his dog bed.

Whew. I cover my chest with my hand. My heart is still threatening to punch a hole in my ribcage.

LEGO letters appear, and they look kind of angry: *You killed him?*

Puck. We did need this guy for information.

But wait.

I check the gun screen and exhale in relief as I show it to Valerian. Luckily for the werewolf, the last time I used the gun, it was in stun mode, and it seems the setting stays the same when you turn on the gun again.

In that case, grab his front paws.

I look at Valerian like he's about to turn into a wolf himself.

He saw us before I made us invisible with my powers. He might tell Icelus.

I go into VR and frantically type out, *So we what? Kidnap him?*

The LEGO text appears even angrier: *We detain him. I'll take him to a Senate facility and wait until he falls asleep again.*

With a sigh, I grab the giant paws. As far as plans go, Valerian's isn't terrible—assuming the werewolf doesn't snap out of his stunned state.

When I mention my concern to Valerian, his reply is: *Just shoot him every few minutes.*

I nod and strain to lift my half of the wolf as Valerian easily lifts his half.

Nope. Too heavy for me.

Grab this paw. Valerian gestures with one of the back ones he's holding. *We'll drag him.*

Dragging works much better. I barely break a sweat by the time we get to the elevator—and we only hit his head on something twice.

Figuring it's as good a time as any, I stun the wolf again.

Once on the roof, we drag our victim to the car and fly toward the city center.

Valerian takes off his mask, but when I reach to do the same, he shakes his head.

I don't want anyone associated with the Senate to see your face.

I nod and shoot the wolf once more.

We fly in a tense silence until the car descends onto a sleek-looking roof.

Shoot him once more and hide the gun, Valerian commands.

I do this, and when we land, I see why.

A vampire dressed in an Enforcer uniform is waiting for us—Valerian must've written ahead. Seeing my mask, the vamp lifts an eyebrow.

If I were him, I'd be more curious about the unconscious wolf.

Before Valerian and I can say anything, the vamp injects our poor victim with something, then hoists him over his shoulder like a sack of flour and strides toward the elevator.

Take my car, Valerian tells me via LEGO text. *I'll get in touch via a regular message. It'll just say, "Ready."*

I bob my head.

As soon as you get that message, go to my place. Don't dreamwalk in the werewolf alone.

Before I can object, he hurries after the vampire.

I tell the car to take me home and close my eyes.

———

I WAKE up from an intense sensation that's flooding my every cell with warm, pleasant energy.

What the puck? Am I having an aneurism?

My breathing quickens and my nails dig into my palms as an even bigger tsunami of pleasure rushes into my body, making my extremities tingle and my toes curl.

Did someone slip me some vampire blood, or did I just have a spontaneous series of orgasms?

Then I realize what it must be.

The game demo. It probably reached a critical mass of users as I was dozing off, and this is how it feels to get the resulting power boost.

Feeling calmer, I close my eyes and do my best to relax and enjoy it. A few blocks later, the sensations abate and my mind clears further. With a surge of excitement, I process the implications.

This is it. This is what I've been working toward with Valerian's team.

I can finally try waking up Mom.

Unwilling to wait even a second longer, I jump into the dream world and check if she's in the tower of sleepers.

To my intense disappointment, she's not.

I instruct the car to fly to Mom's hospital, then open my VR dashboard and write to Valerian: *I need your help. Can you meet me in my mom's hospital room?*

His reply is almost instant: *Where?*

I tell him the address and which room, and he confirms that he'll see me there.

To distract myself for the rest of the ride, I open up Leal's journal and skim through it. A recent entry piques my interest:

Too much evidence points to one unsettling conclusion: There's an Icelus agent right here in the New York Cognizant community. He or she is clearly placed highly enough to spread rumors that generate fears—and thus nightmares. Youngsters seem to be particularly susceptible, so I wonder if the agent is one of the Heralds.

Wow. Heralds are Earth Cognizant for whom the Mandate restrictions are less stringent, so they can speak about the existence of our kind with Cognizant teens who grow up not knowing what they are.

I look for more info on this but only find a few names of Heralds Leal had cleared using dreamwalking. Seems like he didn't have time to find out who the agent was—these last entries happened right before he was murdered.

A slight jolt brings me back to my immediate surroundings, and I realize the car has just landed on the roof of the hospital.

I sprint to the elevator and take it to Mom's floor.

"I'm visiting my mother," I tell the nurses at the station. "Last time, her vitals went haywire; if that happens again, will you be able to handle it?"

The taller of the nurses, the gargoyle whose dreams I snuck into to check on Mom, says, "Does a mooft shit at the zoo?"

Yuck. Fighting the urge to berate the nurse, I charge ahead to Mom's room.

Just as I'm about to step into the room, I hear an unwelcome voice that's too high for all but bat ears.

"Miss Spade. We need to talk."

I spin around and scowl at the billing administrator—or the Horseshoe Bat, as I've mentally dubbed her. "Do you usually patrol this place at night?" I ask, fighting the urge to take out my gun and use it on her.

Her nose goes up. "If you could step into my office—"

"I paid all the outstanding bills. If you didn't get the payment—"

"There's a new policy when it comes to long-term patients," she says nastily. "We need their stay to be prepaid a month in advance."

"Fine." I bring up VR and send over a payment. "Check your account now."

She looks confused. I guess she'd pegged me as broke.

"Will there be anything else?" I snap. "Any other policy you want to make up just for me?"

She blinks. "I—"

"In that case, I'm going to see my mom."

"The visiting hours are—"

"Do *not* test me."

She must not like what she sees on my face because she steps back and says, "The visiting hours are merely a suggestion."

Yeah. I thought so.

She scurries away, and I finally enter Mom's room.

Immediately, my chest tightens. Mom looks the same, all ashen and still. Even some of the old equipment, like the feeding tube, is back. I have to get her out, but since she's not in REM sleep, I'll have to tackle a subdream first. And if I die there, I'll become a crazed killer, and she'll be my first victim. Which is why I need—

Valerian walks into the room with a concerned expression on his face. "What's going on? Is everything okay with your mom?"

I nod. "The demo went live. I'm going to get her out."

He looks her over, frowning. "She's not in REM sleep."

I take out my gun, make sure it's still on stun, and toss it to him.

He catches the gun, looking even more confused.

"The password is yitten," I say.

He looks at the gun, then at me. "What?"

"If I don't say the word 'yitten' when I come out of the trance, stun me and get help."

Before he can argue, I grab hold of Mom's delicate wrist and dive in.

CHAPTER SEVENTEEN

THE SURFACE of the black ocean is serene under my feet. Then a shadow blots out a chunk of the fiery skies. It's a flying creature reminiscent of a turkey vulture, only covered in mucus and brimming with pustules and claws.

A bracelet on my wrist elongates into an eight-foot-long furry spear with a sharp fang-like tip.

The vulture screeches something. An odd intuition tells me it's doing its best to say something that to normal ears would sound like, "The master hates you!"

The vulture dives.

I thrust my spear out.

A claw pierces my shoulder, causing searing pain. I instantly feel faint, but I fight it.

If I pass out, I'll bleed to death.

At least the creature has paid dearly for its bold attack. In the process of getting to me, it shish-kebabbed itself on the spear.

Another wave of dizziness crashes into me. With my remaining strength, I yank the spear out and stab where I hope the thing's heart is.

A guttural screech, and the disgusting vulture expires.

———————

I'M in my dream palace, in agony. Exiting my body, I heal it and go right back in.

Ah, that's better.

Pom pops up next to me, his fur pitch black. "That was too close. You almost died."

"But I didn't. And now I'm here, with enough power to save Mom. Hopefully."

The tips of his ears turn orange. "Can I come see?"

"Sure." I teleport us over to the tower of sleepers.

Lying peacefully in her nook, Mom doesn't have all the tubes and therefore isn't as painful to look at.

Pom perches on my shoulder.

I make us invisible and go in.

———

MOM DIPS A BABY version of me in a wash basin.

Puck. I know where this is going, and I forgot to warn Pom about it.

Yep. Mom puts the baby's head under the water and keeps it there.

What is she doing? Pom asks mentally, his feet digging painfully into my shoulder.

I think it's some weird hell she created for herself in her dreams, I reply. *Now be quiet. I need to concentrate.*

Pom stops talking, and I ponder the situation.

First things first. Gathering my power, I give Mom a jolt that's many times stronger than the one I usually use on people who have trouble waking up after therapy.

Mom continues to drown the baby-me, none the wiser.

Puck. What now? Showing myself is a measure of last resort; I don't want to agitate her if I can help it.

Dr. Cipactli's earlier idea comes to me, that of using a nightmare as a way to wake her up. His actual plan—using a drug to have Mom spiral into worse and worse nightmares—was too risky, but with me here, I can do a more controlled version of what he had in mind and terminate it if I don't like where it goes.

Then again, isn't dreaming about killing me a nightmare? She's not waking up from *that*.

Then I recall another thing Dr. Cipactli mentioned. He said his drug shows people a nightmare related to what last happened to them in the waking world—a car accident in Mom's case. He said that would be a nightmare strong enough to wake someone up.

Yeah, that's it. A nightmare based on a memory might well do the trick. The only thing about it is that I feel bad subjecting Mom to such a painful dream.

You may want to go back, I tell Pom.

He stays on my shoulder. I take a deep breath and remind myself that what I'm about to do is for Mom's own good. Thus determined, I wait for her to finish killing the baby version of me, and then I highjack the next nightmare by pitting her against the grown me in our apartment.

It works. The dream already feels like a memory—with her looking sadly at that version of me with her pretty brown eyes.

In a tired voice, Mom says, "Not this again."

"Your symptoms are worsening," my doppelgänger says. "I heard you screaming at night."

Her face turns ashen. "Did you walk into my bedroom?"

The other me glares at her. "No. More importantly, I didn't break my promise. I didn't invade your precious dreams."

She exhales in relief. "I just had a nightmare, that's all."

"About what?" The other me crosses her arms in front of her chest.

"Can't remember," she says dismissively. "Can we talk about something else now?"

"Was it something to do with my father?" Both of us watch her reaction.

Just like on the day this really happened, an emotion flashes in Mom's eyes, but again so fleetingly that I can't be sure I really saw it, let alone figure out what it was.

"How many times do I have to tell you? I don't remember him," she says. "Nor is it a topic I like to talk about."

"Right. If you don't remember, how do you know you don't want to talk about it?"

She shrugs.

"Fine," the other me says. "Fine. You haven't been eating much, either. And haven't left the house in forever. In fact, this is the first time this week I've seen you in real life." She pointedly looks at the last-generation VR goggles on the end table.

Mom's jaw juts out. "Maybe it's because no one pesters me in VR. I'm the parent, you're the child, remember?"

"Look, Mom. I see your symptoms all the time. If you would just let me into—"

"No!" She beelines for the door, throwing over her shoulder, "Don't suggest that ever again."

"If your symptoms keep worsening, I might not have a choice," the other me yells at her back. "If your life's on the line, I'll break my stupid oath!"

It's painful to see how she freezes and turns to look at that version of me, her expression so full of betrayal I regret those words yet again.

She's been making me swear not to dreamwalk in her for as long as I can remember, yet I'm breaking that promise as we speak.

"You wouldn't," Mom says hollowly, backing up toward the front door. "Please say you wouldn't."

"Fine, but you have to see *someone*," the other me says. "A conventional shrink, perhaps? Maybe make a friend and talk to them? Or—"

"You don't understand!" Her voice rises. "I've tried everything."

"Not everything." There's a determined expression on the face of the other me that I don't recall making, but I must have—this is still a memory.

With a growl, Mom turns on her heel and storms out, slamming the door behind her.

I pay closer attention now, since I've only guessed at what happened after that fight.

Mom sprints for the elevator. Getting inside, she closes her eyes and leans against the wall, muttering under her breath, "She's going to do it. She's finally going to dreamwalk in me."

Puck. I've never heard her talk to herself like this. Our fight had impacted her even more than I thought.

The elevator stops, and she opens her eyes. "I can't let it happen," she whispers. "I won't." The determined expression on her face mirrors the one I saw on myself a few seconds ago.

What does she mean by that?

As I watch, Mom runs out of the building and heads straight for the highway.

No. She couldn't have meant—

But she did.

When the first self-driving car swerves in time to avoid her, Mom throws herself under the next one, then another, over and over, until she finally creates a situation where a car can't dodge her without killing other people.

As the car slams into her body, throwing her in the air, for a millisecond, Mom's face looks triumphant.

Then she crashes onto the pavement in a broken heap.

CHAPTER EIGHTEEN

I SNAP out of the trance and numbly look around the hospital room, the sound of the beeping machines mixing with the cacophony in my mind.

How did I come to be here? Did the nightmare throw me out of the dream world instead of Mom?

"Bailey?"

I follow the voice and see a worried Valerian pointing a gun at me.

"Yitten," I say dully, and he lowers the gun.

I look back at Mom, the computer that is my brain crashing and rebooting.

"Her heartbeat spiked, setting off the machines," Valerian says. "But she's still—"

The gargoyle nurse rushes in and begins adjusting the machines. When the mad beeping stops, she rounds on us. "Whatever you did, don't do it again until Dr. Xipil is here."

I'm still too overwhelmed to speak.

"We won't," Valerian says. "Thank you."

With a huff, the nurse leaves, and I lean on Mom's bed, my knees wobbly.

"Are you okay?" Valerian asks, his voice seeming to come from a distance.

"It wasn't an accident," I say hollowly as the horrible realization fully filters in.

"What?" Valerian sounds even farther away.

I don't know if I can bear to say it out loud, yet the words emerge anyway, as if pulled by a torturer's pliers. "It was… a suicide." I swallow thickly, staring at Mom's ashen face. "She went out of her way to get hit by that car."

Valerian audibly inhales.

An unbearable pressure builds in my chest, my throat cinching tight. Could I have misunderstood what I saw? Or experienced my own nightmare? No, that doesn't make sense. I know it was a memory.

Mom's memory.

Her face blurs in front of my eyes. "It was my fault. I threatened to dreamwalk in her, and she tried to kill herself to prevent it."

"Bailey." Valerian sounds worried.

I sway on my feet. My stomach churns. The back of my throat burns. My heart is hammering in my chest so hard that if I were the one hooked up to all the machines, the nurses would be barging in.

Mom killed herself because of me.

My ribcage feels like the subdream vulture is clawing inside it. Before today, I'd felt guilty about the fight. I'd thought I had upset Mom, which had made her careless.

How stupid. How naïve of me. I hadn't known the true definition of guilt until now. It threatens to drown me, the pressure so crushing I can barely take a shallow breath. Slowly, I sink onto the bed next to Mom, trying to process everything I saw, to make sense of something so incomprehensible.

She'd tried to kill herself.

Because of me.

Is this why she was killing me in her dreams? Because her subconscious knows I'm to blame for her predicament?

Are those nightmares payback for my forcing her to take her own life?

I must make some type of sound—a hysterical laugh or cry—because I suddenly find myself ensconced on a male lap, with strong arms wrapped around me and the pleasant scent of pine teasing my nostrils. "Shh," Valerian murmurs into my hair. "You didn't know what she'd do. How could you?"

He's right, Pom says in my mind. *You can't blame yourself.*

Figures. The rare time Pom is awake, and he's ganging up on me with Valerian. The vulture in my chest claws harder, and the burning sensation in my throat travels higher, concentrating behind my eyelids. Unbidden, a sob escapes, followed by another, and then I'm full-on bawling, the burning tears running down my face, soaking into Valerian's shirt.

He holds me, letting me cry as he strokes my back, murmuring words of reassurance, of comfort. Pom is in on it too, telling me that none of it is my fault, that it was Mom's decision to do this.

Eventually, my sobs ease, and I feel myself being carried somewhere.

I open my tear-swollen eyes.

Valerian is laying me down in the seat of his flying car, considerately making sure not to touch my naked skin with any cooties. Catching my gaze, he waves his hand, and the car interior disappears, replaced with a soothing green meadow.

Wearily, I close my eyes, but the meadow doesn't go away. He's using his power on me.

Valerian appears on the meadow.

I look away, but he shows up there, and the next place I turn, too.

"For your mother's sake, you need to pull yourself together." His voice seems to come from all over the universe. "Once you recover, you'll use your power to wake her and reassure her you'll never dreamwalk in her under any circumstances again. Problem solved."

Exactly, Pom mentally chimes in. *Focus on fixing this.*

I drag in a shaky breath and open my eyes, wiping at my face with my sleeve.

They're right. I don't deserve this self-pity party. Not when I do have a way to undo the damage I've wrought.

Sniffling, I sit up. When Valerian deems me capable of dealing with reality, the inside of the flying car shows up again.

"Why did you take me from the hospital?" I ask, looking at him. "Take me back. I want to go back into her dreams."

He strokes my thigh as if I were a looft on his wrist. "I think it would be best to do as the nurse said."

I want to object, insist that he take me back, but I don't. Because he's right. Instead of relying on the nurse, I should've made sure the doctor was there before I attempted to wake Mom. I was so eager to finally wake her I didn't really consider her safety.

Just like when I'd made that threat about dreamwalking.

The guilt swamps me again, and I wallow in it until we land on a roof.

"We're here." Valerian opens the car doors.

I blink, looking around. "You took me to your place?"

"The car flies here when I don't set a destination," he says. "Do you want to go home?"

"No." I climb out of the car on mushy legs. "I don't want to be alone."

He nods approvingly and climbs out behind me. Placing a hand on the small of my back, he herds me into the elevator, then into his apartment.

"Sit," he orders when we get to his fancy-looking kitchen.

I comply as he uses an old-fashioned kettle to brew an extremely pleasant-smelling tea and places a cup in front of me.

"Want me to hygieia the handle I touched?" He walks over to the fridge, takes two sealed manna packets, and puts one in front of me.

"No, it's fine." I take the cup, the warmth seeping into my chilled fingers.

Valerian sits down at the table across from me. "You can have my bed tonight." Seeing my eyes widen, he adds, "I'll sleep in the guest room."

I mindlessly take a sip of the tea. "I don't think I'll be able to sleep any time soon."

He opens his manna packet. "How can I help?"

I open my packet and devour it as I contemplate the question. "I wish there were something that would make me forget I'm the worst pucking daughter in the world," I finally mutter.

"There could be." His tone is gentle. "I just got a message. The werewolf is asleep."

I finish my food and gulp down the tea. "Good. I'm going in."

He spears me with his intent gaze. "No, you're not. Not alone."

"What do you mean?"

"I'm going into the werewolf's dreams with you," he says. "But only if you're sure you're ready for it."

"I'm ready. I just don't understand." I'm the dreamwalker, not him.

He sighs. "I'll fall sleep. You'll enter my dreams. Then, *together*, we'll deal with Hans the werewolf."

Well, if his goal was to distract me, he's succeeded admirably—only not in the way he thinks. I find the idea of watching him sleep incredibly fascinating. Too fascinating, I'd say.

And that's not all.

Getting access to *his* dreams? He'd refused me that when we first met, but I've been dying to snoop around in there. Hells yes, please. The only thing I'm fuzzy on is how much help he'd be in dealing with the werewolf, but if it means I get those other things, I'll play along.

"Sure," I say, my voice impressively even. "How about you go to sleep now?" *Before you change your mind.*

"Right." He stands up.

"And please, use your own bedroom," I say, recalling his earlier offer—along with the circumstances that prompted it.

The dark vise of guilt squeezes my chest again, but before I can give in to it, Valerian heads out of the kitchen, saying over his shoulder, "Fine. Let's go to my bedroom."

I'm glad his back is to me, so he can't see the coral pink Pom on my wrist. I've been fantasizing about some version of "let's go to my bedroom" for some time now.

I hurry after him, and when I step inside the room in question, I realize I've seen it before.

This is the lush bedroom with the giant bed covered by silk sheets he showed me in a couple of illusions. Only the rose petals are missing.

He takes off his shirt.

I forget how to speak for a second.

Without pause, he takes off the rest of his clothes. And I do mean *all* of his clothes.

I gulp, loudly.

He winks at me, then climbs into the bed and covers himself with a blanket.

Hey, no fair. You can't show me that, then cover it up. I didn't get the chance to properly file away all those hard, perfectly defined muscles in my memory banks. Or touch them. Or lick them.

Who am I kidding? If he let me lick anything, I'd probably chicken out on account of the thousands of different species of bacteria that live on skin.

Valerian's breathing changes.

I creep on over.

Yep. He's now under, but not yet in REM stage. Oh, well. I guess I have to do something not so unpleasant—watch his sleeping face. Those chiseled features are more relaxed than I've ever seen them, and that suits him. He looks like Prince Charming in repose.

Legs growing tired, I sit on the bed and keep watching. And watching. For some reason, I don't get tired of it. I guess I'm one of those creepy people who like to watch someone sleep.

Would it be wrong if I kissed his forehead? Would that wake him up?

The temptation is overwhelming.

Suddenly, I feel the same sensation as I did by the werewolf's door, only stronger.

Could it be?

I lean over him and see his eyes moving rapidly behind the lids.

Interesting. It seems like I'm now able to *feel* someone nearby go into REM sleep.

Useful.

Now an important choice: what part of Valerian do I want to touch? And with what part of myself?

Grinning, I gently pull the blanket down a few inches.

Target acquired.

I reach out and place my palm gently on his chest.

Yummy. Valerian's pectoral muscles are perfectly firm, his skin warm and smooth. I can feel his heart beating, and mine races faster, as if eager to catch up.

Wait, what am I doing?

I need to focus.

Calling on all my willpower, I jump into Valerian's dreams.

CHAPTER NINETEEN

APPEARING in the lobby of my dream palace, I come face to face with a gray-colored Pom, who's looking up at me somberly.

"Guess whose dreams I'm about to walk in?" I say, figuring that will help lift his mood.

The tips of Pom's ears go from gray to a light shade of orange. "Oprah?"

I look at those guileless eyes in confusion. "You mean that nice lady from Earth?"

He nods.

"Why the puck would I dreamwalk in her?"

The orange in the ears reddens. "It was my guess. No need to be mean."

"Sorry." I make Oprah appear next to us, then have her slowly morph into Valerian. "The right answer was Valerian." I resist the urge to snidely add, "You know, the guy I was actually *with* when you were awake."

Pom flies over. "In that case, what are we waiting for?"

Shaking my head, I teleport us to the tower of sleepers and locate Valerian there.

Score. There he is. I half expected to see trauma loop clouds above him—he did mention his parents getting killed—but thankfully, all is clear.

"You mind staying out this time?" I ask Pom, following an intuition.

His ears wiggle. "Okay. But you have to introduce me once he's comfortable in the dream world."

"Deal."

I lean over Valerian, and since there are no cooties here, I give him a not-so-chaste kiss on the lips to enter his dreams.

———

FOR A MOMENT, I think I failed and got jerked out of the dream world because I find myself in Valerian's bedroom.

Then I notice a bunch of discrepancies. One is that both windows leading into the bedroom are black—something to look into later. The other discrepancy is much bigger: There's a second version of me on the bed.

A version Valerian is dreaming about.

A *naked* version who seems to be very bendy and more experienced than I am.

I thank the stars I left Pom out of this; he doesn't need psychological trauma.

Peeling my eyes away from my doppelgänger, I watch Valerian's perfect glutes—which are flexing in action. A part of me wants to use my powers to swap places with the other me; Valerian wouldn't know the difference.

Except we have things we have to do.

I clear my throat.

Valerian stops mid-thrust and looks my way.

"Ah." He makes the naked me go away. "This is a dream."

That was the quickest adjustment to the reality of dreaming I've ever come across.

"Ready to deal with the werewolf?" I ask.

He nods, and without my assistance, he clothes himself.

Second example of his mastery of lucid dreaming. Interesting.

I take his hand—mostly because I want to—and teleport us over to the tower of sleepers.

"What's that?" Valerian stares in fascination at Pom, who lands on my shoulder with a Cheshire cat grin on his face. "A dream manifestation?"

"Not a manifestation. He's real. Sort of. He's my companion." I fluff up the looft's fur. "Pom, meet Valerian."

Pom leaps down and lands at Valerian's feet. Looking the man up and down, he says, "The version you kissed looked just like him."

I redden. "Pom, that was private."

Valerian smirks. "Nice to meet you, Pom."

"What kind of Cognizant are you?" Pom asks.

Valerian uses his power to make our surroundings look like his living room. At least he tries to. I see double: a ghostly version of what he's trying to show me and the tower of sleepers underneath.

The tips of Pom's ears turn purple. "Another dreamwalker?"

"An illusionist." Valerian takes the vision away. "But I'm an experienced lucid dreamer as well." He makes a couple of packets of manna appear in the air before handing one to Pom and another to me.

I taste the treat. Yep. He *is* good at lucid dreaming. So was Hekima, the illusionist behind the New York Council murders. He learned about lucid dreaming because he'd grown up side by side with "my kind" in a mysterious place called Soma.

My heartbeat accelerates.

Could that be where Valerian learned it too? Is that why he got so cagey when I asked him about it?

Pom shovels his manna into his mouth without unwrapping it. After chewing mindfully and swallowing, he says, "Just like the one Bailey made for me when I was trying to understand why everyone in the waking world is so obsessed with eating."

I look at Valerian. "He doesn't need to eat because he gets sustenance from my blood." I make Pom's furry bracelet form temporarily show up on my wrist. "In the waking world, he's a looft."

Valerian examines Pom with even greater curiosity. "You mean like the para—"

"A *symbiont* creature that lives on moofts," I say quickly. The last thing I need is Pom freaking out over the use of the p-word.

Valerian nods sagely, catching on. "That's what I was about to say."

I beam at him. "Exactly."

"And Pom is how you jump into dreams so readily," Valerian says. "Clever."

"Yep." Keeping my tone as casual as I can, I ask, "How did you know?"

Valerian frowns. "A lucky guess."

Right. Sure. Nothing to do with the forbidden topic of Soma.

"The werewolf." Valerian looks around. "He'll show up here when he's in REM sleep?"

"Yes," I say and don't bother adding, "Another very lucky guess?"

"Where would he be?" Valerian examines the sleepers in the nooks around us.

On a hunch, I teleport myself to the floor where the nooks have been empty for a while now.

Yep. "There." I point at the one where Hans showed up, still in wolf form.

Valerian takes the spiral stairs in the middle of the tower, which probably means he can't teleport like I do.

"Do you know how this part works?" I ask when he reaches me.

He smiles. "You touch me and him at the same time, then go in."

More proof he's known some dreamwalkers—and this time, he's inadvertently taught me something I've never tried. Normally, I'd jump into the dream of person A, come back to the tower of sleepers with said person, then jump into the dream of person B.

If this way works, it will be more efficient.

He closes the distance between us and stands in such a way that I can reach him and the wolf with ease.

My heart rate picks up the pace again, my physical awareness of his proximity as intense as it is in the waking world—only here, there are no germs, and I'm fully in control.

I run my tongue over my lips. "So I can touch you anywhere, right?"

His ocean-blue eyes kindle with dark heat as he leans in. "Actually"—his voice deepens—"there's a specific way I'd like you to touch me."

"Pom, sweetie, can you give us some privacy?" I ask, my eyes not leaving those sensual lips just a few inches away. "The thing with the werewolf will be scary anyway."

"Fine," Pom huffs and disappears.

Valerian clasps my hand and places it on the werewolf; then, before I can have a coherent thought, he kisses me.

Wow. It must be the knowledge that he can feel the kiss this time that makes this hotter... because it is. More than once, I feel like we're beginning to float off the ground—a hazard of the dream world.

After what feels like an hour of bliss, he pulls away. "He might leave REM sleep," he murmurs, gazing down at me with heavy-lidded eyes. "It's important that we go in."

Right. Dreamwalking.

Without letting go of the werewolf's fur, I slide my hand under Valerian's shirt and reluctantly plummet into the wolf's dreams.

———

JUST LIKE THE last werewolf I did this with, this one is having two dreams at the same time—one for each of his natures. I'm not sure what Valerian sees, but from my point of view, the two dreams are juxtaposed, like two hologram flicks.

One dream is like a violent nature show. Hans is in wolf form, ripping a mooft into shreds.

What an asshole. Moofts are protected species that are pretty much extinct—no good werewolf would hunt them, even in their sleep.

In the other dream, Hans the man is wearing a mooft mask and is in a meeting room, talking to more masked people.

The interesting thing here is that this feels like a memory.

First things first. I can't deal with two dreams at once.

Just like I did when I fought Hekima, I float out of my body and create a second Bailey, this one with fiery hair. Straining my bodiless self, I will myself to enter both bodies.

Wow. It's easier this time. Much easier. I guess that power boost is a gift that keeps on giving.

Wolf Hans stops eating, raises his bloodied muzzle, and sniffs the air.

Puck. The last time, a werewolf was able to detect me this way.

Luckily, Hans shakes his head and resumes eating.

Valerian appears next to the version of me watching the werewolf.

"I'm making sure he doesn't detect us," he says in a conversational tone.

Right. I almost forgot about Valerian, but he didn't forget to make himself useful.

He gestures at Hans. "Can you make sure he keeps dreaming this for a long time to come?"

I nod and set the dream on a loop.

"Good," Valerian says. "Now can you take me to the more interesting dream?"

So he's only here in the wolf's part of the dream. Interesting.

The me in the conference room dream teleports over to where Valerian and the other me stand.

Looking at my fiery-haired self, I wink.

She/I wink back at me.

The feeling is weird because I'm conscious of both winking and looking at myself doing it.

Then the me who was already here notices a hungry expression on Valerian's face when he looks at each version of me in turn. His purely male thoughts aren't difficult to read: One Bailey is great, two are even better.

Well, if he's a good boy, one day I might use my power to have a sort of threesome with him. It might be fun to enjoy him from different perspectives like this. So fun, in fact, that I feel distinctly warm at the thought.

Suppressing the distracting notion, I leave the fiery-haired me to supervise the wolf's dream and teleport Valerian to the meeting-room dream.

Now that the two-dream juxtaposition isn't confusing things, I get a good look around the room.

Hmm. The masks are all the cheapo crap you can get in any store. All the popular choices at costume parties are represented, from real monsters like drekavacs to fictional creatures like Pac-Man.

One specific mask catches my attention, that of a puck's face.

Could it be?

It is a very common mask.

But it's not just the mask by itself. This man is tall and thin, like the one in the dream of Vas, the orc from the Filthy Bastards gang.

Except that would mean Itzel's grandfather's disappearance is somehow linked to Icelus.

"The High Priest couldn't make it," the guy in the puck mask says in the same creaking-floorboards voice I heard before, confirming it is indeed the same person. "I'll be the one to head today's gathering." He waits to see if anyone has any objections, then opens a hologram map of Gomorrah and waves his hands around until a huge chunk of the map is colored in red.

Everyone's eyes gleam with fear and curiosity.

"As you've probably surmised, this represents the blast radius," the puck-masked guy says. "For the foreseeable future, you'll want to stay far away from those neighborhoods."

My eyes widen. "Blast radius?" I exclaim so that only Valerian can hear. Millions live in the highlighted area, not to mention the Health District is there too—the location where Mom's hospital resides.

Let's talk after, Valerian tells me via LEGO letters.

"Has the date been set?" the werewolf growls.

The puck-masked guy gives him a cold look. "Only the Grandmaster will have that information. What we don't know can't be tortured out of us."

Everyone at the table nods somberly.

"Speaking of capture and torture." The puck mask takes out an unfamiliar device, presses it to his right finger, and winces as the device beeps. "I've just implanted a delivery system." He extends his other hand and taps his index finger and thumb in a Morse-code-like pattern. "That gesture will activate the system. The medicine is painless. Use it if you're captured."

Valerian and I exchange worried glances.

The puck mask walks around the room, implanting the devices into everyone's index fingers. Afterward, he spends a while making sure the group remembers the suicidal finger-tapping sequence.

Returning to his seat, he sweeps his gaze over the room. "I know how committed all of you are to our cause, so stating this is unnecessary." His eyes glint darkly. "If you're captured and don't use the precaution you've just received, Phobetor will deal with you personally."

Everyone looks a lot more frightened than they did at the talk of torture, or when a death-dealing device entered their fingers.

Valerian was right. These people really believe in this nightmare deity, to the point where they might actually kill themselves to avoid its wrath. In fact, the mere mention of Phobetor has a profound impact on Hans. In this dream, his shoulders droop, sweat beads on the back of his neck, and he adjusts his shirt collar.

The version of me who's watching the werewolf notices him reacting as well. He stops eating and tucks his tail between his legs.

Puck. I can tell this thing is about to become a nightmare he'll wake up from. Well, not with me around. I change the dream so that there's a knock on the door leading to the meeting room.

Hans looks in that direction—and I instantly feel the dream is no longer a memory, something I expected.

The door opens, revealing a mooft standing there.

As Hans gapes at the benign cow-like creature, I start to make everyone in the room disappear. Before I get around to the puck mask guy, Hans turns from the mooft, likely to ask his co-conspirators what the hell is going on.

Seeing the puck mask alone, he frowns. "Where's everyone?"

"What are you talking about?" the puck mask asks.

Valerian grabs my elbow. "Use your powers to make our surroundings more generic," he whispers. "We want the dream to merge into the one where the two of them spoke alone."

More proof he knows how dreamwalking works—but I don't have

time to challenge him on it, or ask why he can't accomplish the same thing by using his own powers.

Actually, I think I know why he doesn't do it himself—he's probably too busy making the two of us invisible to Hans.

I cover the room in fog and cross my fingers.

Valerian nods at the guy in the puck mask. "Now have the pucker say something about Erato."

I chuckle internally. Pucker is a great nickname for that guy.

Taking over, I have the pucker say, "The dryad filed patents that could expose everything."

Holding my breath, I watch the werewolf's jaw muscles twitch as the room around us transforms.

Valerian and I look around.

"Is this a morgue?" I ask Valerian in a voice only he can hear.

He nods.

Hans curses under his breath. "I'm going to pay that bitch a visit."

"Discretion is paramount," the pucker says, crossing the room to lean over a corpse. "Phobetor is merciless to those who betray us."

This time, the spooky surroundings and mention of Phobetor have an even stronger impact on Hans. He backs away, his elbows pressing into his sides as if he's trying to make his body as small as possible.

His wolf self stops eating again and whimpers.

Before I can rein in the dream once more, I find myself back in the tower of sleepers, Valerian at my side.

We look at the empty bed where the werewolf was a moment ago.

Well, puck.

CHAPTER TWENTY

"HE GOT SO scared by the second mention of Collywobbles he woke up," I say, though the tightness of Valerian's jaw tells me he's already puzzled that out.

"Wake us up," he orders. "I have to tell the Enforcers to pump his cell with sleeping gas again."

Nodding, I jolt him awake and do the same for myself.

Opening my eyes in the bedroom, I watch in stunned fascination as Valerian leaps out of the bed and starts a hologram call with someone.

The Enforcer vampire I saw earlier answers—and he doesn't lift an eyebrow at either Valerian's nude state or my presence.

"Sleeping gas," Valerian barks. "Pump it into the werewolf's room. Now."

The Enforcer walks over to a screen with a bunch of buttons and frowns. "He's already sleeping."

He gestures to the screen in question, and we see that indeed the werewolf is lying there, as though sleeping.

Or faking.

Or—

"Slice off his right index finger," Valerian orders urgently.

Gruesome, but sure to reveal if the guy is indeed faking.

The vampire moves with the speed of his kind. In a blur, he shows up on the same screen as Hans, curved blade in hand.

Whoosh.

The finger and the werewolf go their separate ways.

The guy doesn't wake up or cry out.

My heart sinks. I suspected this might be the case, but—

The vampire touches the werewolf's throat and looks at the camera. "He's dead."

"Heal him," Valerian says through gritted teeth.

I'm not sure if the vamp heard him or just had the same idea, but he slashes his wrist with the blade and forces some of his blood into the werewolf's mouth.

Nothing happens.

Valerian curses and punches a nearby wall.

The vampire comes back and begins pressing buttons next to the security monitor that shows the inside of the cell.

The security footage rewinds and plays again.

"There," I say when Hans opens his eyes. "That must be the moment he woke up."

What Hans does next isn't a surprise. He looks around the cell, realizes he's been captured and kept under. Then his index finger and thumb tap out a familiar code. As soon as he finishes the sequence, his body slumps —but not in sleep.

Valerian curses again. "How soon can you get a healer there? Or a doctor?"

"Not soon enough to make any difference," the vamp says.

"I'll call back." With an angry gesture, Valerian ends the call.

As he grabs some clothes, I try to get my thoughts in order. "What did the pucker mean by 'blast radius?'" I ask, doing my best to keep my eyes off Valerian's rapidly disappearing nakedness. It's too distracting, and I need to focus. "Did you have any reason to think Icelus would blow up half of Gomorrah?"

Valerian pulls a shirt on over his head, covering his mouthwatering abs. "No. Just that they were going to do *something*."

"My mom is within the blast radius," I say. "I need to move her."

He gestures in his VR. "I just made the arrangements," he says after a minute. "She'll be moved to one of the few hospitals not in the Health District."

I let out a relieved breath. "Thank you." Everything's happening so fast I haven't had a chance to properly freak out, and now I won't have to. Except... "What about everyone else? Will there be an evacuation?"

"That's up to the Senate," Valerian says. "But I doubt it."

"Why not?"

"If Icelus learn about the evacuation, they'll set off the bomb, or whatever it is, right away. Or they'll move it and kill even more people." Grimly, he adds, "Not to mention, the panic such an evac would create would serve Icelus's purposes just as much as an explosion would. Maybe more."

I swallow. "Because fear causes nightmares?"

He nods. "Also, if Icelus are smart, they'll change the plan as soon as they learn Hans has disappeared."

"Meaning Mom won't be safe even at the new hospital?" My stomach tightens with the freakout I thought I'd avoided.

"No one's safe." Valerian's jaw flexes. "Not unless we do something."

To my shame, I fleetingly contemplate getting Mom through one of the gates—and staying off world with her. But such a journey would be risky in her condition. Not to mention, I wouldn't *really* let millions die. However... "What about an evacuation to the Otherlands?" I suggest.

"The hub is in the blast radius," Valerian says. "Also, there's no practical way to get millions through a handful of gates quickly enough."

I blow out a frustrated breath.

"It's not the worst idea, though," he says. "You can go to Earth. Sit this out."

"No," I say with a determination I don't feel. "I'm going to stay, and we'll prevent this thing."

He studies me intently. "You have an idea?"

"Sort of. I didn't get a chance to tell you something. The guy in the puck mask—I've seen him before."

I proceed to tell him about the search for Itzel's grandfather and how it also featured the pucker.

"So we know he met Hans in a morgue, and that he hired Filthy Bastards to kidnap Cadmael," Valerian says thoughtfully. "It's a start."

"Right. And when I last spoke with my friends, Felix was going to see if he could link a purchase of a puck mask to the man."

Valerian looks intrigued. "And did he?"

"I don't know, but there's a way to find out. Give me a minute."

Since Valerian now knows about Pom, I openly touch the furry creature on my wrist and fall into the dream world.

———

"YOU'RE BACK," Pom says. "How did that werewolf dreamwalking go?"

Usually, I wouldn't worry him, but I can't help rattling out the situation as I seek Felix. As my symbiont who can no longer be removed from me, Pom is exposed to all the same risks as I am.

"I'm sorry about that," I tell him.

"Don't be." Turning a brave teal hue, Pom raises his chin. "I'm glad to be your symbiont."

Smiling faintly, I fluff his fur and jump into Felix's dream.

———

FELIX IS BUYING Maya an ice cream cone.

I make her disappear, and he looks around in confusion.

"This is a dream," I say.

Pom lands on his shoulder. "Hi, Felix."

Felix looks at Pom, then at me. "I'm never going to get used to this, am I?"

"I'm here to get some important information," I say. "Did you figure out who the guy in the puck mask was?"

Felix regretfully shakes his head. "Too many stores. Too many purchases."

"And no other leads?"

"Afraid not." His unibrow pulls together. "Why do you look so worried all of a sudden?"

I push back my hair, which I haven't bothered making fiery. "Where are you? In the waking world, I mean."

He looks confused for a second, and no wonder. In a dream, it's difficult to recall where you went to sleep. Scrunching his face, he says, "A hotel near Itzel's place on Gomorrah, I think." Looking more certain, he adds, "Kit and Ariel are in the rooms next to me."

"Good. Meet me at Itzel's, and I'll explain everything."

With that, I wake him and terminate the dream.

———

I COME out of the trance to a sense of movement.

What the puck?

I open my eyes.

Holding me in a fireman's carry, Valerian is entering an elevator.

"Hey!" I push on his chest. "What's the deal?"

"Emergency meeting of the Senate." Turning, he presses the button for the rooftop with his elbow.

"I can walk from here," I say and instantly regret it—it feels nice to be held by him.

He sets me on my feet as the elevator stops at the destination, and we dash to the car.

"Can we stop by Itzel's place on the way to the Senate?" I say as we jump in.

"What's the address?"

I tell him and explain that I want to pick up my friends.

"Fine," he says. "But have them wait on the roof."

I call up Itzel, who answers in a sleep-grumpy tone. I can hear the others in the background as well. I quickly tell them to meet me on the roof and hang up.

Valerian must have some illegal turbo mode on the car because it breaks every speed limit on the planet, getting us to Itzel's roof in record time. Itzel, Ariel, Felix (in his robot suit), and Kit are already there, waiting.

Somehow, they all manage to pile in, suit included, and Valerian tells the car to head for the Senate building while I explain the imminent threat to my friends.

They take it surprisingly well, looking only slightly wild-eyed at the idea that a blast might wipe us out at any moment.

"I don't understand," Felix says. "How is Itzel's grandfather connected to this terrorist act?"

Itzel's eyes look squinty. "What was the blast radius again?"

I tell her.

She does something in VR, mumbling under her breath.

"Is she doing math in the middle of all this?" Ariel whispers.

"Maybe she's trying to triangulate where the bomb would need to be located to create that blast radius," Felix says. "That *would* narrow things down a bit, but not enough for anything actionable."

Kit turns into Itzel but without the mask. In Itzel's voice, she says, "I heard gnomes find calculations soothing."

"Hmm," the real Itzel mumbles. "It just might be possible. And if anyone could—" She yelps and give us all a confused look.

Valerian must've done something startling to her with his power to remind her of our existence.

"Did you figure out the link?" he asks her with exaggerated calmness.

"The Vega reactors," she blurts.

"That's the power source on Gomorrah," Felix whispers loudly to Ariel. "Supplying electricity and such."

"Everyone knows that." Itzel gives Felix a baleful glare, and he shuts up. "Purely in theory," the gnome continues, "that technology could be modified to create a device that would release a surge of energy all at once. The resulting explosion might have the blast radius you described."

I smack myself on the forehead. "Of course. Your grandfather invented the Vega reactors. If anyone could turn them into bombs, it would be him."

Felix's robot hands jam into the armpits of his suit. "But surely those reactors are guarded."

Valerian shakes his head. "If Icelus are smart, they'll make their own reactor from scratch, then use that as the basis for that bomb."

I sure am glad Valerian is on our side; he always seems to know exactly what the bad guys should do.

"Is it hard to make the Vegas reactor thing from scratch?" Ariel asks.

"Vega," Felix corrects.

Itzel gives Felix another glare. "It would usually take a team of engineers, but if a single person could, that would be Gramps. He's done it before."

"Not good." Felix tries to wipe the bead of sweat off his forehead with his gloved hand and nearly gives himself a concussion.

Valerian puts a finger to his lips.

Everyone stops talking.

Valerian messes about in VR for a few seconds, then looks at us in frustration. "I just heard from the team of Enforcers dispatched to capture the Filthy Bastards. The hope was that someone else in that gang knew something." He gestures at something in his VR. "They didn't."

Kit turns into some of the gang members we fought earlier. "That was fast."

"Sometimes even the Senate can mobilize quickly," Valerian says. "Speaking of—I just sent them your theory. They want me to patch them into the car."

"Do it," I say for everyone.

Valerian gestures, and the car windows turn opaque before becoming screens. A second later, Senate chambers—familiar to me from the media —appear on the screens around us.

"Wow," Felix mutters.

You can say that again. All the Senators are perched on gravity-defying throne-like seats—except for the mere-folk, who float inside specially designed water tanks.

Each Cognizant type that officially lives on Gomorrah is represented, except for rare ones, like centaurs and cockatrices. Also missing are the types not allowed residence—like necromancers and giants—but the rest are there, including orcs, dwarves, and elves.

"We didn't see the point of you coming here in person," says an elf Senator I've seen in the media.

Valerian doesn't look the least bit impressed or intimidated. "Do you have an update for me?" he asks imperiously.

"The Enforcers are en route," the elf replies. "They'll watch everyone going in and out of every morgue. We also sent out most of the Senate Guard to help."

Valerian's jaw tenses. "Do *not* let them go in without me." His gaze moves from Senator to Senator. "With my illusion power, I can cloak them. Otherwise, we risk the terrorists committing suicide."

"Would that be so bad?" an orc Senator asks.

"There were many people at the meeting, and they mentioned a High Priest—a leader of some sort," Valerian says. "We know nothing about any of these individuals, so unless we get very lucky and they're all there with the puck-masked one, extracting information has to be our top priority."

"Agreed," a dryad Senator says and gestures in the air. "I'm sending you the list of morgues. We looked into the owners, but no one rang any bells."

Valerian nods. "Can you also let me know which morgues already have Enforcer backup waiting for me?"

"Done," the dryad says, gesturing some more.

"Me?" I whisper to Valerian. "Don't you mean 'us?'"

"Later," Valerian whispers back. To the Senate, he says, "Are you keeping the information contained?"

"It's been classified," booms a dwarf Senator. "Only the Enforcers, the Guard, and the Senate know anything. And we're not even evacuating, as you can see."

"Nor are you helping the Enforcers," is what I don't say. I'm willing to bet they will evacuate before regular people get the chance. They're politicians, after all.

Valerian locks eyes with the dwarf. "Just to confirm regarding my compensation…"

"No taxes for life." The dwarf tugs at his beard. "For you and your companies."

"And my colleagues." Valerian nods my way.

"Fine." The dwarf looks like he's swallowed a particularly scaly ri, living up to the frugal stereotype his kind loathes.

"Also, Gomorrah citizenships," Felix blurts. "For those of us who were born elsewhere."

"Done," the elf says. "Let's not waste valuable time on trivialities."

Grunting in approval, Valerian terminates the call and examines something in his VR.

"What did you mean before?" I ask him. "The whole 'me' business."

"No reason for any of you to go with me," he says, only partially paying attention. "My illusionist powers combined with the presence of the Enforcers should be all that's needed."

Itzel's shoulders stiffen. "My grandfather was kidnapped. I'm going."

"And I refuse to miss the fun," Kit says. "So I'm going as well."

"I'm with Itzel," Ariel says.

"And I'm with Ariel," Felix says, though he sounds a lot less enthusiastic.

"Well, *I* could actually be useful," I say. "If something goes awry, I'll drop a sleep grenade and invade the pucker's dreams to learn what we need."

Valerian finally stops what he was doing and pins me with an intent stare. "You won't put yourself into any danger."

"Deal," I say.

"Fine." He tells his car an address—no doubt our first morgue destination.

As our ride whooshes forward, I tug on Valerian's sleeve and whisper, "Did you move Mom?"

Nodding, he gestures around, and LEGO letters show up:

In your inbox is the address of the new hospital. I chose the second place where her gnome doctor does his rounds.

Wow. I could kiss him right now, microbiome or not. Now it should be easier to focus on the task at hand—which apparently consists of nothing less than saving millions.

Ugh. Since when do I do things like this? Did I catch hero tendencies from Felix, Kit, and Ariel? After all, they did once participate in an epic battle to save multiple Otherlands, including Earth. I wonder… if I do save the day, would that help me forgive myself for Mom's—

"Why the long face?" Ariel asks, yanking me out of my musings.

"Feeling guilty," I reply before I can catch myself.

Felix's unibrow dances a complicated jig on his forehead. "What about?"

After a moment of hesitation, I tell them everything: how Mom always asked me never to dreamwalk in her, our fight, and her resulting attempt at suicide.

Everyone digests the info in silence for a few beats, even the usually carefree Kit.

"You're looking at it all wrong," Felix finally says.

I lift an eyebrow.

"Did you ask yourself why?" he says.

I frown. "What do you mean?"

"I think he's wondering why your mother didn't want you to dreamwalk in her *that* badly," Ariel says.

The question hits me like a centaur hoof to the head.

Why indeed? Before, I figured Mom had forbidden me out of privacy concerns, but I don't think she values privacy to the point of killing herself to maintain it.

It's something bigger. It has to be. But what? Is there something Mom doesn't want me to learn in her dream world? Maybe something to do with those black windows I saw there?

Something from the past she's always refused to talk about?

Then again, if it were related to the black windows, she wouldn't remember whatever it is. And, come to think of it, she always claimed not to remember—about my father and so many other things… In any case, can you really fear someone learning something you forgot? I guess it's feasible. If the memory is horrific enough, Mom might know to keep me away, even without recalling the exact reason.

Valerian places a reassuring hand on my shoulder. I look up at him. Speaking of black windows, I almost forgot about the one I saw in his—

"Ready?" he murmurs.

I look out the window and realize I was too preoccupied to notice our landing.

"As ready as I'll ever be," I reply and follow Felix and Ariel out of the car.

A group of Enforcers and one member of the Senate Guard are already waiting for us.

Dressed in all black, the Enforcers are armed with daggers and swords, while the Senate Guard has both a sword and a gun on his hip that's similar to the illegal one that I still have stashed behind my waistband.

I sneak a peek at Ariel to see her reaction.

Like in New York, all Gomorran Enforcers are vampires, their powers a great fit for law enforcement.

To my relief, Ariel is ignoring the vamps, her full attention on the Senate Guard instead.

Of course. The Senate Guard are not vampires. For many reasons, most of them political, they're ubers—the same type of Cognizant as Ariel herself. Meaning that, like Ariel, this Guard could jump on a cover of any Earth fashion magazine and not look out of place—especially if the issue in question featured Navy SEALs.

This impressive specimen must be extra strong and fast to have gotten the highly sought-after post.

Valerian notices me gawking at the uber and scowls.

What's this? Is he actually jealous?

"The morgue is on the top floor," the uber says—and even his voice is pleasant to the ear. Looking at Valerian, he adds, "I was told you'd be in command."

The unspoken part seems to be that the Senate Guard thinks *he* should be in charge, but the stupid politicians pucked everything up as usual.

"Stay close to me," Valerian growls and strides for the elevator.

Ariel, Kit, and even Itzel give the Senate Guard appreciative glances as we follow.

On the ride down, Valerian shares the info the Senate provided about the mortician in charge of the place, such as his name and how much he paid in taxes last year.

I wonder what use that last part is to us.

When we walk in, the morgue looks exactly how they're portrayed in the media on Gomorrah—which is not at all like the ones on Earth. The bodies of the departed are not kept in metal drawers but on tiers of floating-in-the-air slabs. There's no need for refrigeration, as each has been preserved using a special plastination procedure that keeps them from decomposing for many years.

The three options for burial on Gomorrah are, in order of popularity: cremation, going into the ground at the enormous cemetery on the other side of the planet, or getting eaten by a few Cognizant types that are into that sort of thing—which usually means a financial reward for the departed's family.

The chubby mortician hovering over a not-yet-preserved body isn't aware of us.

The Enforcers and the Guard look at Valerian.

"Not him," Valerian says, and the mortician remains none the wiser.

We check the rest of the morgue to see if there's any other staff we can look at, but find none. Retracing our steps, we leave the Enforcers and the

Senate Guard to watch the ins-and-outs in this morgue and fly to the next location on the list.

Again, we're met with Enforcers and one of the ubers from the Senate Guard, and again the mortician can't be our culprit—he's a dwarf.

No luck in the next morgue either. Or the one after that.

When we land on the next roof, I recognize one of the Enforcers—he's the guy who was watching Hans the werewolf and chopped off his finger.

"Hi again," the vamp in question says to me.

"Virgil, this is Bailey," Valerian says, giving the Enforcer a disapproving stare.

The rest of the Enforcers, as well as the Senate Guard dude, introduce themselves.

Since I'm not good with names, I only remember Virgil's name and that of the uber—Onassis.

Like before, Ariel pretends the vampires don't exist and stares at Onassis's drool-worthy butt as we make our way to the elevator.

"This mortician's name is Wrakar," Valerian says, reading the info in his VR. Everyone looks at him, and he tells us how much money Wrakar made the prior year and other not-so-useful details.

Reaching the floor the morgue is located on, we confidently walk in.

"Wait," Felix whispers when the first body comes into view. "Those marks on the body weren't there in the other morgues."

He's right. The marks are actually carvings in the flesh that are lit from the inside with some strange energy.

Is this some fancy burial procedure I've never heard of? If the intent was to make the departed look more festive, it's an epic fail. The carvings make the body appear macabre instead.

Spotting the markings, Ariel goes vampire pale. "Not again," she breathes, backing away.

I'm about to ask her what's happening when a bolt of energy hits Virgil and the other Enforcers.

For a second, the vampires look stunned. Then, without a warning, the Enforcer closest to Valerian lashes out with his sword.

By some miracle, Valerian dodges to the left—which puts his face right in the trajectory of another Enforcer's fist.

The impact of knuckles striking bone is audible.

Valerian flies up and crashes to the ground in an unmoving heap.

CHAPTER TWENTY-ONE

NO. Not Valerian.

My heart feels like it's imploding.

I can't lose him like this. He's fine. He has to be.

There's no time to check on him or ponder what the puck has just happened. Maybe the Senate has betrayed us, or maybe the Enforcers are somehow part of Icelus—it doesn't matter. Priority number one is survival and helping Valerian.

I yank out my gun and shoot the Enforcer who punched him.

Nothing happens.

I flip the nonlethal setting to kill mode and shoot again.

Still nothing.

Puck. I guess you can't kill a vampire with this tech.

Onassis must know the same thing. Instead of bothering with the gun, he takes out his sword and slashes at the Enforcer I just tried to shoot.

The Enforcer's head rolls away.

Whew. At least the Senate Guard is on our side.

Another Enforcer attacks Ariel. She stabs him with a knife, and Kit morphs into a cyclops and knocks another Enforcer off his feet before he gets the upper hand. At the same time, Itzel grows a ball of lightning on her palms and hurls it at the chest of the Enforcer who tried to behead Valerian earlier, while Felix lowers the faceplate of his robot suit and punches the Enforcer nearest him.

The one Enforcer not attacking anyone is Virgil, Valerian's acquaintance.

He just stands there frozen, a look of intense concentration on his pale face. Catching my gaze, he grits out, "I'm fighting it as best I can. He's incredibly strong. Stay away from me."

Who's strong? What is Virgil talking about?

"So, this is the illusionist who's been snooping around," says a familiar creaking-floorboards voice.

I whirl on the speaker.

This must be Wrakar, the mortician. And surprise, surprise: he looks just like the mystery man in the puck mask.

The mask is missing now, revealing a thin, leathery face contorted in an ugly grimace. Looking at Valerian's unmoving body, he sneers, "He tried to hide you all, but I can see through the eyes of the vampires." He waves at Virgil. "Not to mention, my lovelies." He raises his hands, and that same multi-colored energy streams from his fingers into the bodies on the slabs.

"I knew it!" Ariel shouts. "A necromancer. Again."

She's fought a necromancer before?

Wait. A necromancer? That explains a lot.

Necromancers can reanimate and control the dead, so hanging out at a morgue would be a natural choice for their kind. I also heard a rumor that necros are not allowed to live on Gomorrah—or most worlds where vampires have power—because they can gain control over vamps.

Sounds like that wasn't a rumor, after all. All the Enforcers except Virgil are under Wrakar's spell—and Virgil might lose his fight for freedom any second.

As I process all this, the bodies on the slabs jump down and face us.

Zombies. Freshly made.

My heart rate goes through the roof.

We're so pucked.

CHAPTER TWENTY-TWO

A ZOMBIE who used to be an elderly elf lady rushes my way.

A surge of anger crowds out my fear. Elves live unfathomably long lives, so for Wrakar to disrespect this ancient woman's body feels like a crime against something holy.

No wonder necromancers aren't allowed on Gomorrah. They're the worst.

Though I don't expect it to work, I aim for the elf lady's sagging bosom and pull the trigger.

Nothing happens. My gun can't kill what is already dead.

Having no idea how strong zombies are, I turn to run.

In the corner of my vision, I see everyone dealing with the new threat.

Onassis dispatches an Enforcer with his sword, then slices off an arm from a dryad zombie. The dryad keeps coming. He slices off her head. The headless body keeps moving.

Great. Things are officially worse than I thought.

Two Enforcers and four zombies corner Felix. The chest section of the robot opens up, and two giant guns show up and fire at Felix's attackers.

Boom.

In the enclosed space, the explosion is deafening.

Felix's attackers are in pieces, but the other zombies and Enforcers near him all turn his way.

Puck.

The necro must now consider Felix the most dangerous target—he doesn't realize those guns don't have a reload.

Meanwhile, not far from where I stand, Ariel kicks a dwarf zombie, sending him flying into the air like a giant soccer ball. "Kill the necromancer!" she yells, panting. "That's the only way to stop them."

She must be talking to Felix, who's kind of blown his chance to do what she says by already firing those guns.

Onassis must think Ariel is talking to *him*, though. Pulling out his gun, he tries for Wrakar, but the necromancer is hiding behind a wall of bodies, not allowing the Guard good aim.

Onassis shoots blind. Nothing happens. He shoots again. Same result. Before he can fire another shot, an orc zombie punches him in the face.

I lunge to the right, where I think I can still make the shot. As much as the necromancer deserves my gun's current setting, I switch to the nonlethal mode—a dead necromancer can't tell us where the bomb is. Hopefully if he's knocked out, the zombies will stop as well.

I aim.

A gnarled hand grabs my gun by the barrel. It's a zombie of an elderly uber—who looks hot even now, in a silver fox sort of way. With a jerk, the zombie rips the gun from my grasp.

I was wondering if zombies were as strong as the people they're made from, and what the uber does next confirms my suspicion.

With barely an effort, he crushes the gun into little pieces.

Puck.

Gun destroyed, the uber zombie throws a lumbering punch at my head.

I dodge it with ease. Strong or not, this zombie is not as fast as he was when alive.

Using his lack of speed to my advantage, I jump away.

A thin, elderly female gargoyle zombie rushes me.

Dodging her, I also dive under the outreached hands of the cyclops zombie in the way.

An Enforcer nearly chops off my head when I pass him. Then two zombies try to ram into me with their bodies, and I barely avoid them.

Gritting my teeth, I keep dodging and running around the morgue, feeling like an anorexic elf playing American football with orcs.

When I get a moment of no one trying to end me, I pull out the sleep grenade. My mind spins frantically. Should I do it? In the confined space, all of us would go under, including the necromancer and Valerian—if he's alive. The zombies should stop in that case, but if the necro wakes up first, we'll be worse off than now.

Except there are vampires in play. They don't sleep. Would they become normal Enforcers as soon as the necromancer is under?

That *would* make sense.

In my contemplations, I forget to watch my step—and pay for it dearly. An orc zombie gives me a shove, sending me flying toward Valerian, while the unused grenade slips out of my hand and clanks on the floor.

I land so hard the air vacates my lungs, and a shock of pain reverberates through my entire body.

Stunned, fighting off nausea, I check the battlefield.

Looking increasingly pale, Itzel is shooting lightning balls at the attackers. This is not good. There are only so many times she can use that power before she'll faint.

Felix isn't doing much better. An Enforcer and a zombie are pummeling his broken suit, and he's not responding.

The person doing relatively well is Kit. Now in the form of a giant, she's fending off two orc zombies and four Enforcers.

A shadow covers me, and I look up

An Enforcer sword is swinging down at me.

Well, puck.

The necromancer is about to have a new corpse to raise.

CHAPTER TWENTY-THREE

PAIN EXPLODES in my body as I throw myself to the side, rolling for all I'm worth.

Except I don't roll fast enough. The sword slices through my upper arm, the blade supernova-hot as it parts my flesh.

It takes all my will not to pass out as a wave of nausea crashes into me.

The Enforcer raises the sword again.

A dark patch shimmers in my vision. Before I can make sense of it, Onassis's sword blocks the Enforcer's blade.

Panting, I try to sit up and scoot out of the way of the clashing swords.

My body doesn't cooperate. Must be too damaged.

Fine. Leaving puddles of blood behind me, I crawl. And crawl. And crawl some more. When I can't move another inch, I peek over my shoulder.

The Enforcer headbutts the uber and rips into his throat with sharp vampire fangs.

Onassis staggers back.

"No!" Ariel yells from somewhere nearby.

The vampire thrusts with his sword. There's a sound of breastplate breaking, and Onassis sags to the floor.

Puck. Poor guy.

The Enforcer blurs toward me and raises the sword again.

Only Ariel's already there. Her beautiful face contorted with fury, she beheads him with a sword she must've taken from one of the other vampires.

Blood gushes out of the Enforcer's headless body, spraying my face.

A thousand yucks. Of all the bodily fluids, blood is my least favorite. I can't believe I used to swallow it to stay awake.

Ariel bends to help me up, but a cyclops zombie grabs her by the neck. She spins around and slashes at him, beheading him in one swift move.

The headless cyclops yanks on her sword, ripping it out of her grasp while continuing to choke her.

I grit my teeth. Puck this. I'm not letting Ariel or anyone else die.

I drag my finger through the vampire blood on my face and stick it into my mouth. Fighting my gag reflex, I swallow.

There is no pleasure this time, only the bliss of having my pain go away as my wounds mend in an eyeblink. I'll have to be even more vigilant when it comes to vampire blood addiction going forward, but for now, I have the energy to leap to my feet.

Ariel looks paler than the dead Enforcer at our feet.

Grabbing a sword from the floor, I slice off the cyclops's right arm, then the left.

Freed, Ariel gulps in a breath and grabs a sword, quickly turning the rest of the cyclops zombie into minced meat.

Leaving her to deal with the next zombie, I sprint for the sleep grenade. A reanimated elf lumbers at me, so I chop off his head. A dwarf zombie is next and gets the same treatment. Finally, the grenade is in my hand.

Are things desperate enough for this measure?

I frantically survey the battlefield.

Ariel is bleeding but still fighting off the zombies and Enforcers coming at her. However, Itzel is on the floor, unmoving; she either fainted from too many lightning balls, or was knocked out or killed. Felix's suit looks like a tin can that's been run over by a car, and even Kit looks weary in her giant form.

There's no choice.

I have to act now.

Kit's back is blocking Virgil from my view, but I assume he's still standing where he was.

"Virgil, wake me up," I shout, hoping he can make out my words despite the racket. "And don't kill Wrakar!"

Of course, this assumes a sleeping necromancer will lose power over vampires—a premise I have no evidence for.

Well, here goes nothing.

Holding my breath, I activate the grenade and toss it in Wrakar's direction.

Wrakar must fall under immediately because the zombies and the Enforcers freeze in weird poses. I guess they're waiting for their puppet master to wake up from his nap.

Not good. If Virgil is standing there frozen, my plan is out the window.

Kit succumbs next, her giant form collapsing with a heavy thud.

I can see Virgil now, and my heart sinks.

He's not frozen like his follow Enforcers, but that doesn't matter. Someone has cuffed his wrists and ankles, so all his moving around is just a test of his bindings, which seem to hold his preternatural strength.

Puck. Who's going to wake me up?

Before I can think of an answer, the gas reaches me, and I drop into slumber.

CHAPTER TWENTY-FOUR

MOM and I are standing face to face near a highway, eyes locked like two gunslingers in an Earth Western.

"I won't let you dreamwalk in me," Mom says determinedly.

I cock my head. "Won't *let* me?"

"Yes," she says, her confidence wavering. "I'll stop you by any means necessary."

"Is that right?"

Mom's fists clench. "I'd sooner die."

I roll my eyes. "You don't think that's overly dramatic?"

"I mean it." She glances at the road, then locks eyes with me again. "I'll jump under the first car that comes my way."

I don't believe her.

She jumps.

I stop breathing.

The car rams into her. She somersaults in the air and lands on her back, broken beyond repair.

No! What have I done? The horror is overwhelming.

Shaking, I back away, hand pressed against my mouth. She's dead. Oh puck, she's dead. I killed her.

No, she killed herself. Because of me.

There's a racket behind me.

I spin around and rub my eyes.

Right there on the sidewalk, a bunch of Enforcers are fighting with Ariel, Felix, Kit, and Valerian.

I want to rush to help them, but I'm frozen in place, still not breathing.

Paralyzed, I watch as the vamps kill my friends one by one. When Valerian exhales his final breath, the building behind the massacre explodes. A giant mushroom cloud leaps into the sky, and the wall of heat spreads outward, decimating the vampires and the bodies of my friends in its path.

My paralysis disappears, and I throw my hands up in a shield—as though that will make a difference to the million degrees Fahrenheit rushing my way.

Wait. Something is missing from my wrist.

The furry bracelet.

Pom.

As soon as I realize this, I know what's happening.

I'm dreaming.

I freeze the explosion in its tracks and whirl around.

Mom's broken body is still there, lying on the road, and for some reason, it feels sacrilegious to use my powers to make it go away.

This isn't a dream—not fully, at least. Mom did jump in front of a car. I made her.

She tried to kill herself because of me.

The knowledge hammers at me, stark and brutal, the guilt so heavy that even in the dream world, it makes me sink to my knees. I think some part of me was still in denial before this moment, still hoping that somehow it was all a lie.

"Mom," I whisper, extending my hand toward her corpse. I know that in the waking world, she's in a coma, not dead, but she might as well be.

There's no guarantee that I'll be able to save her, that I'll be able to save anyone. Already, Valerian and my friends might be dead. With my stupid sleep grenade gamble, I probably killed them all—and millions of Gomorrans as well.

"Now that's just stupid," Pom says. "And this is coming from someone who's very familiar with guilt."

I look up at my looft.

Pom's coloring is fluctuating from red to carrot as he jumps into my arms.

I squeeze him so hard I'd probably hurt him if this were the real world.

"I'm sorry," he says, wriggling out of my hold. "I broke two promises at once."

It's true. I've asked him never to appear in my natural dreams because I usually like to enjoy them like a normal person. I've also asked him not to read my thoughts—for obvious reasons.

I give a shaky laugh. "I forgive you. In fact, the next time I have a nightmare as bad as this one, I want you to show up and tell me that I'm dreaming."

"I will." He blinks at me with his big lavender eyes. "Now if only you'd forgive yourself as easily as you forgave me."

I sit back. "You don't understand."

"Don't I?" The tips of his ears turn gray. "That dream was false. You'd never talk to your mom like that."

"So what?" I look at the broken body. "The result was the same."

Pom sighs. "Your mom was a mess. You wanted to help her. Maybe you pushed a little, but you didn't know what would happen. *She* made the choice to jump under that car—end of story."

Rationally, I know he has a point. I *was* just trying to understand why Mom was so depressed and withdrawn, and all I said was, "If your symptoms keep worsening, I might not have a choice."

And I didn't lie. When her life was on the line, I broke my oath—and would again. *Will* do so again, when I'm ready.

I take a deep breath.

This isn't really helping.

No matter what I know rationally, the heavy pressure of guilt refuses to abate.

"Well, it should," Pom says, clearly reading my mind again. "And by the way, you definitely didn't cause the deaths of your friends." Pom nods at the frozen explosion. "Keep in mind that if the bomb had really blown up in the waking world, we'd both be dead now, and thus not talking."

Oh, puck. My friends. The bomb.

In my self-flagellation, I completely forgot about the real danger we're in.

Pom huffs. "You think?"

"You're right on so many levels." I leap to my feet. "If I'm dreaming, that means I'm in REM sleep and thus it's been around ninety minutes since the gas grenade exploded."

The tips of Pom's ears turn purple as I continue. "If Wrakar had woken up, I'd already be dead. That means he's still sleeping. But, like me, he might be in REM sleep. That means a nightmare could wake him up—and then it's game over for us."

"Exactly." Pom bounces from one furry paw to another. "It's almost like you were trying to kill yourself as a punishment."

Puck. Is he right? Did the guilt make me almost give up?

Well, no more. I'm done wallowing. I may never fully let go of the guilt, but I can't let it paralyze me into inaction. If Mom wants to berate me when she wakes up, she has every right to do so, but I have to stop beating myself up. I can't change the past. All I can do is stop this bomb, wake her up, and ask her to forgive me. And with time, maybe I'll learn to forgive myself as well.

"Yes, much better." Pom is fully purple as he hops into my arms. "Now you're talking."

Shaking my head in exasperation—I wasn't talking, I was thinking—I squish him against my chest and take us to the tower of sleepers. I want to spare a precious second to see if my friends are all right.

Instantly, my relief fades, my chest tightening as I survey the nooks.

They're not here.

Pom's fur darkens. "This *could* mean they just haven't reached their REM sleep cycle."

I set him down. "Right. It's also possible they were already knocked out when the gas hit them—unconscious people don't dream."

Suddenly, Kit shows up in her bed.

I almost scream in relief. Without thinking, I leap into her room and jump into her dream.

Naturally, Kit is dreaming of an orgy.

I make all her partners go away and explain that she's asleep.

"Wake me up," she says. "Then wake yourself so we can finish this."

Grinning, I do so.

CHAPTER TWENTY-FIVE

I WAKE WITH A START.

There's a face above my head. A face of a giant—probably the worst way to wake up.

Seeing me blanch, the giant morphs into Kit.

I sit up. "Free Virgil and secure Wrakar," I say urgently. "Don't wake him, but if he wakes up on his own, chop off his right index finger. He still has the information we need, and we don't want him committing suicide like that werewolf."

Eyes gleaming with bloodthirst, Kit hurries to do as I asked, while I leap to my feet and examine my surroundings.

Finally freed, Virgil looks groggy. I shout some orders at him, and that seems to snap him out of his stupor. Rushing toward what's left of Felix's robot, he begins to dig.

Since Ariel is closest to me, I check her vitals, preparing for the worst.

Whew. She's got a pulse.

I sprint over to Itzel.

Another ton off my shoulders. Though Itzel is in even worse shape than Ariel, she will clearly live.

I turn toward Virgil. He's looming over Felix, who looks like one giant bruise under the wreckage of his suit.

"He's going to make it," the vampire tells me, much to my relief.

And now for the check I dread the most.

Sprinting to where Valerian fell, I feel his pulse.

It's faint, but it's there.

I exhale, my knees weakening from relief. He's going to live. I didn't lose him.

Nor am I going to.

Swiping my finger over the vampire blood that's still on my face, I stick it into Valerian's mouth. I know I warned him against this very thing, but desperate times call for desperate measures. Like me, he can go cold turkey starting today.

His breathing improves instantaneously. A second later, his eyes blink open and widen at the sight of me covered in blood.

"It's not mine," I say quickly as he sits up. "There was a battle. Ariel beheaded a vampire. Promise me you'll never drink their blood after—"

"It's okay," he interrupts, and ripping off a sleeve, he wipes the blood from my face.

"There's no time for this," I mutter, pushing him away. "The others—"

"No blood," the now-awake Ariel barks at Virgil. "I'll heal on my own."

The vampire looks insulted. "I wasn't going to give you any. Enforcers don't break the law."

Good points all around. She shouldn't risk the kind of healing Valerian and I have gotten—not after all the rehab. Virgil is right as well: Giving someone his blood is highly illegal. When used in medicinal settings, vampire blood comes from an anonymous donor, and doctors know how to handle it to minimize addiction.

There's a reason I had to get it from the likes of Napoleon.

I catch Virgil's gaze. "Can you get medical help for them?"

"It's en route," he replies.

Valerian leaps to his feet and looks around. "Where's Wrakar?"

"Sleeping," I say. "Hopefully."

As one, we rush to the back of the morgue.

We find the necromancer on the floor, with Kit standing over him, sword ready for a strike.

"As soon as he's in REM sleep, I'm going in," I whisper to Valerian.

"Be careful," he replies in a low voice. "Yours isn't the only way to get the information we need."

I nod and watch Wrakar's closed eyes for any sign of movement. Then loud voices reach my ears.

It's the emergency workers. They've come to take Ariel, Itzel, and Felix.

"Don't worry. I'm blocking his sense of hearing." Valerian nods at the necromancer.

Interesting. I didn't realize his power worked even on sleeping people.

Valerian walks over to pick up Onassis's gun, then approaches an EMT dwarf and chats with him for a few seconds. When he makes his way back, I see he's also gotten himself a hygieia device.

"What was that about?" I ask, glancing at the medical workers.

Valerian hygieias me from head to toe. "I made sure they'd take Felix and company to the same hospital as your mother. And I told them to put the bills on my tab."

If we were alone, I'd probably kiss him twice—once for the disinfecting and once more for taking care of my friends.

And then maybe a third time for being alive.

And a fourth, just for me.

"Can I at least chop off that finger now?" Kit pipes up.

I round on her. "Don't. That would wake him up."

She frowns. "He hurt my friends. He has to pay."

"And he will pay," Valerian says darkly. "Don't you worry about that."

After that, everyone watches the sleeping Wrakar in sullen silence until I feel that strange sensation again, the feeling of a nearby person going into REM sleep.

I check Wrakar's eyes to be sure.

Yep. He's dreaming.

Taking the hygieia device from Valerian, I clean a spot on the necromancer's wrist and touch it with great reluctance.

A moment of concentration later, I'm in the dream world.

CHAPTER TWENTY-SIX

"WELL?" Pom demands. "How's—"

"Still working on saving Gomorrah," I reply and rush to the tower of sleepers.

Locating the necromancer, I breathe a sigh of relief when I see the lack of clouds over his head; the last thing I want is to deal with a necromancer's trauma loop.

"Will this be scary?" Pom whispers.

I shrug, my gaze not leaving my target. "I'd sit this one out if I were you."

"Okay, I will," Pom says and starts his Cheshire cat disappearing act. When only his mouth is visible, he throws out, "Good luck."

Inhaling a deep breath, I touch Wrakar's wrist and dive in.

———

MY SURROUNDINGS ARE FAMILIAR—AND make no sense.

Under my feet are the calm waters of an endless black ocean and above me are angry, fiery skies.

This looks just like the place where all the subdreams take place, except it can't be: I double-checked to make sure Wrakar was in REM sleep, and more importantly, when inside subdreams, I never realize that's what's happening.

Why and how would Wrakar be dreaming of this? Did a dreamwalker describe subdreams to him? That would imply other dreamwalkers see the black ocean and fiery skies when they end up in subdreams, and I thought that was just my subconscious at work.

Something else occurs to me, something even stranger.

I don't see Wrakar anywhere.

Odd. Can a dreamer be missing from his own dream?

Looking around, I realize the necromancer isn't completely missing. As I concentrate, I feel a presence.

A presence that's slowly congealing out of nothingness to stand on the ocean in front of me.

When I can make it out, I realize that he—or it—looks nothing like the necromancer, even one distorted by the most nightmarish imagination.

The creature is humanoid but taller than the biggest giant. Even without that size, it would be the most frightening thing I've ever gazed upon—yet paradoxically, I can't explain what scares me about it so much. His face is beautiful, but in a terrible, overwhelming way.

If I had to pinpoint what makes it so, I'd say it's those eyes. They make me think of black holes. Looking into them is like seeing every nightmare I've ever experienced. Like looking under a dark bed as a small child. Like licking the floor in a public bathroom. Like—

"Begone," the creature booms, its melodious voice conjuring my every fear.

An image of my friends dying before reaching the hospital flits through my mind. Then one of Mom never waking up. Then—

"Begone!" the voice repeats, and just like that, I'm kicked out of the dream.

CHAPTER TWENTY-SEVEN

"WHERE'S THE BOMB?" Valerian demands as soon as I come out of the trance.

I shake my head, my heart hammering in my chest as I back away from the necromancer and nearby bump into Virgil.

"What happened?" Valerian growls.

"I don't know." I gulp in a breath. "He took on a scary guise inside his dreams, and somehow that threw me out—but I'm going back in."

Valerian steps in front of me before I can touch Wrakar again. "He's not in REM sleep anymore. I don't want you to risk your sanity—not when there are other ways to make him talk."

Sure enough, that sense of having a sleeper nearby is gone, and the necromancer's eyes are no longer darting about behind his lids.

I take a breath to settle my still-racing pulse. "So how are we going to do this?"

Valerian takes out the gun, switches it to nonlethal mode, and shoots the necro in the head. "Remove the finger," he says to Kit. "Then I need him in my flying car."

Kit smiles grimly and cuts Wrakar's entire hand off at the wrist.

Virgil creates a tourniquet from a sleeve to stop the bleeding and heaves the necromancer over his shoulder like a sack of rotten potatoes. We follow as he carries him to the car, Valerian shooting the necro with the gun every couple of minutes.

Once Wrakar is in the car, Valerian gives Virgil an apologetic look. "You can't come with us."

Right. In the air, far from vampires and corpses, Wrakar will be as good as powerless.

Virgil grudgingly nods.

Kit and I enter the car after Valerian, and we take to the air as I try to understand what happened in the necromancer's dream. I'd never seen anything like it before. He must have a horrible imagination to manifest such a creature.

Just as we clear the clouds, Wrakar moans, then opens his eyes and screams in pain.

"Ah," Kit says nastily. "Someone's finally awake."

"Stay back," Valerian says to us and points his hands at Wrakar.

Previously, his illusions would happen stealthily; he never had to show the arcs of energy like Hekima did. But this time, the energy is on display. He's either putting more illusory power into whatever he's about to do, or he just wants to show off.

Wrakar's screaming grows louder. Instead of pain, there's fear in it now, the kind of fear I felt inside his dream. His body jerks spasmodically, and he claws at himself with his one remaining hand, as if killing something visible only to him.

Whatever Valerian is making him see, it must indeed be horrific.

The scream goes on and on, for what feels like an hour. Finally, Valerian stops the energy flow, and evenly, almost conversationally, says, "Where's the bomb?"

Wrakar shakes his head.

Valerian shoots him with the energy again. The screams and clawing spasms go on for even longer.

"Where's the bomb?" Valerian asks again. "Tell me, and this can all stop."

"Hub building," Wrakar croaks out. "The hundredth floor."

"The hub building is near the center of the blast radius," I say. "He might be telling us the truth."

"It's a good location," Kit says, turning into the necromancer, but with the hand attached. "There's a convenient escape to the Otherlands just an elevator ride away."

Valerian levels a menacing glare at our captive. "Who's guarding the bomb?"

Wrakar doesn't answer.

Valerian repeats the torture illusion.

"Everyone," Wrakar rasps when he finally stops screaming. "I was about to head there myself."

Valerian implements the illusion again, waits for the necromancer to stop screaming, and asks, "When is the bomb set to explode?"

Wrakar glances at the time on the car dashboard and grins maniacally. "Twenty-seven minutes."

My heart sinks.

I'm not sure we can even get to the hub building by then, let alone stop something from happening.

"Car, activate turbo mode," Valerian barks.

Turbo mode? Is that why we were going so fast before?

Valerian shoots more orders at the car, including the address of the building in question. With a jerk, the car dives below the clouds and zooms in the direction of the hub with a speed that presses me down into my seat.

Puck. *Turbo mode* should be called *rocket mode*.

Ignoring Wrakar's pained whimpers, Valerian gets in touch with the Senate in his VR and tells them where to send people. Then he curses up a storm.

"What happened?" I ask.

He gestures to terminate the conversation with the Senate. "The pucking morons don't think they can get anyone there within the allotted time."

Kit rubs her hands together. "Seems like it's up to the three of us to stop the bomb. What fun."

When this is all over, I'll have to give Kit the bad news: She seems to have replaced her sex addiction with a craving for violence. And while we're at it, I'll make her aware of the real definition of the word "fun."

Valerian shoots Wrakar with his mojo again. After he deems the screaming sufficient, he stops the torture and asks, "How do we deactivate the bomb?"

"I don't know," Wrakar croaks. "Only the High Priest knows."

Frowning, Valerian shoots Wrakar with the illusion energy a few more times, but the answer stays the same.

Valerian looks at Kit. "Do you have a way to disable him, temporarily? If we walk into that building and it turns out that he lied, I want him alive to regret it."

Kit looks thoughtful for a second, then grins. "If you don't like spiders, you might want to look away."

I don't know about Valerian, but I jerk my gaze away and put my hands over my ears for good measure.

Even through my palms, I can hear Wrakar yelling in horror. He swears on everything from his mother's remains to his own life that he didn't lie to us, and begs for Kit to stop whatever it is she's doing.

Eventually, Wrakar's vocal cords must give out, because instead of screaming, he just produces a prolonged hoarse croak.

"There," Kit says eventually. "He's not going anywhere."

When I turn, I see what I sort of expected—and it's still extremely disturbing. The necromancer's ghost-pale face is sticking out of a giant silk cocoon of the type spiders use to wrap their prey.

"So," I say, my voice shaky. "What's the plan?"

"We go in," Valerian says. "I make sure they can't see us. When we know which one is the High Priest, we apprehend him while I make sure the others are none the wiser. I then make him tell us how to disable the bomb, and we do just that. Afterward, I can make it so that Icelus kill each other, or maybe we knock them out one by one." He looks at me. "Which do you prefer?"

"Knocking them out is safer," I say. "We don't know what powers they have. They might hurt us in the process of attacking one another."

Nodding, Valerian lands the car smack in the middle of the hub, which I'm pretty sure is illegal. Ignoring the gates all around us, we sprint for the elevator, where I smash the button for the hundredth floor.

A quick ride later, the elevator doors ding open and we exit—straight into a horde of Icelus.

CHAPTER TWENTY-EIGHT

THIS FLOOR IS CLEARLY MEANT to be rented out for big parties, like weddings and Jubilees, but that's not how it's being used at the moment. Far from it.

A row of hospital beds stands where dining tables usually would. On the beds are comatose people who must be sleeping—I know because my newfound REM sleep sense can detect many of them dreaming.

Next to each bed stands an Icelus member. They're all wearing the masks from the werewolf's dream and holding intricately designed daggers, their attention on the podium where the wedding band would typically be.

Following their gazes, I audibly exhale.

A black-clad figure stands with his or her back to us, fiddling with an unfamiliar device.

My heartbeat skyrockets.

It's not that hard to guess what's happening. The figure is the High Priest, and the beeping device is the reactor-turned-bomb. Most concerning, on the screen where the married couple would usually watch a video collage is a digital clock counting down seconds.

Everyone stares at the remaining time.

Ten minutes and ten seconds.

Do you think it's until the explosion? I message Valerian. *Or the moment they should run upstairs if they mean to escape via the gates?*

Let's assume time to explosion, he replies. *I wouldn't put it past these fanatics to blow themselves up for their deity.*

Oh, yeah. I forgot about the deity part. These idiots worship Phobetor—or Collywobbles, as far as Valerian's concerned.

The countdown hits ten minutes exactly.

It must be some critical milestone in whatever's about to happen because the walls all around the room turn into screens displaying a slideshow of horror-movie-worthy images.

Wait a second. I've seen something like this before. It was—

The black-clad High Priest turns from the bomb to face the Icelus members and announces in a booming voice, "The first sacrifice."

A thin elf in a drekavac mask stabs the sleeper nearest him.

My jaw drops open—but not from the violence I've just witnessed.

I know the High Priest, know that Darth Vader-like mask and voice.

It's Doctor Cipactli, the gnome who works at the sleep clinic I nearly put Mom in.

Puck.

She could've been that sacrifice.

Speaking of sacrifices, they now make a macabre kind of sense. The sleepers must be having nightmares, so the Icelus fanatics probably think that killing someone in that state will bring them closer to the nightmare deity, or some nonsense like that.

Cipactli's clinic is where I've seen those subdream-like images, too.

Hold on.

I scan the sleepers.

Yep. Gertrude, the gangrene-giver from the New York Council, is right there. Poor wretch. We're not exactly pals, but I don't want her to be a sacrifice to a made-up god.

Another sleeper, on a bed near Gertrude, catches my eye.

It's Cadmael, Itzel's grandfather.

Focusing my REM sleep radar power on him tells me he's dreaming, so he's alive for now.

I wish Itzel were here so I could reassure her.

Frantically opening my VR, I write everything I've just realized for Valerian, adding that Doctor Cipactli studies nightmares—a natural subject of interest for a worshiper of a deity like Collywobbles.

Valerian pulls out a gun just as LEGO letters show up in front of me, chilling me to the bone: *He's a gnome!?*

Pucking puck. Most powers don't work on gnomes.

Valerian takes aim, but he's hesitating and I can understand why. We need the gnome conscious to tell us how to disable the bomb. The stun of the gun might knock him out for longer than the time we have left. An equally good question is *how* we'd make him talk in the first place. Valerian can't use his illusion torture on a gnome—and even if we magically got the High Priest to sleep, I wouldn't be able to get the answers either; as I recently learned, I would need the gnome's consent.

I glance at the stage.

Crap. The High Priest is looking right at us, a lightning ball already in his hands.

Valerian seems to finally come to a decision, but before he squeezes the trigger, the High Priest launches his projectile.

The ball of energy zooms toward us with the speed of light—and smashes straight into Valerian's chest.

CHAPTER TWENTY-NINE

NO. Not again.

Spinning on my heel, I lunge toward his fallen body.

From behind me, a giant's voice booms, "I'll hold them off!"

That must be Kit. No doubt she's changed to match that voice.

A second later, the sound of her enormous fist slamming into someone's flesh confirms it.

I block out the sounds of the fight, focusing on the prone figure in front of me. Valerian's clothes are singed where the ball hit him, but the skin underneath isn't charred, just reddened, like after a bad sunburn.

The breath I've been holding escapes my lungs. He must know how much of a trouble magnet he is, and wore protective gear.

I check his pulse. Faint but there.

My own pulse settles into a steadier rhythm. Swiftly, I scan myself for any hint of vampire blood from earlier. I know I said he needs to abstain, but I'd rather he live as an addict than not at all.

No blood left. All cleaned up by Valerian himself.

"Crap." Kit's voice sounds tiny this time, as though she's inhaled a bunch of helium.

It jerks me back to what's happening. As much as I want to fuss over Valerian, there's an impossible task before us: stop the bomb before the timer runs out.

I pry the gun out of his fingers.

The gun is dead. The electricity of the High Priest's projectile must've fried something. Holding the useless weapon, I leap to my feet and face Kit.

She's a giant again—and kicking a gargoyle Icelus in a harlequin mask.

The High Priest hurls another lightning ball at Kit.

She turns into something small with wings—either a pixie or a hummingbird.

The projectile whooshes through the empty air.

The elf in a drekavac mask, the one who made the sacrifice earlier, runs under tiny Kit and heads straight for me.

Kit turns back into a giant, preventing any other Icelus from coming this way.

I aim at the elf. "Freeze!" I order in my best imitation of a cop's voice. "Drop the knife, or I'll shoot."

The elf keeps coming, his face unreadable under that mask.

Puck. He's calling my bluff. Gulping in a panicked breath, I wait until he's almost upon me before I hurl the gun at his head.

The elf must've had some training. He dodges the projectile with ease and sneers, "Did you bring a broken gun to a knife fight?"

Crouching, I sweep at his legs. He jumps over my foot and slashes at me with his dagger.

Pain sears through me. The knife has just sliced through my forearm.

I grit my teeth, ignoring both the pain and the panic I feel at the thought of the earlier victim's blood mixing with mine. If I freak out, I'm as good as dead. Even without the freak out, there's probably less than nine minutes left to live.

Hoping it's the last thing he'd expect, I uppercut the elf with my injured arm.

The injury makes my swing clumsy, and the elf jerks his head back before coming at my throat with a dagger.

I catch his wrist before the blade connects.

He goes to punch me, but I catch that wrist as well.

Thank puck he's especially skinny.

He tries to twist out of my grip, but I hold on with all my strength, ignoring the blood spurting from my arm.

Eyes cutting to my injury, he hisses, "How long do you think you can keep this up?"

I headbutt him in reply, my forehead smashing into the drekavac mask. The mask splits. Stars explode in my vision—but hopefully even more in his.

He kicks me in the knee. My kneecap screams in agony. He jerks on his wrists again and pushes me with his whole body.

I lose balance, taking him with me as I fall.

Ouch. I land on my back, air whooshing out of my lungs. To my shock, I'm still gripping his wrists.

He aims the dagger at my neck and presses down. I let go of his left wrist and grasp his right one with both hands to keep the knife from reaching me. The blood from my forearm drips onto my face, but I ignore it, straining with all I've got.

He grabs the knife with his free hand and pushes harder.

I do my best to hold him, but a male, even a skinny elf, is stronger than me.

Inch by inch, the knife descends.

CHAPTER THIRTY

AN INSANE IDEA occurs to me, and there's no time to figure out if it will work or not.

I unclasp my left hand from his wrist.

Now that it's his two arms against one of mine, the knife descends faster.

I regrasp, putting my left hand around his right.

His teeth audibly grind together. "No way you'll snatch my dagger."

If I had any breath left for trash talk, I'd tell him that I don't need to. Instead, I reach for his index finger with mine and tap out the Morse-code-like pattern I saw in the werewolf's dream.

At least, I hope it's the pattern. Stress could've messed with my memory, or for that matter, they could've already disabled the "don't get taken alive" device.

Behind his cracked mask, the elf's eyes widen—then go blank.

When he slumps, I roll him off me and extract the dagger from his grasp.

Sucking in shallow breaths, I sit up. My head spins, my vision spotty with black. Fighting not to faint, I struggle to my feet and nearly cry out at the pain in my knee.

My legs hold me, but just barely.

According to the countdown clock, we have five minutes left. Even if I knew how to disable the thing, I doubt I'd make it through the Icelus in time.

Then again, there are fewer Icelus alive, thanks to Kit. And another bit of good news is that the High Priest must be tired of generating all that lightning because instead of hurling another ball, he shouts, "Free the sacrifices! Some of them sleepwalk. Might keep that giant busy."

Puck him. It's a good plan. If other sleepers are anything like Gertrude, the last thing we want is for Kit to face them. Though... in their sleepwalking, they're just as likely to hurt the bad guys as they are us.

Hopefully.

A dwarf in a Pac-Man mask rushes to execute his leader's order. One by one he unbinds every sleeper, even Cadmael. Right away, some of them—Gertrude included—rise from the beds and start walking aimlessly.

Itzel's grandfather stays put. Unlike the others, he has no sleep disorders and is just drugged. In fact, I can still feel him in REM sleep.

Limping, I move forward, step after agonizing step. My vague plan is to somehow make it to that stage and force the High Priest to stop the bomb by holding my knife to his throat.

No idea how I'll make it so he doesn't fry me with his power, or what I'll do if he's willing to die for his beliefs—which is clearly the case.

"Cover me," I say to Kit as I close the distance between us.

In reply, she stomps and punches everyone near her, clearing me a path.

I limp farther.

Kit clears the path again.

We're a sprint away from the stage, only I can't sprint even to save all those millions of lives.

The High Priest must not think me a real threat because the next lightning ball he hurls flies at Kit. She does the turn-to-pixie trick again and remains unscathed.

I clench my teeth and stagger forward—only to realize Gertrude has wandered my way.

Arms flailing in random movements, she's nearly upon me.

CHAPTER THIRTY-ONE

PUCK. All she needs to do is touch me, and whatever body part she gets, I'll lose.

Except she's dreaming, so she can't see me.

Gambling on that, I turn sideways moments before she can brush her fingers over my face. She passes right by. However, if she keeps heading in that direction, she's going to be a problem for Kit.

I recall something from the time I had to sleepwalk in her during my Council investigation.

Touching her *hair* is okay.

Without giving it too much thought, I whack the back of her head with the knife handle. Then, for good measure, I do it again.

As she drops like a stone, I realize this is the second time I've knocked her out under dire circumstances. One more, and the universe should let me punch her out for free.

I turn back to the stage—and come nose to nose with the High Priest, who promptly aims a kick at my injured knee.

It buckles underneath me, and I fall onto all fours.

Through the haze of pain, I realize this is it.

I've blown my only chance to overpower the gnome.

But hold on. The High Priest isn't the only gnome here who has the information I need. As the inventor of the reactor, Cadmael was the one who'd turned it into a bomb. I bet he can help disable it too. With all the fighting for my life, I didn't get a chance to think of this earlier.

Above me, the High Priest forms another lightning ball and shoots it at Kit.

Kit transforms before getting hit.

I look at the far, far away bed where Cadmael is. If I were there, I'd jump into his dream and wake him up—I can still feel him in REM sleep. But given the state of my leg, I'd have to crawl, which means there's no way I'd make it there in time.

Maybe Kit could throw me. But no, she's too busy with her own battle. Besides, who says I'd land in any condition to dreamwalk? I can barely stay conscious as is.

Then I remember it.

Touchless dreamwalking.

I haven't tried it since the beta testers gave me a boost of power. There's a chance I could make it work now.

Closing my eyes, I extend my hand in the direction of Cadmael's bed and strain to make the connection.

It doesn't work.

I strain harder.

Nope.

I take another route. I imagine standing there, above the elderly gnome's tiny body. I imagine touching his wrinkled forehead, picture how I'd want to clean my hand afterward.

The exercise is effective in that I can almost feel the germy skin under my fingers.

Still, nothing happens.

No, wait.

Something *is* happening.

Something both odd and familiar.

There's a small voice in my head, a voice that seems to be saying, *Who are you, and what do you want?*

Of course. He's a gnome, so I need his consent.

My name is Bailey. I'm a friend of Itzel, your granddaughter. I'm trying to help you. Please let me in.

No mental reply comes, but something yields and I enter the gnome's dream world.

CHAPTER THIRTY-TWO

IGNORING a barrage of questions from Pom, I teleport to the tower of sleepers as soon as I appear in my palace. Swiftly, I find Cadmael and leap into his dream.

A dream that is clearly a nightmare.

Icelus agents are cutting Itzel into small pieces with their ceremonial daggers while Cadmael is tied up and powerless to save his granddaughter.

Not bothering with subtlety, I evaporate Icelus, make Itzel whole, and have her kiss her grandfather on the cheek before sprinting out of the room. Finally, I free the gnome from his nightmare bindings.

He rubs his rope-burned wrists and stares at me with utter incomprehension. "How?"

"You're dreaming," I say calmly. "That was a nightmare. I'm a dreamwalker. My name is Bailey."

"Bailey," he says, still looking stunned. "Itzel mentioned you."

"Great," I say quickly. "Sadly, we don't have time to get better acquainted. Icelus kidnapped you. They made you build a bomb from Vega reactor technology."

He looks like I've slapped him.

Good. I need him to snap out of the dream haze and smell the apocalypse.

"Did it go off?" he asks, his voice small. "How many dead?"

"It hasn't exploded yet, but it could at any moment. Which is why I need you to wake up and disable it."

The gnome's back straightens. "Where is it?"

I turn the room around us into the hundredth floor of the hub building—with Icelus, the bomb, and the rest of it.

"You're here." I point at his bed. "The bomb is there." I point at the podium. "Make sure to avoid him." I point at where the High Priest stands over my body.

Eyeing the High Priest warily, Cadmael nods. "How do I wake up?"

"Just wish to do so," I say.

He closes his eyes.

I help him with a jolt of my power.

He stays, eyes still closed.

Whatever they gave him to make him sleep is strong.

Only I'm stronger. Quadrupling my usual jolt, I shoot Cadmael with it. It works.

He disappears and I find myself back in the tower of sleepers, where Pom stares at me with an unblinking gaze.

"We might survive this yet," I tell him and terminate the dream.

CHAPTER THIRTY-THREE

I COME out of the trance to the sound of a lightning ball smashing into a distant wall.

Kit is in pixie form, which is how she's dodged the projectile again.

Sneaking a peek at the beds, I see Cadmael get up.

Yes! Now we just need to keep the High Priest from noticing this development.

Kit spots Cadmael too and reaches the same conclusion. Abandoning her pixie shape, she turns into a drekavac.

Now we're talking. All she needs is to touch the High Priest with one of those pustule-covered tentacles, and the evil gnome will be writhing on the floor in pain.

Realizing the same thing, the High Priest dodges Kit's appendage and sticks his hand into his pocket.

With all my remaining strength, I grasp my knife. Before I can summon enough energy for a stab, the High Priest notices my intent and jerks his hand out of his pocket.

In his grasp is a vaguely familiar device.

There's a hiss.

I blink in confusion. My knife is in the hands of the High Priest.

Pucking blood loss. It made me miss the moment he took that from me.

Drekavac Kit whips another tentacle at the High Priest.

He slices at it with the dagger.

The tentacle drops to the floor.

Kit's scream is as horrific as her drekavac form's appearance.

Seizing the moment, the High Priest hurls the knife at Kit's head and follows up with a lightning ball.

The blade enters Drekavac Kit's eye. She screams even louder—which is when the lightning ball smashes into her chest.

The drekavac becomes Kit once more, only with a missing hand and a charred hole in the middle of her chest; her clothing wasn't as protective as Valerian's.

The High Priest shoots her with another lightning ball. Then another.

Kit collapses, now a charred corpse.

No. Not Kit. I can't lose—

The High Priest turns to the stage.

Puck. He wasn't supposed to notice Cadmael. But he does—and shoots the older gnome with a ball of lightning.

Cadmael drops to the floor.

Puck, puck, puck.

He was but a few feet away from the bomb. It might as well be thousands of miles now—the digital countdown on the screen reaches zero.

I gasp in horror as the bomb explodes, the wave of heat spreading in a vaguely familiar fashion.

Suddenly, Pom shows up between me and the approaching demise.

His fur is pitch black, his lavender eyes wild. "You said to let you know if you're having a nightmare," he pants. "I'm letting you know."

A nightmare? As in, a dream?

I stop the explosion. Exiting my body, I heal it and jump back in.

Wow. I *am* dreaming. But how? Or the better question is: When did it start?

For a second, I entertain a fantasy that this whole thing, the bomb and Icelus, was a bad dream. But no. Now that the pain isn't clouding my mind, I know exactly what happened.

That device and that hissing sound—I remember them both. When I met the High Priest as Dr. Cipactli, he used this very thing to put himself into REM sleep in order to sample my powers.

Koshmar, he called the drug. He said it creates nightmares that get progressively worse. He also said that the first one always features whatever the sleeper experienced right before falling asleep—in this case, the continuation of our fight.

I float up in relief.

Everything I experienced after that hiss, including Kit's death and the explosion, was a nightmare.

Kit is still alive out in the waking world.

The bomb didn't explode.

Cadmael might still make it.

Maybe. Hopefully.

Regardless, I can't believe Dr. Capactli was offering to use this drug to wake Mom. I'd dodged a huge bullet when I rejected his help. If I'd let Mom be his patient, she'd be in this room as one of the sacrifices.

The bastard. He clearly lied about the most important aspect of this drug. He claimed that if a nightmare gets bad enough, the sleeper wakes up. That's obviously not how it works, else I would've woken up as soon as Kit was killed—and Cadmael when Itzel was tortured. It seems like the real way this Koshmar works is to keep someone in nightmares indefinitely, an evil only a follower of Phobetor would dream up.

I wonder what would've happened to me if I'd accepted his job offer.

Nothing good, I'm sure.

On a hunch, I teleport to the tower of sleepers—specifically into Kit's nook.

It's as I thought.

She's here, dreaming.

"Dr. Cipactli—that is, the High Priest—didn't just spray me," I explain to Pom, who appears beside me. "I need to wake her first."

Grabbing Kit's hand, I jump into her dream.

———

KIT IS in the same cursed room on the hundredth floor—no surprise there. She's watching as the High Priest disembowels me. The me in Kit's dream, that is.

The grief on her face is touching. I didn't realize she cared that much about me.

I freeze the scene, turn the High Priest into a toad, and stand so she can see me.

"What's this?" she asks, eyes rounding.

"A nightmare, and you better wake up." I quickly explain what's happening.

She strains to wake up. I help her with a strong jolt, and she disappears.

As soon as I'm back in the tower of sleepers, I wake myself up.
Time to deal with the High Priest in the waking world.

CHAPTER THIRTY-FOUR

I LOOK up through my half-closed eyelids.

The High Priest clearly doesn't think me and Kit a threat. A lightning ball leaving his hands, he's focused on the stage, where Cadmael is approaching the bomb.

Puck. My nightmare is threatening to become reality.

Itzel's grandfather must remember what I told him about the threat of the other gnome. With surprising speed for his age, he turns and shoots a lightning ball into the path of the one flying at his head.

Boom.

Colliding just a few feet from the stage, the two lightning balls violently explode, the blast knocking Cadmael off his feet.

I glare at the High Priest.

Pucking bastard. He's ruined everything.

There are mere seconds left on the timer—no time for the older gnome to get up and disable the bomb.

Well, if I'm going to die, I'm going to hurt the one responsible before I go. Gritting my teeth at the pain, I raise my knife and stab the High Priest in the foot with all that remains of my strength.

He yells in pain and swings back his other foot to kick me—which is when Kit's giant fist smashes into his jaw.

The devastating punch causes the High Priest to fly up into the air, and as he lands, I make sure my knife is waiting for his heart.

His body jerks on top of me, a wheezing gasp exploding from his lips, and then he slumps, moving no more.

Kit rushes forward and yanks the bleeding gnome off my body.

For once, I'm not bothered by the bodily fluids on my skin.

Barely conscious, I glance at the stage.

Cadmael is on his feet again, but it's too late.

The countdown has reached zero.

Sucking in a breath, I brace for the explosion.

CHAPTER THIRTY-FIVE

THE BOMB KEEPS on beeping but doesn't explode.

I lock eyes with Kit, who looks as confused as I feel.

Then I recall my own question to Valerian: I wasn't sure if the countdown was to the explosion or to the moment the Icelus should leave to escape via the gates. Valerian thought it was the former, but it looks like the Icelus cult isn't suicidal.

The countdown was there to let them know when to bolt.

Which means we have time.

Some time. It's unclear how much.

Luckily, Cadmael isn't looking a gift centaur in the mouth. As soon as he realizes we're alive, he sprints over to the bomb and fiddles with it.

The longest minute of my life passes.

Twenty thousand gray hairs and a pint of my blood later, the reactor-bomb stops beeping. At the same exact moment, the elevator doors open, and a squadron of Senate Guard rushes into the room.

Weakly, I look up at Kit, who's turned into herself. "We're going to live?"

"Hush now." Kit crouches next to me and plants a soft kiss to my forehead. "All will be well."

Good, because I don't think I can hold on much longer.

Exhaling what I hope isn't my last breath, I pass out.

CHAPTER THIRTY-SIX

I COME TO.

Well, that's a relief. I half expected the afterlife, but I doubt this is it. I can hear familiar voices arguing in the distance—not something I'd expect after passing on.

I open my eyes. The hospital room is too bright, so I shut them again.

"Guys," Felix says. "I think she woke up."

I attempt Project Open Eyes once more. The faces of Ariel, Kit, Felix, Itzel, and Valerian are all within sneezing distance from my face, and all are speaking at the same time.

"You're okay." My voice is hoarse as I force out the words. "I was wor—"

"Here." Valerian grabs a glass of water from a table by my bed and places the straw sticking out of it into my mouth.

I take a small sip.

My throat feels better, and I realize I have an IV in my arm, along with tubes in other places and monitoring equipment attached to my chest.

How bad was my condition for me to need all this?

"You're going to be fine," Valerian says as if reading my mind. "You had a nano surgery on your knee, and you should be able to walk on it, no problem. They didn't use any vampire blood during treatment, just pumped you with fluids. You lost so much blood you're bound to be weak."

"What about you?" I croak out, indeed feeling so weak the question takes an effort.

"All fine," he says, his sensual lips curved in a warm smile.

"The doctors here rely on vamp blood too much," Ariel grumbles. "I had to tell them repeatedly not to use it on me."

"Same," Felix says.

"I didn't need medical help." Kit winks at me. "Unlike some, I can handle myself in a fight."

Ariel and Felix object loudly, but I miss what they say due to a bout of dizziness. Breathing deeper, I crane my neck forward to catch the straw and suck in another sip. The cool water makes me feel a little better—until I accidentally spill some.

"You made her wet," Kit says to Valerian and pantomimes lasciviously with her eyebrows.

"Seriously?" Itzel asks at the same time as Ariel rolls her eyes and Felix slowly shakes his head.

"Did I hear you arguing earlier?" I ask, my voice finally my own. "You were loud."

Valerian gives everyone a narrow-eyed stare. "We don't want to worry her."

I feel all the blood drain from my face. "Is it Mom?"

Itzel shakes her head. "She's in the room next door, next to my grandfather."

Her grandfather, of course. I almost forgot. "Is he okay?" I ask.

"Fine, tell her," Valerian snaps. "All this guessing is worse."

"It's not Gramps," Itzel says. "Check any media feed. You'll understand."

I enable the VR and skim the headlines. "Oh. They know about the bomb."

Know is an understatement. The news outlets are reporting every tiny detail, and I soon learn why. Wrakar, the necromancer, scheduled a message to go out. In what they've dubbed the Necromancer Manifesto, he lamented that his kind were second-class citizens on Gomorrah and waxed poetic about how the bomb was justice for his people.

"What a pile of mooft crap." I turn off the VR. "Icelus didn't create the bomb for the necromancer kind. They did it to give people nightmares."

"Which they've succeeded in doing despite our efforts." Valerian's face looks so thunderous the others take a step back.

"I blame the Senate," Itzel says. "When the media asked them if the

Necromancer Manifesto was true, they confirmed it, adding that they thwarted the plot."

Ariel curls her upper lip. "Typical politicians. Taking credit for our work."

Felix lifts his hand, as if to touch Valerian's tense shoulder, then decides against it. "Just give me the word, and I'll hack into—"

"No," Valerian says, noticeably calmer. "Icelus won this round. Messing with the media or the Senate would just make things worse."

I suck in another sip of water with a slurp. "They didn't win. Millions didn't die. We didn't die. True, this news will give some nightmares, but not nearly as many as would be the case if the bomb had actually gone off."

"Which is exactly what we were arguing about," Kit says. "Your boyfriend disagrees. He thinks the situation is worse now. The millions we saved are just more people to dream the nightmares."

Boyfriend? Is that what they all think?

Okay, I'll take it.

Valerian's jaw remains tight. He doesn't seem to have noticed Kit's premature labeling of our relationship—or if he does, he doesn't care. "What I'm saying is that Icelus succeeded," he says grimly.

"Only if you believe that nightmares really do feed some deity of theirs," I say. "But since all that is baloney, *we* won."

His stormy expression softens. "You're right," he says, though I don't think he means it. "More importantly, you need to rest."

Ah, that. He might be right there. The effort of talking does make me feel like I've just completed a triathlon. Still, I'm not ready to get tucked in yet—not until I erase that worry from his gorgeous face.

"Can we talk in private?" I whisper, holding his gaze.

In an eyeblink, our surroundings change to a soothing meadow. My friends are no longer visible. Only Valerian is here, gazing down at me with those ocean-deep, hypnotic eyes.

"Can they hear us?" I ask.

He approaches the bed. "No. Can't see us either, at least not this version of us."

I try to sit up, but a wave of dizziness undercuts my efforts, so I settle for frowning up at him. "You almost died. Twice."

"We both did." His face twists with regret as he leans over me. "I'm sorry. I should've never gotten you involved."

"Then you'd be dead." If I had the energy to smack some sense into him, I would, but my arms feel too heavy at the moment.

"You don't understand," he says, frowning. "I—"

I push up onto my elbows and kiss him smack on the lips. His soft, yummy lips… My breathing quickens, a wave of heat chasing away the worst of the weakness as I—

An angry beep sounds, and Valerian abruptly pulls away. The illusion disappears, revealing the faces of my worried friends and the source of the noise—my heart monitor.

An uber nurse rushes into the room, moving almost too fast for my eyes to track. With the same speed, she examines me and adjusts the monitors before declaring that I'm fine but shouldn't be overstimulated in my current state.

I'm not sure I agree with that assessment. I'm not a doctor, but I feel like if Valerian stimulated me properly, I'd be good as new.

Unfortunately, that's not to be. The nurse herds everyone out of the room and goes to town on my IV, saying, "That should help you relax."

If by "relax" she means "go under," sure.

As my lids grow heavy, I realize something.

I kissed Valerian. In the real world. Without worrying about microbes.

That's huge. I can't wait until I'm all better, so I can make sure that wasn't just a fluke. There's going to be vigorous testing. Maybe double-blind control studies as well—as in, with both of us wearing blindfolds, and maybe handcuffs in his case.

With a smile on my face, I let the drug drag me under.

———

I WAKE UP FEELING BETTER. Infinitely better. The doctors must agree, as I only have some of the medical paraphernalia attached to me now.

Sitting up with ease, I look around.

The only other person in the room is Valerian. He's sleeping in a chair.

Aww. He stayed with me. That earns him another kiss. Maybe several.

My bladder yanks my mind from sexy thoughts to mundane reality.

I swing my legs down and see if I can stand up.

Yep. The knee is as good as new. I detach the heart monitor and the rest, and go into the bathroom to take care of business.

As I exit, I come face to face with Dr. Xipil.

"Ah, good. You're awake," he says.

I nod at the sleeping Valerian, then put a finger to my lips and gesture for the door. The gnome doctor nods, and we tiptoe out, closing the door behind us.

"I wanted to apologize," he says in a low voice. "I had no idea Dr. Cipactli was involved in a terrorist plot. Had I known—"

"Don't mention it." I beam a reassuring smile at him. "How's my mom?"

He glances at the nearby door. "We've just brought her back from the other hospital. Sadly, there's no change in her condition."

I walk over to the door in question and open it.

Seeing Mom hooked up to all those machines is again a punch to the heart—doubly painful now that I know she got this way because of me. I try not to dwell on that last part, though. Not when I can do something a lot more practical.

"I'd like to walk in her dreams again," I tell Dr. Xipil.

"Now?" He looks at the clock.

It's just past midnight.

I nod. "I'm feeling very strong. Can you get someone to help you subdue me in case I die during the subdream stage?"

He gestures in his VR, and a minute later, the uber nurse from before steps into the room.

We tell her what's what, and I approach Mom.

No touchless business now. I reach out and place my hand on her forehead.

"I'm sorry," I whisper. "I'll fix this."

Closing my eyes, I fall in.

CHAPTER THIRTY-SEVEN

A BLACK OCEAN is under my feet, and fiery skies are above my head. A huge creature is flying at me. It looks like an eyeball, but its eyelashes are snakes the size of anacondas—with fangs ready to bite.

A furry pitchfork grows out of my wrist.

The pupil of the giant eye dilates, and I get the strange feeling that a malevolent intelligence is examining me, scanning and filing away my every molecule.

The snake closest to me strikes at my neck. The fangs bite into my flesh, and I feel the poison beginning to spread through my bloodstream.

I thrust with my pitchfork.

The furry weapon enters the eyeball like a fork into jelly.

The snakes/eyelashes yelp in pain before slumping as one, creating the illusion of the eye closing.

———

I'M in my dream palace, blood gushing from the wound and my consciousness flickering in and out from the poison. I escape my body, heal the wound, and force the poison out, causing it to hang like a black cloud above me. Jumping back in, I dissipate the cloud and exhale a sigh of relief.

"Another close call." Pom's furry face is grim, his color black. "You need to stop doing this."

"I will as soon as Mom is out of her coma," I say and teleport to her nook in the tower of sleepers.

Making myself invisible, I touch Mom the same way as in the waking world.

———

A TEENAGE me is on the bathroom floor somewhere on Earth, if the primitive toilets are anything to go by. Her/my head is bashed in, brains spread out on the white tile. The windows in the place are black, so the only light comes from the flickering halogen lamps that add a macabre touch to the crime scene.

Mom stands above me holding a heavy porcelain toilet tank cover that's covered in blood.

Ugh. She couldn't bother to kill me in a more hygienic manner? I think I'd rather get my throat sliced with a scalpel—assuming it's sterile.

Ignoring Mom's nightmare, I gather all my power into a massive "wake up" jolt.

She doesn't wake up.

I close my eyes and strain so hard my nails pierce my palms.

This jolt doesn't work either.

Healing my wound, I try the jolt again. And again. And again.

After what feels like a thousand attempts, I have no choice but to give up.

The disappointment is bitter on my tongue. Only the knowledge that the *Lucid Dreamer* project isn't complete yet keeps me from utter despondency. I should get a much bigger boost when the game goes live, and I'll try it again then.

It's bound to work when I have more power. I have to believe that.

For now, I might as well jump out and let Mom be.

I'm about to do just that when my gaze lands on the black windows.

The secrets behind them call to me like sirens to lonely sailors.

Was Felix right? Is there something horrible Mom's hiding? Could she have tried to kill herself so I wouldn't learn whatever is behind one of these windows?

More importantly, could I use that secret to make her wake up?

Like the proverbial cat who bites the dust due to its overpowering curiosity, I float toward the nearest window.

Below me, Mom is too busy with her daughter slaughter to notice.

Before I can talk myself out of doing it, I fly into the onyx-like glass.

CHAPTER THIRTY-EIGHT

JUST LIKE BEFORE, I plunge into an icy black lake.

Previously, my powers couldn't help me swim to the shore, but what about now that I've gotten a boost?

I will myself to become lighter than water so I can float.

It doesn't help.

I will the water to become saltier, but that doesn't work either.

Fine. I'll swim.

Stroke after stroke, I edge closer to the nearest shore. I focus only on swimming. And swimming. And swimming. My breathing grows labored, yet the shore is still far away.

After what feels like hours, my every muscle starts to ache.

The shore is still a mile away.

I can't sink. If I do, I'll be kicked out of the dream world with my powers depleted. At least, that's what happened the last time I drowned under similar circumstances.

Desperately gulping in air, I swing my arms and kick with my legs, letting the motions become my only reality.

When a stray thought arises—like the one about the black windows I saw in Valerian's dreams—I banish it and refocus on the swim. When I'm about to give up, I meditate on a simple truth: My muscles are not really tearing into bits. It's not oxygen that I lack. This is just a dream.

This seems to help for a while, and eventually, I spot the shore nearby.

Harnessing all my willpower, I speed up so much Michael Phelps would be jealous.

As soon as my hand touches the dirt of the shore, the lake and the muscle spasms in my legs vanish without a trace.

———

MOM IS in a spacious room with three other people. There's a bathtub made of crystal in the middle, and she's floating in it.

Oh, and she's pregnant. More than pregnant—she's in the process of pushing the baby out.

Wow. Since this is a black-window memory, that means Mom doesn't remember giving birth to me. That must be odd.

Greedy for all the info, I examine the man holding Mom's hand. He's got bronzed skin, amber eyes, and my chin.

My breath hitches.

Can it be?

"Push, honey." He kisses the back of Mom's hand. "That's it. I love you."

It has to be him. My father. The man I don't know anything about.

"Push!" the second person in the tub, the midwife, orders, staring intently at the crowning baby head.

Wait a second. The language they speak—I don't remember hearing it before, yet I understand perfectly.

"You're doing good," says an older woman holding Mom's other hand. "Almost there."

She looks just like Mom. A grandmother or an older sister, maybe—as in, my aunt?

The baby screams.

The midwife hands the gooey newborn to my father with a wide grin.

"It's a girl," he says, his eyes shining with joy. "A baby girl."

To my surprise, the midwife tells Mom, "Keep pushing."

Pushing after giving birth? Is it to get the placenta or something?

A second baby crowns.

Wait, what? I stare uncomprehendingly as the midwife goes through all the motions.

The second baby screams.

The midwife gives the second newborn to my mom.

What. Is. Happening?

"Do you know what you're going to call them?" the aunt/grandmother asks my father, taking the first infant from him.

He beams at her. "Asha, for my late mother." He looks at the baby in Mom's arms. "And Bailey, after her grandmother." He winks at the older woman—who must be the grandmother in question—and lifts the baby dubbed Bailey as if he were the monkey shaman presenting the new lion king.

My grandmother grins in delight and coos at the infants, but I don't register what she says.

My mind is spinning, my invisible mouth wide open.

A sister.

A twin.

Where is she? How come I don't remember anything about her? For that matter, where is my father? Or this namesake grandmother? Why don't I know anything about them either?

"Let me hold one," Mom says hoarsely, reaching for the baby-me when the memory transforms into another one.

———

MOM AND A MUCH OLDER ME—AROUND seven—are walking through the hub on Gomorrah.

Since the hub is on top of the skyscraper, there's a great view down below, and both Mom and little me are staring at it as if they've never seen it before.

In fact, they look as though they've never seen a skyscraper before.

"This will be our new home," Mom says to little me, gesturing at the picturesque view.

"Our textile?" little me asks, eyes glued to the skyline.

"The word is *exile*. And we're never to speak of what happened before we came here."

Little me gives Mom a somber glance. "We're not?"

Mom crouches so our eyes are at the same level. "We've always lived here. Our lives before today were just a dream that we created using our powers."

The little me nods, her chin quivering.

I stare at them, stunned.

Could what Mom says be true?

Was the birth of two girls a memory of a dream?

No. My powers knew it was a real memory. Just as this one is.

"Let's go." Mom grabs little me by the hand, and the dream jumps to another memory.

———

WE'RE in a room covered from floor to ceiling with pottery paraphernalia, everything from wheel to kiln. Bailey, my grandmother, is molding a vase on the wheel. Looking on with a serene expression is Mom, who's holding two little girls by their hands.

Both resemble me, and I realize that my twin is of the identical variety —and that we were still together at this age, which must've been four or five.

That's definitely old enough to form memories, yet I don't recall this at all.

Oh, and it's clear that these memories are coming to me out of order: birth, seven, now four.

"Come, dear ones," the grandmother says.

The two little girls shuffle over.

"You can touch," she tells them.

Grinning mischievously, the twins leave palmprints on the sides of the vase.

The grandmother smiles in approval and deposits the vase into the kiln.

Wait a second.

I know that vase.

I broke it years later, on Gomorrah.

Mom was sad when it happened, as if it had sentimental value. Yet she couldn't have remembered this moment when the vase broke, not when the memory was locked in the black window.

Maybe these memories aren't as locked away as I thought—or the vase was precious simply as a memento from the forgotten past.

When the grandmother gives the vase to Mom as a gift, the memory terminates.

———

THIS ROOM IS the one where Asha and I were born.

Mom is holding my father's hand. Around them are a few adults I haven't seen before, though one man looks vaguely familiar. At their feet, my twin and I are about six years old and playing with two boys of similar ages. One of the boys also reminds me of someone, in the same indefinable way as the older man.

"I'm sorry, Davu. I don't think there's a choice," my father says to the familiar-looking man. "The prophecy—"

"Was vague," says Davu dismissively. "If—"

One of the boys pulls on his sleeve. "Dad, can Bailey and I go to the garden?"

Davu nods, and little me and the boy race out of the room.

"Mommy, can Kojo and I also go?" Asha asks.

Mom smiles. "Of course."

Giggling maniacally, my twin chases after the boy—Kojo—as if she were a werewolf and he a tasty hare.

As soon as they're out of the room, the memory terminates.

"WHERE'S BAILEY?" Asha asks Mom as they walk through alien-looking vegetation. Some of the enormous blue-green trees remind me of Earth's baobabs, others of sea coral.

"She's got an upset stomach," Mom says. "Daddy is with her."

With that, the memory ends, but another starts right away, a birthday party where my twin and I are playing with the boys from before, plus a dozen other children.

The next memory is of Mom tucking in the two twins, her face soft as she croons to us.

As I witness it all, I can't understand why Mom would want to forget all of this. Unless… is this black window something someone did to her? But if so, who? And why?

The common denominator in all these recollections seems to be Asha, my twin.

The next memory is of Mom, Dad, my sister, and me on a hike through a forest with that same alien vegetation. This time, I catch a glimpse of the sky—and exhale in wonder. Up above, besides clouds, are forests and buildings. The ground seems to warp upon itself, as if the planet we're on is not a sphere but an odd pretzel.

The next memory starts before I can puzzle out the strange geometry of the surroundings. It's of the four of us playing some game with cards made of an exotic material that reminds me of ivory.

Another memory follows, where Mom and the twins are watching the same strange sky at night. Not surprisingly, the star constellations are completely unfamiliar.

The peaceful stargazing shifts into yet another memory—and as I realize what I'm seeing, the pit of my stomach turns to ice.

CHAPTER THIRTY-NINE

MY SISTER and I look to be about seven. We're running through a clearing in the woods populated by the plants from the earlier memories.

Both girls are screaming in terror, and for a good reason.

Our parents are chasing after them with machetes made out of strange, non-shiny, ceramic-like material.

No. This can't be what it looks like. Surely the machetes are just for clearing vegetation, and this is some weird game. But the girls' terror seems all too real, and the weapons aside, something isn't right with our parents.

It's their faces. There's a magma-like fire in their eyes and a complete lack of emotion on their features.

Still, could this be a game regardless? Something to do with a holiday like Halloween?

A whole crowd of people is chasing after my parents. In the front, I spot my grandmother, Davu with his wife and son, and Kojo and his parents.

"Stop!" Davu screams at my parents.

They don't respond, just keep chasing the girls.

One of the twins trips over a root.

The other keeps running for a few moments, then looks back, panting. "Asha, no!" my younger self gasps and rushes to her.

Asha is crying.

Little Bailey tries to lift her.

The parents close in.

Our father faces the crowd while Mom raises her machete.

"Mommy, no!" little me screams.

The machete whooshes by little Bailey's cheek and bites into Asha's neck.

Blood gushes out of the wound, spraying little me all over.

Asha's severed head rolls away.

Little Bailey screams.

I don't want to believe my eyes—except my eyes have nothing to do with what I've just witnessed, only my powers. And though I want to deny it, my powers leave no room for doubt.

This is a memory.

A memory that explains why I don't know my sister.

Numbly, I watch as Mom's strange eyes gaze at little me, who's sobbing uncontrollably. Then Mom's entire body tenses, her face twisting with alternating expressions of blankness and horror. Her eyes flicker between magma-like fire and normal brown, and her left hand grabs her right, as if trying to steal the machete from it. Finally, her eyes stay brown, and the horror eclipses all else on her face.

She looks at the bloody machete in her hands. Then at headless Asha.

With a raw, guttural moan, she spins around—just as my father smashes a fist into her temple.

The memory terminates.

THE NEXT MEMORY is of Mom reading a bedtime story to the three-year-old twins.

The one after that is another hike, but I barely pay attention to it.

I'm reeling, unable to process the impossible.

I had a sister, a twin, and Mom killed her.

That must be why she wanted to forget everything to do with Asha, and why she was so terrified to have me dreamwalk in her. Some part of her must know that she forgot something awful—and this might even explain the dreams where she was killing me. I look just like Asha would if she were alive.

Those nightmares echoed the terrible truth.

Mom killed my sister.

No wonder she's been depressed for as long as I've known her. Even without recalling the details, she must've been in constant psychic pain.

And is this why I don't remember Asha either? Because I witnessed her murder at the hand of our mother? I'm no shrink, but children have been known to block out traumas far less significant than this.

Why did Mom do this? And what was the deal with her eyes at the time of the murder? That magma I saw in her gaze was weirdly familiar. It's almost like—

The memories halt, and I find myself in an environment that reminds me of those eyes.

Black ocean is under my feet, with skies that seem to be on fire up above.

It's the place where subdream monsters attack, only I'm not in a subdream.

In fact, I've only seen this backdrop outside of subdreams once—when I dreamwalked in that necromancer.

Puck. I completely forgot about that until now.

A presence congeals out of nothingness to stand on the ocean in front of me, a humanoid creature of enormous proportions.

It's a frightening sight, even if it's hard to pinpoint why. The face looking at me is just as beautiful as the last time, with features that have a supernatural kind of symmetry.

It's the exact same face as in the necromancer's dream, though logic states he and my mom shouldn't be dreaming the same thing.

Not unless they both somehow saw it.

The black holes on the terribly beautiful face scan me more carefully this time, and all I can do is stand there and stare up at it, paralyzed.

"You're you. And alive." Like in the necromancer's dream, its booming voice conjures my every fear.

I swallow hard. "Who are you? What are you?"

"I'm Phobetor." The vibrations of the being's reply make the blood freeze in my veins, even before I comprehend the significance of that name. "Your existence is a blight."

My stunned mind latches on to the strange phrase. A blight—that's what the subdream monsters said to me earlier. This must be the master they were talking about, not Mom.

Phobetor's black-hole eyes narrow, and its truck-sized arm reaches for me.

With an impossible effort of will, I snap out of my paralysis and jolt myself awake.

———

BACK IN THE REAL WORLD, I hold myself together long enough to reassure the uber nurse and Dr. Xipil that I'm not homicidally insane. Then I rush into the bathroom and empty my stomach.

When I can breathe again, I let myself process the last thing I saw.

The terrible, beautiful being called itself Phobetor—same as the deity Icelus worship. A god of nightmares, said to benefit from all the misfortune in the Cogniverse.

It's impossible.

Unthinkable.

Utterly ridiculous.

I can't believe I'm even entertaining this idea, but... are Icelus right?

Does Phobetor really exist?

If so, what does he have to do with me and my mom?

I stare at my ashen face in the mirror, the damning memory-dream I just witnessed playing in front of my eyes. Asha and me, our parents with machetes... the strange hue of their eyes...

And Phobetor, right there in Mom's dreams.

A million questions race through my mind, but I can only latch on to one.

If Phobetor is real, is he the reason for the horror I witnessed?

Is he why Mom killed my twin?

DREAM CHASER

BOOK 3

CHAPTER ONE

I STUMBLE out of the bathroom in Mom's hospital room and nearly collide with Dr. Xipil.

"Are you okay?" the gnome doctor asks.

I'm far from okay, but if I tell him why, he might want to have me talk to a shrink. The injuries I suffered during the fight with Icelus are healed, but mentally and emotionally, I'm a wreck.

Case in point: I'm seriously considering the existence of Phobetor, the god of nightmares Icelus worship. Worse yet, I'm wondering if said deity made my mom kill my sister.

What little blood had returned to my face rushes away again.

I had a sister. A twin.

It's as hard to wrap my mind around that fact as it is to fathom my mom killing her.

Her name was Asha, and I watched her die before I'd even accepted the fact that she'd existed.

What I wouldn't give for a chance to have met her, or to at least remember her.

"Do you want to lie down?" Dr. Xipil asks, sounding more worried. "You look like you're about to pass out."

I give him a forced smile. "I'm fine. Just disappointed I failed to rouse Mom."

Dr. Xipil glances at the bed where Mom lies and sighs. "You'll try again. You're bound to succeed eventually."

Not ready to discuss an evil deity that might be waiting for me in Mom's dreams, I simply nod.

Mom looks serene in her comatose state. Calm, even. But that has to be a lie. Her dreams are of killing a daughter—because that's what she'd done in the waking world.

In a very real way, I don't know my own mother. Makes me wonder if you can know anyone, or trust them.

The doctor clears his throat. "You have loyal friends."

Puck. I have to snap out of this, or the good doctor will insist I go back to my hospital bed.

I head for the door, and as casually as I can, ask, "What makes you say that?"

"They all recovered much faster than you did, but they wouldn't leave your side until your husband chased them away." He opens the door for me.

"My husband?" I'm too shocked to walk through.

Dr. Xipil gestures at my room across the hall. "Boyfriend?"

"Oh, you mean Valerian." I step out into the hallway. "He's neither my husband nor my boyfriend."

Not yet—but fingers crossed.

The corners of Dr. Xipil's eyes crinkle. "Are you sure he knows that? Because he definitely acted like a significant other while you were under. The nursing staff and I had to walk on eggshells."

Really? Aww. "Sounds like I should check on him."

"Good idea. If he wakes up and you're not there, he'll freak."

"Oh, come on, that doesn't sound like him."

"You didn't see what I saw," the doctor says. "If you need anything else, let me know tomorrow afternoon. My shift is now officially over."

I thank him, and he hurries away as I head over to my room.

Sticking my head in, I see Valerian slumped in a chair, his dark, thick hair disheveled around his beautifully symmetrical face. His intense ocean-blue eyes are closed, his kissable lips slightly parted.

Quietly, I tiptoe in. He's in REM sleep, according to my newfound REM-sensing ability and the fact that his eyes are moving behind his eyelids.

Hmm. Maybe I don't need to wake him. The fact that he's dreaming is an opportunity. I could, for example, talk to him in his sleep… or snoop in those black windows he's got.

Yep. I'm going for it.

Resisting the temptation to walk over and touch his chiseled face, I initiate the dreamwalk remotely. Might as well practice the new power.

Just as I did with Itzel's grandfather, I imagine standing next to Valerian, close enough to breathe in his clean pine scent. I imagine touching his carved jaw and picture how that hint of stubble would feel under my fingers. I imagine how my heart would beat faster and heat would spread—

To my disappointment, I don't need to imagine this further, because with the familiar whiff of ozone and the sensation of falling, I drop into his dream.

———

AS SOON AS I appear in the surreally colored, manna-scented lobby of my dream palace, Pom shows up—and between the expression on the looft's furry face and his deep black coloring, I can tell he knows a lot of what I've learned in Mom's black window.

Taking the scenic route to the tower of sleepers, I fill in any details Pom doesn't know and reassure him that I don't magically have the answers to his million questions—and that I'd like to know the why and how of Phobetor and my twin as much as he does.

"Ah," Pom says sagely when he spots Valerian sleeping on his bed. "You're here looking for a distraction."

I brush my fingers over Valerian's dimpled chin without willing myself to go in yet. "I guess you could say that."

Pom's triangular ears take on a light orange hue. "And how are things going between the two of you?"

"What?"

The pupils in his lavender eyes morph into red hearts. "Are you in love?"

I jerk my hand away from Valerian's face. "Are you crazy? I don't even know what that would feel like. We barely know each other. Plus—"

"You might be overthinking it." Pom perches on my shoulder. "Is it because you've never had a boyfriend?"

I shoo him off. "I'm thinking just the right amount. You should give that a try someday."

He lands on the edge of Valerian's bed. "Just don't go looking for reasons not to love him. We both know you want to."

It's official. I'm getting love-life advice from a looft, a creature that reproduces by asexual budding.

Shaking my head, I dive into Valerian's dream.

CHAPTER TWO

VALERIAN IS SITTING on the floor in a dingy room with paint peeling off the walls. There are folding chairs and a strong aroma of stale coffee. One of the windows is black, but I don't go for it yet. This dream is a memory, and I'm curious to learn about Valerian's past.

Making myself invisible, I let the dream progress.

All the chairs except one are occupied by teenagers, and everyone is unaware of Valerian, which means he's making himself invisible with his illusionist powers. The only adult in the room is a person I've met—Princess Peach, Felix and Ariel's roommate.

Speaking of Felix, his girlfriend, Maya, is here too, sitting next to Princess Peach.

Then another familiar person shows up, someone I never wanted to see again.

Hekima, the illusionist murderer who nearly cost me my life, walks in.

He doesn't notice Valerian either, so an illusionist can fool another illusionist. Good to know.

"Today we continue the subject of the Otherlands," Hekima says as a way of introduction. "Let's begin with a quick review of last week."

He then goes over what everyone should already know—that there's such a thing as Otherlands and that they are what Earth humans would call "universes." He explains that these worlds have different stars and galaxies, and even the flow of time can vary among them. There's an infinite number of them as far as anyone knows, but the gates Cognizant use lead to only an insignificant subset.

This must be Orientation, a kind of school where Earth Cognizant teens learn about secret Cognizant stuff. On Gomorrah, we just call that school, but I can see why they'd need a special class on Earth, what with the Mandate and all.

"I alluded to the dangers of the Otherlands the last time we met," Hekima says when he's finished with the basics. "Today I really want to drive home that point."

He raises his arms, and pulsing red energy streams from his fingers into everyone's heads—including Valerian's.

The room goes away, replaced with what looks like a radioactive wasteland.

Everyone except me starts gasping for nonexistent air. Hekima snaps his fingers once again, causing the world to change to that of a lush forest.

"There are Otherlands where the environment itself will kill you," he says. "But even seemingly friendly ones like this world can have creatures so dangerous no Cognizant would dare to live or even travel within it."

A cute deer-like creature runs out of the forest, followed by one of the worst monsters in existence.

"That's a drekavac," Hekima explains, but what he says next is lost on everyone because the drekavac catches up with the deer and touches it with one of its pustule-infested limbs.

The deer screams and collapses to the ground.

The drekavac looms over its victim, but Hekima snaps his fingers again, and the classroom comes back.

Why show these children such horror? And why is Valerian here?

"Getting killed by a drekavac is the worst fate that can befall anyone," Hekima says. "Their mere touch brings about such debilitating pain that weaker victims die from it." He looks over the horrified faces. "The environment, the flora, and the fauna are just a few of the many ways you can perish in the Otherlands. Some gates are one way only—so no one knows what happens there—and other gates lead to worlds that we, the Cognizant, turned into deathtraps."

He snaps his fingers again. The classroom morphs into a deserted landscape, where two scary-looking men are chasing someone.

"This is what's left of the world where Tartarus last ruled," Hekima says just as the two men catch their prey.

Tartarus? Now there's a figure you bring up if you want to give people nightmares.

"The humans on this world know about the Cognizant and rightfully blame us for the desolation," Hekima continues, pointing at the endless dunes. "They wait by the gates to catch one of our kind, and if they succeed, they do horrific things to them."

Right on cue, the two men start to cannibalize their catch.

That's just great. The nightmares are guaranteed now. At school, we also learned to be careful traveling in the Otherlands, but it didn't require such theatrics.

Hekima keeps on talking about the doom and gloom of the Otherlands as I walk over to where Valerian is sitting.

"The point I'm trying to make is really simple," Hekima is saying when I pay attention to him again. "Be very careful when traveling to the Otherlands, and do not enter any gates unless you're absolutely sure where they lead." The horrific scenes repeat in quick succession. "Even if you think you know the gate is safe, I strongly advise you think twice before entering, and definitely wait until—"

I ignore the rest.

There's a folder next to Valerian I hadn't noticed before.

Icelus Suspects, the label says.

When Valerian opens the folder, a picture of Hekima is on top of the papers inside. Looking between the picture and the real man, Valerian writes on the paper below, "Eighty percent sure."

Wow. Hekima was Icelus? It would explain why he made this lesson so scary—and is consistent with his murdering personality.

"We're almost out of time." Hekima looks at his watch. "Does anyone have any questions?"

Valerian leaps to his feet.

Princess Peach raises her hand, nearly jumping out of her seat in excitement. Hekima calls on her.

Someone whispers something like "teacher's pet," but she ignores them as she rattles out, "Who made the gates? Who discovered the Otherlands? When? How? Could—"

In reply, Hekima goes into the same theory we learned on Gomorrah —that the gates were made by legendary, powerful teleporters dubbed *the gate makers*. He then suggests the obvious—that there are probably worlds without the Cognizant, left as sanctuaries, or worlds where Cognizant exist but don't have gates that allow them to leave.

Finally, he gets up and walks to the door without waiting for any follow-up questions. Princess Peach raises her hand again but puts it down when Hekima leaves the class, with Valerian following.

Outside the classroom, Valerian stalks Hekima to his destination, a small apartment.

Checking his watch again, Hekima plops into his bed.

Wait, what? Why was he in such a rush to take a nap?

Valerian shakes his head, takes out his folder, and changes the probability to ninety percent.

I almost reveal myself so I can ask Valerian why sleeping on a tight schedule might make someone more likely to be a part of Icelus, but I resist.

And it's a good thing I do.

The Orientation dream stops, but another one begins, again a memory.

————

A NEARLY NAKED Valerian is sitting on a wooden slab in a large windowless room, with sweat beading on his hard-muscled body.

Yum. I like where this is going. Not that I have many options but to keep observing what happens next—the black window is missing. Then again, it might be around, but I can't see it. It's so steamy in the room—in the literal sense—that it's barely possible to see a foot away. This is clearly a sauna, a nightmare invention for those of us who care about proper hygiene.

"Illusionist," says the vapor around the room in a melodious, Russian-accented masculine voice.

"Seer," Valerian replies, looking around. "You might want to show yourself."

With a *whoosh*, the vapor gathers in a single spot a few yards away from Valerian.

Valerian wipes a stream of sweat from his eyes, and by the time he completes the gesture, the vapor is gone, replaced by a man covered only by a small towel.

Tangled blond hair and wild beard aside, this man is almost as impressive as Valerian himself. If I hadn't heard him be referred to as a seer, I'd guess him to be an uber.

Wait a sec. *A seer.* There are a couple of different varieties of them, but all are among the rarest Cognizant types—up there with dragons and healers.

The seer tugs on his beard. "You're wise to heed my summons. I have to repay the favor I owe you today."

Valerian wipes a rivulet of sweat from his brow. "You do?"

"After this conversation, you and I will never meet again," the seer says solemnly.

"Right." Valerian shakes his head. "And I take it you already know what I'm going to ask?"

"I know all the things you considered asking." The seer grabs a nearby ladle, dips it into a water bucket, and pours water into a stove-like contraption nearby. With a hiss, more vapor fills the room. "You want to know how to get rid of Hekima, the newest Icelus agent you've found," the seer continues. "And you want to do it in such a way that it can never be linked back to you—which is difficult due to your obvious ambition to take Hekima's place on the New York Council."

"I can see why your kind has the reputation it does." Valerian pushes back his sweat-soaked hair. "You know my questions. Do you have an answer?"

"Send an anonymous email to Kain, the new head of the New York Enforcers," the seer says. "Tell him you know of the murder investigation Kain is leading, and that you have a perfect candidate for him."

Despite the room's heat, I feel cold.

It can't be.

He wouldn't.

He didn't.

Valerian frowns. "Who?"

"The dreamwalker who's done a few jobs for you," the seer says. "Suggest her, and you'll get what you want."

"You've got to be pucking kidding me," I mutter.

Valerian looks right at me.

Puck. I didn't mean to say that out loud.

Valerian's frown deepens, and he must assert the reality of his dream the way Hekima once did, because I become visible against my will.

He squints at me. "Bailey? How are you here?"

My disbelief transforms into fury. "You threw me under the bus, didn't you?" I advance on him. "Kain and his vampires kidnapped me and forced me to work for the Council because *you* suggested it. How could you do that to me?"

He blanches. "I'm sorry." He stands up, sweat dripping everywhere. "I didn't know you when I spoke to Yaroslav. We'd only emailed each other."

"And you think you know me now? Because I certainly don't know you."

And before I do something I'll later regret, I jolt myself out of his dream.

CHAPTER THREE

I EMERGE from the sleepwalking trance in utter fury. It's a good thing I did my dreamwalking from a distance. I don't want to be touching him right now.

Valerian's eyes pop open.

I narrow mine.

He jackknifes to his feet.

I turn and sprint to the door.

There's a sound of footsteps behind me, so I slam the door in his face and run down the corridor.

"I have as much right to be angry with you as you do with me," he shouts from behind me.

Reaching the elevator, I stab the button and glance back.

He's twenty feet away but gaining on me quickly.

"Why were you in my dreams?" he yells. "Were you hoping to find something about Soma? You know how I feel about that!"

The elevator doors open, and I leap inside, smashing the button for the ground floor. "Your whole 'I didn't know you' excuse is weak," I yell back as the doors slide closed. "The first time we met face to face was in that castle."

He lunges at the doors, hand extended, but doesn't make it.

Whew.

The last thing I want is to continue that conversation—or look at his gorgeous, traitorous face.

He's mad at me? Our crimes can't even compare. True, he was cagey when I asked him about Soma—the place where his and my kind seem to live—but I didn't even know his black windows and Soma had anything to do with each other. He, on the other hand, was directly responsible for that whole mess with the New York Council.

The elevator doors open, and I dart out and grab a car, directing it to take me home. Settling comfortably into the seat, I touch Pom's furry body on my wrist.

The dream world is where I have the best chance of calming myself.

———

POM GREETS ME, his fur black and his expression worried. "What's wrong?"

Pacing between the impossible shapes populating the lobby of my palace, I fill him in on Valerian's betrayal.

As I speak, Pom's fur lightens to a mixture of blue and light orange. "Well," he says when I'm done, "it *is* true. He didn't know you yet."

My hair turns fiery without my willing it to. "If you like him so much, why don't you attach yourself to *his* wrist. Or ass. Or—"

Pom disappears in his signature Cheshire cat style. When only his mouth is left, he says, "You might want to visit your memory gallery to calm down."

"Coward," I mumble when he's gone.

I contemplate creating a version of Valerian I could scream at, but I decide against it. Going to the memory gallery might actually be a good idea, since it's a bit like opening a photo album but on steroids. It's bound to distract me from my crazy thoughts, but I know Pom is still watching and I feel like being contrary, so I teleport to the tower of sleepers.

Aha. I'm in luck.

Ariel, Kit, Itzel, and Felix are all dreaming at the same time.

I pull them all into one dream, take us to my cloud office, and fill them in on everything, from my discovery about my twin sister and the encounter with Phobetor to Valerian throwing me under the bus with the New York Council.

"Wow," Felix says, his unibrow bunching on his forehead. "You've been busy."

I sigh. "Understatement."

Kit shakes her head. "I can't believe Valerian was after Hekima's

Council seat. When we offered it to him, he seemed so genuine when he pretended not to want it."

"The Council offered him a seat?" I exclaim. "Already?"

Kit bites her lip. "He was the natural choice. Hekima showed us how useful an illusionist can be and—" She stops. "Never mind that. I can't believe you had a twin. Must be hard learning that you lost her, and in such a way." As she speaks, she morphs into a copy of me.

Ariel gives me a worried glance. "How about we talk about something else?"

"It's okay. I didn't really know her." As I look at my face on Kit, all I feel is a peculiar type of numbness. "Hard to grieve someone you didn't know existed."

What I *am* mourning is my perception of my mom as someone who'd be unable to kill her daughter, even under the potential influence of an evil deity.

Seeming to understand, Ariel squeezes my shoulder.

Itzel looks uncomfortable with all this. Adjusting her breathing mask, she asks, "What did that world look like? The one you saw in your mom's memories?"

Glad to have something to do, I recreate the clearing where I saw my sister killed. I place the tall forest around us just like it was in Mom's memory, with the blue-green trees shaped alternately like baobabs and coral reefs, and I even add in the odd skies that imply the planet is an odd pretzel shape instead of a sphere.

Everyone looks around, mouths agape.

"That sky…" Felix exhales in awe. "So cool."

Ariel turns to Itzel. "Is this a ring world? Built by your kind, maybe?"

Itzel shakes her head. "It could be gnome built, but the structure isn't a ring. It must be two counter-rotating cylinders. Reminds me of a spaceship design I've read about on Earth—O'Neill colony."

She clears the grass at our feet and draws a rough sketch of the design in the dirt.

Everyone stares at it blankly.

Itzel huffs in frustration and gives Felix a defeated look. "You need an Earth pop-culture reference, don't you?"

"No," Felix says.

"Yes," Ariel says at the same time.

"*Interstellar*," Itzel says. "Cooper Station, at the very end."

"Oh, yeah," Felix says, looking up with even greater wonder. "So you think this is a spaceship?"

"That's a philosophical question," Itzel says. "Any planet can be said to be a spaceship, especially if the planet was artificially created the way this one must've been."

Kit loudly yawns. "I'm dreaming, yet you're about to put me to sleep."

"Guys." I snap my fingers to get their attention. "There's one thing we haven't touched on yet—the most worrisome aspect of what I've learned." I look at each of them in turn. "Do any of you know how a god of nightmares could be a real thing?"

"Maybe he isn't a god, per se," Felix says. "Not in the way humans think of them. Maybe he's just a powerful dreamwalker or something similar who was worshipped. With enough mojo from human faith, many of us can become like gods."

"He might be right," Ariel says. "There was a Phobetor in Greek mythology, and he had the same job. If more worlds have the same myth about a specific Cognizant, his powers would've grown beyond anything we can imagine."

I look around furtively. "How about we call him Collywobbles going forward? Especially when in the dream world?"

Valerian was insistent that we shouldn't say Phobetor's real name, and now that I've encountered him, I can no longer dismiss his concern as paranoia.

Kit nods. "No problem. Can you show him to us? Collywobbles?"

"I don't think I want to do that here either," I say. "I have this bad feeling. Like if I bring him about, he'll actually come to life."

"Hmm." Felix picks up a fallen leaf from one of the trees. Weirdly, it's shaped like a hexagon. "Could that be why he appeared to you in the first place?" he asks. "If your mom was taken over by him, as you theorized, that means she must've—"

"We agreed not to talk about that," Ariel snaps at him, casting a cautious look in my direction.

"I'm okay." I square my shoulders, ignoring the painful tension in my neck that somehow persists even in the dream. "If he's right, how about we don't talk about Collywobbles at all? At least not here."

Everyone falls silent.

"Maybe we should all sleep on this," I say. "If anyone has good ideas in the morning, get in touch."

They agree, so I let them go on sleeping and return to my cab.

When I get to my apartment a few minutes later, I collapse into my own bed. But I can't sleep, my mind replaying everything in a nauseating loop.

Finally, after what feels like hours, I drift off.

———

I'M WALKING through Times Square, doing my best not to touch the thousands of tourists and natives, which is harder than it should be. Above us loom skyscrapers adorned with screens playing flashy videos, most of them advertisements. All seems ordinary—until a vaguely familiar music begins playing.

It's "Dance of the Sugar Plum Fairy," the melody from a famous ballet here on Earth. In New York, they play it a lot around Christmas.

The screen nearest me stops showing the soda commercial, and a creepy-looking wooden soldier glares at me with a gaping mouth full of black teeth.

No, not a soldier. The Nutcracker—which is the name of the ballet where that music is from.

Unlike the usual depictions of this character, this one has real brown eyes inside a wooden head. Further adding to his creepiness is the way the face is painted, with a blood-colored grin framed by a tentacle-like mustache.

I stare at it, unable to look away.

The screen shimmers, and the Nutcracker is no longer inside it.

He's three-dimensional now.

Real.

My instinct for self-preservation kicks in, and I back away.

He leaps down, landing on a bent wooden knee, like some superhero.

I gape at the crater he's created in the spot where I stood a moment ago.

Suddenly, Pom shows up between me and the Nutcracker. His fur is black, his eyes wild. "Did you still want me to tell you when you're having a nightmare?"

A nightmare? As in, a dream?

I look at my empty wrist.

Of course. Pom is walking and talking—he can't be on my wrist.

"Thanks," I say to Pom, and will the music and the Nutcracker to disappear.

The music stops, but the Nutcracker stays where he is, the evil grin spreading wider. "It would've been easier to kill you if you didn't know you were dreaming," he says in a creepily melodic voice that reminds me of the music I just stopped. "Still, one has to make do."

What the hell? How is my own nightmare creature refusing to go away? Unless—

Extending his wooden, fingerless hand, the Nutcracker charges at me.

CHAPTER FOUR

INSTINCTIVELY, I duck.

The wooden ball of his hand smashes into a tourist, ripping through him and punching out his heart from his back.

"I'm sorry. This is too scary," Pom says and disappears.

Hey, that's a good idea.

I try to jolt myself awake—but feel a tug of power in the opposite direction. It's a bit like when I tried to wake up Mom, only I'm the one I can't rouse.

This supports a theory I've already started forming. "You're a dreamwalker."

The Nutcracker aims another punch at me.

I dodge it and two following swings, then smash a fist into his right eye.

He cries out but heals the damage I made instantly. With renewed fury, he lashes out, and his fist smashes into my shoulder, dislocating it.

Hot nausea sears through me, but before it can disable me, I leap out of my body and heal myself. I also consider doubling myself but decide against it for now—it's good to have an ace in my back pocket.

Returning to my body, I punch the Nutcracker's midsection. It hurts me more than him—his body doesn't just look like wood, it feels like it too. Note to self: Figure out how to make myself a dream body from something sturdier than flesh. It would be a lot like the fiery hair project, only bigger. For now, I make a blowtorch appear in my hands and aim it at my opponent's wooden chest.

A ten-foot cockroach materializes in the path of the flame, giving up its dream life to save my foe.

A yellow cab careens toward me.

I take flight—which is when the nearest skyscrapers grow taller, then fold sideways, creating a square box in the sky.

He thinks that will stop me?

I crash through the glass, steel, and concrete, and look down.

The Nutcracker is flying after me.

Stealing his own strategy, I make the One Times Square building lengthen and spear him with the spire from which the iconic New Year's Eve ball drops.

An elephant takes the strike.

Not wanting to be outdone, I make a great white shark appear, its jaws closing on the Nutcracker's head.

It doesn't get a chance to bite. In a blink, it explodes into a cloud of butterflies that flutter away.

I change our surroundings to that of another NYC tourist spot—the South Street Seaport.

Great. He hasn't stopped me yet—though I still don't know if he's fine with the change of scenery, or if he can't stop me.

Regardless, he takes advantage of it swiftly. A ship rises from the waters and nosedives at my head.

I try to make the ship disappear. His power annuls my attempt. I will the ship to morph into a ball of cotton candy. Nope.

Fine. I teleport behind the Nutcracker and make a baseball bat appear in my hands. As the ship crashes into the pavement where I stood, my bat breaks over the Nutcracker's head.

"You bitch!" he cries out.

I make the cobblestones levitate out of the walkway and fly at his head, one after another. As he dodges, I try jolting myself awake once more.

This time, it works.

———

SITTING UP IN MY BED, I order the lights on and frantically scan the room.

Nobody is here.

Leaping to my feet, I examine the whole apartment, just in case.

Empty.

I can't believe I now have yet another thing to worry about. I pace the living room for a few minutes before I decide that I must talk to someone about this. Maybe one of my friends is still dreaming? If they're on Gomorrah, it's still nighttime here and will be for a while.

The question is, do I dare go back into the dream world? What if the Nutcracker is waiting for me there?

It feels unlikely. It seems that part of his strategy was to catch me while I was still unaware of my dreaming, and for that to happen, I'd need to be dreaming naturally. Besides, if I give up dreamwalking completely, I'll be powerless.

And there's an extra precaution I can take—if Pom is willing.

Touching my looft's fur, I dive back into the dream world.

———

BEET-COLORED Pom appears at my feet as soon as I pop into my dream palace.

"I'm sorry for being such a coward," he says, his ears droopy.

"Don't say that." I muss the fur on top of his head. "That thing could've killed you. Then where would I be?"

Pom's fur darkens. "Killed?"

"Well, yeah. And I have no clue what that means for you. If he'd killed *me*, I'd have gone homicidally insane." I frown at him. "Can *you* go insane?"

He turns full black. "No idea."

"Then let's not find out. If the attack happens again, run away, exactly like you did."

"Okay." His fur lightens a bit. "But I will keep warning you about nightmares—else that thing could get a jump on you."

"Perfect. And there's something else I need you to do. If the Nutcracker shows up while I'm dreamwalking inside *your* dreams, you have the power to wake me up, so I'll need you to do that after you disappear."

"You got it." Pom turns teal and gives me a crisp army salute.

"Let's test it now."

With a nod, he disappears, and I find myself back in my apartment.

I touch Pom again, and once I greet him in the palace, I teleport us to the tower of sleepers and check the surrounding rooms.

Out of everyone, only Felix is here, so I connect with him.

He's dreaming of working with Itzel on a new robot suit. It's a memory, actually.

Banishing Dream Itzel, I explain to Felix that he's asleep and take him to my cloud office, where he paces the cloud as I tell him about the fight, finishing with, "When I woke up, there was no one there, which means this dreamwalker—if that's what that was—didn't touch me to get in. He or she either had a connection with me already, or set up one remotely, from outside my apartment."

Pom, perched on my shoulder, turns pitch black.

Felix stops pacing the cloud. He might already know what I'll ask, but I say it anyway. "If it's the latter, there's bound to be security footage of him—or her—creeping by my door."

His unibrow does a little dance. "I'll check on this as soon as I wake up. But are you sure this was a dreamwalker and not Pho—I mean, Collywobbles?"

"Well, the latter is extremely powerful and would've ended me quickly… Unless the idea was to just toy with me."

"And you don't know any other dreamwalkers, right?" Felix asks.

"If I did, I'd ask them to teach me how to wage a battle in the dream world. I got lucky this time."

Felix looks around, eyes bulging. "Can he show up here?"

"Should that happen, I have a plan." I pat Pom's furry feet, and he proudly puffs up. "Besides, I think the Nutcracker needs me dreaming naturally, to catch me unaware."

"How about doing something proactive in case he does show up again?" Felix asks. "I can help."

Good idea. I could, for starters, make my body more solid.

Gathering my power, I attempt to turn my flesh into metal.

Only my pinky solidifies—and I can't feel it at all.

With another effort, I force the metal pinky to bend. It does, and some feelings go back into it. It's a start. I bend the pinky some more, until it eventually feels like a regular one, only slathered in Novocain.

My index finger is next, then the whole arm, then finally my torso.

"What do you think?" I try to ask. The question doesn't come out. I guess the metal exterior is messing with the function of my throat.

It takes me a few minutes to fix that problem. When I finally master my newly metallic body, I ask, "Can you attack me?"

Felix walks over and gingerly pokes my midsection.

"You've got to do better than that." I create boxing gloves around his hands. "Punch me."

He does.

I feel the punch, but the impact is definitely dampened.

"The problem is that this takes up a lot of concentration." I create a baseball bat to replace Felix's gloves. "Hit me with that."

He smashes the bat into my midsection.

I barely feel it.

Felix smacks me again. "This is cool," he says when I don't flinch. "What's next?"

"Your call. What do you need?"

He grins. "Guns. Lots of guns."

I take us to a blank room with rows upon rows of weapons inspired by his movie reference.

Grin widening, he picks up a Beretta, loads it, and points it at my chest. "Are you sure?"

I inhale a big breath. "Shoot."

Bang.

My chest hurts as if I were punched, but the bullet just falls at my feet.

This is a workable strategy.

Arming Felix with other weapons, I experiment with different ways of fighting a dreamwalker—melting a katana instead of letting it slice me, increasing gravity to prevent a cannonball from smashing into my metal chest, messing with the chemistry of gunpowder to prevent an Uzi from firing, and so on.

"Those video game design courses have clearly given you an advantage," Felix says after we both tire of the exercise. "Practice like this some more, and I'm sure you'll defeat that Nutcracker—assuming he or she dares attack you again."

If only I were that optimistic.

"Thanks for the help. I'll let you sleep normally now," I say and leave Felix's dream.

Too wired to go back to sleep, I brew myself a soothing herbal tea and sip it leisurely for a while.

When I catch myself yawning, I get back into bed. It takes a while, but eventually, I go under, and this time, my slumber is dreamless.

———

IN THE MORNING, a message from Felix is waiting for me in VR:

Nothing in the security footage. The Nutcracker must've made a connection with you before.

Hmm. That does limit the pool of suspects somewhat, and is worrying. Some creepozoid touched me while I slept. Just thinking about it makes me want to hygieia myself.

With a slight pang of disappointment, I don't find a gushing apology from Valerian in my inbox—nor a message of any kind. Not even a "you suck." Oh, well. Sounds like that's it between us. I just hope he doesn't stop the development of the *Lucid Dreamer* game because of this—I need the power boost from that to rouse Mom.

At least I think I do. With Phobetor as a variable, having more power might not be the only thing I need. Still, it should help with the Nutcracker situation.

Unsure of what to do next, I check in on my rehab job and find a big backlog of clients waiting for my unique form of therapy, so that's what I do for the rest of the day.

OVER THE NEXT THREE WEEKS, I continue catching up on my workload at the rehab clinic. The Nutcracker doesn't show in my dreams, and Valerian is incommunicado.

Things get so routine with my clients that I wonder, not for the first time, if I should start a VR company to carefully craft VR experiences for common phobias that would mirror my dream therapy. It's actually one of the reasons why I took the game design classes in the past.

Maybe this is a project to look into after I save Mom. Especially if I patch things up with Valerian, a VR guru.

No, scrap that last bit. Valerian is not going to be in my life anymore, either as a love interest or a business partner—and I don't care how much I dream about his stupid, pretty face.

By the fourth week, I start to worry about the *Lucid Dreamer* project. If Valerian could throw me under the bus as he did with the Council, why would he continue all that expensive video game development for me?

To that end, I stalk the tower of sleepers until I catch Bernard there. Swiftly, I jump into his dream.

BERNARD IS DREAMING of a trip to the zoo with his daughter.

It's a memory, which means they've reconciled to the point of daytrips. Good for him.

I let him enjoy the dream, and when the next one starts, I direct it to a memory related to my query.

——————

BERNARD—OR Bernie in this context—is sitting at the table with Ratridevi Bhairava, a.k.a. Rattie.

Today, Bernie looks more like Wario than his nemesis Mario, while Rattie is as attractive as he was when I saw him last, his symmetrical masculine features and strong dark eyebrows not at all rat-like despite the nickname.

"Let's talk replayability for *Lucid Dreamer*." Rattie activates the screens around them, and his Bangalore team joins the conference. "We want our user base to play the game over and over."

Bernie frowns. "Our plot is too linear, and that's hard to change. Nor do we have that many alternating paths or endings."

"Right. That's why I think the easiest way we can add some replay value is with multiple characters," Rattie says, and everyone on the screens nods.

Bernie twirls his mustache, villain style. "Maybe we use a character that's already in the game?"

"We could," Rattie says. "Our big bad would be a cheap option. He's got the same powers as—"

I tune the rest of it out. The villain in the game is the Rat King. I even tried fighting him in VR, though in that case he took on the guise of a spider with the head of a clown wearing a surgeon's mask. The playable version would probably look more like Rattie himself—as that's what his mischievous Bangalore team often makes their monsters' faces look like.

"And we don't need to involve another model," Bernie says, echoing my thought process. "If needed, you can just pop into the motion capture lab and—"

At the mention of the motion capture lab, I vividly recall being there with Valerian and the way he attached those dots to my face. Also, the way he—

Wait, why am I fantasizing about that traitor?

"—and the best part is that the release date won't change," Bernie says. Everyone nods approvingly.

That is indeed the best part. Depending on how far back in the past this meeting was, the game might come out very soon.

"Now, if that's settled, we should talk about the feedback from the testers." Bernie opens a folder. "The most recurrent note is: Too many clowns and spiders."

The Bangalore team start laughing, and when Bernie gives them a questioning look, one of them explains that the clowns and spiders are Rattie's fault. Apparently, he has them overuse those elements in all the projects they've created.

Not interested in hearing more, I exit the dream and find myself back in my office at the rehab facility.

Doesn't seem like Valerian has halted the game design. Maybe he's not as much of a jerk as I thought.

As if waiting for that moment, a message shows up in my VR inbox.

It's from Valerian.

If you recall, I offered to take you out of the castle when we met.

What? He disappears for weeks, and his idea of groveling is that? Pom turning red on my wrist, I compose my reply:

You offered to rescue me out of self-interest. If you recall, the vampires kidnapped me before I finished that job with Bernard. I guess your seer miscalculated—or it was all part of the big plan. Your offer to rescue me was as hollow as your current apology, and you know it. The vampires had my DNA, so taking me out of the castle would've only delayed the inevitable.

I wait for him to prevaricate his way out of that, but he doesn't reply.

Nor is there a reply on the next day, and the one after that.

Just as I figure he's done talking to me forever, I find a bouquet of flowers in my office with a small note:

I'm sorry.

The gall of the guy. He thinks he can kill some plants and make everything okay?

Still, I put the flowers into a vase and catch myself smelling them for the rest of the day with a dumb grin on my face.

The next day, I get a box of candy with the same note.

Unlike its Earth cousins, Gomorran candy is actually good for one's teeth, and is many times more delicious, which goes doubly so for the extremely expensive brand Valerian got for me.

Still. Just because I'm gobbling down the candy doesn't mean I'm ready to forgive and forget.

The next day, a box is waiting on my desk. There's a bracelet inside.

I put it on. It's pretty, even if it looks nothing like Pom's furry body on my other wrist. And no, just because I'm wearing the bracelet doesn't mean we're okay now.

By gift number seven, my resolve wavers a bit. That is, until I get a new message from Valerian the next day:

Felix told me everything. Can you put aside your silly misconceptions long enough to talk to me?

Silly misconceptions?

I remove his bracelet and toss it into the garbage disposal.

The nerve of that man.

And what was Felix thinking, talking to the enemy? He's lucky I'm not evil enough to sneak into his dreams and have him take a swim in a lake filled with blood. Or make him and Valerian screw themselves—and each other.

That last bit heavily inspires my reply, which, not surprisingly, is:

You and Felix can go puck yourselves.

Valerian doesn't write back, and there's no gift on my desk the next day.

Okay, so maybe I could've replied with something a bit more ladylike.

The rest of the morning passes in a blur of therapy appointments. Finally, feeling like I should treat myself, I go for lunch at White Fang, a restaurant run by a werewolf that serves various meat tartar and has a nice ambiance. Today, it's pretty much empty, which suits my mood just fine.

I'm halfway through my ri sashimi when someone sits down at my table.

It's Valerian, looking as unrepentant as can be.

CHAPTER FIVE

TALL AND BROAD-SHOULDERED, he's wearing a gnome-designed tunic that looks to have been tattooed on his muscled body. His expression is unreadable, the ocean-blue eyes serene, with not a twitch of emotion visible on those carved features.

Pom's fur turns coral pink.

Damn hormones. I forgot just how attractive Valerian is. He looks yummy enough to end up on the menu, and it's distracting me from my anger.

A server robot rolls over to the table, a plate of sashimi on his head. Valerian must've ordered it while I was staring.

I glare at him. "You're kidding, right? One of us is not staying."

He picks up a piece of sashimi with his bare fingers—proper werewolf table manners. Putting it in his mouth, he chews exaggeratedly slow.

I get up. "Fine. *I'll* go."

Suddenly, the other tables around us disappear, along with the restaurant's windows and entrance.

Valerian leans back in his chair and swallows his morsel. "We need to talk. What can I do to lower your hostility so you'll listen?"

Pom's fur is now the angriest red. "You can build a time machine and not puck me over."

He heaves a sigh. "Anything else?"

"Tell me everything you know about Soma. Let me see the precious black windows in your dreams, and maybe I'll hear you out."

His hands curl for a moment, but there's no hint of emotion on his face—that or he's tricking me with his illusion powers to think so. Sitting up straighter, he says, "This is important. I'm working with the Gomorran Senate and the Councils on Earth."

I plop back into my chair. If I try to flee now, I'll knock over a table or walk into a wall. Besides, if he's telling the truth, I don't want to anger the Senate or any of the Earth's Councils. Instead, I give him my most seething stare. "How many times do I have to get nearly killed before you leave me alone?"

He narrows his eyes, his serene mask gone. "I'm here to save your stubborn hide. You know you're in terrible danger, as much as you pretend otherwise. And I have arranged for your protection." He makes the illusion go away, returning the tables, windows, and entrance to visibility.

"Danger?" I ask, the sashimi feeling like a stone in my stomach. "What danger?"

"Seriously?" He shakes his head. "The one you call Collywobbles. You got on his radar—and lo and behold, someone is hunting you in your dreams. How long do you think it'll take before trouble comes for you in the waking world?"

That's an interesting point. Even I wondered if those events were related. But—

A strange duo walks into the restaurant. One of them is a man with dark glasses and one of those special walking sticks the blind use to navigate the streets on Earth. Next to him is a giant canine wearing a guide-dog getup—a job a robot would do here on Gomorrah.

Only that's not a dog.

It's a werewolf, in his or her animal form.

The maybe-blind man beelines for our table without using his stick and doesn't touch a single obstacle in his path, his guide werewolf lagging behind.

Without much ado, he sinks into the chair to my left and takes out a pair of tighty-whities from his pocket.

In a flash, the werewolf turns, becoming a naked man with sad eyes and unkempt facial hair that makes it difficult to determine his age. He snatches the underwear, robotically puts it on, then sits on the remaining chair and looks blankly into the distance.

The maybe-blind guy turns my way. "Hi, Bailey." His gaze cuts to my companion. "Hi, Valerian."

"Nostradamus," Valerian mutters, looking as discombobulated as I feel.

This is Nostradamus?

A legendary figure, he's said to be one of the most powerful seers in existence, and has been instrumental in saving all of the Cognizant kind at least once.

"At your service," Nostradamus replies. "And my companion is Marius. Nice to finally meet you both—outside of visions, that is."

Valerian glances at Marius. "Pleasure." Then his attention homes in on Nostradamus. "Everyone thought you disappeared with the rest of the seers."

The rest of the seers disappeared?

What's going on?

"I'll be gone too, after we talk," the seer says sagely. "But first, I'm here to tell you how to save Bailey's life."

CHAPTER SIX

SAVE *ME*?

No. Not again.

Valerian looks at the werewolf as if for an explanation, and when none comes, he says, "I'm here to protect her."

"Sadly, the protection you plan will doom her, and everyone else." Nostradamus grabs a piece of sashimi off my plate and tosses it into his werewolf friend's mouth.

The werewolf catches it and swallows without chewing, his sad eyes staring into the distance.

On autopilot, I move my plate toward Nostradamus and open VR to order the same thing again.

Valerian rubs the bridge of his nose. "The safe house the Senate prepared—"

"Will get broken into, the Enforcers overwhelmed," Nostradamus says. "And though my powers aren't as good when it comes to events that happen in dreams, I can tell you that most versions of the future you planned for her end with Bailey going homicidally insane."

I blink. "As in, the Nutcracker kills me in a future fight?"

"Not if you avoid sleep," Valerian says. "There's—"

"She'll refuse to live on vampire blood," Nostradamus says, and I nod emphatically. "But even in the rare futures where the choice is not hers, things end just as tragically."

Wait a second. He saw futures where someone force-fed me vampire blood? Who'd be—

"I hate seers," Valerian growls. "I assume you're going to tell us what to do?"

"I can show you a path." Nostradamus snatches another sashimi piece and eats it with an impressed look. "Take her and her friends with you to Necronia."

"And?" Valerian prompts.

"What's Necronia?" I ask.

Nostradamus rises to his feet. "Valerian will explain shortly."

Valerian jumps up too, his muscles bunching tight. "Wait, that's it?"

Shreds of tighty-whities fly everywhere as the werewolf morphs back into a shaggy beast and places himself between Valerian and Nostradamus.

Nostradamus lays a hand on the snarling wolf's head, scratching him behind the ear. "He's upset. It's understandable."

Valerian sits back down, all but vibrating with tension. "Why won't you tell us what we need to do in exact detail? Why this charade?"

"Well, for one thing, if you know the future, you can change it," Nostradamus says.

I blink. "We can?"

"Sure. For example, what if I told you 'don't get dessert after I leave?'"

"If you said not to, we wouldn't," Valerian says.

"It's not that simple, though," Nostradamus says. "You'll see." He turns to leave.

"Wait!" I call. "Can you at least give us a few tips?"

"Sure," the seer says over his shoulder. "Take Chester with you—or another powerful probability manipulator. If the other side recruits one of his or my kind, he'd be a good counterbalance."

The other side? Does he mean the Nutcracker?

"Wouldn't Chester make it impossible for you to know our future?" Valerian asks.

"I don't know your future exactly anyway," Nostradamus says. "I'm here to offer you a path that doesn't lead to certain doom for you and everyone—but that doesn't mean I can guarantee a positive outcome."

Ugh. No wonder everyone dislikes seers.

A robot rolls over to the table with my new serving of sashimi. I take it on autopilot and put it on the table.

"Farewell," Nostradamus says. "Oh, last but not least, if you hear the

Fate Motif, play the detective." With that, he strolls out of the restaurant, his werewolf on his tail.

I face Valerian. "What just happened?"

He scrubs a hand over his face. "I think we've officially gotten in over our heads. The Earth Councils have been trying to locate Nostradamus without any success—and he just waltzes in here, spouting prophecies like it's nothing."

"Uh-huh. Why are the Councils looking for him? Why did he keep hinting at some kind of apocalypse? What the puck is a Fate Motif? And what's Necronia?"

"First things first," Valerian says. "What do we do about the pucking dessert?"

I frown at him. "Didn't Nostradamus say not to get it?"

My appetite is history, and I bet the same is true for Valerian. Still, I summon VR and scan the menu. Today's only options for dessert are chef's choice of kibble with freeze-dried innards or a glazed *cheburashka* ear. No, thanks. The first option will no doubt taste like gourmet dog food, and the second sounds as appetizing as a baby koala ear would on Earth.

Valerian gestures in his own VR and wrinkles his nose. "Nostradamus's exact words were 'don't get dessert after I leave.'"

I dismiss the VR interface. "But he prefaced that with 'what if I told you.'"

"Right. That implies that merely saying the phrase 'don't get dessert after I leave' could, by itself, alter our future somehow. But that makes no sense. The only way it could be true is if we ordered the dessert out of spite."

"Which you won't do, right?"

He narrows his eyes. "I'm not the spiteful one."

"What's that supposed to mean?"

"Where do I start? You threw away the bracelet I gave you. Ignored—"

"You spied on me?"

Valerian doesn't reply. He's staring at the restaurant entrance.

Following his gaze, I gape at the dozen new arrivals—Cognizant of various types. Some are naked, some are only wearing underwear, and the rest have on a mix of nightgowns and pajamas.

All of them are armed with objects found in a typical kitchen: a few people with knives, a large female elf with a colander, a male dwarf gripping a spatula, a gargoyle with skewers, a dryad with scissors, and so on.

But it's not their clothing or weapons that make my insides freeze-dry like the dessert we'll probably never get the chance to order. Nor is it the lack of emotion on their faces.

It's their eyes.

There's a magma-like fire in all of them—the same exact peculiarity that Mom displayed when she killed my twin.

"Cast an illusion!" I whisper harshly as all fiery eyes lock in on us.

Valerian shakes his head. "Their condition makes it hard to fool more than one, and to stop them, I'd need to fool all of them—or more precisely, the one controlling them. The one who sees through their eyes. If I had a team of illusionists to help me, that would be a different story."

His explanation raises many questions, but I don't get to ask them because at that moment, acting as one, the motley crew pounces.

CHAPTER SEVEN

A KNIFE whooshes by my ear, causing me to duck. A colander flies at my midsection, so I sidestep. A meat tenderizer smashes into Valerian's shoulder. He grunts, then leaps between me and a rolling pin, taking the blow on his chest.

"Stop getting hit!" I shout.

"Thanks," he pants. "I'll get right on that."

I pick up the tenderizer and launch it at the head of the dwarf with a spatula. It smacks him in the face, hard, but he keeps on coming. Not good.

Valerian catches a knife in mid-air and sends it flying into the eye of the elf woman. She drops her colander and collapses on the floor, presumably dead.

That's something. Seems like they can be defeated.

If we had a squadron of fighters with us, we'd stand a chance. As is, not so much. Not with their seeming imperviousness to pain, sheer numbers, and our lack of any weapons or useful powers.

A pair of skewers zoom by Valerian's head, then scissors. I curse myself for not carrying a sleep grenade to work as I dodge a dirty frying pan. Of all the unsanitary ways to go. Could this get any more nightmarish?

Valerian flips over our table and uses it as a shield. Good idea. That should buy us a minute, maybe two. Kitchen tools pound at the table like hail.

I cautiously peek out.

A new group of people zooms into the restaurant. Given their all-black outfits, super-fast movement and fangs, I have to assume they're Enforcers, or at least vampires impersonating them.

If this lot is with the weird-eyes group, we're going to be even deader.

But they don't seem to be. At least not the one I recognize. His name is Virgil, and he was Valerian's ally before.

Yep. Virgil disembowels a dryad while another vamp rips out an elf's heart.

A massacre follows. Soon, Valerian and I are the only people in the restaurant left alive, not counting the vampires. Their aliveness is a matter of debate.

"Why did it take you so long?" Valerian barks at Virgil.

Virgil licks a rivulet of blood from his hand. "You said you wanted privacy. Asked us to stay outside of the hearing range. That's a mile for me."

He can hear us from a mile away? Surely that's with a sound amplifier?

Then something clicks.

I round on Valerian. "You had them spy on me. Is that how you knew about the bracelet I tossed away?"

"They merely protected you," he says. "I knew about the bracelet because the rehab facility gave us access to the security camera in your office."

This is some Big Brother mooft dung. The folks at the rehab facility and I will have words.

Virgil hides his fangs. "You'd better take her to the safe house."

"There's been a change of plans on that front," Valerian says. "Instead of staying under your watch, she's going to come with me."

Virgil lifts an eyebrow.

Since it sounds like I might finally get some answers, I replace my initial angry retort with, "Where are we headed?"

Valerian looks at the bodies of our attackers. "Not here."

"Take that van." Virgil gestures at a vehicle nearby. "It's been vetted."

Nodding, Valerian strides to the car, and I follow.

This is one of those luxury limo-type rides that take people to weddings and the like. There's a bar and fridge here, a couch, and space enough to stand and move around.

As we get rolling, Valerian pours two drinks at the bar and hands me one of the glasses.

I take a small sip. Delicious. "Did that make any sense to you?"

He sits opposite me. "I'm sure you see what Nostradamus meant about the dessert. He mentioned it, and we started to argue about it when he left. If he hadn't said anything, we probably would've been out of the restaurant before the Overtaken arrived." At my blank stare, he explains, "The Overtaken is what I call the people with the strange eyes."

"The dessert is not what I was asking about. It's everything else. Who are the Overtaken?"

"It's only a theory." He puts his drink down on a small table nearby. "I believe they're possessed and controlled by Collywobbles." He makes air quotes around Phobetor's nickname. "As I was saying before, you're on his radar now."

Uh-oh. "So those eyes—"

"Are what reveal the control," he confirms.

"Which means my mom—"

"I'm sorry." He gently squeezes my knee.

I let out a shaky breath. Though I'd suspected something like this myself, I find it difficult, if not impossible, to accept that Mom was controlled by a god of nightmares. And killed my twin—let's not forget that impossible-to-process factoid.

"—Overtaken have started to appear in bigger numbers recently," Valerian is saying when I pay attention to him again. "That's what helped me convince the Senate and the Earth Councils to act."

Shoving aside all thoughts of my mom and my dead sister, I leap to my feet and begin pacing in the small confines of the car. "Start at the very beginning. Why did the Councils look for Nostradamus? When he hinted at doom and gloom, did it have something to do with the Overtaken? And what's Necronia?"

Valerian picks up his drink and takes a large sip. "Right. From the beginning. You remember Wrakar?"

I stop. "The necromancer who nearly killed us?"

I wish I could forget him. The last time I saw the guy, Kit had him cocooned in a spiderweb.

"The Senate had him questioned," Valerian says. "We learned a lot."

Ouch. *Questioned* is a polite way of saying *tortured*.

"According to Wrakar, Icelus is a multi-world organization," he continues, "all united in one goal: to make *you know who* stronger. Though we stopped the attack here on Gomorrah, the Cognizant in countless Otherlands weren't so lucky."

I sit back down, my knees suddenly feeling weak. "They blew up people?"

"On some worlds. On others, they instigated a war. And on some, they worked in a subtler manner. Remember Koshmar, the drug that gives nightmares?"

I nod.

"On one world that's a lot like Earth, they managed to start a pharmaceutical company and distributed a more lethal version of that drug as a sleeping aid. This has led to millions of deaths and billions of horrific nightmares."

I pinch the bridge of my nose. "I didn't realize Icelus is so widespread. How many members are there? How do they coordinate these atrocities across the Otherlands?"

"Many of the cataclysms were caused by the same cell. As for world-to-world communication, Wrakar claimed they have a dreamwalker among them for that. At first, it seemed farfetched, but after that attack inside your dream, I believe him on this, too."

Another dreamwalker.

An Icelus dreamwalker.

That must be who the Nutcracker is.

"How do you know it's a person?" I ask. "Couldn't a nightmare deity personally help them coordinate?"

He shrugs. "Seems like overkill. Besides, I think the Overtaken is what happens to people who get too chummy with the one you mention. Most Icelus are independent agents, not puppets with fiery eyes."

"Right. So you questioned the necro and told the Councils on Earth about your findings?"

"And the Councils on other easy-to-reach Otherlands," he says. "The idea is to coordinate a defense. This is why we looked for seers. Besides the obvious usefulness of their visions, they can communicate inter-world, albeit only with each other."

I recall Nostradamus saying how Valerian will never meet him again. "Let me guess. The seers foresaw your interest in them and ran away before they could get pulled into this mess?"

Valerian rakes his fingers through his hair. "Exactly. Which is when everyone started to *really* worry."

"What about that cryptic Fate Motif thing he said last? And, relatedly, how do I play detective?"

His upper lip curls. "Seers. I've heard of the *Fate Motif* in the context of music. Specifically, Beethoven's *Symphony No. 5*, also sometimes called the *Fate Symphony*."

I know the music piece he's talking about. It's one of the best-known compositions of classical music on Earth. One where the opening bars—and the motif—are Da-Da-Da-DUM.

"But what does it have to do with anything?" I ask. "And how do I play the detective?"

Valerian shrugs. "Let's hope you figure that out when the time comes. Playing the detective might mean using your reasoning skills or something like that."

"And Necronia?"

"That's Wrakar's home world—or more precisely, the world he was exiled from. He and the dreamwalker—whose identity he doesn't know—discussed that world at length, and Wrakar is convinced that it'll be attacked by a particularly nasty Icelus cell called the Pales. I decided to head up a team to go there to prevent the attack and capture the Pales."

I rub my temples. "And I wasn't going to be a part of this team, was I?"

He shakes his head. "I wanted to keep you safe on Gomorrah, but that's out the window now. Nostradamus is not a seer you can ignore."

Great, just great. If that dessert thing's taught me anything—besides a fear of seers—it's that I'd better go on this stupid mission. "Did the necromancer say what kind of attack to expect?"

Valerian grimaces. "You won't like it. He thinks it'll be via a vicious virus, one that affects humans and Cognizant alike. The Pales apparently specialize in bioweapons and have used viruses on other worlds already."

A virus.

I can feel all the blood draining from my face.

Why couldn't it be anything else?

"You don't have to go," he says gently.

"He said I'd die if I don't."

"Actually, he said my current plans would lead to your death, but what about new plans? What if you stay on Earth?"

I stand up and pour myself a stiffer drink.

I have no idea what to do. Do I trust a seer? And if so, can I physically make myself go to a world where a scary virus is running amok?

What's really odd is that the idea of traveling with Valerian terrifies me almost as much as catching this virus. I don't know if I'll be able to stay mad at him while spending so much time together.

A part of me is already weakening. He did, after all, want to keep me safe before the seer messed it up.

Well, if I do go, I'll stay extra vigilant when it comes to Valerian. Surely, I can stop myself from lusting—or worse—with sheer iron will.

Yeah. Right. And maybe I can fight the virus with my willpower while

I'm at it. Even now—though it could be the alcohol talking—I want him to hug me and kiss me and tell me everything will be okay.

As if sensing that, he comes to stand next to me by the bar. "You barely survived the last encounter with Icelus," he says softly. "Think hard before you make your choice."

I down my drink. "There's not really a choice, is there? Nostradamus has spoken. Besides, if Collywobbles was behind my sister's death, I want to thwart him and his minions."

Valerian nods solemnly. "This will be a long journey. How about we start over?"

And so it begins. "Nice try. You know my price to let bygones be bygones." I face him squarely. "Tell me everything about Soma and let me into the black windows in your dreams. I want no more secrets."

He turns away. "That's too much."

A hysterical chuckle escapes my lips. "You served me on a platter to the New York Council. Now you want me to go to a virus-infested world, and you have the nerve to say *I* ask too much?"

"It's not me who says you should go. In fact, I'm still wondering if there's a way you *don't* have to go."

"There isn't." Not according to a legendary seer, untrustworthy though he might be.

Valerian exhales audibly. "Fine. You win. After we're done with this mission, you'll get what you want."

The car stops.

I look up at the hub building. "We're going to Necronia already?"

"Earth first." He exits and holds the door for me. "You'll be safer there."

As we cross through the lobby of the building, I spot Enforcers—no doubt our bodyguards in case the Overtaken strike again.

"How does Collywobbles Overtake people, exactly?" I ask.

Valerian gestures for me step into the elevator and presses the button for the top floor. "No one knows for sure. So far, the one thing all victims had in common is recurrent nightmares and other sleep problems."

"Do they retain their powers?" I ask when we come out of the elevator and head for the blue shimmering plasma gate that leads to Earth.

"Seems like it," he says. "And, as I mentioned, I can only fool a single one with illusions, which makes my power useless when dealing with a team of them."

We step through the gate and come out on the Earth side. The JFK hub is underground, so my voice echoes as I say, "I wonder if my powers would work on them."

"I wouldn't go into the dreams of the Overtaken," Valerian says. "*You know who* might be waiting for you there."

Right. I wonder if Mom counts as one of the Overtaken. She clearly did at one point. And I did face Collywobbles in her dreams.

We enter the corridors, but instead of leading me to the secret door that opens into the JFK airport, Valerian takes a different turn.

"What's there?" I ask.

"A lab." He goes into a room at the end of the corridor.

I follow him.

A lab? More like a mad scientist's lair.

If a medical supply company were to battle a hardware store inside a space station, this might be the aftermath. A mix of Gomorran and Earth tech is everywhere, but particularly on a table where Itzel is building something, her attention fixed on her task.

Ariel and Felix are here too, engaged in an animated discussion.

"—no way Batman would beat Iron Man in a fight," Felix is saying. "Not unless they didn't have any gear on."

Ariel frowns, managing to still look uber-attractive while doing it. "If Batman had enough time to prep—"

"Hi, guys," I call. "What's going on?"

All three look at me as though I've appeared out of thin air.

Valerian smirks. He must've hidden us with his powers until now.

"I was working on something important," Itzel says, raising her head to pin me with a grumpy stare. "These two were supposed to test my work, but are really just interrupting."

I walk over to examine Itzel's "work." She's made a number of masks that are reminiscent of the one she always wears, being a gnome with breathing problems and all.

"I commissioned Itzel to make equipment for our Necronia trip." Valerian takes out a phone and types as he talks. "The Enforcers will take the prototypes to human labs and test them out."

I look around in confusion. "And she's working on a backwater world like Earth because…?"

"There's never been a major pandemic on Gomorrah. When it comes to virus protection and the like, this place is actually ahead." Itzel gestures at a nearby hazmat suit.

"Oh, please," I say. "We don't get pandemics thanks to the likes of hygieia and better sanitation. Earth is *not* ahead."

"We'll take hygieia devices with us," Valerian says. "But since the virus in question will most likely be airborne, we need masks too." He turns to Itzel. "Bailey needs a mask now as well. So do the rest of you."

"What?" Felix asks just as Ariel bursts out, "Why? Who?"

Valerian and I fill them in on our encounter with the seer.

"I can't believe things are so bad that Nostradamus got involved," Felix says. "The proverbial shit is about to really hit the proverbial fan. On an epic scale."

Ariel nods grimly. "Some kind of apocalypse is coming."

Itzel looks like someone crashed her favorite spaceship. "I should've known that being your friend would one day bite me in the ass," she says glumly.

Of course. Nostradamus said my friends need to come with us on this mission. I've been too self-absorbed to realize what that means for the people in this room.

"I doubt he meant you," Felix tells Itzel. "Seers can't predict a gnome's future."

"Not directly," Ariel says. "But should we risk everything by *not* having her come?"

Wow. They're taking Nostradamus's words even more seriously than I did.

"I'm sorry about that," I say. "He didn't elaborate much, so if you guys don't want to—"

"I'm going," Ariel says firmly.

"It's a chance for me to test out my new suit," Felix says, a lot less firmly.

"If you *do* go, you'll be handsomely rewarded," Valerian says to Itzel before turning toward Ariel and Felix. "That goes for the two of you as well."

Itzel perks up. "Rewarded by you or the Senate?"

"Both," Valerian says. "And the Earth Councils too."

Felix and Ariel exchange impressed glances.

"I have a feeling we'll be able to work something out." Itzel bends over the mask in front of her with renewed enthusiasm.

Valerian checks his phone. "I have to go make some arrangements. The Councils have assigned you protection. They're waiting in a limo outside." Turning, he heads toward the exit.

"When do we start the trip to Necronia?" I call after him.

"In a few days," he replies over his shoulder.

"What?" I look at Ariel and Felix. They both shrug. "Where do I stay in the meantime?"

Valerian stops and gives me an exasperated look. "Your bodyguards should keep you safe anywhere."

"How about you crash with us?" Ariel suggests excitedly. "We have an unused room at the moment."

"And there's a domovoi at our place who can kill anything that might get inside," Felix adds. "Also, our doors and windows are bulletproof."

Huh. I wonder if the latter is something Bowser set up for Princess Peach, the original occupant of the room in question.

"Perfect," Valerian says. "We'll meet back here. I'll text you the details."

With that, he strides out.

"Text who?" I ask the remaining crew.

"Me," Felix admits. "We've been working together the last few weeks."

I level a look at him filled with pretend annoyance. "So that's how you had the time to spill all my secrets to him."

Ariel grins. "You've known Felix long enough to realize how big of a gossip he is. If there's something you don't want the world to know, don't tell him."

"I can *totally* keep a secret." Felix's unibrow seesaws on his forehead. "I never told anyone about—" Noticing Ariel's death stare, he swallows audibly and mumbles, "Never mind."

"Can you shut your pieholes?" Itzel growls. "I'm working."

Ariel rolls her eyes. "Let's go see who the Councils assigned as protection."

She leads us out of the room and through the labyrinthine corridors into JFK, where an anorexic-thin woman is waiting for us.

"Thalia!" Ariel exclaims. "Great to see you again."

"Thalia is a nun from the Jinto mountains on Voikomlya," Felix whispers into my ear. "They're amazing fighters."

"Nice to meet you, Thalia," I say reverently. "I've been to your world and met some of your sisters." More specifically, I made dream connections to a couple of the warrior nuns so I could learn a bit of their fighting style, but since I never asked permission, I don't mention that part.

At the mention of her order, Thalia's thin face saddens.

"She's exiled and lives here on Earth." Felix further lowers his voice. "The reason she doesn't say anything is that she's under a vow of silence."

"See? Gossip," Ariel says.

Thalia takes out a phone and frantically types something out.

Ariel's phone beeps. Looking at it, she smiles and says, "Thalia said something not-so-flattering about Felix, then suggested we follow her to the limo."

The trip through the airport is uneventful, and when we exit, the palest woman I've ever seen is waiting for us outside. If she were human, she'd look to be in her late sixties, but I doubt human is what she is, as they rarely have such an unfathomable look in their eyes.

Nodding at the woman, Thalia takes out her phone and types up a storm.

Ariel checks the text and shows me the screen.

This is Edith. She's the oldest vampire on Earth. She's your protection. I'm just the driver.

A vampire, and the oldest on Earth to boot? Impressive. Given the woman's wrinkles and frown lines, I never would've guessed her nature—though it does explain those eyes and the paleness.

Cognizant who can become vampires upon their death are called pre-vamps. Not all of them turn, though. I've heard that drinking blood from a more powerful vampire helps their odds—with the side-effect being that they become sire-bonded to the donor vampire and have to do their bidding for a while. Living on Gomorrah hurts those turning odds, so you never meet pre-vamps there, only full vampires. Before they turn, pre-vamps are extremely long-lived, so Edith must've been ancient before her "death."

"You must be Felix, Ariel, and Bailey," she says with a slight German accent.

Felix and I reply that it's very nice to meet her, and Ariel just mumbles something unintelligible. Though she's kicked her vampire blood addiction, she doesn't feel comfortable around walking, talking sources of her drug of choice.

Getting into the limo, we pull out of the airport and promptly get stuck in traffic—New York at its finest. After a few minutes of the car alternating between crawling along and standing still, Edith stiffens and sits up straighter.

What the puck?

A woman in a nightgown steps onto the road. Then a man in silk boxers. Then more and more people in sleepwear.

My heartbeat picks up speed.

Their eyes are fiery, just like the Overtaken on Gomorrah.

This group is better armed, though.

As one, they raise their guns and fire at us.

CHAPTER EIGHT

I CRINGE, my eyes squeezing shut as the bullets slam into the limo, the deafening noise of gunfire blending with Felix's shrill screams.

Silence falls, followed by another round of gunshots.

By all rights, I should be holey, but I feel okay.

I open my eyes.

There isn't even a crack in the windshield.

"Bulletproof," Felix explains hoarsely, wiping the sweat from his brow.

To the side of me, Ariel is holding a gun. I have no idea where she pulled it from.

Thalia sets the car in "park" and reaches for the door handle.

"No," Edith says, her fangs extending. With a lisp, she orders, "Stay!"

Before we can argue, the vampire whirls into too-fast-to-track motion. I assume she opens the limo door, exits, and closes the door behind herself, but it's done with such speed I barely catch it—and not a single bullet has the chance to fly in.

Oblivious to the spray of bullets, she lunges at the nearest attacker.

The Overtaken fire again.

Edith doesn't seem to care.

An eyeblink later, the first Overtaken is a pile of gore.

A millisecond after that, another one is ripped apart. Then the next.

Two heartbeats later, all that's left are assorted body parts.

Edith turns away from her victims, her face taking on a strained, constipated look. Before I can wonder about vampire digestion, a bullet emerges from a bleeding hole in her neck and clanks onto the pavement.

Edith relaxes, and the hole heals right away.

"Wow," Felix mutters.

You can say that again. I knew that older vampires were powerful, but this is scary.

Edith's eyes take on the mirrored look of glamour, and she flashes to the nearest bystander car. She performs her vampire mind trick on everyone inside, then glamours all the rest of the bystanders as far as the nearest exit.

The glamoured drivers start their engines and head straight into the ditch by the side of the road, clearing it for us.

Edith whooshes back into the limo and orders Thalia to drive.

The nun floors the gas, and we leave the highway before anyone can say "dial 911." Edith takes out a phone and orders someone to "clean up" near the exit we've just left.

At triple the speed limit, we fly through the city streets until a police officer stops us—which is when Edith glamours him to be our escort. The cop gets back into his car, starts the siren, and clears the way for us until we turn onto the Brooklyn Bridge.

From there, the ride to Felix and Ariel's downtown building is uneventful. Leaving Thalia in the car, we step into the lobby. I half expect more Overtaken to attack again, but none do.

An elevator ride later, we reach the bulletproof front door of the apartment, and Edith says, "I'll wait outside."

Felix and I shrug while Ariel looks relieved.

As we step inside, two familiar furry creatures come to greet us: a chinchilla and a cat.

Hi, the chinchilla—Fluffster, who's really a type of Cognizant called domovoi—says in my head. *Good to see you again.*

The cat gives me and everyone else a once-over, then pretends she happened to check on the front door by accident. Her attitude seems to say, "A purebred Persian with a face as flat as mine doesn't *really* care if plebeians such as you exist."

Ariel scoops up Fluffster and hugs him to her chest. "Bailey is going to stay with us for a bit. Isn't that awesome?"

The chinchilla looks at me unblinkingly, his eyes too intelligent for a rodent. *Are you going to be helping out with rent?* he asks mentally.

"Dude." Felix rolls his eyes. "If you must know, thanks to Bailey, Ariel and I are going to be 'handsomely rewarded' soon."

Fluffster demands to know why, so I bring him up to speed.

If I know Felix, he's not going to ask for money, Fluffster says mentally when the story is over. *This household could go completely bankrupt, and he wouldn't bat an eye.*

"I'll get money, don't worry." Ariel rubs the fluffy, frugal creature against her cheek.

"And I plan to ask for something that can totally be monetized," Felix says. "I want to start a VR game company on Gomorrah."

"Wait, don't tell us." Ariel lowers Fluffster to the floor. "You're going to build the Matrix."

"The Matrix was a prison," Felix says defensively. "I want to build a fully immersive VR game environment that people would want to visit voluntarily and stay in for months on end."

"Potato, potahto." Ariel saunters over to a linen closet and pulls out a set of sheets and towels. "Both are simulated worlds with lots of action and adventure." She glances at me. "Come, let's get you settled in."

She leads me into an empty room with a bed, table, and bookshelves filled with paper books. Stripping the current sheets from the bed, she replaces them with the new ones and hangs the towels on the back of the chair.

I scan the books. They're all about magic—the performance art, that is, not powers. Makes sense. This is Princess Peach's room—or was—and she's really into this stuff.

"Is it okay that I'll be using her bed?" I ask Ariel, nodding at a nearby picture of Princess Peach herself.

"Oh, yeah," Ariel says. "She's on Atlantis, a world where time flows much faster than here. My math isn't so good, but I think in the time we've had this conversation, she's experienced a whole day of honeymoon bliss."

"So, if you know where she is, could we—"

"No. If Valerian were to go there with the intention of asking her for a favor, she'd see him coming and not be around when he arrives. And that's the best case. If he's not lucky, Valerian would catch her—which is when her hubby would kill him in the most spectacular manner. He really wants them to have this time to themselves and specifically warned against interruptions."

Right then. No help from Princess Peach or her "hubby." Not that either of them could help with the biggest problem of all— Collywobbles, who doesn't even exist in the waking world.

Unless he does. What does anyone really know about a god of nightmares?

"You hungry?" Ariel asks.

I reply in the affirmative, and she drags me to the kitchen before I can clarify my dietary hesitations.

I needn't have worried. Grinning like a maniac, Felix puts a large bunch of bananas into a salad bowl and places it ceremoniously in front of me.

He and Ariel get what he calls "his special," and the domovoi a bowl of oats with nuts. The cat receives a can of food that says "Fancy Feast" on it and has a picture of a feline very similar to her—but I think that's just weird marketing and not proof that cats are cannibalistic.

Is it true all you eat is bananas, like a monkey? Fluffster mentally asks me when I peel my first one.

"When on Earth, yes," I say with my mouth full. "It's the food I trust the most." And not very much at that, but I don't add that bit; Felix is already having too much fun at my expense.

I can live on oats and hay, Fluffster says. *Which, like bananas, is inexpensive.* He looks meaningfully at Felix, Ariel, and the cat.

Felix nearly chokes with mirth. "Don't worry," he says when he catches his breath. "If finances get tough, Ariel and I promise to live on bananas as well."

"And don't forget oats," Ariel says.

The cat gives everyone a look that seems to say, "If you don't get me my special food, I'll feast on your not-very-fancy eyeballs instead."

They tease me more with each banana I peel, and when I finish the whole bunch, Felix gets up, goes over to a cupboard, and takes out a couple of familiar packets.

I narrow my eyes at him. "You have manna?"

"Got a taste for it when we stayed on Gomorrah, so I smuggled in a bunch," Felix says. "It's all yours. I just wanted Ariel to see the banana eating at least once."

"Evil," I mutter, reaching for a packet.

"Genius," Ariel says, grinning.

Glaring at her, I dig into the heavenly food as they finish their boring, unsanitary Earth dishes.

For the rest of the day, I make myself comfortable in my new environment. We watch a movie and play violent video games, and I finally crash in the borrowed bed.

Nutcracker doesn't appear in my dreams, which is a relief.

The next couple of days pass by quickly; having roommates who aren't your mother can be pretty fun. On the third day, Felix gets a text from Valerian:

Be at the lab at 5.

When we notify Edith about this development, she's not surprised in the least.

Our limo ride to the JFK airport is blessedly uneventful. No Overtaken attack, and when we stop at the passenger drop-off point, Ariel asks Thalia, "You're not coming with us, right?"

The nun shakes her head.

"She's made a vow to stay on Earth or some such," Felix whispers.

Of course. I can see how staying on Earth is a form of penitence, on par with a vow of silence or fasting. When I share this opinion with the others, Ariel starts violently defending her home world, and we argue about it all the way to the lab.

Valerian is already waiting for us when we walk inside, and he's not alone.

A number of unfamiliar people are here, along with some I've met before—besides Kit and Itzel, that is.

One such person is Chester, a probability manipulator who looks like a satyr. Another one is Nina, a woman with facial piercings and extremely powerful telekinesis abilities. Also here is Colton, a giant who is a small enough example of his kind to be able to live on Earth. All three of them are members of the New York Council.

"Welcome," Valerian says. "Let me make the introductions." He proceeds to name me and everyone I know, along with our powers. When he gets to the first stranger, I pay closer attention.

"This is Fabian," Valerian says, nodding at a man only slightly smaller than Colton. "He's the Alpha of the Berlin pack."

Impressive. A werewolf Alpha is as powerful as an ally can get.

"He's famous for his martial arts," Ariel whispers reverently.

"You're too kind," Fabian growls with a heavy German accent. "I invented wolfu, the first martial art performed in wolf form."

Nina tugs on her nose ring. "A wolf fighting? How would that even look?"

"Let's hope we don't get into enough danger to find out," Itzel grumbles.

"That's Stanislav," Valerian continues, nodding at a gray-haired man wearing all black. "Head Enforcer of the Saint Petersburg Council."

Felix eyes the man warily. "A chort?"

"*Da*," Stanislav says with a frown. With a thick Russian accent, he asks, "You have a problem with that?"

"*Nyet, nyet*," Felix says quickly. "It's nice to meet you."

It is indeed. Chorts can mess with their victim's organs and turn parts of their own anatomy insubstantial when attacked. Stanislav might be even more useful than an Alpha werewolf, and definitely scarier to touch.

Edith examines Stanislav very carefully, and he glares at her in return. I wonder what's up with that. I've heard something about vampires and chorts being at each other's throats but don't recall the details.

"Last but not least is Dylan." Valerian gestures at an attractive young woman in a leather jacket. "Though Cognizant, she doesn't have a power in a traditional sense. She'll be our science adviser."

Dylan lifts her chin. "If knowledge is power—and it is—I'm the most formidable Cognizant here."

"Don't forget the most modest," Itzel says with an eye roll.

Valerian gives Itzel a stern look. "Dylan has a genius-level IQ and doctorates in multiple disciplines—including virology."

"And don't forget my knack for languages," Dylan says. "I'm your translator as well."

"Gnomes are good with languages," Itzel objects. "I speak several."

"Yes, but unlike you," Valerian says, "Dylan was willing to spend the time to learn the language of Necronia from our necromancer prisoner."

Itzel stiffens. "I needed to design the masks."

"Which I helped with," Dylan says. "If you—"

"Speaking of masks," Valerian says. "Those of you who haven't, please try on yours."

All of us hustle over to the table where the masks await.

"I used hygieia on yours already," Valerian says, pointing at the middle one. "Go ahead and put it on."

I examine the mask. It looks overdesigned—like it might help out against a poison gas attack, not just a virus. A strap goes over the top of my head, and two others loop around my ears, creating a snug fit. When I put it on, I can smell something chemical and metallic, but my breathing doesn't slow down.

"This is an amazing design," I say, my voice muffled.

Ariel snatches her mask from the table. "It *is* really cool. Bailey looks and sounds like Bane."

"That's Batman's nemesis," Felix explains. "Leave it to Ariel to link anything and everything to her favorite caped crusader."

Ariel lightly punches his shoulder and puts on her mask. Immediately, she looks like a gnome. So does Felix when he tries on his.

Nina levitates her mask onto her face while everyone else puts on their masks more traditionally.

As if it's the most natural thing in the world, Fabian starts to strip, exposing rows upon rows of muscles that only the most potent of steroids can conjure up in non-werewolf folks. When he's down to his boxers, he turns his back to us and finishes stripping.

At the shameless display of his glutes of steel, Itzel looks away, Kit whistles like a cartoon wolf, Ariel waggles her eyebrows, and Dylan blushes like a medieval maiden. Conscious of Valerian's narrow-eyed stare on me, I pretend to be swooning as well.

"My mask is a special design," Fabian says without turning, his German accent even deeper. "Just wanted to test it one last time."

With a flash, he turns into his wolf form. The size of a bison and even more muscular than in humanoid form, it's a shaggy thing of terrifying beauty. And indeed, his mask has elongated to accommodate his canine face, making him look like a muzzled hellhound.

When he switches back to his man form, the mask contracts, but no one pays attention to that because this time, he's facing us, his family jewels and other bits out in full force.

Kit whistles again, Ariel fans herself, and Dylan looks on the verge of fainting.

"Great job, Itzel," the werewolf says, ignoring it all.

Itzel looks him over, swallows very loudly, and averts her eyes. I, on the other hand, gape for all I'm worth to annoy Valerian.

It must work, because his chiseled jaw tightens and he uses his powers to shield Fabian's bits with a fig leaf until the werewolf puts his boxers back on.

Acting disappointed, I turn to look at the leftover masks. There's at least a dozen of them.

"What about those?" I ask, nodding at the stash.

"They're for the second part of our team," Valerian says, still sounding irritated—much to my delight. "We're meeting them en route."

Puck. We've already got an ancient vampire, a giant, a telekinetic, an uber, a chort, a shapeshifter, an alpha werewolf, an illusionist, and a robot suit. Now it sounds like there are more reinforcements. By the time we get to our destination, we'll be a freaking army.

Grunting, Colton collects the remaining masks and stashes them in his ginormous backpack.

Itzel shows us some of the mask features—like being able to eat and drink without taking the mask off—and Dylan makes sure to point out which features were her contributions.

"You still have to make sure the food and drink aren't contaminated," Itzel says apologetically when she's done with the demo. "If I'd had to build a decontamination chamber, the project would—"

"No worries," Colton booms and turns to show us a bag the size of an industrial refrigerator. "I'm carrying the supplies."

"Careful," Valerian says. "There are grenades in there."

Kit slides her mask up her forehead and transforms into a creepy plant-like creature without a mouth and nose, and with green cactus spines instead of hair. Returning back to her anime-character self, she says, "In a pinch, I won't need the supplies or the mask and could live off photosynthesis."

"*Nyechist*," Stanislav mumbles under his breath.

"That means something like *evil forces*," Felix whispers into my ear. "Usually said about chorts."

Stanislav's hearing must be good—he gives Felix a withering glare.

Chester also takes his mask off, revealing a devilish grin. "Shall we go?"

"Just one thing." Valerian unfurls a big hand-drawn map on the table. "Memorize the path to Necronia, in case we get separated."

"Done," Dylan says instantly. "I have a photographic memory."

"I hope you have the patience to wait for the more mentally challenged among us," Fabian growls through his mask, and Dylan takes a step back, proving she's got enough street smarts to be wary of an annoyed werewolf.

I memorize our path with ease; making sense of such maps is a course taught in middle school on Gomorrah. Felix and Ariel take the longest, and no wonder: Their teacher was Hekima, whose primary objective in his classes turned out to be causing nightmares.

"Now grab a weapon and let's go," Valerian says when everyone recites the map from memory to his satisfaction.

Ariel sprints over to the farthest corner of the room with all the excitement of a kid on Christmas morning. There are two piles there—one of blade weapons like knives, swords, and the like, and the other of guns.

"Remember, firearms don't work on every world," Dylan says as she watches Ariel cram pistols into every crevice of her outfit.

With a shrug, Ariel picks up a knife and a scabbard with a sword in it.

"I've got my own," Chester says and pulls out what looks like a sword handle from the back of his pants. He presses something, and the handle turns into a weapon I've never seen before—a sword made from a substance that looks just like the shimmering plasma of the gates.

"Wait," Felix says. "Isn't that—"

"A family heirloom." Chester winks and retracts the blade.

When it's Colton's turn, the giant picks up a claymore, which looks like a dagger in his massive hand.

Itzel forms a lightning ball on her palms. "I'm good."

Nina makes a scabbard and a scimitar fly into her hands and attaches them to her waist. "I probably won't need these, but it doesn't hurt to have them."

Edith grabs an ax and straps it to her back, while Stanislav does the same with a saber.

Spotting a few Gomorran guns, I grab one, and Valerian and Dylan do the same.

"Should I distribute the grenades?" Colton booms.

"Not yet," Valerian says, picking up a pair of sai—pointy dagger-like weapons.

"What kind of grenades are we talking about?" I ask as I strap a dagger to my waist and a katana to my back. I'm no expert on the daggers, but I've studied how to wield the katana in the dreams of two Kendo masters who'd hired me to help them dream-spar 'to the death.'

"Sleep and poison grenades," Valerian replies. He seems to have finally gotten over his irritation with me. "The first in case we want you to dreamwalk in a group of enemies, the other in case we need a weapon of mass destruction."

"Wouldn't the poison kill us along with the bad guys?" Felix asks.

"Not if you keep the mask on," Itzel says.

"Got it." Felix walks over to a big contraption I hadn't noticed before. It must be a new version of his robot suit, and it boasts four arms, Hindu-goddess style.

"Keep the mask on," Itzel says when Felix starts to take his off.

"She's right." Dylan straps a rapier to her waist. "A virus can penetrate the robot faceplate. If I had designed the suit for you, I would've—"

"We made the suit before we knew about this mission," Itzel says. "Besides, who cares? His head will fit, even with the mask on."

"Well, I care," Felix grumbles, climbing into the heap of metal. Through a speaker in his chest, he says, "I can barely breathe."

"You'll survive," Valerian says, then packs away the map and leads our ragtag procession to the hub room.

"How about I go first?" Chester says when we all approach the purple gate that is step one of our journey.

No one objects. His chances of getting randomly attacked are minuscule compared to those of us without his probability manipulation powers.

Once Chester steps through the shimmering plasma, the others follow. When it's my turn, I step in with some excitement. The one thing I've never really done much is Otherland spelunking, since that's more dangerous than visiting dream worlds, yet not that much more entertaining.

Or so I thought.

When I come out on the other side, I exhale in wonder.

CHAPTER NINE

THE SKY above us is a fluorescent purple, with pink cotton-candy clouds—a combination I've never used in my dream world creations because, ironically, I thought it was too unrealistic to exist in nature. There's also a Saturn-like ring around this planet, and two moons—one slightly smaller than Earth's and one twice that size.

As we hurry to the next gate, I notice that my steps are lighter, indicating a different gravity from that on Earth and Gomorrah.

The most worrying part is the air. Even through the mask, it feels unusually thick and sweet—but I figure if it were poisonous, Valerian would've planned for it.

"I've been on this Otherland before," Ariel whispers. "There's a gate to the Las Vegas airport nearby."

Felix glares at her. "You go into Otherlands to end up on the same world? The risk—"

"Beats an eight-hour plane flight," she mutters back.

Chester lets out a sigh. "Too bad Vegas isn't where we're headed. I love that place."

I'm sure he does. He can win at any game of chance, no matter how much the odds are stacked in favor of the house.

Felix is staring at the yellow shimmer that is our destination. "You know the gate we're about to take was on Hekima's list of 'dangerous ones to avoid,' right?"

"I'm sure that asshat was exaggerating," Valerian says coolly.

"Let's hope so," Itzel mumbles under her breath.

Oblivious to any possible danger, Chester steps into the new gate like I'd step into my favorite restaurant. The rest of us follow more cautiously. And it's a good thing we do.

When we emerge on the other side, Hekima's description doesn't seem all that exaggerated. For starters, the temperature and heat make the bathhouse from Valerian's dream seem chilly in comparison. Then there's the pterodactyl-like birds that circle in the sky like vultures above a desert.

Before I can ask Valerian to make us invisible to the fauna, a pterodactyl dives for us.

Almost casually, Nina extends her hand. With a pained shriek, the flying creature stops mid-flight and slams into a nearby cliff.

Stanislav mutters something in Russian in an impressed tone, and Felix replies, "*Da, da.*"

The rest of the flying creatures must not be choosy eaters; they swarm around the body of their fallen comrade with loud shrieks of glee.

My enthusiasm for Otherland spelunking fades a bit as we continue. The next world is a never-ending desert with a strangely starless night sky. The one after that is a gray tundra.

"What are we expecting on Necronia?" I ask, the tension in my shoulders easing when nothing attacks us for another two worlds.

"It's run by necromancers," Dylan says, taking on a professorial tone. "They have a religion that revolves around souls, and they use reanimated corpses to run their economy. That keeps humans grateful by letting them live in luxury. According to—"

"That reminds me." Valerian looks at Kit. "They have some sexual taboos I wanted to warn everyone about."

Everyone who knows Kit well follows Valerian's gaze with curiosity, while the woman herself minces forward as if "everyone" didn't mean "her."

"They are deeply homophobic," Valerian says, and Kit slows her pace. "Also, there's a strict anti-adultery law."

"Which is why Wrakar was exiled," Dylan chimes in. "He had an extra-marital affair."

Kit stops and morphs into an androgynous person of unspeakable beauty. "What if they're single?" she asks in a voice that's as masculine as it is feminine.

The corners of Chester's eyes crinkle. "How about you just keep it in your pants?"

Pouting, Kit looks at Dylan. "Fine. But maybe someone can help me scratch the itch on the way?"

Dylan's ears turn a deep red, and she gracelessly sprints into a blue gate in front of us.

Fabian growls something in German, and Itzel replies in kind.

"Well, I just figured sex is something else she might have a doctorate in," Kit says defensively and steps into the gate after Dylan. The rest of us follow, and I can't help but notice how Ariel is doing her best never to be near Edith.

Speaking of Edith… Isn't she going to be a problem on a world of necromancers? In our morgue encounter with Wrakar, a group of Enforcers was a major hindrance.

I mull this over for a couple of worlds before sharing my concern with the team, Edith included.

She huffs. "I'm too powerful for any necromancer to control."

"I'm sure," I say. "But won't they know what you are and get upset? Didn't your kind drive them off most worlds?"

"They won't even sense that I'm a vampire," Edith says. "The plan is to say that I'm an uber. My lack of youthful looks should help with the deception."

Chester smirks. "True. Vamps aren't known for their need of Botox injections."

"Still," I say. "It's a little worrying."

Falling into step beside me, Valerian places a hand on my shoulder and squeezes lightly. My treacherous stomach feels wobbly all of a sudden. "Edith's ability to glamour necromancers overrides the risk of discovery," he murmurs in my ear. "You don't need to worry."

Ignoring the warmth spreading through me, I remove his hand from my shoulder and turn to Edith. "Is that true?"

"It's how we got so much information out of our necro captive," she says proudly.

Hearing this, Ariel backs away from the vampire and changes the topic by asking about the team that Valerian mentioned will be waiting for us.

Oh, yeah. I almost forgot about that.

"Since Icelus is operating on multiple worlds, we're trying to organize a cross-Otherland defense," Valerian replies. "The people you're asking about are from the worlds that have decided to participate thus far."

"Wow," Ariel says.

"That's cool," Felix says.

Itzel bobs her head. "A historical achievement, indeed."

If I weren't mad at Valerian, I'd join their praises. Cognizant worlds usually stay out of each other's business.

Falling into step beside me again, Valerian touches my arm. "There's actually someone waiting for us who you might be interested in."

I not-so-subtly step out of his reach and lift an eyebrow.

Annoyingly, Valerian doesn't look put off. "Since Icelus uses a dreamwalker to coordinate across worlds, we decided to do the same and located a willing one on a world called Raira."

My second eyebrow joins its twin, and they both shoot up my forehead. "You know another dreamwalker, and you're just telling me now?"

His lips press together. "We just recruited him a few days ago."

"You might want to give Valerian a break," Kit says just as I'm about to say something snide. "The Council of Councils wanted to use *you* to coordinate across worlds, but he said it was out of the question."

I blink up at Valerian's ocean-blue eyes. "You did?"

"I wasn't going to throw you under the bus for a second time," he says, his face unreadable.

"Hmm," is my genius reply. I look at my friends, but they all avoid my gaze.

Fine. I jump through the next gate and end up on an icy plain under a toxic-looking green sky.

No one bugs me for the next two gates. Felix and Stanislav speak Russian; Itzel, Edith, and Fabian banter in German; then later, Felix and Dylan discuss computer science in what might as well be a foreign tongue.

And surprise, surprise—Dylan has a doctorate in that too.

The next world is a green savannah with waist-high grass.

Ariel catches up with me. "Am I the only one who thinks Necronia sounds like Narnia's dead sister?"

"Hush," Edith hisses. "Something's coming."

Everyone stops talking.

Thunder—or something like it—rumbles in the distance. The grass vibrates as the ground shakes.

"An earthquake?" Felix whispers.

"Run!" Chester yells and hoofs it to the gate.

I finally see the danger—a herd of mammoth-like creatures, only bigger and fiercer-looking. If they reach us, we're all meat tortillas.

As one, we launch into a sprint. Edith, Ariel, and Fabian are soon in the lead. The herd is gaining on us. To my shock, Nina sits down on the ground in a lotus pose and closes her eyes, a serene expression appearing on her face.

What the—

Everyone, Nina included, floats up off the ground.

Ah. She's using her powers again.

Floating like this is an eerie feeling that I've experienced once before and hoped never to feel again, but it beats the alternative.

The creatures stampede under us.

When they're gone, Nina gently lowers us back down. "You guys might want to start pulling your own weight," she says, jumping to her feet.

Ariel follows her into the gate, and the rest of us walk in after them.

"Is this your home world?" Chester asks Colton after I exit on the other side.

It takes me a second to figure out why he singled out the giant.

The primitive huts in the distance are the size of four-story buildings on Earth. Oh, and there are a dozen giants behind Chester. They're coming toward us from the direction of the next gate we need to take.

All are big but one is especially so.

A giant giant.

Itzel gasps. "Look at their eyes!"

"Crap," Felix mutters.

You can say that again.

That fire in the giants' eyes means only one thing.

They're also Overtaken.

CHAPTER TEN

BEFORE ANYONE CAN BLINK, Ariel is already holding a gun in her hand. Aiming at the giant, she presses the trigger.

An empty click sounds.

Puck. A world where firearms don't work. Isn't Chester's luck supposed to rub off on us?

But hey, that's Earth technology. I yank out my Gomorran gun, set it to stun, and shoot the giant giant.

Nothing happens.

Heart racing, I switch the setting to lethal and shoot again.

Still nothing. I guess since giants aren't allowed on Gomorrah, no one bothered to calibrate these guns to impact one.

One of the giants stoops to pick up a stone.

Puck.

He hurls it at me. I duck. Colton catches the stone and pelts it back at the bigger giant. The Overtaken giant stumbles but keeps on coming.

"Stay back!" Valerian jumps in front of me, as if he can somehow shield me from giants. Inspired by his example, Felix steps protectively in front of Dylan, who looks paler than Edith.

Edith herself, along with Chester, Stanislav, and Ariel, charges forward, and Colton follows, while Fabian strips off his clothes and morphs into his impressive wolf form before joining the fray as well. Kit, too, shifts into a copy of the giant giant and lumbers after everyone.

"Valerian, use your powers to hide us from them!" Dylan shouts.

He grimly shakes his head. "I can't. I'd need to trick them all, but I can only handle one. Best I can do for you is make you not see the violence."

"No, thanks," Dylan says, but I can tell she's tempted.

I'm tempted too, but I'd rather know what's going on, so I can help.

Itzel, who's stayed by my side, shoots the smallest of the Overtaken with a ball of her gnome lightning. It smashes into his forehead, and he drops to the ground.

Score.

Itzel tries doing it again, but her new target dodges the projectile.

To my right, Nina extends her hand and visibly concentrates.

The second-smallest giant lifts off the ground an inch, then plops back down, which causes him to stumble. The ground shakes as he crashes down, nearly squashing Fabian—who jumps away on hind paws with a grace I wouldn't expect from an animal his size.

A rock smashes into Nina's head, and she drops to her knees, blood trickling down her temple. "Seriously, start pulling your own weight, people."

Ignoring her, Edith swings her ax at the giants, who try to grab her.

One loses an arm, another a finger. But her victory comes at a cost— the giant giant grabs Edith by her legs and yanks hard. Her ax drops to the ground as she curses and flails.

Ariel throws a dagger at the giant giant's head.

Bullseye. Or rather, giant's eye, as that's exactly what the dagger pierces.

The Overtaken giant doesn't react to the injury. He simply grabs Edith's head with his free hand and pulls with a twisting motion.

Fearing for her, I leap out from behind Valerian and throw my own dagger at the giant's other eye. Sadly, my aim isn't as good as Ariel's. I hit the wrong giant, and in his shoulder, not the eye.

Activating the gate sword, Chester slices at the giant giant's leg.

The leg is severed, but it's too late for Edith.

By the time the giant crashes to the ground, the vampire's head and body separate and fly in different directions, spraying blood and bits of flesh everywhere.

Valerian yanks me behind him with a curse as I gape at Edith's remnants, my stomach churning with equal parts horror, pity, and disgust. No matter how ancient, a vampire can't survive a beheading.

Stanislav slashes at the next biggest giant with his saber, slicing off a chunk of his leg. Seemingly oblivious to the injury, the giant swings a massive arm at the chort, but his grasping hand goes through Stanislav's suddenly incorporeal torso—which is when Ariel chops it off at the wrist with her sword.

Oblivious to the fountain of blood gushing from his injured limb, the giant pivots to snatch up Ariel with his remaining hand, but Kit finally catches up with everyone and smashes a car-sized fist into the attacker's face.

The giant crashes to the floor.

With a roar, Colton beheads another one with his claymore. Fabian and Stanislav help Ariel down another, while Chester and Kit get yet one more.

At that point, the fight turns, and one by one, our allies kill or incapacitate the rest of the Overtaken giants.

When it's all over, Nina makes her way to Edith's remains, her expression somber. "To live so long just to perish here," she murmurs, shaking her head. "What a shame."

Equally grim, Colton scoops up nearby dirt, his enormous hand creating a hole worthy of a shovel. He keeps digging until the pit is six feet deep. At that point, Fabian picks up Edith's head and removes the mask, while Kit, still in her giant form, lifts the torso. Gently, they lower the vampire's remains into the grave.

Kit and Colton cover Edith with dirt as Fabian puts on his clothing. Then Fabian hands Edith's mask to Colton, who wipes the blood and stashes the mask in his backpack.

"Anyone want to say anything?" Valerian asks, sweeping a grave gaze around our congregation.

"More giants might be on the way," Itzel says. "We should go."

I approach the grave on unsteady legs. I feel sick, both from the adrenaline overdose and the senseless slaughter I just witnessed. Bending down, I find a patch of ground that *isn't* soaked with blood and toss some dirt into the grave. "Phobetor has a lot to answer for."

Though my voice is barely above a whisper, Valerian's jaw tenses. "Don't say his name." He walks over and hygieias my hand before I can do so myself. In a softer tone, he adds, "But you're right. He does."

"We should listen to the wise gnome and go before more trouble catches up to us," Chester says.

Everyone mutters their agreement, and we plod to the gate, disinclined to talk for the next six worlds.

"I'M STARVING," Fabian says when we enter a hub located in a lush forest meadow. "As the German proverb says, 'Hunger leads the wolf to the village.'"

Kit morphs into an adorable girl wearing a red riding hood. "I'm also hungry… like a wolf."

"Let's make camp," Valerian says. "I'll make us invisible to any predators that might lurk in the forest."

"I doubt they'd dare show up here." Removing his boxers again, Fabian takes on his wolf form and stalks into the bushes.

"I'm also going to get something to eat," Stanislav says, holding his saber. "Anyone care to join?"

Chester, Kit, and Nina tag along with the chort while the rest of us build a couple of fires.

Felix steps out of his robot suit and plops in front of the largest fire. "Am I the only one who finds the idea of a necromancer world creepy?"

I crouch to Felix's right. "I do too."

"It could be worse." Ariel folds her legs into a lotus pose across from me. "It could be a world full of vampires."

"That wouldn't be sustainable," Dylan says, joining us. "I've run the numbers. If a world has a greater than five percent vampire population—"

I don't hear the rest because Valerian strides over and takes a seat next to me.

I scooch away from him.

Shaking his head, he walks over to Colton's backpack, gets something out, and sits next to me again.

"Seriously?" I scoot away once more.

"Here." He slides next to me yet again and hands me a packet of manna, along with a water bottle from Gomorrah.

I snatch the food and drink without a thank-you, which is harder than it sounds. Mom raised me to be polite.

Valerian starts to say something, but Stanislav and his group of hunters show up, carrying a bleeding furry creature.

Gross. They're going to skin it and actually eat the meat. Did they forget all the gore we just saw on the giants' world? Leaning toward Valerian, I whisper, "Can you use your powers to prevent me from seeing their meal?"

Smirking, he does as I ask. After that, I can't bring myself to chase him off, so we sit side by side as I eat and drink through the special openings in the mask—a task that requires a surprising amount of concentration.

When I finish, I tell Valerian I don't need the illusion anymore, and he removes it. Through the mask, the smell of charred flesh isn't as bad as I feared, though watching everyone shove that unsanitary meat into their masks is nauseating.

"What do you think the Overtaken want?" I ask, mostly to distract myself.

Dylan lowers her meat skewer. "I guess they want whatever *you know who* wants."

"We call him Collywobbles." Felix wipes his greasy fingers on his shirt, and I almost ask Valerian to reapply the illusion. "But yeah, what does he want?"

Valerian tosses a log into the fire. "In the long run, more nightmares. Or more precisely, power."

I frown. "But how does killing my sister accomplish that? Or attacking us?"

"Not us." Valerian's forehead creases. "So far, I'm only aware of the Overtaken attacking you and Maxwell."

"Who's Maxwell?" Ariel asks at the same time as I exclaim, "Me?"

"Maxwell is the dreamwalker with the other team. We're going to meet him soon," Valerian says. "As to why—something about dreamwalkers must be a threat to Collywobbles, and he doesn't seem to trust Icelus to deal with it."

I turn to him—and can't help but notice that we're close enough to kiss, or would be if I were ever insane enough to let that happen. Well, and if there were no masks in the way. "How do you know it was me the Overtaken want?"

Valerian heaves a sigh. "The mess in the werewolf restaurant wasn't the first time they came after you. The Enforcers thwarted five attempts prior to that—two by your apartment and three near your work." Eyes gleaming, he places a hand on my knee. "That's why I wanted to put you in a safe house."

"Great." I not-so-gently remove his hand. "Now I'm on the priority kill list of a god."

No one replies. They just sit there, looking at me with pity.

I shiver, and not just because of the brisk evening breeze. As if to make things worse, I overhear Chester telling a scary story to his fellow New York Council members at the nearby fire. On the word "eviscerate," I tune the rest out.

"I wonder how many Overtaken there are?" Ariel asks after she finishes with her hunk of meat and tosses her skewer into the fire. "Also, do we know *how* Collywobbles turns people into them?"

"Maxwell might know the answer to the latter, but I can tell you about the former," Dylan says, again taking on that professional tone. "Thousands of people on Gomorrah have reported symptoms consistent with what we've dubbed the Overtaken. But the number of the affected is harder to puzzle out on Earth and other similar places since the condition has only affected the Cognizant thus far, and we can't report supernatural-sounding details like fire eyes to human doctors. So we still don't know if humans are immune, or if Collywobbles just hasn't bothered with them."

Ariel shakes her head, her expression subdued. "So many people turned into mindless puppets."

"That's not exactly what happens," Dylan says. "When awake, the Overtaken are actually normal. Even at night, they only get up and sleepwalk on rare occasions—when Collywobbles has something for them to do, we think."

Felix's eyes widen. "So if we'd woken up the giants and the other people who got killed, they—"

"Those deaths are on Collywobbles's conscience," Ariel says sharply. "When it comes to self-defense, don't second-guess yourself or you'll be the next corpse."

On that cheerful note, the conversation peters out until Dylan yawns loudly, creating a chain reaction with the rest of us.

"Someone should watch me at night," I say, not meeting anyone's gaze. "If the Nutcracker attacks and wins, I might be a danger to you all."

"I'll take the first shift," Ariel says. "Felix can go next, then—"

"No." Valerian crosses his arms over his chest. "I'll watch her."

I open my mouth, then close it. I'm not sure how I feel about Valerian watching me sleep. Definitely *not* aroused. Or intrigued. Also, why does he want to do this? Is it because he doesn't trust me to be asleep at the same time as him—worried I'd waltz into his dreams and steal his precious secrets?

When no one argues with him, he puts out the fire, fishes out a sleeping bag from Colton's backpack, hygieias it, and puts it a perfect distance from the coals.

I stomp over to the sleeping bag and climb in. Puck him and these little acts of kindness. If he keeps this up, I'll feel like a jerk holding on to my grudge, which I bet is his evil plan.

Before I can stop him, he zips up my makeshift bed. "Sweet dreams," he murmurs, gazing down at me. "I'll be here if you need me."

"Whatever," I say, glad he can't see Pom turning coral pink on my wrist.

Closing my eyes, I instantly drift off.

CHAPTER ELEVEN

I'M STANDING in front of my video game design class, naked as a mole rat.

Everyone stares at me, some giggling and some rolling their eyes. My left hand moves to cover my groin area, and as my right one goes to hide my breasts, I realize something is missing from my wrist.

The furry bracelet.

Pom.

In an eyeblink, I use my powers to clothe myself and make the audience disappear.

Ah, the good old 'naked in public' dream. If I had a gold coin for every time I've stumbled into one of these, I'd be richer than a dragon.

Speaking of dream invasion—no Nutcracker here. Does he need me unaware that I'm dreaming for his strike? Just in case, I turn myself metallic before teleporting to the tower of sleepers.

"Hi," Pom says, appearing next to me as I examine the people whose dreams I could potentially sneak into.

"Hey, bud. Hope you weren't awake during that fight with the giants."

When he says he wasn't, I update him on what's happened so far.

"So what now?" he asks when I'm done.

"I want to check on Mom," I say, spotting the gargoyle nurse I've been using for this purpose. "Want to join?"

He turns gray. "I don't like seeing Lidia like that."

He doesn't like it? It's *my* mom we're talking about.

Biting back an unnecessarily sharp retort, I touch the nurse and nudge her into a dream memory about Mom.

In this one, she's making sure there's enough goop available for Mom's feeding tube. Mom herself is lying there ashen and unmoving, for all intents and purposes a living corpse.

A hollow ache takes residence in my chest, and I let the nurse slip into her next dream while I teleport to my memory gallery. I know replaying a memory where Mom is fine doesn't change the reality of her current situation, but it's comforting nonetheless.

Once I'm calmer, I walk around the paintings depicting events from my life to see if there was any hint that I'd had a sister. I locate only the one that I already knew about, where I break a vase on which my twin and I had left our handprints.

I replay the memory.

Mom was sad, but it's unclear if she knew *why* she was sad. Thanks to a black window in her mind, she doesn't consciously recall killing Asha—or that Asha existed at all.

I strain to recall something—anything—else, but there's nothing. My theory is that seeing Mom kill Asha in front of me was so traumatic that I blocked the whole thing out, along with the majority of my childhood. But shouldn't there be at least a few stray memories?

Feeling heavier than before, I leave the memory gallery and reunite with Pom in the tower of sleepers, where I locate a few of my patients and provide some therapy sessions.

Making others feel better is a mood booster for me.

"You might want to create some exposure therapy for yourself," Pom says as we fly into the lobby and hover below a mosaic depicting an archery-target-like mandala made out of multicolored glass. "Your adrenaline levels are through the roof."

I grimace. "That would be tricky. The main source of my fear is going to a world with a nasty virus."

Pom nods sagely. "Of all the ways to perish, that one would be the worst for you."

"You can say that again." I swoop down and land on my metallic feet with a thud.

"Won't you be safe with the mask Itzel made?" Pom asks, following me down.

"No mask is perfect."

He wiggles his ears. "So how about that therapy then? To calm you down?"

I roll my eyes. "What would that even entail?"

"You can have a dream where you lick doorknobs in a bathroom."

Ugh. I suppress a shudder at that mental image. "No, thank you. And in any case, this is a deadly plague. I'm justified in my paranoia. Any other bright ideas?"

"We can talk about you and Valerian," he says hopefully, his coat turning a light orange hue as his pupils transform into hearts.

"Nope," I say and jolt myself awake.

—

UNDER THE LIGHT of four moons, I see Valerian sitting there, vigilantly guarding my slumber.

For some reason, the sight makes me smile.

Closing my eyes, I drift into sleep again—this time without any dreams.

—

IN THE MORNING, we have a hearty breakfast—another Valerian-smuggled manna for me, leftovers from dinner for the rest of the crew—and continue on our journey.

"Maxwell and the others are just through there," Valerian says as we approach a pink gate that, according to the map we memorized, leads to the world just before Necronia.

When we step through, we end up in an underground hub that looks just like the JFK one we started from.

Instead of a team, one person is waiting here for us. He's wearing a surgical mask with a plastic face shield on top. He looks us over with sad eyes, his forehead creasing in worry.

"Maxwell?" Valerian asks.

Nodding, the man turns away. "Those masks look like good ones, but it'll still be safer if we talk outside."

He hurries out of the hub, and we follow him through a maze of corridors right into what looks like a train station on Earth.

Except there aren't usually any corpses on Earth train stations, and I spot a dozen here. The dead—at least I assume that's what they are—are all dressed in odd clothing, their skin a strange purplish hue.

I suppress a shudder.

"What happened here?" Dylan asks, looking at a nearby man, whose face looks to have been contorted by agony before he perished.

Maxwell doesn't stop to explain. He carefully circles around the corpses in his path and picks up the pace again as we near an exit.

We follow him out. The buildings and the storefronts outside remind me of Midtown in Manhattan—except there are no people here at all, just more corpses.

"Stay there." Maxwell walks about fifteen feet away from us, looks back, and backs up one more step. "This should do it."

"Do what?" I shout. "Where's your team?"

He takes out a handkerchief and wipes at his eyes.

Puck. Is that blood on the handkerchief?

Before I can ask, he pockets the hanky with a somber expression. "They're dead."

On some level, I expected him to say something like that, yet it's still a shock. They must've been as formidable as our team, so for all but one to be dead—

"Dead?" Fabian steps toward Maxwell, but Dylan grabs his shoulder.

"Keep the distance," she says tensely. "If this is what I think—"

"They're not the only ones dead." Maxwell gestures at the nearest corpse. "The majority of this world's population are doomed too. Just as I am." He wipes his eyes with his bare hand and displays his fingers.

Yep. It was blood I saw.

Blood from the eyes.

If I were Maxwell, I'd be hysterical now.

"Haemolacria," Dylan mutters. "It's usually benign."

"It's the first symptom." Maxwell wipes the blood on his shirt. "Soon I'll have heart palpitations, then upset stomach, then just around the time my skin turns purplish red, I'll perish."

Pucking puck. Itzel's masks have a huge design flaw. There's no way to puke without taking them off—which is why I just swallow the bile down and do my best to even out my breathing.

"When?" Valerian asks, his brow furrowed.

"Depends on one's immune system," Maxwell says. "The orc from my party lasted four days while the elf was dead the day after."

Slow breathing is out the window. I begin to hyperventilate.

"Does anyone else find it suspicious that he's the last person alive?" Chester asks conversationally. "Or that he has whatever the plague is, yet has a mask on? Or is it not airborne?"

"No, the virus transmits through air droplets," Maxwell says. "My team and I wore protective gear as we waited for you, but then the Overtaken attacked." He takes out the handkerchief again and dabs some of the new blood away. "It's my fault. It's me the Overtaken wanted, and everyone protected me as well as they could. The Overtaken killed some of them outright, and ripped off masks from the faces of the others. I was the only one who managed to keep my mask on. And one of the Overtaken must've been sick because the team displayed symptoms soon after."

"Then how did you catch the virus?" Dylan asks.

He shrugs. "Perhaps the virus can penetrate a mask like this, or maybe I caught it when I ate or drank. I was staying at the hospital with my team"—he gestures at a building across the street—"and in hindsight, that might've been a bad idea."

I'm only partially listening as the word *virus* repeats on a loop in my mind. I want to run until my legs cramp up, then take a hygieia device and use it from head to toe, over and over and over again.

"So that's why you wanted to keep the distance?" Itzel asks.

Maxwell nods.

"This has to be the same virus we came to prevent on Necronia," Dylan says. "Icelus must've already let it loose on this world."

"That's what we assumed." Maxwell rummages through his pocket and takes out a couple of beakers. "These are blood samples from my team. Do you think you can figure out a cure using them? There's a lab at that hospital and—"

"Where?" Dylan's eyes gleam with excitement.

Maxwell tells her how to locate the lab in question, and Dylan sprints across the street.

"I'll make sure nothing attacks her," Fabian says and rushes after her.

I try to rein in my panic. "We should give Maxwell one of the better masks. This way, when he goes to the lab with Dylan, she's less likely to get infected."

Everyone likes the idea, so Valerian takes out a mask from Colton's bag and places it on the pavement.

We all step away as Maxwell approaches. Keeping his back to us as a precaution, he swaps his old mask for Itzel's design. When he's done, we return to our previous positions and wait for Dylan.

"We have a question for you," Valerian says after a period of uncomfortable silence. "How do the Overtaken come to be the way they are?"

"It's also a virus, of sorts." Maxwell's voice sounds muffled by the new mask. "A person somewhere—let's call him Dreamer Zero—had a very special nightmare, one that allowed *you know who* in. Thus, Dreamer Zero was the first Overtaken, most likely without knowing it. Then, because the special nightmare was so memorably nasty, Zero felt obliged to tell a friend, or a relative, or a therapist about it. What he probably didn't know was that this particular nightmare is unique—hearing its details plants something like a virus in the subconscious in such a way that when the person who hears it goes to sleep, they *also* dream the exact same nightmare, thus giving access to *you know who*. From there, the nightmare spreads exponentially, far and wide."

Chester casts a nervous glance at Kit, Colton, and Nina, who look shell-shocked.

"How long between the nightmare and the sleep walking?" Nina asks in a strangely unsteady voice.

"A couple of nights," Maxwell says. "Why?"

"What was the nightmare about?" Chester asks, sounding equally strange.

"I'm not one of the Overtaken, so I haven't seen this particular nightmare," Maxwell says. "But even if I had, telling you about it would mean I'd turn you into an Overtaken, so I'd have to keep quiet."

Valerian examines the New York Council members with a frown. "Why are you asking all this?"

Colton shifts from foot to massive foot. "Chester told us about a nightmare he had last night. Then, when I went to sleep, I had the dream myself."

"So did I," Nina says grimly.

"Same," Kit says, glaring at Chester with narrowed eyes. "I can't believe you infected me—and not with something sexually transmitted at that."

Chester shakes his head. "My daughter couldn't sleep because of a nightmare." His voice is hollow. "She told me what it was, and I thought it curious when I dreamed the same thing."

"How long ago?" Maxwell asks sharply.

Chester scratches behind the back straps of his mask. "Two days. I've had the nightmare twice so far—which made it more notable and is the reason I told others about it."

Maxwell shakes his head. "You have two more days before you need to take precautions. I suggest having someone lock your room for the night." He looks at the other Overtaken-to-be. "You have three more days—unless you start messing with your sleep cycles to stall it."

"We have experience with people who are dangerous when they sleep,"

Nina says. "Gertrude, our fellow Council member, is a gangrene-giver who sleepwalks."

At the prospect of being treated like Gertrude, Colton, Kit, and Chester look glum.

"How much of the nightmare story do you need to hear to get into trouble?" I ask, recalling my eavesdropping from the other day. "I think I overheard Chester talk about his nightmare, but only caught a few words."

"If you didn't have the nightmare, you're fine." Maxwell gets his hanky out and dabs at his eyes again. "Make sure not to hear any more, though."

Puck, yeah. The idea of getting a mind virus, or whatever the term, has never even occurred to me, but now that it has, it goes to the top of my things to avoid, up there with crunching on kitty litter.

Kit morphs into Chester but with fiery eyes. "How could this even happen? Isn't your luck power supposed to protect you?"

Chester shrugs. "Bad things still happen to me. The universe is too chaotic to avoid that."

"Guys. Isn't that a person?" Ariel points into the distance.

Everyone looks.

A woman in a surgical mask is creeping around a block away from us. When she sees us looking, she bolts as if worried we'd catch her and turn her into soup.

Maxwell follows the woman's retreat with his sad eyes. "Not everyone here is dead. There are whole continents on this world where the governments shut down all incoming travel. The virus hasn't spread there as much."

Valerian's eyebrows meet in the middle of his forehead. "More like Icelus hasn't yet spread it everywhere."

Felix's robotic neck turns with a screech. "If Icelus are still here on this world, it gives us a chance to help the people on Necronia save themselves."

"Ever the optimist," Itzel says. "Icelus might've infected this world by accident—and could already be done with Necronia by now."

"Nostradamus didn't think so," Felix says defensively.

"He also wanted us to take Chester, yet look what happened," I say.

"Whatever Nostradamus said will no doubt benefit *him* most of all," Chester says. "Seers can't be trusted. I bet he never said the people of Necronia will be saved."

That's true. He didn't. The only clear-cut thing the seer said was that I will perish if I don't go to Necronia. Given the virus situation, I'm tempted to take my chances with not going and let the chips fall where they may.

"We're not just trying to save Necronian lives." Valerian's eyes gleam with menace. "We have to catch Icelus agents so they can be questioned."

Kit morphs into a giant spider I've seen once before. "Questioned, tortured… who wants to split hairs?" she growls through a set of mandibles.

Seeing Maxwell's terrified reaction, Kit becomes herself again and winks at the poor guy.

"Our walking-talking encyclopedia is done," Stanislav says, looking across the street.

Sure enough, Dylan is sprinting toward us, Fabian on her tail.

"So," Maxwell says when she reaches us. "Can you cure me?"

Panting, she shakes her head. "That lab isn't equipped for research. If I already knew the chemical formula for the cure, maybe I could make it there. As is, it would take longer than the time you have left. I think we'd better follow the protocol we established in the case of contamination."

Ariel lifts her eyebrows. "We planned to get sick?"

"A medical team of vampires and quarantine rooms are waiting for us at the hub on Gomorrah," Dylan says. "If Maxwell rushes back, he can be there in a day."

"Unless the Overtaken kill him," Itzel says. "Or the virus makes him too weak."

"He'll need an escort," I say. "Which could actually solve our other problem." I wave at Chester, Kit, Nina, and Colton.

"I agree," Valerian says. "Chester has a day before he turns, the others even longer. That gives them time to escort Maxwell to Gomorrah."

"Good plan." Kit transforms into that creepy plant-like creature without a mouth and nose.

"It's an outstanding plan," Nina says. "Except for the part where we walk with the sick guy."

"Kit and I can stay close to him while you and Colton keep your distance," Chester says. "With two masks and my luck, I shouldn't catch the virus."

No one has the heart to tell him that if his luck had worked, it would've protected him from becoming an Overtaken.

"Here." Chester hands Ariel the handle of his gate sword. "Your group will need this more than ours."

Ariel takes the artifact reverently and gives Chester her own sword in return.

"This actually works out," Felix says.

Everyone looks at him like he's lost some mission-critical marbles.

"Maxwell will take himself and samples of infected blood to Gomorrah." Felix folds his pinky. "They develop a cure." He folds his ring finger. "We tell Necronians how to make it." He folds his middle finger. "Then all we have to do is catch Icelus and go back." He triumphantly folds his index finger.

"How simple," Itzel says with an eye roll. "Maybe it should've always been the plan to kill half our party?"

"We'll need a way to stay in contact," Maxwell says. "To that end, can you please lie on the ground?"

Everyone looks at everyone else. No one wants to say what we're all thinking—the virus has clearly gotten into his brain.

"I meant Dylan," Maxwell says. "Please, I don't have much time."

Gingerly, Dylan lies on the ground.

Maxwell extends his hand and closes his eyes.

Instantly, Dylan's eyes also close, and her body relaxes.

Wait. She can't be—

But she is. My new senses confirm it. Maxwell has not only made Dylan fall asleep; he's put her right into REM cycle.

"How did you do that?" I exclaim excitedly.

Maxwell doesn't reply. He's clearly setting up a dreamwalk session with Dylan.

Would I meet him if I set up a link myself? I've never dreamwalked in someone who already had another dreamwalker in their mind, and the idea sounds interesting.

If it weren't for the virus, I'd try it. As is, though, I feel irrational repugnance at the idea of ending up face to face with Maxwell, even in the dream world. It's probably my fear of germs, but I can't help feeling that there's more to Maxwell than it seems, that he's hiding some secret.

Hold up. He's a dreamwalker. Could *he* be the Nutcracker? His job is to coordinate communication between Otherlands the way the Icelus dreamwalker does, so how ironic would it be if they were the same person? He could then anticipate every move against Icelus—the perfect spy.

I need to talk to Valerian about this. Soon.

"Done," Maxwell says, bringing me out of my suspicion-filled fugue.

Looking disoriented, Dylan gets up from the ground.

"Let's go," Maxwell says.

"How did you put her into REM sleep like that?" I ask.

Maxwell looks at me as though for the first time. "That's something we dreamwalkers can just do."

"Not me, and I'm a dreamwalker."

"No one taught it to you on… your home world?" he asks haltingly.

"You mean on Soma?" I ask on a hunch.

Maxwell's eyes nearly bulge out of their sockets. "We really have to make haste," he says hurriedly. "It's literally a life-and-death situation."

With that, he rushes into the station.

"Good luck," Chester says to us and follows the dreamwalker.

Colton takes off his backpack and hands it to Fabian, the only member of the party big enough to carry it. With a farewell, the giant lumbers after Chester. Lacking a mouth in her plant form, Kit blows us an air kiss before she goes, while Nina just waves and follows the others.

As soon as they disappear into the station, I notice Valerian glaring at me.

Of course. I said the forbidden word. *Soma.*

Was that why Maxwell bolted so fast too? Is Soma something you never talk about—like Fight Club from that Earth movie? Or is it because Maxwell is the Nutcracker and didn't want to teach an enemy dreamwalker any new skills?

Puck. If he *is* the Nutcracker, what if his whole team hadn't died of the virus?

What if he'd killed them?

I rattle out my concerns out loud, ending with, "Should we run after them?"

Fabian shakes his head. "They have Chester's probability manipulation to keep them safe."

"But he couldn't keep *himself* safe," Itzel says.

"Maxwell was vetted," Valerian says with finality. "I say we've wasted enough time on this world. Let's head to Necronia."

"What?" Itzel exclaims. "We're still doing that? Our group is half the size we were supposed to be, and we just lost our most powerful allies."

"Bullshit," Stanislav says, his accent thicker than usual. "Your most powerful ally is still here."

"The chort is right," Fabian says. "Assuming he means me, of course."

"We can't not go," Felix says, almost regretfully. "Nostradamus's prophecies are not something you want to mess around with."

"Fine." Itzel readjusts her mask. "I just want to go on record saying this is a bad idea."

Felix mimes writing something in an imaginary notebook. Pretending to close it, he says, "Noted."

Valerian turns on his heel and strides into the train station. The rest of us follow, vaulting over corpses when necessary. I do my best not to think about dead bodies decomposing and whether the virus is still live in the air around them. Because terrifying. And super gross. A sprint down the corridors later, we find ourselves in the hub and in front of the purple gate that is our destination.

"Ready?" Stanislav asks.

Everyone nods, though some, like Itzel, less enthusiastically than others.

"Let's go then," the chort says and enters the gate.

Fabian and the others follow, and I go last.

Stepping out on the other side, I realize Chester's probability manipulation powers hadn't failed him. Far from it.

If this is Necronia, he's lucky to have missed it.

CHAPTER TWELVE

WE'RE INSIDE A SMALL CANYON, surrounded by gray mountains, with a sky blocked by gloomy clouds up above. My eyes have to adjust to the lack of light, and when they do, I realize a legion of people are crammed into the hub like rotten sardines.

They're wearing masks with nightmarish designs and loin cloths, along with itchy-looking bras on what might be the females. Their skin is ashen, and they have tattoo-like carvings all over their bodies that glow from the inside.

The only place free of these people is a two-foot-wide tunnel that leads from the hub canyon into a crack in a mountain ridge—a crack that looks like a gap in the teeth of a dead titan.

My teammates gingerly advance into the people-tunnel. Behind us, the tunnel fills with silently moving bodies, cutting off the way back—which doesn't fill me with warm fuzzies, not even a little bit.

"These must be corpses," Ariel whispers. "I can't believe this is happening again."

She's probably right. Now that she's said it, I could swear there's a stench of death seeping through my mask's powerful filters.

"For their sake, I hope they're dead." Felix points at one of the carvings. "Doing that on a live person would be against the Geneva Convention."

"We're far from Geneva," Ariel mutters.

"Well, yeah," Felix says. "Nor are we in Kansas anymore."

Nobody replies to him, and we continue through the tunnel in silence until Felix speaks again in a loud whisper. "Those masks look like they were designed by H.R. Giger." Without waiting for a follow-up question, he explains, "He did design work on *Alien*."

I know the artist he's talking about and have to agree. The masks depict people and steam-powered machines interlinked in an eerie, almost sexual symbiosis.

Dylan says something in an unfamiliar language, seemingly addressing the corpses.

"What did you say?" Felix asks her. "That sounded like a mix of German and Vietnamese, with some Klingon thrown in."

"It sounded nothing like German," Fabian says, giving Felix a cold look. "If anything, it reminded me of Russian."

Stanislav glares at the werewolf. "*Sobaka*. That's nothing like Russian."

Stern-looking LEGO letters appear in front of my eyes, and I assume in front of everyone else's also:

Let's stay quiet and figure out what they want.

We follow Valerian's suggestion, and it soon becomes clear that what the corpses want is to herd us through the crack in the rock.

When we step out of the crack, we find ourselves in a bigger canyon, which is filled to the brim with more animated corpses, thousands upon thousands of them.

Valerian's LEGO letters appear again:

Dylan, try speaking with them.

She begins yelling in the same language, facing this way and that.

At first, there's no response. Then every single one of the thousands of corpses replies in unison. Their speech—a strange dry rustle, like dead branches rubbing against each other—creeps into my bones, chilling them below zero kelvin. This is what hell would sound like, I imagine, and though the corpses seem to be using the same language as Dylan, through their withered vocal cords, it sounds exponentially uglier and more terrifying.

"They asked why we're here," Dylan announces.

Tell them, Valerian commands via LEGO letters.

Dylan shouts in Necronian for a few seconds.

Almost anticlimactically, the corpses respond with just two words.

"You lie," Dylan translates.

"Ungrateful bastards," Fabian growls.

Persuade, Valerian orders. *Tell them about Icelus and the virus. Tell them what the symptoms are.*

Dylan tries—or at least, she speaks in Necronian for a while.

The reply from the corpses is a little longer this time, but given how Dylan whitens, I doubt we'll like the translation.

The corpses step aside, creating a tunnel, this time leading back the way we came.

"They said this is our last chance to go back and never return," Dylan says, her voice shaking. "If not, and I quote, 'I'll turn you into helpers.'"

"Helpers?" Felix asks.

Ariel examines the masked corpses with a shudder. "I bet it's a euphemism for *zombies*."

"I say we do leave." Itzel glances the way we came. "We told the necros about the threat, so our consciences are clear."

Valerian glares at Dylan. "Tell them we'd like to talk to someone in charge."

Felix chuckles humorlessly. "Good old 'may I speak to the manager?'"

"More like 'take me to your leader,'" Ariel says.

"Shut up," Stanislav says. "They might speak English."

Ignoring everyone's back-and-forth, Dylan yells out a short phrase.

The response through the zombie mouths is curt.

"Time's up," Dylan says with a stutter.

Her translation wasn't necessary. With a shuffling of naked feet, the tunnel leading back to the hub closes, and the so-called helpers assume aggressive postures—ready to leap and claw at our faces.

In a coordinated move, the zombies attack.

CHAPTER THIRTEEN

"WEAPONS OUT!" Ariel shouts, pulling out a big gun with one hand and her plasma sword hilt with the other. Without a second of hesitation, she shoots the zombie closest to her in the middle of his mask.

Boom.

Mask in tatters and face a mangled mess, the zombie stumbles back before recovering and lunging at her.

Ariel activates her sword and slashes at her attacker. The gate-like substance of the blade effortlessly cleaves the zombie from head to groin. Not surprisingly, the already-dead creature doesn't die, but since each half can't balance on one leg, they fall and get trampled by the next set of zombies who attack Ariel.

She shoots one and slices another in half with all the speed and grace of an uber while I unsheathe my katana. My heart drums furiously in my chest as I swivel my head from side to side, taking in the battlefield.

To my left, Dylan fires her Gomorran gun. The zombies are unaffected, as I knew they would be, having once tried this move on their kind myself.

"Valerian, do your illusion thing!" Dylan shouts.

He's already got his sai out and is stabbing both of them into the throat of the zombie nearest to him. "Necros can see through the eyes of all the zombies," he yells back as he yanks the weapons out before plunging them back into zombie flesh. "My powers won't work here!"

Back to back with Valerian is Felix. With his upper right robotic arm, he catches a zombie by the throat and keeps her there. His upper left hand grabs the zombie's head, while the lower arms hug the zombie's torso.

Metal creaks, and the zombie's head separates from her body.

Another zombie lunges at my throat, but a ball of lightning hits him in the chest, sending him flying.

"Thanks!" I shout to Itzel, who blasts another zombie with a second lightning ball.

One more zombie leaps at me—a female one, if the bra is anything to go by. I swing my katana and slice her hand off before it reaches me, then behead her with a strike I've practiced in my dream.

To my surprise, it works from the first try. Whatever this katana is made of is amazing. It goes through flesh and bone as if through sponge cake. Whoever provided these weapons knew what they were doing.

To my right, a male zombie with talon-like nails takes a swipe at Stanislav's arm. All the nails get is empty air—the chort uses his power to make his flesh insubstantial just in time.

The zombie swipes again, aiming at Stanislav's head. His nails scrape the mask as the chort makes his head insubstantial and sidesteps the next strike.

The zombie is left holding Stanislav's mask. With a twist of his wrist, he tosses it like a frisbee back at the chort's head. Stanislav's face phases in and out of substantiality, and the mask whooshes through him to the other side of the canyon. A moment later, Stanislav retaliates, beheading his opponent with his saber.

Two more zombies attack Stanislav.

He phases over and over, slicing with his saber all the while.

In the meantime, Fabian is already naked, the backpack at his feet. With a flash, he morphs into his wolf form and starts hopping from paw to paw as though dancing, while at the same time swinging his limbs around. Each time one of his massive paws connects with a zombie, the zombie loses an important part of his or her anatomy. It must be the wolfu martial art he mentioned. It's deadly, and probably would be more so if it weren't for his muzzle-like mask.

A large male zombie jumps at me. I slice at his Adam's apple with the katana. The head rolls at my feet, and I do my best to catch my breath. This beheading felt harder. My arms are growing tired.

A few more zombies later, my arms feel like lead, my muscles screaming in exhaustion. The most discouraging part is that no matter how many reanimated corpses I or my teammates dispatch, there are thousands more to take their place.

Puck this. I'm not giving up. Panting, I swing harder, beheading another zombie just as a squadron of shadows appears in the sky.

What the puck?

They're flying creatures, each the size of a roc bird, but they look like a hybrid between a pterodactyl and a bat. In the claws of each flying creature is a masked person.

In a blink, the squadron swoops down, delivering more zombies into the already-impossible battle.

We are beyond pucked.

CHAPTER FOURTEEN

GRITTING MY TEETH, I will my leaden arms to move. *Swing, swoosh, don't think about gore and germs.* I'm a zombie-beheading machine, taking out one after another, not thinking about how sweaty and numb my palms are getting or how my lungs are struggling to drag in enough air through the mask.

Still, no matter how determined I am, my body is beginning to give out. I stumble, nearly dropping my katana as a zombie lunges at me, teeth snapping like a rabid dog. Gasping, I lop off its head, and as I pivot to face a fresh onslaught of attackers, I realize none are coming.

The attack has suddenly stopped.

The zombies open their mouths and begin to speak.

All eyes swing toward Dylan, staring at her with hope.

"That's odd," she pants, wiping the sweat from her forehead. "They're asking what the first symptom of the virus is."

"Tell them." Stanislav's Russian accent is thicker than ever.

Dylan shouts a reply in Necronian.

The zombies speak once more.

"They said his name is Nulen. He swears that if we put our weapons down, he'll talk to us face to face."

Everyone exchanges worried glances.

"I don't see harm in it," Valerian says, tossing his sai on the ground. "It's only a matter of time before we lose."

Everyone solemnly nods. I guess I wasn't the only pessimistic one.

The zombies back away, creating a wider circle around us.

I toss down my katana, then the gun.

Ariel drops empty gun after empty gun on the ground. Then she disables her gate sword and gently places it on the rest of the weapons.

When everyone's disarmed, the zombies speak again.

"He's asking Fabian to turn back into man form and for Felix to be turned off," Dylan says.

In a flash, naked Fabian stands before us. He picks up his clothes and starts to dress.

The robot suit opens up, and Felix reluctantly steps out of it.

Stepping aside to create a tunnel, the horde speaks again.

"Step away from the weapons," Dylan translates.

"I have a better idea." Felix shoots the robot with a ray of magenta energy. The robot starts to move of its own accord. It picks up the backpack and stashes it inside itself, where Felix's body would usually be.

Catching on, we help the robot stash the other weapons inside it. When our armory is hidden, the robot closes shut, and Felix makes it walk through the tunnel the zombies created. It reaches all the way to the edge of the nearby mountain, and when the robot gets there, it sits on the ground and grabs its legs with all four arms, slumping forward.

We wait in tense silence. And wait. And wait. After what feels like an hour, a new zombie tunnel opens up, and a man steps out of it—presumably Nulen. As pale as a pre-vamp, he's dressed in strange leather clothing and has lines of black paint on his face.

He walks over to us, and when he's within touching distance of me, he stares me in the eyes so intently, it's as if he's trying to see who blinks first. But no. He just steps over to Itzel and does the same thing, then repeats the process with everyone else.

A weird greeting ritual perhaps?

Finally, he opens his mouth and speaks.

"He's asking what kind of Cognizant we are," Dylan translates. "Should I tell him?"

Valerian nods, and Dylan speaks for a few seconds.

Nulen frowns and replies in rapid-fire Necronian.

Dylan pales. "He's asking which of us can make someone cry blood."

"Tell him the truth," Valerian says. "Such power doesn't exist, and he probably knows this."

As Dylan speaks in Necronian again, Nulen's frown deepens.

This is when I notice it—and realize the reason we're still alive.

In the corner of Nulen's right eye, a red droplet is gathering. A bloody tear that can only mean one thing.

The virus we came to stop is already here.

CHAPTER FIFTEEN

"STANISLAV NEEDS TO put his mask back on," Dylan blurts, her gaze following mine.

The chort touches his face as if realizing its nakedness for the first time. "It flew there." He points at the other side of the canyon.

"Do we have another mask in Stanislav's size inside the backpack?" I ask urgently.

Eyes wide with horror, Dylan shakes her head.

"What about one for him?" I gesture at the necromancer.

"Maybe," she says, helplessly glancing toward the robot.

I take a breath, trying not to panic. "Tell him to get his 'helpers' to bring Stanislav his mask and to let Felix go get one for him."

Dylan and Nulen go back and forth, looking increasingly agitated. Finally, the necromancer nods, and the zombies reopen the tunnel that leads to the robot.

As Felix sprints for the backpack, the zombies pass a mask over their heads is if it were a stage diver at a rock concert.

Stanislav's mask arrives first, luckily intact. He carefully puts it on, letting the necromancer see how he works the back straps.

Felix comes back and throws Nulen his mask.

The necromancer puts it on and speaks in a muffled voice.

"He asked about a cure," Dylan says. "I told him we don't have it yet but are working on it. He then stated that we're lucky. He indeed has never heard of a Cognizant power that would cause blood tears, particularly at a distance, so he has to give us the benefit of the doubt. Ultimately, it's up to the Parliament to decide if we're telling the truth. He'll take us to them."

"Good," Valerian says. "Let's hope Maxwell survives his trip back, and that the scientists on Gomorrah work out how to make the cure posthaste."

If we're throwing around hope, mine would be *please let us not get sick*. No, make that *pretty please, with a cherry on top*. Valerian still has a good point, of course. Without a cure or some other counterbalance to bad news, the Parliament might well treat us as the proverbial messengers to shoot.

Nulen strides toward a big opening in the canyon, and the zombies part for him in the widest tunnel we've seen yet. He waves for us to follow.

"What are the chances Stanislav caught the virus?" I ask in a low voice as we walk after him.

"Depends on a lot of factors." Dylan's professorial tone is back. "We're outside, and Stanislav and Nulen didn't stay close together for long. Also, chorts have excellent immune systems—though not pre-vamp levels, of course. If I had to guess, I'd say infection is unlikely."

"I'll keep my distance from everyone, just in case," Stanislav says and falls back.

Valerian looks at Dylan. "Did you ask Nulen how *he* might've gotten sick?"

Dylan smacks her forehead, then talks to Nulen for a few seconds.

"He doesn't know," she says when they finish. "He'd never heard of a virus like 'ours' before today."

"Did he talk to anyone else who came through the gates?" Valerian asks.

Dylan checks.

"No," she translates a moment later. "The reason he was there by the hub was to enforce the policy their Parliament put in place many years ago. No one from the Otherlands is allowed on Necronia."

Not friendly, but understandable in light of how necromancers are treated on vampire-biased worlds like Earth and Gomorrah.

We don't talk the rest of the way, and when we exit from the canyon, it's into yet another canyon that's big enough to fit a small city. Once we're out of that canyon, a big herd of zombies spills out of there, following us.

Glancing to make sure Nulen isn't looking, Felix turns back and sends a blast of magenta energy behind us.

A few seconds later, his robot suit crawls out of the canyon on six limbs.

Without turning, Nulen shouts something.

"Leave that there," Dylan translates.

"Dude." Ariel waves at the hundreds of corpses all around. "He can see through the eyes of his dead minions."

With a sigh, Felix makes the robot sit on the ground by the smaller canyon's entrance.

"You think it'll be safe?" Ariel looks wistfully at the robot. "I want the gate sword back."

Felix gives Nulen a suspicious once-over. "Depends on whether they have any high-end blowtorches on this world."

Fabian places a hand on the small of Dylan's back and loudly whispers, "Tell our necromancer friend to be careful of the self-destruct mechanism inside that machine. That should keep our stuff safe."

"You want me to lie?" Dylan asks, her face flushed.

The werewolf pulls his hand away and tilts his head like a curious puppy. "You can't lie?"

"Of course I can," Dylan mumbles. "Just prefer not to."

"Well, it's not really a lie," Itzel says. "If they were to apply a blowtorch in the wrong place, the suit *could* explode."

Placated, Dylan delivers the message to Nulen, and he doesn't respond with so much as a grunt, just keeps on heading toward a large contraption that resembles a wooden raft, only large enough to carry an army.

Odd. Is there a river I'm not seeing?

Reaching the "raft," Nulen and two dozen of his helpers step onto it. Looking at us, he shouts a command that Dylan translates as "get on."

After everyone cautiously steps onto the wooden platform, its purpose becomes clearer. Zombies walk over and grab what turn out to be wooden handles, lifting us and the "raft" off the ground.

"A zombie-powered carriage," Felix mutters as we begin to move.

"A litter," Dylan says. "I'd get used to zombie-powered things if I were you. We'll see a lot of it soon."

At first the ride is rocky, but then we reach a relatively even terrain and it feels like we're floating. When we exit the big canyon, we gape at the gray mountains around us like a bunch of tourists.

"What the hell?" Ariel exclaims, looking at Nulen.

I follow her gaze, trying to make sense of what I'm seeing.

If you unfocus your eyes, Nulen is just on a chair. But if you look closely, it's clear that his chair is made entirely of people. Dead people. Each zombie must've twisted like a contortionist to make the structure.

Noticing our attention, Nulen speaks in Dylan's direction.

Before she can translate, the zombies that aren't part of his chair begin to move. Some kneel, some twist around, and soon, eight more macabre chairs join Nulen's human throne.

"He said 'take a seat,'" Dylan says. "In case that wasn't obvious."

We all stare at our "chairs." I don't know about the others, but if it were a choice between a gun to the head and this furniture, I might just opt for the gun.

Like it's the most natural thing in the world, Stanislav plops onto one. "Clever," he says. "The soft belly of that woman makes a cushion."

Right. I'd *gladly* choose the gun.

Stepping as far away from the "furniture" as I can, I pointedly stand and watch the mountains to keep my mind off my battle-fatigued muscles.

"I have a surprise," Valerian says, approaching me.

Startled, I turn and see him holding a hygieia device.

Wow. I can't believe he's managed to keep it through the whole ordeal. I've got to say, he's good at the suck-up game. If it weren't for the masks, I think I wouldn't kick him in the balls if he tried to kiss me right now.

Eyes crinkling above his mask, Valerian sterilizes a large circle of the platform beneath us.

"Thanks." I sit cross-legged in the middle of the circle. "If you want, you can join me here."

Is he looking smug? It's hard to tell with the cursed masks.

He sinks to the floor a perfect distance from me, and just like that, the landscape around us seems more romantic than gloomy. That is, until we leave the mountains and see a field of some kinds of native vegetables.

A field that's crawling with the masked dead.

I guess if you don't care about the eek factor—and that's a big if—it makes sense to use this free workforce on difficult agricultural tasks.

As we keep riding, we spot a herd of goat-like animals that graze inside a pasture that's walled off by zombies. Later, we see zombies performing even more functions: fixing roofs, chopping down trees, and even building a pyramid the size of the ones in Giza, but with creepy designs carved into the sides that remind me of the masks that the zombies wear.

An hour after the dirt road underneath us becomes paved, we enter a village.

A big village.

"Are all those pale people alive?" Ariel asks, studying the crowds that stare at us with unabashed wonder.

Dylan exchanges some quick words with Nulen. "He says they're predominantly human, with just enough necromancers to keep things running. You can recognize his kind by the leather clothing they wear. The humans revere them—hence all the waving."

Indeed, the majority of the people are wearing clothing made of cotton-like material, with only an occasional leather-clad figure here and there.

Nulen says something else.

"We're stopping for a meal and a sleepover," Dylan explains. "He'll stay in special necromancer quarters, while we'll rest in an inn designed for humans."

No one objects, and when we reach the town square, our zombies lower the litter to the ground, allowing us to step off.

Dylan has another quick exchange with Nulen. "We go there." She points at a large structure to the side of the square.

Felix looks around dubiously. "Don't we need money or something like that?"

When Dylan translates this question to Nulen, he looks at Felix disdainfully and delivers what sounds like a tirade.

"We won't need money to stay at the inn," Dylan says. "The owner is a necromancer, and the staff are helpers. That means that food and drinks are free, as are the lodgings. In general, all basic human needs are provided for on Necronia, free of charge."

Around us, I spot people reverently nodding when they see Nulen's outfit. Not surprising, given what we've just learned.

"They really love their necros here," Fabian says, echoing my thoughts.

Stanislav nods. "There's a good word for that: necrophilia."

We chuckle as we head for the inn, but then we spot a herd of zombies on our tail.

"Seems like Nulen wants to make sure we stay at the inn and nowhere else," Felix says.

Valerian lifts his broad shoulders in a shrug. "Since we weren't going anywhere else anyway, let him."

When we step into the establishment, a leather-clad woman looks warily at our masks, but is overall cheerful. However, when Dylan speaks up, the cheerfulness disappears. I guess she's detected an accent and doesn't like strangers.

Still, she has a zombie seat us in the restaurant area, and I thank the stars for the wooden table and chairs.

Valerian uses hygieia on my chair and part of the table, and I reward him by not telling him off when he sits by my side.

The other patrons sit far enough away that I can't tell what they're eating or hear their speech. Like most humans I've seen here, they're pale, wear cotton clothing, and seem to be really happy considering they live on such a dreary world.

Masked "helpers" bring out appetizers in the form of a big bowl of fruit.

Valerian examines the fruit, then samples one, peeling and stuffing pieces into the proper section of his mask. He repeats this a few times, and when he comes across one that reminds me of a yellow orange, he catches Dylan's gaze. "Can you ask the innkeeper for a whole bowl of these for Bailey?"

When the bowl arrives, Valerian hygieias one fruit and hands it to me.

I gingerly peel the thing and stick a piece through the mask's opening.

It reminds me of a slightly tart banana, only fruitier.

"Thanks," I say and pick up another.

After about seven more of the round banana approximations, I feel full. These must be more nutritionally dense than my favored Earth fruit.

My teammates, in the meantime, are much more adventurous/suicidal with their food choices. They gobble down bowls of pink soup made from who knows what, skewers of an unknown meat that smells like feet, and bread from a mystery purple grain. Oh, and they chase all that down with fermented drinks that make the meat smell like flowers in comparison.

For everyone's sake, I hope Dylan can make antibiotics in a pinch.

Bellies full, everyone yawns.

Dylan compliments the innkeeper, and the woman smiles and replies in rapid-fire Necronian.

Stammering something back, Dylan reddens and looks at us with a horrified expression.

Before she can translate whatever was said, a group of strange zombies steps into the room. Their masks don't have the scary imagery. Instead, they depict very generic, good-looking human faces. Their bodies are atypical too: The men are muscular and cut, and the females have curves in all the right places—and no bras.

"She's offering them to us as, um… bedroom companions," Dylan says, reddening further.

Okay. I'm starting to really want that gun to the head.

"You were wrong before," Ariel whispers to Stanislav. *"That's* necrophilia."

Felix eyes one of the bustier zombies. "In a way, they're like sexbots, so…"

Ariel rounds on him. "Seriously? Did you forget about Maya? Plus the whole necrophilia thing?"

Felix draws back, offended. "I wasn't going to say yes. I was just comparing—"

"Please thank our host and tell her we're all too tired for companions today," Valerian says with a straight face.

When Dylan conveys this, the woman shrugs, and her bizarrely sexualized zombies scram.

She then has a regular male zombie show us the bathroom facilities, which are primitively water-based, like those on Earth. After that, the zombie leads us to a cluster of rooms. To my huge relief, the open doors reveal beds made from wood instead of dead people.

The zombie leaves us in the hallway, and Valerian points to a room with a chair. "This will be Bailey's. I'll be standing watch."

Oh, right. I completely forgot. I could get killed by the Nutcracker in my dreams and go homicidal on everybody's ass. A gift that keeps on giving.

"I'll take that one." Stanislav points at the room farthest from us. "And I'll keep the mask on as I sleep."

"Everyone should keep their masks on," Dylan says. "I get that it's uncomfortable, but we know the virus is already out on this world, so why take any chances?"

I don't know about anyone else, but taking my mask off was never on the agenda.

As the other rooms are chosen, I clear my throat. "I need a volunteer."

Fourteen eyebrows and a half of a unibrow lift in unison.

"Remember how Maxwell was able to make Dylan fall asleep?" I ask.

Reluctant nods.

"I want to do that too… to one of you."

Silence.

I put my hands on my hips. "You're going to sleep anyway."

Ariel steps forward. "Fine. I'll be your guinea pig."

Grinning maniacally under my mask, I follow Ariel into her room.

"Do you mind waiting outside?" she says to Valerian.

If he minds, he doesn't voice it.

As soon as she shuts the door in Valerian's face, Ariel strips, revealing a body that's impressive even for an uber. Talk about an unattainable standard of beauty. I don't exactly have poor self-esteem, but if I stare at her enough, I'm certain to develop it.

With a yawn, she gets under the covers. "This might actually work out. Sometimes I have trouble falling asleep."

"Okay," I say. "Close your eyes."

She does.

Now what? I had no idea dreamwalkers could do what I'm about to attempt. Now that I know it's possible, I still have no clue as to how.

I start by looking intently at Ariel and wishing her to sleep with all I've got.

"Is this going to take long?" she says, yawning again.

"No clue."

Extending my hand, I picture Ariel sleeping in as much detail as I can, a bit how I initiate dreamwalking from a distance.

Nothing.

Then it hits me. Before I could make dream connections from afar, I needed skin-to-skin contact. Maybe this power works the same?

I carefully approach the bed. "Do you mind if I touch you?"

Ariel opens her eyes. "You're lucky I'm not Kit. Or Felix, for that matter."

Chuckling, I gently put my hand on her wrist and wish her asleep.

Nothing happens. I try an imagination exercise. I picture Ariel sleeping so vividly I could create a painting of it in my memory gallery. Still nothing. I'm about to pull away in frustration when I do something purely on instinct, calling on a strange hint of a feeling, one that reminds me of having a word on the very tip of my tongue.

It works.

Ariel is asleep. No, not just asleep. I can feel that she's in the REM stage of sleep, which she wouldn't be in if she just fell asleep out of boredom.

With a fist pump, I tiptoe out of the room.

Now if I only knew what I did so I could repeat it. It would mean the end of subdreams, just to name one huge benefit off the top of my head. And if I do this quickly enough, I would be like a sleep grenade myself.

Walking into my room, I catch Valerian waving his hygieia device over my bed.

Wow. And he didn't even know I'd see him being super nice like this.

Walking over, I place the hand that touched Ariel under the sterilizing rays.

The problem is I get too close to Valerian and my treacherous heartbeat speeds up. "Thanks," I say breathlessly, nodding at the bed.

"I'll do the same to your clothes after you take them off," Valerian says, his voice husky.

I step back, ignoring the flush spreading over my skin. "Nice try. Turn around."

With a sigh, he obliges.

"Actually, leave the room."

He walks out the door.

"How do I know this isn't just an illusion?" I ask the empty space around me. "For all I know, you're standing there staring at me."

The empty air doesn't respond, so I undress, put my clothes on Valerian's chair, and hide under the blissfully sterilized blanket. "You can come back in."

Valerian returns and cleans my clothes as promised, ending with my underwear.

"Perv," I mutter when he hangs the last article—my bra—at the head of my bed. "You liked touching my undies. Admit it."

His eyes crinkle above the mask. "I admit that and more. For instance, I'd like for my hands to do the job your bra usually does. Panties too."

I'm speechless—and so hot I may combust on the spot.

"What would you say if I took off my clothes?" he asks softly.

The heat inside me intensifies.

"I can hygieia every single part of my body and get in there with you," he says temptingly.

"Um, no…" I clear the hoarseness from my throat. "I don't do that with people I barely know."

He strides over to the chair and sits. "You know me."

"No," I say pointedly. "I don't know where you grew up, or if you have siblings, for that matter. I don't know if—"

"Nice try," he says in a perfect imitation of my tone. "I'm not ready to speak about Soma. If that's all you want, you should just go to sleep."

"Fine." I close my eyes and turn over, giving him my back.

Then something dawns on me. Did he just admit that Soma *is* where he was born?

I lie there, unable to sleep, my mind churning. Eventually, I feel someone in the distance go into REM sleep. Lucky for them. I want to be dreaming right now.

Since I can, I make a connection to whoever it is. Then I use Pom to visit my sleep palace and find that it's Stanislav I've just connected with.

Awesome. My remote connect range is farther than I thought.

Since I'm here, might as well sneak a peek at the chort's dream. I've never dreamwalked in his kind before.

Making myself invisible, I dive in.

CHAPTER SIXTEEN

STANISLAV'S current dream is a memory. He's standing in front of a round-faced woman who must be the descendant of whoever was the original model for the matryoshka dolls. In Stanislav's hands is a tiny kitten of the Siberian variety. It's not as cute as Pom, but extremely close.

It's clear the chort is loath to let the little creature go, so the woman eventually snatches it away with a wide grin.

He marches over to the fridge, opens it, points at the milk, and says something in Russian. Grinning even wider, she nods and replies placatingly in the same language. Stanislav grabs her hand and leads her to an adjacent room, where he points at an enormous box of kitty litter.

She nods solemnly, then pantomimes putting the kitten into the box.

"*Molodetz*," Stanislav says. He then pecks the woman on the cheek and the kitten on the top of its head and walks out of the apartment.

I decide this is as good a moment as any to tell him he's dreaming, so I make myself visible and do just that.

"What are you doing here?" he asks once he adjusts to the idea of talking to me in a dream.

"Wanted to ask you how you're feeling." I take us to a white-sand beach. "Didn't want to put you on the spot in front of everyone."

"I'm healthy as a bull." He takes off his shoes and buries his feet into the sand.

"Okay then. I'll leave you be."

"Wait. You saw my earlier dream, right?"

I smile sheepishly. "Yep. Sorry about that."

"Can you walk into my girlfriend's dream? That's who the woman was. I want to know how Murzik is doing."

"Is Murzik the kitten?" I ask.

He nods, a tender expression stealing over his face.

"Sadly, I can't just dreamwalk in a random person," I say. "I have to make a connection with them first, and that requires proximity."

"Ah," he says, looking extremely disappointed. "Then go."

I wave and leave his dream.

———

I LIE in bed for a while longer, making connections with the rest of our party, just in case. I don't invade their dreams, though. Stanislav took it well, but I'm not sure if some of the others would. Plus, Fabian, being a werewolf, would be way too difficult.

Finally, I fall asleep.

———

I SIT on a throne made of bones. There's an army of vampires kneeling at my feet.

"Next," I say imperiously.

A vampire crawls over to the throne, slashes his wrists with a ceremonial dagger, and squirts blood into a glass chalice.

A servant picks up the chalice and hands it to me.

I gulp down the liquid like a Slurpee. A wave of pleasure smashes into my every nerve cell with the force of an opiate concentrate.

"Next," I say again, my voice somehow steady despite the bliss.

Another vampire worshipper makes a donation.

I drink this too. The pleasure grows stronger. I say "next" again and again. When the pleasure blurs into pain, I notice something odd as I raise the chalice to my lips.

No furry bracelet.

No Pom.

This is a dream.

Obviously a dream, now that I think about it.

I will the pleasure away.

The pleasure doesn't leave. If anything, it gets *more* intense. Less like the vampire blood effect and more like an orgasm, but not quite. It feels as though my whole body has turned into an erogenous zone, and someone is stroking me all over.

What the puck?

I exit my body the way I do when I want to heal it.

The pleasure doesn't stop.

I duplicate myself and put my consciousness into the two bodies. Both of me feel the pleasure now, but it doesn't stop.

Going back to a single body, I try counterbalancing the pleasure with some pain. I make a thick needle appear in my hand and stab my palm with it.

I might as well try to stop a hurricane with an umbrella.

Puck. What a weird predicament.

Can intense enough pleasure kill? And if so, could this be a very unusual form of attack from the Nutcracker?

Pom appears in front of me, his fur black and his face worried. "What's happening?"

"I have no idea," I try to say, but it comes out as a moan.

"Ah, you want privacy," he mumbles and disappears.

I want to call him back, but I just moan again.

Fine. It's not like he could've helped with something like this.

Impossibly, the pleasure intensifies again.

That does it. If this is a dream attack, waking up should snap me out of it.

Gritting my dream teeth, I jolt myself awake.

<hr>

I'M BACK at the inn, but the pleasure is with me, stronger than ever. It now feels like some energy is pouring into me—an energy that brings pleasure as a side effect.

I soon discover that here in the real world, it's harder to keep my responses under control. Case in point: A moan escapes my lips without my consent. Then another one. Then a scream.

I'm vaguely aware of Valerian rushing to my side.

Writhing, I groan louder.

Strong arms wrap around me and soothing words are whispered into my ears, but the pleasure assault continues.

"You're going to be okay," I hear Valerian whisper before something finally short-circuits in my brain and my consciousness winks out.

CHAPTER SEVENTEEN

I COME to my senses on the bed, where I'm held in a spooning position. Valerian's arms are wrapped around me, his hands on my belly.

Whew.

I feel better.

I never thought I'd find a *lack* of pleasurable sensation a relief, but here we are.

A part of me knows I should wriggle out of Valerian's hold, but a much bigger part of me needs the comfort and thus tells that first part to shut up and enjoy this.

"What just happened?" I whisper—and realize my throat is hoarse, presumably from all the moaning and screaming.

"Did you feel really good for no apparent reason?" Valerian asks, his breath tickling the back of my neck.

I exhale, trying not to react to *that* pleasurable sensation. "Understatement of the year."

"I think I know what happened," he murmurs into my ear. "The game must be in the hands of the players."

The game. Of course. How could I forget?

Last I checked, Bernie and Rattie had kept working on the *Lucid Dreamer* project. The game features me as the heroine who openly uses her powers, and the hope was that it would leverage human belief mojo to make me a stronger dreamwalker.

Seems like the game has been released, and our idea has worked.

When beta testers had first used the game, I'd also felt pleasure, just less of it. If the intensity of what I experienced tonight is anything to go by, this was a more significant boost.

"What now?" I ask hoarsely. "What can I do that I couldn't do before?"

"No idea." Valerian's breath tickles my ear again. "But hopefully you can jolt your mom awake the next time you try."

Right. With my pleasure-addled brain, I hadn't thought of that yet, even though that was the whole point of the project.

I cover his hands with mine. "I want to hurry back to Gomorrah."

Valerian stills, then exhales slowly. "I'm sorry. Even if we didn't care about this world dying from the virus, Nulen would fight us again—and we'd lose."

I do my best to conceal my disappointment. "Of course. Need to finish saving Necronia first."

"That's right. Besides, it will probably take you a few days to internalize your new power. Also, as more users get the game, you'll grow stronger yet."

I stiffen. Experiencing the boost isn't something I want to relive.

"Don't worry," Valerian says softly. "My guess is, now that you've achieved a certain threshold, adding more will feel like a good mood, or even nothing at all."

Huh. Is that why I'm in such a good mood right now? Or is it because of the spooning?

An unexpected yawn tugs at me, and I hear a soft chuckle against my hair.

"Go back to sleep. You need it."

I close my eyes, though I'm doubtful I'll be able to fall asleep after all that's happened—not to mention, with his arms around me.

Wrong.

The sleep is instant, dreamless, and extremely deep.

———

WHEN I WAKE in the morning, to my huge disappointment, Valerian isn't spooning me anymore. Instead, he's back in his chair, watching me with an unreadable expression.

Did I dream the whole power boost and his comforting me?

He moves to the edge of his seat, his gaze warming slightly. "How are you feeling?"

I sit up, holding the blanket against my chest. "Was it all a dream?"

A faint smile touches his eyes. "No. It happened."

I check to make sure Pom is on my wrist.

He is. Not dreaming *now*.

"Look away," I say and realize my throat feels better.

He complies, and I quickly put my clothes on, then head for the door.

"Breakfast is already downstairs," he says. "You're the last to wake up."

I guiltily examine the dark circles under his eyes. "Did you get any sleep?"

He shakes his head. "I stood watch, as promised."

"Then you'd better get some sleep soon. I can tell you from experience, sleep deprivation blows."

He cocks his head. "I *could* sleep on the litter. But you'd have to promise not to sneak into my dreams without my permission."

I place a hand over my heart. "I swear not to go into your dreams without your permission when you sleep on the *litter*. But if you don't let me in soon, eventually I'll catch you sleeping elsewhere and not be able to help myself."

He nods, eyes gleaming. "I'll take that under advisement."

————

THE BREAKFAST IS identical to dinner, with banana-like fruit for me and questionable items for the crew. As we eat, Dylan tells us she was visited by Maxwell in her dream. He and the others have reached Gomorrah safely, and the scientists there have started working on a cure.

"In the meanwhile, a healer is keeping him alive," Dylan says as we get up from the table. "In hindsight, maybe we should've brought one with us as well."

"Isis refused to go," Valerian says. "Same with the others we asked."

"What about Kit and the rest?" Ariel asks. "Did they become Overtaken?"

"They did," Dylan says somberly. "But with proper care, they can continue to lead normal lives."

Valerian holds the door for me. "So long as they sleep under lock and key, and stay far away from Bailey."

"Well, yeah," Dylan says. "That's what I meant."

When we get outside, Nulen's zombies are still there. They escort us to our strange transport, where the necromancer himself is already lounging in his zombie chair.

Upon Dylan's request, Nulen makes a bed of zombies for Valerian.

Valerian sterilizes a spot for me on the wooden floor, then stretches out on the bed and closes his eyes.

Ariel comes up to me and nods at Valerian conspiratorially. "Someone had serious fun last night," she whispers.

I give her a blank stare. "I don't know what you're talking about."

She rolls her eyes. "Your moaning and screaming was loud enough to wake me up."

I fight a flush. "It's not what you think." I tell her what really happened, and she seems to believe me. *Barely.*

When she leaves, I examine myself to see if I feel any different now that my power is boosted.

I don't, at least not much.

Touching Pom, I go into the dream world and experiment with my powers there.

Still no difference. Maybe I can make more sleeper connections per day now, but that's not something I need at the moment.

Back in the waking world, I sense it when Valerian enters REM sleep. The feeling that informs me of this is stronger now, but not qualitatively different.

It takes all my willpower to resist the temptation to dreamwalk in him. Stupid conscience. If I were a sociopath, I'd break that promise in a heartbeat.

To distract myself, I observe our surroundings. We pass by a coal mine where a zombie strapped with dynamite is blown to bits—presumably not for fun but in order to break solid rocks into pieces. Later, we pass another large pyramid construction site, and after that, more farms. At some point, I spot a steam locomotive in the far distance. No doubt zombies are the ones tossing coal into the furnace there, too.

I'm diverted from sightseeing when Dylan asks Nulen something. The necromancer replies in a sharp tone that wakes Valerian and makes Dylan pale to pre-vamp levels.

Looking at her, Fabian frowns. "What was that?"

Dylan darts a furtive glance at Nulen. "I was wondering how his virus is progressing, so I asked if he felt any heart palpitations or had an upset stomach."

"And?" Fabian asks, his frown deepening.

"And he said never to ask again. Also threatened me."

Fabian looks on the verge of turning into his wolf form when Valerian puts a hand on his shoulder and whispers something into his ear.

"Fine," Fabian growls. "Don't ask the asshole again. It's *his* health, after all."

Dylan nods.

We ride in dour silence for a while after that. Eventually, we reach a town that's at least twice the size of the village we visited. We have lunch at another inn and resume our journey.

In the evening, we reach an actual city and eat dinner at the nicest inn thus far.

"Thank you," I tell Valerian after he sterilizes my bed yet again.

His eyes gleam above the mask. "Don't make me turn around or leave the room, and we'll call it even."

Heat floods my cheeks, making me grateful for my mask. Worse yet, I suddenly don't know what to do with my hands—they're itching to take off my top.

"Hey, I'm kidding." He turns around, giving me his back. "We'll pick this up when you're ready."

Whew. I can't believe I was actually considering getting naked for his viewing pleasure.

What is wrong with me? Why do I keep forgetting what he did?

Stripping as quickly as I can, I dive under the covers before he gets any ideas, such as turning around.

"You can look now," I mutter.

He goes to sit in the chair, where he winks at me.

Huffing, I close my eyes.

As is usual in Valerian's presence, sleep eludes me for a while, but eventually, I drift off.

———

I'M in the Intro to Programming class, and the professor slaps a final on my desk.

Puck. I thought I dropped this course, but I was mistaken. A couple of minutes ago, I realized I forgot to actually drop it. Now I have to somehow pass this exam even though I didn't attend a single lecture or read a page of course material.

Dread spreading through my very being, I open the paper and Pom pops out.

"You're dreaming this again?" His fur turns light orange. "Why?"

Oh. He's not on my wrist, so this is a dream—one I've had countless times for some reason.

Out of the corner of my eye, I see the professor throw an eraser at me.

Odd.

Instinctively, I dive under the desk—and it's a good thing I do. On the way to my head, the eraser becomes a foaming-at-the-mouth pit bull.

What the puck?

Leaping from under the desk, I glare at the professor—who morphs into the dreaded shape of the Nutcracker.

"You're hard to ambush," the creepy creature says in his melodic voice. "It won't save you, though."

A gun appears in his hand.

Leveraging my earlier practice, my body becomes metal.

Bang.

My shoulder screams in agony, but the bullet falls at my feet.

"Oh, that won't work," he says. "I know what you actually look like."

He does something, and my metallic body turns back into flesh.

Oh, puck.

He aims his gun again.

CHAPTER EIGHTEEN

AS FAST AS I CAN, I mess with the chemistry of the gunpowder in the Nutcracker's weapon.

He squeezes the trigger.

The gun clicks, but no bullet comes out.

He hurls the gun at my chest.

I sidestep and make his feet heavy while weakening the structure of the floor underneath him.

The Nutcracker crashes through the floor.

"This is too scary," Pom says and disappears.

I change my surroundings to those of the lobby in the gorgeous Harpa Reykjavik concert hall located in Iceland. If the Nutcracker isn't from Earth—or is but has never visited this place—I might have an advantage.

He doesn't appear.

Score.

I try to jolt myself awake.

It doesn't work, and I soon hear why. It's that cursed music—*Dance of the Sugar Plum Fairy*—blasting from all around.

He must be here and is somehow preventing me from waking up.

But how? I'm supposed to be more powerful now. Has the Nutcracker also gotten more power since our last encounter? That doesn't seem likely. Valerian was probably right when he said I need to internalize what I've gained.

Assuming I survive this encounter, that is.

In an eyeblink, the Nutcracker appears ten feet away from me and launches an angry tarantula at my face.

I leap to the side, then run up the wall, changing gravity and the traction of my feet as needed.

The Nutcracker chases after me with the clickety-clack of wood hitting metal and glass.

When I reach the windows facing the harbor, I make the glass melt under my feet. Swiftly, I fly out, landing on the cold waters of the Atlantic Ocean.

The Nutcracker lands on the water nearby with ease. I guess he's practiced walking on water as much as I have, or is a natural at it.

Without much ado, he throws a scorpion at my head.

I make a katana appear in my hand, a replica of the one I fought zombies with the other day. With a *whoosh*, I slice the scorpion in half, then lunge at my opponent.

My hope is that by walking on water and having to defend a close-up attack, he won't have the bandwidth to mess with our environment.

My plan almost works. The katana strike lands, but the metal only cuts a shallow gash in the wood that is his chest.

Right. Wood is harder to penetrate than flesh.

A saber appears in the Nutcracker's wooden hand just in time to parry my next strike. Puck. My own strategy is working against me now. When I try to melt his weapon, it doesn't work.

A close-up fight was a mistake; unlike him, I'm made of flesh.

Maybe I can turn him corporeal to even the score? He gave me a clue as to how when he said he knows what I look like.

I swing the katana. He sidesteps and unleashes a barrage of his own attacks.

As I parry the onslaught, I realize I have a slight problem when it comes to making him corporeal.

I have no clue what he looks like.

Or do I?

The last dreamwalker I met was Maxwell, and he seemed suspicious to me.

Could this be Maxwell?

Parrying the next attack, I will him to take Maxwell's shape—sad eyes, the mask, and all.

Nope. He's still in the Nutcracker guise and must know what I failed to do because his already-evil grin looks infinitely more wicked.

Okay. Either this isn't Maxwell, or I misunderstood how this works.

Or he's just more powerful. Or I need to know what Maxwell's face looks like to get this right.

Ow!

All my ruminations have made me lose my battle concentration, giving the Nutcracker a chance to slice open my right forearm.

Ignoring the bleeding, I parry another dozen strikes as I attempt to control the environment again. Except a whale I try to conjure up doesn't swim from under the water, nor does the water itself want to turn into magma under the Nutcracker's feet.

Pucking puck.

My muscles are tiring from all the frantic Kendo moves I'm using. If I don't do something soon, I'll make a fatal mistake and that'll be that.

No. Not when Valerian is guarding me in the outside world.

Not when I have a real chance to wake Mom.

Exiting my body, I play an ace I've been saving for the right moment. Instead of wasting time on healing my wound, I duplicate myself and jump into both bodies.

The me that is behind the Nutcracker slashes at his saber-holding wrist, effortlessly cutting through the wood. The Nutcracker's human eyes widen—which is when both of me try the wake-up jolt.

It works this time.

A single me opens my eyes on the bed inside the inn.

Panting, I sit up.

Valerian leaps to his feet. "What's wrong?"

Wiping the cold sweat off my brow, I tell him.

"That bastard," he says through gritted teeth when I'm done. "This is why we need to catch a leader of one of the Icelus cells. They meet via this dreamwalker, so they should know his identity."

"Unless he disguises himself even with them," I say, still shaken.

He waves dismissively. "One leader would lead us to another, until eventually we'd find him."

"The Nutcracker said he knew what I look like. That narrows our list of suspects drastically."

"Right." His dark eyebrows furrowed, Valerian adjusts his mask. "Either Icelus have a dossier on you, or someone you know is a dreamwalker who's hiding that fact."

"Or it's Maxwell," I say.

"He didn't see your face, so he doesn't *really* know what you look like."

Oh, yeah. I had the mask on when I met him. But wait— "He could've seen me in Dylan's dreams. Or yours if you connected with him."

"Highly unlikely. Maxwell hates Icelus even more than I do."

"How do you know?"

"The vetting," Valerian says. "During it, Maxwell allowed himself to get glamoured by an ancient vampire and was thoroughly questioned. I don't know of any way to fool that."

The adrenaline is leaving my body, and the tiredness is kicking in. "Fine," I say with a half-yawn. "But I can't help the feeling that there's more to Maxwell than meets the eye."

Valerian peers at me intently. "You think you'll be able to fall sleep again?"

"I can try." I close my eyes.

Minutes later, I'm out.

AT BREAKFAST, Dylan tells us she saw Maxwell in her dreams again, and he informed her that the work on the cure continues. He also said he dreamwalked in his contacts on all the collaborating Otherlands, and the news he got there is mixed. The deadly Icelus virus hasn't shown up anywhere, which is good, but the Overtaken threat is spreading exponentially everywhere, which is not so good.

"That tells me the Icelus cell we're after is the driving force behind the spread of the plague." Valerian gesticulates with a breakfast sausage made out of a local creature. "We stop them, we stop it."

"And then we'll 'only' have to deal with legions of the Overtaken," Itzel says.

We all ponder Itzel's point for the rest of breakfast, but no one comes up with anything good enough to share with the group.

The rest of the day is identical to the one prior; we ride through the countryside and witness ever more ingenious uses for a zombie labor force. By the next day, the roads become better, and in the afternoon, we see a city that sprawls from horizon to horizon in the distance.

Nulen says something.

"That's Necropolis," Dylan translates. "Our destination."

The city looks more curious the closer we get. There are flying creatures crisscrossing the skies, tall trees that have somehow been made part of the skyline, and skyscraper-high gothic-looking buildings.

Soon, though, the city isn't what draws everyone's attention. What we're gaping at is the truly mind-boggling number of zombies in our way.

Not thousands but millions, they surround Necropolis like an impenetrable wall. Their faces are covered by the same masks as Nulen's zombies, but these specimens were clearly taller and beefier people when they were alive.

"Cream of the undead crop," Ariel says, awestruck.

"The best of the zombie best." Felix's tone echoes hers.

Everyone else stays mute.

When we approach the zombie wall, the dead clear a path for us and close ranks behind us once we get through.

"Even less chance of going back now," Fabian mutters.

"Great," Itzel says in that grumbly manner she's adopted for most situations on Necronia. "We're even more screwed than before."

Further debate is drowned out by a horrible screeching sound as the gates of Necropolis are drawn apart by thousands of zombie arms.

Inside the city, we see that we're not the only ones using zombies for transport; a lot of Necropolis residents seem to be doing the same. Some ride piggy-back on zombies, like overgrown children, while others sit inside a single-person palanquin or hammock.

What's different in this city is that there don't seem to be any humans in sight—only leather-clad necros.

When I ask Dylan, she confers with Nulen and confirms my supposition.

Necropolis is a necromancer-only city.

We ride through the streets until we reach a gloomy-looking building. A zombie opens a door for us as Nulen says something to Dylan.

"He's asking us to wait here," Dylan translates. "He'll go to explain the situation to the Parliament."

Felix clears his throat. "Does he look purplish red to anyone else?"

We all stare at the necromancer with varying degrees of concern.

Puck. He does indeed look purplish red—like Pom would if he were equal parts happy and mad.

"There's not much we can do for him," Valerian reminds us, stepping into the house.

We follow his example, and as soon as we're all in, the door to the house closes and locks from the outside.

"Are we under house arrest?" Ariel asks.

"More like jail," Felix says, looking around.

He's right. Our surroundings are more reminiscent of a dank dungeon than a house.

As he usually does, Stanislav walks as far away from everyone as he can—since we still don't know if he's infected and all. "At least we get a reprieve from the constant presence of zombies," he says, perching on a chair in the corner.

"And there's normal furniture," Itzel says, plopping on an ancient-looking chair.

Valerian sweeps away cobwebs and dust from another chair, hygieias it, then gestures for me to sit.

Gratefully nodding, I do so.

"I guess we wait," Ariel says to no one in particular.

So we wait again in a tense silence.

And wait.

And wait some more.

At some point, I have to use what passes for the bathroom in this house—and experience another bout of gratitude for Valerian's hygieia device.

After about four hours, I'm both thirsty and hungry. An hour after that, I start complaining, and soon after, I have to explain to Felix that I'd rather die of thirst than drink the water of questionable potability that comes out of the faucet in the grimy bathroom.

Two hours after that, Valerian captures some of said water, waves the hygieia device over it, and convinces me to drink.

Four hours later, I haven't developed dysentery, but I'm hungry enough to gnaw on my own arm.

"Should I break a door or a window?" Fabian asks, yawning.

"Let's play nice for a while longer," Valerian says. "There are millions of zombies outside. We don't really stand a chance."

And the interminable waiting continues, with more yawns coming in, followed by naps.

"You should also sleep if you can," Valerian says to me. "I'll make a clean surface for you."

He does, and I drift off—luckily without a visit from the Nutcracker.

———

WHEN I WAKE UP, our situation is unchanged, my hunger is stronger than ever, and the question of breaking out is at the top of everyone's agenda.

Just as Fabian walks over to test the strength of the door, the lock clicks.

We all leap to our feet, eyes glued to the door as it opens.

The person who walks in isn't Nulen. It's a good-looking young woman with heavy eyeshadow and a black line drawn horizontally across her face below the eyes. Her leather outfit has a worn look to it, as though she got it from a necromancer thrift store. Half of her hair is jet black, while the other half is bleached white, and it's all held back by a pair of goggles on her head—an accessory that wouldn't look out of place at a steampunk convention.

"You're not Nulen," Dylan says to her, forgetting to switch to Necronian.

"Amazing powers of observation," the woman says in unaccented American English. "Anyone want to say something even more obvious?"

"Who are you?" I blurt.

"Where's Nulen?" Valerian says at the same time.

"My name is Rowan," the newcomer says. "Nulen is dead."

"Dead?" we exclaim in unison.

"Well, yeah," she says. "I figured you'd know, seeing as how the Parliament are convinced it was your evil schemes that killed him."

CHAPTER NINETEEN

EVERYBODY STARTS SHOUTING AT ONCE, with Dylan babbling in Necronian.

Rowan frowns at her. "Did you not hear me speak your language a second ago?"

Dylan winces. "Sorry. All the stress is getting to me."

Stepping up to her, Fabian places a comforting hand on her shoulder.

Rowan scratches the bleached side of her head. "Stress sucks. I heard that when an octopus is overstressed, she'll eat herself, and sadly, not in a dirty way."

"That's not actually accurate," Dylan mutters under her breath while I grin internally. The necromancer seems to share my often-inappropriate sense of humor.

"I have a question of my own," Rowan says, ignoring Dylan. "What's with the masks? Are you all gnomes?"

"I'm the only gnome," Itzel says. "With the others, it's a long story, which will have to wait until you've answered some of our questions."

"Right, about that." Rowan shifts from one booted foot to the other. "I don't have many answers for you. I'm only here because I speak your language—and because the Parliament wouldn't be too sad if you killed me." She looks us all over. "With that in mind, how about you don't kill me? Please?"

Everyone continues to shower her with questions, but they speak too fast for anyone to understand anything, plus Stanislav and Fabian might actually be speaking their native tongues.

Rowan loudly clears her throat, and silence finally falls. "I wouldn't recommend you make the Parliament wait."

"They want to speak with us?" Dylan asks.

"Right. I think I'll call you Ms. State-the-Obvious." Rowan glances at Fabian, then at Dylan. "Or is it Mrs. State-the-Obvious?"

"Why does the Parliament want to talk to us?" I ask. "Or is that also obvious?"

Rowan's expression turns more serious. "From what I've been told, Nulen died in the process of explaining your visit to them. They questioned his corpse afterward as well. I wasn't given any details; it's not as if I need to know who you are to bring you to them. Or how much danger I'm in. Or—"

"If Nulen told them everything, they should be glad we're here," Dylan says.

"Sounds like someone wants to be renamed to Ms. Naivete." Rowan looks at Fabian. "Or is it Mrs.?"

Ariel's pretty eyes turn flinty. "Her name is Dylan. And remember how you asked for us not to kill you just seconds ago?"

Looking more intrigued than intimidated, Rowan examines Ariel. "With that bravado, I take it your name isn't Ms. Hotness McSexyBod either? Because that's what I have in my head."

Ariel stands up from her chair and gives its seat what seems to be a light squeeze.

With a loud crack, the wood shatters into tiny splinters.

Rowan's eyes widen. "You're one of those Strongmen types, aren't you?"

"An uber," I say. "And I wouldn't piss her off. Or any of us for that matter."

As if to highlight my words, Fabian crushes his chair as well, while Stanislav passes his hand through his.

Valerian must also show her something really impressive because her eyes widen and she mutters, "Is it possible to learn this power?"

A smile touches Felix's eyes as he deadpans, "Not from a Jedi."

Rowan grins. "I like you. What are you called? All I got so far is Skinny McUnibrowPants the Second Jr."

He rolls his eyes. "I'm Felix." He points at his roommate. "That's Ariel. And that's Valerian, Bailey, Itzel, Stanislav, and Fabian." He points at each of us in turn.

"Well," Rowan says, "now that I know your names, I feel more invested in your fate—which is getting more dire with every wasted second."

"Right," I say. "How about we go?"

"Hakuna Matata," Rowan says and exits through the door.

"Do we trust her?" Dylan asks.

Everyone shakes their heads.

"Do we trust this Parliament?"

The shakes are even more vigorous this time.

"Great," Dylan says. "But I guess we have to go anyway."

We head out of the prison-house one by one. Once outside, I spot Rowan standing next to a group of drab-looking zombies, plus a creature that reminds me of an Earth's opossum, only creepier and cuter at the same time.

"Say hello to my little friend," Rowan says, following my gaze.

The creature scurries over and grins toothily at me.

I step back.

"Oh, don't worry. Frank won't hurt you," Rowan says. "He's under my control, like the rest of the helpers. Aren't you, Frank?"

Frank scurries back to Rowan's side and looks exaggeratingly zombie-like.

"You have a dead pet?" Dylan asks.

"Are you sure you'd mind if I called you Ms. State-the-Obvious after all?" Catching Fabian's narrow-eyed stare, she quickly adds, "Or it could be Mrs. State-the-Obvious, of course."

Our translator visibly bristles. "I insist you call me Dylan. But allow me to state more obviousness. You lived on Earth?"

Rowan brushes imaginary dust from her leather jacket. "What gave it away: my skills with the tongue or my amazing mastery of American pop culture?"

"But isn't your kind banned?" Dylan asks.

"I was incognito," Rowan says. "Kept my head down. Pretended to be human. Didn't raise corpses and have them stroll down 42nd Street willy-nilly. That sort of thing."

"Aren't we in a rush?" Valerian asks, looking impatient.

"Right." Rowan's face grows serious, an expression that I suspect doesn't show there much. "Follow me."

Briskly, she strides northward, and we follow.

Over her shoulder, Rowan asks, "Do you want me to play the tour guide?"

No one replies.

"That"—she points at a magnificent castle-like structure to our left—"is the church of Mor. He's the god everyone here believes in. Oh, and they worship him hard, so don't say things like *Mor be damned*, or *by Mor*, or *Mor take me*, and so on. Especially not in front of anyone in the Parliament. They don't like it. I speak from experience."

Stanislav groans. "Do you ever shut up?"

Rowan turns and peers at him intently. "Something's off about your eyes. I can't quite put my finger on it."

The chort snorts, and Rowan proceeds to explain the local religion, which, among other things, preaches that when a soul leaves the body, the proper way to revere the leftover shell is to turn it into a helper.

"How convenient," Felix says. "I bet humans willingly bring you corpses to turn into zombies."

"Don't use the z-word in front of the Parliament," Rowan says. "They don't like that either."

Two good-looking women in nice leather clothing cross the road and give Rowan the evil eye. When she ignores them, they say something in Necronian—and though I'm no linguist, I catch a distinct nasty undertone.

Rowan smirks and responds with something equally snide.

The two women upgrade their evil eyes to death glares. One even goes as far as to spit in Rowan's direction—a gesture that should be outlawed throughout the Cogniverse, as far as I'm concerned.

Frank, the weird opossum, rushes at the spitter and promptly bites her toe.

The woman shouts something, grabs her friend, and rushes away.

"What was that about?" Felix asks Dylan.

"Something about some person named Keyser making a huge mistake. What she"—Dylan nods at Rowan—"replied with must've been some slang I didn't recognize."

Rowan wrinkles her nose. "They were talking about their husband and my betrothed."

Felix stares at the escaping women openmouthed. "You guys have polygamy on this world?"

"Polygyny, to be exact," Dylan says.

Rowan's upper lip curls as she looks at Dylan. "You're so useful. Mor forbid we use the wrong term."

"But is it true?" Felix demands, and I recall that Uzbekistan, the country on Earth that his family's from, is supposed to have something along those lines. Or had—what little I know about this is from Ariel's teasing.

Rowan bares her white teeth. "To put it in terms you can understand, members of the Parliament and other powerful male necromancers take multiple wives under the pretext of a eugenics-like program to increase the number of powerful necromancers overall. For better or worse, my own necromantic potential is high—which is allegedly more important than, say, intellect or looks. So yeah, I drew the short straw. And no, I can't have multiple husbands; that would make some minds implode."

Ariel stares at her in fascination. "And your hubby-to-be is named Keyser?"

"Yeah. I know. Like from *The Usual Suspects*," Rowan says. "You're about to meet him. He isn't as cool as his name would imply. Kind of the opposite."

No one speaks as we walk a few more blocks—that is, until Valerian's LEGO letters appear, presumably for everyone except Rowan:

If things go south, we take one or more members of this Parliament hostage and get the puck off this world.

Fabian flexes his fists. I guess he realizes that with our current lack of weapons, he's the most dangerous in the group.

We step onto a large circular plaza where a large building stands in the middle, and ten mansions are located along the plaza's circumference.

"This is Decagon Square. The Parliament meeting room is in there." Rowan points at the middle building. "And each member of the Parliament resides in one of those." She gestures at the surrounding mansions.

As we head to the center building, I overhear Dylan talking to Fabian about the word *decagon*. She mentions such practical pearls of wisdom as "a decagon is a figure with ten straight sides and angles," and "the name 'decagon square' is a contradiction of terms," and last but not least, "each mansion is inside an angle that is exactly 144 degrees."

The biggest zombies I've seen yet open the doors of the center building for us, and Rowan leads us down a posh corridor with walls decorated by creepy art à la the zombies' masks.

"Through here is the Parliament meeting room," Rowan says, nodding at a set of ornate doors. She peers at Stanislav again. "Seriously, what's going on with your eyes?"

I follow her gaze and see what she's talking about.

My heartbeat skyrockets.

There's a tiny gathering of red moisture in the chort's tear ducts.

Stanislav must see me whiten because he wipes at his eyes and stares at his fingers in horror.

It's blood.

CHAPTER TWENTY

I BEGIN HYPERVENTILATING as a million thoughts rush through my mind.

I want to run. Barring that, I want to grab Valerian's hygieia device and use it until its batteries run out—even though the rational part of me understands that we have our masks for exactly this reason. Both my mask and Stanislav's should prevent any viruses from going in or out, so there's double protection.

In fact, everyone—besides Stanislav—should be fine, even the maskless Rowan.

Still, it's hard not to spiral. Stanislav was only briefly without the mask, yet he's already having his first symptom.

The virus is extremely contagious.

I'm not the only one freaking out either. Everyone on the team is a little wild-eyed, their foreheads clammy. The only person looking more confused than scared is Rowan. Staring at the blood on Stanislav's fingers, she asks, "Is that normal for your kind?"

Stanislav ignores her. I imagine he must be in shock.

"What do we do?" Dylan's voice is barely above a whisper.

LEGO letters instantly appear in the air:

There isn't much we can do. Let's talk to this Parliament.

"Seriously, what's going on?" Rowan demands.

"Long story," Valerian says. "Just stay as far away from Stanislav as you can."

"Uh-huh, sure." She stares at us, and when no explanations are forthcoming, she heaves a sigh. "Fine. Ready to go?"

At our nods, Rowan has her zombies open the doors for us.

Stanislav trudges into the room. Rowan waits a few seconds to let him get far enough away, then follows—with the rest of us on her tail.

We end up in a room large enough to play football in, with a neck-straining, sixty-foot-tall ceiling.

Rowan's zombies close the doors behind us.

Like the surrounding square, this room is decagon shaped, and in each of the ten angles stands a massive throne with a masked figure.

"These helpers were giants in life," Rowan whispers, in case we couldn't guess by the zombies' size. "The masks are designed to look like each member of the Parliament."

Sure enough, the masks have people's features depicted on them, a bit like the sex-worker zombies' masks did.

"So the members of the Parliament aren't here in person?" I ask, my eyes darting from giant to giant.

"Nope," Rowan says. "Each Parliament member sees through the eyes of the helper dedicated for his use and hears through his ears. Think of it as a videoconference, only designed to make you feel small and insignificant."

Felix whistles. "Zoom has nothing on this."

Puck. There goes Valerian's plan to kidnap one of these people in case things go south. Despite Rowan saying she's engaged to one of them, it's clear that kidnapping her wouldn't do much good; as she said, they don't seem to care about what happens to her. If they did, they would've asked her to use a zombie proxy instead of dealing with us face to face.

The best we can hope for now is that things don't go any more south than they already have.

One of the giant zombies stands up and says something in a booming voice.

"Should I translate?" Rowan asks Dylan.

Dylan shrugs.

Taking it as agreement, Rowan points at the zombie with a mask that has a hawkish nose. "That's Keyser, and he insists I use the word 'demand' when I ask you why you came to this 'magnificent' world."

We all look at Dylan.

"That's pretty much what I heard," Dylan says. "Except the original had more aggrandizements and flowery language."

Valerian steps forward. "We came to help. An organization called

Icelus is trying to rouse fear throughout the Cogniverse. Their agents are on this world, trying to infect your citizens with a deadly disease."

Rowan's shoulders tighten. "Is that what the masks are for?"

"Exactly," Dylan says.

Rowan rounds on her. "And *that's* the long story? I could've made time for that—especially since it took you all of two seconds to explain." She pivots to stare at Stanislav with widening eyes. "Is he—"

"We learned that at the same time as you," Dylan says. "He caught it from Nulen. You should be safe because he has a mask on."

Keyser's booming voice drowns any further discussion.

"He demands to know what we're talking about," Rowan says.

Valerian plants his feet wide. "Translate what I said, but not a word about Stanislav."

"Disobey him, and I'll rip you to shreds," Fabian adds, his German accent stronger than ever.

"Since you ask so nicely, how can I refuse?" Rowan says and starts to translate, with Dylan hanging on to her every word.

I feel a little guilty about the threat on Rowan's life, but desperate times and all that.

Keyser's reply is curt and loud.

"You lie," Rowan translates. "I assume you want me to skip the accompanying insults."

Valerian's hands flex as he looks up at the giant. "You saw Nulen die of the virus with your own eyes."

"They saw him through their helpers' eyes, but I'll translate," Rowan says and speaks Necronian for a few seconds.

Keyser's reply is a bit longer but no less angry.

"He insists you killed Nulen with your vile otherworldly powers," Rowan translates.

"Why would we come here, putting ourselves at your mercy, and do that?" Valerian shouts.

A giant with a small goatee replies this time.

"Even if there is a virus, how do we know the organization you're talking about exists? How do we know you didn't bring the disease with you?" Rowan darts a furtive glance at Stanislav as she says this last bit. "Most importantly, what do you want?"

Valerian looks at Stanislav, then at the currently standing giant. "I want you to capture the Icelus agents and give them to us. In exchange, we'll provide the cure for the virus."

"Wait, what?" Felix says. "Didn't we want to catch Icelus ourselves?"

"These necros seem to hate outsiders too much to let us do that," Valerian says, and Rowan nods in confirmation. "More importantly, we need to take Stanislav back to Gomorrah as soon as possible. As much as I hate Icelus, they're not worth his life."

"Must be nice to have friends," Rowan mutters. Louder, she asks, "Can I translate now?"

"Please," Valerian says.

Rowan speaks Necronian.

The giants begin a discussion among themselves.

As they go on, Dylan whitens. I'm guessing we won't like the translation when it comes.

Indeed, Rowan gives us an uncomfortable look when the giants stop speaking. "Some of them say your deal is so outrageous, they don't see why you'd come here to make it," she says. "Keyser, on the other hand, says you're either crazy or very clever—and has called for a vote to decide your fate."

"A vote?" Ariel adjusts her mask.

"If the majority of them stand up, you're going to be killed," Rowan says, not meeting our eyes. "Otherwise, they'll hear more about your deal."

How fun. My fate is again tied to a ruling body's vote. I'm definitely getting the next one for free.

Keyser's giant stands up.

The one with a small goatee follows.

Then another. And one more.

When the fifth one stands up, everyone tenses.

If one more joins them, that will be a majority against us.

The sixth giant stands.

Puck.

We're officially screwed.

CHAPTER TWENTY-ONE

SOMEBODY LOUDLY KNOCKS on the doors that lead into the meeting chamber. The pattern of the knocks is strange, something like *Da-Da-Da-DUM*.

The giant zombies and the rest of us look at the door.

The banging repeats, again going *Da-Da-Da-DUM*.

Wait a second. Isn't that how the *Fate Motif* from Beethoven's *Symphony* goes? My arms prickle with goosebumps. This must be Nostradamus's cryptic prediction finally coming into play. Which means I'm supposed to play the detective—whatever that means.

Keyser barks an order at Rowan, and a moment later, she has her zombies open the doors.

A man rushes into the room. He looks haggard, with black bags under his eyes. More notably, his skin is purplish red, and there are steaks of blood on his face.

Rowan wisely backs away from the guy. Without her mask, she's in mortal danger from him.

Ignoring us, the newcomer haltingly monologues in Necronian.

LEGO letters appear in the air in front of me:

Are you playing the detective?

So Valerian has also noticed the connection to Nostradamus's words. Good. For a second, I was worried the adrenaline spike was making me hear things that weren't there.

I nod at him, then close my eyes and do my best to "play the detective."

Except I don't know where to start, and the presence of yet another victim of the virus is making me want to run away screaming.

Hold on.

The virus.

I bet playing the detective implies I should figure out who or where the Icelus are.

Assuming they're on this world in the first place.

No. They have to be. Nulen was sick when we met him, so he must've gotten infected by someone before we arrived, thus proving Icelus presence on this world. Not much detective skill required to figure *that* out.

Although… when we met him, he had only the very first symptom. That means he'd gotten infected recently. Also, the Parliament doesn't believe us about the virus, so they couldn't have heard reports of it, which also points to it being a recent arrival on this world.

So what does Nulen being one of the first cases tell me? Not much yet —but hold on. Going back to Icelus being on this world… Wasn't Nulen guarding the hub with a force of zombies to prevent any arrivals?

Another round of goosebumps ripples down my spine. That's exactly what he was doing. Which means one of two things: Either Nulen let Icelus agents in and was infected by them in the process, or someone else let them in and that someone else got Nulen sick too. Given that Nulen is dead, the only useful option is the second one. Which means—

The newcomer collapses, seemingly mid-sentence.

"Dead," Rowan says somberly. "I can feel it."

The six standing Parliament members sit back down.

One of the ones who didn't vote to kill us—a giant with a mask that features a cartoonishly strong chin—begins to speak.

"He wants me to bring the messenger back," Rowan says. "If that sort of thing is going to make you puke, I suggest you look away." And as I look on, Rowan shoots the dead guy with a stream of multicolored energy.

A moment later, the messenger is back on his feet.

Members of Parliament attack him with questions, and the messenger answers in a robotic monotone.

"What did he say?" I hiss at Dylan.

Dylan looks to be in shock, so Rowan answers in her stead. "There was an outbreak of the virus in the province he's from. Humans and necromancers are dying in droves."

"And what's the Parliament talking about now?" Valerian asks.

"Shegan is asking the messenger if the eight of you have been seen in the province," Rowan translates. After the messenger zombie replies something, she adds, "Apparently not."

"Of course not," I say. "Nulen brought us here straight from the hub."

Rowan chuckles humorlessly. "Silly rabbit—you expected the Parliament to use logic?"

"Kind of," I say. "Can you translate something for me?"

Rowan nods.

"Was Nulen the only person guarding the hub against newcomers?"

"I can answer that myself," Rowan says. "There's a whole team of us who share that particular chore. Right now would be my turn, but I'm not at my post thanks to all this brouhaha you've created. Thanks for that—and I mean it."

My pulse speeds up in excitement. "How long do each of you spend on your post?"

"A few days," she says. "Depends on weather and things like that."

"And whose turn was it right before Nulen?"

"Exozar's," Rowan says.

"Then logic says this Exozar is working with Icelus," I announce triumphantly before explaining my deductions.

Just as I finish, the Parliament demands to know what we're talking about, and Rowan loops them in.

As she speaks, Dylan looks at her admiringly, but it's unclear why.

After Rowan is done explaining, Shegan speaks up.

"If you can get proof of what you say, they'll take your deal," Dylan translates.

Keyser speaks up next—and talks for a while.

Rowan rolls her eyes when he's done. "The great humanitarian that is my husband-to-be says you can't be trusted, and that the proof wouldn't prove anything as far as he's concerned. He also says the virus isn't such a big deal; it will just grow the number of available helpers, thus improving the quality of everyone's life. He also says we can use helpers to quarantine impacted areas—which is no doubt a euphemism for 'burn everything to the ground' and contradicts his 'more helpers' point."

Shegan speaks again.

Rowan nods approvingly. "This more reasonable dude says their job as the rulers is to do everything they can to get people the cure. He also worries the virus might be spreading through Necropolis now, thanks to this messenger. Finally, he says they should vote on this."

Yay. Another pucking vote.

The Parliament confers, and Rowan explains that if the majority of the giants remain seated, we'll be allowed to get the proof we need. Otherwise, the default ruling stands—as in, we get killed.

We all watch with baited breaths.

Keyser stands up.

A colleague of his does the same.

This is it.

History is about to repeat itself.

CHAPTER TWENTY-TWO

NO MORE GIANTS STAND UP.

The vote has just gone in our favor.

A relieved exhale escapes my lips as Shegan speaks rapid-fire Necronian at Rowan, who nods and replies in a respectful tone.

"I'm to head the investigation," she translates. "Let's go before they change their minds."

We hurry out of the room and head down the corridor in silence.

When we enter the lobby, Dylan looks at Rowan. "You didn't have to put your neck on the line for us in there."

"What are you talking about?" Felix asks.

"When she told them Exozar was guilty, she said she was suspicious of him too—that he's been acting strange lately," Dylan explains.

"As in, I lied," Rowan says. "Exozar and I haven't spoken in months."

Dylan nods. "And after she said that, Keyser told her to be sure she means what she says and made it clear that by doing this, she's aligning her fate with ours."

"I'm beginning to have a feeling that he doesn't want me even as a seventh wife," Rowan says ruefully. "I don't know if I should cheer or be insulted."

Ariel stares at the necromancer as if seeing her for the first time. "You shouldn't have done that. Our chances aren't good."

"But thank you," I say hurriedly. "I bet you helped the vote."

"Yeah, well, I wasn't as self-sacrificing as you might think. I can use logic just as well as anyone—and it says my fate is already tied to yours." She nods at Stanislav. "More precisely, his."

"You think the messenger has gotten you sick, so you want the cure," Stanislav says, wiping at his slightly bleeding eyes.

Rowan nods. "Bingo."

"That room was spacious and you stood far away from the messenger," Dylan says reassuringly. "Your viral load would've been small and chances of infection insignificant."

Stanislav holds out his bloody fingers. "Isn't that what you told me at the hub?"

"And I wasn't wrong," Dylan says. "Given how long it took you to develop your first symptom, the viral load you must've inhaled *was* small."

He glares at her. "Yet I'm still sick."

Rowan bends down and scratches her dead pet under his whiskery chin. For a zombie, Frank looks too much like he's enjoying the grooming —but what do I know of such things?

"There's something more important we should discuss," Rowan says after she's done with her pet therapy. "How are we supposed to figure out if Exozar is guilty or not?"

Everyone exchanges startled glances. Everyone except Valerian, that is, who pointedly looks at me.

"If you could get me access to him, I could determine his guilt," I say, doing my best to sound more confident than I feel.

Felix and Ariel still look confused, so I say, "I'm supposed to be playing the detective right now, and in the past, that's always involved my powers."

Rowan has her zombies hold the doors as we exit. When we're outside, she says, "What's your power?"

I explain about dreamwalking as we make our way south, with Rowan's helpers lumbering after us like extras in a horror movie.

"New question," Rowan says when we stop next to a drab building that looks eerily like the one we were imprisoned in. "How will you understand his dreams if you don't speak Necronian?"

I grin under my mask. "Good point. You or Dylan have to volunteer to go in with me."

"Rowan volunteers," Valerian says firmly. "She's more familiar with local customs and such, so she'll make a better translator."

LEGO letters show up in the air as he speaks, and they say:

Also, this way we can check two necromancers for the price of one.

I nod. "Rowan it is."

"And I guess Rowan agrees," she says dryly. "Though the word 'volunteer' clearly means something different in English than it does in Necronian."

"Is this our target's home?" I ask, looking at the drab structure in front of us.

"Yep, that's Exozar's quarters," Rowan says. "Now what?"

Valerian looks at the door. "Can you get him to open up for you?" he asks Rowan.

"Sure," she says.

Valerian turns to me. "And could you do that sleep-at-a-distance trick Maxwell performed on Dylan the other day?"

I bite my lip. "Maybe. When I pushed Ariel into REM sleep that time, I was touching her skin. But that was before the power boost…"

"I don't understand," Rowan says.

"Sounds like we need a plan B," Dylan says, ignoring her.

"Plan B will be for me to knock the guy out," Stanislav says. "Then tie him up so Bailey can touch him as much as she needs."

"Touch him where?" Rowan asks with a smirk but is ignored again.

"I really hope we don't have to resort to plan B," I mutter under my breath. "I'm not eager to touch a stranger who might be spreading the virus." Or any stranger for that matter. Or even people I know.

"I'll hygieia his skin if we end up going that route," Valerian says. "That will kill anything." He looks at Dylan, who vigorously nods.

I still don't want to touch anyone, so I'm going to do my best to get plan A to work.

"Don't we need a way to make sure he doesn't see our team as a threat?" Felix asks.

"We can disguise you all as helpers." Rowan gestures at her zombies.

"I'm not putting on a mask that's been on a corpse," I say with a shudder. "There's a limit."

"You don't have to do that," Rowan says. "Follow me."

She leads us a couple of blocks over, where we enter an empty store filled to the brim with brand-new masks and different clothes, all designed for zombie wear. We pick masks big enough to fit over our current ones and robe-like garments to hide our non-Necronian attire.

After Valerian sterilizes my choices, I put them on.

The rest of the team does the same, and we totally end up looking like a bunch of zombies—a pretty eerie development.

"The helpers wear these masks to spare the family of the deceased the pain of seeing their loved ones walking around," Rowan explains as we walk back. "Not sure who decided the design should be this disturbing, though—or why."

When we get back to our original destination, Rowan gives us a thorough once-over. "Don't draw attention to yourselves," she says. "If Exozar puts his mind to it, he could figure out that you're not helpers."

I guess I'll have to do my part quickly.

"Ready?" Rowan asks.

I nod, and she knocks on the door.

A minute passes.

The door opens. A pale, disheveled head peeks out and says something in Necronian. Rowan replies in kind. The guy steps out, and they begin talking.

I close my eyes and concentrate. I don't bother wishing my target asleep or doing any imagination exercises. Instead, I try to replicate what I did to Ariel on instinct.

Nothing happens.

Maybe the wishing and imagining helps?

I do both while seeking the tip-of-the-tongue sensation. Still no results. Meanwhile, I can hear the necromancer conversation petering out.

I open my eyes and see Rowan darting glances at Stanislav, who's standing near Exozar.

Catching her drift, Stanislav sends his fist at Exozar's chin.

Bam.

Stanislav's strong arms catch Exozar before he falls.

"Finally," Rowan says. "I was seriously running out of things to say to the guy."

Grunting, the chort drags the necromancer inside, and the rest of us follow.

"Let my helpers do the rest," Rowan says. She has her zombies put Exozar on his bed, locate a rope, and tie up his arms and legs. "Your turn," she says to me when the bondage is complete.

True to his earlier promise, Valerian sterilizes a patch of skin on Exozar's wrist.

I touch the area gingerly, doing my best to suppress a strong desire to gag as I seek the prerequisite feeling.

It takes me a couple of minutes, but eventually, I get that sensation.

I metaphysically push.

Finally. Exozar is in REM sleep.

I switch gears and drop into his dream. As soon as I appear in my palace, I exit my trance.

There's one more step before I can properly dive in.

"Your turn," I tell Rowan in a low voice. "Oh, and you might not want to be standing next to sharp objects for this."

Rowan stretches out on the floor at the foot of the bed. She gives Valerian a caustic look when he cleans her wrist with the hygieia device.

I approach and make skin contact again. Rowan makes a goofy face and closes her eyes. I also close mine and search inside myself. The feeling is a little easier to locate this time; practice makes perfect and all that. When I catch it, I push, and Rowan is in REM sleep immediately.

I grin. I've officially mastered a new dreamwalker power. At least the touch version of it.

Without removing my hand, I enter Rowan's dream.

Time to see if our alleged ally can be trusted.

CHAPTER TWENTY-THREE

FINDING myself in my dream palace lobby, I gape at the scene in front of me with a mixture of fear and confusion.

Two feet from me stands a frozen-in-place Nutcracker, with pitch-black Pom glaring up at him.

What the puck?

"Pom!" I shout. "Get away from him."

The Nutcracker disappears and Pom turns toward me, the fur on the tips of his ears going from black to beet. "You weren't supposed to see that."

"See what?" I ask, though a part of me already knows.

"That wasn't the real Nutcracker," Pom says, confirming my suspicion. "He just scares me so much, I figured I'd use exposure therapy to become braver." The beet color moves from his ears to the rest of his body.

I smile and fluff up his fur. "It's brave of you to even try. Especially on your own."

Pom's ears take on a brown tinge. "You mean it?"

"Sure. I usually have to badger my clients to try exposure therapy, and once they agree, I have to hold their hand every step of the way."

He hugs my leg and grins. "Thanks. Maybe I'll join you in whatever you came here to do—no matter how scary."

"Good idea."

I don't tell him that my investigation isn't likely to uncover frightening dreams. Let him believe he's being brave. Besides, one never knows what can come out of other people's subconscious.

Pom perches on my shoulder, and I make us invisible before teleporting to the tower of sleepers. Locating the nooks of both of my new necromancer connections, I enter Rowan's. "We'll start with her."

———

A MAN WEARING a Necronian zombie mask is chasing Rowan through the streets of Manhattan. Though this isn't a memory dream, it does prove she's been to New York City.

I make the pursuer evaporate, more for Pom's sake than Rowan's.

As Rowan stops running and looks around in confusion, I debate how to proceed. What I'm about to do works best if I have something like an alibi to check. Answering a question such as "is this person part of Icelus?" is much harder and therefore time-consuming. Basically, I have to put Rowan—and later Exozar—in different dream scenarios, and as they fill in the details from their memories, I might spot something incriminating.

Or I might witness them knitting socks.

The worst part of this is that I can never prove anything with one-hundred-percent certainty. Even if I spend days without discovering an incriminating memory, it could just be due to bad luck.

Oh, well. All I can do is my best.

I start with the simplest trick I know. I make a random stranger on the street whisper the word "Icelus" and watch Rowan's expression.

She looks confused for a second. Then her mind takes over, and she strolls right into a nearby cinema to get a ticket for a movie in *The Fast and the Furious* franchise.

I switch to mental communication and tell Pom, *So far, this doesn't look suspicious.*

I don't think this woman is evil, Pom replies as a voice in my head. *And my intuition is never wrong.*

I'm not staking our safety in the real world on anyone's intuition, so I change the surroundings to a warehouse, a setting where I imagine shady conversations might occur.

Rowan's mind doesn't generate anything suspicious in response.

I put her in a few more shady places, with a similar lack of results.

After more futile digging, I recall an extra clue that I have in this case. The Nutcracker is someone who knows what I look like—and if he's the Icelus dreamwalker, Icelus members might know him in the real world.

Excited, I have Rowan meet dream versions of anyone I can possibly think of, from nurses at Mom's hospital to all of my rehab clients.

Nothing.

Then I get an idea. If Rowan is in Icelus with Exozar, putting them together in a dream might yield memories of them conspiring.

When Rowan is not paying attention, I change her current surroundings from a back alley to Exozar's house, then add Exozar himself.

Rowan's subconscious takes over, and suddenly, the room looks different, though clearly, we're still on Necronia.

My guess is this is Rowan's own living room. Her pet, Frank, is here as well, and Exozar is smiling and pointing at the creature.

They speak Necronian for a bit.

Puck. Valerian and I hadn't thought this through. In hindsight, I should've brought Dylan in too. Though it's pretty clear the conversation is about the pet; they're not looking anywhere else.

As I watch, Exozar crouches and feeds the creature a couple of local nuts. He's rewarded with a lick from Frank and a grin from Rowan.

This must be from a time when Frank was alive—that or I've just learned something new about the zombie diet.

I think she's clean, Pom mentally informs me.

You're probably right, I reply.

Since we're still in a memory dream, I let it play out.

Exozar leaves, and Rowan plays with Frank for a while longer.

We should play more, Pom says in my head.

I pet his furry foot. *You're right. Once I'm out of deadly peril, we'll make playing a regular thing.*

The door Exozar left through opens again, and a new person steps in.

The hawkish nose and the other facial features match those on the mask that a giant zombie wore when we faced the Parliament.

Of course. This is Keyser, Rowan's betrothed.

And he doesn't look pleased. Quite the opposite.

Turning, Rowan asks him something, her tone playful.

He shouts at her.

Eyes narrowing, she shouts back.

His nostrils flare, and he grits something out—clearly an insult.

Rowan looks like she's been slapped.

Frank advances on Keyser, baring his very sharp teeth.

Keyser shouts again and kicks the poor creature like a football as Rowan lunges forward with a cry.

Frank smashes into the wall and slides down in a limp heap.

Pom's feet dig painfully into my shoulder.

Rowan rushes over to her furry friend, her face a mask of such grief that I almost make myself visible and give her a hug. I can't even imagine what she's feeling. If I ever lost Pom—

No, I can't even think about it.

Looking unrepentant, Keyser shouts one more time and slams the door on the way out.

Rowan kneels next to her pet, tears streaming down her face.

"Please, please, please," she whispers in English. "Don't be dead."

There's no response from the creature, and from the way Rowan's face crumples, it's obvious her plea wasn't answered. Bending over the pet, she sobs, rocking back and forth and muttering a mix of English curses and harsh-sounding Necronian words.

Then her sobs cease and her jaw sets in a stubborn line. "I'm going to bring you back," she whispers raggedly. "It'll be our little secret."

Standing up, she extends her hands, pointing at the little corpse. A blinding energy beam shoots out of her fingertips, one that looks very different from what she used when she resurrected the messenger earlier.

Frank stirs.

Kneeling over him again, she pets his fur, a watery smile appearing on her face.

Frank's gaze is unfocused, but he's clearly not dead anymore.

"Thank goodness," Pom exclaims. "I was worried she'd lost him for good."

Dude, you spoke out loud, I mentally answer.

Rowan looks up from Frank, wiping the wetness off her cheeks. "Is someone here?"

I debate if I should answer.

"Can the books be true?" she asks Frank. "Is Mor already punishing me for my sin?"

Frank doesn't reply, but I've made my decision now, so I make myself visible and clear my throat.

She looks at me, eyes wild. "By Mor, where did you come from?"

"You're dreaming," I say soothingly. "Remember how I was going to pull you into Exozar's dreams to help me translate? Well, I'm here, and I caught you reliving a painful memory, that's all."

She rubs her forehead. "You saw the whole thing?"

I nod somberly. "Sorry about Frank."

"Me too," Pom says.

Her gaze darts to my shoulder, and her eyes widen to comical levels.

I explain what Pom is in the simplest terms I can. When I finish, Rowan gives me an imploring look. "Please don't tell anyone what you saw."

"I'm not actually sure what I saw," I say. "Is Frank an unusual zombie or something?"

Rowan bends down and grabs the opossum-like creature off the floor. "He's not a zombie at all."

"I meant a helper," I say.

"He's not really a helper either." She strokes Frank's fur. "Only the most powerful necromancers can do what I did, and all of us are forbidden from doing it. Usually, when we raise a body, the soul—or consciousness—is gone from the resulting entity, letting the necromancer have control. But it *is* possible to do something different with a very fresh corpse. You just bring the life back without taking control. It's forbidden, but I'm a horrible excuse for a necromancer." She glances at the door, and I get the feeling that must be one of the things Keyser yelled at her.

"As far as I know," she continues, "Frank is the only being that has been brought back in this forbidden way. If the others found out about it, they'd kill me and destroy Frank."

Pom eyes Frank warily. "Is he the same as he was before he died?"

Averting her gaze, Rowan sets her pet down. "There *have* been changes. I'd rather not talk about it, though."

"It's fine," I say before Pom can insist. "We should jump into Exozar's dreams."

I teleport us to the tower of sleepers, leaving Frank behind.

"Wow." Rowan twirls in place, gaping at our surroundings. "Where is this?"

I explain it as well as I can and fill her in on how the investigation is going to proceed.

"Wait," she says. "You did that to me, didn't you?"

"We've just met," I say unapologetically.

"Fair enough. But won't Exozar see me? Or hear when I translate for you?"

I mentally say, *How about we talk like this?*

She doesn't look as shocked as I expected.

"That's cool," is all she says. "Are you hearing me do the same?"

Pom giggles. "You're still talking out loud."

"I was trying something," Rowan says defensively. "How about you tell me what to do?"

"Try to have a dream where you can talk to me telepathically," I say. "I'll help you."

She strains until her face turns red, and Pom helpfully informs her that she looks like someone dreaming about pooping rather than speaking mind-to-mind.

How about now? Rowan asks mentally.

There you go, I reply in kind. *In dreams, the impossible becomes possible.*

I was the first to get this to work, Pom chimes in.

You were. I tickle his paw. *But you're going to stay silent the whole time we're in Exozar's dreams, or you have to stay behind. Okay?*

Deal. Pom hops over onto my other shoulder.

I grab Rowan's hand, make all of us invisible, and touch Exozar's forehead.

A moment later, we're in the necromancer's dream.

CHAPTER TWENTY-FOUR

EEK. Exozar is having a wet dream.

This isn't scary, but I'm out, Pom informs me, and I can no longer feel his paws on my shoulder.

Well, this is awkward, Rowan announces.

No kidding. The woman bent over in front of Exozar is none other than Rowan herself.

She must notice that bit only now because she adds, *This never actually happened, but it does put a new spin on the phrase 'in your dreams.'*

Yep. I can confirm this isn't a memory.

Since Exozar's attention is on the naked Rowan, I change the environment from that of a bedroom to a shady warehouse.

Maybe he's dreaming this because you were the last person he saw before falling asleep? I ask.

I think he's fancied me for a while. That's why he opened the door so readily for us. And it's partly why Keyser was so jealous when he walked in on us on that fateful day. He must've passed Exozar on the street and guessed where he was coming from.

I ignore what she says next because Exozar grunts in pleasure, pulls away from his lover, and starts to dress.

When he's looking away from the naked and blissed-out dream Rowan, I swap her for a broken wooden mannequin.

I can't believe he hasn't noticed that switch, the real Rowan complains. *Maybe he doesn't like me as much as I thought.*

This is just the way dreams work, I reassure her.

I wait a few beats, but Exozar's subconscious doesn't fill in any details. If he had shady conversations with Icelus, it didn't happen in a place like this.

Then something occurs to me. Unlike with Rowan, I actually know one place where Exozar would've had to meet Icelus at least once. Smiling in anticipation, I change the surroundings to the Necronia hub—canyon, zombies, and all.

Now for the tricky part.

To really jar Exozar's subconscious, I make a figure step out of the gate we came from. I don't give this mystery person any distinct facial features or anything—the hope is that Exozar will.

Eureka. The newcomer suddenly develops a pale thin face, a pointy chin, and pitch-black eyes.

Another person follows him out of the gate, then a bunch more.

All are dressed in black leather outfits, and all look relieved when Exozar approaches them.

"Percival," Exozar says to the pointy-chinned one and follows it with a Necronian phrase.

Percival must be that guy's name, Rowan translates. *Exozar is happy to see him 'again.'*

Percival takes a backpack off his shoulders and rummages inside. Taking out a gallon-sized flask, he hands it to Exozar with a few words in Necronian.

Percival's accent is barely noticeable, Rowan comments. *He says the flask contains vampire blood, and that Exozar has to drink a glass per day to keep the virus at bay.*

Huh. *Could this Icelus cell be vampires?* I ask, eyeing the flask warily.

I doubt a vampire would show up on this world, especially if they're trying to stay incognito, Rowan replies mentally. *Any necromancer worth the title would feel them from a mile away. Not to mention how much vampires fear our ability to take them over and make them do our bidding. There's a reason they made sure we're unwelcome on worlds like Earth.*

Exozar takes the flask and says something.

He's asking if vampire blood is how the rest of Percival's team will keep themselves alive while they infect people, Rowan translates.

Carrying on in Necronian, Percival continues to rummage in his backpack.

He says his team are all pre-vamps, Rowan says. *Their immune systems can keep this virus at bay indefinitely, which is why they've been chosen to spread it.*

Pre-vamps. I wasn't that far off. I examine the pale faces of the arrivals. *I take it your kind can't detect or take control of one of them.*

Nope, Rowan replies. *Only once they turn.*

Percival hands Exozar something that looks like a cross between a syringe and a throwing dart. After the necromancer examines the device, Percival pulls out a heap more of them and they have a brief conversation.

Percival says the vampire blood will make sleep a problem, but that it's mission-critical for Exozar to be dreaming at noon after a night with a full moon, Rowan explains. *Apparently, in those things is a drug that can facilitate this—the only problem being a nightmare side effect.*

Ah, so it's that Koshmar poison again, the one that makes you see a nightmare based on whatever happened right before you got dosed. It was used on me by the late Dr. Cipactli, also known as the High Priest of the Gomorran Icelus cell. Valerian mentioned that Icelus had many uses for it, and here's one. I guess they now have a quick-acting version and utilize it a bit like how I plan to use my newfound power to put people into REM sleep.

Percival shouts something to one of his pre-vamp companions. The guy comes over and lies on the ground. Aiming the gizmo at his face, Percival presses on the top of the device, and an odorless spray escapes with a hiss.

It seems to take effect immediately; the pre-vamp's eyes start to move rapidly behind their lids.

You know, Rowan chimes in, *last night was a full moon, and it's about noon now.*

Puck. If they needed him to sleep for the reason I think—

As though to confirm my concerns, I hear the dreaded music from the *Dance of the Sugar Plum Fairy.*

Instantly and without explanation, I jolt Rowan awake. Then I do the same to myself—and disappear just as the Nutcracker appears smack in the middle of Exozar's dream.

CHAPTER TWENTY-FIVE

WE'RE BACK in Exozar's bedroom.

Looking disoriented, Rowan sits up.

"The Nutcracker. He's in his dreams right now." I point at Exozar's head.

Valerian narrows his eyes. "That hints he's guilty."

"We don't need hints," Rowan says, all signs of sleepiness gone from her face. "We saw him meet with the pre-vamp Icelus group. He's as guilty as—"

"Wait," I say, holding up a hand.

Something's wrong, but I can't figure out what.

Fabian's ears prickle. "I hear shuffling footsteps in the other room."

At the same exact time, I understand what's bugging me.

It's a specific feeling—or lack thereof.

"Exozar's awake," I exclaim, finally putting my finger on it.

Though the necromancer's eyes are still closed, I can no longer feel him in REM sleep. The Nutcracker must've woken him up with a jolt.

As if waiting for me to say that, a handful of zombies rush into the room, no doubt under Exozar's control.

Stanislav swings a fist at Exozar's face, but the necromancer rolls off the bed, yelps in pain as he hits the floor, and rolls under the bed before anyone can get to him.

Ariel gives the bed frame a hard kick. The wooden structure collapses on top of Exozar, and we hear the necromancer grunt in pain.

"This is not good," Felix says in a frightened voice.

I follow his gaze.

Puck. That's a major understatement.

One of the attacking zombies is strapped with dynamite, and another has just lit the fuse.

Before my life can flash before my eyes, Rowan shoots multicolored energy at the zombie-bomb. The zombie stops in his tracks and swiftly backs away from us. However, a fellow zombie kicks the dynamite carrier's leg, breaking it like a twig, and another zombie breaks the other leg as two more tackle the wounded bomb-zombie to the ground.

"Run!" Rowan bolts for the door.

Fabian grabs Dylan, throws her over his shoulder like a sack, and sprints after Rowan. Stanislav snatches up Felix and Itzel, and Ariel grabs me, whooshing out of the house before I can so much as think "holy uber."

As soon as we're outside, she puts me on my feet and shouts for me to run.

I instinctively launch into a sprint, then stop and spin around, eyes widening in horror as I register the lack of a tall, broad-shouldered figure behind me.

Valerian.

He's not here.

He's still inside that house—and there can't be much length left on that fuse.

CHAPTER TWENTY-SIX

I LUNGE TOWARD THE HOUSE, but strong arms grasp my shoulders, yanking me to a stop.

"Let me go!" I yell, struggling with Ariel.

She doesn't listen.

After what feels like the longest second of my life, Valerian flies out of the house.

Boom.

The blast sends him flying.

I twist out of Ariel's grasp and sprint toward him. But before I can get to him, he sits up, brushing the dirt and gravel off his clothes.

"You okay?" I pant, crouching next to him.

He nods and gets to his feet. "I got lucky." He looks at the house on fire and curses under his breath. "There goes our chance to question Exozar."

Exozar, right. Rising to my feet, I try to get my frantic heartbeat under control. Valerian is fine. He made it. We all did. Still, my hand is unsteady as I push back my hair and readjust my mask. That second when I thought he wasn't going to make it—

Nope, not going there. Got to focus on the situation at hand. Exozar must've done this on purpose, sacrificing himself for the Icelus cause—or to avoid getting tortured for information.

"Maybe we can question his corpse?" I ask Rowan when she runs up to us. Whew. My voice is finally steady.

She shakes her head. "I need something left of him to resurrect."

A necromancer dressed in red rushes past us in the direction of the house. Behind him is a group of about twenty zombies, also wearing red.

"The fire brigade," Rowan says, and indeed, the zombies are already tossing buckets of water and bags of sand at the burning house.

Once the fire is out, we go over to assess the damage.

There are no discernable pieces left of Exozar, nor can we locate the flask with the vampire blood, or Koshmar sprayers, or any other evidence.

Rowan kicks a charred and mangled soup pot. "I guess we have to hope the Parliament takes our word on this."

Stanislav clutches his chest. When he notices me staring, he jerks the hand away.

Puck.

"Are you having heart palpitations?" I ask cautiously.

"Isn't everyone?" he replies gruffly. "We were nearly blown to pieces."

Dylan eyes him worriedly but lets it slide.

"Let's go back to the Parliament," Valerian says. "The sooner we explain what happened, the sooner we can go back."

Assuming we *can* go back. I don't say it, though, because it's clear from everyone's grim faces that they're thinking the same thing.

———

AS WE WALK to the Parliament building, I tell everyone what Rowan and I discovered.

"I'm not surprised Icelus pre-vamps are behind the spread of the virus," Valerian says. "Vampires and pre-vamps hate necromancers, so they have an extra motive to want to destroy this particular world."

"Let's hope the hatred is mutual," Ariel says. "It might increase the odds that the Parliament goes after Icelus for us, even though we can't provide any evidence."

"Oh, it is mutual," Rowan says. "But can I ask a dumb question? What is Icelus, exactly?"

Valerian tells her about Collywobbles and how Icelus are an organization that worship him, while the Overtaken are people who were taken over by him while they dreamed a very specific nightmare. He then warns her about letting people share their dreams with her.

"We should spread that advice through as many Otherlands as we can," Felix says. "Talking about nightmares might become as impolite as showing off your toenail fungus at the dinner table."

Dylan chuckles. "I'll mention this to Maxwell the next time I see him in my dreams. Assuming he's not reached the same conclusion independently."

We enter Decagon Square and march into the Parliament building.

"Take the helper masks and clothes off," Rowan says. "They might not like the disguises."

We comply, leaving everything in the corridor before entering the meeting chamber.

Rowan strolls into the center of the room and confidently gives her spiel.

Immediately, Keyser begins shouting, while Shegan speaks in a calmer voice. The rest of the Parliament fall somewhere in the middle. When the most vocal Parliament members settle down, Rowan speaks some more, and the reactions repeat.

"My husband-to-be clearly hasn't taken his afternoon nap yet," Rowan says to us when the Parliament quiets again. "He's pricklier than a hedgehog cactus."

Dylan rolls her eyes. "What she's trying to say is he doesn't believe us, nor her for that matter."

"Shegan does, though," Rowan says. "Some of the others might also."

I don't like where this is heading.

"Why would we lie?" Ariel asks, exasperated. "More importantly, why concoct such a story?"

"Don't forget the blown-up house," Felix says.

Rowan sighs. "I raised all those points. Let's hope that helps us when they vote."

I knew it.

Another vote.

Shoot me now.

CHAPTER TWENTY-SEVEN

KEYSER STANDS up from his chair.

I grit my teeth.

A long second passes.

Keyser looks around in confusion.

Not a single other Parliament member stands up.

Rowan grins from ear to ear and says something in Necronian.

Keyser's giant collapses back into his throne and monologues for a couple of seconds. Then his limbs hang lifelessly, as if a puppeteer had given up control of a marionette.

Rowan rolls her eyes and addresses the other giants.

Shegan gives her a curt reply, and they go back and forth for a few minutes.

"Let's go," Rowan says to us and strides for the door.

"We're not getting killed, right?" Itzel asks.

Rowan waits until we're in the corridor. "Not only are we not getting killed," she says proudly, "but after Keyser had his tantrum and left, I got a chance to negotiate on your behalf."

"She got them to make Icelus their top priority." Dylan looks approvingly at Rowan. "She then gave them some sensible quarantine procedures to follow while they wait for the cure, and she even got us access to the Parliament's own personal supplies for our trip."

Rowan has her zombies hold the doors for us, and after we exit, she says, "I assume we want to travel to the hub without stopping?"

Dylan cuts her eyes toward Stanislav. "Time is not our friend."

Nodding, Rowan leads us to a storage facility, where she recruits particularly strong-looking zombies and gets us a raft-like platform twice the size of the one Nulen used to bring us to Necropolis.

Laying the platform down in a nearby yard, she asks us about food preferences. To my relief, she doesn't bat an eye at my request for copious amounts of the banana-like fruit and distilled water.

"Also, can you get us real beds instead of the usual zombie contortions that pass for furniture on the road?" Valerian asks. "Or at least one real bed, for Bailey."

Great. I'm beginning to sound like a prima donna.

Rowan is totally fine with this request as well, and thanks to the zombie labor force, getting the beds and chairs only delays us an extra couple of minutes.

In the end, we have everything, even a leather canopy for the zombies to hold over our heads in case of rain.

Rowan gives us a speaking glance. "If you don't like going into a chamber pot held by a helper, use the facilities now and do your best not to drink too much."

"She's talking to you," Felix whispers, winking at me conspiratorially.

I pinch his side, eliciting a loud yelp, but I do take advantage of the nearby restroom facilities, as advised.

Everyone settles into their chairs, and we head out.

As we navigate the streets of Necropolis, necromancers follow us with curious eyes. After a few minutes, we spot a dead bird by the side of the road, the kind that had brought zombie reinforcements for Nulen when we first arrived on Necronia.

"Poor thing," Rowan says and shoots the dead creature with multicolored energy.

The bird flies up and perches on the platform by Rowan's side, right next to Frank.

I have to admit, her power is rather useful.

"You did a great job back there," Valerian tells Rowan when we go through the Necropolis gates and start making our way through the zombie wall that surrounds the city.

She smiles. "Thanks. I have to admit, I've been trying to get on your good side before asking for a favor."

We all look at her with varying degrees of wariness.

"You've all met Keyser." She leaps out of her chair and begins to pace the wooden platform.

I wrinkle my nose. "We've had the displeasure of making his acquaintance, yes."

"Well, not marrying him isn't an option for me," she says. "Nor is moving to another world with necromancers. They're all friendly with Necronia and would locate me for a big shot like Keyser." She stops pacing and looks at me pleadingly. "I was hoping you could put in a good word for me with the authorities on Earth, so I'd be allowed to immigrate."

Huh, okay. I look at Valerian. "If anyone could make that happen, it would be you."

He frowns at Rowan. "That's an enormous ask. Why didn't you negotiate freedom from Keyser when you had the Parliament by the shorthairs back there?"

She examines the wood at her feet. "It's not just about the marriage. I got spoiled when I lived on Earth. I could bore you for hours talking about all the freedoms I wish I had, but if I'm honest, I just as much want to move because I love everything about Earth—its human cultures, the internet, music, movies, video games…"

"Not a single necromancer has ever been allowed to do what you're talking about," Valerian says. "Vampires are a powerful voice among the Earth Cognizant. And they live such long lives, some of them have grievances with your kind from personal experience."

She sighs. "I knew it was a long shot."

I make a mental note to talk to Valerian some more on Rowan's behalf. I like her, and her request doesn't seem so unreasonable to me—except for the part where she wants Earth, instead of a more civilized world, like Gomorrah.

Rowan sits back down, and we ride on the nice road for a while without talking. I must zone out for a bit because when I refocus on the path ahead, I see a group of people in the distance.

I jump up from my chair and approach Rowan. "What do you think that's about?" I ask, nodding at the crowd.

Our zombie bird takes flight and swoops down to take a look at the newcomers—and as it does, Rowan's forehead creases with a frown.

"It's Keyser," she says. "He's waiting there with a warrior-helper contingent. We could try going around, but it might be wiser to hear what he's got to say."

Valerian's already on his feet, peering intently at the obstacle. "Do you think the Parliament have changed their minds?"

"I doubt it." Rowan has the zombie bird land by her feet. "This might just be about me—in which case, I'll go with him willingly, then urge the Parliament to assign you another necromancer guide posthaste."

I don't want to give her back to that pet-killing brute, but on the flip side, a delay might cost Stanislav his life.

Judging by my friends' expressions, they're having similar thoughts.

We continue toward Keyser and his helpers, and it's only when we're right next to them that I realize he isn't here for Rowan at all.

I also realize we're in big pucking trouble.

It's Keyser's eyes.

They have that telltale magma in them—like those of the rest of the Overtaken.

CHAPTER TWENTY-EIGHT

PUCK. He must've taken that nap Rowan briefly mentioned and never properly woken up from it. Exozar—or one of the Icelus—must've shared the viral nightmare with him, and here we are.

"Maybe he can't use his powers in that state?" Felix says, his voice shaking.

No such luck. His warrior zombies—big, beefy individuals—mobilize and rush toward us.

Valerian steps forward, shielding me with his body. "My illusions aren't working," he says tensely. "He's seeing through zombie eyes, like a regular necromancer."

Rowan's zombies lower our riding platform to the ground and rush at Keyser's troops.

It soon becomes clear that we have a twofold problem with this form of defense: We have fewer zombies to start with, and each of Keyser's beefier specimens is worth two, if not three, of ours.

Zombie arms are ripped from sockets, and zombie heads are bashed with them. The sounds of tearing flesh and breaking bone are nauseating, as is the sight of all the gore.

Dylan raises her voice to be heard above the clamor. "Knocking out Keyser is our only option."

Rowan grimaces, muttering, "Mrs. State-the-Obvious nails it again." But she makes her dead bird take flight and swoop at Keyser's head.

I watch with bated breath. If this works, we win.

Unfortunately, Keyser shoots the bird with his necromantic mojo, and the thing flies back at us. Rowan shoots the bird again, taking it over. Keyser wrestles control back—and they keep going back and forth.

"We need to distract him," Dylan says.

Fabian strips off his pants before turning into a huge wolf. His shirt rips to pieces in the process, but he's already leaping into the zombie melee with graceful wolfu-powered moves.

The beefy zombies swarm around him—and pay dearly.

"He'll take too long to get through," I say. "Itzel, can you do your thing?"

A lightning ball forms inside Itzel's palms and flies at Keyser.

A beefy zombie throws himself in front of his master, taking the projectile in the chest.

Itzel hurls another lightning ball.

Another zombie sacrifices himself.

In the distance, a crowd gathers. Judging by their clothing, they're human, so I doubt they'd help us even if they wanted to. In fact, seeing how our enemy is on the Parliament, there's a higher chance they'd help *him* if they could.

Itzel shoots futilely again.

Fabian's claws tear through Keyser's zombies like recycled tissue paper, but there's only one of him and scores of them.

"Are you able to fight?" Valerian asks Stanislav.

With a string of Russian curses, the chort rushes forward. He doesn't do nearly as much damage as the werewolf, but whenever a zombie takes a swipe at him, they find incorporeality where flesh should be.

"Can you take care of the Mordamned bird?" Rowan shouts at Ariel.

Ariel grimly nods.

Rowan stops the necromantic push-pull of the bird and aims her fingers at a particularly muscled zombie near Keyser.

Her plan is clear: She's going to try to have Keyser's own zombie knock him out.

The bird dives at Rowan.

Ariel leaps into the air with uber speed and strength, catching the bird by the tail.

Pucking puck. The feathers rip out of the bird's tail and stay in Ariel's hand while the bird's beak smashes into Rowan's forehead.

Ariel curses bitterly as Rowan's eyes roll into the back of her head and she collapses.

Dylan sprints over and kneels next to the necromancer. Frank, Rowan's zombie pet, hisses at Dylan but lets her get close to his mistress.

Keyser has the bird fly up again, but Ariel leaps up and grabs it again, this time by the sides. Unable to flap its wings, the bird stays put. The reprieve only lasts a second. Keyser shoots at our zombies one by one, and they start to switch sides.

"Give that thing to me," Valerian barks at Ariel, and she does—but the bird is so big and strong I have to help Valerian keep it immobilized. Panting, I wrestle with its clawing feet while he constrains its wings, preventing it from taking flight.

In the meantime, Itzel launches another lightning ball that a zombie takes for his master. Itzel herself collapses, having overused her power.

Ariel leaps off the platform into the fight, but as more and more of our zombies switch sides, she, Fabian, and Stanislav have a harder time keeping them at bay.

Ten zombies jump onto our platform.

Felix rushes at them, fists raised, and is knocked out immediately.

Exchanging a grim look, Valerian and I let go of the stupid bird and take fighting stances.

The bird takes flight in the direction of Keyser. A zombie closes the distance between us and swipes at my head. I duck and deliver a flawless uppercut at my opponent's jaw. My knuckles sting, but the zombie shows no sign of having felt the blow.

Another zombie joins the already-hopeless fight. I sidestep her punch and sweep the legs of the first zombie. He jumps over my sweep and grabs my right hand. His friend does the same with my left.

Not good.

A third zombie lunges at me and rips off my mask. I gulp in a breath, only to realize the mask has been greatly dampening the stench of the battle. Gagging, I try not to hyperventilate as the zombie throws down my mask and stomps on it until it's all but useless.

I flail and kick at my captors. Two zombies dive for my legs, grasping them and holding them in place. To my left, Valerian is bashing a zombie on the head with an arm he must've ripped off from another attacker. An armless zombie—presumably the owner of Valerian's makeshift club—takes a swing at Valerian with its remaining hand.

A dozen more zombies gang up on Valerian, and I lose sight of him for a few terrifying seconds. All I hear are thuds of flesh beating flesh. I struggle harder. For some reason, the thought of him perishing is infinitely worse than the thought of myself dying in this putrid mess.

Some of the zombies shift aside, and I catch sight of him—bruised and battered but alive. My breath escapes in relief. Two zombies are holding his left arm and three his right, with each of his legs also meriting a couple of zombies.

For a guy with no supernatural speed or strength, he's certainly holding his own.

The zombie who destroyed my mask lunges at Valerian and gives his mask the same treatment. Puck. This mask-stealing is deliberate.

There's a flurry of movement from where Dylan stands over Rowan, but before I can make out what's happening there, a shadow blots the sky, stealing my attention.

I look up as far as I can, nearly dislocating something in my neck.

It's the bird, and it's holding Keyser in its talons.

Puck. He's found a way to bypass Fabian, Stanislav, and Ariel.

The bird deposits Keyser in front of me, and we lock eyes.

My heartbeat skyrockets.

His eyes aren't just fiery. They're rimmed with bloody tears.

Whoever made him the Overtaken also made sure he was infected with the virus.

I rip at the zombie hands holding me with renewed vigor, but I might as well try to move a concrete wall.

Keyser closes what little distance was between us, makes a disgusting hawking sound in his throat, and spits a large wad of mucus straight into my face.

I reflexively cringe, closing my eyes, and feel viscous liquid cover every inch of my face. My stomach heaves and my skin prickles as though it wants to crawl away from my body. This is worse than the dive into the moat sewer where I nearly got eaten. I'm so grossed out I think I might go into shock of the type people get when they lose a limb.

I crack open my lids in time to see Keyser spit at me again. It lands on my chin and drips down, sending a surge of bile up my throat.

"An agonizing end for you, child of Soma," Keyser says in a gloating voice, killing what little hope I had that the splatter of blood under his eyes wasn't the symptom of the virus.

CHAPTER TWENTY-NINE

BEFORE I CAN RECOVER from the gross assault or process his words, Keyser turns to face Valerian, who's putting up a solid fight with the zombies trying to pin him down. As I realize Keyser's intention, all blood drains from my face.

"No!" I yell—just as Keyser makes the same awful hawking noise and spits in Valerian's unprotected face.

"I haven't forgotten you either," the necromancer says gloatingly.

My heartbeat is nearing lightspeed, and my vision is red from anger. I strain against the zombie hands holding me in place, but to no avail.

If I were free, I would rip Keyser into little pieces with my bare hands. I really would.

Through the haze of fury, I catch another sign of movement near Dylan.

It's Rowan. She's sitting up and looking around, her gaze unfocused.

Spotting Keyser, she shoots multicolored energy at one of the zombies holding Valerian's right arm. That zombie releases Valerian and smashes a fist into Keyser's face.

The bird takes flight and dives for Rowan. She shoots necromantic energy at it, while her zombie punches Keyser in the stomach. Air audibly whooshes out of Keyser's lungs.

In the meantime, Valerian yanks on his partially freed right arm and twists it out of the other zombies' grip. With a murderous look in his eyes, he punches Keyser in the temple.

The bird swoops, snatches Keyser with its claws, and takes flight. When they're some twenty feet off the ground, Keyser shoots the bird with his energy. As an Overtaken, he seems oblivious to pain, which allows him to recover impossibly fast.

Rowan shoots the bird also, wrenching the control away long enough to force the bird to open its claws. Keyser plummets. With a desperate twist in the air, he takes over the bird and makes it swoop after him, but Rowan steals the bird back and makes it fly up.

They ping-pong like that until Keyser lands on his back with a loud splat, his arms and legs splayed in unnatural positions.

Shockingly, he's somehow still alive and in control of his zombies.

Leaving Rowan's side for the first time since the battle began, Frank scurries over to Keyser and covers the necromancer's face with his furry body. Keyser's arms must be too broken to move because he just lies there as the opossum-like creature slowly smothers him into oblivion.

With Keyser unable to interfere, Rowan takes over the zombies around us. She starts with the ones holding Valerian. As soon as he's free, he rushes to my side and pries away the hands of the zombies holding me.

"Thank you," I say, panting, when the last zombie is off me.

"Here." Valerian rips off his sleeve, wipes the gross spit off my face, and holds the hygieia device over it for triple the required time.

In the periphery of my vision, I see Rowan taking over the zombies that our friends are fighting. My full attention is on Valerian, though. He cleans himself in the same fashion, then pulls me to him and holds me tight, his strong hands stroking my back as if I were his pet cat.

I'm grateful for the kindness. Though I'm mostly numb, I can feel the horror gradually creeping in, and I wrap my arms around Valerian's waist, pressing harder against him.

A flash captures my attention, and I turn around in Valerian's embrace to see Fabian back in his human form—and completely naked. Casually, he locates his pants on the platform and struts over to check on the rest of us.

I step out of Valerian's embrace and start toward Felix, but Ariel is already checking on him.

"He's fine," she says, seeing my concerned face.

"So is she," Stanislav reports, kneeling over still-unconscious Itzel.

Ariel, Fabian, and Stanislav appear uninjured also, apart from some minor cuts and bruises.

Fabian peers into the distance with a frown. "We'd better go. The spectators are moving in."

Sure enough, the humans who were watching the battle from afar are starting to draw nearer.

Rowan, who's having a zombie help her get to her feet, eyes the approaching mob with a gloomy expression. "Frank," she calls out. "Enough!"

Unpeeling himself from Keyser's face, her pet skitters over to Rowan's side with what seems to be a smug expression on his furry face.

"Is he dead?" Ariel asks, looking at Keyser.

In lieu of a reply, Rowan shoots Keyser with her necromantic energy and his eyes reopen.

The fiery glow is gone.

"Oh, good," Ariel says. "It would suck if a corpse stayed Overtaken even after becoming a zombie."

Rowan looks to be straining, but Zombie Keyser can't seem to stand up.

"Too broken," she says through her teeth, then has a couple zombies pick up Keyser's corpse and place it on the platform where we're all gathered. The rest of her helpers lift our platform and launch into a run, leaving the mob of humans behind us.

After a few minutes, Itzel comes to, as does Felix, and Ariel and Dylan render what first aid they can.

As I take all of this in, Valerian stands by my side, stroking my back—which might be the only reason I'm keeping it together.

"I don't understand something," Ariel says, looking from Keyser to Frank. "Why didn't he take over your pet to save himself?"

Looking uncomfortable, Rowan nevertheless shares the secret about Frank—how she broke the most sacred taboo of her kind and created an atypical zombie with free will.

"Oh, I get it now," Felix says with a faint smile. "Frank is short for Frankenstein, isn't it?"

"That would imply that I fear and hate my creation," Rowan says. "But I love my fuzzy-wuzzy."

"Please keep this a secret," I tell everyone. "If the rest of the necromancers find out, Rowan is screwed."

"Oh, it's too late for that anyway," Rowan says. "I killed my betrothed. A member of the Parliament. In front of witnesses. I'm already beyond screwed."

"You got his body." Ariel nods at the reanimated Keyser corpse. "No body, no crime."

"No, I'm as good as dead," Rowan says, then walks over to her chair and collapses into it.

"I don't mean to add to your distress, but you'd better stay away from Bailey and Valerian," Dylan says to Rowan in a low voice. "They may be infected."

May be infected. My heart skips a beat, and my legs begin to shake as I gulp in shallow breaths. I've been desperately trying not to think about the implications of my mask being gone and that glob of spittle landing on my face, but I can't ignore it any longer.

"Shh, don't panic." Valerian pulls me to him, but my shaking only intensifies, and after a moment, he picks me up and carries me to the bed farthest away from Rowan's.

I curl into a ball on my side.

"It's going to be okay," Valerian's voice states in my ears. He must be using his power to make it sound as though it's coming through headphones.

If I could summon the will to speak, I'd tell him it pucking isn't going to be okay.

He may be infected.

I may be infected.

Those two thoughts buzz around my head like angry bees.

Valerian murmurs more reassuring words that I ignore. At some point, he must tire of talking and lies next to me, wrapping his arms around me.

Eventually, I pull myself together enough to get up and force myself to eat a couple of pieces of fruit. I think I'm still numb, and I hope to stay that way.

As I trudge back to my chair, I see Stanislav. Clutching his stomach, he tosses a piece of dried meat off the platform.

"What's wrong?" I ask.

He shrugs. "Necromancer food not good for my digestion."

Before I can press further, he turns his back to me and stomps over to the other side of the platform.

I let him go, though I don't buy what he said. Not after I saw him clutching his chest before. The virus symptoms in order are tears of blood, heart palpitations, upset stomach, and purplish-red skin.

He seems to have had three out of the four.

In fact, is it my imagination or is his skin already a smidge purple?

I hurry over to Valerian. "Can you use your powers to give us privacy?"

"Sit in your chair," he says, and I oblige.

He tells Itzel to stay far away from us, then plops in his own chair. Suddenly, our surroundings change. I find myself in the same chair but in the middle of a gorgeous garden filled with plants from both Gomorrah and Earth.

"Now the others can't hear us," he says. "Not unless you want me to pull someone in, that is."

I take in a calming breath. "Does Stanislav look purplish-red to you?"

Valerian peers in the direction of the cherry blossom tree, his forehead creasing. "Maybe."

"Can you pull in Dylan?" I bend down and pick up a daffodil. The flower has the texture and scent of the real thing. Sometimes I forget how impressive Valerian's power really is. If I were to make this flower in a dream, I'm not sure I'd be able to give it as much detail.

A second later, Dylan appears in the garden with us, her chair right next to me even though in the real world, it's about twelve feet away.

I tell Dylan about my observations of Stanislav, and she looks progressively gloomier as I list all the symptoms I've observed.

"I'm afraid you're right," she says. "His infection seems to have progressed."

Valerian's hands squeeze the arms of his chair. "How long does he have?"

"Depends on the chort immune system in general and his in particular," she says. "I'm sure the exertion of our recent fight didn't help."

"Are we talking hours, days, or weeks?" Valerian presses.

Dylan fiddles with her mask. "I don't think he'll make it to Gomorrah. My hope is that the cure is simple to make, so I can do it on the world where we met Maxwell. The hospital next to the hub there has a rudimentary lab."

Pom's fur is pitch black on my wrist as I pet him in order to self-soothe. "I thought the cure hasn't been developed yet," I say quietly, trying not to give in to the panic beating in my chest.

She sighs. "They've made progress. The best minds are on it. Hopefully they'll have it by the time we need it."

That's a lot of life-critical outcomes riding on mere hope.

Though on some level I'd rather not know, my mouth forms the words. "What about us?"

Valerian glances at me sharply. "You sure you want to talk about it?"

"I'd rather know," I lie.

"Then tell it to us straight," Valerian says to Dylan. "I saw the look on your face when you told Rowan we may be infected. Your poker face is crap."

Dylan flushes. "I'm sorry. I just didn't want anyone to panic. The sad truth is that you received a massive viral load. Unless your immune system is like that of a pre-vamp, you're going to show symptoms soon."

I cover my face with my hands as my carefully nourished numbness gives way to unbridled existential dread.

I'm not ready to die.

And I'm even less ready for Valerian to die.

"Thanks, Dylan," he says, his voice coming as if from a distance. "Go to sleep now, okay? We don't want to miss the moment when Maxwell tries to dreamwalk in you."

"On it," she replies, and when I lower my hands, Dylan is gone and Valerian is standing next to me with an unreadable expression on his face.

Anger, sharp and irrational, surges through me. "How are you so okay?" I demand, jumping up. "Why aren't you freaking out?"

He gives me a crooked grin. "I'm obviously freaking out too. Having the power of illusion helps when you're trying to look cool, though." As if to highlight his words, stylish sunglasses appear on his face, and his nondescript traveling outfit transforms into a skintight bodysuit.

A reluctant smile tugs at my lips. "That outfit is more sexy than cool, you know."

He grins back at me. "As long as it's distracting you from germ worries, who cares?"

To my surprise, it *is* distracting me. His face has been covered by the mask for so long, I'd forgotten the effect it has on me. Now it's all coming back with a vengeance.

Wait, what am I thinking? Is my body going into some kind of "procreation before death" mode? Clearly, being as sex deprived as I am is throwing my priorities out of whack.

"There's more we can do to distract you," he says, as if reading my mind.

I stare at his lips, then slowly lick mine.

His gaze darkens, and he clasps my hand, pulling me closer.

Gazing up at him, I trace my finger over his sensuous lips. "Is this the real you?"

"An illusion," he says hoarsely. "Despite what Dylan said, there's always a small chance I'm sick and you're not. I'd never forgive myself if I infected you."

I'm perversely disappointed.

He leans down and kisses me. Hard.

All my troubling thoughts evaporate as I return the kiss, my core turning into a geothermal spring as his tongue brushes over my lips.

Panting, I make my tongue dance with his.

Or do I?

I pull away. "You're not really feeling this, are you?"

His sexy lips curve. "It's fun to make *you* feel things. Besides, if I got to *really* taste you, my ability to maintain the illusion might be compromised."

Is that a compliment? It sure feels like one.

"Why don't we take this into the dream world?" I bite my lower lip. "I want you to feel things too."

His nostrils flare. "Does this mean you've forgiven me?"

I freeze, having forgotten all about the grudge until now.

Have I forgiven him? I guess I have. It seems petty to hold on to anger given the danger our lives are in right now—and everything he's done to keep me safe. Actually, if I'm honest, I probably forgave him the very first time he used that hygieia device on my behalf.

Another thought occurs to me. Have I been using my grudge to avoid thinking about my feelings for him? And what exactly are those feelings?

No, I'm too overwhelmed to think about *that* pesky question.

Realizing he's waiting for my answer, I say quietly, "I think I have forgiven you." Seeing his cocky smile, I quickly add, "But I still want to learn about Soma, especially given—"

"That child of Soma bit Keyser spouted?" His face is serious now. "I've been pondering that too."

"And did you figure it out?" I ask, not bothering to hide the eagerness in my voice.

"I was allowed to keep very few of my memories." He looks like it pains him to utter every word. "Everything to do with Soma is secret, so if one wishes to leave it and go to the Otherlands, the way I did, the price is the very memory of Soma. Only a powerful dreamwalker can break a black window, and the most powerful of your kind live on Soma, making this a perfect security system." He pauses, looking at me. "Well, almost."

"So one of the windows is all your memories of Soma?" I ask, aghast. "As in, your whole childhood?"

"Young adulthood too," he says with a wince. "But think about how effective the system is. Even if tortured, I wouldn't be able to reveal anything about my home—not that I would. I'm allowed to remember how much I loved it… and how much I want to keep it safe."

He looks like he's in pain, so I squeeze his hand—that is, until I realize he can't feel that either.

"I saw two black windows," I say softly. "If one is Soma, what about the other?"

He pulls his hand away. "I don't know. Obviously, it's an important secret, but I wasn't left any hints as to what it is."

"Maybe you'd know more if you got your Soma memories back?"

"Possibly. I genuinely have no clue."

I touch him—or his illusionary form—again. "How about you remove the illusion, and I touch you for real, putting you in REM sleep?"

He sighs. "You need to rest. So why don't we agree to this: I go to sleep, and you do as well. Then, when you dream naturally, we break the Soma window."

"I don't know if I'll be able to fall asleep with everything that's happened," I say.

He smiles ruefully. "Which is why I wanted to properly motivate you to rest."

"Evil. Where's my bed?"

"There."

The bed materializes in the middle of a flower meadow, surrounded by forty-two different species of dahlias. I tiptoe over the flowers as though I could actually break them. When I lie down on the bed and close my eyes, the sound of a gentle ocean surf caresses my ears.

"What if the Nutcracker comes and kills me this time?" I ask without opening my eyes.

"I already spoke to Fabian," the wind replies in Valerian's voice. "He'll subdue you if necessary."

Fine. I do my best to even out my breathing. The scent of salty ocean air conspires with the sweet aroma of flowers to calm me.

It takes an hour or so, but eventually, I drift off.

CHAPTER THIRTY

ARMS OUTSTRETCHED, I'm flying in the skies on Gomorrah, dodging skyscrapers in my way.

Wait a second. When did I learn to fly? This must be a dream.

I check my wrist. Yep. Pom is missing.

I halt my flight and take myself to my dream palace.

Pom is here, his fur a happy purple.

"Hey, bud," I say. "How are you?"

I don't tell him our lives are in danger, but there's a chance he knows via an unauthorized snooping inside my mind.

"I just finished some exposure therapy." His fur turns brown. "It goes better and better each time."

Whew. He hasn't yet picked up on the danger. "Excellent. How about you work on it some more while I take a trip into Valerian's dreams?"

"You want privacy?" he asks, the tips of his ears turning a jealous green.

"It's not what you think," I say, though I hope that we do find time for what Pom is alluding to. "I'm trying to learn a secret from Valerian, and if he sees you, he might get skittish."

His fur takes on a light orange hue. "You'll tell me the secret though, won't you?"

"I will," I say solemnly.

"Unless it's gross or scary," he amends.

"Sure. I doubt this one will be, though."

He nods, ears flopping, and I teleport into the tower of sleepers, right into Valerian's nook.

He's here. It's now or never.

I place my lips on his to make contact and dive in.

———

VALERIAN IS MAKING out with a dream version of me. She's really into it, and so is he. We're in his bedroom, and both of the windows are black—which is what I'm here for.

"Great job with the dream," I say after I've watched my fill. "They say when you practice something while sleeping, you get better at it in the real world."

He looks at me—a second version of me from his perspective—and recovers from surprise with record speed. "You think I need to get better at this?"

"No. You're a sex god," his dream version of me says in a sultry voice.

Though feeling jealous in this case doesn't make sense for multiple reasons, I still take perverse pleasure in making her disappear.

Valerian looks vaguely disappointed. Heaving a sigh, he points at the black window nearest us. "That's the one with Soma memories. It's one of the few things I know."

I head toward the window in question.

"Wait," he says. "We want to break it so that I get the memories back when you're done."

"I have no idea how to do that."

"I do." He comes up to me and takes my hand, his touch giving me warm tingles even in the dream world. "Just bring me with you when you go."

Oh. I can do that. I think.

I make us both fly into the window, and he squeezes my hand tighter as I make contact with the black glass.

———

I PLUNGE into icy black water.

Two problems are apparent right away.

First is that a rope is wrapped around my waist. It attaches me to a rickety boat, inside which is an unconscious Valerian. This must be the side effect of dragging him with me.

What's more worrying is the size of the body of water around us. It's either a sea or a small ocean—I can't see a shore in any direction. The last time I tried to swim through something like this, I drowned, and that time, I didn't have to drag a boat with Valerian along.

Then again, I'm supposed to be more powerful now. Maybe that could give me an edge?

I try to use my powers, willing myself to become lighter than water so I can float. This didn't work before and doesn't now. I will the boat to fly like a balloon, but it doesn't.

All right. I'll swim the old-fashioned way.

I swim for what feels like an hour with a freestyle stroke, then switch to breaststroke and swim some more. Still can't even see the shore. The rope makes it awkward to do a backstroke, so I switch to butterfly and swim that way for a while.

After what feels like a day, my every muscle aches and the irritation from the rope burns messes with my concentration.

I keep on swimming. It becomes a meditation, with my movements as the mantra. One arm after another. I think only about swimming. And swimming. And swimming. My breathing grows more labored, yet the shore is still nowhere in sight.

A part of me wants to give up and sink, but I can't. If I do, I'll be kicked out of the dream world with my powers depleted. More importantly, I want to learn about Soma and give Valerian his missing years back.

At some point, the exhaustion and pain grow unbearable, but then, to my surprise, I get a second wind.

Is it my newfound powers kicking in? Maybe I've manipulated the balance of oxygen in my body to somehow counteract the buildup of lactic acid in my muscles. Or maybe I've just figured out a way to boost the endorphin production in my brain. Whatever it is, I'm not complaining.

I swim and swim and swim, and finally, I spot a distant shore.

Gulping in air, I kick harder, ignoring the fact that the distance I have left is greater than any I've tried to swim in prior black windows.

Just as I did before, I remind myself of a simple truth: My muscles are not really tearing into bits. It's not oxygen I lack. There's no lactic acid in my muscles, and the rope cutting into my waist isn't real. This is just a dream construct that makes it difficult for weaker dreamwalkers to access the locked memories.

That last bit helps perk me up. Surely I'm not weak with the boost I got.

The second wind lasts halfway through my desperate sprint to the shore. The pain returns, infinitely worse, and my strength flags. Still, I refuse to give up. I just swim as though my life depends on it.

As though if I drown, that is it.

Something shifts then. My arms and legs move without my conscious control. I begin slicing through the water like a shark, and keep this up all the way to the shore.

My feet brush the sand, and the ocean around me disappears.

————

I FIND myself in a familiar clearing in the woods populated by alien trees, some resembling coral reefs, others baobabs. The surreal, forest-filled sky is familiar as well and implies that this planet—or spaceship—is a pretzel shape instead of a sphere. Or, as Itzel put it, it's a structure made of two counter-rotating cylinders known as the O'Neill colony.

This clearing is also the very place where Mom killed Asha.

If I had any doubts that I was born on Soma, they're gone now.

Setting that aside, there are two Valerians here, and one of them looks noticeably younger than mine. The young Valerian is shirtless—a great look on him—and is fighting with a tall, striking stranger, while the regular Valerian is standing right by me, looking awestruck by the scene.

"I can't believe I forgot this," he mutters. "I know that's how black windows work, but now that I'm here, it's hard to believe I couldn't remember this."

"Why are you fighting this guy?" I ask.

"I'd never fight Kojo," he says with a faint smile. "We're just sparring."

Kojo. Where have I heard that name? I don't get a chance to ask because the memory changes.

————

THIS TIME, Valerian and Kojo are young teens, both climbing a baobab-like tree.

Aha. Just like in Mom's black window, the memories are coming at us out of order. What's different is that this memory plays out fast, like a slightly sped-up video. Or maybe the boys are just fast climbers?

"Isn't it dangerous to climb that quickly?" I say to grown-up Valerian, who's next to me again. "Or is something else going on here?"

"The memories will speed up as my presence compromises the black window's integrity," he says. "What I want to know is, how do I remember this factoid already? I don't think I knew this before we started."

"Integrity?" I ask as Kojo and Teen Valerian reach the top and sit on a thick branch.

"At some point, the black window will shatter," my Valerian says. "After that, we'll get kicked out, and I'll have the memories back."

I start to reply, but the memory changes again.

———

VALERIAN LOOKS to be two or three, and is as adorable as a toddler can be. His ocean-blue eyes are twice their current size, and his cherubic face already shows a hint of adult Valerian's striking features.

A woman is holding the toddler, and it doesn't take a rocket scientist to figure out it's his mom. Her loving expression and their resemblance make that clear.

"This is my earliest memory of her," my Valerian whispers reverently. "I think she's about to sing."

She does, and even sped up, the song is beautiful and serene. Soon, toddler Valerian's eyelids begin to droop, and the memory flips again.

———

WE'RE in an achingly familiar room.

Grown Valerian gapes at the people here, and so do I.

The young Valerian is about six, and so is Kojo. To my shock, I recognize both of them at this age. I've seen them in another black window—my mom's.

But what stuns me most is the sight of the two girls playing with the boys.

Two identical twins.

Bailey and Asha.

Little me and my dead sister.

CHAPTER THIRTY-ONE

MY PARENTS ARE THERE TOO. In fact, I think I saw Mom's memory of this exact event. Young Valerian was there; I just didn't yet know that's who he was. At that point, I just thought the boy looked familiar.

My breath catches in my chest.

Valerian and I knew each other as kids. In Mom's memories, I played with him a lot.

I suppose I should've anticipated that this could be the case. He's from Soma. I've been suspecting that I'm from Soma. The possibility of us knowing each other in the past was there.

I turn to the grown Valerian, who's staring at the scene openmouthed. "The first time we met, I thought you looked familiar."

He nods, still looking stunned. "I felt the same. I even told you, remember?" He shifts his gaze to the little me. "I must've recognized you even with the black window blocking the memories."

I also look at our younger selves.

Why can't *I* remember this?

I glance at my mom for answers, but that's useless. Like in her version of this event, she's just holding my father's hand.

I turn my attention to the other adults in the room. One man looks particularly familiar, just as he did when I first saw this in Mom's window.

Now I understand why that is.

"That's your father, isn't it?" I point at the man. "Davu?"

Valerian nods, his jaw tight. "That's him."

"I'm sorry, Davu. I don't think there's a choice," my father is saying as I tune in to the adults' conversation. "The prophecy—"

"Was vague," Davu says dismissively. "If—"

Little Valerian pulls on his sleeve. "Dad, can Bailey and I go to the garden?"

Davu nods, and little me and the boy race out of the room, ending the memory.

————

THIS NEW MEMORY is of a birthday party.

Valerian, Kojo, my twin, and I are playing together with another dozen children.

I'm barely following the events, in part because I'm still reeling from what I've just learned, and in part because the memory is replaying even faster.

"I thought you were older than me," I say to grown Valerian as a new memory starts, one where he loses his front tooth and puts it in a little box, like treasure.

"Time runs faster on Soma than on Gomorrah," he says. "Since I stayed there longer than you, I've lived longer."

Yet another memory starts, now with everyone moving comically fast. In it, Kojo, Valerian, Asha, and I are playing hide-and-seek and yelling in sped-up, chipmunky voices.

Then a memory of a funeral whizzes by. "My parents," Valerian explains when I look at him questioningly. "The only thing I was allowed to remember about my family was the name of the group responsible for their deaths." His voice roughens. "Icelus."

The next memory passes in an eyeblink, showing Kojo, Valerian, Asha, and me running barefoot outside.

"The window is about to break," Valerian says, and two memories flash by in the time it takes him to finish that sentence. In one, his father is chastising him for something, and in the other, he and Kojo are playing a sport the rules of which are impossible to figure out at this speed.

The next dozen memories go by so quickly I only make out snapshots. In one, he kisses my five-year-old self on the cheek; in another, he's holding her hand.

No wonder I react to him as I do. He was probably my first crush—

The world explodes around us, jolting me awake.

I OPEN my eyes in the real world. I must've slept for a while. It was still daytime when I fell asleep, but it's sunrise now.

Recalling what I've just discovered, I leap to my feet.

Valerian is already coming toward me, hair disheveled and eyes wild. "I remember everything."

Something about his eyes stops me dead in my tracks.

He's got droplets of red moisture near his tear ducts.

Blood tears.

I want to scream, but no sound comes out of my lips.

Valerian's face goes ashen.

Can he see the terrible news on my face?

But no. He points at my eyes, and I know what he's looking at without him saying anything.

I rub at the moisture gathering in the corners and look at my trembling hand.

There's blood on my fingers. Like Valerian, I have bloody tears.

The scream that I'm suppressing grows louder.

Valerian pivots to face the other side of the platform. "Dylan!"

She rushes over, then notices our eyes and freezes. "The massive viral load," she whispers. "I was hoping I was wrong about the implications."

"The cure," Valerian barks. "Do you know how to make it?"

She cringes. "Maxwell says they're close but not yet."

"Go back to sleep and tell him to have a vampire meet us at the nearby world," Valerian orders. "That or a person with a jar of vampire blood."

Dylan bites her lip. "I think I know where you're going with that, and I have bad news. The experts on Gomorrah have done a lot of testing on animals infected with Maxwell's virus. When given vampire blood before any symptoms, the symptom onset is delayed. But if taken after the symptoms show up, vampire blood actually accelerates the progression of the disease. There's a reason they have extremely expensive healers keeping Maxwell alive."

Valerian's hands turn into fists. "We should've made Isis or another healer join this expedition."

Dylan backs away. "Isis refused, remember?"

"I could've dragged her by force," he growls. Taking a deep breath, he says in a calmer tone, "Do you have any tips for slowing down the progression of the disease?"

Dylan looks uncertain. "One thing that might help is to take it easy. As we saw with Stanislav, exerting oneself lowers your body's defenses."

"Right," he says, sounding even calmer now. "When will you be able to go to sleep again?"

"I just woke up," she says. At the narrowing of his eyes, she quickly adds, "Bailey can use her powers to put me into REM sleep at any time, though."

"Bailey is going to take it easy," Valerian says firmly. "How about you do some exercises to tire yourself out, then eat a heavy meal and attempt a siesta?"

"Sure, I can do that," Dylan says. "I warned Maxwell to—"

"I'm sorry to interrupt," Felix says, approaching with a grave expression. "There's something you need to see."

He motions toward Stanislav's bed.

I look at it—and immediately wish I hadn't.

Stanislav's skin is a deep purple with just a touch of red. Eyes closed, he's thrashing like a man possessed by a demon with ADHD. Under his breath, he's mumbling something in Russian, but the only word I recognize is Murzik, the name of his kitten.

"How long has he been like this?" Valerian asks, his voice roughening as he walks over to the unfortunate chort.

On leaden legs, I follow.

"Don't know," Felix replies, joining us. "I just noticed it."

Rowan, Ariel, Fabian, and Itzel rush over as well, and deny knowing anything when Valerian barks the same question at them.

Stanislav's thrashing slows, and he begins whimpering something in Russian.

"It hurts," Felix translates, his voice pained. "He can't hold on anymore."

Ariel grabs Stanislav's wrist. "Fight it. You're a chort. What's a measly virus to you?"

"Can she get sick from touching him?" I whisper into Dylan's ear.

"Not according to Gomorran experts," Dylan whispers back. "Her mask will keep her safe."

Stanislav stops thrashing. In a few seconds, he stops whimpering also.

"I'm sorry," Rowan says, her expression solemn. "It's over. I can feel it."

Ariel doesn't seem to accept that. She checks Stanislav's pulse—only his dead body turns ghostly and disappears in her grasp, leaving behind nothing, not even the clothes.

She draws back, startled, and Felix puts a hand on her shoulder, squeezing lightly. "Chorts phase one last time when they pass."

CHAPTER THIRTY-TWO

VALERIAN WHIRLS ON DYLAN, his face a mask of fury. "It happened overnight. You said he'd make it to that nearby world!"

Dylan staggers back. "I hoped. I'm sorry."

Fabian steps between Valerian and Dylan, his expression grim. "We're all upset," he growls. "Let's remember it's Icelus we're upset with."

Valerian unclenches his fists. "I didn't mean… This is a lot to process."

You can say that again. During our travels, I'd grown to like Stanislav quite a bit. He wasn't at all how I'd expected the infamous chorts to be like—in a good way.

"Felix," I say unsteadily, thinking back to when I dreamwalked in Stanislav. "You have to tell his girlfriend."

"Of course," Felix murmurs.

A droplet of something slides down my cheek—probably blood—but I don't check. "Make sure to tell her to take care of the kitten. She'll understand what that means."

Felix nods somberly.

"She'll be taken care of," Valerian says. "Both of them will be."

Ariel looks around. "Does anyone want to say anything?"

Fabian turns to the now-empty bed. "I'll start. I've known Stanislav for…" And as he goes on, reality presses on me from all sides.

This is a eulogy.

Stanislav is gone.

My heart squeezes painfully in my chest, my emotions in turmoil.

Grief is there, for sure, but also a good dose of guilt. There's a selfish part of me that grieves Stanislav's passing for the wrong reasons: Now we see how precarious Valerian's situation is. And mine.

"You should rest," Valerian's voice intrudes into my mental fog.

He takes me by my elbow and leads me away from the makeshift funeral. As soon as my rear hovers over the edge of the bed, my knees give out. I end up hunched over in an awkward position, but I don't care.

Valerian sits by me and gives me a bear hug.

His scent and warmth provide a tiny bit of relief—that is, until I allow myself to really assess my situation.

Despite a lifetime of obsessively using hygieia and hand sanitizer, of sacrificing touching, kissing, and even hugging, I got sick. And not just sick. Infected with a deadly virus for which there's no cure yet.

Phobetor truly is the god of nightmares. He found a way to make my worst one a reality.

And what a nightmare it is. I can almost feel the virus releasing its unholy genetic instructions inside my cells, can sense my cells getting overpowered and starting to work for the enemy, creating enzymes that help the intruder make more copies of its disgusting self. I can picture new copies of the virus ripping out of the cells like nightmarish creatures from the *Alien* movie. Even as I'm thinking this, more cells are falling victim. And more. Until—

"Look at me," Valerian demands.

I obediently shift my gaze to his face.

"You're going to be fine." The words sound more like an order than reassurance.

I swallow the thick lump in my throat. "How could we possibly be fine?"

"Dylan will get the recipe for the cure in her next dream," he says confidently. "It will be easy to make. We'll rush to the nearby world, and she'll make the cure there, no problem."

I stare into his ocean-colored eyes. "If you're trying to pass for a seer, your fortune-telling needs to be more oblique."

He puts a finger to his temple and with mock concentration says, "I see you in a different bed. There's moaning. A pond is nearby."

I smile weakly. "That vision isn't all that mysterious. There's a pond in your apartment on Gomorrah."

He leans in, eyes gleaming. "It doesn't change the fact that there's moaning in your future." And closing the remaining distance, he presses his lips to mine.

Holy puck. I'm kissing in the real world—and it's magic. Amazingly, bacteria and viruses couldn't be further from my mind. Instead, all my senses are focused on him, on the way his lips feel, how his breath is warm and faintly sweet… how anxious butterflies in my stomach are now flapping their wings in a mating dance.

Deepening the kiss, I grab his hand and slide it under my shirt.

He stiffens and pulls away.

I eye him in hurt confusion.

"We can't," he says raggedly.

"You can give us privacy with your powers," I protest.

"It's not that. You need rest, and taking this further would be just the opposite."

Taking this further.

Is that what I want?

Incredibly, yes. All the way yes.

"Why don't you lie down," he says. "I'm going to go see if Rowan can speed up her zombies some more."

"But—"

He's already on his feet, striding away.

Ugh. Stupid Dylan and her "take it easy" advice. If the virus kills me, I'll be really pissed I didn't seize the moment just then.

My heart is still fluttering like a leaf in a tornado, and I take a few calming breaths—though what I actually need is a cold shower.

My pulse continues racing despite the relaxation attempt.

Wait a second. Aren't heart palpitations a symptom?

No. No way. Too soon. Besides, that way lies another freak-out.

I'd better distract myself—and I know just the thing.

Stretching out on the bed, I touch Pom's fur and go into the dream world.

———

AS SOON AS I appear in my dream palace, I leave my body, even out my heart rate, and jump back in.

Pom appears in front of me, his expression subdued.

I came here to level with him, but he might already know something.

"Is everything okay?" he asks instead of his usually cheerful hello.

"It's not," I say and tell him about the virus situation.

As I talk, his fur turns black.

"I'm sorry," I say when I finish. "In hindsight, I'm a terrible host."

The tips of Pom's ears redden. "That's stupid. Even with the virus in mind, I wouldn't want to be anyone else's symbiont."

"Thanks." I grab him off the floor and press him against my chest. "On the bright side, this virus has shown me what a true parasite is like. I never should've called you anything but a symbiont."

Pom wiggles his ears. "I've been trying to teach you."

"You have," I say. "And now I'm telling you how I really feel."

He wriggles out of my grasp and lands gracefully on the floor. "How about Valerian? Did you tell *him* how you feel?"

I hesitate, then shake my head. "I'm sure he knows."

"How? I don't think even you know."

I heave an exasperated sigh. "What does it matter if we're both going to—"

"You can be so stupid sometimes." His fur is deep red now. "Sometimes I worry I use too much of your brain."

I narrow my eyes. "What do you mean, *use my brain?*"

His angry red hue morphs into a guilty beet. "Well, yeah. I don't exactly have my own head in the real world, do I?"

"You don't, but—"

"As part of our symbiotic bond with the moofts, we loofts borrow some brain cells to be able to expand our consciousness. Later, we stimulate neurogenesis to compensate for the—"

"You know what, I don't think I want to know." I fold my arms across my chest. "Just tell me one thing… When I talk to you, am I talking to myself?"

"My neurons have very limited interaction with your own." His fur is a kaleidoscope of colors. "I'm a separate entity, just one that happens to share things with you."

"Yeah," I say sarcastically. "Things like my blood, and as it turns out, my brain as well."

"I thought you knew. How did you think I was able to use your powers? Or pick up your thoughts?"

I pinch the bridge of my nose. "You must've stolen the part of my brain that was responsible for asking those very questions."

"Like I said, neurogenesis—"

"And like I said, I'd rather not know the details. How about we play a game instead?"

When I see how quickly he turns a happy purple, I feel a pang of guilt that I haven't offered this to him more often.

Better late than never.

We play every game I've ever heard of, then invent some of our own and play those.

"I'm tired," he says after I beat him thrice at our latest invention: tic-tac-toe but on a three-dimensional array of cells, using kittens and puppies instead of naughts and crosses.

"How about you rest?" I say. "I was thinking I'd give a free therapy session to all my clients."

"Smart," Pom says sagely. "They say helping others can make you feel better."

"Nice. So altruism is selfish."

He grins and does his Cheshire cat disappearance.

"I could use feeling better, that's for sure," I mutter and teleport to the tower of sleepers.

Of course. Just as I'm in a giving mood, not a single one of my patients is asleep.

Fine.

I go to the memory gallery and recreate my first kiss in every juicy detail. If I do survive the virus, this is an experience I'll want to enjoy again and again.

Since I'm here, I replay some of my other favorite memories—especially those with Mom.

Poor Mom. Bad luck has a sense of irony. Just as I've hopefully gotten the power to bring her out of her comatose state, a virus is going to stop me from doing so.

Nope, not going there. Dwelling on bad outcomes isn't part of "taking things easy."

For Mom's sake, I create the most soothing environment around myself that I can muster, then meditate for what feels like days. Eventually, I grow very, very bored of taking things easy. At least the dream-world kind of easy.

In any case, I should check on how Valerian is doing.

To that end, I jolt myself awake.

BEFORE I EVEN OPEN MY eyes, I realize this was a bad idea.

Out here, in the real world, my heart is hammering irregularly in my chest.

There's no doubt now.

It's a symptom of the virus.

Opening my eyes, I see Valerian stretched out on his bed. Someone dragged it over to be next to mine.

Valerian notices me looking and sits up with a grunt.

I look at his chest area. "Is your heart—"

"Yours too?" he asks worriedly.

I nod. "Also, I think I'm starving."

His face darkens further. "Are you sure it's hunger?"

I examine the gnawing sensation in my belly.

Puck. It might well be the third symptom. If so, purple skin will be next, and after that is the end.

"There's good news," Valerian says, gesturing in the direction we're moving toward. "We're almost there."

I sit up.

Yep. I recognize the mountain ridge in the far distance.

Still, given how quickly the virus has been progressing with that insane viral load we got, we might not make it to the gates. And even if we did make it, last I checked, Dylan doesn't have the cure.

Speak of the devil. Dylan walks over, an excited expression on her face. "I just woke up. Maxwell explained how to make the cure. It's simple. I can do it at that lab at the hospital on the nearby world."

Okay. Now we have a chance. A small one but still.

"What do you think are the odds we'll last that long?" Valerian asks, echoing my concerns.

"It's hard to say for sure," Dylan says. "My hope is that you make it."

She also hoped Stanislav would make it, and that didn't turn out so well.

"I want more than hope," Valerian says. "Rowan," he yells. "Can you come here?"

Rowan hurries over, a curious expression on her face.

"Is there any way we can speed up this ride some more?" Valerian asks.

"I've stolen all the helpers from the fields we've passed," Rowan says. "Short of helping them carry this thing myself, I'm not sure what else I could do."

"Shouldn't there be some zombies by the gate?" I ask.

Rowan rubs her forehead. "Sleeping beauty has a point. Let me check."

The dead bird Rowan found earlier takes flight and zooms ahead of us.

As I wait, I carefully examine Valerian's skin.

There's the slightest tinge of purple there—though it could be the stress playing tricks with my vision.

Looking at the back of my hand yields the same result. I think my hue is a little purple, but I'm not certain.

Rowan frowns, her gaze distant.

"What's wrong?" Dylan asks.

Rowan's tone is grim. "Let me make the bird dive down to be sure."

She concentrates for the next minute, then turns a pained gaze on us. "It's Icelus. They're blocking our way to the hub."

CHAPTER THIRTY-THREE

WE START PEPPERING her with questions, but she winces and exclaims something in Necronian.

"Mor blast them," she growls in English. "Apparently, pre-vamps are expert jumpers. The helper bird was caught."

"Back up," Valerian says. "Are you sure this is Icelus we're talking about?"

"It's the pre-vamp Percival who did the jumping," Rowan says. "The others are also from Exozar's dream. I've never been surer."

"And they got your bird?" I ask, feeling sick. Aside from the danger posed by Icelus, the delay doesn't bode well for Valerian and me. "As in, they know we're coming?"

"They might not know the bird was a helper," Rowan says without much confidence. "As soon as they caught it, I withdrew my control, so they might think it croaked from the fright of being caught."

"Everyone," Valerian shouts. "We need to talk!"

Fabian, Ariel, Felix, and Itzel rush over, and Rowan tells them what she just discovered.

Some of the same questions as earlier get asked all at once.

"Guys, shut up," I say sternly. "We need a plan, not a game of twenty questions—and I think I have one. Felix, what's the reach of your powers?"

He looks like a lightbulb has just lit up above his head. "I'm on it," he says and shoots an arc of magenta energy into the distance.

Soon metal glints in that direction, proving Felix and I are on the same page.

Rowan cocks her head. "Is being coy part of the plan?"

"Felix is about to reunite with his robot suit," I explain. "Inside the suit are our weapons, including poison grenades. My plan is inspired by what Exozar did to us. You send in a zombie with a grenade and—"

"When pre-vamps die, they turn into vampires," Ariel says with distaste. "We'll just be facing more powerful enemies."

"But we have a necromancer." I nod at Rowan. "She can take over vampires and make them do her bidding. Can't you?"

"It's a good plan," Rowan says. "Unless the wind blows the poison toward us, that is."

"The masks block poison," Itzel chimes in.

"That's great for those with masks," Rowan says. "What about me, sleeping beauty"—she looks at me—"and her beau?"

My beau?

"We have spare masks that were meant for members of the team that didn't make it," Itzel says. "Those masks might not fit the three of you well enough to wear for long, but if you hold one tightly against your face, you'll block the poison."

"Why would we get close enough to Icelus to be in danger of the poison in the first place?" Felix asks.

Rowan scratches the bleached side of her head. "I've only taken over a vampire once. It was in self-defense when I was on Earth. I'm pretty sure I need to be nearby to do that."

"It doesn't matter," Valerian says. "Pre-vamps or vampires—I can make us invisible to their eyes."

Rowan looks skeptical, but Valerian must show her a quick demonstration of his power because her eyes widen and she gives an impressed whistle.

"I like this plan," Fabian says. "Especially if Rowan can make one or more of the Icelus come with us to Gomorrah for questioning."

"Seems feasible," Rowan says. "At least in theory."

"I also like the plan," Valerian says, darting me an approving glance.

Something flutters in my belly in response, almost making the virus-driven stomach upset recede.

"That doesn't look like Earth technology," Rowan says, looking at the four limbs of the approaching robot.

"I helped Felix build that," Itzel says proudly. "A lot of the parts are from Gomorrah."

"Please," Felix says. "I could've built it on Earth if—"

"Open the thing and let's get to business," Valerian says sternly.

Looking sheepish, Felix stops the robot and has it open its shell.

Ariel rushes over and reverently grabs the handle of the gate sword Chester gave her. She then examines the guns and throws them in the backpack, muttering about the lack of ammo.

Fabian pulls out a Gomorran gun and Stanislav's saber, and hands both to Dylan. When their fingers touch, Dylan blushes.

Valerian repossesses his sai, and I get my katana and Gomorran gun.

"You shouldn't have gotten up," Valerian says as I secure my weapons. "Take it easy."

I lift my chin. "You got up, so I got up."

He shakes his head, walks over to his chair, and demonstratively plops into it.

I mime his actions, and as soon as I do, I realize how weak the virus has already made me.

Sitting is a relief.

Felix removes the backpack from the robot and sets it on the ground before letting the suit envelop him.

Itzel rummages in the backpack until she locates three masks that look to be about the size required, along with a set of tools.

When we try the masks on, not a single one fits.

"That's what the tools are for," Itzel says, unperturbed, and starts messing with the masks.

Meanwhile, Fabian takes out a poison grenade from the backpack and hands it to Rowan, who gives it to a zombie with particularly muscular legs.

"Here," Itzel says, handing me just the front of a mask. "Hold it tight against your face."

I do, and the ad-hoc scents of the mountain air go away.

Nodding approvingly, Itzel gives the hacked masks to Valerian and Rowan as well. Like me, they press the masks against their faces and hold them there, their muscles tense.

Fabian strips but doesn't turn into his wolf form, creating a distraction for the female part of the team, especially Dylan.

The rest of the way to the canyon, we ride in tense silence. Eventually, we arrive at the entrance where Felix left the robot before.

"Icelus are just through there," Rowan whispers, pointing toward the smaller canyon.

"Is this close enough for you to take them over?" Valerian asks in a low voice.

"Should be," she replies. "Can you make us invisible from here?"

"No," he says. "But I don't think we should get any closer."

Rowan nods, and the grenade-carrying zombie rushes into the canyon. The rest of the zombies put down our platform, and we get our weapons ready, just in case.

Rowan's brows furrow. "Percival is missing, but the rest of them are there."

We survey the canyon we're in. It's big enough for someone to hide behind the rocks.

Our zombies scatter.

"I'm going to have them look for him," Rowan explains.

"Don't forget to throw the grenade," Valerian says. "If you take over the newly formed vampires, you'll have more resources to search for the missing Percival."

"Already done," she says. "They're choking to death as we speak."

A few minutes later, a squadron of vampires rushes out of the canyon —clearly under her control.

A shadow blots the sky for a second.

I look up sharply, expecting another bird, but it's a person plummeting toward us.

"Percival!" I shout, pointing at him.

All heads tip back, following my gaze. They must be wondering the same thing I am: Where did he come from? Did he jump from the cliff above us? Or leap from behind a rock forty feet away?

In either case, Rowan wasn't kidding.

These pre-vamps can jump.

I aim my gun and shoot.

I must've missed. Percival lands, his legs miraculously unbroken, and before anyone can so much as blink, he hurls something at Valerian and Rowan.

Rowan collapses, the mask in her hand rolling to the side.

The vampires she was controlling are blinking and shaking their heads in confusion.

Not good.

Valerian also hits the ground, his mask rolling away.

Puck!

I aim my gun just as Fabian shifts into his werewolf form. Swiftly, I change the setting to nonlethal; if I kill Percival, I'll make yet another vampire for us to deal with.

I shoot.

I must miss again.

Percival hurls something at me just as Fabian's claws swipe at his neck.

I feel a sharp prick in my neck, then blackness.

CHAPTER THIRTY-FOUR

I COME to my senses just as Fabian's claws miss Percival's neck. Either their fight has gotten repetitive, or whatever Percival used on me hasn't taken effect.

I don't have time to dwell on it long, though, because the newly made vampires are here and beginning their attack.

Four jump at me, and I swing my katana in wide circles to keep them at bay. One vampire from the core group leaps at Itzel but gets a lightning ball in his chest.

Two attack Ariel. She punches one, but that gives the second one a window—and he sinks his fangs into Ariel's neck.

Puck, no.

Ariel drops to her knees, her skin paling with each pint of blood the vampire steals.

I slice at one of the vampires attacking me, and in the periphery, I spot a vampire ripping off an arm from Felix's suit.

Felix's shriek chills my blood. That metal arm must've contained his actual arm—no other way to explain the fountain of blood that gushes out of the broken suit.

This can't be happening.

But it is. Another vampire punches a hole through Dylan's chest, rips out her heart, and sucks it dry of blood.

The vampires attacking me get bolder, and I slash ever wider circles with my katana in a frantic effort to keep them away. My arms are tiring, though, and I don't know how long I can keep this up.

Then I notice another horror in my periphery. Valerian is thrashing around, just like Stanislav did at the end. His skin is a deep purple with just a touch of red.

No. Please no. Anything but this.

I redouble my efforts against the vampires, even though my strength is waning with each second. I can't let Valerian die. I refuse to. He has to live. He has to make it, even if I don't. He can't die so horribly, so—

A pitch-black Pom shows up between me and the vampire nearest me.

"You wanted me to interfere if there's a nightmare," he says, ears flopping. "Here I am. This is a bad one."

I look at my wrist.

Pom's not there.

But how?

Then it hits me. The thing that pricked my neck was an injector dart with that Koshmar drug. Of course. I saw Percival give a heap of these to Exozar. He obviously kept some for his own use.

In the heat of the battle, I didn't recognize the cursed injectors for what they were.

A breath of relief whooshes out of my chest. Ariel and Dylan were not killed. Valerian didn't go into the last stages of the virus, and Felix didn't lose his arm—that was all a nightmare.

Then again, who knows what's happening in the outside world. It's feasible that they *are* dead, just in a different way from what the drug made me see.

"Shouldn't you wake yourself up?" Pom asks, echoing my thoughts.

"Not yet," I say and teleport to the tower of sleepers. "I need to wake up Rowan and Valerian. He can make us invisible to the vampires, and she can take them over completely."

Whew. Rowan and Valerian are here. For a second, I was worried they got hit with something other than Koshmar—or worse, were killed while I dreamed.

"What's that?" Pom asks, his ears pricking. "Are you making that music?"

Pucking puck!

It's the *Dance of the Sugar Plum Fairy* again.

"The Nutcracker," I say through gritted teeth.

CHAPTER THIRTY-FIVE

MOTHERPUCKER. The enemy dreamwalker couldn't have attacked at a worse time—and that's probably the point.

Since going to a random locale on Earth seemed to help me battle him the last time, I do so again, teleporting to the entrance of the insectoid-looking Opera House in Sydney, Australia.

At the same time, I try to jolt myself awake.

It doesn't work, and the reason why is clear. The Nutcracker appears in front of me, his clown-like painted mouth twisted in a sneer.

Puck. He's still able to prevent me from waking up.

When we faced each other the first time, I was pre-boost, and we were evenly matched. Then, when we fought after I'd gotten the boost, things stayed the same. At that point, I thought that maybe I just hadn't internalized the boost. Now there's been enough time for that, and I have to consider a theory I dismissed the last time: that he's somehow gotten a boost that matches mine.

A bazooka appears in his hands.

I fiddle with the gunpowder.

He must've planned for this somehow, because when he squeezes the trigger, a rocket whooshes out.

I dodge.

The rocket hits the Opera House, and a huge explosion levels the place.

Pom, who's managed to stay with me until now, disappears without so much as saying the word *scary*.

I take flight toward the Sydney Harbour Bridge. An orca jumps out of the water below. There's no way something that big can jump so high, so I normalize the gravity below the orca just enough so that its teeth miss me by a nanometer.

Reaching the bridge, I alter the gravity and turn the soles of my shoes into magnets, so I can run on the side of the bridge, parallel to the water.

None of my shenanigans slow the Nutcracker. He's either practiced dream fighting for ages or has a background conducive to it, like me with video game design.

"The more time you waste, the higher the odds that Percival will kill you in the real world," the Nutcracker says in his creepily melodic voice. "After he's done with all your friends, that is."

I turn and manifest a massive anvil right above his head, as if we were in a roadrunner cartoon. "I'm pretty sure Fabian and his wolfu have made mincemeat out of that pre-vamp already."

He dodges the anvil and throws a cloud of spiders at me. "A pre-vamp? In your dreams. Percival is one of the most ancient vampires. Your werewolf is as good as dead."

Oh, puck. That explains that superpowered jump. With a shudder, I recall what Edith, another ancient vampire, was able to do. If Percival is as powerful, Fabian is indeed in trouble.

All of us are.

If the Nutcracker's goal was to throw me off my game with this revelation, it works spectacularly. I miss my chance to destroy the spider horde, and now they're creepy-crawling all over me—and biting.

Acting purely on instinct, I dive into the water below, turning my body into metal on the way. The Nutcracker knows what I look like and can turn me back, but hopefully not before I get rid of his arachnid friends.

With a loud splash, I hit the water and sink like the chunk of metal that I am.

The spiders drown, as I hoped, but my reprieve is short. The Nutcracker shows up, incongruently standing on the ocean floor despite his wooden body.

With a flick of his hand, he returns my body to its flesh-and-blood form.

I begin to resurface, so I quickly adjust the density of the water around me, allowing me to stay put.

With a smirk, the Nutcracker creates a giant bubble of air around us, then manifests a saber in his hand and lunges at me.

My katana shows up in my hand just in time to parry.

This isn't good. Our sword fighting didn't go so well the last time. At least not until I played my secret weapon—the multiple body technique.

In a blink of an eye, I exit my body, create a duplicate of myself, and leap into both. The two of me raise our katanas—and are blocked with two sabers in the hands of two Nutcrackers.

"Fool me once, shame on you," the Nucrackers say in unison. "Fool me twice…"

I don't listen to the rest. I let one of me parry the thrusts of the two Nutcrackers, while another me exits her body and creates a third copy of me.

It works—but the Nutcracker does the same, and there are now three of him fighting three of me.

Desperate, I create a fourth copy.

He does as well.

Fine.

Each version of me teleports to a different location on Earth—one to Big Ben, one to the Eiffel Tower, a third to the Leaning Tower of Pisa, and the fourth to the Brandenburg Gate.

The Nutcracker joins us in each location, his saber clashing with our katanas in a furious assault.

Each me has the same problem: Our slices don't hurt his wooden body as much as his injure our regular flesh.

Still, we battle on.

That is, until the Big Ben Nutcracker says, "Screw this." He turns himself into a nuke and kabooms with a mushroom cloud over all of London.

Puck.

The Big Ben version of me is gone now.

The rest of us fight harder, but the Nutcracker likes his nuke strategy, so he blows up his Eiffel Tower and Leaning Tower of Pisa selves in the same exact way.

We're down to one on one again.

If he commits suicide one more time, we're both going to be insane in the real world. Maybe it wouldn't be that big of a change for him, but I don't like that option.

Calling on my last remaining strength, I speed up my attack. The plan is to keep him too busy to turn himself into a bomb.

His saber nicks my wrist. Blood spurts out, but I'm fighting too hard to leave my body and heal the wound. Lunging forward, I slice his right shoulder, but my blade doesn't hurt the cursed wood.

If I don't figure out who he is, I'm going to lose. Soon.

He's not Maxwell, but he *is* someone who knows me. Maybe someone I don't think of as a dreamwalker. Someone who might've boosted his power recently and—

The puzzle pieces crash into place.

Parrying a saber slice, I allow myself a moment of distraction, willing my opponent to take the form I've just guessed to be his real one.

To my shock, it works.

The nightmarish face turns attractive, with symmetrical masculine features and strong dark eyebrows. Only the eyes stay the same.

I should have recognized those eyes the first time we met.

The Nutcracker is Ratridevi Bhairava, Valerian's head of development.

Or as he likes to be called, Rattie.

CHAPTER THIRTY-SIX

"WHAT GAVE ME AWAY?" Rattie asks in his own voice, skillfully parrying my next attack.

"I should've seen it sooner." I keep talking in the hopes I'll distract him enough to pierce his flesh. "Your development team teased you for overusing spiders and clowns, and the Nutcracker's face is very clown-like. Not to mention, I've lost count of how many spiders you've thrown my way."

As I speak, I parry and slice, but he's too fast.

"Now that I think about it," I continue, "an important character in the Nutcracker story is called the Rat King—not a far cry from Rattie."

I block his counterthrust and cut his wrist, which bleeds in a mirror of my own injury.

Score. Talking works.

Encouraged, I go on. "The power boost is what *really* gave you away." I glide out of his attack like a Kendo master. "You like to make the villains in your games look like you, and the big bad in the *Lucid Dreamer* project —who's also called the Rat King—had your face in the demo that I tried."

I see him slowing down from his wound, so I ignore my own blood loss and attack with renewed vigor. "You pretended to make yourself a playable character in the game 'for replayability,' but really, it was to get as much power as me."

I don't remind him about the other clue—how his video game design background makes him so formidable in the dream world. Why boost his ego? Instead, I execute a truly awe-inspiring set of moves that end with the tip of my katana pressed against his throat. "The problem for you is that I'm better than you."

"Are you?" he sneers, and I realize his saber is in the same position against my neck.

Puck.

When I press the tip of my blade deeper into his neck, he does the same to me.

We're back to the mutual suicide scenario—and I see determination in his eyes.

He might actually be willing to go insane together.

CHAPTER THIRTY-SEVEN

DEADLY TENSION BUILDING, we stare at each other like two gunslingers.

Suddenly, Pom appears behind Rattie and sinks his teeth into the dreamwalker's ear.

Wow. I guess all those bravery practice sessions haven't gone to waste.

Rattie's eyes widen and his head whips around, but Pom is already gone. There's brave and there's suicidal, and my little symbiont knows the difference.

It doesn't matter, though. You snooze, you lose.

With deep satisfaction, I bury my katana in Rattie's neck.

He makes a gargling sound.

I don't bother trying to figure out what he's attempting to say. Ripping the katana out, I slice his head clean off.

As life leaves Rattie's body, a shockwave hits me, like the aftermath of a massive explosion. It's raw dream manipulation energy—and it twists everything around me, threatening to tear apart the very fabric of this world.

Only it doesn't.

Instead, it forces me awake.

CHAPTER THIRTY-EIGHT

I WAKE up to a gnawing pain in my stomach and an irregular heartbeat in my chest.

Puck. The virus is progressing.

Then again, there's great news. Thanks to my newfound REM detection sense, I can feel that both Rowan and Valerian are still alive and asleep, no doubt dealing with Koshmar-induced nightmares.

Gathering my strength, I open my eyes, sit up, and take in as much information as possible in the span of a few eyeblinks.

Despite Rattie's dire predictions, Percival hasn't defeated Fabian. At least not yet. They're fighting so preternaturally fast it's hard to follow what's happening. The vampire moves with a savage brutality, while the wolf is graceful, with copious hopping from paw to paw in the dance that is his martial art.

Felix and Ariel are back to back. He's beating up a vampire with his suit's four arms, while she's slashing a different vampire with the gate sword. Judging by the pile of severed vampire body parts near them, things are going well there.

Itzel and Dylan, likewise back to back just a leap away from me, are also holding their own.

Itzel throws a ball of lightning at a vampire who tries to grab her. Her attacker flies back almost to where I sit, lands on his head, and doesn't get up. Great result, but I can see Itzel is weakened by the use of that power.

At the same time, Dylan is waving Stanislav's saber wildly, and without any technique. The freshly made vampires attacking her don't seem to realize that the saber isn't all that dangerous in Dylan's hands and are keeping out of the thing's reach. At least, for now.

My gaze falls on Valerian and Rowan's unmoving bodies.

I need to wake them, starting with Rowan. If she takes over the vampires again, our problems will be—

A vampire leaps at Itzel again. She shoots a ball of lightning at him. The vampire flies back, landing next to me. His leg is clearly broken, with bone sticking out, but he doesn't pass out like the guy who landed on his head. Instead, he locks eyes with me—and I see the thirst gleaming in his bloodshot orbs.

Puck.

I frantically pat the ground for my katana.

The vampire crawls toward me, fangs out.

My hand lands on the hilt. I grab it, leap to my feet, and swing.

My attacker's head separates from his body, and the world spins around me as if it were my head rolling on the ground.

Must be weakness from the pucking virus.

Another vampire lunges at Itzel. She gets this one smack in the face with the lightning ball—only to fall to the ground herself, unconscious from power overuse.

The vampire she blasted flies toward me.

I sidestep and slice with my katana, beheading him mid-flight.

The vampire is no more, but my wooziness worsens.

I pull myself together as best I can. With Itzel on the floor, Dylan's back is exposed, and she doesn't seem to realize this.

"Dylan, behind you!" I yell hoarsely.

But my warning is too late. A female vampire grabs Dylan's saber hand from behind and twists, causing the blade to fall. She then covers Dylan's nose and mouth with her hand, blocking her airflow.

Staring at us with wild eyes, the vampire hisses, "If you don't put down your weapons, she's dead."

CHAPTER THIRTY-NINE

NEITHER ARIEL nor Felix put their weapons down, and Fabian doesn't stop fighting Percival—not that he's got weapons besides his claws.

The vampires who were circling around Dylan spin around and leap at me.

I tighten my grip on the katana. If I put it down as the hostage taker demanded, we'll all get killed anyway. As is, Dylan should have a minute or two before she suffocates. I need to dispatch the group of vampires rushing at me and wake up Rowan before that happens.

I don't let myself dwell on the alternative. Because if Dylan doesn't survive, any chance of getting the cure in time is out the window. Even if we beat the vampires, Valerian and I will perish from the virus.

The first vampire lunges at me but stays out of the reach of my katana.

"Coward," I mouth and go on the offensive.

The gash I slice across his torso would fell a man, but this is a freaking vampire, so he keeps on coming—and is joined by two others moments later.

Being outnumbered generates enough adrenaline to make my wooziness subside, and I cleave the wrist of the next vampire who tries to get me, then behead the next.

"Jump on the katana!" I hear Percival yell from a distance.

No one is going to obey that. Unless… are these vampires sire-bonded to Percival? That happens if a pre-vamp drinks the blood of a vampire before they turn.

That must be the case here. The vampire without the hand leaps forward and shish-kebabs himself on my sword.

Puck.

He lets his body go limp and drops to the floor, taking the katana with him. Before I can so much as take a fighting stance, the vampire right behind the sword-jumper grabs my throat.

"Now!" he bellows triumphantly. "If you don't put down your weapons, this one will suffocate too."

CHAPTER FORTY

MY LUNGS ARE on fire and my head feels like someone took a bat to it.

All my instincts scream for me to thrash and fight, but I go limp instead. Let my attacker think he's won. I have only seconds of oxygen in my system, and I intend to make them count.

First, I attempt remote-entering Rowan's dreams.

Nope. That technique is too novel for me to execute in this state.

Hoping the vampire doesn't notice or care, I touch Pom's fur—and because I've done this a million times, I catch a whiff of ozone and plummet into the trance even while being choked.

———

I APPEAR in the dream palace lobby and realize I have a problem.

Lack of air is pulling me out of the dream world.

I strain my powers to stay in, the reverse of jolting awake. It seems to work, so I teleport right into Rowan's room in the tower of sleepers.

Pom shows up, but I ignore him. Slapping my palm on Rowan's forehead, I leap into her dream.

———

NOT SURPRISINGLY GIVEN the Koshmar dart, Rowan's dream is taking place in the canyon battlefield that would be our waking world.

Every single one of us is already dead here, clearly of hideous causes.

"This is too weird and scary," Pom says when he sees what's happening to Rowan, and promptly disappears.

I can't blame him. Covered in blood and gore, Rowan is lying among our body parts, the top of her skull opened as if in the middle of a neurosurgery. Frank is here, and he's eating Rowan's brain as she convulses from time to time—I guess when he chomps on the parts responsible for movement.

That's gross and disturbing. Then again, I've recently learned that my own pet had done something like this to me for real—stealing some neurons instead of eating them, but still.

I make Frank disappear, heal Rowan's brain and skull, and remove all the gore from our surroundings.

"This is a dream," I tell her. "You need to wake up and save everyone, starting with me and Dylan."

She looks at me with bulging eyes.

"This. Is. A. Dream," I enunciate. "Save me and Dylan first. Got it?"

She gives me the smallest nod but doesn't speak, a bad sign.

I have to trust she understood what I said. There's no time to waste.

I jolt her awake.

Now Valerian.

I teleport to the tower of sleepers again, but before I can touch him, the lack of oxygen yanks me out of the dream world.

CHAPTER FORTY-ONE

FOR A SECOND, everything is black, and my lungs feel like they're bursting.

Then the hands around my neck let go, and as I greedily gulp in air, I'm gently lowered into a sitting position.

Rowan's clearly come through.

Remaining in a sitting position is a struggle, but I force myself to stay upright and survey the battlefield.

The vampire suffocating Dylan has already let her go as well, and she's lying on the ground, hopefully just resting.

Felix and Ariel dispatch the vampires they were fighting without realizing it's no longer needed. Then they gape at the rest of their opponents—who are standing unnaturally still, ready to follow Rowan's commands.

But not all of them are subdued.

Percival is still fighting Fabian, and Fabian is clearly getting tired.

"I can't take over Percival!" Rowan shouts. "I've been trying."

Right. Edith was immune to necromancer powers as well.

"Help Fabian!" is what I try to yell back, but nothing comes out.

Percival must realize the direness of his situation—and tries a desperate maneuver. He allows Fabian's claw to enter his shoulder, then smashes a fist into the werewolf's jaw.

Fabian flies up and lands in an unmoving heap.

Percival's wound would kill anyone else, but he's not even paying attention to it. What's worse, the wound is healing. Rowan sends her vampires toward their sire, and in the distance, I see her zombies. She's bringing them back from their search for Percival.

The first Rowan-controlled vampire reaches Percival and is ripped into pieces in an eyeblink. The second one gets the same treatment. The third one gets his neck snapped.

All this happens insanely fast—that or my brain is slowing.

Rowan makes the rest of the vampires and the newly arrived zombies attack Percival en masse. At first, it seems like an easy win, but vampire blood and zombie limbs are flying all around Percival, and he's no worse for the wear.

Moving preternaturally fast, he rushes at Felix and Ariel.

Puck. He'll rip them apart. I need to do something.

I concentrate like I've never done before. I picture myself touching Valerian in every detail possible—and because it's him, my imagination has no trouble with this at all.

Percival smashes a fist into Felix's chest just as I connect with Valerian and fall into his nightmare.

VALERIAN IS KNEELING in a puddle of blood and gore, holding my lifeless body in his hands. Bloody tears stream down his cheeks, and the expression of sorrow on his face wrenches at my insides.

I evaporate my corpse and loudly clear my throat.

Valerian looks up at me, wild hope flashing in his eyes.

"This is a dream?" He looks around. "That drug?

"Time is of the essence," I say quickly. "As soon as you wake up, help Felix and Ariel with Percival."

He leaps to his feet.

I jolt him awake and leave the dream world.

PUCK.

A lot must've happened in the brief time it took me to wake Valerian.

Felix is lying a few feet away, a huge dent in the chest of the robot suit.

Ariel is in trouble too. Percival's fangs are in her neck, and he's draining her at the same time as he's trying to rip the gate sword from her grasp.

Amazingly, Ariel is not letting go of the weapon.

I look for my katana. Maybe if I could—

Valerian sits up.

Normally, when he uses his power, it's invisible. But this time, an arc of pulsing red energy streams from his fingers into Percival's head.

Belatedly, I realize that making Ariel invisible isn't going to help her.

But that doesn't seem to be what Valerian is doing.

Releasing Ariel, Percival whirls around with a war cry.

Whatever Valerian has made him see must be frightening indeed, because the ancient vampire is trembling as he faces it.

Ariel comes to her senses and swings the gate sword.

"Wait!" Valerian yells.

He must want the leader of this Icelus group for questioning—and the sort of questioning Valerian has in mind is exactly what Percival deserves.

Ariel doesn't hear or care if she does. Her sword slices through the vampire's neck as though it were made of vapor. Percival's headless body collapses, the head rolling to the side.

Valerian curses up a storm.

Ariel faces him unapologetically. "You're too sick to safely contain him and you know it."

Valerian glares at her, but the cursing stops.

She's right, I realize with a sinking feeling. Valerian's color is a deadly shade of purple.

I glance at my hands.

So is mine.

Rowan rushes to check on Itzel while Ariel begins peeling Felix out of his ruined suit.

"The gnome is okay," Rowan says to my relief.

"So is Felix," Ariel says, lifting another weight off my shoulders.

Rowan checks on Fabian next while Ariel approaches Dylan.

"The werewolf's heartbeat is strong," Rowan says—and just to confirm her words, Fabian morphs into his naked human form, jumps to his feet, and scans his surroundings with an impressively alert gaze.

Rowan glances mournfully at Ariel.

She must already know what Ariel is about to say. After all, she can feel corpses.

My breath seizes in my lungs.

Ariel looks up, subdued.

"I'm sorry," she says gravely. "Dylan didn't make it."

CHAPTER FORTY-TWO

VALERIAN'S GAZE homes in on Rowan. "I want you to resurrect her." He jabs a finger at Frank. "Do to her what you did for your pet."

Rowan backs away. "Impossible."

"You've done it before, so it's clearly possible," Fabian growls.

Rowan darts Frank a quick glance. "That was a crime of passion. I shouldn't have done it."

"But you did, and he's back." Fabian's face twists as he looks at Dylan's body. "How could that be a crime?"

"You don't understand what you're asking," Rowan says. "This is my people's biggest taboo for a reason. Dylan wouldn't want this."

Fabian advances on her. "Dylan took a big risk helping us with this mission. She deserves to be brought back."

Rowan backs farther away.

Fighting a bout of nausea, I drag in a deep breath. "Please, Rowan. If you don't want to do it for Dylan, do it for me and Valerian. She's our only chance of surviving the virus."

Rowan looks at Valerian, then at me, no doubt noticing our skin coloring and the fact that we're barely able to remain sitting. "Why don't I bring her back as a regular zombie? She could then talk you through making the cure."

Fabian glares at her. "We don't just need a chemical formula. We need a scientist. Dylan has multiple PhDs. She's a virologist. None of us can do what she can, especially not by playing a game of Simon Says with a zombie. By not bringing her back, you're signing Valerian and Bailey's death warrants."

Rowan's face tightens as she glances at her pet. "Frank's not the same person after what I did."

"He wasn't a person to start with," Ariel says. "He's an opossum or whatever."

"You know what I mean," Rowan says. "His personality—"

"Is his memory intact?" Ariel cuts in.

"I guess." Rowan grimaces. "But there were other side effects that—"

Valerian's hands begin trembling. Catching us looking, he balls them into fists. "We don't have time for this. You said you're no longer welcome on this world and want asylum on Earth. Do this, and I'll see to it personally that you get it. I'm on the New York Council and have favors I can cash there. You know how much vampires despise your kind. I'm your only chance."

Rowan lets out a defeated sigh and gingerly approaches Dylan's body. "This can go apocalyptically bad. That's a lot to have on my conscience."

Valerian's eyes glint coldly. "How about I help you deal with your conscience. Tell yourself you have no choice—because if you don't do this willingly, I'll be forced to use my power to make sure you do it." He must show her a taste of what he means because she pales to a nearly translucent hue.

"Don't do that again, please," she says unsteadily. "And promise me this: If Dylan asks afterward, you tell her I didn't have a choice. Also, whatever she does, it's on you."

"Done," Valerian says, his tone gentling.

Rowan kneels next to Dylan's body, and a blinding energy beam shoots out of her fingertips, just like when she did it to Frank in her dream memory.

I desperately need to lie down, but hope and curiosity keep me in a sitting position.

Dylan stirs. Rowan soothingly strokes Dylan's hair as she opens her eyes. Her gaze is unfocused, but she's clearly not dead anymore.

Beaming, Fabian rushes over to her. "Dylan. Are you okay?"

Dylan looks at the naked werewolf uncomprehendingly. "I... am Dylan."

"Do you remember the cure?" Valerian asks her. "The virus?"

A hint of recognition sparks in Dylan's eyes, and she rattles out a chemical formula, as well as what must be Earth-specific scientific words that don't ring a bell for me, like Erlenmeyer flask.

"Can you walk?" Rowan asks her.

Dylan slowly stands up and makes a circle around the necromancer in halting, awkward steps.

Fabian looks at Ariel. "Can you carry Bailey? I can grab Valerian and the gnome, and Dylan can drag Felix."

Felix sits up. "I don't think I need to be dragged."

"Me neither," Itzel says, but without sitting up.

I ignore the rest of the logistical chatter and allow myself to lie down.

It's a mistake. The mother of all post-adrenaline crashes allies with the weakness from the virus to make me woozier than a drunk hippopotamus on ice. My consciousness cuts in and out. At one point, I open my eyes long enough to see Ariel carrying me into the gate. The next time I have the strength to peek at the outside world, we're in the hospital near the hub, the one that has a lab where Dylan can make the cure.

Assuming the resurrected Dylan can do it. She's not exactly her usual self.

The next time I come to, my limbs are trembling, and no matter how much I want to know Valerian's status, I don't have enough strength to roll over and check on him.

Sometime later, someone gives me a gentle shake.

With a monumental effort of will, I open my eyes.

It's Ariel. She's got a beaker in her hand.

"Drink this," she croons, placing it against my lips. "Dylan came through with the cure."

"Valerian," is what I try to say, but only a gasp comes out.

She must know what I mean because a smile touches the corners of her eyes. "Felix is giving Valerian his dose as we speak. Now drink."

I painfully swallow the bitter substance she pours into my mouth.

"There's something in there that should help you sleep," Ariel says from a long distance away.

Whatever substance she meant was probably overkill.

As soon I close my eyes, I'm out.

———

I AND A DELEGATION OF DWARVES, elves, and other Cognizant from Gomorrah come through the gate and take in the world of Necronia. We're all carrying jars labeled "The Cure," but written in English for some reason.

That's odd. Shouldn't that have been written in Necronian? Also, shouldn't we be wearing masks? Also, why—

I glance at my wrist.

Pom is missing.

Of course. This is just a dream.

I'm probably in a hospital bed right now, the cure hopefully eradicating the virus in my system. That is, if Dylan didn't accidentally make a laxative drug instead. She did seem pretty loopy after her resurrection.

Still, in this dream I feel great, a positive sign.

When I teleport to the tower of sleepers, a multicolored Pom is already in Valerian's nook.

"I knew you'd come here," he says, ears flopping.

I pick him up and squeeze him in a hug. "How are you feeling? Do you think we're getting cured?"

His voice is muffled against my chest. "I hope so. Hard to say."

I set him back down. "As you so insightfully predicted, I'd like to talk to Valerian now. Want to join?"

"Nah. I'm going to invent a game that we can play. Something that I can always win."

"Good luck with that." Grabbing Valerian's wrist, I dive into his dream.

———

LITTLE ME AND little Valerian are sitting in a dark closet. He has a mischievous expression on his face, and I'm giggling.

This is an actual memory. Must be from the batch that flashed too fast for me to register.

Before I can let my presence be known, the kids clasp hands and run out of the closet into a room where one of the windows is black.

"Ah," I say out loud. "More unexplored secrets."

Little Valerian halts, looks intently at me, and morphs into a grown version of himself.

"I'm sleeping?" he asks, his tone dreamy.

I point at the black window. "Ready for total recall?"

He nods, and before he can come to his senses enough to change his mind, I grab his hand like the child version of me did, and launch us into the black glass.

———

I'M BACK in the black ocean, and Valerian is in a boat, like before.

The swim is just as hard, only it doesn't bother me as much this time around. After everything I've been through recently, a swim, no matter how difficult and long, is a vacation in comparison.

After what feels like a day of swimming, I touch the shore, and the flood of memories begins.

————

VALERIAN AND I show up in a large meeting room.

A dozen adults are sitting in a circle, Valerian's and my parents among them. In the middle of the circle is a person I did not expect to see in the context of Soma.

It's Nostradamus, the seer, with his werewolf lying at his feet like a dog.

Kid Valerian is here too, standing to the side where nobody seems to pay him any attention.

"Oh, right," my Valerian says. "I remember this now. I snuck in and used my powers to make it so that the others couldn't see me."

Nostradamus begins to speak. "If Phobetor isn't stopped, he'll destroy everyone, not just your little world."

"We know this," my father says. "Tell us something we don't."

"There's one thing that will give you a chance at victory," Nostradamus says. "A minuscule chance."

Mom looks at the seer skeptically. "What is it?"

"Only Two working as One can defeat the god of nightmares," Nostradamus says. "Remember, only Two working as One."

Everyone, including me and grown Valerian, gazes at him in confusion.

"That's much too vague," my mom says. "Who are the Two? How do you work as One?"

Nostradamus stands up. "I might've already said too much."

Everybody starts shouting questions, but the werewolf growls at them and leads the seer out of the room.

With that, the memory ends, and a new one begins.

————

VALERIAN'S PARENTS are standing next to a glass door that leads into a padded room. My mom is in there, with the signature fiery eyes of the

Overtaken. She's yelling obscenities and literally climbing the walls.

Is the memory speeding up already, or is Mom just acting crazy?

Young Valerian is here again, spying.

"Clearly, they weren't the Two," Valerian's mother says. "Else Phobetor wouldn't have been able to take them over, would he?"

"I think it's clear who the Two are," Davu replies. "Why else is Phobetor trying to have their parents murder them so desperately?"

"Poor twins." Valerian's mom shakes her head. "To have—"

She stops and narrows her eyes directly at where little Valerian is standing.

"You forgot to control my sense of smell," she says sternly. "What have I told you about—"

The memory cuts off.

———

DOZENS OF PEOPLE are gathering in a large room. Young Valerian isn't the only child this time—a bunch of them are here, looking bored.

Since nothing interesting is happening in the memory, I spin around, facing grown Valerian. "Does any of this make any sense to you?"

"Some," he says. "I was young when this went down. As you saw, what little I do know was via spying."

"The twins your father meant are me and Asha?" I look around to see if they're here at the gathering. They're not. "Phobetor took over my parents and murdered my sister because he thinks we might bring about his downfall?"

"Call him Collywobbles," Valerian reminds me. "And I have no idea what he thinks, but your parents did try to kill the two of you while under his control. That's why they were locked in padded rooms."

I rub my eyebrows. "How did they get Overtaken? Did someone describe that viral nightmare to them?"

"I don't know."

"And what the puck did Nostradamus mean by Two as One?"

"I don't know that either," Valerian says. "Though in that case, I doubt anyone does."

Before I can pepper him with more questions, his mother addresses the gathering. "Dear illusionists, we gather here with heavy hearts to discuss the fates of Bailey and Asha."

Everyone falls silent, giving her their full attention.

"I propose a simple plan," she continues. "Phobetor wants their parents to kill them, so we must do what we do best. We must create an illusion that will make them—and the one controlling them—think they succeeded. After that, we'll send them into exile and raise the girls in secret."

I look at Valerian, my eyes widening.

Before I can say anything, the memory terminates.

———

THIS NEW MEMORY runs much faster, but I'm still able to follow.

Valerian's parents are standing next to another glass door that leads into a padded room. Only it's my father inside this time, and he's not thrashing around.

He's hugging his knees, catatonic.

"I don't know how Lidia escaped," Davu says. "And it was pure bad luck that she saw Bailey on the way out."

Valerian's mother is frowning. "Any idea where she went?"

"No clue," he says.

"Well, all we can do is pray she's banished Phobetor for good," she says. "Else the next time she goes to sleep, he'll learn of our deception and have her kill Bailey for real."

Again, the memory terminates too fast for me to say something.

———

A FAMILIAR SCENE BEGINS, set in the fateful clearing on Soma. In the version I saw in Mom's memory, Asha and I were about seven, and we were running and screaming in terror.

But my sister and I aren't here.

It's just my parents chasing nothingness with machetes, their eyes those of the Overtaken.

The crowd that was chasing after my parents in Mom's memories is here too. In the front, I spot my grandmother, Davu with his wife, little Valerian, and Kojo and his parents.

"Stop!" Davu screams at my parents.

They don't respond, just keep chasing what they must think are the twins.

I have to use my recollection of Mom's memories to fill in the details.

Illusory Asha trips over a root.

The illusion of young me keeps running for a few moments, then looks back, panting. "Asha, no!" she gasps and rushes to her.

At least that's what my parents must be seeing—and so must Phobetor through their eyes.

This is the moment illusory Asha started crying, and I tried to lift her.

Our parents close in.

Our father faces the crowd while Mom raises her machete.

This is when the illusory me screamed, "Mommy, no!" in Mom's memory.

Mom slashes with the machete through empty air—though of course, she thinks she's just beheaded Asha.

Numbly, I watch as Mom's strange eyes gaze at another spot. One where the illusion of me must be sobbing uncontrollably.

Just like in her own memory, Mom's body tenses, her face twisting with alternating expressions of blankness and horror. Her eyes flicker between magma-like fire and their normal brown hue, and her left hand grabs her right, as if trying to steal the machete from it. Finally, her eyes stay brown, and horror eclipses all else on her face.

Wow. This is what Davu had meant in that out-of-order memory that preceded this one.

Somehow, Mom has banished Phobetor from her mind, reversing her Overtaken status.

She looks at the bloody machete in her hands, then at where the headless Asha would be if she were real. With a raw, guttural moan, she spins around—just as my father smashes a fist into her temple.

Having knocked Mom out, my father sprints over to where the illusory version of me would be and slashes at the empty air with his machete.

The memory terminates.

———

IN THE NEXT MEMORY, Valerian's parents are speaking too fast for me to comprehend their words, but I think they're explaining the need to forget the incident at the clearing and the associated memories via a black window.

I'm only half listening anyway, as I'm desperately trying to make sense of what I've just learned.

Mom didn't actually kill my sister, just like my father didn't kill me.

They were made to think that they did this by the Soma illusionists.

But that means—

The world explodes around us, instantly jolting me awake.

———

BACK IN THE REAL WORLD, I open my eyes.

The room is too dark to see anything.

I sit up.

Someone turns on the light.

It's Valerian. His skin isn't purple anymore.

I look at my own hands and see they aren't purple either.

My eyes fly up to his face. "My sister is alive?"

He comes toward me. "First, how are you feeling?"

"Peachy," I snap, and it's the truth. No sign of earlier weakness or stomach pains. "My heart is beating fast, but that's normal given what I've just learned."

Looking relieved, he reaches over and clasps my hand in his large palm. "Bailey—"

I glare up at him. "Answer me. My sister—"

Smiling warmly, he squeezes my hand. "She's alive."

"And you had no idea?"

"Not the slightest. They left not a single clue."

"But wasn't she in your memories of Soma? Your parents said we'd be raised there."

"She wasn't. I suspect that after your mom's escape and before making everyone forget, my parents took Asha to the part of Soma that's separate from the rest. That's what I'd have done in their shoes."

Holy puck. I stare at him, my heart skipping around as if the virus were back. My mind races furiously, flipping through all the memories I've seen.

My sister is alive.

Mom didn't kill her.

I have a living sister, a twin.

And there's apparently a prophecy about us… and Phobetor.

The implications of it all are overwhelming, and as I stare into Valerian's eyes, the words tumble out of their own accord. "I need to speak to Mom about this. If my powers aren't able to snap her out of her coma, this news—"

"I'll take you to her," Valerian says softly, and leaning down, he presses his lips to mine.

DREAM ENDER

BOOK 4

CHAPTER ONE

I'M KISSING VALERIAN.

This is my second time kissing in the real world, and it's glorious. The hospital room around me spins on its axis. My fingers are buried in his thick, silky hair, and his lips are soft and smooth, his tongue skillfully—

Someone rudely clears his throat.

I stiffen. Before that moment, the thought of bacteria and viruses couldn't have been further from my mind, but now, images of post-nasal drip invade my consciousness, ruining the mood.

Valerian draws back from me and glares at the intruder—a bashful-looking Felix, who looks extra thin without his robot suit.

"I'm sorry." Felix backs out of the room. "I—that is, the others... If you're up, we should head back."

Head back. To Gomorrah. Right.

As much as I hate to have been interrupted from what Valerian and I were doing, going back is an excellent idea. Between the boost to my dreamwalker powers and the revelation about my not-so-dead twin, getting to Mom is at the top of my priority list.

"We're on a post-apocalyptic world ravaged by a deadly virus," Felix says, still sounding defensive. "It's not exactly a place to Netflix and chill."

Valerian must show Felix something with his powers because he pales, turns on his heel, and sprints away.

"We should go," I say reluctantly, my eyes on Valerian's sensuous lips.

"To be continued," he murmurs into my ear and strides out of the room.

With a sigh, I follow.

When I was brought to this hospital from Necronia, I was barely conscious. Now that I'm walking through the white corridors with my awareness intact, I wish someone would knock me out again so I wouldn't see all the dead bodies sprawled around.

The virus Icelus had planned to unleash on Necronia had made its way here first, with deadly results.

The dreariness follows me all the way outside, where our team is waiting inside a circle of corpses that are standing upright. That's thanks to Rowan, the necromancer who left Necronia with us.

As we approach, she pushes her signature steampunk-style goggles higher up on her head to combat a few unruly strands of her strangely colored hair—half of her head is bleached white, the other half is jet black. Behind her is Fabian in his musclebound man form, dressed for once. Next to him is Dylan, her long brown hair uncharacteristically disheveled and her blank eyes lacking the razor-sharp intelligence that always made them so lively. Itzel, our gnome friend, and Ariel, Felix's uber roommate, are with them also.

Spotting me, Ariel flashes a radiant smile that shows off her uber-perfect teeth.

"Finally. Sleeping Beauty awakens," Rowan says to me. "I bet there was a kiss involved." She winks at Valerian.

Felix reddens and Valerian shakes his head, while Itzel just huffs into her breathing mask.

"Newly made zombies?" I ask Rowan, glancing at the upright corpses.

She nods. "I gathered some *helpers* for our trip." She emphasizes the preferred Necronian term.

Ariel looks worriedly down the street. "It's a good thing she did. The Overtaken attacked us twice while you were out."

I scan the zombie herd, but of course, in death, the Overtaken look identical to other corpses. "Twice? I didn't realize there were enough people left alive on this world to Overtake."

"There are," Felix says. "In fact, while you were out, I was able to locate a computer in the hospital and use my powers to get into this world's equivalent of the internet. I spread the formula for the cure as widely as I could. Should give the survivors a chance."

Ariel smacks Felix approvingly on the shoulder. "I wonder if the Councils could leave some ready-made cure here when they bring it to Necronia."

"I'll tell them to do so," Valerian says. "Now we should head out before more Overtaken attack. We have no cure for *that* problem."

Fabian pushes the zombies aside and hands me and Valerian our Gomorran guns. Once we have those stashed, he also gives me my katana and Valerian his sai.

Dylan is still standing there, her gaze unfocused.

"Dylan," I say formally. "I wanted to thank you. If you hadn't come through with the cure, Valerian and I would be part of Rowan's zombie herd."

At the mention of her name, Dylan looks in my general direction but doesn't meet my gaze. Nor does she acknowledge the thanks.

Weird.

She hadn't acted like this before.

Is this one of the side effects of Rowan bringing her back from the dead? With a pang of guilt, I recall Rowan saying Dylan wouldn't be the same, yet Valerian, Fabian, and I pressured her to perform the special resurrection anyway.

Then something else catches my attention. With the exception of Itzel, no one is wearing masks anymore—despite the fact that we're on a virus-infected world.

When I ask about it, Dylan seems to perk up a little. "The cure isn't just a cure," she says with a hint of her usual professorial tone. "It works prophylactically as well."

Ah, so they all drank it. Smart.

Rowan runs a hand through the bleached side of her hair. "Let's go."

She and Fabian cross the street, with zombies and the rest of us close behind.

We enter the train station again, and thanks to Rowan, the purplish corpses lying around join our herd of zombies.

Due to sheer numbers, our procession takes a while to navigate the maze of corridors into the hub, where I watch Rowan do something strange: She grabs the nearest zombie by the hand, that zombie grabs the hand of another, and so on. They daisy-chain like that until everyone is holding hands, like a bunch of macabre kindergarteners.

"It's the only way I can get them through the gate," Rowan explains. "This way, they register as my possessions."

I dart a guilty glance at Dylan.

Rowan bends over and places Frank, her resurrected opossum-like pet, in a sack hanging crosswise over her body. "Dylan is still Cognizant. I think she'll be able to get through without me. Hopefully."

Fabian extends his hand to Dylan. "How about we don't take any chances."

If I were Dylan, I'd make sure to point out that I'm not Fabian's possession, but she just meekly grabs his hand while avoiding the werewolf's eyes.

Puck. I really hope this odd behavior is temporary.

Valerian looks at Rowan. "Where's the body of your betrothed?"

"We questioned him while you were out," she says. "Keyser didn't know much. The ancient vampire had glamoured him to thwart anyone who mentions the word 'Icelus.' That was also when he'd gotten infected and was told about the nightmare that made him into an Overtaken."

"What about all the vampires we killed on Necronia?" Valerian asks. "Could you bring them back for questioning?"

"I tried," Rowan says. "I guess it doesn't work with dead vampires—which kind of makes sense, seeing how it's their second death and all."

Valerian curses under his breath. "We desperately need intelligence on our enemy."

I put a hand on his shoulder. "Maybe Maxwell will have something for us when we get to Gomorrah." I look at Dylan. "Did he tell you anything on that topic in your dreams?"

Dylan doesn't respond.

"Dylan," Fabian says soothingly. "Did you sleep?"

She shakes her head.

Rowan pats the sack where she's stashed her pet. "Frank doesn't sleep either."

Neither do vampires—another type of the undead—but it wouldn't be courteous to mention that.

"Let's go," Rowan says, and before anyone can object, she leads her zombie train into the pink plasma gate.

We step out on a hub located in a lush forest meadow where we'd camped on the way to Necronia.

"This time, let everyone else go first," Valerian says to Rowan as we approach the next gate. "That way, if there's an attack, we can cover your arrival."

With a barely perceptible eye roll, Rowan gestures for everyone to go ahead, like a doorman.

Ariel, Fabian, and Dylan take the lead, Itzel and Felix step in next, and Valerian goes right before me.

When I come out on the other side, it's to the sound of battle.

CHAPTER TWO

FRANTICALLY, I take in the situation.

There are about a hundred enemies swarming the hub, all in various sleepwear. Their fiery eyes make it clear why they're trying to kill us.

They're the Overtaken.

Great. Just great. All I want is to get to Mom and try to wake her up, but pucking Phobetor isn't going to make it easy, is he?

Whipping out my gun, I hold it so tightly my knuckles whiten.

Time to fight.

But first, I flip my gun to the nonlethal setting. The Overtaken aren't bad people; they're being used by one. Or more specifically, by a bad god of nightmares.

A woman in her nightie hurls a skillet at my head.

I duck, and the lead projectile whizzes by my ear.

Without taking time to aim, I shoot my attacker in the chest.

She collapses.

A burly man rushes at me, arms outstretched. I take a fighting stance, but before I can so much as block a hit, Valerian puts my attacker down with his gun.

Fabian is now in his wolf form. Swinging his massive paw, he smashes it in the face of one of the attackers, breaking the woman's skull into pieces.

Puck. So much for sparing lives.

One of the Overtaken stops attacking and looks straight at me and

Valerian. "I wanted the two of you to suffer from the virus," he snarls. He doesn't feel that way, of course; it's Phobetor speaking through his mouth. "Since you're so stubborn, I'll have to dispatch you like this, with violence."

"You can try," Valerian grits out and shoots the speaker.

The guy drops.

"Resistance is futile," Phobetor says through the mouth of a large man and has him lunge at Itzel.

Puck.

I aim at him but miss.

Backing away, Itzel launches a lightning ball at her attacker. He flies back and lands on his back.

Yes! We might just get out of this yet.

"Did the god of nightmares just quote the Borg?" Felix asks, panting. "Does that mean he's seen *Star Trek*?"

Phobetor must not like it when mortals criticize the authenticity of his villainous quips or his taste in TV shows. A thin woman leaps at Felix with a meat tenderizer.

Puck. Without his robot suit, he might not be able to take her on.

She swings the tenderizer at his head.

Felix sidesteps, but just barely.

Heart pounding, I aim and shoot.

The woman drops to the ground.

Ariel knocks out the Overtaken next to her, then casts an exasperated glance at Felix. "*Star Trek*? Seriously?"

Felix shrugs and dodges a colander flying at his head while I shoot the person who threw it.

Behind me, Rowan appears with her daisy chain of zombies.

Finally, some reinforcements.

Problem is, the zombies are still clearing the gate, and I don't think Rowan can let go of their hands, else she'll lose most of them.

For now, we're still on our own.

Phobetor must see the writing on the wall because the Overtaken attack with renewed vigor. My teammates retaliate. Ariel knocks a woman out with a blow to the temple, while Fabian breaks a few arms and legs. Through all this, Dylan is staying back; she appears to still be coming to terms with the shock of her second chance at life.

Rowan's last zombie clears the gate, and she has them unlock hands and leap at the Overtaken.

I shoot a few of our enemies to help, but it's no longer necessary.

Within seconds, the Overtaken are on the ground, held down by zombie hands.

Wiping the sweat off my forehead with my sleeve, I lower my gun and turn to Dylan. "We should give these Overtaken the cure for the virus. Our zombies might be contaminated."

Dylan's face doesn't change in any way to indicate that she's heard me. However, she takes out an ampule and proceeds to pour the liquid down the throats of Phobetor's victims.

After the cure has been distributed, Valerian walks around and methodically knocks them all out with his gun.

Meanwhile, Dylan trudges over to the body of the Overtaken whose skull Fabian crushed. Once there, she kneels, as if in mourning.

Felix cocks his head. "Has her resurrection made her more compassionate?"

Rowan sucks in a breath. "I hope it's not what I think."

We rush over to where Dylan is kneeling, and just as slurping sounds reach my ears, I realize this must be what Rowan was hoping against.

Dylan isn't mourning the woman.

She's eating her brain.

CHAPTER THREE

I FIGHT A GAGGING SENSATION. So, so gross. "Brains can contain infectious prions," I say out loud. "Think mad cow disease and the like. Eating is how you get them into your body."

Felix tears his gaze away from Dylan. "Is that the only reason not to eat them?"

"Well, no." I shudder. "I'd rather starve to death."

Fabian turns back into a person and looms over Rowan in all his naked glory. "What's happening?"

Rowan steps back. "I didn't want to bring her back, remember? Sometimes taboos exist for good reasons. I told you there would be side effects."

"That's not a side effect," Fabian growls. "That's a full-blown effect."

Rowan glances at the sack where she's keeping her pet. "Frank's appetites also changed in that direction. He prefers the brains of his own kind, but since those are hard to come by, I substituted the brains of domesticated animals and he's been thriving on that."

Ariel runs her hand through her shampoo-commercial-perfect hair. "Monkey brains are eaten as a delicacy in some places. This isn't that different, I guess."

Yep. And that's the reason I only eat bananas when I'm on Earth.

Frank sticks his head out of the sack, the curious expression on his furry face seeming to say, "Did someone say yummy brains?"

"I can see why your people don't like to call them zombies." Itzel nods toward Rowan's helpers. "They want to save that term for where it's more applicable." She looks pointedly at Dylan.

With a growl, Fabian rushes over to where his clothes are, puts them on, and sprints over to Dylan.

Gently, he puts a hand on her shoulder.

Did Dylan just growl at him?

Nah. Must be my imagination.

"We did this to her," I whisper, looking up at Valerian.

His chiseled jaw tightens. "Don't beat yourself up. I was the one who pushed Rowan, and I'd do it again if I had to. So Dylan has an eccentric diet now. Still better than being dead."

The slurping noises stop, and Dylan stands up.

Fabian rips a chunk of cloth from the dead woman's nightgown and wipes the remnants of brain matter from Dylan's face.

"Thank you," Dylan says haltingly.

"Are you okay?" Ariel asks her, looking remarkably ungrossed out.

"I feel very strange." Dylan's tone is robotic, though a hint of her former intelligence glimmers in the empty pools of her eyes. "I see a lot of potential for research in this area, and that pleases me."

Uh-huh. Is she talking culinary research?

"We're going to get you a top-of-the-line laboratory," Valerian tells her. "Whatever you need. You'll be taken care of, I swear it."

Despite his earlier words, he must also feel guilty about his role in Dylan's fate.

Felix clears his throat. "If something happens to me, I want to go on record saying that I do *not* wish to be brought back like this. Maybe as a helper, if you really need one."

"Why would we need such a puny one?" Ariel retorts, and he sticks his tongue out at her.

Rowan glares at Valerian. "I'm not doing that again anyway. Not even with a gun to my head."

"Doing what?" Dylan asks.

No one replies, and Rowan sullenly collects her zombies.

"We'd better go," Valerian says and strides toward the next gate.

No one speaks, and nothing attacks us for the next two worlds.

When we get to the third hub, all seems quiet there as well. However, when we're halfway to the gate we need, the Overtaken leap out of the surrounding gates.

Puck.

Here we go again.

A cleaver flies at my shoulder.

I sidestep it and shoot the Overtaken responsible.

A wok careens at Valerian.

Double puck.

Valerian isn't dodging, nor am I going to be able to push him aside in time.

Smack. The wok hits one of Rowan's helpers in the head.

Whew. She must've made it jump in front of Valerian.

An Overtaken leaps at Fabian, an ax in his hands. Fabian dodges the weapon, then knocks his attacker out without bothering to shift into wolf form.

Ariel is attacked next. A blur of movement later, she has her opponent in a chokehold.

"Why don't I tell you about an interesting nightmare," says one of the Overtaken. "It all started—"

I shoot the speaker. "Don't listen to that," I tell the others urgently. "He's trying to plant the Overtaken nightmare into your subconscious."

"Bailey's right." Valerian's voice booms in my ears as though it's coming from the center of the universe. "I'll use my powers to block his future attempts, but if I forget or get knocked out, sing loudly or shove something into your ears."

"We can just shout *hoorah*," Ariel says, and does so as she leaps at an Overtaken, knocking him out with a blow to the head.

"My turn," Rowan says and sics her entire undead army on our attackers.

I dodge a few more hits, but before long, our zombies triumph over the Overtaken, and we stun them again with our Gomorran guns.

Felix looks over the battlefield, then glances at the gates the Overtaken came from. "Did Phobetor take them over in each of those worlds?"

"Doubt it," Ariel says. "I bet they're local, and he had them exit through those gates to create an ambush. That's what I would've done."

"Right," Itzel mutters. "Let's hope he never overtakes you."

Amen to that.

Valerian's jaw tenses. "Either way you look at it, Collywobbles's vile influence is spreading."

I reach over and squeeze his forearm gently.

The tension drains out of his body as he looks at me, a now-familiar heat kindling in his gaze.

My breathing speeds up. This is so not the time for this.

As if to emphasize that, Dylan asks tonelessly, "Was it a dream, or did I eat a brain on the other world?"

Yep, that's a definite mood killer.

"You did," Fabian tells her softly. "But that's okay. In wolf form, I eat all the organs."

Dylan stares at him uncomprehendingly.

"You know what happened to you, right?" Fabian asks. "You know that Rowan—"

"I was dead, and now I'm not," Dylan says, sounding less robotic. "I think it's starting to sink in."

Valerian and I exchange a meaningful glance.

"The more you become your old self, the better," I say. Hopefully that also leads to fewer eaten brains, but I keep that to myself.

"Right," Dylan says distantly. "But who or what was my old self?"

Shooting Rowan a death glare, Fabian grabs Dylan's hand and drags her toward the next gate.

"Hold up," I say before they cross over. "The next world is the one where the Overtaken giants attacked us. Can we handle it if they do it again?"

They stop as Rowan scratches the jet-black side of her hairdo. "You killed them the last time, right?" she asks.

"We had no choice." Ariel glances at our current batch of unconscious attackers. "The guns don't stun giants."

"Not judging. In some situations, you don't have a choice." Rowan darts Fabian a dirty look. "I was just thinking that I might be able to recruit the bodies of your kills."

"They were mostly in pieces," Valerian says. "Besides, I'm sure their friends and family have buried their remains by now—and probably not by the gate."

Rowan takes out Frank and strokes his matted fur. "That's not good. Giants are powerful."

Valerian examines the knocked-out Overtaken in front of us. "We *could* make some more zombies for you."

"Dude," Felix says. "That's cold."

Ariel activates her gate sword. "I can take on a giant."

"Me too," Fabian growls.

"I have a better idea," I say and tell them what it is.

"It could work," Rowan says. "I can't help but notice that I'll be assuming all the risk, though."

Fabian crosses his arms over his chest. "Do you have a better plan?

Maybe there's someone else's life you'd like to ruin?"

Rowan heaves a sigh and has the zombies gather in one group near our destination gate. Then she makes some of the smaller ones climb onto the shoulders of the bigger ones, thus forming zombie pyramids.

She then clasps the hands of the bottom zombies of two of the pyramids and leads them to the gate. When she gets there, she sticks her head and arms inside, which lets the zombies clear the gate completely.

Rowan herself stays without crossing, with only half her body in the world of the giants.

My hope is that she'll make a much smaller target for any attackers this way.

"Dude." Ariel tugs on the back of Felix's shirt. "Are you checking out Rowan's butt?"

Reddening, Felix shifts his gaze from Rowan's leather-clad posterior to his shoes. "It's not what you think. I was just—"

"Don't." Ariel grins. "I'm just looking out for you. You know how jealous Maya gets. You're so close to finally losing your virginity, I'd hate for you to blow it now."

Impossibly, Felix reddens more.

I suppress a grin. Maya is his young girlfriend, and I'm not sure it would be Earth legal for them to do what Ariel suggests. I also make a mental note to keep my lack of real-world sex experience to myself—I don't need Ariel to label me a virgin.

Especially since I probably won't stay one for long with Valerian around.

Suddenly, Rowan's body tenses.

I hurry toward her. "Rowan? Are you hurt?"

Valerian catches up to me. "I think she's fine."

Sure enough, Rowan pulls her arms out of the gate, grabs another set of zombie hands, and shepherds through yet another pyramid—all the while keeping her head in the giants' world.

Through all this, Felix keeps his gaze anywhere but on Rowan's tush.

When all the zombies have crossed over, I expect Rowan to return to us, but she maintains her stance, her muscles coiled tight, as if for battle.

Finally, she steps fully into the gate, which is our cue to follow.

When we come out on the other side, it's to a scene of a massacre.

Ninety percent of Rowan's zombies are in pieces on the ground. However, a dozen or so giants are unconscious too, and three appear to have been killed, because they're now zombies at Rowan's command.

"Once my helpers had smothered that one, I took him over as you suggested." Rowan gestures at the largest zombie giant. "Then I had him knock out his brethren, and when a few punches proved fatal by accident, I didn't let the bodies go to waste."

I dart a worried glance at Dylan.

There's a lot of brain matter scattered about.

To my relief, she's just looking around blankly. If she's got any cravings, she's not giving into them—a good sign.

Fabian sniffs the air and grabs Dylan in a fireman's carry. "We'd better leave before more giants arrive."

Sure enough, in the distance, near huts the size of four-story buildings, are new figures—and they're headed our way.

Without further delay, we sprint for our destination gate.

With a roar, the giants launch into a sprint as well, gaining on us quickly.

Ariel and Fabian, with Dylan draped over his shoulder, dive into the gate first, followed by Rowan and her remaining zombies.

"Hurry!" Valerian yells and all but throws me into the gate as the giants' pounding footsteps shake the ground around us.

Flying out the other side, I stumble, nearly faceplanting, but before I can panic about Valerian's fate, I feel his hands on my waist, steadying me.

"Everyone good?" Ariel asks, panting as we run for the next gate, and we all reply in the affirmative, not daring to slow down in case the giants have followed us in.

Around us is a green savannah with waist-high grass—not super conducive to a run, but we do our best. And it's a good thing, because thunderous sounds reach our ears and the grass around us vibrates as the ground shakes.

Did the giants follow us?

How many are there?

"Crap," Felix breathes. "It's those mammoths again."

Oh, right. On the way to Necronia, we nearly got trampled here.

"There!" Fabian points to our left.

Puck. The fierce mega creatures are stampeding our way once again.

Can Phobetor take over animals, or is this bad luck? Or did he Overtake a person who's scared these animals into running toward us?

No time to stick around and find out.

We further pick up our pace, but our target gate is too far.

"Rowan," I shout. "Slow them down!"

The necromancer is already on it. The biggest zombie giant lumbers forward and firmly plants his feet between us and the mammoths.

The herd smashes into him, sending him flying—but moments are all we need to leap into our destination gate.

————

THE NEXT WORLD LOOKS SAFE, but we rush through it anyway, in case the Overtaken jump out of the gates. Nothing attacks us, though. We clear the world after that without incident also, and same goes for the one with a toxic-looking green sky.

"No wonder Nostradamus got involved," Ariel says as we get to the following gate. "Phobetor—I mean, Collywobbles—seems to be a threat to everyone everywhere."

Itzel adjusts her gnome mask. "I wonder what his end goal is?"

"To kill me, that's for sure," I say. Then, realizing I never told them about the things Valerian and I discovered in his black windows, I do so, just glossing over the Soma bits since everything to do with that place is so hush-hush.

"So Nostradamus has shown up twice in your life," Ariel says, frowning. "That can't be good."

Felix's unibrow dances on his forehead. "I agree. What I don't understand is Collywobbles's actions. Even if killing you is one of his goals, there has to be more. Otherwise, why Overtake so many? Why start Icelus groups?"

Valerian squeezes my shoulder. "According to the lore of our people, his end goal is for every sentient being to end up in a state of perpetual nightmares. Thanks to Icelus activity, he's stronger than ever, and closer to realizing that objective."

We all mull this over until we get to a blue gate. It leads us to a never-ending desert with a strangely starless night sky and no Overtaken. The one after that is a gray tundra—again blissfully empty.

The next world is hotter than a bathhouse, with pterodactyl-like birds circling above us like vultures over a roadkill. When one dares to dive down, Rowan makes one of the giant zombies swat it away like a fly. After that, the rest of the birds decide to wait for easier prey.

"After the next world, we'll be on Gomorrah," I tell Rowan. "Earth is just a gate away from there."

The necromancer perks up, then gives Valerian a worried glance. No doubt she's wondering if he'll keep his promise to get her citizenship on Earth—especially in light of Dylan's new situation.

I'm pretty sure he will, but if he doesn't, I'll speak up on Rowan's behalf.

The pre-Gomorrah world has a fluorescent purple sky with pink cotton-candy clouds, a Saturn-like ring, and two moons.

Forgetting her worries, Rowan cranes her neck to stare at the heavens in openmouthed fascination.

We speed up, our steps lighter thanks to a difference in gravity.

"I don't think we should bring the zombies to Gomorrah," Valerian says, turning to Rowan. "In general, we can't have you stay there long—and what little time you spend there, you must keep your nature hidden. Vampires have a lot more pull on Gomorrah compared to Earth. They might well kill you first, then apologize after."

Rowan audibly swallows, and her zombies fall lifelessly to the ground.

I hadn't realized vampires had that much influence on Gomorrah, but Valerian is probably right. They're our police force and the army rolled into one.

Rowan definitely made the right choice with Earth.

We go through the gate.

At the sight of the Gomorrah skyline, Rowan's eyes widen to comical levels.

I can't blame her. It's cooler than all the Earth cities combined, and certainly bigger than anything I've seen on Necronia.

Valerian leads us away from the gates, then stops in the center of the skyscraper roof hub and begins making VR gestures in the air—probably checking on Senate business and summoning us a ride.

There aren't many people around, but something catches my attention in the periphery.

Heartbeat picking up, I spin around.

Five people step out of the gates nearest us.

Familiar people.

Four of them are former members of our Necronia delegation, and all five are on the New York Council.

There's Nina, a black-haired telekinetic with facial piercings; Kit, a shapeshifter who currently looks like her anime-character self; Chester, a probability manipulator with a satyr-like face; Colton, a rather tiny giant; and last and my least favorite, Gertrude, a gangrene giver who hates my guts for no good reason.

Felix and the others spot them too, and at first, they smile.

The smiles quickly turn into furrowed brows when they get a closer look.

Everyone but Gertrude sports the fiery eyes of the Overtaken.

CHAPTER FOUR

"HELLO AGAIN," Phobetor booms through Colton's giant throat. "Gertrude and I made a deal. I rid her of her sleep problems, and in exchange, she unlocked the bedrooms of your friends." Colton's mouth curves in a macabre grin. "How about you and I make a deal also? Hand over the dreamwalker, and I let you go."

Valerian responds with a rude gesture—hopefully speaking for everyone—and I narrow my eyes at Gertrude. The woman once came to me to solve her sleeping problem, and I couldn't. She sometimes kills people with her power when she sleepwalks, but still, working with Phobetor isn't a good solution.

It's a stupid one, in fact.

Valerian's thoughts must flow along the same lines. "Traitor," he mutters, glaring at her. "You'll lose your Council seat over this."

Gertrude smirks. "Who's going to tell them once you're dead?"

Eyes narrowing, Valerian shoots an arc of pulsing red energy into Gertrude's head.

The gangrene giver's pupils dilate, and her head swivels from side to side, her face a mask of horror. Whatever experience Valerian has just created for her must be bad, because she screams, as if in pain.

Is it wrong that I feel just a touch of joy at Gertrude's misfortune—or schadenfreude, as Fabian would call it?

"I take it you know this motley crew?" Rowan asks, surveying our opponents.

"We do, and that's the problem." I take out my gun and verify that it's still on a nonlethal setting. "We don't want to harm them."

"I'll take on Colton," Fabian growls. "A giant can take a few punches." He morphs into his wolf form, his clothes ripping into confetti in the process. With a howl, he rushes at Colton.

"I'll help," Ariel says, leaping after Fabian.

Dylan doesn't say anything, just follows Ariel and Fabian with halting steps.

Everything happens almost at once.

Chester runs at Rowan, while Kit morphs into a cheetah and leaps in Felix's direction. Itzel shoots a ball of lighting at Chester but misses. I shoot him with my gun and miss as well. Itzel throws another ball of lighting. Still misses.

Puck.

Chester's luck powers must be in play.

Fine. Felix needs help too.

I shoot at Kit, but my feet lift off the ground and I miss her as well.

Puck. There can be only one reason why I'm flying outside the dream world.

Nina's telekinesis.

I can't believe this is happening to me again.

Within seconds, I'm hovering five feet off the ground. Fighting nausea, I twist in the air until I'm upside down—and see Cheetah Kit mid-leap at Felix's throat.

Without aiming, I shoot twice.

Oops. Both Felix and Kit fall—but at least she never made it to his throat.

Nina lifts me another foot, and I flail desperately but without much to show for it. My breaths speed up. I think a part of me hopes I'll magically turn into a helium balloon that will stay up when Nina inevitably drops me.

Below me, Ariel grips Colton's right leg, and Dylan does the same to his left.

With another howl, Fabian smashes a paw into the giant's solar plexus.

Colton falls with a loud boom.

My relief mixes with concern. I hope Fabian was right, and Colton can handle this abuse.

My worry deepens when Chester reaches Rowan and knocks her out with a backhanded slap.

Nina lifts me another few feet. As I fly, I try flexing my core and twisting.

Score.

I'm facing the direction I want.

I aim my gun at Nina and do my best not to dwell on the fact that once I press the trigger, I'm going to plummet.

The hesitation costs me. The gun is wrenched out of my hand by a telekinetic pull, and a moment later, Nina's aiming it at me.

Gertrude's screams cease, and I see Valerian aiming his gun at Nina's head.

Nina collapses.

Valerian blurs into motion.

I drop like a granite statue of an obese elephant.

CHAPTER FIVE

I SQUEEZE my eyes shut so I don't see the ground rush toward me. If I were a cat, I'd twist in the air so I can land on my feet. Then again, wouldn't that break my feet? My heart tries to evacuate my body through my throat, and I can't exactly blame it.

I land on something hard, but in a strange way, with my butt sinking deeper.

I open my eyes.

Valerian's face is above me. He's caught me in his outstretched arms.

He's saying something soothing, but the hammering pulse in my ears makes it hard to make out his words.

Gently, he sets me on my feet. I grip his biceps as I catch my breath and scan the battle scene.

Colton is unconscious or worse, and Chester must've knocked out Itzel after he was done with Rowan because the gnome is lying there, unmoving.

Gertrude is on the floor, whimpering, and Chester is near her, fighting the trio of Ariel, Dylan, and Fabian.

To my utter astonishment, Chester is holding his own. Without super strength or speed, he's able to dodge Fabian's wolfu moves, as well as Ariel's lightning-fast kicks and punches. When Dylan occasionally tries to grab Chester, she doesn't succeed either.

Valerian aims his gun at Chester. Nothing happens. Valerian curses.

There's an error code on the gun's screen, something about it needing a battery recharge.

Probability manipulation is a useful power.

"Can't you use an illusion on him?" I ask urgently when Chester dodges yet another round of attacks. "You can handle a single Overtaken, can't you? Without his other minions, Phobetor won't know what the true reality is."

"Let me try." Valerian points his hand at Chester.

"Wait. You need to show him something pleasant and fun. Something his powers will welcome."

Nodding, Valerian shoots his energy at Chester's head.

At first, Phobetor screams obscenities through Chester's lips. Then the fire disappears from Chester's eyes, and a dopey grin contorts his face, making him look even more like a puck or a satyr.

The crazy thing is that Ariel still misses when she tries to punch him in the face. Same goes for Dylan and Fabian.

"I got him," Valerian yells to them. "He won't fight back."

He's right. When Ariel and Fabian stop, Chester keeps standing there, absorbed in whatever pleasant vision Valerian has put him in.

Suddenly, there's a blur of movement at Fabian's feet—and blood ices over in my veins as I realize what it is.

CHAPTER SIX

GERTRUDE GRABS FABIAN'S hind paw.

Puck. How did we forget about her?

The rot is instant. Within an eyeblink, Fabian's leg looks as if it's been infected for weeks.

He licks the poor leg, then begins to howl. The gangrene spreads and spreads, until his howling turns to whimpers… and ceases.

No. Can't be. Please—

Fabian collapses in a rotten heap.

Dylan stares at Gertrude's hand, then glares unblinkingly at what's left of Fabian. Finally, her eyes narrow on Gertrude's throat, and a terrifying expression appears on her previously blank face.

"You want to be next?" Gertrude asks hoarsely.

Dylan lunges.

Ariel tries to catch her, but it's too late.

Dylan's hands are already squeezing Gertrude's throat.

In a moment, she'll be a rotting pile, like Fabian.

CHAPTER SEVEN

EXCEPT DYLAN'S hands don't rot. Her knuckles whiten as she squeezes Gertrude's throat, and that's it.

"Must be a side effect of her resurrected state," Ariel mutters in awe.

That makes some macabre sense. Gangrene happens when tissues die, but Dylan's tissues have been there, done that.

Realizing that her powers are useless, Gertrude flails. Dylan gives her a vicious jerk, smashing the back of her head into the roof. Gertrude's body goes limp. Dylan bashes her head into the roof again and again. Eventually, the gangrene giver's skull breaks.

I look away as slurping sounds begin.

Catching Valerian's gaze, I debate if I want him to blot out my senses.

"Serves Gertrude right," he says coldly. "Don't feel bad for her."

Seeing my miserable expression, he envelops me in a tight hug, and we stand like that while a montage of my interactions with Fabian plays in my mind. I haven't known the werewolf for long, but we've been through so much together that I've grown to think of him as a friend.

If not for his selfless bravery, I might not be alive today.

"Did he have any family?" I whisper, my voice catching as I lean deeper into the hug.

Valerian's lips brush my ear. "Don't worry about them. The Councils will take care of everything."

Swallowing the lump in my throat, I pull away.

I have to check on my friends.

Ariel must be on the same wavelength. She's already kneeling next to Itzel. Seeing my concerned expression, she gives me a thumbs up. "Felix is just out as well," she says. "And Rowan will live. Same goes for the giant."

A Colton-sized weight lifts off my shoulders, even as my gaze finds the pile that was Fabian, and dark anger surges through me.

I thought I hated Phobetor before, but I didn't understand the subtleties of hate until now. It's heart-wrenching to see Dylan standing over Fabian's remains, looking completely lost. She must've felt something for him, something that transcended her resurrection. And now she's lost him.

I look at Valerian, and my heart squeezes painfully in my chest.

I could've lost him too.

I still might.

"I'll take Dylan to Earth and get her settled," Valerian says. "You focus on your mother."

My mom. Of course. I almost—

A flying car lands on the roof.

"If that's more Overtaken, I give up," I mutter.

Fortunately, it's not.

Virgil, a vampire I've met before, comes out of the car, along with a score of other Enforcers.

Vampires don't need to sleep, so I doubt they make good targets for Phobetor.

"These Overtaken need to be taken back to the New York Council," Valerian tells Virgil.

"And Felix needs medical care," I say.

Valerian nods. "I'll take them all to Earth."

"What about him?" Virgil looks questioningly at Chester, who's still standing there, staring at some alternate reality brought about by Valerian's powers.

"That's one of the reasons I'm coming with you," Valerian says.

I bite my lip, staring at him. "I want to be with you." It's illogical, irrational, but I can't help the feeling that if he leaves, I might never see him again.

"What about your mom?" he asks. "Besides, I just got a message. There's a pandemic on Earth. A virus. And though it's not as deadly as the one we've just been cured from, I know how you feel about germs, and there isn't a treatment so far, so…"

I stare at him in horror. "Did Icelus cause this pandemic too?"

"No evidence of that," he says. "Might just be a coincidence—but it benefits Collywobbles nevertheless. With no treatment in sight and billions of lives at risk, there'll be plenty of nightmares for him to feast on."

Dylan looks up from her grisly meal. Her eyes are glimmering with pain and a fraction of her old intelligence. "A virus?"

Valerian tilts his head. "If you're interested, I'll make sure you have whatever you need to develop a treatment or a vaccine."

Dylan wipes what must be bits of Gertrude's brain from her mouth with a sleeve. "I think I'd better focus on my impulse control and dietary requirements first and foremost."

Smart. It wouldn't help anyone if she accidentally ate the brain of a colleague.

Valerian locks eyes with me. "I'll come back as soon as I can."

I almost ask him to take me with him, virus be damned.

But no. I can't delay visiting Mom's dreams any longer.

"Be careful," I tell him, and he smiles.

"We have hazmat suits waiting, don't worry."

"Fine. I give you two hours," I say gruffly. "Three at the most."

"Your wish is my command," he says, and stepping up to me, he slants his mouth over mine.

My body instantly ignites. Mighty hormones, what is he doing to me? The world around us disappears as fireworks explode in my belly—and maybe in the sky.

"There's no time for that," Dylan's voice says from somewhere.

Ugh. Can't she just go and eat another brain so we can have a moment?

To my immense disappointment, Valerian pulls away.

"To be continued," he says with a cocky smirk.

Virgil strides over, Itzel in bridal carry in his arms.

All amusement vanishes from Valerian's face, and he narrows his eyes at the vampire. "If something happens to Bailey, I will hold you personally responsible. Understand?"

"We've taken all the precautions," Virgil says. "Everyone around her with the exception of the gnome doctor will be a vampire. Even though we don't need to sleep, some of us choose to do so on occasion, but I've forbidden everyone from dreaming until this whole mess is resolved. The new safe house is a veritable bunker that no—"

"Just know that your existences are intertwined," Valerian says grimly. "This isn't just me speaking. She's the highest priority for the Senate."

I am?

Virgil nods. "Let's go."

I don't move. I guess I still haven't fully recovered my wits.

Valerian grabs my hand and shepherds me to the flying car.

Virgil slides Itzel onto the seat next to me, while Valerian kisses me once more, then closes the door before I can clutch his shirt and refuse to let go.

As the car ascends, I spot Felix sitting up.

He's definitely okay.

We torpedo forward, accompanied by a squadron of flying cars.

"My team," Virgil explains when he sees my concerned glance at the other vehicles.

After we traverse a couple of city blocks, Itzel comes to her senses and peppers me with questions about what happened after she passed out. As I explain, Virgil listens on, but keeps his expression blank. My voice cracks as I tell Itzel about Fabian's demise, and we fly the rest of the way in a mournful silence.

When we reach the southernmost district of Gomorrah City, we land on a roof of a mega skyscraper I've never visited before. Virgil leads us to an elevator, where he swipes his comms over a special reader, and we begin to descend. And keep descending for an obscenely long time.

If we step out into the iron core of the planet, I won't be surprised.

I turn to Virgil. "When you mentioned a bunker, you meant it literally, didn't you?"

He nods. "The Senate built it a while back for themselves. Valerian convinced them to let us use it for a while."

The elevator finally stops, and when the doors open, it's to a room filled to the brim with vampires, all dressed in riot gear and armed to the teeth.

One of them hands Itzel some strange headgear contraption and steps back, aiming a gun at the poor gnome. "Put it on."

"What is that?" I ask.

The vampire who provided the contraption looks at Virgil.

"That's a security measure," Virgil says patiently. "Though we haven't seen a single Overtaken gnome, it doesn't hurt to be careful. This device will detect it if you fall sleep—and it'll alert the team."

Itzel takes the gizmo, examines it approvingly, and puts it on her head like a crown. "It's gnome designed, isn't it?"

"Indeed," says a familiar voice from behind a wall of vampires. "I made it."

The vampires let the gnome through.

He's wearing the same headgear as Itzel, and I recognize him instantly. It's Mom's doctor.

"Hi, Dr. Xipil," I say. "Let me introduce you to Itzel."

Itzel extends her small hand in an almost coquettish manner. "A pleasure."

A smile touches the corners of Dr. Xipil's eyes as he shakes the proffered hand. "The pleasure is all mine. I've done much in the past few weeks that I wanted a fellow gnome to appreciate."

Itzel points at her head. "That's some interesting work. And I've never met a gnome doctor before. What made—"

"How about you flirt on the way?" Virgil says with an eye roll, then herds me and the chatty pair down a corridor. A labyrinthine walk later, we enter a large room where another strange contraption stands, with Mom inside it.

If Felix's old robot suit had a baby with a hospital bed, and if that baby mated with a tank, this is what the offspring would look like.

"That's my pride and joy," Dr. Xipil says. "Valerian wanted to make sure your mother is safe, and can be moved around freely. My design was inspired by—"

"Does it open?" I cut in, my eyes not leaving Mom's placid face behind the thick glass. "I need to touch her for what comes next."

Nodding, Dr. Xipil takes out a remote screen and hits a few icons on it.

The contraption rolls up to us, and the thick glass opens like a clam shell.

"Amazing work," Itzel says, but I'm no longer paying attention to her. Walking over to Mom, I place my fingers on her forehead. Two questions swirl through my mind as I prepare to use my powers.

Is it finally going to happen? Will I be able to bring her out of the coma?

CHAPTER EIGHT

EVEN WITHOUT DR. XIPIL'S equipment, my senses tell me Mom isn't in REM sleep. That means that if I were to simply jump into her dreams, I'd end up in a subdream and risk my sanity.

Why do that if I can put people into REM sleep with my powers?

I try that now, but it doesn't work.

Odd.

I attempt it again. Still nothing.

"Is she on any stimulants?" I ask Dr. Xipil, interrupting his bragging.

"No. Why?"

"I can now put people into REM sleep, except it's not working on her."

"No stimulants," Dr. Xipil says. "Just fluids and nutrients."

Itzel's eyebrows furrow. "Could your powers be malfunctioning after all that stress?"

"Lie down on the floor," I tell her.

"What?" The gnome steps back, but Virgil is already in her way.

"I'm just going to test my powers on you," I say. "Please."

Reluctantly, Itzel lies on the floor.

"Her hat is about to tell you she's asleep," I tell Virgil. "Make sure your people don't panic."

With a loud sigh, Virgil makes a few gestures in his VR.

"Don't fight it. I need your consent," I tell Itzel, and she sighs before nodding in agreement.

I bend down, touch her forehead, and do the exact same push as a second ago.

Itzel is in REM sleep instantly, and her headgear begins to buzz and flash with lights, waking her up.

I wince, rubbing my ears. "Seems like this hat is an alarm in more ways than one."

Virgil shrugs. "Waking up is preferable to what my team and I might do to a suspected Overtaken."

Itzel sits up. "I started to have a very nice dream," she says groggily, then looks up at Dr. Xipil. "You were there."

"Were you playing doctor?" Virgil asks.

Itzel gets up, her ears reddening.

Having made sure my powers are in good working order, I try to push Mom into REM sleep once again.

It still doesn't work.

I turn to Dr. Xipil. "Do you have something that can put her into REM sleep?"

He shakes his head.

I face Virgil. "Do we have any of that Koshmar drug the Icelus use?"

"I wouldn't recommend giving that to Lidia," Dr. Xipil says sternly.

"We don't have it anyway," Virgil says.

I scratch my chin. "What about Maxwell?"

"Who?" Dr. Xipil asks.

"Another dreamwalker," Virgil says. "What about him?"

"Can you bring him over here?" I ask. "Maybe he can do this?"

Virgil makes VR gestures again. "My people are on it."

Belatedly, I recall my suspicion that there was more to Maxwell than met the eye. At the time, I thought he was the Nutcracker, but that turned out to be Rattie.

Still, is it safe to have him so close to me and Mom?

"Keep an eye on him when he comes," I tell Virgil. "Give him one of those hats too."

Virgil flashes his fangs. "You don't need to tell me how to do my job."

Just my luck. I'm stuck in the middle of the planet's core with a thin-skinned vampire.

"Is there a place I can sit as I wait?" I ask.

Virgil leads me into something like a waiting room, while Itzel and Dr. Xipil remain behind, chatting about their designs.

Getting comfortable in a chair, I touch's Pom's fur and, with the familiar falling sensation and a whiff of ozone, enter the dream world.

————

WHEN I SHOW up in my impossibly colored, manna-scented palace lobby, Pom is standing in front of a pyre of wooden logs, holding a lit match.

"Playing with fire?" I ask.

The pyre and the matches disappear, and Pom's fur turns a deep purple. "You're here! I've missed you. What's new?"

He seems so happy that I'm loath to tell him about the recent events. But he insists, so I recount everything.

By the time I'm done, Pom's fur is a washed-out gray. "I don't like Phobetor. He's a major meanie."

"I'd use much stronger language, but I agree with the sentiment." I stroke his head until his triangular ears regain a hint of purple.

"Can we play again?" he asks, blinking his huge lavender eyes at me.

"Does practice count as play?"

He turns a golden hue. "I think it does. Depends on what we're practicing."

I change our surroundings to a recreation of the environment where subdream battles occur.

An ocean of black water is now under our feet, and a magma sky is above. Not for the first time I notice that the sky is a lot like the eyes of the Overtaken—and the water is not that different from the kind inside the black windows, except I have no problem standing on subdream water.

Pom warily examines the new environment. "What kind of practice did you have in mind?"

"If Maxwell doesn't know how to put Mom into REM sleep, I'll have to get to her via the subdream again. It occurred to me that we can practice some skills that might help us survive in that scenario."

Pom's ears wiggle slightly. "How would that work?"

"I'm making this up as we go. For starters, do you think you could somehow realize a subdream is a subdream and tell me?"

His ears droop and take on a beet color. "Every subdream looks like this, yet I don't realize it. Too lost, like your clients before you tell them they're dreaming."

"The same happens to me. Maybe if we hang around here long enough and keep reiterating that this is where subdreams take place, something will stick?"

He perks up. "Maybe. Also, you're a more powerful dreamwalker now. Maybe that'll help you the next time."

I sigh. "I hope so."

"So we just run around here?" His ears take on a carrot hue. "That doesn't sound like fun."

"You know how you've been turning into weapons for me when subdreams happen?"

His fur turns brown, and he lifts his chin. "I do it instinctively. It's what saves our lives."

"Exactly. And you've been all kinds of different weapons. But I think my preference would be a katana."

Pom leaps at my wrist and becomes a bracelet, as if this were the waking world. He then extends and turns into a furry blade.

I touch the edge of the Pom katana, and my finger starts bleeding. In this form, my symbiont is surprisingly sharp.

I slash the furry katana through the air a few times. "This is awesome. Let's practice you doing that. Hopefully you'll get so used to it you'll do the same in the subdream."

Pom separates from my wrist and expands until he becomes his cute self again. "To make it more fun, we need something for you to slay."

Genius.

I manifest a creature that attacked us in a subdream once. It looks like twenty ant mandibles grew to the size of a truck, then sprouted antennae and legs.

Pom shudders. "Creepy. Could probably also work as exposure therapy."

"Less talking and more turning into a katana, please."

With a grin, he leaps onto my wrist again, then extends and becomes the blade I favor.

I jump up and slice the mandible creature's head clean off. As it evaporates, I remind myself that monsters plus black ocean and fiery skies means a subdream. I want it to become a strong enough association that I might think of it when in a real subdream.

Pom transforms back into himself. "That was fun. Let's do it again."

This time, our opponent resembles a giant spiral worm—or syphilis bacteria, but with centipede-like legs ending in knife-sharp talons.

As soon as Pom becomes the katana, I behead the spiral worm with a flick of my wrist.

My looft is right. This is kind of fun.

Wait, almost forgot to remind myself that this is what a subdream looks like.

Before Pom can stop being a blade, I bring forth another monster from our subdream past—a ten-foot-tall monstrosity that reminds me of a tardigrade, a micro animal that lives in water, has no discernible eyes or nose, a hole for a mouth, and eight limbs that end in claws attached to a fat, sea-cow-like body.

Leaping off the water, I somersault in the air as I swing Pom.

Tardigrade's head separates from its body.

This is a subdream. The thought pops into my head almost on autopilot this time—a great sign.

As I'm landing, I create the next target: a hairless and earless humanoid figure with one huge mouth where the face should be. It's got a sword-like claw growing out of its right index finger, and I make it take a swing at me. I dodge the strike, then behead it like the others—while reminding myself of subdreams.

Now I'm really getting into the spirit of this exercise.

I recreate another monster I've met in subdreams, a pair in fact: a mount that looks like a warthog crossed with a spider and its rider, a giant naked mole rat with tentacles.

I leap off the water and swing my sword once, twice.

Both the warthog mount and the mole rat rider lose their heads at the same time.

"Subdream," I mutter.

Pom morphs into a talking version of himself. "These are so scary, yet I'm okay."

I grin at him. "The exercise is working. Now if only it were this easy in the real subdream."

Shrugging, Pom becomes a katana again.

I make our next opponent a turkey vulture, only skeletal and covered in pustules, with a featherless body and claws. Feeling bold, I let the monster fly at me while I wait in a samurai stance, with Pom above my head.

The vulture dives. As I wait, I think the magic word: *subdream.* Just as the vulture's claws are ready to rip into my flesh, I slice.

Score. Another successful beheading.

I create more creatures and practice beheading them, all the while repeating the phrase "this is a subdream" like a mantra.

For the next phase of the training, I animate the monsters and make them even more aggressive with their attacks. Next, I create them in groups—first pairing the tardigrade with the nail-sword thing, then the ant with the spiral worm, then the vulture with the warthog and its ugly rider. Finally, I throw them all into a fight and behead them until my Pom katana feels like a real extension of my hand.

The world around me vibrates.

Someone is trying to wake me from my trance in the real world.

"Pom, train without me for a bit," I say and jolt myself awake.

I WAKE to the sight of Virgil's pale face a foot away from mine.

"What?" The question comes out sharper than is wise when dealing with a killing machine that is a vampire.

To my relief, he doesn't bat an eye at my rudeness. "Maxwell has arrived. Shall I take you to see him?"

I stand up, eager to see the other dreamwalker. "Let's go."

Virgil leads me down a corridor. Stopping next to a metal door, he unlocks it and ushers me in.

There's a man inside.

I stare at him.

Specifically, at his familiar features.

"Is this a… a joke?" I stammer.

Virgil frowns at me uncomprehendingly, and so does the man.

"Valerian?" I spin in a circle. "Is it you doing this?"

Virgil presses his finger to his temple and makes a circling motion.

The man is also looking at me like I've gone crazy. "I'm Maxwell," he says slowly.

His voice is also familiar, and not from when we met near Necronia. That time, it had been out of context and muffled by his mask, so nothing had clicked. That same mask had also concealed his features—just as my mask must've concealed mine, preventing him from recognizing me.

But now he *should* know who I am. Yet he's acting as if we're strangers.

"Don't you recognize me?" I ask breathlessly. "I'm Bailey."

"I figured." Maxwell stares at me with a deepening frown. "You do look vaguely familiar, though I've only seen you in a mask. In fact—" His face twists. "No, I can't place it, I'm sorry."

He can't, but I can.

Because I saw him recently without a mask, and more than once.

It was in Mom's black window memories, and Valerian's as well.

Maxwell isn't just a random dreamwalker.

He's my father.

CHAPTER NINE

I WANT to lunge forward and embrace him. I also want to lash out, yelling questions like "where the puck have you been all my life?" and "why don't you recognize your own daughter?"

But I don't say anything.

I can guess what happened. He's forgotten me, same as Mom has forgotten Asha, my twin, and for the same reason. Soma illusionists made him—and Phobetor, who took him over—think that he killed me.

Yet even if I'm right, it doesn't make this feel any better. His lack of recognition feels too much like rejection. Like I don't matter to him… which I guess I don't.

Maxwell nervously brushes the gray stubble on his chin. "Bailey, is everything okay? You look upset."

I pull myself together, ignoring the pitch-black Pom on my wrist. "There's a dreamwalking problem I need your help with," I say, my voice impressively even.

His amber eyes brighten. "What's the problem?"

"It's my mother. Her name is Lidia."

He shows almost no reaction to the name, except maybe a slight widening of his pupils.

Seems like he's forgotten more than just little old me.

Could he be missing all the memories related to Soma, like Valerian was? If so, he wouldn't even recognize Mom—assuming Soma is where they met.

"She's in a coma," I continue and explain the strange state Mom is stuck in and how I need to push her into REM sleep so I can jolt her awake from inside her dream world.

"Sure, I can try to put her into REM sleep." He rakes a hand through his salt-and-pepper hair. "Where is she?"

I glance at Virgil, who turns around and leads us down the corridor.

The two gnomes are still in Mom's room, still chatting after all this time. I ignore them, my attention on my father's face as he looks at Mom.

"Have you met her before?" I ask, gesturing at the rolling-bed contraption. "She's a dreamwalker like us."

Maxwell stares at her, his forehead creasing. "She does look familiar..." Stepping closer, he scans her face. "The two of you share some features."

So that's that. He's missing *a lot* of memories.

Knowing that I'm not the only one he's forgotten should make me feel better, but it doesn't. All I feel is sadness... and under it, my anger at Phobetor expands. He's pucked up the lives of everyone in my family.

He's torn us apart.

Reining in my emotions, I ask, "Do you need to touch her? I saw you do this from afar with Dylan..."

Maxwell keeps staring at Mom's face as if he's planning to carve a statue of her later. "Doing it with touch is the more conservative approach," he responds absentmindedly.

Dr. Xipil opens the clamshell again, and Maxwell hesitantly reaches out, placing his hand on Mom's wrist.

Closing his eyes, he stands there for a few seconds. Then he opens his eyes and gives me a regretful look. "I'm sorry. It didn't work for me either."

Puck. "Would it help if we did it together?"

He shrugs. "Doesn't hurt to try."

I walk over and touch Mom's other wrist.

This time, we both close our eyes and push.

Nope. Even with our joint effort, Mom doesn't go into REM sleep.

I open my eyes. "I guess I'm going in as is." Hopefully all that training with Pom will help.

Maxwell jerks his hand away, eyeing me like I've already been killed in the subdream and have gone homicidally crazy. "You can't."

I lift an eyebrow.

"It's extremely dangerous. If you get—"

"I've done it many times," I say curtly. "I know what to expect."

"But—"

"I appreciate your concern. How about you wait behind Virgil… just in case."

Taking it as his cue, Virgil strides over.

"If I try to kill you, you have my permission to restrain me," I tell him.

Virgil grimaces. "How about you wait until Valerian is back? If I do have to restrain you, you could get hurt. I don't want an awkward conversation with your lover."

I flush.

I wish Valerian were really that.

Maxwell looks even more worried now. "Don't do this, Bailey. Can't Lidia get to REM sleep on her own?"

Dr. Xipil clears his throat. "That never happens."

"I'm going in," I say firmly. "Don't distract me."

Before anyone can stop me, I grasp Mom's wrist and dive in.

CHAPTER TEN

SOMETHING IS VAGUELY familiar about the black water under my feet and the magma sky.

A gang of creatures is attacking. Their bodies are semi-humanoid, but their heads don't even try—with rows of shark teeth, small beady eyes, and a tentacle with a light on its tip, these heads look like they belong to anglerfish, or some other deep-water monstrosity.

Shouldn't these guys live under this ocean? No time to figure it out. One of the anglers is almost upon me.

A furry appendage snakes from my wrist and turns into a katana.

Something feels right about the whole situation. The katana feels natural, like a best friend.

The closest angler screeches in a voice as ugly as its face, "You're the one the master hates!"

I teach it the mistake of chatting during a battle. With a whirl of my katana, the fishy head is separated from the body.

"Your existence is a blight!" the next one screeches as it leaps at me.

Whoosh. Another head severed.

Without any further talking, the rest of them attack en masse. A claw scratches my cheek. I yelp in pain and behead the attacker almost on autopilot. Saber-like teeth tear into my left shoulder. Ignoring the pain, I swing my katana. The biter is no more.

The rest circle around me warily, no doubt biding time until I weaken from the blood loss, which sadly isn't going to take long.

Desperate, I go on the offensive. With a leap, I behead the largest surviving angler and, landing on the ocean water, take a samurai stance.

The rest of the anglers back away. When I rush at one, it retreats faster. I don't give it chase because I'm feeling more and more faint. My shoulder is bleeding too much. I have minutes, maybe seconds before I faint—which is when they'll pounce.

Puck. I'm screwed, and they know it.

There's got to be something I can do.

It's on the tip of my tongue—or mind. Something about this scenario. Something about this sword. Something I trained myself to remember.

Wait. I trained *with* someone.

My eyes drop to my furry katana, and it finally clicks.

That's Pom—and since he isn't a bracelet on my wrist, I must be dreaming.

That's it.

Not that this is a dream, exactly. It's a subdream, and for the first time in my life, I'm aware of the fact that I'm here.

Giddily, I test out my usual powers by leaving my body.

It works!

I effortlessly heal myself, then jump back in.

The beady eyes of the anglers widen, and their retreat speeds up.

"Pom," I say to the katana. "You know this is a dream, right?"

At first, nothing happens. Then the blade morphs into Pom's usual dream form. His fur is black and his eyes wild as he takes in the anglers before poofing out of existence.

I can't blame him. This is almost too scary for me.

Oh well. Now that I have my powers, I manifest another katana in my hands.

The anglers turn and flee.

Taking to the air, I torpedo at the nearest angler and turn it into mincemeat without breaking a sweat. Grinning, I point my hand at my next victim and simply wish him out of existence. Then I land and dispatch another one. And another.

Then something odd happens.

A presence slowly congeals out of nothingness to stand on the ocean in front of me.

It's the nightmarish being I've seen before.

Phobetor.

CHAPTER ELEVEN

BIGGER THAN THE TALLEST GIANT, he's the most frightening thing I've ever seen—even if it's hard to say why. There's something ineffably horrific about him. Something that I feel with my dreamwalker senses instead of my vision. His face is actually beautiful, if in a terrible, overwhelming way that doesn't seem to be meant for mortal sight. Maybe it's his eyes. They look like black holes that contain every nightmare anyone has ever had. Looking into them is like walking in a dark forest as a child. Like having germs multiply inside your body. Like—

"Kneel." Phobetor's melodious voice conjures my every fear. "Become my servant."

Every cell in my body demands that I give in. In his embrace, there will be peace. Mom and I will reunite. I'll no longer feel this overwhelming fear. I'll—

"Puck. You," I grit out as I use all my power to throw off whatever spell he's trying to cast on me.

The black holes that are his eyes widen before narrowing dangerously. "Those who don't join me willingly, I can claim by force."

He advances toward me, hand outstretched.

There's a fiery flash in the magma sky above me, spiraling down.

A deep intuition tells me that if that tendril were to reach my head, that would be it. I would be one of the Overtaken.

Backing away, I hurl my katana at his face.

The blade melts and evaporates before it gets halfway to its destination, but killing him wasn't my goal anyway. I just wanted to distract him long enough to jolt myself awake.

It's the biggest jolt I've ever created.

And, to my shock, it works.

—————

OPENING MY EYES, I jerk my hand away from Mom's wrist.

I'm not ready to go back.

Maybe I'll never be.

"Do I need to restrain you?" Virgil asks. "Valerian is on his way here, so I'd rather not."

My frantic heartbeat eases. "He is?"

Virgil's smile shows off his fangs. "He's just arrived at the hub. My people are picking him up."

I wipe the sweat from my forehead. "I guess I won't go on a killing spree then. As tempting as it is."

"That was reckless," Maxwell says sternly. "You could've—"

"There's something you need to know," I blurt.

He frowns in a way I've sometimes seen in the mirror.

"It's private," I say. "We should talk in the dream world." I cast an apologetic look at Dr. Xipil and Itzel, but don't bother with Virgil.

Maxwell's frown deepens. "Your dream world or mine?"

"How about yours," I say, feigning a casual attitude.

In fact, it must be his. My aim is to check his dreams for the presence of black windows—but I don't tell him this in case he's touchy about this topic, like Mom was.

Maxwell surveys the room. "Is there a bed around here?"

"This way." Virgil leads us into a room with a gurney and a wheelchair next to it.

What is this, a horror movie set?

Getting on the gurney, Maxwell extends his hand.

I take a seat in the wheelchair, clasp his fingers, and try to push him into REM sleep without further ado.

For a second, I worry that it might not work, like it didn't with Mom. But it does. His eyes start moving under his eyelids, and I can feel him in REM sleep with my special sense.

"This will be safer, so no need for subduing," I tell Virgil.

The vampire cocks his head. "So if you attack me, I should just let you?"

"Anything to avoid that awkward conversation with Valerian," I say and jump in.

———

I APPEAR in my dream palace in front of Pom.

My looft's ears are beet-colored while the rest of him is gray. "I'm sorry I left during the subdream. I got too scared."

I pet the fur on the top of his head. "I also bailed—and for pretty much the same reason."

He gives me a quizzical look, and I tell him what happened as I make my way to the tower of sleepers.

When I locate my father, I tell Pom, "You can join this, but please stay incognito. Explaining you isn't on the agenda."

He leaps onto my shoulder and becomes invisible. *If we need to talk, let's do it mentally.*

Making myself invisible as well, I reach out and grab my father's wrist.

———

RIGHT AWAY, my senses inform me that this dream is a memory.

I let it play out, curious about my father's life.

He's sitting on the floor next to a coffee table in the middle of a sea of empty food containers, beer bottles, and piles of newspapers that span many years. The rest of the living room reminds me of Earth shows set in the fifties—with a tiny TV that looks like an astronaut's helmet, a phone with a cord attaching it to the wall, and uncomfortable furniture that was brightly colored once but is washed out now.

Maxwell is either playing solitaire or randomly moving playing cards around the table. His movements are sluggish, his expression that of bored despair.

Is he suffering despite having blocked out the painful memories? Pom mentally asks. *I think that's what happened to Lidia.*

This is just one dream, I reply. *Besides, this could just be the way life was before internet was invented.*

Despite my words, I suspect that Pom is right. This Maxwell seems like a broken man—and it's not unreasonable to think that his past is the cause.

Remembering my original goal, I look at the dusty shades blocking the two windows.

Hard to say if the glass behind the shades is black.

Moving softly to avoid detection, I walk over to one of the shades and lift it up. The city outside is dirty and dark, the building across covered in worn-out graffiti and rust streaks.

I walk over to the second window.

Not surprisingly, underneath this shade is black glass.

Suddenly, I become visible, and a voice booms through the room as though from a giant speaker. "Just what do you think you're doing?"

Okay. It's official. He's as touchy about this as Mom.

I feel myself jerked away from the black window and dragged five feet in my father's direction.

Pom's feet dig into my shoulder. He might be about to bolt.

"Maxwell, this is Bailey," I say soothingly. "We decided to have a talk in the dream world. Remember?"

He thrusts his hand at the black window, and metal blinds with spikes appear there, hiding it from view. "I don't remember giving you permission to sneak around."

I gesture at the metal blinds, and they melt into a puddle on the floor. "That black window is what I came to talk to you about."

"No!" He makes a sweeping gesture, and all the objects in the room fly at me.

Pom's feet are no longer on my shoulder.

As I suspected, he's found this too scary.

I try not to tense up as I increase the gravity in the room, causing all the projectiles to drop before reaching me.

Immediately, they rise up off the floor. I put them down again and round on Maxwell. "Stop fighting me! It's time for you to remember what you forgot."

His nostrils flare as he gestures at me, and I feel myself getting wrenched from the dream world.

Though I've never countered such an attack, I *have* forced myself to stay in the dream world through sheer willpower, and I do so now.

With a growl, he tries to jolt himself awake. I can feel him doing it.

Puck.

Remembering that the Nutcracker—Rattie—was able to prevent me from jolting, I do my best to guess how he did it. Maxwell's breathing grows louder, and he begins to sweat as I strain my powers, keeping him in the dream world with everything I've got.

Panting, he loosens his collar. "I don't want to harm you."

I grit my teeth. "More like you can't. Let's just go into that window. You'll see that I—"

He flexes and unflexes his fingers, and I get drenched with something like liquid nitrogen. The frostbite that covers my body feels like a burn—though that could in part be because I'm sizzling with anger.

Maxwell looms over me. "The only way I'm going into that window is if—"

I exit my body, but instead of healing, I create two duplicates of myself right behind Maxwell and jump into their bodies.

By the time his eyes widen, we already have him in our grasp.

He tries jolting awake again, but it's too late.

We all smash into the black glass.

CHAPTER TWELVE

AS USUAL, I plunge into icy black water.

There's only one of me here; the other remains in the room we were just in. Since I don't need to be in that room, I dispel that me and focus on my surroundings. Just like when I did this with Valerian, there's a rope attaching me to a rickety boat.

Inside is Maxwell.

If I make it to the shore, he's going to recall whatever this black window is blocking.

With no shore in sight, I swim.

After what feels like two days, my every muscle screams in pain, and the irritation from the rope burns is about to drive me mad.

Ignoring it all, I keep swimming. I remind myself this isn't real. This is just a trial of my strength, a way to make sure only the worthy can give my father his memory back.

Well, I'm worthy. If I was able to give back the memories of Soma to Valerian, I should be able to do this too.

Soon, swimming becomes a type of water-based yoga, my breath and movements synchronized perfectly and my mind purely in present moment.

This helps for a few hours, but then thoughts of quitting return. To battle them, I glance back at Maxwell's face and fantasize about how it'll look when he learns the truth.

This keeps me going for what feels like another day.

At some point, the exhaustion and pain grow completely unbearable. Then, just like last time, I get a second wind. I swim and swim until I see a distant shore on the horizon.

Yes!

My lungs begin to work overtime as I kick harder. I slice through the black water like an orca until my feet finally touch the sand—which is when the water and the boat disappear.

———

WE'RE in a familiar clearing in the woods with trees that look like a mix of coral reefs and baobabs. The sky is that of Soma—two counter-rotating cylinders of an O'Neill colony.

A younger Maxwell is sitting on the grass with my mom, who looks to be in her late teens.

"So, Max, what did you want to do?" she asks teasingly.

Max, huh? I guess that's short and sweet. Max doesn't yet have any gray in his hair, and his skin is more bronze than Maxwell's—probably from spending time outside like this.

Seeing my parents together makes my whole body feel tingly and warm—that is, until they begin kissing, much too passionately for my comfort.

Maxwell gapes at them, blinking rapidly.

I clear my throat.

Maxwell rounds on me. "I can't believe I forgot Lidia."

There's a dullness in my chest. "You forgot more than just her."

"Still, you shouldn't have done what you did." He rakes his hands through his hair. "There's got to be a reason I gave up something so wonderful."

"I know what happened," I tell him. "All is not as it seems."

He's not listening, though. He's staring at Mom, his gaze unfocused. She, in the meanwhile, is sucking on the neck of his younger self with an enthusiasm a vampire might envy.

Has my father just recalled being given a major hickey?

"I hope you're right," he says after a moment. "I never want to forget Lidia again."

I sigh. So he was listening. "No hope necessary. I know I'm right."

The memory changes.

———

SOMETHING I'VE EXPERIENCED in Mom's black window begins to play out.

Three people are in a spacious room, with Mom in a bathtub made of crystal.

Like in Mom's memory, she's pregnant and in the process of birthing me and my twin.

Maxwell's mouth slackens as he stares at his younger self, who's holding Mom's hand like his life depends on it.

"Push, honey." Max kisses the back of Mom's hand. "That's it. I love you."

Maxwell looks at me, his eyes widening beyond what's possible outside the dream world. "I had two daughters!"

I feel a burn behind my eyelids. "You still have them."

His mouth opens and closes, like that of a fish.

"Push!" the midwife orders in the memory.

The crowning baby's head shows up.

Maxwell stares at me unblinkingly.

"You're doing good," says my grandmother in the memory. "Almost there."

The newborn starts screaming.

Maxwell steps toward me, his eyes darting between me and the baby. "Are you…?"

The midwife hands over the gooey newborn to his younger self with a wide grin.

"It's a girl," Max says, his eyes shining with joy. "A baby girl."

The stinging behind my eyes intensifies. "I am."

"Keep pushing!" the midwife orders.

"Which one?" Maxwell asks achingly as the second baby crowns.

"Bailey," I say through the knot in my throat.

"Bailey?" It's as if he's tasting the name.

The second baby screams, and the midwife gives the newborn to my mom.

"Do you know what you're going to call them?" my grandmother asks.

Max gestures at the baby in Mom's arms. "Asha, for my late mother." He looks at the other newborn. "And Bailey, after her grandmother."

With that, Max beams at my namesake-grandmother and lifts baby-me proudly, à la Lion King.

My current-day father finally snaps out of his stupor and closes the distance between us, enveloping me in a hug that's decades overdue.

A tension I've carried since I was a child eases, the hollow ache inside my chest receding. My heart feels full and tingly, expanding until it threatens to burst out of my ribcage.

My father.

I've found him.

Maxwell squeezes me tighter. It's a good thing I don't need to worry about my ribs in the dream world.

In the distance, my grandmother coos at the infants.

"Let me hold one," Mom says hoarsely, and the memory shifts.

———

AN ALL-TOO-FAMILIAR SCENARIO STARTS, playing out a little faster than the prior memories—the beginning of the speedup.

Maxwell, the one I brought with me, wipes away the moisture on his face and shifts his gaze from me to the clearing in the woods where the memory is taking place.

His eyes widen again, and he turns ashen.

My sister and I look to be about seven. We're screaming in terror because our parents are chasing after us with machetes.

"This didn't happen," I tell Maxwell quickly. "You've got to keep that in mind."

But he's already reeling. "No. I was Overtaken. I remember that now." He points at the magma-like fire in the eyes of his younger self.

"Okay, that part happened. But not everything you're about to see did."

He pivots on me, eyes full of old horror and disbelief. "What are you talking about?"

"Do you see those people?" I point at the crowd that's chasing after my parents. "That's Davu and his son, Valerian. You remember what their power is, right?"

Maxwell stills, his jaw working. "Illusions… A lot of people in that crowd are illusionists."

"Stop!" Davu screams at my parents in the memory.

They don't respond, just keep chasing the girls.

Asha trips over a root.

Maxwell reels. "Please, no."

The young me keeps running for a few moments, then looks back, panting. "Asha, no!" she gasps and rushes to her.

Asha is crying.

Little Bailey tries to lift her.

The parents close in.

"This is all an illusion," I say as current-day Maxwell continues to fall apart. "It was meant to fool Phobetor through you."

Max faces the crowd while Mom raises her machete.

"Mommy, no!" the little me screams.

Maxwell clamps his hands over his ears and squeezes his eyes shut, as if that can block the events from playing out in his mind.

The machete whooshes by little Bailey's cheek and slices into Asha's neck.

Blood gushes out of the wound, spraying my young self all over.

Asha's severed head rolls away.

Little Bailey screams.

Maxwell drops to his knees, mumbling something unintelligible as he rocks back and forth.

I reiterate that this is an illusion, but I can't blame him for freaking out. I've experienced this twice now and I know it's fake, yet it still makes me feel nauseated.

Mom's strange eyes gaze at the young me, who's sobbing uncontrollably. Her whole body tenses, her face twisting with alternating expressions of blankness and horror. Then her eyes begin to flicker between the magma fire and her normal brown, and her left hand grabs her right, as if trying to steal the machete from it. Finally, her eyes stay brown, and horror eclipses all else on her face.

"She banished Phobetor," Maxwell mutters, confirming my earlier suspicion. "Same thing happened to me... after I..."

Mom looks at the bloody machete in her hands. Then at headless Asha.

With a raw, guttural moan, she spins around—just as the younger version of my father smashes a fist into her temple.

"Don't do it," Maxwell yells at Max in a hoarse voice.

His younger self doesn't listen. He stalks over to little Bailey and swings the machete.

A primal scream is wrenched from Maxwell's throat.

"It didn't happen," I say as soothingly as I can—though, having never seen this part of the scenario, I'm a little shaken by the fact that he actually went through with it. He killed me.

Phobetor or not, illusion or not, he swung a weapon at my neck. The neck of my more adorable seven-year-old self. If he were to become Overtaken again, he'd probably kill the grown me in a heartbeat.

Was it too much to wish that parental love would somehow triumph despite all the odds? Did he not love me enough to snap out of it? Did Mom not love Asha enough?

Max's body tenses the way Mom's did, his face also morphing from blankness to horror as his eyes begin to flicker between fiery and amber.

He's beating Phobetor, like she did. Only he, too, has done it when it was too late. Or maybe Phobetor has released them both, thinking that the twins are dead.

That's a scary thought, actually. Could he take over Maxwell again now that he knows I'm alive?

In the memory, Max falls to his knees and screams—which is when the crowd reaches him and Davu knocks him out.

———

THIS NEW MEMORY RUNS FASTER.

Max is hugging his knees, catatonic. He's inside a padded room while Valerian's parents are standing outside, behind a glass door. Whatever they're saying to each other is impossible to hear. If this is the time when Valerian spied on them, they're talking about how my mom has escaped from a similar room, grabbing me along the way.

"I remember being in that cell," Maxwell says, glaring at his younger self.

"Why a cell?" I ask, though I can guess.

"They didn't trust that I'd beaten Phobetor for good," Maxwell says, confirming my suspicion. "I didn't trust myself either."

"But you did beat him, right?" I ask warily. "You're not a ticking bomb?"

His gaze loses focus. "As you've probably guessed, when a dreamwalker is Overtaken, we're fully aware of what Phobetor makes us do. After I did…. what I thought I did, the pain drove me to banish Phobetor from my dream world."

I shift from foot to foot. "Or maybe he just didn't need you enough to push the issue?"

His shoulders slump. "That's also possible, but I doubt it. He's been trying to get back in. In fact, it's been a battle to keep him out all these years—a battle I've gotten better at with time. But you're right. There are no guarantees. It might be wise to always keep a careful eye on me."

That's exactly what I plan to do, but there's no reason to belabor it. Instead, I say, "He's back in Mom's dreams."

Maxwell lifts a shaky hand to his forehead. "Of course. That was Lidia in a coma. How could I have forgotten about that?"

I pat his shoulder. "It's a lot to take in."

"So Phobetor has her?"

"I'm not sure," I say and explain what happened in the subdream.

Maxwell frowns. "That doesn't prove he took her over. In fact, if she never goes into REM sleep, he'll have a hard time making her an Overtaken. I think he just took advantage of an opportunity. Bailey..." He looks at me pleadingly. "Promise me you won't go back into Lidia's dreams."

"But the coma—"

"Let me think on that." He shifts his attention to his unmoving younger self.

Davu opens a small window. "Are you hungry?"

Max doesn't reply.

"I remember this," Maxwell says. "It was a month before I escaped."

Before I can ask how he escaped, or anything else, the memory changes.

———

THINGS SPEED UP EVEN MORE.

We're in a large meeting room. A dozen people are sitting in a circle, Valerian's and my parents among them. In the middle of the circle is Nostradamus and his werewolf.

I happen to know kid Valerian is here too, but he's hiding using his powers, so he's not part of my father's memories.

"The prophecy," Maxwell says darkly. "That cursed thing cost me everything."

Nostradamus begins to speak. "If Phobetor isn't stopped, he'll destroy everyone, not just your little world."

"We know this," Max says. "Tell us something we don't."

"There's one thing that will give you a chance at victory," Nostradamus says. "A minuscule chance."

Mom looks at the seer skeptically. "What is it?"

"Only Two working as One can defeat the god of nightmares," Nostradamus says. "Remember, only Two working as One."

Everyone gazes at him in confusion.

"That's much too vague," my mom says. "Who are the Two? How do you work as One?"

Nostradamus stands up. "I might've already said too much."

Everybody starts shouting questions, but the werewolf growls at them and leads the seer out of the room.

———

THIS MEMORY LOOKS like a movie on fast-forward.

Mom and Max are watching Asha and me play in the distance.

Maxwell gazes longingly in the same direction.

"Two working as One doesn't have to mean the twins," Mom says, sounding like a chipmunk. "You and I are soulmates—that's a type of two working as one, isn't it?"

"You can make that argument, true," Max says, also sounding funny due to the speedup. "But let's be honest with ourselves. Without ever having heard of the seer, the girls play a game they call 'two as one.' Are we to ignore that?"

Mom twists a ring on her finger. "That game could be a coincidence. Even if it's not, are we really going to allow our children to fight Phobetor?"

Max squeezes her hand. "That's a different conversation altogether. Whether or not us being soulmates means we're Two as One, I'd rather defeat Phobetor myself than have my daughters be forced to do it."

She nods. "Everyone says we're the most powerful dreamwalkers they know. The girls don't seem to be stronger. At least, not yet."

"I guess that's that," Max says. "We're going to tell everyone that we're certain the prophecy is about us."

Mom squares her shoulders. "We're going to battle Phobetor."

———

IN THE NEXT MEMORY, Max is a young child. He's playing a game with other boys, the details of which are hard to make out due to the speedup.

The memory that comes after this takes place in the padded room again, only this time Max isn't catatonic. He stares intently at the corner of the room. Thanks to the speedup, what must've taken a long time for him happens almost in an eyeblink.

A shining plasma gate opens in the corner of the room. It looks like the gates at the hubs, only smaller and fainter.

A woman steps out of the gate. "You have only two favors left. Use this one wisely."

In lieu of an answer, Max leaps into the gate.

Before I can ask Maxwell pertinent questions about his unusual form of escape, the next memory starts. In it, my parents are battling in the dream world—at least I assume that's where they are, since when Mom punches a wall behind Max, it shatters into pieces.

"Training for the big battle," Maxwell says without being prompted.

I guess he doesn't want me to think he beat his wife.

When I refocus on the memories, Max is at a funeral, and the memory after that looks like my parents' wedding.

Now things begin to move so fast I can only guess at what I see. It seems like the next memory is that of a battle happening in a subdream-like space. I get a glimpse of Phobetor, as well as Mom and Max.

The next thing I catch is the end of the battle. Both my parents have fiery eyes.

What follows flashes by so fast it's impossible to make out, and then the world explodes around us, jolting me awake.

CHAPTER THIRTEEN

I OPEN my eyes in the waking world.

Virgil looks at me curiously as I lean back in the wheelchair to catch my breath.

That was a lot of information all at once. It's a good thing I'd sat down before I started, as my legs are actually feeling weak.

Maxwell sits up on the gurney. He looks at his empty palms, then touches his fingers to his lips while looking at me as if for the first time.

"Do you remember now?" I ask cautiously.

"I remember everything." His voice is choked with emotion.

For a few moments, we just stare at each other. Then Virgil coughs theatrically.

I have no idea what the vampire thinks is going on here, but I don't care. I stand up as Maxwell slides his legs down the gurney.

As soon as he's off the bed, he envelops me in a fierce hug.

My heart flutters even more rapidly here in the real world. My father's scent, clean and woodsy, tugs at something in the back of my mind, evoking a feeling of comfort and safety. My usual germ fears are far from my mind, and even after we pull apart, I don't feel the slightest urge to hygieia.

"Your mother," Maxwell says raggedly. "Can you please take me to her?"

I glance at Virgil, who's watching us with a puzzled frown. Catching my gaze, he nods and leads us out.

I use the time as we walk to compose myself. Just because my father now remembers me doesn't mean all our problems are solved.

When we get to Mom's room, the two gnomes are still chatting. Ignoring them and Virgil, Maxwell rushes to Mom's tricked-out bed and stares at her greedily, eyes gleaming with moisture.

"Open it," he says. "Please."

Dr. Xipil pauses his animated discussion with Itzel, touches the remote, and the clamshell glass opens up. He and Itzel then tactfully step away, while Maxwell grabs Mom's hand and closes his eyes.

"Are you going into her dreams?" I ask softly, coming up to stand next to him.

He shakes his head. "I'm no use to anyone if Phobetor takes me over again. Or makes me go insane."

I lay my hand over his palm, which is still squeezing my mom's hand. "How do we save her then?"

He looks at me. "We need to go to Soma to reunite with Asha."

I gape at him, struck speechless.

I'm still wrapping my mind around finding my father. To also gain a sister? My twin? I can't even—

"Once you and Asha meet, you'll have to decide if you're willing to follow the prophecy," Maxwell says, and his words hit me like a bucket of crushed ice. "Once Phobetor is defeated, any of us can go into your mother's dreams, give her back her past, and jolt her awake."

Phobetor defeated.

Prophecy.

Until this moment, these were merely abstract concepts.

Now I have no choice but to consider them, even though my brain refuses to compute it all.

"I don't know about my sister, but I'm not a hero from some fairy tale," I say slowly. "Even if I were, how would I defeat a god?"

"By, among other things, believing in yourself," Maxwell says solemnly.

Pom's fur turns pitch black on my wrist. "Sure. Why didn't you say so before? I'll just believe in myself all the way to a miracle. Maybe I'll turn lead into gold while I'm at it."

My father shakes his head. "Even before Nostradamus, our people believed we would have to deal with Phobetor one day. Believed that he *could* be defeated."

I take a step back. "I saw him close up."

"And he had me under his power," Maxwell says softly. "I understand the magnitude of this task better than anyone."

I begin to pace the room.

Can I do this?

No clue. Probably not, though. My parents tried, and that didn't work out so well for them. It would be a shame to find my twin, just to have Phobetor Overtake us and have us kill each other.

Still, going to Soma and meeting my sister is the first step in this insane plan, and it's something I'd want to do even if Phobetor didn't exist. Once there, if there's no other way to wake Mom, and if Asha's on board, we can revisit the whole battling Phobetor idea.

Who knows? I may not be a hero, but if I train a bit, maybe I could at least bluff Phobetor into letting me into Mom's dream world. I did manage to jolt away from him the last time. That's something.

I stop pacing and face my father. "Let's do it. Take me to Soma."

CHAPTER FOURTEEN

MAXWELL SMILES PROUDLY. "That's my girl."

I'm not sure how to respond to that—or to the warm glow his words generate in my chest—but I don't have to because Valerian walks into the room.

His gaze falls on Maxwell's face, and his eyes widen. "Max? Max Spidi?"

Spidi? Is that my real last name? It makes sense that Mom would take on our current one—Spade—as a way to stay more incognito in her exile.

Maxwell's jaw hangs open. "Valerian? Valerian Bale?"

Aha. Seems like between their black windows and the masks we were all wearing on our journey to Necronia, neither my father nor Valerian had realized they knew each other.

That's good. If I'd found out that Valerian knew about my father and didn't tell me, I'd have trouble forgiving that kind of betrayal.

Valerian's stunned gaze shifts back and forth between us. "Does Bailey know that you're her—"

"Father? Yes," Maxwell says.

"Her father?" Itzel exclaims, finally tearing herself away from her conversation with Dr. Xipil.

Speaking over each other, Maxwell and I explain our recent revelation. As we speak, the puzzled look on Virgil's face transforms into one of understanding and relief.

I don't know what he thought when Maxwell and I were hugging, but I wouldn't be surprised if he was worried about having an even more "uncomfortable" conversation with Valerian.

When the explanations are over, I take Valerian aside. "What took you so long?"

He rakes his fingers through his dark, thick hair. "I had to make sure everyone was all right, then clean up a huge mess you made at my VR company."

Puck. With all the family drama, I'd forgotten about the people who got knocked out on the skyscraper roof hub. "How's everyone?"

"The members of the New York Council woke up and are as good as new," he says. "More measures will be taken when they sleep now, so even if Collywobbles wants to bribe anyone else into releasing them, they'll have a devil of a time dealing with all the security precautions."

I nod approvingly. "What about Felix and Ariel?"

"Never better. I also got the ball rolling to get Rowan settled on Earth —which wasn't an easy conversation. Finally, I made sure Dylan has a lab and financing to do any research she wants."

"Fine," I say with mock grumpiness. "I guess you didn't completely waste the hours I gave you. Now what is that mess you claim I made? Is the video game I'm starring in selling poorly?"

Valerian's face darkens. "The game is fine, but Rattie was sleeping in one of our office's napping units when he attacked you."

Ah, right. I myself slept in one of those once—which is when I'd actually made a dream link to Rattie. I bet he'd done the same with me around the same time; that's how he was able to attack me.

Then Valerian's meaning dawns on me.

Rattie's attack. I killed him, a dreamwalker, during a dreamwalk. That means—

"He went homicidally insane," Valerian says grimly, confirming my suspicion. "The security footage was brutal. He slaughtered everyone on his way out of the office building, and some pedestrians after that."

Bile rises in my throat. "Anyone I know?"

"I'm not sure who you know at the company," Valerian says and rattles out a bunch of names that don't sound familiar.

"What about Bernard?" I ask. Having dreamwalked in the man and nudged him to reunite with his estranged daughter, I feel invested in his fate.

"He was one of the lucky ones," Valerian says. "He had plans with his daughter that evening."

Whew. That's something. Still, I can't help but feel awful—especially since I hadn't given the consequences of defeating Rattie a single thought. Then again, I was too busy dying of the virus shortly after that battle, and then dealing with a score of Overtaken attacks and a family reunion.

Swallowing the lump in my throat, I ask, "Where's Rattie now?"

Valerian frowns. "No one knows, and not for a lack of trying. He took a cab to JFK without killing the driver. Felix helped us get the airport security footage, and we saw Rattie heading toward the hub. His eyes were those of an Overtaken. The theory is that he fell asleep after his murder spree, and Collywobbles took over his body."

"What's a Collywobbles?" Maxwell asks, approaching us.

"That's what we call the god of nightmares," I explain. "Valerian believes that calling him by his real name gives him more power."

Valerian takes my hand and rubs my palm with his thumb. "Not a lot of power, mind you, but why give him any? Also, I kind of like the idea of using a disrespectful nickname for him. I bet it would infuriate him if he knew."

Maxwell glances at our joined hands, a faint smile touching the corners of his eyes. "We always knew the two of you would end up together. That you found each other in exile is extraordinary."

Are we together? I guess it's close enough. I contentedly squeeze Valerian's hand. "Don't forget we also did it without any memories of our past. It boggles the mind if you think about it."

The look Valerian gives me makes something inside me melt into a gooey puddle.

"It's very romantic," Itzel says, coming up to us with Dr. Xipil—whom she looks at meaningfully for some reason.

At the mention of romance, my father's gaze falls on Mom's contraption, and his expression turns somber. "We need to talk." He gives the gnomes and Virgil a hard look. "In private."

Itzel and Dr. Xipil nod and step out of the room.

Virgil doesn't.

"Go," Valerian orders, jabbing his thumb at the door.

Virgil exits with visible reluctance.

"Don't bother eavesdropping," Valerian says as the vampire begins to close the door behind himself. "I'm going to be using my powers to shield us."

"Fine," Virgil says over his shoulder. "If Maxwell or Bailey attack you, don't come crying to me after."

Before Valerian can answer, the vampire is gone.

Valerian looks at Maxwell. "This is about going to Soma, isn't it?"

Maxwell nods solemnly.

"I've been thinking along the same lines," Valerian says. "But it's impossible to get there."

My heart sinks. "Why?"

"The trip from here to Soma goes through extremely dangerous Otherlands," Valerian says.

"Mom and I must've made the journey once," I say. "And you did too."

"That was before all the Otherlands started teeming with the Overtaken," he says. "If we were to try to go to Soma now, our trip from Necronia would seem like a leisurely stroll in comparison."

The sinking sensation intensifies. "What if we brought an army of vampires with us?"

Valerian shakes his head. "Still too dangerous. Also, we're trying to keep the location of Soma a secret."

Maxwell nods. "Soma's very existence must stay a secret."

I look at him. "How can a world's existence ever be a secret? Isn't there a hub that some Cognizant could accidentally stumble onto?"

"Soma is special," Maxwell says. "There's only a single gate leading to and from it. The entry gate for Soma is hidden on a nondescript world, far from the regular hub."

"So that's it?" I don't bother hiding the disappointment in my voice. "I don't get to meet my twin?"

"I'm sorry," Valerian says, and looks it.

"There is a way," Maxwell says. "Otherwise, why would I suggest we go to Soma?"

I belatedly recall a memory of his. "Of course. You want to use that woman who sprung you from Soma."

"She owes me one last favor," Maxwell says. "And I'm glad I didn't use up that favor when I was sick with the virus. I suspected I might have to return to Soma one day."

Wow. Talk about self-discipline. When I had that virus, I would've called in every favor and spent every penny to get closer to the cure.

"What are you two talking about?" Valerian asks.

"A teleporter," Maxwell says. "A world jumper at that."

I wanted to ask him about that when I first saw the memory, but things moved too fast, so I didn't get a chance. Teleporters are among the rarest Cognizant types, and the most powerful of them—a tiny minority of an already small group—are world jumpers. It is said that world jumpers can create personal gates to Otherlands.

Personally, I've never met any of them. If it weren't for the hubs, I would doubt that world jumpers exist. Legends say the gates in the hubs were created by a mix of gnome technology and a group of ultra-powerful world jumpers, sometimes called the gate makers.

"I thought world jumpers were a myth," Valerian says, echoing my thoughts.

"They're real," Maxwell says. "They prefer to live on worlds that don't have hubs—because they can. So, naturally, they're hard for the rest of us to come across. The jumper who owes me needed a dreamwalker, so she found me, not the other way around."

Valerian frowns. "But if she's on another world, and without a hub, how are we going to recruit her?"

"Dreamwalking isn't constrained by Otherland boundaries," Maxwell says. "If it were, Phobetor wouldn't be as big a problem as he is."

"Call him Collywobbles," Valerian says, almost on autopilot. "Do you think your world jumper is sleeping right now?"

"There's only one way to find out." Maxwell looks at me. "Can you put me in REM sleep?"

"You don't need me to put you to sleep to get to the dream world." I wave my wristband as its fur turns brown. "You can use Pom instead."

"What's a pom?" Maxwell asks, then looks at my pet, eyes widening. "Oh, wow. That's a creature, and it's in REM sleep."

"*He* is," I say, and explain that Pom is a looft, a symbiotic creature that lives on moofts.

Maxwell takes a half step back. "How did you get him in the first place? Dream world access is nice, but to willingly let a parasite leech your—"

"He's a symbiont." The defensiveness in my voice is ironic, given how much I've teased Pom about this very thing.

"I was wondering about this too." Valerian looks at Pom. "How did the two of you end up together?"

Smiling, I pet Pom's fur. "A patient of mine was badgering me to go to the South Gomorran Petting Zoo. She said it was the most soothing experience she's ever encountered, and that I could use it as dream therapy. I eventually gave in." I look at Valerian to make sure he appreciates what a great sacrifice that was for someone as wary of germs as I am. "According to my extensive research, moofts were the only creatures at that zoo that were never featured in an article about cross-species transmission of disease. So at the urging of my patient, I reached out to touch one. My hand landed on the most colorful and furry section of the creature—which turned out to have been a budding looft. The looft got attached to my wrist. Naturally, I freaked out at first. But then I learned about loofts and that they spend the majority of their lives in REM sleep, so I realized the potential. Long story short, I met Pom in the dream world, fell in love with his cuteness, and now he's my best friend."

A best friend who recently admitted to using a section of my brain, but still. What's a few neurons among friends? I was probably too smart for my own good.

Maxwell wrinkles his nose. "If you don't mind, I'd rather just go into REM sleep from my own dreams."

Huh. Is my father wary of touching Pom for the same reason I'd be—a totally reasonable and rational fear of viruses and bacteria that everyone else in the world lacks for unfathomable-to-me reasons?

Nah. He'd hugged me without a second thought.

Then again, I'd also hugged him without hesitation.

"Lie down on the floor," I say, figuring if he's really like me, he'll object to that unsanitary instruction.

He lies down. He either doesn't share my qualms or the prospect of touching Pom was the worse evil. "I'm ready."

Figuring this might be a good time to practice using my sleep-inducing power remotely, I try it out.

It works. My father is instantly in REM sleep.

Seizing the moment, I turn to Valerian. "Did you miss me?"

His ocean-blue eyes glimmer. "What do you think?"

The room around us shimmers and becomes a lush bedroom once more, the one with an enormous bed swathed in silk sheets and scattered with rose petals.

I swallow hard, my pulse picking up. "I think you couldn't stop thinking about me."

He closes the distance between us and brushes his fingers along my jaw. His touch sends an electrical jolt through my body, making my skin prickle and my breathing hitch in my throat.

Biting my lip, I reach out to squeeze his muscular forearm. "Am I touching the real you?"

He nods, his eyes falling to my mouth.

Without a second thought, I rise on tiptoe and kiss him.

He returns the kiss hungrily, his tongue sweeping over the closed seam of my lips—which part of their own accord. He immediately takes advantage, deepening the kiss, and my mind goes pleasantly blank, empty of thoughts about germs or nearby parents or anything else. All I am is blissful awareness of how soft his lips are, how—

He picks me up and strides toward the bed.

Wow. Some of this can't be real.

"You think you can handle more?" His voice is like heated molasses.

I nod as our eyes meet, my racing pulse making it difficult to speak.

His clothes disappear, and I no longer care if this is real or not. Pom's fur turns coral pink on my wrist, and my own clothes feel like a straitjacket as heat thrums under my skin, making me feel like I'm melting. Breathing raggedly, I reach out to stroke the smooth, hard muscles of his chest and—

Valerian curses, and his clothes reappear as the bedroom poofs out of existence, revealing the reason.

Maxwell has just sat up.

Puck. Did he have to finish his dreamwalking so quickly?

I fight the urge to fan myself. How embarrassing would it be if I asked Valerian to use his powers to give me a cold shower?

"Later," Valerian promises in a soft whisper, and I nod, flushing.

"It's a date," I whisper back. "And when it happens, I don't want any illusions. Not the first time."

Valerian's eyes darken. "Your wish is my command."

"It's done," Maxwell says, scrubbing a hand over his face. "We have a few minutes before she arrives."

I look around the room, forcing myself to focus on something other than Valerian. "We're taking Mom with us, right?"

"Of course," Maxwell says.

"And leaving as soon as the jumper shows up?"

He nods. "Why wait?"

"In that case, we need the remote for Mom's bed."

Valerian's already on it. "I'll go talk to Dr. Xipil and tell Virgil we're leaving."

"But don't tell them where we're going," Maxwell says.

Valerian opens the door. "I'm not the one who blabbed about Soma's location to a random teleporter."

My father stiffens. "I didn't have a choice."

"Well, I do, and I don't intend to say anything." Not waiting for a reply, Valerian walks out.

Maxwell turns to me. "He's different than I remember him. Tougher. More like his father."

"What about me?" I ask. "Am I different?"

"I don't know yet." He smiles. "Ask me again once we get to know each other a little better."

I grin back at him. "Deal."

"Actually, would you mind telling me something about yourself?" he asks. "You mentioned patients earlier. Are you a doctor?"

I tell him about the dream therapy I pioneered, and as I do, I can see his shoulders straighten with pride.

"Is that your main passion?" he asks after I'm done.

"There's also virtual reality games," I say. "I hope to use that technology to create something similar to dream therapy, but more accessible."

He smiles. "You're a lot like your namesake grandmother. She, too, is a healer in her heart of hearts."

"I can't wait to meet her," I say, then frown. "She's alive, right? She was already old in your memories, and Valerian said that time flows faster on Soma."

"Dreamwalkers live very long lives," Maxwell says. "Barring some unfortunate accident, Mama B should be alive, and in good health."

"How long is long?" I ask. This is something I've always wondered but couldn't ask Mom, who disliked any topic having to do with our powers. "Is it centuries, like ubers, or—"

"That's about right. And before you ask, so do illusionists." He gives me a wink.

I try my best not to flush again. How much did he hear and see of my makeout session with Valerian? "How about you tell me about your life in exile?" I ask, both to change the topic and because I'm genuinely curious.

For all I know, I might have a stepmom—or half-siblings.

My father sighs. "There isn't much to tell. For a while, I abandoned dreamwalking completely and became a musician."

Huh. That's random. "Which instruments did you play?"

"Whichever I could get my hands on. Eventually, I became a conductor. I'm still famous on the world I exiled myself to."

I bite my lip. "Were you lonely?"

"I didn't remarry, if that's what you mean." He looks down. "I didn't remember you and Lidia, but on some level, I think I knew something. It's hard to explain. The very thought of starting a family was abhorrent."

Mom didn't date either. Her life was pretty miserable, in fact. I hope I brought her some happiness, but he didn't have even that much.

"I'm sorry," I say.

He looks up. "Don't feel sorry for me. I channeled all those pent-up emotions into my music. In a real way, a lot of people got joy from that pain, and I'm okay with that."

The door opens again, and Valerian walks in. "All set." He hands Maxwell the remote for Mom's bed.

Maxwell presses a button, and the clamshell closes. "Do we need to change some nutrition bag or anything like that?"

"I have all the instructions," Valerian says. "This is something we'll be able to do easily on Soma."

My father inclines his head. "Thank you so much, Valerian. Davu would be so very proud."

Eyes gleaming, Valerian mumbles a thanks.

A shining plasma gate suddenly opens in the corner of the room. It looks like the one from Maxwell's memory—similar to the ones at the hubs but smaller and not as bright.

The woman from the memory steps out of the gate. Her face is classically beautiful, and her highly intelligent eyes dart around the room worriedly until she catches sight of Maxwell.

Relaxing, she makes the gate she came from disappear, and two more gates show up, one on each side of her.

"This is your last favor," she says to Maxwell, her voice more melodic now that it's not sped up.

"Thanks, Karina," Maxwell says. "You might've just saved the Cogniverse."

"Sure," Karina says with a heavy dose of skepticism. "Just remember, regardless of how the world saving goes, we're through. If I see you in my dreams again, my next gate will open under your feet, and it will exit above an erupting volcano. On a world with no oxygen."

Before anyone can comment on her threat, she steps into one of the gates, and the gate shimmers out of existence.

Well, okay then. That's one way to have the last word.

"We must hurry," Maxwell says and fiddles with the controls on Mom's bed.

"Can we trust this Karina?" I ask. "What if she's done the whole top-of-volcano gate preemptively?"

Maxwell smiles. "Karina is a woman of her word. This gate leads to Soma. And if I do visit her dreams again, a gate will indeed open under my feet and plunge me into a volcano, on a world without oxygen." On that cheerful note, he rolls Mom's bed into the gate and steps through himself.

"Your father has always been a good judge of character," Valerian says, and before I can reply, he also enters the gate.

I take a breath and glance down at my wrist, where Pom's fur is turning black.

Here goes nothing.

Volcano, here I come.

CHAPTER FIFTEEN

I STEP out into a padded glass room, where there's definitely oxygen.

I recognize it immediately, and judging by Maxwell and Valerian's faces, they must as well.

This is where my father was being held when he escaped with Karina's help.

Maxwell curses. "I should've been more careful. One of Karina's least endearing qualities is her sense of humor. I asked her to bring me back to Soma. I bet she thought it would be funny to bring me back exactly where she'd sprung me from."

Valerian knocks on the glass. "Feels bulletproof."

Maxwell yells out loud.

Since there's no one around, no one answers.

I scan the corners where the walls meet the ceiling until I hit jackpot—a gizmo that could be a camera.

I wave at the hopefully-camera like a maniac.

Nothing happens.

Valerian examines the door lock and curses in frustration.

We wait.

Valerian starts to pace.

No one comes.

"If Lidia were awake, she might know how to beat that lock," Maxwell says. "She was good with such things."

"If Mom were awake, we might not even be here," I mutter.

Maxwell slides down a soft wall until he's sitting on the floor in a pose that reminds me of when he was locked in this room in his memory. "No one knows we're here. We could starve."

"I wouldn't worry about that," I say. "We'll die of thirst long before that."

Valerian casts a furtive glance at Mom's bed.

"We're not stealing Mom's nutrients, if that's what you're thinking," I tell him sternly. "And if it is what you're thinking, shame on you."

Valerian folds his arms across his chest. "I fleetingly considered using the contraption as a battering ram but instantly dismissed the idea."

I pinch the bridge of my nose. "That's even worse than stealing her food."

"Well, I wasn't going to steal her food in the first place," he says.

"Children," Maxwell mutters. "Focus on workable solutions. Please."

Stroking Pom's fur to calm myself, I thoughtfully study my father. "You're from here. You must have dream connections with someone. Why don't you dreamwalk in a local and ask them for help?"

Maxwell theatrically smacks himself on the forehead. "How did I not think of that? My only excuse is that I've only recently remembered that I know people who live here."

I scratch my chin. "I hadn't thought of that before. Who did you think they were when you saw them in your tower of sleepers? I bet even *I* was there..."

"What's a tower of sleepers?" Maxwell asks.

As I explain, a slow smile spreads over his face. "What you call a tower of sleepers is just your own personal dream construct to deal with the problem of dreamwalking in someone you've made a connection with. Mine is just a room with paintings of the people whose dreams I'd like to visit."

"I use paintings too," I say. "But for my memory gallery, which is a way to revisit the memories I like."

"There you go," Maxwell says. "But to answer your original question, if you don't remember someone, they won't appear as a dream contact, regardless of how you represent such things in your dream world. It's not like a phone that has a list of contacts stored in its memory. Dream constructs use your mind—so if you forget a person, they won't appear in your tower of sleepers."

"That makes sense," I say. "Mom must've had a dream connection with both me and Asha, but I bet that after her exile, she never saw the two of us in her version of the tower of sleepers, only me."

"All that is fascinating," Valerian says. "But could you shelve dreamwalk theory until after we're freed?"

Maxwell stretches out on the floor. "Put me in REM sleep."

I do, and Valerian and I both pace as we wait.

After what feels like many hours, my father sits up. "I just spoke with your grandmother. Help should be on the way."

My grandmother.

I'm about to see her.

The idea makes me breathless—that or we're running out of oxygen in this room.

After what feels like a few more hours, a man walks up to the glass. Wearing a helmet and a chrome bodysuit, he looks like he's stepped off a set of a show about deep space exploration. He even holds what looks like a space gun—a long, sleek rifle-like thing.

Valerian makes LEGO letters appear in my line of vision: *That's one of the guards. Most of them are illusionists and therefore don't usually need to use weapons. Do you have any idea why your grandmother would send one to escort us out like this?*

I shrug, as does Maxwell—who must've seen the same question.

"Stay away from the door," the guard says.

As we back away, Maxwell explains about Mom's bed.

The guard unlocks the door and orders us to walk in front of him in the direction he says.

We oblige, with my father controlling the bed to make it ride ahead of us.

As we walk, I can't help but notice something I didn't realize when experiencing other people's memories of Soma. The surroundings have a definite spaceship vibe. I don't know if it's the silvery walls that lack any decorations or the very basic furniture and the guard's uniform.

When we exit the structure with the "jail," the spaceship feel grows stronger. The buildings around us are silvery and overly geometric in their shape—like someone had printed them out in one shot instead of building them with metal and cement, the way it's done on Gomorrah and Earth.

Spotting Valerian looking up at the sky, I follow his gaze.

How cool. Though I've seen this sky arrangement in the memories, looking at it live is that much more surreal. The road we're currently walking on seems to lead into the sky that looks like a circle. To the side of us, the ground seems to slope up, with forests and more buildings above our heads.

"So trippy," I breathe, my neck aching from the strain of looking up at such a steep angle. "I avoid these types of environments in the dream world because they seem too unrealistic."

"That's one of the reasons we need illusionists on Soma," Maxwell says, taking on a professorial tone that reminds me of Dylan. "Soma founders expected people to go crazy from staring at the weird sky. Illusionists can make it all look normal."

As if to illustrate the point, Valerian uses his powers to unfold the environment around us, making the sky look all-encompassing, as usual. The houses that were in the sky show up as distant structures on the horizon.

"Don't." I touch his elbow. "I'm not stir crazy yet."

The surreal reality comes back.

I gape at everything until we walk into a cuboid structure, where the guard leads us into what looks like a cafeteria. There are shiny metal tables and chairs all around, but only one of them is occupied.

It's an older woman with white curly hair, and I recognize her immediately.

It's Bailey, my grandmother.

CHAPTER SIXTEEN

DROPPING something that looks like a toothpaste tube onto a silvery tray, my grandmother leaps to her feet and rushes over to Mom's bed. Lips trembling, she stares down for a long minute as I watch her, my chest heavy.

Somberly, my father opens the clamshell-like top of the contraption, and my grandmother bends over her daughter and kisses her gently on the forehead.

I can't even imagine what she must be feeling.

When she looks up at my father, her eyes are swimming with tears. "It's as you said. Not even a hint of sleep. My poor Lia."

Lia? I've never heard anyone call Mom that. I like it, though.

Blinking a few times, my grandmother straightens her spine and turns to the guard. "Please take Lia's bed to the medical bay."

The guard glances at us uneasily. "They haven't been cleared."

"Leave me the gun then," she snaps.

The guard walks over and hands her the gun, which she accepts with obvious distaste.

My father gives the guard the remote for Mom's bed and explains how to use it. Reluctantly, the guard makes Mom's bed roll out and follows behind it.

My grandmother stares after them with visible longing. When the guard is completely out of sight, she composes herself and turns to Valerian. "You've grown to be a fine young man," she says, her voice softening to a kind, motherly tone. "Can you be a dear and make sure no one can overhear us?"

Looking a little taken aback, Valerian nods and presumably does as she asks, while my grandmother turns her razor-sharp gaze on me.

"Come, child. Let me take a look at you."

I take a reluctant step in her direction.

Will she hug me or shoot me with that gun?

Her gray eyes—identical to mine—moisten again as they scan me from head to foot. "You're so much like your sister," she says softly. "Yet so unlike her at the same time."

"You have some of Mom's features," I say with a shy smile. "And mine."

Laugh lines appear at the corners of her eyes. "Are you sure it's not the two of you who have my features, little bee?"

Was that my nickname? If so, I don't remember it at all.

"Where's Asha?" Maxwell asks.

"All in good time," my grandmother says, her face smoothing out. "You'll have to forgive me for the security measures. We've had the Overtaken try to sneak into the gate." Her hand tightens on the gun.

Valerian's expression darkens. "Overtaken here, on Soma?"

"I'm afraid so. And not just from the Otherlands either. Some Soma citizens have been succumbing. That's why the guards now walk around armed at all times."

"But how?" I ask. "Is anyone dumb enough to listen to other people's description of nightmares?"

She shakes her head. "Phobetor's power has now grown to the point where he can work his vileness through a regular nightmare, especially if the sleeper's guard happens to be down."

"Call him Collywobbles," Valerian says, and explains why.

"That's like trying to stop an ocean with a dam, but I'll do as you ask," she says. "Now, please, let's get the unpleasantness taken care of. Lie down." She gestures at the nearby benches.

Valerian pulls out a hygieia device and waves it over a bench for me.

I lie down, and he does the same.

My grandmother points a hand at Valerian and his body slumps. She does the same to my father next.

I feel them both in REM sleep and realize how the clearing works. If we've been Overtaken, dreamwalking in us will reveal it.

She points a hand at me, and I instantly fall asleep.

————

VALERIAN AND I are in his bed, making out. Suddenly, he disappears and I find myself clothed and standing in a cafeteria-like room.

My wrist is lacking Pom. This, combined with the sight of prone Maxwell and Valerian, informs me of two things: I'm asleep, and my grandmother is dreamwalking in me at the moment.

Probably.

"Where are you?" I ask, looking around.

With a satisfied chuckle, she drops her invisibility. Here, in the dream world, she looks to be about my age, and our resemblance is even more noticeable.

"So, you and Valerian," she says with a mischievous grin. "Unless that dream was more along the lines of wishful thinking?"

I flush. "It's in the early stages. Let's not jinx it by talking about it, okay?"

"Sure thing. For what it's worth, his dream of you leaves me little doubt about his feelings." She winks.

My blush intensifies, and I do my best to change the subject. "You've cleared Valerian, right?"

"And you," she says.

I jerk my chin at Maxwell. "What about him?"

Her expression turns more somber. "He's keeping the beast at bay. I will look out for him."

I'm glad she's spared me from having to suggest the same thing.

With his best Cheshire Cat impersonation to date, Pom appears on my shoulder.

"Hello, Bailey's Grandmother," he says, his fur morphing from light orange to teal. "It's nice to meet you. I'm Pom."

Her eyes grow cartoonishly wide. "That's not a dream construct, is it?"

"I'm not," he says.

"He's my best friend," I say, and explain about my symbiotic relationship with the looft.

"Well, now I've seen everything," she says, shaking her head in amazement. "It's a pleasure to meet you, Pom."

He turns a deep purple. "The pleasure is mine."

"Now, if you don't mind, I want to catch up with my grandchild."

"Of course, Grandmother," Pom says.

"Call me Mama B," she replies with a grin. "Everyone else does."

"Later, Mama B," Pom chirps and disappears—but his paws are still digging into my shoulder, so I know he's just turned invisible.

"He's a charmer," she says.

"That he is."

She makes the room around us change to a forest meadow, gracefully sinks onto the grass, and pats a place next to her.

Since we're in a dream and therefore without germs, I sit.

"Tell me a little bit about yourself," she says. "Where do you and Lia live?"

I tell her about Gomorrah, my job, and my recent misadventures, but I don't go too much into Mom's troubles before the coma.

"What about you?" I ask when I'm done. "Tell me what your life has been like."

"In a word, busy," she says with a sigh. "My typical day consists of running around Soma like a madwoman. I don't spend nearly as much time with my great-grandchild as—"

"Wait." I stare at her openmouthed. "My sister is—"

"Married and has a daughter." She makes two people appear in front of me, an attractive, strong-featured man who looks familiar and a girl about eight years old.

I peer at the man, picturing him without his dark, neatly groomed beard. "That's Kojo, isn't it?" I say, remembering the name of another one of our childhood friends.

"It is, and the name of that precious one is Chloe," she says with great-grandmotherly pride. She grins at me. "You're an aunt."

I look Dream Chloe over. With that mischievous smile and the halo of curls that make her look like a dark-headed dandelion, she might just be cuter than Pom. "Where is she? Out there, in the real world, I mean? And where's Asha?"

I'm dying to meet my twin.

My grandmother sighs. "I think we'd better wake up so I fill you in along with everyone else."

Huh, okay. I wonder what the mystery's all about. "Before we go, do you want me to call you Mama B or Grandmother or—"

She beams at me. "When you and Asha were small, you called me Bebe."

"Bebe it is," I say and jolt myself awake.

———

FEELING GROGGY, I get up from the bench, and my father and Valerian do the same.

Bebe walks over to a nearby machine and presses a couple of buttons.

The machine dispenses three silver cubes, and she sets them on the table near her tray. "Might as well eat while we talk."

"Eat?" I examine the cubes for any sign of edibleness.

She unfolds one cube until it becomes a tray like hers, with clear tubes of some gray substance inside. She squirts the paste-like stuff into her mouth and swallows. "These will serve every nutritional need."

"And they're sterile," Valerian says reassuringly. Under his breath, he adds, "Perhaps too much so."

I take a seat and squirt a tube into my mouth, half expecting the minty flavor of toothpaste.

Nope. There's no taste. I've never eaten something this neutral before. There's no flavor whatsoever, and even the texture of the substance is bland.

Oh, well. I don't care as long as it's really sterile. The last thing I want is to come all this way just to die of salmonella poisoning before I even meet my twin.

Bebe looks at Valerian. "Can you be a dear and use your powers to make me think I'm eating something more palatable?"

He nods, and the next time she squirts the goo into her mouth, she looks a lot happier.

"I didn't realize your kind could create the illusion of taste," I say.

"Of course," Valerian replies. "If we couldn't, you'd be able to use the sense of taste to know you're being fooled."

That makes sense. When I kissed an illusory version of him, I couldn't tell the difference. Taste was involved.

Oops. Pom is turning coral pink on my wrist.

I wave my tube at Valerian. "Can you make mine taste like manna?"

"I can do better." He rummages in his pocket and hands me a familiar manna packet. "I picked up some before we left."

I beam at him. "Thank you." As I take the gift, my fingers brush his skin, and Pom's coral-pink color deepens.

Bebe and my father exchange a knowing look.

I stuff the manna into my mouth and enjoy it as the others swallow their goo.

Then I turn to Bebe. "So. Where is my sister?"

CHAPTER SEVENTEEN

BEBE PUTS down her tube and sighs. "Asha lives with the Escapists."

"I thought so," Valerian says grimly.

"It makes sense," my father says with a frown. "But I don't like it."

"Who or what are the Escapists?" I ask, puzzled.

Bebe looks at me, then at Valerian and Maxwell.

"Bailey doesn't remember much about her life here," Valerian explains.

"A black window?" Bebe asks.

"I couldn't locate one," I say.

Bebe strokes her wrinkled chin. "Asha also has a memory gap. She doesn't remember Bailey—and more importantly, Max and Lia—and we couldn't locate a black window in her case either." She studies my father with an unreadable expression. "My theory about Asha's memory loss is that it was caused by the pain of having seen both her parents become Overtaken." Her gaze shifts to me. "That's probably the case for the both of you."

She might be right. That could indeed be the reason for my memory loss. My parents suddenly became slaves to an evil deity who wanted me dead. I'm an adult, and I wish I could forget all about it.

I pick up my tube and squirt some of the goo into my mouth. "Let's get back to the Escapists."

Bebe looks at Valerian. "Any suggestions on how to best explain them?"

"Start earlier." He swallows some of the goo. "Maybe tell her the ancient history of Soma."

Bebe looks thoughtful. "I can do that. Just bear in mind, this history is more like a legend. We don't know how much is fact or fiction."

I nod.

She waves her hand to encompass our surroundings. "As should be abundantly clear, we're a space colony."

"So it *is* a spaceship," I say.

"Of sorts," she says. "It was designed to sustain a population indefinitely, so in that way, not very different from a planet. Just smaller."

I look around in wonder. "Is Soma flying somewhere specific? Is the plan to arrive at a distant star?"

"Sadly, no," Valerian says.

"We're orbiting a planet," Bebe adds.

"A dead planet," Maxwell says darkly. "Our ancestors' home and the first world that Collywobbles destroyed."

My head spins.

Bebe eats more of her food, the form of which makes more sense in the context of a spaceship. "Some legends also say our world is where he's from," she says. "They claim he was a dreamwalker who made humans worship him—and that the purpose of Soma was not just to escape, but to produce a dreamwalker powerful enough to defeat him one day."

I realize my mouth is open, so I shut it before some space bug flies in.

Maxwell finishes his tube of goo. "They say the way Collywobbles became what he is today was by building a device that locked his brain in a state of perpetual REM sleep. His body was discarded in the process— and therefore, should he die in the dream world, he'd be gone."

Well, that's good to know. "What's the best way to kill him?" I ask eagerly.

"Beheading would do it," Bebe says.

"Except that anyone who's gotten close enough to try that trick has been Overtaken," Maxwell says bitterly.

Right. He's speaking from personal experience. "Then what's the solution? How do you behead him if it's not safe to get close to him?"

"Something to do with that business of Two as One," Maxwell says. "Hopefully."

"Right," I say. "And that brings us back to the original question of Asha."

"I'm almost there," Bebe says. "Early Soma colonists wanted to return home, and that meant defeating Collywobbles. There was a lot of training to that end, and some even married in ways that led to boosting dreamwalker powers in their children. After a while, a group of Soma residents got sick of such an onerous life. They didn't want to deal with the big goal. They felt cooped up by the size of the colony, sick of the bland food and everything else. They decided it was unfair to be born into such a life, and that the rest of the Cogniverse should deal with Collywobbles on their own. As a result, they created a solipsistic dream world for themselves, and they live out their lives in there instead of the real world. Whenever they wake up, a group of illusionists use their powers to make the whole thing seamless for them, and they themselves use memory erasure to forget that the rest of Soma and Collywobbles exist. If they had a motto, it would be 'ignorance is bliss.'"

I scratch my head. "And they're the Escapists? Why would Asha want to live with them?"

"She didn't. We put her there," Bebe says. "The story we wanted everyone to believe was that the two of you were killed. We couldn't maintain that falsehood if she were prancing around Soma."

That makes sense. When I was in Valerian's black window, he told me he hadn't seen her growing up and that she probably was in a part of Soma separated from the rest.

He was right.

I leap to my feet. "Can we go get her now?"

Bebe squeezes the last of her tube into her mouth and stands up as well. "Let's."

She hands the gun to Valerian and leads us out of the cafeteria building. As we walk, she tells us how the ranks of the Escapists have grown recently and warns me about what to do when we reach them, which basically boils down to avoiding mentioning anything unpleasant that could turn a dream into a nightmare.

"Why does the rest of Soma put up with them?" I ask as we get to the forest area.

"They go out of their way to avoid nightmares, so they never get Overtaken," Bebe says. "Basically, they're harmless, so nobody minds their existence."

We walk onto a clearing, and I swallow my next question, too fascinated by what I see.

A large squadron of guards with guns stands around a circular moat dug up in the soil. All their guns are pointed at the very center—where a single gate stands, one that looks just like the ones at the hubs, only lonesome.

I step on a dry branch, and they turn, pointing the guns at me.

"At ease," Bebe says.

"Yes, ma'am," they reply in unison, then turn back and point their guns back at the gate.

"Keep up the good work," Bebe tells them and waves for us to follow her.

As we proceed deeper into the forest, I recall her saying that the Overtaken have come from the Otherlands. Sounds like they arrive to a warm reception. Bebe explains that the guards don't even bother shooting if only one or two Overtaken come through the gate. Since every guard is an illusionist, they work together to make the Overtaken—and their master—see something that isn't there. Something that makes them kill each other.

Eventually, we come out to an area that appears to be a clone of the place we came from—which is now in the sky from this vantage point.

A guard is patrolling nearby.

Bebe points her hand at him, and he falls down, instantly in REM sleep.

Valerian raises an eyebrow.

"Just so they don't ask too many questions," Bebe explains and heads toward a small spherical structure.

When we get there, she plays with some machine, and when I ask what she's doing, she says, "Disabling the cameras. Again, don't feel like answering questions."

How crappy is the security here that she can just turn off cameras willy-nilly? Unless she's a hacker, like Felix?

Bebe leads us farther in until we stop next to a chrome door with controls similar to those for the cameras. I can feel three people in REM sleep inside the room.

Bebe points her hand at the door. There's a thud, and I can feel a fourth person enter REM sleep.

She fiddles with the controls, and the door slides away. We step over a sleeping illusionist that Bebe has knocked out with her powers and walk inside—only to stare at my sister and her family in horror.

Asha, Kojo, and their daughter, Chloe, are hooked up to a web of machines that look like close relatives of the ones that keep Mom alive.

Except this family isn't in a coma. They're just sleeping.

I fight the urge to rip the tubes and cables away from them. "Is this the medical bay?"

Bebe shakes her head. "The equipment is here to feed them and make sure they're hydrated."

The gear hooked up to Asha begins vibrating and jostling her around.

I look at our grandmother.

"That equipment was originally used to stave off muscle degeneration when the colony's artificial gravity wasn't on," she explains. "Without it, they wouldn't be able to function upon return to the real world."

"I hope they have this in the medical bay," I say. "Mom could use it."

"Don't worry, they'll build up her muscles there," Bebe says confidently. "The one positive side effect of dealing with the Escapists is our competence in this area."

I examine my sister with concern. "Do they never, ever wake up?"

Bebe gives me a confused look. "They couldn't have exactly made a baby in the dream world, could they?"

Great. I almost walked into the-birds-and-the-bees talk with my grandmother.

I scan the gear attached to my twin. "Why use the machines then?"

"Prophylactic," she replies. "They take a cocktail of substances to stay in the dream world for as long as they can, so muscle atrophy and nutrient deficiency can become a concern."

"I see. And she agreed to this life?"

"It's better than exile from Soma," Maxwell says softly.

I could argue but opt not to.

"They're there willingly." There's a note of defensiveness in Bebe's voice.

I scratch the back of my head. "What I don't get is how they keep the whole 'ignorance is bliss' attitude while they're awake."

"That was a challenge, but they solved it. In exchange for being able to visit the dream world, Escapist illusionists do their best to make the awake time—what they call Contemplative Domain—go smoother for the dreamwalkers. For example, they make sure no Escapist sees Soma as it really is, with the unusual sky and all."

Right. She's already mentioned something like that. "How do they maintain a dream world that's shared by so many people?" I ask.

"Actually, the dream changes, but there's still coordination involved. It's one of the things they also deal with while awake."

"I'm glad we came while they're asleep," I say. "I'm curious about their world."

Valerian squeezes my shoulder. "Careful, now. I don't want you to like it so much you'd abandon reality."

I laugh. "Even if it's the most utopian heaven imaginable, the machines would be a deal breaker for me. Besides"—I make eye contact with him—"there are things in the real world I wouldn't want to leave behind."

"That's sweet," Bebe says. "Now, is everyone ready to go in?"

We all nod.

She gestures at nearby cots. "Valerian, you should lie down."

Valerian obeys, and she puts him into REM sleep. Then she lies down on the nearby cot and extends her hand toward him. "See you in my dreams."

"I'm going in," my father says, gesturing toward Bebe.

I also make a remote dream connection with my grandmother and dive in.

———

WHEN I SHOW up in my dream palace, Pom is there, waving his furry paw at me.

"You're in for a treat," I say. "We're about to meet my twin."

He flies up to my shoulder, his fur turning a deep golden color. "Let's hurry up."

I get us to the tower of sleepers and turn my head to look into Pom's guileless eyes. "Would you mind staying invisible?"

"Why?"

"I don't know what the Escapists might find unpleasant."

The tips of his ears redden. "You think they might find *me* unpleasant?"

"I doubt it," I say, making him invisible myself. "But they do seem crazy, so who knows."

"I'll be quiet," he says solemnly.

"Thanks."

I locate my grandmother in the tower of sleepers, touch her forehead, and prepare to see the dream world that the Escapists prefer to reality.

CHAPTER EIGHTEEN

WE'RE on the bottom of the ocean.

Bebe, Valerian, and my father are breathing effortlessly, so I let myself inhale the water. Instead of causing pain to my lungs, as it would in the real world, this liquid pleasantly fills me up and leaves a scent of salty ocean surf in my nostrils.

"I guess it's nice to completely forget reality sometimes," I say, and my voice sounds normal despite the liquid around us.

Valerian looks up. "You can say that again."

I follow his gaze, and my breath catches as I take in the view above us.

If this were a real ocean bottom, everything would be pitch black. These depths, however, are lit up like a shallow coral reef on a sunny day.

But the light—and the lack of crushing water pressure—are just the beginnings of the wonders. There's an underwater city here, and it sprawls from horizon to horizon. With its floating castle-like skyscrapers and mind-numbingly large scale, it puts even Gomorrah to shame.

"Welcome to the Water Domain," Bebe says. "It's Asha's favorite."

"There are other domains?" I strain to see above the water.

"So many I've lost count." Bebe raises her arms above her head like a diver and launches up, torpedo-style.

Valerian, my father, and I follow.

Bebe stops her ascent next to one of the largest castle-like buildings and floats there until we catch up.

"This is Asha's home," she says, gesturing for us to get inside.

We end up in a room the size of a large theme park—much larger than the castle was from the outside.

"They're probably in the living room," Bebe says and zooms through the water toward a pair of doors the size of five-story buildings.

She pushes them open, and I'm startled to see that the next room lacks water.

"The Escapists don't bother with realism," Bebe says when she notices me staring at the spot where a wall of water simply stands in defiance of common sense.

Without comment, I step from the watery room into the air of the next one.

Consistent with the lack of realism Bebe mentioned, I'm not wet in the slightest. Nor are the others when they join me.

Apart from being waterless, this room is just as big as the prior one, making it even less likely that it could be inside the castle we entered. Oh, and the views from the floor-to-ceiling windows are those of a desert, not of any kind of watery domain.

There's also another city in the distance, one that looks like a mirage come to life.

"That's the Sand Domain," Bebe explains. "Kojo's favorite."

She takes a leisurely step forward but somehow ends up miles away from us.

I step forward as I would in the real world and end up next to Bebe.

Forget realism. It's actually possible the Escapists go out of their way to defy it.

The next room's windows must look out onto the Snow or Winter Domain, on account of all the frozen wilderness and the city made of ice in the distance. After that, we're back in the Water Domain, swimming in a "room" the size of Manhattan.

"This is the living room," Bebe says two rooms later. The view out of the window here is that of breathtaking volcanoes.

Is this the Seismic Domain? Through several enormous windows, I can see a floating city in the clouds, right in the path of volcanic eruptions that don't seem to harm it one bit.

But not all windows are see-through here.

Some of them are black.

Interesting.

"Bebe," says a child's voice. "You're back!"

My niece appears in front of us not unlike Pom sometimes does. Her adorable curls defy gravity, making the top of her head look like a perfect sphere. On the very top of the hairdo is a tiara with diamonds so big a royal family would kill to possess it, and a few inches above the tiara hovers what looks like a halo, but in the shape of an infinity symbol.

"Hi, honey," Bebe says, smiling at her. "Where's Mommy and Daddy?"

Chloe closes her eyes for a second, then grins as she opens them. "Now they know you're here."

Does she not see the rest of us?

I wave a hand.

No reaction.

"Thank you," Bebe says. "How are things going?"

Still ignoring us, Chloe takes off her tiara and bites into it, gleefully crunching on a large diamond and some of the metal. "I'm studying elliptic geometry."

"And?" Bebe asks.

The missing piece of the tiara grows back, and Chloe puts it back on her head. "On a sphere, the sum of the angles of a triangle is not equal to one hundred and eighty degrees." As she speaks, a large sphere appears in front of us, with a triangle outlined.

"That's right," Bebe says, nodding approvingly. "And, if memory serves, there are no parallel lines."

I scratch my head, and that seems to finally draw my niece's attention.

"Such strange constructs," she says, looking at me and Maxwell. "She looks identical to Mommy, and that man also shares a few of her features. But that last one"—her gaze shifts to Valerian—"doesn't look like her at all. Is it an art project?"

"They're not constructs." Bebe playfully pinches Chloe's cheek. "They're real people."

My niece's amber eyes widen. "Newbies?"

"Even better," Bebe says. "They're guests."

Now we have Chloe's complete and undivided attention, especially me. "Why did you decide to look like Mommy?" she asks, examining me like a bug under a microscope. "Do you admire her that much?"

I give Bebe a questioning look. Is saying "I'm your aunt" considered unpleasant information that we're supposed to avoid in this world? Or is the unpleasant info bit only meant for any non-family Escapists?

Two new people poof into existence between us and the girl.

My pulse leaps.

It's my twin and her husband, Kojo, both also with infinity halos above their heads—must be an Escapist thing.

Smiling at Bebe, Asha looks everyone over curiously, her gaze lingering on me.

"Nice choice of face." Her voice sounds just like mine, only a little uncanny in the way voice recordings are. "What do you really look like?"

Bebe's eyes are misty as she steps forward and clasps my twin's hands. "Asha… I want you to meet your father and twin sister."

CHAPTER NINETEEN

CHLOE'S MOUTH SLACKENS, Kojo's eyes widen, and Asha is blinking so fast her lashes look in danger of falling off.

"Father?" my twin repeats, her gaze darting between me and Maxwell as she twists out of our grandmother's hold. "Sister?"

Bebe solemnly nods.

My throat feels swollen and tight, so I just stand there, taking in Asha's reactions.

A diamond throne appears behind her, and she sags into it.

Kojo steps forward, recovering from shock. "Valerian. Long time no see."

That's right. They were besties.

Valerian claps him on the shoulder, and they embrace while Asha darts a glance at one of the black windows. "Why don't I remember them? Did I lock them away?" You can almost hear the unasked, "And why?"

My throat tightens further. On some level, I was hoping that seeing each other would unlock the memories we seem to be missing, but I guess no such luck.

"I told you about them," Bebe says. "You must've locked those conversations away."

The throne disappears as Asha pushes up to her feet. "I don't understand. How can this be real?"

"I remember Bailey, hon," Kojo says, turning toward her. "And your father. I also told you about them…"

She swallows. "Must've locked that away, too."

Bebe nods at the black windows. "How about you and Kojo unlock all your memories and wake up so we can talk?"

"I guess," Asha says, looking shaken. "Is he a relative too?" She points at Valerian.

Kojo frowns. "You don't recognize him, either? That's Valerian, our friend from childhood. I mention him all the time."

Her jaw firms. "You're right. I've locked too much away."

Bebe and Kojo exchange a knowing look, then Kojo says, "We'll be out in a few."

Clasping his wife's hand, he leads her to one of the black windows, and as they disappear into it, Bebe jolts everyone awake.

———

BACK IN THE REAL WORLD, I wipe sweat from my brow.

Maxwell stands up, looking equally devastated. "That didn't go as I expected."

"What did you expect?" I ask.

Bebe also gets to her feet. "Give them some time. In fact, why don't we wait outside the building?"

I let them herd me out, my mind still spinning from everything that happened.

Once outside, I pace until the door creaks open, and Asha and her family step out. Here, in the real world, she looks a little bit older, her body a little rounder than mine. Stepping up to me, she touches my face, like a blind person.

Not sure what to do with my hands, I touch her face too, my heart thudding with bittersweet pain.

"All I remember is what Kojo and Bebe told me about you," she whispers, staring into my eyes. "They said our mother stole you away. I don't doubt we're sisters, but I still don't remember you and I don't know why."

My mouth feels as dry as the Sand Domain. "I don't remember anything either. All I know about our childhood is what I've seen in other people's memories."

She drops her hands and steps back. "Did we lock it away?"

"Not through a black window," I say quietly. "At least none that I've found."

She faces our father. "They said you were Overtaken."

Maxwell winces. "I beat it. I'm sorry I didn't come back. I made myself forget everything. I now see how much of a mistake that was."

Asha's face looks just like mine does in the mirror when I'm on the verge of a mental breakdown. "What about our mother?" she demands. "Did she beat it? Is she here too?"

"She's on my side of Soma," Bebe says.

For the first time, I realize no one is making Asha and her family think Soma doesn't exist, and they're okay with it.

"You know about the real world?" I ask my sister.

Bebe stands up straighter. "Asha and her family aren't your typical Escapists."

"We let ourselves recall Soma and the rest of it when we're awake," Asha says. Looking at her daughter, she sternly adds, "And we tell no one about it, understood?"

"Yes, Mommy." Chloe winds a curl around her little finger. "I've never told anyone anything and never will."

"That's a good girl." Asha looks back at me. "Why didn't our mother come with you?"

"She couldn't." I dampen my lips. "She's in a coma."

Asha's eyes widen.

"How about we explain more on the way to the medical bay?" Bebe says.

No one objects, and we head in the direction of the nearby forest.

"Valerian, can you make Asha and her family invisible to the guards?" Bebe asks. "Still don't want those questions."

Valerian—who's been talking in hushed tones with Kojo—nods and presumably does as Bebe asks.

Maxwell chats up Chloe while Asha and I fall back a little.

"Tell me about your life," we say in unison.

After a chuckle, we say, still in unison, "You first."

I stay silent this time, but she does as well.

We both laugh.

"You're a guest here," Asha says, finally breaking the strange synchronicity. "I'll go first."

I listen greedily as she tells me about her life as far back as she can recall.

She and our grandmother lived in an apartment on the Escapists' side of Soma. In the beginning, my sister would visit their dream world without the use of drugs and machines—mainly to kill the time as she waited for our grandmother to come back from her business on the other side of Soma.

At some point, Kojo started visiting. Our grandmother arranged it so that he was one of the few people on Soma who didn't believe Asha dead. With time, she and Kojo found the Escapists' world a fun getaway and spent more and more time there, eventually using all the methods to extend the stay, just like the rest of the Escapists.

When they were old enough, they got married, and sometime later, their love gave them Chloe—who Asha thinks is the brightest and cutest being in the universe.

"That sounds like a charmed life," I say. "Like a perpetual honeymoon."

Asha agrees but reiterates the difference between her family and "normal" Escapists. She and Kojo don't permanently forget everything about their pre-Escapist lives; they do it selectively, and only when asleep. Also, they visit the other side of Soma on occasion, with the help of a Bebe-approved illusionist who makes them invisible.

"I'm really sorry I knew nothing about you when we met in the dream world," she says. "I locked away the memories of our grandmother telling me about you and our parents because it's just too painful to know you have family you can't remember."

"I don't blame you," I say. "If I knew how to create black windows, I'd probably lock away a thing or two."

She stops and gives me an incredulous look. "You don't know how to lock away memories?"

"I probably don't know a lot of basic dreamwalking techniques," I say and launch into my own story—one that starts with our mother not teaching me anything about dreamwalking or speaking about the past.

Since Asha does seem able to handle "unpleasantness," I don't sugarcoat anything. I explain how Mom thought she'd killed Asha, so she locked away those memories. I go over my theory as well: that on some level, though Mom couldn't recall why, she'd feared I'd dreamwalk in her and stumble onto this horrible secret.

Asha grimaces. "Our poor mom. If I thought I'd killed Chloe, I'd end myself right then and there."

"She couldn't," I say. "She had me. Well, she couldn't until I was old enough." Chest tightening, I explain about Mom's suicide attempt and my inadvertent role in it.

We pass by the moat-ringed gate and the squadron of guards protecting it in a heavy silence. Meanwhile, the conversation between

Valerian and Kojo grows more boisterous, and I overhear Chloe grilling Maxwell with endless random questions.

"Tell me more," Asha urges, so I do. I tell her about the good memories with our mother on Gomorrah and about my efforts to keep her alive and undo the damage done by the car accident.

"What about him?" Asha asks in the middle of my story about Necronia. She nods in Maxwell's direction. "You didn't mention our father at all."

"Right. That's a whole other thing. We met only a few days ago, but it wasn't until earlier today that I realized who he is." That leads into yet another complicated story, which I do my best to cover as we step out of the forest and walk toward the structure we visited earlier.

"Bebe did mention something about a prophecy," she says when I finish telling her about why we came to Soma. "It just never made sense to me. You and I are supposed to defeat Phobetor?"

"Call him Collywobbles, but yes."

"How?"

"I don't know. That's just the prophecy. I'm not sure how I feel about it. I don't think of myself as a hero. Do you?"

She chuckles and shakes her head. "Hardly. So you have no idea what Two as One means?"

"In our father's memories, he and Mom talked about something we did as kids that sounded like it. The hope was that you'd remember what it was."

She frowns. "I have no clue."

"Me neither," I say.

Bebe holds the door for us, and we begin to navigate the corridors to the medical bay.

Asha lets everyone go ahead again and falls into step next to me. "You know," she says quietly, "my whole life I've felt like a piece of me was missing."

A bittersweet ache pierces my chest. "Me too."

"Could the act of our reuniting be Two as One?" she asks hopefully. "Is there any way we can consult the seer about it?"

"He foretold that Valerian and I would never see him again. So unless he talks to us via proxy, I don't see that happening."

We enter a room covered to the brim with medical equipment. Must be the medical bay. And indeed, I spot Mom here. She's out of her portable bed and hooked up the way Asha and her family were.

Asha walks over to peer at Mom's face, her expression so full of longing it gives me a knot in my throat.

Chloe tugs on Bebe's shirt. "That's your daughter who's my grandmother?"

Eyes puffy, Bebe nods.

"And she's asleep but not dreaming?" my niece presses.

"Something like that," Bebe says thickly. She looks at Asha. "Can *you* push her into REM sleep?"

My sister lays a hand on Mom's arm and closes her eyes, visibly concentrating.

"She's one of the best dreamwalkers on Soma," Bebe whispers into my ear. "Living with the Escapists has allowed her to hone her skills to perfection."

Asha opens her eyes. She looks beyond disappointed. "It didn't work. Should I risk going in like this?"

"No," Bebe, Maxwell, and Kojo say at the same time.

She rounds on them, eyes narrowing. "Then what do we do?"

"You and Bailey need to prepare," Bebe says. "Work together to figure out what Two as One could be."

Asha scoffs. "Prepare to defeat Collywobbles? You don't ask for much, do you?"

I put a hand on her shoulder. "How about we start by filling in gaps in my dreamwalking techniques?"

A faint smile touches my sister's lips. "All right."

"I'll help," Maxwell says.

"And me," Bebe says.

"I'll take all the help I can get," I say. "When do you want to start?"

"Now." Asha lies down on a nearby cot. "I go first."

Nodding approvingly, Bebe puts her into REM sleep, while I get comfortable on a nearby cot.

"See you later," I tell everyone and eagerly jump into my sister's dreams.

CHAPTER TWENTY

AS SOON AS I show up in my dream palace, I make my hair fiery, grab Pom, and teleport to the tower of sleepers.

"She looks just like you," Pom says, flitting around as I lean over my sister.

"Want to come meet her?" I ask.

He turns purple and nods so vigorously I worry he might hurt his neck.

Smiling, I take his paw in my left hand and touch Asha's wrist.

———

I STARE AROUND IN CONFUSION.

Instead of Asha's dreams, I'm back in my dream palace lobby.

Or not.

The colors differ, my collection of impossible shapes isn't here, but the basic layout is the same.

Also, Asha is here, gaping at Pom, who's hovering over me.

"Where are we?" I ask her.

"I call this my dream castle," she says proudly. "Now what the heck is that?" She points at Pom.

I hastily explain about Pom and then say, "Your castle looks just like my palace."

"Your what?"

"The place I appear when I first go into the dream world of another person," I say. "It's also where I go when I realize I'm dreaming myself."

She blinks. "It's the same for me. I realized I was dreaming, remembered why, and waited for you here."

I take a closer look at my surroundings.

Colors and shapes aside, every tile and every piece of marble is the same as in my dream palace. Up in the ceiling is the exact same mosaic depicting an archery-target-like mandala made out of multicolored glass.

The main difference is that she calls hers a castle.

"We must've designed this together as children." I stroke Pom's fur as he lands on my shoulder. "Before the memory loss."

She hesitantly approaches and touches Pom's ear. "It has to be that."

"Does yours also have a tower of sleepers?" Pom asks, his huge lavender eyes glued to my sister. "And a memory gallery?"

I explain what those are, and Asha grins widely, then takes us to a clone of my tower of sleepers, only larger.

"That's a lot of connections," I say, examining the never-ending floors. "And they're all asleep right now."

"Those are my fellow Escapists," she says.

Ah, right. She woke up ahead of schedule.

I take her to my tower of sleepers, and she can't believe how alike they are, size aside.

I show her my memory gallery next, and she takes us to her version.

The paintings are obviously different, as are the memories they replay, but the layout of the room itself is the same. Ditto for the style of the frames and the floors.

"Can I experience some of your memories?" Asha asks shyly.

My pulse speeds up. "Can I see yours?"

She nods excitedly, and we spend a while sharing our best memories. I get to experience some truly amazing things—like giving birth and nursing a baby—as well as countless precious moments with Bebe.

"Thank you," Asha says after she's done with the last memory in my gallery, the one where I broke a vase that later turned out to have prints of both Asha's and my hands. "I feel like I just got to know our mother."

I pet Pom's furry feet. "And seeing your memories made me feel like all those things had happened to me."

Grinning, she makes her hair fiery to match mine. "Seems like being twins, our experiences are that much more compatible. Kojo and I experimented with this a bit, and when I saw some events from his point of view, it was jarring."

"I'm not surprised," Pom chimes in, his fur turning golden. "You have the same mannerisms, and the way you talk is the same. Even little things like your smiles are—"

"We're monozygotic twins," I say. "We have the same exact genes, and we lived together for the first few years of our lives. I'm surprised we're not finishing—"

"Each other's sentences," Asha says with a wide grin.

Pom rolls his eyes with a melodramatic sigh. "Even what passes for your sense of humor is similar."

I grab him by the feet and tickle his chin until he apologizes.

"He reminds me of Chloe," Asha says with a grin.

"Oh yeah?" Ears turning a light shade of orange, Pom escapes from my clutches and lands at her feet. "Can I meet her?"

"She'd love that," Asha says, grinning down at him. "But business first."

"Right," I say. "You're supposed to be teaching me something I don't know."

She nods. "How about you tell me what you can already do?"

I start by explaining how I use my powers for therapy, and how I take jobs pulling out memories from people. I then tell her about my fight with the Nutcracker and what I've learned more recently—including how to unlock black windows, duplicate myself, enter dreams from a distance, and push people into REM sleep.

"That's pretty solid." Asha makes the room around us match her enormous living room in the Escapist world. "I think we'd better start with the more difficult tricks and work our way down."

"Like what?" I ask.

"Voila." She shrinks until she's the size of Pom. "Have you ever played with perspective like this?"

Pom and I just gape at her diminutive form.

"I'm ashamed to admit this idea has never occurred to me," I say. "Not even after reading *Alice in Wonderland*."

Asha gives me a confused look and in a high-pitched voice asks, "Who's Alice?"

"Oh, just a book on this primitive world I frequently go to," I say. "Don't worry about it."

"Ah, okay," she says. "I wouldn't beat yourself up for not trying this particular idea. It's not very practical, especially given how you've been using your power. Besides, if you did try, you'd find it harder than it seems. Chloe hasn't been able to master it, and even Kojo is terrible at it."

Really? She's right in that it doesn't seem that hard, in theory.

Asha grows back to her normal size—and keeps growing until she's a giant.

I look up enviously and will myself to grow as well.

Nothing happens.

Asha shrinks to her normal size. "To do this, you have to picture yourself made out of molecules."

Closing my eyes, I do as she says, visualizing myself as made from molecules of water, oxygen, DNA, hemoglobin, ATP, digestive enzymes, cholesterol, and as many other things as I can recall from my chemistry and biology classes. My fear of germs works to my advantage here. There have been times when I've pictured getting attacked by bacteria and viruses in a mental exercise that's quite similar to this.

"Now grow the molecules as you would a random object," she instructs.

Hmm, okay. The number of cells in the body is something like thirty trillion, and each cell can contain up to two trillion molecules. That makes the total number of my molecules something unfathomable, like a septillion.

I will those septillions to grow.

When I open my eyes, I'm the same size.

I repeat the exercise, but it doesn't work on the second try either. Or third.

"Use your emotions to your advantage," Asha says.

Pom turns light orange. "Emotions help with dreamwalking?"

"Of course." Asha shrinks to his size, then goes back to normal. "There's a strong connection between dreams and emotions in general."

Of course. I can't believe I haven't figured this out on my own. It makes so much sense. "You're right. I did some of my best dreamwalking when I was fighting the Nutcracker, and I was teeming with emotions that time. Well, one specific one: fear."

Asha smiles mischievously, and we appear in a new room, one that looks like the largest dojo in the history of martial arts. "Let's leverage your fear."

Before I can say anything, a throwing star pierces my shoulder.

"Hey, that hurts!"

With a speed almost too fast to perceive, Asha manifests another throwing star in her hand and launches it at me again.

I dodge, then materialize a hundred-pound jar of coconut pudding above my sister's head and let it fall.

She neutralizes my delicious attack and makes a sword telekinetically jump into her hand from the nearby displays.

Pom watches us, his fur pitch black. But hey, at least he hasn't disappeared on me this time.

Asha leaps at me, sword raised.

With a move we practiced for the subdream battles, Pom jumps onto my wrist and becomes a furry katana—just in time for me to parry Asha's thrust.

She delivers a flurry of attacks.

My breathing speeds up.

"Are you scared yet?" she asks.

"A little."

She stops and grows to the size of a giant, sword and all.

"Grow if you want to live," she booms and slashes down with her sword.

CHAPTER TWENTY-ONE

RATIONALLY, I know Asha must be bluffing. Yet I'm afraid. Very afraid. I think it's a combination of the adrenaline coursing through my system from the fight and the lizard part of my brain reacting to a being that large swinging a sword at me.

A horrific thought flits through my mind. What if she doesn't know I'll go insane if she kills me? Could that knowledge be something she'd locked away and didn't recover today?

Okay, if fear was the desired goal, I've got plenty of it now. Maybe too much.

Channeling it as well as I can, I will my molecules to grow.

There's a moment of vertigo, then I find myself blocking Asha's sword with my Pom katana.

We're the same size.

I look at the room around us. Yep. Everything else is tiny.

Suddenly and without my willful participation, I shrink back to my usual size.

Asha does as well, then changes the dojo to the previous living room and evaporates her sword. "I'm so proud of you. Few people manage to do this on their first day."

Pom separates from my wrist and lands on my shoulder. "You grew me too," he says excitedly. "That was awesome."

I wipe sweat from my forehead and jump out of my body to heal my shoulder. "You're a part of me, so that was a freebie," I tell Pom when I return. I look sheepishly at Asha. "Despite all that fear, I couldn't stay big for even two seconds."

My sister manifests a throne for each of us and plops into hers. "Part of the reason staying big is so tricky is that it's not rooted in everyday experience. On top of that, when you're big or small, you have to keep worrying about proportions at all times—which is a lot of complicated math. Don't worry, though. Over the coming days and weeks, we'll have you practice holding size variations."

I sit down on my throne. "Will you need to nearly kill me each time?"

She shrugs. "What other emotions do you want to leverage?"

"I don't know. But you do know actually killing me would be bad, right?"

"Of course," she says. "You weren't in any danger. I'm just that good of a dreamwalker."

"Modest too." I grin at her. "Can the great dreamwalker master teach the lowly student something else?"

She rubs the diamonds in the armrests of her throne. "Have you ever tried pushing people into REM sleep from inside the dream world? Or across large distances?"

Pom flies onto my lap, lavender eyes wide. "You can do that?"

"Yep," Asha says. "I can put anyone on Soma to sleep from here."

"How?" I ask.

She shrugs. "Just focus on the person in question and do what you would do from nearby."

"Wow," I say. "Can I try?"

She grins. "Do it to Bebe. That shouldn't be too challenging. She's in the same room with us, just in the waking world."

Rubbing my hands together, I close my eyes and picture my grandmother in enough detail to create a dream construct. But instead of making a fake Bebe, I will the real one to go into REM sleep.

Did that work?

"You girls miss me already?" Bebe's voice says.

I open my eyes.

Score. My grandmother is here. I can't believe this worked on the very first try. And it's even better than I expected—instead of appearing in my dream palace, Bebe is right here.

She shifts her appearance to that of her younger self. "I assume you bothered me because you figured out how to be Two as One?"

Asha and I exchange guilty glances.

"They didn't really talk about that," Pom says.

"Traitor," I mutter.

Asha jumps off her throne. "How about we work on that now?"

"I'm game. What do we do?"

"I have no idea." Asha quirks an eyebrow. "Bebe, do you have suggestions?"

"I think you should start with the most direct understanding of Two as One," Bebe says.

"And that is?" Asha asks.

"Become a single being," Bebe replies.

We gape at her.

"Can that even be done?" Asha asks.

Bebe shrugs. "Your parents tried it."

"And?" I ask.

She closes her eyes, and a second later, Maxwell joins us.

"Tell them how you and Lia tried to become a single being in the dream world," Bebe orders.

Maxwell frowns. "It never worked. We'd just get punishingly tired after each attempt."

"What fun," Asha says. "Can't wait to experience that."

"Where we failed, you two may succeed," Maxwell says. "After all, at one point in time, you were the same being—a single fertilized egg."

"That was before we could dream," Asha says.

"Exactly," I chime in. "Let's not forget how that egg split into two separate embryos, and how those embryos eventually ended up living pretty different lives. Even if this is something we did as kids, there's no reason to think it will still work."

"Well, I'm curious to see how it goes," Bebe says.

Asha approaches me. "What do you think?"

"For Mom, I'll try anything. Even if it seems kind of weird."

"And creepy," she says. "But let's try it."

"How?" I ask.

"Let's do that same molecule trick from earlier, but tell yours to mix with mine."

"You should hug as you do it," Pom suggests.

Shrugging, I hug her—which feels nice and soothing.

I close my eyes and do my best to imagine us becoming a single person. I visualize the molecules intermixing as Asha suggested, a task made easier by the fact that our DNA is the same.

Nothing happens. That is, until I feel really woozy.

Asha's arms are no longer around me, and someone audibly gasps.

I open my eyes—or maybe our eyes.

Nope.

Asha is still separate from me. She's just stepped away and is dry-heaving.

I also feel sick but hold myself together better.

"Did it work?" I ask Maxwell and Bebe when the worst of the nausea passes. "Did we merge even for a moment?"

"No," he says.

"Not even a little bit," she says.

"Don't do that again." Pom's fur is a dingy yellow. "It made me sick."

Asha inhales a deep breath and lets it out slowly. "There's no way we did that successfully as children."

A wave of exhaustion hits me. To make sure I don't fall on my butt, I make a lounge chair and plop into it. Before Asha's knees buckle, I make a chair appear under her as well.

"Thanks." She sinks into it and looks at Maxwell. "When you said it would be punishingly tiring, you weren't kidding."

"Sounds like that will be the end of training for today," Bebe says. "Bailey should rest."

"I agree." Maxwell looks at me worriedly. "You've had a crazy day."

I chuckle humorlessly. "Oh, I've been merely saved from a deadly virus just in time to fight hordes of the Overtaken. I call that Tuesday."

"I've arranged a room for you," Bebe says. "You should go and rest."

"I will," I say. "But could you two teach me something else first? Something quick and easy?"

Bebe gives Maxwell an expectant look.

"How about we start with some theory?" he asks.

I shrug.

"As you probably know, keeping track of details is one of the hardest parts of dreamwalking," he says. "You're building worlds in your mind, so your ability to remember details is one of the limiting factors."

"She's just played with growing big and small," Asha chimes in. "So we've touched on what you're talking about."

"Good," Maxwell says. "So here's a practical tip: You can find ways to make it easier on your mind while you expand your power."

I eye him in confusion. "Are you talking about mnemonics?"

"Something even more natural," Maxwell says. "Being social beings, we're already very good when it comes to our memories of other people."

"Right. And?"

He waves a hand, and we find ourselves in a valley where a crowd of people stands. "One way for you to use a lot of your power yet not overtax your mind is to utilize dream characters of people you know to help you."

I scan the crowd and whistle. "If I'd used something like this on the Nutcracker, I would've beaten him that much quicker."

"There you go," Maxwell says. "Keep in mind the constructs can be friends, enemies, or even fictional characters—so long as you can imagine them being real and therefore give them a dream life that would feel almost independent from you."

Asha nods approvingly. "This isn't something I've experimented with, but I will now."

I consider what Maxwell is saying. I've used dream characters as dream lovers and in other ways to entertain myself, but I've never thought about weaponizing them.

But why not?

With barely any effort at all, I manifest as many people as I can, starting with those closest to me—like Valerian, Felix, Ariel, Itzel, and Kit.

As soon as they appear, they begin to talk among themselves as dream characters often do.

Maxwell is right. I don't feel any drain on my attention.

Okay, let's push this. Since they don't even have to be among the living, I manifest Fabian, Edith, and Stanislav.

They appear and join the conversation with Felix and Ariel.

Seeing them makes me a little sad, but I busy myself with adding some of my patients and favorite celebrities to my growing army.

It works just as well as with friends. Each new person greets the others, and they gleefully join forces.

This could be fun.

I begin to manifest fictional characters from different media on both Gomorrah and Earth. Soon, the likes of Joygasm Troglodyte, Dracula, Robin Hood, Frankenstein, Zorro, and Tarzan join the fray, followed by whichever other heroes and villains come to mind.

Next, I throw in gods of different mythologies into the mix, like Thor, Athena, and Morrigan.

Last but not least, I add my favorite video game characters.

"Good," my father says. "Let's see if you feel any strain on your resources as the battle ensues."

Before I can ask what battle, his crowd of characters roars a war cry and rushes at mine.

I watch the clash yet feel no more tired than I already am—which is, granted, pretty tired.

In mere seconds, his army slaughters mine.

I look at the dead and vow to practice this skill a lot more... but after some rest.

"Your turn," I tell Bebe. "I think I have energy to learn one more thing today. Maybe."

She smiles impishly. "Have you ever jolted more than one person awake?"

"You mean at the same time?" I ask.

She nods.

"No, I've never tried that. I usually only dreamwalk in one person at a time."

"Well, it can be useful," Bebe says. "Why don't you see if you can manage it with all three of us?"

"All right. But don't resist me. I don't think I can handle all three if you do."

"I bet you can, but I'm game to save it for more advanced lessons," Bebe says. "Now less talking and more jolting."

Taking in a calming breath, I try it.

They're still here.

Is fatigue an emotion? I think it is—so I channel it into my task as Asha suggested.

Boom.

My family is gone.

I jolted them awake.

Bursting with pride, I wake myself up as well.

CHAPTER TWENTY-TWO

I COME to my senses in the waking world.

"Hey," I say, opening my eyes. "I feel much less tired here. Usually, the reverse is true."

"You don't typically attempt to become a single entity with anyone in the waking world." Asha steals a glance at Valerian and winks at me. "Not outside of the bedroom, that is."

I nearly choke.

Valerian grins wickedly, and I hope he isn't comparing our sense of humor, the way Pom did.

"How did it go?" he asks me.

I can't help but smile. "I learned a lot. Can't wait for the next lesson."

"Which will be tomorrow," Bebe says with mock sternness.

"At the soonest," Valerian says, and he seems to mean it.

"Yes, bosses," I say.

A guard walks in, salutes Bebe, and hands her a bundle.

"It's clothes for the three of you." She distributes the bundle into three piles and gives each to Valerian, Maxwell, and me.

I pick up my bundle. The outfit is the same as everyone else's on Soma —silvery and plain.

"Let me show you your rooms," Bebe says and walks out of the medical bay.

Maxwell, Asha, and I happen to glance at Mom at the same exact time, and as our eyes meet above her, our expressions are equally grim.

The machines are exercising her muscles—which looks disturbing, at least to me.

"We'll get her out." I make the words sound like an oath.

They nod, and we follow Bebe.

Maxwell's room is at the beginning of the next corridor, Asha and her family's is across the tower from him, and Valerian and I get the two rooms next to them.

Bebe accompanies me to explain how to use the shower. She then assures me the bedsheets are sterile and self-cleaning, due to a technology that sounds a lot like hygieia.

"Thank you," I say earnestly.

Her eyes gleam with wetness. "It still feels like a dream to have you back here."

"I feel the same." I have a sudden urge to kiss her papery cheek, but the thought of germs stops me. "See you soon."

She leaves, and I test out the shower. Then, feeling nice and clean, I put on my new clothes and step out of the bathroom.

Valerian is waiting for me in the middle of my room. Like me, he looks freshly showered and is wearing the Soma outfit Bebe provided us.

My heartbeat picks up pace, and I suddenly feel warm all over. The silvery material clings to every muscle on his tall, broad-shouldered frame, highlighting the perfection that is his body. And his face... Puck, that face of his is enough to make a girl lose her mind—especially given the dark heat in those ocean-blue eyes.

I fight to get my breathing under control as I close the distance between us. "To what do I owe this pleasure?"

His sensuous mouth quirks. "There was talk of a date.... unless you're too tired."

My pulse spikes further. Holy puck, it's happening. Finally happening. I dampen my lips. "Remember what I said. I don't want any illusions."

His eyes are glued to my mouth. "Not even for a more romantic setting?"

Gathering my courage, I take off my top and toss it on a nearby chair. "I meant you. I want your body and my reactions to it to be real, but you can do what you want with our surroundings."

His gaze roams over my exposed flesh, all but scorching it with its intensity. "And you're sure you can handle this?"

I bite my lip, trying to keep my mind off all the viruses and bacteria we'll be exchanging. "I think so. But just in case, you can also hide bodily fluids from my sight." And blood, should there be any, with this being my first time and all.

"You got it." Eyes gleaming, he takes his own shirt off.

Oh. My. Estrogen. I've seen him naked before, but knowing this is real, and that I can do what I want to him, makes me feel like my body is going into total meltdown.

I may not be a traditional virgin, having had all kinds of sex in the dream world, but the real thing is brand-new to me, and it's hotter than anything my imagination has conjured up so far.

I channel my dream world self, the one that's completely in control. "Take it all off," I order huskily, and show him what I mean by removing what remains of my clothing.

He obligingly strips, a sexy smirk playing on his lips as he pushes his pants down.

My breath catches in my throat, and Pom's fur turns a deep coral pink on my wrist.

He really *is* gorgeous—all parts of him. Surging forward, I rise on tiptoes just as Valerian dips his head, and we lock lips.

This kiss is better than all the prior ones combined. A tingling electricity spreads through my body, and my knees begin to buckle. His strong hands catch me before I can fall, and in an eyeblink, we're on the bed.

Wow.

He nibbles on my neck. The room around us goes away, replaced with the most majestic nebula in the Cogniverse—and we're flying through it at lightspeed without a spacecraft.

He moves his attention to my clavicle. Double wow. My pulse breaks the sound barrier.

Slowly, torturously, he explores every part of my body until his tongue finds what it must've been searching for.

A thousand wows.

I gasp.

His tongue works relentlessly—until pleasure explodes in my core, and I arch my back.

A star goes supernova in the nebula around us.

His tongue retraces its route back to my neck, and after another nibble, he lifts his head to gaze down at me. "You okay?"

"Continue," I whisper. "Please."

His pupils dilate, and he proceeds, very gently. There's a moment of pain, but soon, it's a distant memory. Instead, a pleasure spreads through me that puts anything I've experienced before—even the high from vampire blood—to shame.

Bigger and more colorful supernovas erupt in the nebula around us, like fireworks, each one coinciding with my orgasms.

He tenses and then relaxes in my arms to one final supernova explosion, and I hug him tight, though my muscles feel like jelly.

"You should rest," he murmurs, brushing the hair off my forehead, and I nod, smiling up at him.

We turn, getting into a spooning position, and he wraps his arms around me, holding me like he'll never let me go as I close my eyes contentedly and fall into the deepest sleep of my life.

CHAPTER TWENTY-THREE

I WAKE up to the realization that I slept and didn't have a single dream.

Then I remember what had happened just before I fell asleep, and my heart rate picks up. We finally did what I've been yearning for from the moment I met Valerian. But what now? What does it mean? Are we—

My stomach loudly grumbles, and I realize I'm so famished I'd probably risk Earth street food.

Valerian is still spooning me, so I gently wriggle out from under his heavy arm and tiptoe into the bathroom. After a shower, I sneak back into the room and put on my clothes.

Valerian opens one eye. "You heading somewhere?"

"Hungry," I say, something warm and soft filling my chest at the sight of him lying there, all sleep-mussed and sexy.

Yawning, he gets up also and begins to dress.

As I watch, my hunger for food transforms into a different kind of craving, but before I can act on it, Valerian finishes dressing and says, "Let's go. I'm also famished."

Oh, well. Hopefully we can get right back to it after we eat.

We locate the cafeteria from earlier, and Valerian figures out how to use the dispensing machine to get two silver cubes and a clear container with water. We take a seat at a table, turn the cubes into trays, and I squirt the food from a tube into my mouth without bothering to ask him to make it palatable. After I chase the paste with a few gulps of water, I finally feel like myself again—and questions from earlier resurface.

"Can we talk?" I ask, heat filling my face.

He puts down his tube, a wicked gleam appearing in his eyes. "What's on your mind?"

I reach deep for my courage. "It's about what happened. I just wanted to—"

A loud sound pierces the air, startling the puck out of me.

"Is that you?" I ask Valerian.

Frowning, he shakes his head.

Maxwell rushes into the cafeteria, white as a ghost. "Come with me, now."

He runs out, and we chase him into a room with a wall covered by a floor-to-ceiling screen. With the exception of Mom and my niece, my whole family is here—all staring at the currently blank screen with grim expressions.

"Did something happen to Chloe?" I ask, my mouth going dry.

"We took her to the daycare in this building," Asha says. "She's fine... for now."

Well, that's ominous. So much for going right back to bed activities.

Bebe fiddles with some controls. "I'll show it to you from the beginning."

The screen comes to life, displaying a feed from a drone that seems to be hovering above the entry gate to Soma.

A person steps out of the gate.

It's a large male elf with the fiery eyes of the Overtaken.

CHAPTER TWENTY-FOUR

A TALL GUARD at the gate sends an arc of illusionist energy at the newcomer. The elf looks around in confusion, then dives head first into a nearby moat, breaking his neck in the process.

Before I can let out a relieved breath, another Overtaken steps out of the gate.

And another.

This time, two guards shoot them with illusionist mojo, and the Overtaken start savagely fighting each other.

Another Overtaken emerges from the gate.

And one more. Then two at the same time. And three.

Most of the newcomers are wearing nightwear, and some are armed with things you'd find around a kitchen—tools they cleave and chop each other with, covering the ground with gore.

When there are more of them than there are illusionist guards, the guards raise their guns and begin shooting.

Another dozen Overtaken leap out of the gate and kick their fallen comrades into the moat.

The guards shoot them too.

More Overtaken emerge.

The guards keep on shooting.

One of the Overtaken hurls a colander at the guards before she gets gunned down.

The moat is beginning to fill up with bodies.

The stream of the Overtaken intensifies to the point where they seem to show up faster than the guards can shoot them. The moat is completely filled up now, and one of the newly arrived Overtaken takes advantage of this and lunges at the closest guard with a knife.

The guard shoots the attacker, but it's too late.

The knife is in his throat.

In my periphery, Bebe grimaces, muttering a name.

Seeing one of their own killed seems to bolster the rest of the guards. With grim efficiency, they gun down the Overtaken killer and his comrades.

But more Overtaken take the place of the fallen ones, and another round of slaughter ensues. Then another.

Bebe rubs the back of her neck. "Do you understand now?"

"The Overtaken came for me," I say, my voice catching in my throat.

"They came for all of us," Bebe says darkly. "I'm going to fast-forward so we can see what's happening right now."

She fiddles with controls, and the video of the battle speeds up until all I can make out are waves after waves of Overtaken arriving and getting shot down. When the recording resumes playing at normal speed, it's to show the guards putting down yet another score of attackers.

Except the gun of one of the guards doesn't fire when it should—costing him his life.

"Chigi." Bebe's face is a mask of horror. "He'd just joined the guards. What am I going to tell his mother?"

"Why did his gun not shoot?" I ask over a lump in my throat.

"Ran out of charge." Bebe pushes back her white curls. "I was afraid of that."

A man limps into the room.

We all give a start. Given what's happening on the screen, we half-expected him to be one of the Overtaken.

But no. This man's eyes aren't fiery. They do look familiar, though.

"Here are the weapons you requested," the newcomer says and dumps a heap of guns that look just like the ones the guards carry. There are also strange non-shiny swords that clank more like ceramics than metal, and a bunch of wicked-looking machetes.

"Thanks, Idi," Bebe says as I figure out whose eyes Idi's remind me of: Kojo's.

Now that I think about it, they share other features as well.

As if to confirm my theory, the newcomer faces my sister's husband. "Hi, son. Good to see you awake."

Kojo solemnly nods. "I wish we were meeting under better circumstances."

Idi limps over to the only chair in the room and sits with a wince—something is clearly wrong with one of his legs.

On the screen, another guard's gun loses charge, then another.

"We need to do something. Let's take those"—I gesture at the heap of weapons—"and get over there."

Valerian steps in front of me. "It would make more sense to dispatch additional guards."

Bebe rounds on him. "You think that wasn't the very first thing I did?"

She did? That almost makes it sound like she's in c—

A large green figure steps out of the gate on the screen, and my heart rate doubles as I realize it's an orc with fiery eyes. A big specimen that looks like he's been caught in a blast of gamma radiation and now no one likes him when he's angry.

The surviving guards react admirably.

Raising their guns as one, they shoot the orc.

Yes!

Except nothing happens.

Asha gapes at the screen. "Maybe the guns aren't designed for something that big?"

Whatever the reason, the orc rushes the guards, breaking through them like a linebacker from hell as Bebe gasps in horror.

All the nearby Overtaken use the opportunity to leap at the knocked-down guards.

Four people die.

Bebe looks on the verge of weeping as she recites each of their names under her breath.

A new group of guards emerges from the forest, each armed with two guns and either swords or machetes. They begin to fire at the Overtaken, and once they're done with them, they help their surviving comrades to their feet.

The guards then form a wider perimeter around the gate and gun down the next wave of the Overtaken.

Bebe manipulates the controls again, and a smaller square appears on the screen, showing the Escapist side of Soma—with a green figure of the orc running through it.

"Someone put me under." Kojo lies down on the floor. "If the Escapists don't wake up, he'll kill them."

Asha immediately gestures at him, and I feel him entering REM sleep.

Meanwhile, another orc—a smaller specimen—rushes out of the gate with a bunch of elves, gnomes, and a couple of ubers. The guns don't work on this orc either, but four of the guards attack him with their swords and machetes.

A few bloody slashes later, the orc is dead—and I exhale a breath I didn't realize I was holding.

Meanwhile, the guns of the other guards work just fine on the elves, gnomes, and ubers.

On the smaller screen, the big orc runs at a nearby building, but a guard steps into his path, shooting in desperation.

It's as futile as before.

"Use your illusionist powers," Valerian mutters at the screen. "He's alone."

The guard must realize the same thing. An arc of energy hits the orc on the head, halting him in his tracks.

The orc looks around in confusion. Then, seemingly recovering, he runs right into the nearby wall, bloodying his forehead.

He does this over and over, until he drops to the floor.

I guess that's the silver lining of the fact that the Overtaken feel no pain. They can clobber themselves like that.

Meanwhile, on the larger section of the screen, another big orc jumps out of the gate. Then another. When there are four of them, they rush the guards.

Two orcs get chopped into pieces with the swords, but two make it through.

Again, they run for the Escapist side of Soma, where the guard who just defeated their big cousin bravely faces them.

Jaw clenched tight, he shoots them with his mojo.

Nothing happens.

"His powers won't work against the two," Valerian says despairingly.

Realizing the same thing, the guard flings his useless gun at the nearest orc's head.

It doesn't slow his onslaught in the least.

Grabbing the guard by his throat, the orc squeezes his green fingers.

"Fight, Jahi!" Bebe yells, her eyes glued to the small screen.

But Jahi's kicks make no impact on his bulky attacker, and he slumps into a dead heap at the orcs' feet.

Jumping over Jahi's body, the orcs run into the building, and an ashen Bebe turns the controls again, switching the camera view to the inside.

Huge eyes shining like flames, the orcs break into the first apartment.

There's a family inside—a mother, father, and two children—hooked up to the machines the way my twin was.

I want to look away, but something forces me to keep on watching.

At my side, Asha is weeping quietly, her hand covering her mouth.

One by one, the orcs choke the parents, then the children.

"Put me under," Asha says frantically, stretching out on the floor. "I need to see what's taking Kojo so long."

I move to do it, but Maxwell gets to her first, swiftly sending her into REM sleep.

On the bigger screen, the guards put down two more waves of the Overtaken.

Bebe rounds on Idi. "We need to warn my people. The guards may not be able to contain this."

He nods tersely as I stare at my grandmother. "Bebe, are you Soma's leader?"

She gives me a distracted glance. "I'm the Elder. Idi here is my second-in-command."

Aha. That's why she was able to override security cameras willy-nilly. But there's no time to dwell on it because a group of naked Overtaken exit the gate on the screen.

In a flash, they turn into wolves and leap at the guards.

Idi thrusts a microphone-like device into Bebe's hands.

Her spine turns ramrod straight as she lifts the device to her mouth. "Citizens of Soma." Her voice booms out of the ceiling in the room—and presumably everywhere. "We are under attack."

I stop paying attention to her as the fight on the screen escalates.

Though the guns do work on the werewolves, the canine Overtaken are just too fast. In an eyeblink, ten guards are ripped into shreds.

At the sight of the massacre, tears stream down Bebe's face, but her voice doesn't waver as she explains the situation to the rest of Soma.

The remaining guards on the screen finally contain the werewolves, but at a cost. Their perimeter is noticeably sparser.

"—Soma shall prevail," I catch Bebe saying before she hands the microphone back to Idi.

Asha suddenly sits up, cursing—and Kojo jackknifes to his feet, talking over her.

"Speak one at a time," Bebe orders. "What happened?"

Kojo moderates his tone. "They refused to believe us. They won't wake up."

"More like won't face reality," Asha says, jumping to her feet. "Even to save their lives."

Bebe looks like she's aged another couple of years during that exchange. "So be it. The guards will do the best they can for them."

As if to illustrate, two guards armed with swords attack the orcs on the smaller screen.

Kojo and Asha stare at the larger screen with despair and fury.

One of the Overtaken that's not an orc remains standing when a guard shoots him. Two more guards aim at him, but also fail to bring him down.

A female guard dives out of the perimeter, slashing her sword at the stubborn invader. The blade enters the Overtaken's shoulder—but comes out on the other side as if he were made of vapor.

"A chort," I say, watching in horror. "They can phase."

The female guard must realize this too, because she retreats. Only it's too late. The chort kills her with a single touch, then grabs her sword and tosses it to the next person who steps out of the gate.

I gawk at the newcomer.

Those symmetrical masculine features and strong dark eyebrows are unmistakable.

It's Rattie—the person who was secretly the Nutcracker, a dreamwalker I vanquished in the dream world and thus made homicidally insane.

Right now, his eyes are filled with fire, which means that instead of his damaged mind, he's being controlled by Phobetor's no less dangerous intelligence.

Valerian narrows his eyes at the screen. "So this is where he went. I hope the guards get him."

The guards do not. They're too busy with the chort.

Asha curses again as a giant jumps out of the gate.

At first, I think it's Colton, but no. This one is female, and she's at least two heads taller.

The guards not too busy with the chort shoot at her. Just like with the orcs, the guns don't seem to work due to the female giant's size. With steps that shake the forest around them, she lumbers toward the guards nearest her.

Rattie hangs back, as do all the regular-sized Overtaken as they stream in through the gate.

Before the giant gets to her destination, the guards in her way drop their guns and ready their swords. She smashes into them without any attempt at self-preservation. Ignoring the sword a brave guard sticks into her left thigh, she grabs him and uses him like a club to bash the others.

A couple of swings later, a dozen guards are on the ground.

Rattie and a small army of the Overtaken must've been waiting for just this opening. Without bothering to finish off the downed guards, they vault over them and launch into a sprint.

When I realize which way they're headed, ice fills my stomach.

They're running to our side of Soma.

CHAPTER TWENTY-FIVE

"WHAT DO WE DO?" Idi gasps out.

"Make a stand." Bebe rushes to the nearby table and takes out small earplug-like devices.

Idi limps over to the weapon pile, but Bebe grabs his shoulder. "We need someone to stay back and update us on the developing situation."

She thrusts an earpiece into Asha's hand, and my sister shoves it into her ear, then grabs a gun and a sword.

Kojo frowns at the weapons in his wife's hands. "Why don't you stay with Idi?"

There's a ferocious gleam in Asha's eyes. "My child is in this building. The only way the Overtaken are getting in is over my dead body."

Mine too.

I snatch up an earpiece for myself, then stride over to the weapon pile and pick up a gun and a sword.

Valerian grabs my wrist. "I want you to stay with Idi."

I twist out of his hold. "I'm going to protect my family."

He stares at me for a tense second, then sighs. "I had to try."

He takes up weapons of his own, and Bebe, Maxwell, and Kojo do the same.

With grim determination, we sprint out of the building.

Once outside, I discover we're not the only ones who've gotten this idea. A group of armed people are already here, as well as more teams by the entrances of the other buildings nearby.

Bebe's rousing speech must be the cause.

"We need to form a tactical formation," Bebe says and orders us to stand like a firing squad, backs to the building and guns pointed at the edge of the forest.

I end up on the rightmost end of the line, with Bebe on my left, Asha on her left, then Valerian, then Kojo, then Maxwell, then people whose names I don't know.

A second later, a pair of elves dash out of the forest—a male and a female, both dressed in sleepwear, as most Overtaken are.

"Illusions!" Bebe shouts.

Valerian and one of the other defenders shoot the Overtaken with arcs of energy.

The elves freeze. Then the female attacks the male, tearing out his hair. He smashes a fist at her face, shattering her nose. She gouges out his left eye—which is when another pair of Overtaken appear out of the forest.

An uber and a dwarf.

"We don't have four illusionists," Bebe shouts. "Fire on my command!"

The elves stop fighting. Now that the Overtaken outnumber the illusionists, Phobetor can't be fooled.

The four race at us, the gravely injured elves oblivious to pain.

When they're fifteen feet away, Bebe hollers for us to fire.

I shoot the rightmost Overtaken—the dwarf.

He collapses, tripping one of the wounded elves in the process.

I shoot the downed elf as my allies take care of the rest.

"The giant is finally dead," Idi's voice says triumphantly in my ear. "Oh, wait, now there's an orc."

"Give us tactically critical information only," Bebe barks into her earpiece. "Can't afford to be distracted."

"Understood," Idi replies.

Another group of Overtaken—all naked—streak out of the forest, so we gun them down. An even larger group barrels out next, but we destroy them too. This pattern repeats until my trigger finger is cramping from all the squeezing.

A pair of dwarves fly out of the forest like birds.

I resist the temptation to rub my eyes.

It soon becomes clear that they're not actually flying. More like hovering ten feet off the ground. Under them is another motley crew of Overtaken.

They all charge at us.

"There's a telekinetic in that group." Idi's voice is somber. "He's caused chaos back at the gate and is now causing the dwarves to float."

Not just float. Whoever the telekinetic is, he catapults the dwarves at us.

I fire upward—as does everyone else.

A lifeless dwarf whooshes over my head and smashes into the ground. Another one slams into one of the men in the middle of our formation, knocking him off his feet.

"Fire!" Bebe yells.

My finger spasms over the trigger. The others shoot as well. Five Overtaken collapse, but clearly not the telekinetic—who must be the one launching the limp bodies of our enemies toward us.

I sidestep, and an elf crashes into the wall behind me.

To my left, Bebe ducks to avoid a dwarf. So do Asha, Kojo, and Maxwell.

I shoot at the Overtaken again—dropping an uber.

There's a sudden telekinetic jerk on my gun.

Oh, puck. I grip the handle as if our lives depend on it, since they do. The force of the next pull drags me forward, my feet skidding on the grass.

Nope. I'm not giving up my gun.

The handle begins to jerk up and down, lifting me off the ground, then smashing me back down.

I dig into the grass with my heels and hold on for dear life. I'd shoot too, but aiming in this situation is impossible. I could hit myself or my allies.

"Use your sword!" Bebe shouts. "We can't allow them to get that gun."

Puck, she's right.

Unclenching my fingers, I slice with the ceramic sword. There's a screech as the cleaved-in-half gun careens toward the Overtaken.

Pivoting, I dash back to rejoin my squad, but the telekinetic has already moved on to the next victim.

Maxwell gets dragged forward by his gun. He copies my earlier maneuver by slashing his gun in two before he lets the telekinetic have it.

If this keeps up, we'll be defenseless.

Kojo is pulled out of the ranks next, but by his sword instead of his gun. He releases the hilt, and the weapon whooshes over the heads of the Overtaken and disappears into the forest.

Well, at least the telekinetic didn't take it.

Valerian aims carefully at someone behind me and pulls the trigger.

The others do the same. Reaching my spot in the formation, I spin around to see what they've accomplished.

All the Overtaken are now down. The telekinetic shouldn't be bothering us anymore.

I feel a spurt of hope, but in the next moment, Rattie steps out of the forest, a sword in each hand.

Unbelievable. How did I manage to forget about him?

The situation quickly worsens. Hundreds more attackers follow Rattie, and instead of running for us right away, as the others have done, they stay near the forest, gathering forces.

"Shoot!" Bebe orders.

Everyone on our squad fires, but they only get a couple of Overtaken at this distance.

As the enemies gather, I miss my gun more and more. I'm also increasingly concerned about the guns running out of charge.

The Overtaken assemble for a few more seconds, oblivious to the loss of the ones we've taken out. Then, as one, they begin their assault in a massive horde.

Our makeshift troops fire, over and over. The Overtaken fall, but their comrades simply vault over their bodies and keep on coming.

And it's bad.

Halfway to us, a whopping ninety percent of the Overtaken are still in the running.

When they're forty feet away, our guns make a bigger impact, but there are still at least two dozen Overtaken barreling toward us, with Rattie in the lead. His eyes darts between me and Asha before finally settling on me.

Everyone fires desperately.

They miss Rattie and a few others, who are almost upon us.

"Prepare for close-quarters combat!" Bebe shouts needlessly.

I grip my sword handle until my knuckles whiten.

When he's about ten feet away, Rattie shouts, "Die!" and hurls one of his swords at me.

There's a blur of movement.

No.

Not this.

I gape at Bebe.

The sword meant for me is protruding from her stomach.

CHAPTER TWENTY-SIX

WHEEZING, my grandmother slumps.

Though she's clutching the grievous wound with both hands, it doesn't stop the gushing of her blood.

My heartbeat pounds deafeningly in my ears. Through the haze of shock and fear, I realize two things.

First, Bebe jumped in the path of the flying sword to save my life.

Second, and more importantly, Rattie is almost here, so unless I act this very instant, Bebe's sacrifice will have been for naught.

Shaking off the haze, I leap over Bebe, putting myself between her and Rattie. Out of the corner of my eye, I see the Overtaken reach the rest of my family and allies. In the span of an eyeblink, Valerian beheads an elf, and Kojo shoots an uber.

Rattie lunges at me with the sword.

I dodge, but his blade nicks my upper arm. The pain is sharp and stinging, but I recover quickly and parry his next hit.

He slashes at me again.

I block instinctively, and sparks fly where our two ceramic-like blades clash.

We end up in a lock with the swords crisscrossed in a horizontal position.

I push against the clinch to try to knock him off balance.

He doesn't budge.

When he does the same to me, I somehow manage to stand firm, feet rooted to the ground. Even with him being waif thin, as a guy, he has the advantage of strength, but I have desperation on my side.

Still, with me bleeding, I won't last long and he knows it.

I give him my best death glare. It's probably my overactive imagination, but I feel like I see Phobetor's face deep in those fiery depths. A sadistic part of me I didn't realize existed wants to reach into those eyes and choke the god of nightmares with my bare hands for hurting Bebe.

Rattie pushes with renewed force, an ugly expression contorting his handsome features.

I push back, matching his strength.

"Tick-tock," he sneers. "Your grandmother is bleeding out, like a stuck mooft. And so are you."

I'm so angry I feel like my own eyes might burst into flames.

Baring my teeth like an animal, I growl, "If she dies, I will hunt you down to the ends of the dream world. God or not, I will end you." Leveraging my fury, I strain my quivering triceps to shove again with my sword—and at the same time, I kick his shin, hard.

Though there's no sign of pain on his face, he does lose his balance for a second—which is all I need to open a deep cut in his shoulder.

Is that concern in those fiery eyes? Can't be. Phobetor doesn't care about losing this one body.

His next thrust is at my neck.

I parry, then hack and slash at him viciously, eager to draw more blood.

He counters every slice.

I block his strikes as well, but my muscles are growing tired, and the loss of blood is making me woozy.

Rattie's shoulder wound is bleeding too, but I doubt it'll mess with his concentration.

He lunges at me again, leaving a gash in my side.

Puck.

I need to win and soon.

Somehow.

The next round of attacks is brutal, but I'm beginning to notice something.

There's a pattern to Phobetor's movements.

A pattern I can exploit.

I block and dodge the next couple of strikes and wait for my moment. If I'm right, there will be an opening soon.

There. I stab his thigh as he prepares for the thrust part of his pattern.

Again, there's no sign of pain on his face, but there's more anger there. More importantly, his footwork is now compromised, so I must've done some real damage.

Is he going to continue the pattern? It might be all he knows.

And he does keep going in the same vein. Except when I exploit it again, I miss his neck and only nick his ear.

Puck.

His eyes narrow and the fire disappears from them, replaced by madness.

Double puck.

Without Phobetor's control, Rattie has reverted to what he's become after I killed him in the dream world—a homicidal maniac.

I attack, hoping I catch him off guard.

Nope.

He blocks, and with an animalistic roar, he swings the sword wildly. I barely dodge the attack, and the onslaught that follows. In theory, Rattie is vulnerable to illusion powers once more, but I don't dare distract Valerian for that. Instead, I attempt to push my opponent into REM sleep, figuring that will bring Phobetor back in the worst case, or make Rattie sleep in the best case.

It doesn't work. Either he's in a strange dream-like state already, or I have too much adrenaline to work my powers.

Doing my best to ignore the weakness and cold brought about by the blood loss, I attack him, then defend myself as I study his repertoire of movements.

Aha. Rattie's attacks begin to remind me of the time I fought him in his Nutcracker guise in the dream world, but remixed through insanity. Going on a hunch, I raise the sword above my head and slice down with all my strength.

He blocks just in time, and a flash of sparks later, we're in a carbon copy of our prior crisscrossed sword lock. Except this time, things are different. Insane or not, he's more able to feel pain than Phobetor—so I smash my knee into his groin.

Rattie screams like a wounded boar.

I shove harder, and his own sword slices his face.

His eyes widen, and fire returns to them—but too late.

I pierce his chest, my blade penetrating breastbone and entering his heart.

CHAPTER TWENTY-SEVEN

RATTIE'S BODY COLLAPSES, eyes lifeless.

Panting, I whirl around and scan the rest of the battlefield.

An Overtaken has his hands wrapped around Asha's throat. My sister's eyes are wild with panic, but she's struggling valiantly.

I dash over there and chop off the enemy's hands at the wrists. Freed, Asha gasps for air and shoots the crippled Overtaken in the head at the same time.

Then we join forces and help Valerian with the uber he's been fighting.

Next, we look over to where Maxwell and Kojo are fighting a werewolf in animal form. Both dreamwalkers have gashes from claws and teeth, and are bleeding profusely.

Asha and Valerian shoot the werewolf in the head at the same exact time.

The beast collapses.

We help everyone else next, dispatching the rest of the Overtaken one by one.

"Bebe," I pant when the last of the enemies is no more.

Tossing our weapons aside, Asha and I rush over to her and kneel on either side.

Her face ashen, Bebe lies in a pool of blood. Her breath is shallow, coming out in pained gurgles.

"I couldn't allow you to be killed," she chokes out, her gray eyes glued to my face.

"Hush," I whisper raggedly. "Save your strength."

"Take her to the medical bay," Valerian says urgently, coming to kneel at my side. "Kojo, Maxwell, and Asha can help you make sure she isn't jostled. Once she's safe, you all should patch yourselves up as well."

I throw a frantic glance at the forest. "What if there's another attack?"

As if to confirm my fears, an Overtaken elf steps out, then an uber.

"We'll handle them," Valerian says and tosses Asha's gun to a dreamwalker who needs it. "Go."

With a heavy heart, I work with the others to carefully lift Bebe.

As we step into the building, her breaths grow more labored, and her gaze struggles to focus on Asha and me.

We hurry as gently as we can, leaving a trail of Bebe's blood behind us.

Midway to the medical bay, the sound of her strained breaths stops.

Ice coats my chest, and my throat feels like it's being squeezed in a brutal fist. "Please hang on," I whisper to my grandmother. "Please, please, just hang on."

The rest of the way is a blur.

Once inside the sterile room of the bay, we lay Bebe's frail body on a gurney.

A woman wearing all white dashes over. "I'm the doctor on duty," she says quickly, already feeling for my grandmother's pulse.

Her face goes carefully blank, and she does several more checks as I watch, Pom's fur the dullest gray it's ever been.

I know what she's about to tell us before she turns to face us, pain and regret gleaming in her eyes. Even so, I need her to spell it out because a part of me refuses to believe it. Doesn't want to believe it.

"I'm sorry." The doctor's voice wavers. "She's gone. The sword went straight through—"

I don't hear the rest.

My knees give out, and I sink to the floor. On the other side of the gurney, Asha does the same, her face—a mirror image of mine—a mask of anguish.

I can't process this, can't deal with the grief that feels like a giant sitting on my chest. Numbly, I watch as Kojo crouches next to Asha and gathers her into his embrace.

She starts to cry.

I wish I could as well, but I barely knew my grandmother—and that's what hurts the most. It's all the years we didn't get to spend together, all the hugs that were never given, all the wisdom I'll never learn from her.

The doctor shakes off her own grief and begins applying first aid to everyone as Maxwell approaches me uncertainly.

"Bailey," he says hoarsely. "Are you okay?"

I nod. What else can I say? Everyone here has way more reason to be grieving than I do.

I've never felt more like an outsider in my life than I do in this moment, surrounded by family I don't remember and don't really know.

Eyes somber, my father squeezes my shoulder, and I draw in a steadying breath, shoving down that hollow, choking feeling. "Valerian," I say thickly. "He's out there. We have to help him."

With his life on the line and Soma on the brink of destruction, I can't just sit and wallow.

Maxwell frowns. "You're injured. He can—"

Idi clears his throat in the earpiece, reminding me the device is still in my ear. "An Overtaken necromancer has just arrived at the gate. He's resurrecting the fallen on both sides. I'm sending the rest of the guards down there. It's our only chance."

The faces of everyone around me reflect the same despair I'm feeling.

A necromancer is bad news. Horrific news.

I need to do something. *We* need to do something. But what?

"I'm going to take her to the morgue," the doctor says somberly, and starts wheeling the gurney out.

No one stops her, though a part of me wants to.

"This is all my fault." The words escape my mouth as if of their own accord. "Phobetor is after me. If I'd stayed away from Soma, Bebe would still be alive."

Asha stops crying and gives me an incredulous look. "Two as One, remember?" she says with a hiccup. "He wants me just as much as he wants you."

Maxwell nods grimly. "Asha's right. This attack was carefully planned. He wouldn't have had time to set it up *after* we arrived. If anything, your presence saved some lives."

I shake my head, my throat tight again. "It was me she jumped to protect."

"And I'm sure she'd do it all over again, as would I," Maxwell says. "And it wasn't because of the damned prophecy. She loved you and couldn't let you die."

The prophecy. How could I have forgotten about that?

A true hero destined to destroy an evil wouldn't have forgotten. If we needed more proof that I'm not it, here it is.

Puck that.

My spine straightens, a burst of anger chasing away the hollow grief and guilt.

I don't care if the prophecy is about me, or if it's even true.

Things are much simpler now.

Bebe is dead, and I made Phobetor a promise about this exact outcome —and as the god of nightmares is my witness, I will keep my promise.

I will either destroy him or die trying.

The pressure in my throat eases a smidge, and a dark smile crosses my lips, even as the scope of what I plan to undertake sends tendrils of fear throughout my body.

I catch my sister's gaze.

They say twins can read each other's minds—and I feel it in this moment.

I know she's arrived at a conclusion similar to mine.

I leap to my feet. "There's a way to save everyone on Soma. A way that doesn't require the use of swords and guns. Not real ones, anyway."

Asha also jumps to her feet, the determined expression on her face mirroring mine. "Yes. We take the fight to Phobetor."

"We kill him in the dream world," we say in unison.

CHAPTER TWENTY-EIGHT

MAXWELL DRAWS BACK, staring at us in disbelief. "You're not ready. You need months of training first. If—"

"We don't have a choice." I begin to pace. "A necromancer is a formidable foe, and who knows what other surprises await us in the real world."

Kojo catches my sister's wrist. "You haven't figured out the Two as One technique."

"We'll just have to do without it," Asha says. "Our parents didn't have a technique, and they took him on."

"And got Overtaken." Maxwell darts a glance at Mom's comatose body. "You need to do better than we did."

I stop. "We *are* doing this. From here on out, we only talk logistics."

Maxwell opens his mouth, then closes it, a defeated expression stealing over his face. "We need allies. Dreamwalkers and illusionists ideally, but any Cognizant could help—especially if they have powers."

"Why?" Asha asks. "If it's the dream world…"

Maxwell winces. "Phobetor always has an army of creatures with him." He looks at me. "Subdream monsters, you call them."

That makes sense, and my father's idea of bringing in allies could help face such an army. Someone comfortable with their powers can use them in the dream world as a form of lucid dreaming. A dreamwalker would be able to annul their powers, of course, but I don't think subdream creatures would have that power.

The best part is, those who aren't dreamwalkers have one huge advantage in a fight like this: If they get killed, they'll simply wake up, as if from a nightmare.

The doctor comes back in, but we ignore her.

Kojo doesn't look happy as he says, "Let me speak with the Escapists again. Maybe they'll—"

"It's worth a shot," Asha says. "But first, I have a question. How do we actually find Phobetor in the dream world?"

"Me." Maxwell's eyes gleam. "I'm always fighting him off. If I give up that fight, you'll face him. When your mother and I—"

"Hold on." Kojo looks at Maxwell as if he's grown a set of antlers. "Won't you become one of the Overtaken in the process?"

Maxwell's expression is pained. "I should be tied down. In fact, all of us should be. Just in case…"

Asha turns to the doctor and explains the part of the conversation the woman missed. Then she asks, "Do you have something we can use to restrain ourselves?"

"The Overtaken aren't a new problem," the doctor says and sprints over to a cabinet. She returns with thick, bandage-like ropes that she attaches to special grooves in the four nearby gurneys.

She then gestures for us to lie down.

Reluctantly, I stretch out on a gurney, and the others do the same.

"Ready?" the doctor asks.

Half-hearted agreements all around.

She restrains us.

No one brings up an obvious point. If an Overtaken—even a weak one—gets past Valerian and the others, we're toast.

"Now," Maxwell says, pulling me out of my dark thoughts. "I'll put Asha under, and she'll bring the rest of us in from the inside."

"I'm ready," Asha says.

I can feel her go into REM sleep, followed by Maxwell and Kojo.

How will it feel when she drags me in like that? Maybe like anesthesia or—

———

I FIND myself standing on a gelatinous surface inside a canyon of chocolate mountains, with the sky above reminiscent of cotton candy.

Is this another Escapist Domain? Maybe Food or Dessert?

My family are already here, so I don't waste time asking about the environment.

"A good place to gather all the forces," Maxwell says, gesturing at the delicious landscape.

As if summoned by those words, Pom appears in the middle of our gathering, his fur a light shade of orange. "What's going on?" He looks at Kojo curiously. "Who's that?"

Speaking fast, I explain that introductions will have to wait for later because we're in a life-and-death situation and about to face the god of nightmares himself.

As I speak, Pom's fur turns darker and his ears take on a beet hue. "That sounds beyond scary."

I pet the top of his head. "We can do this without you. In fact, it might make it easier for me if I don't have to worry about you getting hurt."

He shakes his head, his ears turning teal. "I want to help."

"Fair enough. How about I'll mentally call for you if I need you? That way, you can gather your courage in the meanwhile."

Pom turns a dark purple and gives me a military salute with his paw. "You got it." He performs his best Cheshire Cat disappearance.

"I'm off to recruit the Escapists," Kojo says and disappears as well, without fanfare in his case.

"What about me?" Asha asks. "I don't really know anyone that Kojo doesn't."

"Remember the dream constructs from my earlier lesson?" our father asks.

Asha's eyes brighten. "I did want to experiment with that."

A unicorn with humanoid arms appears in the distance and shouts something to Asha.

"A character from the Escapist myths," she explains. "Let me make more."

Different people and creatures begin to show up, along with a version of Kojo that looks more noble and buff than the real thing.

"We'll do this too," Maxwell says to me. "But after we bring in the real people, since they need to be briefed."

I nod, already thinking along the same lines. "This is where your status as an ambassador between worlds could pay off. You must've gotten to know many powerful Cognizant."

Asha quirks an eyebrow, and I explain how Icelus used Rattie to coordinate between worlds, and how Maxwell was chosen to do something similar for the good guys.

"The problem is that I don't know those powerful Cognizant too well," Maxwell says. "I hope I'm convincing enough to get them to join our dream battle."

"I believe in you," I say.

"Thanks." He smiles and disappears.

"Later," I tell Asha and take myself to my tower of sleepers.

Looking around, I debate my first choice of an ally.

A lot of the people from New York are asleep right now. It must be nighttime in that part of Earth. Sadly, some Earth Cognizant with the best powers—like Nina, Kit, Colton, and Chester—are Overtaken and therefore not available.

On the bright side, Ariel is here, and so are Rowan and most of the rest of the New York Council—people who are presumably grateful to me for finding a murderer in their midst.

I decide to start with Rowan, figuring it would be fitting to get help from a necromancer in the dream battle while another necromancer threatens us in the real world.

The question is whether Rowan will be able to use her power here.

Only one way to find out.

I jump into Rowan's dreams.

—————

ROWAN IS SITTING in front of a glass-covered display with a variety of spiders, flies, and other creepy-crawlers inside. Lifting the glass, she starts pinning a cockroach into an empty slot.

Gross. Those things live in garbage and spread all the worst germs of Earth. I wouldn't touch one even in the dream world.

Pointedly clearing my throat, I wave to get Rowan's attention.

She drops both the pin and the cockroach and rubs her eyes—without first sanitizing her hands.

Wrinkling my nose, I make the critters disappear. "I didn't realize you were an entomologist. Unless this is a creepy hobby?"

"Sleeping beauty," Rowan exclaims, grinning. "Am I dreaming you, or are you dreaming me?"

I return her smile. "How would you be conscious of yourself if I were dreaming you?"

She shrugs. "Your awesome power?"

"I'm actually in a rush," I say and rattle out what I want and why.

Her eyes grow ever wider as I go on.

"So," I say in conclusion. "Will you help us?"

"I guess," she says. "Especially if you can tell me how I'm supposed to use necromancy in my dreams."

I create zombies for her, specifically her macabre entourage from Necronia, masks and all. The zombies begin to move around in strange patterns, and Rowan grins at this like only a necromancer would.

"It works just like if I were awake," she explains. "So cool. I've already grown to miss this."

Miss it? She must not be allowed to use her powers on Earth. I want to ask her, but there's no time. The fates of Valerian and all of Soma are on the line.

"Let me take you to our meeting place," I say. "Once there, do your best to summon even more corpses. My sister can help you with it."

"Your sister?" she and her zombies ask at the same time.

Instead of answering, I take us to the yummy-looking canyon and quickly introduce her to Asha.

"This is another way you can help us," I tell my twin as I examine the thousands of dream constructs she's already manifested. "How about I bring people here, and you explain what's what to them?"

She grins mischievously. "I could even pretend to be you to make it quicker."

"Suit yourself," I say and return to the tower of sleepers.

After a second of deliberation, I decide to dreamwalk in Ariel next.

I find her dreaming about chopping off vampire heads with her gate sword. I watch for a second, worried that without my supervision, she'll succumb to the temptation to drink vampire blood.

Nope. She ignores the blood completely. This must be about violence, which, though a little disturbing, is still healthier than the addictive alternative.

Revealing my presence to her, I deliver her to my sister for explanations.

The next person I recruit is Vickie, the siren from the New York Council.

"What about Felix?" Ariel asks when she sees me show up with the siren. "I think he'd want to help."

"I didn't see him sleeping," I say.

Ariel chuckles. "He had his girlfriend over. I bet there's a pillow fight going on right this moment."

"You can put your friend into REM sleep from here," Asha says. "Remember what I taught you?"

"He's on another world," I say. "There's no way I—"

"You can," Asha says. "Use your emotions."

My emotions are still in such turmoil I don't know which one I should utilize. Settling on fear, I close my eyes and picture Felix in every detail, from his unibrow to his thin, lanky frame.

"Here goes," I mutter and will Felix into REM sleep.

"What the hell?" Felix's voice is panicked. "Where am I?"

I open my eyes and grin at him. "I drew you into the dream world with my mighty powers."

He looks at our surroundings, then at some of the fantastical constructs Asha created, then at her face. "Either I'm crazy, or this is a dream."

"Or both," Ariel says with a grin.

Felix suddenly blushes like a maiden. "What happened to my body in the real world?"

"It's asleep," I reply.

Even his ears redden now. "Any chance you can jolt me awake so I can explain this to my date? Afterward, you can bring me right back."

I nod toward Asha. "My sister will help you. She'll also explain what we're doing and help you recreate your robot suit."

Without waiting for anyone to object, I return to the tower of sleepers and dreamwalk in another member of the New York Council. Then another—until I get them all in the chocolate canyon, practicing their powers.

From there, I start pulling in people more indiscriminately, even going as far as asking some of my patients to help out.

On a hunch, I leap into the dreams of Napoleon, the lutin who's my Gomorran underworld connection. He helped us during the Icelus investigation.

As often happens in his dreams, instead of looking like the little red devil that's his awake form, he's in the guise of a short man wearing a bicorne. And like the last time I was in his dreams, he's walking on a beach on an island called Elba.

"You're in luck," I say without preamble. "You get to help with a battle that might put the best of Earth military history to shame."

Battles are a fetish of his, so much so he forced me to recreate them in his dreams as a form of payment.

Napoleon's deep-set gray-blue eyes gleam with avarice, and I take him to our scrumptious place of gathering.

He whistles when he spots all the people already here.

"Is this all of your army?" he asks with his signature French accent.

"Only the start of it," I say. "More is coming." Hopefully.

"Who's the foe?" he asks.

"My sister will explain," I say and introduce them.

"Wait, this is Napoleon?" Ariel asks when she overhears the introduction. "Isn't he supposed to be smaller and redder?"

Felix—who has on his robot suit—lifts his face plate. "More importantly, why has Mr. Nain Rouge made himself look like *the* Napoleon?"

"I am *the* Napoleon," the lutin says. "Now tell me about the opposing army. *Hâte*."

I leave Asha to explain everything, and go on to recruit whoever I can.

When I get back, Maxwell and Kojo are still off recruiting, so I work on my own army of dream constructs, starting with versions of some of the people already here, including Felix and Ariel. Next, I manifest Valerian, hoping the entire time the real one is okay. Itzel is constructed next; with her being a gnome, I couldn't push her into REM sleep.

After this, I create dream versions of our Necronia travel companions, both the ones who are currently Overtaken—like Kit, Colton, Nina, and Chester—and the departed, a.k.a. Fabian, Edith, and Stanislav.

That team joins the conversation with Dream Felix and Dream Ariel, and I work on the copies of my patients and celebrities, starting with Joygasm Troglodyte, Dracula, Robin Hood, Frankenstein, Zorro, and Tarzan. I continue until every comic book hero and god I know is present, ending with Zeus.

"Hey now, where's Batman?" Ariel demands. "How could you skip the best hero in the history of fiction?"

"Forget him, he has no powers. Where is Neo?" Felix asks indignantly. "Dream world is close enough to the Matrix that—"

"It has to be a character I'm familiar with," I reply.

"Batman is the best," Ariel says.

"No, Neo is," Felix retorts.

I open my mouth to shut them up when Maxwell shows up with an army larger than mine and Asha's combined. He must've gathered his team elsewhere and teleported them all at once—a feat I'll have to attempt someday.

"Maybe it's for the best that we're challenging Phobetor after all," he says. "The situation all around the Cogniverse is dire. The Overtaken are attacking people at random now. Trillions are dying. Countless

Cognizant fail to wake up from nightmares. On some worlds, even humans are—"

Kojo suddenly appears, and with him, yet another army.

All the Escapists have the infinity halos above their heads like Asha's family did when I first met them, and some of their faces are identical to Asha's dream constructs, which makes sense since she's lived in that community most of her life.

"You came," Asha exclaims, looking at them excitedly. "Thank you."

"Your husband is persistent," says an Escapist woman with noble features.

"That he is," my sister confirms with a smile.

"What now?" I ask Maxwell.

He averts his gaze. "I'll make it so that Phobetor and his minions appear."

I frown. "What about the part where you sacrifice yourself to our enemy?"

"It will be temporary," Maxwell says. "Once you win, I'll be myself again."

"If," Felix mutters, and Ariel gives him a glare.

"We'll make sure that we do." I pat Felix's robot suit on the back. "Now let's delve into the nitty-gritty of our strategy."

CHAPTER TWENTY-NINE

EVERYONE'S MOOD seems to lift, so I must've said the right thing. Napoleon jauntily strides over, as do Asha, Kojo, Ariel, Felix, Rowan, the Council members from the different worlds, and a few leaders from the Escapist horde.

Maxwell gestures at a nearby chocolate mountain, and it melts away, replaced by a football-field-sized structure that looks like the biggest snow globe in history. Inside it is the familiar subdream sky that looks to be made from magma, with black water below it.

"Here is his army—at least as much of it as we experienced before he took us over," Maxwell says and populates the subdream simulation with millions of monsters. Some are those I've encountered, but many are new to me, though just as horrific.

"The cavalry," Napoleon says, nodding at the army of warthog-spider mounts and their tentacled naked mole rat riders. "And that's air support." He points at the cloud of skeletal turkey vultures and other flying abominations that fill the air between the sky and the ocean. "Lots of infantry." He gestures at the various beasts, among which I recognize the monstrous versions of tardigrades, spiral worms, ants, nail-sword critters, and anglers.

"All formidable," Maxwell says grimly. "Yet all of them combined don't come close to the threat that is Phobetor." He makes the dreaded figure appear behind the troops as everyone stares in horror. "If a dreamwalker gets beyond this point"—he draws a line halfway through the battlefield—

"they risk becoming one of the Overtaken. From there, the closer to Phobetor, the higher the risk."

Napoleon scratches his chin. "What are the capabilities of our troops?"

Maxwell points at the dream constructs. "They're the weakest—merely extensions of the dreamwalker who created them."

"Cannon fodder." Napoleon's eyes narrow. "Can you make more?"

In answer, countless more dream constructs show up, all a lot like Asha's, which means it's the work of the Escapists.

"What about me and the other dreamers?" Napoleon asks. "What are our capabilities?"

Asha tears her gaze away from Phobetor and faces Napoleon. "Unless you're familiar with lucid dreaming techniques, your powers will roughly match those you have in the real world."

"That's if you don't get on Phobetor's radar," Maxwell says. "If you do, you'll die instantly—or be turned into an Overtaken, depending on his whim. Either way, you'll be out of the battle."

"You will wake up, though, if you die," Asha chimes in before anyone panics. "Like from a nightmare."

"Exactly," Maxwell says. "Death here means rude awakening for anyone who isn't a dreamwalker. But for us, it's insanity—assuming we don't turn into the Overtaken. Understand?"

Everyone solemnly nods.

"What about those?" Napoleon wrinkles his nose at Rowan's masked zombies.

"Part of my power," Rowan says. "I'm a necromancer."

"Zombies." Napoleon examines Rowan with keen interest. "Even better cannon fodder. Can we bolster their numbers too?"

The zombie army grows exponentially in an eyeblink.

Wow. Escapists are very good at this dreamwalking business. I'm glad they're on our side.

Napoleon clears his throat. "I propose the following high-level plan: Break their ranks with cannon fodder, then hit their infantry with ours, while some portion of our dreamwalkers take care of their cavalry. The rest of the dreamwalkers take to the air."

"What about him?" Felix thrusts a metal finger in Phobetor's direction.

"He expects the sisters to attack him, right?" Napoleon asks.

"Yep," I say. "Did Asha tell you about the prophecy?"

"She did," he replies. "Can you teleport over to the target?"

"That doesn't work on the battlefield," Maxwell says. "It's possible to teleport away, but then when you teleport back, it would be to the farthest edge of the field."

"So it's a lot like a normal battle," Napoleon muses. "In that case, given that he's expecting you, the last thing we want is for you to approach him head on."

"But if we don't, we can't win," Asha says, and I can tell she almost adds, "Assuming there's any way we *can* win."

"As dreamwalkers, you can change your appearances, can't you?" Napoleon asks. "For what I have in mind, I'd want the sisters not to look like themselves. Two other dreamwalkers will pretend to be them."

Asha and Kojo exchange a glance, and she morphs into him while he turns into her.

I make myself look like Valerian, and in his voice say, "We need one more me."

The Escapist woman with noble features morphs into another Asha—which is the same thing as me.

"Make your hair fiery," I say and demonstrate.

A second later, she's a dead ringer for me.

"Excellent." Napoleon gleefully rubs his small hands together. "The two decoy twins will openly go for the big target by air, while the camouflaged ones can travel on foot—as it should be easier to get lost in the sea of infantry."

"The twins shouldn't use their powers either," Asha—who's really Kojo—says. "If Phobetor doesn't realize you're dreamwalkers, the camouflage will be that much better."

Maxwell nods approvingly. "It's a much better plan than when my wife and I tried to defeat Phobetor. Maybe you will actually succeed."

"We'd better get started," Kojo—who's really Asha—says. "At any moment, someone can kill us in the real world."

As if to confirm her words, one of the Escapists poofs out of existence, and with him, a small army of dream constructs as well.

My chest tightens. "It must've been the orcs. They're still on the loose on the Escapist side of Soma."

"It's time then," Maxwell says. "Get in position."

We do our best, but due to the size of our army, this takes a while.

"Let's arm the troops," Napoleon says.

"Guns won't work," Maxwell says. "Bows and arrows might, and something like a ballista, but the most effective will be close-range weapons, like swords, axes, and machetes."

That makes sense, at least given my own experience with the subdreams.

After a quick deliberation, the dreamwalkers among us arm anyone who needs it, then manifest weapons for themselves.

I end up with a perfectly balanced katana on my back and a bow and arrow in my hands. My sister (as Kojo) manifests herself a crossbow and a sword that's a copy of the ones we use on Soma.

When all the preparations are complete, Maxwell comes over to where camouflaged Asha and I stand among the non-dreamwalkers.

"Are you sure about this?" I ask him. "You've been free all these years…"

Maxwell nods, face taut. "Farewell."

With that, his face muscles go slack, and his posture softens, as if he's removed the weight of the world from his shoulders.

The dessert-themed environment around us is replaced with that of the subdream, with the magma sky above and the black ocean below.

Like a bolt of lightning, a tendril of magma strikes Maxwell's head. Then it swirls and grows until it looks like a tornado of fire. From his eyes streams a fiery light, forming a strange hologram in the air as if the eyes were some weird movie projectors.

It's a representation of a brain, I realize, staring at the hologram in shock. His?

At first, the brain is a healthy pink, but then fire spreads through it, taking over the neurons. At the same time, an army of subdream creatures appears in the distance in front of us—a million times more frightening now that they're their usual size.

Behind them, far in the distance is Phobetor, his beautiful face both terrifying and unreadable as the fire consumes the rest of the hologram brain.

An inhuman wail escapes Maxwell's lips—and just like that, my father disappears.

CHAPTER THIRTY

"ZOMBIES, ATTACK!" Napoleon screams from his position in the back.

With a slight eyeroll, Rowan gestures at the monster horde, and her zombies charge.

There's a second of eerie silence, and then the zombies and the subdream creatures clash.

Now one can hear body parts getting ripped off, tentacles slashed, and mandibles broken—and fountains of sticky green goop and blood float on top of the black water like macabre modern art.

"Make more zombies," Napoleon orders when the first wave is all but gone—after barely destroying one percent of the enemy army.

The other dreamwalkers make more corpses, but my sister and I abstain so as not to reveal our powers.

This second group of zombies charges, but we're on the radar of the subdream monsters now.

A group of flying creatures whoosh in our direction. They look like a hybrid between heavy-duty excavators and condors, and their shrieks make even Vickie, the siren, cringe.

Ariel aims her bow at the sky and looses an arrow.

"Anyone know what a group of condors is called?" she asks as the arrow hits one of the flying creatures in the eye.

"A condo," Felix says and launches the four giant rocks he's been holding in each of the hands of his suit.

One of the rocks bashes the condor that Ariel already wounded on the head, and the thing drops, squashing some of the enemy troops as a bonus.

The ballista fires with a loud snap, dropping a dozen condors.

Moving with uber superspeed, Ariel grabs another arrow from her quiver and downs another bird. "Is that short for condominium?"

Rowan shoots her crossbow, hitting another condor in the chest. "I actually think the term is 'scarcity.'"

Ariel looses yet another arrow, finishing the monster Rowan hit. "That's dumb. What we have is an abundance of condors, or the opposite of a scarcity."

That's an understatement. The condo or so-called scarcity of these monsters is a hundred thousand strong.

"Everyone, fire!" Napoleon shrieks.

We obey, releasing a cloud of arrows and rocks so thick it blots out the magma sky.

Most of the condors get pierced by the projectiles, but a few manage to survive.

They dive for us.

The siren shrieks upward, and two seconds later, any birds within earshot are stripped to constituent parts. Still, some are mid-dive, including one that seems to be headed for—

I swing my katana just as a beak smashes into my temple, nearly blinding me with pain as I slice the creature in half.

Staggering, I prepare to leave my body to heal myself, then remember that the plan calls for hiding my powers.

Kojo—the real one—must've been keeping an eye on the proceedings. He waves his/Asha's hand, and my wound instantly heals.

"Air support!" Napoleon yells as another condo/scarcity of flying monsters swoops our way.

A large portion of the Escapists take flight, including the fake twins. They start shooting multicolored lightning bolts at the horrific birds, lighting up the sky like fireworks.

Some condors make it through and dive down at us again.

"My zombies are gone!" Rowan yells. "Make more."

Before anyone can do that, a condor smashes into Napoleon's head, and the general disappears.

"Should I bring him back?" I urgently ask my sister. "I'm the only one who has the link."

"It's not worth revealing yourself," she replies in Kojo's voice. "Instead, help me make sure the monsters don't kill my husband."

Of course. If that happens, Kojo will turn homicidally insane—not something I want for my sister and niece.

Before I can reply, yet another condor swoops down, and I cleave it in half with my katana.

Horrific shrieks emanate from the battlefield. It's a squadron of tardigrade-like beasts; they're slithering toward us with a speed one wouldn't expect from their ten-foot-long sea-cow bodies.

Both Rowan's zombies and our dream constructs rush to intercept.

In the distance, the warthog/mole rat cavalry mobilize, so the remaining Escapists take flight and rush over there, as per Napoleon's plan.

The tardigrades slam into our forces and kill a bunch of my patients, as well as the dream construct of Napoleon, before anyone can react. Moments later, a large contingent of zombies are also torn apart by tardigrade claws, and one large monster manages to bite off Frankenstein's head.

A condor gets too close to Kojo. Moving in unison, my sister and I launch arrows at the monster, piercing it in the chest and the head.

Robin Hood avenges his fallen dream-construct comrade by turning the large tardigrade into a pincushion with his arrows, but he pays with his life when eight claws of another rip him into shreds.

In the sky, a cloud of skeletal turkey vultures comes to the aid of the condors.

Ariel takes one of them out with her bow. "I think a group of vultures is called a kettle," she says, eyes narrowed.

Felix hurls a stone but misses his vulture. "Or a committee."

Rowan chuckles. "My favorite collective noun for vultures is a wake. Now, what do you call a group of collective nouns?"

Ariel dispatches a condor and a vulture. "Maybe a glaring of nouns, like with cats?"

Ignoring the rest of that insane conversation, I check on our Escapist air support, particularly my brother-in-law.

Though they're making decent progress with the bird menace, I can't help the feeling that their colorful lightning attacks aren't as imaginative or effective as mine would've been. Kojo is probably the most effective fighter among them—which might be why the birds attack him more often. That or the fact that he looks like Asha and is therefore on Phobetor's hit list.

I explain my observations to Asha, ending with, "I expected more from the Escapists, given their extensive experience with dreamwalking."

Kojo's eyebrows furrow on my sister's face. "Violence isn't something they've ever encountered. That's the cost of living a sheltered life."

"What about splitting into multiple selves?" I get a clear shot and down one of the vultures. "That's something they could try to speed things up."

She also shoots down a bird. "That technique is taboo in Escapist society. I've learned how to do it, but I'm not typical."

A kettle of vultures breaks through the wall of the Escapists, and Asha and I focus on shooting them down.

When we're done, I turn my attention to the battle being waged in the distance.

The Escapists' sub-squadron smashes into the warthog/mole rat cavalry, pulverizing mount and rider alike. The battle with the tardigrades is also going well for our cannon fodder troops—that is, until the arrival of nail-swordsmen, humanoid creatures with claws as long and sharp as my katana.

Two of these newcomers rend Joygasm Troglodyte and Tarzan apart before either can so much as throw a punch.

With a sonic boom, Zorro's whip wraps around the neck of one of the nail-swordsmen. Then Zorro beheads the thing with his sword before slashing his signature Z on the defeated foe's chest. But in the process, he turns his back on one of the surviving tardigrades—and is instantly gouged by eight of the monster's claws.

Two vultures career at my sister's husband. She and I move in sync, releasing arrows at the same time.

Two dead vultures spiral down, leaving streaks of goopy blood in their wake.

Kojo is safe for now.

Meanwhile, nearby, Zeus smites the tardigrade with a bolt of lightning not unlike the ones the Escapists are shooting at the birds in the sky.

A nail-swordsman hurls Dream Chester at Zeus, giving another one of his kind a chance to chop both Chester and Zeus into kebabs.

Moving with vampire speed, Dracula dashes for the nail-swordsman and rips the monster's throat out with his fangs. He then tears the claws from his victim's hands and hurls them at a tardigrade nearby as if they were blades.

A thin nail-swordsman leaps into the air, beheading Dracula mid-flight—which is when Dream Itzel hurls one of her lightning ball projectiles at him, leaving behind nothing but ashes.

"Bailey's constructs kick ass," Ariel exclaims.

"You're just saying that because that version of you is the best of the bunch," Rowan says with a hint of jealousy. The construct version of her is already dead, though I have no idea how or who took her out.

And indeed, Dream Ariel moves with uber speed, slashing off mandibles and tentacles from every creature that comes her way.

Our attention must be a jinx. Dream Ariel miscalculates a leap at a nail-swordsman and gets disabled.

Itzel avenges Ariel with a lightning ball, but is then beheaded herself.

"Dream me is also doing well," Felix says. "Much better than the dream constructs the Escapists created."

Both statements are true. His robot suit is covered in subcreature goo as Dream Felix rips other creatures into pieces. In contrast, the Escapists' creations are having their asses handed to them. Most are just copies of the Escapists themselves, but without dreamwalker powers. They're basically engaged in fisticuffs. However, they're still not as bad as their creatures from myths; those are almost comical. Case in point, the unicorn with humanoid arms—a being that a lot of them manifested. Its modus operandi is to try to tickle enemies to death, with predictable results.

Meanwhile, another vampire I made—Edith—rains havoc on the enemy forces, making me wish I'd manifested more vampire-based dream constructs. But it's too late now. I can't use my powers—especially not when condors and vultures keep swooping in, trying to kill Kojo. Two pairs of them do this now, and my sister and I are joined by Felix and Ariel as we down the monsters, then preemptively kill a few nearby vultures as well.

Spiral worms, ants, and anglers join the cannon fodder battle. Soon, the zombies are all dead—or whatever the appropriate term is—and all the Escapists are too busy with their own fighting to make more.

The Escapists in the sky are being herded back toward Phobetor, while the ones attacking the cavalry are doing a bit better. They've defeated about half their targets and are battling the rest.

It's getting harder to defend Kojo from this distance.

At least for me. Ariel looses an arrow at a condor who's flying at the fake me—and she's farther from us than Kojo is. The arrow hits the creature's heart, slaying it instantly.

"Anyone who can fly should boost our air support!" Ariel yells.

"Smart," my sister says. "I should've given that command."

I tell her not to beat herself up; after all, Ariel is former military and my sister was almost as sheltered as the Escapists.

On Ariel's command, some of the superheroes and gods from the dream construct troops launch into the sky, as do some of the dreamers that Maxwell recruited from the Otherlands.

I was right. He's gotten to know some powerful people.

With the superheroes and gods away, the battle gets tougher for our cannon fodder.

Kit turns into a copy of Colton, and the two of them stand back to back, stomping on any monster brave or foolish enough to come at them. This goes on for a while, until two enormous condors swoop down and smash into the giant figures' heads.

The condors die on impact, but they stun Kit and Colton long enough for a colony of ant monsters to swarm them, their mandibles leaving nothing behind.

A pang of anxiety washes over me as I watch a nail-swordsman behead Dream Valerian.

Though it may not be rational to retaliate for the killing of a dream construct, I put an arrow into that nail-swordsman's eye. Watching it die is satisfying, so I figure it's good for my morale.

How is the real Valerian doing in the waking world?

No time to ponder that. The ground battle is escalating. A spiral worm leaps on Dream Felix, peeling him out of his suit so that an angler can pierce his neck with those shark-teeth.

At the same time, a tardigrade slashes the throat of the construct-siren mid-shout, just as a turkey vulture swoops in and takes out Dream Maxwell.

A whole committee of vultures somehow gets past the Escapists and swoops down. The ballista takes out four of the birds, and I join everyone in slaughtering the rest.

It's hard to keep track of the battlefield now. Superheroes and gods take the brunt of the attacks, but their ranks are thinning. The dream constructs that are most effective are duplicates of the New York Councilors and their equivalents from the other worlds. Dream Nina works closely with Fabian in wolf form and with Stanislav, who's armed with a saber. She throws half the creatures in her way onto Fabian's teeth and claws, and the rest onto Stanislav's saber.

That is, until a turkey vulture fractures the telekinetic's spine with its beak, and an angler finishes her.

Fabian leaps at the vulture, rending it with his claws. Somehow, the vulture stays alive long enough to drag the werewolf twenty feet into the air before dying—at which point, Fabian crashes into a tardigrade and also perishes.

Thanks to his phasing, Stanislav is like a mini-army. He pierces two foes—an ant and a spiral worm—with his rapier, phases when a nail-swordsman tries to shear off the top of his head, then kills the monster with a touch.

Forget vampires, I should've manifested more chorts.

Still, the cannon fodder troops are dwindling fast. Eventually, even the likes of Stanislav can't manage the onslaught. An angler gets the chort near the end, and the rest of the monsters finish off anyone left.

"Infantry, attack!" Ariel shouts.

Pucking puck.

Infantry is us, and unlike the dream constructs, my sister and I will face dire consequences if we die.

CHAPTER THIRTY-ONE

WE SMASH into the enemy army before they can regroup from the fight with our cannon fodder troops.

The New York Councilors and their Maxwell-recruited equivalents from the Otherlands are in front, displaying a staggering assortment of powers.

In the span of mere seconds, subdream monsters are torched, ruptured from the inside, split into atoms, pulverized, exploded, imploded, torn into large and small pieces, slammed into each other, and hurled at the other side of the battlefield—all with minor losses on our side.

Occasionally, a monster breaks through, and those of us in the back ranks have to dispatch them. At first, I cut them down with my bow, but then my quiver runs empty, so I toss the bow aside and slice the monsters with my katana.

It's frustrating not to be able to use my power. Here in the dream world, I could be more destructive than any of the Councilors.

Suddenly, I hear a strange sound from our flank.

The Escapists battling warthog/mole rat riders must've lost or given up because a significant portion of the cavalry is galloping our way.

A telekinetic slings Vickie, the siren, in front of the newcomers. With a mighty shout, she rends fifty riders apart. But then one of the surviving warthog creatures pierces her chest with its spider-like legs, and she dies.

Well, "wakes up in a cold sweat" is more accurate. Either way, she's no good to us anymore unless I manage to push her back into REM sleep, which would involve using my powers.

A woman I don't know shoots black energy at a warthog, and the thing's spidery eyes instantly go blank.

Ariel downs a mole rat rider with her last arrow. "Fighting on two fronts can be a problem."

"Make me more zombies!" Rowan shouts. "I can help."

Again, if I could use my powers, I'd do better than make more zombies. Same goes for my sister.

Yet, a fresh batch of zombies shows up in the path of the cavalry. Since we're now below our air-support Escapists, I have to assume someone up there—probably Kojo—heard Rowan's plea.

As the cavalry and the zombies face off, the rest of us carve through monsters, slowly advancing toward Phobetor.

Every inch forward thins our front lines more. If this keeps up, my sister and I will be in the thick of it by the time we cross the midpoint of the enemy forces.

My body tingles with nervous anticipation, and I squeeze the hilt of the katana harder.

The last New York Councilor dies shortly; soon after that, the final one of Maxwell's recruits is killed as well.

"This is it," Ariel says with an excitement I don't share.

Then again, her sanity isn't on the line, like mine is.

With mandibles clacking, a colony of ant monsters crashes into our ranks. A big ant lunges at me, so I cleave it in two and get sprayed with disgusting gore. It takes all my willpower not to vanish the foulness using my dreamwalking skills.

Like a war goddess, Ariel races forward, chopping mandibles left and right and cleaving insectoid bodies into pieces. Felix's four arms move like a silvery blur, his upper hands tearing off antennas while his lower hands rip off ant legs at the same time.

A lot of my patients die, some in such horrible ways that I'll have to provide them with free therapy.

There's a guttural cry to my left. A spiral worm has just sliced off Rowan's head with its knife-sharp talons. Ariel dashes toward it, but I don't see what she does because a giant tardigrade looms over Asha, ready to smother her with its bulk.

Without coordinating, she and I move in unison, slashing the thick trunk of the monster from each side.

The fragmented thing dies, but two anglers take its place.

Asha slices hers into quarters as I behead mine.

Another angler attacks me. As I dodge its tentacles, I have to remind myself that the disgusting viscera covering me is part of a dream and therefore lacks viruses and bacteria.

Shark teeth pierce my left shoulder.

Yelping in pain, I cleave off the angler's head. As it drops, a wave of nausea washes over me at the rotten-fish stench of the angler's blood and the burning agony of my wound.

A nail-swordsman rakes his claws over Asha's back. She gasps in pain, and the thing lifts another sword-like claw for a death strike. I leap forward and slice off the creature's arm before it can descend.

"Thanks," Asha pants. Then her eyes widen at something behind me.

I whirl around.

A spiral worm is corkscrewing headfirst at my chest—something or someone must've launched it, like a lance.

With a shout, Ariel jumps into its path. The thing smashes through her chest and comes out on the other side—which is when I behead it.

Ariel dies.

Gritting my teeth, I chop a nearby worm into pieces, then kill a dozen more in a haze of pain and fury.

When I slow down, I realize I've been hemorrhaging all over the place, and so has my twin.

I glance up to see why her hubby or one of the other Escapists hasn't healed us yet—just as an inhumanly beautiful voice carries across the whole battlefield, conjuring terror with each syllable it utters.

"I grow bored," Phobetor says. "Now that you're firmly within my reach, behold."

Within his reach? He must mean the invisible line through the battlefield that Maxwell drew for us earlier.

We did cross it, some time ago. There wasn't a choice. To kill him, we need to get close to him.

Phobetor waves his gargantuan hand.

Like the bolt of magma lightning that struck Maxwell, a tendril from the sky leaps into the head of the fake me—an Escapist woman whose name I didn't even learn.

The tendril then swirls and grows, until it looks like a tornado of fire. A fiery light streams from my duplicate's eyes, forming a brain hologram in the air.

Within seconds, the fire takes over the brain, and she disappears.

Phobetor's voice takes on a new inflection. "Interesting. That wasn't who I thought it was."

Another tendril careens toward the head of fake Asha, who's really Kojo.

Without losing his wife's guise, Kojo extends his hand, and even from this distance, I can see his/our features contort with strain.

The tendril meant for him shimmers in the air, then dissipates.

"Wow," I breathe. "Kojo is able to resist Phobetor."

"Perhaps at this distance," my sister whispers. "If he were closer, I doubt—"

Phobetor waves again.

All the remaining condors and vultures morph into shards of obsidian that careen at the heads of Kojo and the Escapists too fast for my eyes to track.

Bam. The projectiles bash against all the heads as one, leaving the stunned dreamwalkers floating in the air.

Suddenly, every molecule in my body feels heavy, as if gravity has quadrupled. And that must be exactly what's happened. Blood gushes faster from my shoulder, and it's a struggle to remain on my feet.

Kojo plummets from the sky, along with the other Escapists.

Puck. If they hit the ground, their minds will be broken beyond repair.

"No!" Asha yells and extends her hand toward her husband.

There's a blur of movement in my periphery.

I twist for it, sword ready—but it's too late.

The moment of distraction has given a nail-swordsman an opportunity, and the beast has cashed it by burying its sword-like claws in my sister's stomach.

CHAPTER THIRTY-TWO

AS I BEHEAD my sister's attacker, I make the fastest decision of my life.

If I don't use my powers, Asha and her husband will end up homicidally insane, as will their fellow Escapists.

No. Not on my watch.

Feeling like I'm throwing off shackles, I summon my dreamwalking ability and heal Asha's wound. Then I counter Phobetor's gravity reversal with one of my own, adding in extra air resistance for good measure.

Kojo's lethal plummet slows to the gentle downward drift of a feather.

I start to jolt him awake, but another tendril leaps out of the magma sky and strikes his head. Again, a brain hologram shows up, and as I watch in horror, my brother-in-law is Overtaken.

Then this happens to another Escapist.

And another.

I shake off my stunned paralysis and channel all of my terror and grief into jolting the rest of the Escapists awake.

To my shock, it works, though this is exponentially more people than the maximum I've jolted before.

Asha must realize our power embargo is at an end because my shoulder heals, as do the other aches and pains in my body.

Phobetor gestures again.

Felix's suit melts around him until nothing is left as every single one of our remaining allies dies in similarly torturous ways—and no matter how much I push back with my power, I'm unable to stop the slaughter.

Soon, Asha and I are the only ones left, and our disguises disappear, leaving us looking like twins again.

Staring at the monsters around us with anguished eyes, Asha jerkily makes a circle with her hand.

The nearby monsters turn into vapor mid-leap.

I do the same, trying to ignore the fear squeezing my chest, the awful certainty that we are losing.

"We need to keep fighting," I tell Asha when her gaze meets mine, but I can see the same despair written on her face.

Still, her back straightens, and she nods grimly.

We turn to attack a new crop of monsters, but we don't get far.

Two new bolts of magma snake from the sky toward us.

Asha extends her hand, her features contorting in an echo of Kojo's strained expression.

The fiery tendrils shimmer in the air and dissipate.

Two more show up, and Asha destroys them too.

In the distance, Phobetor's figure grows impossibly larger. "End them!" his terrifyingly beautiful voice booms, and millions of his minions close ranks around us, like a hangman's noose.

CHAPTER THIRTY-THREE

"MULTIBODY TECHNIQUE!" I shout as I leave my body.

Leveraging my panic and desperation, I make two of me, then the two make four, and those four make eight, and so on until my powers fail on the twentieth split—but by then, there are more than a million me, for such is the power of exponential growth.

Asha has done the same, but faster and one extra time, so there are over two million versions of her on the battlefield now.

Each of us is hungry for battle.

The only problem with splitting so many times is that it leaves very little power to do anything flashy to the monsters. No matter. We kill them with our katanas, while Ashas do the same with their swords.

One of me kills a vulture and an angler in a single strike.

Nearby, a version of my sister beheads a tardigrade and disembowels a nail-swordsman.

"How about you and I act as generals from my dream palace?" I pant. "I think the rest of us won't miss us."

She nods, and I use what little power I have left to teleport the two of us into that very familiar environment as the legions of ourselves continue cutting through the monsters toward Phobetor.

Once inside the dream palace, I face her. "What's the new plan?"

In the time I ask the question, hundreds more monsters are slain by us on the battlefield.

"I don't know." Asha looks hunted. "Maybe we figure out the Two as One thing?"

"Even if we do, then what?"

She chews on her bottom lip. "The copies of us could hold back the subdream monsters as we approach Phobetor and use the mystery skill to kill him."

As she speaks, the other us advance toward our enemy.

Worryingly, Phobetor doesn't look at all intimidated.

"We're overleveraged on dreamwalker powers," I say. "I could barely teleport the two of us here."

Asha squares her shoulders. "Let's think positive. Maybe the mystery technique needs only a little power. If so, I could spare that."

"Fine. Let's focus on figuring out the Two as One bit." I rake my fingers through my fiery hair. "The stress isn't helping jog my memory at all."

Asha nods grimly. "I'm drawing a blank too—exactly as if there were a black window blocking my childhood from me. Except I could never locate one, same as you."

Even though I know it's pointless, I look around.

Nope.

No black windows have magically materialized.

Feeling silly, I even look up.

Nope.

Just the usual decorative mosaic depicting an archery-target-like mandala made out of multicolored glass.

My stomach drops.

Glass.

Multicolored.

"It can't be," I mutter.

Uncomprehending, my sister follows my gaze.

I jab my finger at the mosaic. "The bullseye. There, in the very center. It's the darkest piece. Isn't it black?"

"It is," she breathes, awed.

"Isn't a window a piece of glass?" I press on. "Maybe they're usually bigger, and on walls, but—"

Asha extends a trembling hand, a glimmer of hope returning to her eyes. "I might have enough juice to take you through it."

I clasp her hand, and she rockets up.

As the bullseye nears, I realize that it isn't even all that much smaller than a window. Being a piece in a mosaic makes it appear that way, especially from the very bottom of the lobby.

It has to be the black window we've missed all these years—we just didn't see it as such because we've grown to see the mosaic as a whole, not a sum of its parts.

It must be what's hiding our childhood memories.

It's our only chance.

Sure enough, as soon as the top of Asha's head touches the bullseye, the dream palace around us evaporates.

———

WE'RE in a room covered from floor to ceiling with pottery paraphernalia, everything from wheel to kiln.

"We made it," Asha exclaims, looking around in wonder. "For a moment there, I thought I was going to drown in that black water, towing you along."

That's right. This time, I was the unconscious one inside the boat. "This is my first time experiencing this from this end," I say. "What should I—"

I don't finish the sentence because memories flood in, just as this particular one starts playing in front of our eyes.

Bebe is molding a vase on the wheel.

Seeing her unlocks a cascade of recollections: her lovingly calling me "her little bee," the countless hugs she gave me, the priceless wisdom she imparted, the stories she told to lull me and Asha to sleep...

It's almost unbearable, and the tears that I couldn't shed for her earlier begin streaking down my cheeks. But they're not just tears of sadness. Though I lost Bebe today, I've just regained a part of her as well.

A part that I will now carry in my memories.

Asha's eyes are also on Bebe, her cheeks as wet as mine.

The memory continues to play out.

Mom is sitting there with a serene expression on her face.

Seeing her triggers its own rollercoaster of childhood memories, each more treasured than the next.

The countless times she tucked me into bed.

The way she'd make the boring Soma food seem fun.

The love and warmth she'd given me.

Next to me, Asha drags in a shaky breath.

Mom is holding the young versions of us.

The recollections of my sister at that age flow in, and I feel like my mind might burst from it all.

Focusing, I strain to catch one particular memory among them—of the Two as One game—but it's too hard. Things are too jumbled at the moment.

"Come, dear ones," Bebe says in the memory.

As the two little girls shuffle over to her, I realize I've seen this very memory in Mom's black window. Except now I remember it in every detail, down to how it felt, and it's so much more vivid than when I was an observer.

"You can touch," Bebe tells the girls.

Grinning mischievously, the twins leave palmprints on the sides of the vase.

Bebe smiles in approval and deposits the vase into the kiln.

"Isn't that the vase from your memory gallery?" grown Asha asks. "The one you broke years later, on Gomorrah?"

Before I can reply in the affirmative, Bebe gives the vase to Mom as a gift, and the memory terminates.

———

THE NEW MEMORY RUNS FASTER.

We're in a different room, and I recall that it's the living room of our Soma dwelling.

I've seen this room in memories of others.

It's where Asha and I were born.

"Did anything about Two as One come back to you?" grown Asha asks.

"No." I greedily scan the room in the hopes that something here will trigger the memory we seek.

Mom is holding Dad's hand, and seeing him opens a new tsunami of recollections.

The piggyback rides.

The itchiness of his stubble when he'd kiss my cheek.

The loving way he'd gaze at us.

The feeling of safety in his embrace.

I can only think of him as Dad from now on, not father—and certainly not something as impersonal as Maxwell.

The memory continues.

Six-year-old versions of me and Asha are playing with Valerian and

Kojo while our parents converse about the prophecy.

Valerian pulls on his father's sleeve. "Dad, can Bailey and I go to the garden?"

Davu nods, and little me and little Valerian race out of the room.

Again, I can't help but remember more than the content of the memory provided.

Valerian and I were best friends, inseparable companions. He was also my first crush—and at the ripe old age of six, I made a vow to myself that I would marry him one day. There was even a chaste kiss once—our true first kiss, as it turns out.

The sweet memories stoke my fears about Valerian fighting the Overtaken in the waking world. With effort, I shake it off. I have to believe he can handle himself—and that Asha and I will be able to defeat Phobetor in time.

Young Valerian chases the young me all the way to the garden.

Asha and Kojo soon show up as well, and we play a Soma version of tag until the memory terminates.

———

THIS IS IT.

In this sped-up memory, Asha and I are in the dream world, in her childhood version of the memory gallery.

"Two as one, remember?" young me says to Asha with a small pout. "You and Kojo ran away for a whole hour. I want to know what happened."

I remember what's about to happen, and stagger as if from a blow. "We're so pucked," I say in horror as everything to do with the game clicks back into place.

Young Asha creates a painting so that the young me can leap into it.

"This is all there is to that game," I say to the wide-eyed grown Asha. "We made a pact to share every single breath with each other, so when circumstances tore us apart for a few minutes, we'd create the memory of what the other missed." As I say the words, dozens of super-cute memories of Asha's experience paintings replay in front of my mind: her playing doctor with Kojo, her getting a stubbed toe healed in the medical bay, and on and on.

Grown Asha's face blanches. "How can this help us with Phobetor?"

"It can't." I look at her mournfully. "This *is* the game our family heard about—and it has nothing at all to do with the god of nightmares."

CHAPTER THIRTY-FOUR

ASHA'S EYES ARE ENORMOUS. "But the prophecy—"

"Must be about someone else. Or 'Two as One' means something else that we didn't discover."

The memory of the game terminates, and the ones that follow are too fast to register. I don't need them, though. I remember everything. In a way, locking away my childhood preserved the memories for me. Usually, people remember only bits and pieces of theirs, but I recall it all. It just doesn't help with our predicament.

Still, if we survive, I intend to enjoy savoring each memory, finding a place for them in my palace. Then again, surviving is a big if—

ASHA and I are back in my dream palace lobby.

The bullseye in the middle of the target in the ceiling is no longer black.

"Should I unlock yours?" I gesture up.

"Later," she says. "After we make sure there *is* a later."

"Smart. Do you have any semblance of a plan?"

She begins to pace. "Some of our selves have reached Phobetor. Why don't we have those selves become singletons once again? This way, we'll be near him, and with our powers intact."

"But the monsters will tear us to shreds," I say.

"We'll recreate our constructs and have them protect us. Hopefully they'll last long enough for us to do the next part."

I arch an eyebrow. "And that is?"

"We attempt to become a single being again," she says in a matter-of-fact tone. "That has to be what the prophecy was about."

"You mean that technique we tried during the training? We failed at it, remember?"

"We're more motivated now," she says grimly. "And have more emotions we can channel into it as well."

That last bit is true. If emotions were electricity, I could power a small town with mine.

"Hold on," I say. "The last time we tried that trick, we got insanely tired."

"I know." She scrubs a hand over her face. "It could be our last move. Do you have a better idea?"

I shake my head.

"Then let's do it. Remember, start with the molecule trick you used to grow big, then tell your molecules to mix with mine as we hug."

"Got it," I say and teleport back to the battlefield.

———

ASHA JOINS ME IN A SECOND.

As Dad had warned us, teleporting back here puts us at the edge farthest from Phobetor.

But that is only true for these versions of us.

In the far distance, millions of others are much closer to the looming target, and two of us are exactly where they need to be.

"Time to make some of ourselves disappear," Asha says and poofs out of existence next to me.

This version of me does the same thing, as does one that's just finished killing an extra-large tardigrade. Same for a nearby me who's just beheaded a nail-swordsman.

Millions of poofs later, only one of me and Asha remain—the ones closest to Phobetor.

My full dream power is coursing through me now, no longer used up by the multibody technique.

"We need to stall the creatures," my sister shouts. "Quick!"

The creatures in question turn our way and prepare to attack en masse.

Channeling the pleasant emotions from the memories I've just recovered, I recreate every single one of my dream constructs in one giant use of power, bringing back both fictional characters and people I know in real life.

Asha does the same—but even with her additions, there aren't enough allies, not by a long shot.

"I got this." I channel my strongest emotion—anxiety over Valerian's fate—into pushing everyone I know back into REM sleep.

By all rights, this shouldn't work. I've just learned this skill, and I've only been able to do this to one person, not hundreds.

Yet it happens.

Felix, Rowan, Ariel, Napoleon, the siren, and the rest of the New York Council reappear in the path of the subdream abominations—and recover their wits quickly enough to attack.

This might buy us a little time.

"Now or never," Asha says, echoing my thoughts.

Dropping our weapons, we hug.

I close my eyes and visualize myself made from molecules. Then I will them into becoming a single person with Asha.

"How touching," Phobetor's booming voice intrudes, but I banish it from my mind, instead visualizing our molecules intermixing. "A hug and a chance to see your friends for the last time," he continues mockingly. "What's next, the last meal?"

I channel all my emotions into the desperate merging attempt.

Nothing happens at first.

Then I feel a familiar wooziness.

Asha's arms are no longer around me.

I open my eyes—or, hopefully, our eyes.

Nope.

Asha is still separate from me. She's just stepped away to dry-heave, like the last time we tried this.

I also feel sick, but I hold it in as a wave of exhaustion smashes into me.

"This is as far as your parents got," Phobetor says, and I have to crane my neck to see the malevolent expression on his ethereal face far above me. "You know what happened after that."

As a macabre underscore to his words, Rowan and Napoleon get disemboweled by the nail-swordsmen.

I glare up at the god of nightmares. "Shut the puck up. I have a promise to keep."

He scoffs. "This is your last chance to become my servants willingly." His voice evokes all my fears, like it did when I faced him in Mom's dreams. "Kneel."

Like that time, my whole being demands that I give in—only this temptation is exponentially worse. In his embrace, there will be solace. Our whole family will reunite. I'll no longer feel this overwhelming exhaustion. I'll—

"No!" both Asha and I exclaim at the same time.

I channel my wrath into my power, and just like that, I throw off his vileness and feel like myself again—except completely drained and on the verge of a panic attack.

Judging by my sister's angry glare, she's also thrown off his attempt.

"So be it." Phobetor advances toward us, hand outstretched.

Two massive bolts of magma snake down toward our heads.

Asha lifts her hand, her features contorting again, and I mirror her gesture, though I have no idea what I'm doing.

I focus on the tendril that's coming my way, willing it out of existence with all my might.

The fiery tendril shimmers in the air and dissipates.

Only mine, though.

The second one smashes into Asha's head and swirls, growing to tornado proportions until my sister's eyes begin to stream a fiery light that forms a brain hologram in the air.

No. Please no.

I strain my power to sever the horrible link for her—but to no avail.

All the parts of Asha's brain are taken over by the fire, and a pained cry escapes her lips as she disappears.

I stare at the empty spot uncomprehendingly.

On some level, I must've believed the cursed prophecy.

I thought—or hoped—that the two of us were somehow *destined* to win.

Meaning we'd find a way, against all odds.

My heart feels like it's imploding as I lift my gaze to meet Phobetor's black-hole eyes.

The prophecy was a pleasant fantasy.

Now it's just me, alone with the god of nightmares.

In a moment, he will kill or Overtake me—and that'll be the end.

CHAPTER THIRTY-FIVE

PUCK THAT.

I'm not letting that happen before I at least smack the bastard in the face.

I visualize myself as made out of molecules again, then will them to grow, channeling everything into this last-ditch attempt: the weariness, the agony of defeat, the desire to save Valerian and my family, the grief over Bebe's demise.

To my shock, I grow to Phobetor's size in an instant.

Here we go.

Balling my hands into fists, I lumber toward him.

"Nice try." He gestures at me.

This time, the fiery strand isn't a bolt but a twister. Swirling like a tornado of fire, it leaps for my giant head.

I extend my own ginormous hand and will the strand out of existence.

It reaches me anyway.

A searing pain smashes into my nerve endings.

Whatever I did to thwart this attack before clearly didn't happen this time. Unless… I didn't do anything, and it was Asha.

She protected me instead of herself.

That's why Phobetor was able to Overtake her.

Too bad her sacrifice was in vain.

Fire streams out of my eyes and forms an epic hologram of my jumbo brain behind Phobetor.

It looks odd, different than the others—and not just because of the size.

There's a network of vein-like tentacles inside my brain. *Furry* tentacles.

I try to lift my arm and find it paralyzed.

I will myself to shrink, but that doesn't work either.

The fire spreads through my holographic brain's neurons—but this, too, doesn't go as it did for everyone else.

Whenever the fire meets the furry parts of my brain, it fails to take them over.

I blink at the image, and suddenly everything slides into place.

Of course.

"Two as One" didn't refer to me and Asha. It was about me and someone else.

Someone who is closer to me than any sibling.

Someone with whom I share all my nutrients.

Someone who feels my emotions.

Someone who's always there for me in the dream world.

Someone who shares my brain—and is thus the obstacle Phobetor's power has just encountered.

Pom and I live as a single symbiotic organism.

We're Two as One.

Pom! I mentally shout. *I need you. Please be brave. I know you can do this.*

In the hologram, the furry tentacles turn from black to teal and begin pushing the fire back, clearing the other portions of the brain.

I regain the feeling in my arm, but I remain still, not letting Phobetor see it.

Let's end this, I shout inside my head.

Like we've practiced. Pom's voice is filled with determination.

What?

Phobetor's eyes narrow. He's realizing something is wrong.

A furry bracelet appears on my wrist, and I understand what Pom means.

We've trained together to defeat the monsters in the subdreams.

He's been my weapon all along.

He elongates into a furry katana, one proportional to my enormous size.

My enemy is finally within my reach.

With all my might, I slice with my furry weapon—and in the black pools of Phobetor's enormous eyes, I see both horror and surprise.

My blade bites into his neck, cutting through skin, muscle, and veins, severing cartilage and spinal cord.

As it comes out on the other side, the pull of his hypnotic stare disappears, and his head separates from his giant body, rolling over to my feet.

"I keep my promises." Vehemently, I kick the ginormous head in the face, launching it in the air like a soccer ball. "That's for my grandmother."

I feel it then.

I feel the being that was Phobetor evaporate out of existence—and as he does, a shockwave of power is unleashed.

Like a nuclear blast, it crashes into me, and everything goes totally dark.

CHAPTER THIRTY-SIX

I COME TO.

I'm alive. Yay. It would've sucked to have killed Phobetor but paid for it with my life—like a true hero of legendary prophecy.

There's a tiny, warm hand on my wrist.

I open my eyes.

I'm in the medical bay, with Chloe, my niece, at my bedside.

Seeing me awake, she springs to her feet.

"You're finally up!" she shouts with childish exuberance. "Stay there, I'm going to get someone."

"Wait, is your mommy—"

She's already gone.

Questions swirl through my groggy brain.

Where is everyone? How long was I out? Is Valerian alive? Is Dad still Overtaken? Is Asha? Is everyone else?

I push up to a sitting position and look around.

The gurneys that we were strapped to earlier are now empty—a good sign.

Mom is still here, but someone moved her onto a bed.

My heart leaps. With Phobetor gone, I can finally go into her dreams and try to get her out—but I'm going to wait for some answers before I attempt it.

My gaze falls on my furry bracelet.

Wait, Pom. That's who I need to check on first. He was there when the blast of power knocked me out, so he could've also gotten hurt.

A touch and a moment of concentration later, I'm in my dream palace once more.

Pom is here, grinning at me, his fur a deep purple.

"You're okay." I grab him in a hug and squeeze for all I'm worth.

He grunts comically, so I put him down.

He floats up to be eye-level with me. "Never been better. How about you?"

"I'm fine. Just clueless about the others."

Speaking of the others, what happened to Felix, Ariel, and the other people who kept me safe from subdream monsters?

I take Pom to the tower of sleepers to find out.

Felix and Ariel are asleep, as are the members of the New York Council.

I check on Ariel first. She tells me she's great, and that the whole thing was actually fun. I make a mental note to reject any future invitations to do something "fun" with her.

Felix is also okay, and a lot more healthily unenthusiastic about the violence he lived through. Same with everyone else I check on.

When I exit the siren's dreams, I spot a person in the tower of sleepers that I haven't seen here for a long time—not since the beginning of all my misadventures, back when she was Ariel and Felix's roommate.

Is it a coincidence that she's here now that I've thwarted an apocalypse?

No way. Given everything I know about this one, she's dreaming at just the right moment so we can chat.

Pom points at her. "Isn't that Princess Peach? Haven't seen her in forever."

Nodding, I approach the pale-skinned, black-haired woman and touch her forehead, leaping into her dreams.

———

AS I TAKE in the dream, I do a double take.

We're in my dream palace lobby.

How does she know what it looks like? I don't usually take people there.

She's standing in front of a dream version of me, who's saying, "Fine, let's talk here." And the mind-boggling part is that this dream feels like a memory.

Except I never said those words to her. Unless...

Of course. This is a seer vision of a conversation we'll have at some point in the future. Probably the very conversation I came here to have.

I dismiss the other me and change the environment to that of a desert, mainly to be contrary.

"Hey," I say. "Were you expecting me?"

A deck of cards appears in her hands as if by magic, and she gives them a practiced shuffle. "Come on. You know where this conversation is supposed to take place."

With a sigh, I take us back to my palace.

She grins. "You also know your next line."

"Fine," I say with an eye roll. "Let's talk here."

The cards disappear from her hands, again as if by magic. "I wanted to thank you and Pom for a job well done. Phobetor was a threat to my family's future—everybody's future, really—so I'm pleased he's gone."

Pom perches on my shoulder. "I'm confused. If you didn't like him, why didn't you help us?"

"Nostradamus was on it," she says with a shrug. "When that guy has a plan, it's better to stay out. I know this from personal experience. Besides, I couldn't just tell you the future. If I did, it wouldn't happen." She examines her nails. "Also, I promised my hubby not to get myself embroiled in any shenanigans—particularly of an apocalyptic type—for at least a few centuries. He would've been growly if I'd lied."

A strong headache begins to thud in my temples, so I quickly jump out of my body to cure it.

I think if I talked to seers more often, I'd lose my pucking mind.

"You're welcome," Pom says in the meanwhile.

I sigh again. "Was there anything else?" I ask her. "I need to wake up to check on more people."

"Here's a little gift," she says. "The people you want to check on are all fine, and most of your possible futures are long and happy, especially for you and your husband." She makes an oops face. "I meant, your boyfriend. No, wait, is it too soon even for that? Your hookup?"

Pom's eyes widen. "Is she serious?"

I don't answer because my headache is returning again. My mind reels. As a seer, she knows what the future brings, but she's also a mischievous jokester, so how can I know if she's telling the truth? Especially that bit about Valerian and me getting married? By telling me this information, she may well be starting a chain of events that leads me to do her a favor in a "few centuries," when her "hubby" lets her get back to "shenanigans."

"They're waiting," she says with a smirk. "I feel like I've done my part."

With that, she wakes up.

Exchanging an exasperated glance with Pom, I return to the real world.

———

"I'M TELLING YOU, she was up," my niece is saying.

I open my eyes again.

Besides Chloe, surrounding my bed are Dad, Valerian, Kojo, and Asha.

My chest feels warm and tingly.

"You're okay, right?" Chloe asks. "Say yes."

"Yes," I say, smiling at her. I look around. "What about all of you?"

Valerian nods, his eyes gleaming brightly. "As soon as you won, the Overtaken became themselves once again. I had the good fortune to last until then."

I leap off the bed and tackle-hug him. Then I hug everyone else.

Pom's fur is the deepest, happiest purple I've ever seen.

Though the seer had just told me they're fine, I had to see it with my own eyes, feel them with my own hands.

Not for a second does my worry about germs kick in with all this touching. It was like that with Mom, my only other family until now, so I guess it makes sense.

My heart expands at the thought.

I have so much family!

"How long was I out?" I ask, trying to contain my excitement.

"Almost a day." Valerian frowns. "Got me worried."

"I got *you* worried?" I exclaim. "I wasn't the one fighting an army of the Overtaken."

"No one has been able to do what you did," Dad says. "We didn't know what to expect."

"Right," I say. "So what happened while I was out?"

Valerian clasps my hand with both of his, his palms big and warm around my fingers. "The newly freed Overtaken helped us with the wounded and the dead. The necromancer was especially useful."

Asha looks at our joined hands and gives me a surreptitious wink.

"Afterward, we escorted them all far away from Soma and locked away their memories of it."

"That's a busy day." I glance at Mom's unconscious body. "What about her?"

Dad follows my gaze. "I waited for you, so I could ask for a favor."

I look at him.

"I know you've worked really hard to bring her out of that comatose state—and I'll be forever grateful to you for that. But I was wondering if you'd let me do this last part. She might be more receptive if—"

"Of course." I actually feel a little relieved. A part of me was dreading trying this again—and possibly failing. "I just want to get her back."

"I'll do it now," Dad says solemnly. "And I'll make sure she's got all her memories back while I'm at it."

I face Asha. "Speaking of memories... Did you—"

"Yes," my sister says. "I remember you now. As soon as there was a quiet moment, Kojo unlocked the black window for me. I now remember you, Dad, Mom, and Valerian."

My eyes sweep over everyone in the room. "I also got it all back," I say softly. I meet Valerian's gaze. "And I mean, *everything*."

His ocean-blue eyes are warm and bright, like tropical waters. Suddenly, the medical bay morphs into Valerian's living room—and the illusion makes it so we're the only ones there.

"You're giving us privacy?" On my wrist, Pom's fur turns coral pink.

He nods, squeezing my hand tighter. "Before the Overtaken attacked, you wanted to talk," he murmurs. "What about?"

"Ah, that." I give him a mischievous grin. All my uncertainty about us is gone. "I think I've figured it all out. Memories of us as kids really helped."

He arches an eyebrow. "Care to include me in your revelations?"

"If I must." My grin widens. "I know you're crazy about me. I'm beginning to warm up to you also. What do you say we see where that leads us?"

I decide not to tell him about the seer's "husband" prognostication. She said knowing the future could change it, so why tempt fate?

A slow, dangerously sexy smile curves his lips. "Are you saying you want to go steady?"

In answer, I rise up on tiptoes and kiss him. There are no thoughts of germs in my mind, no thoughts of anything but the man in front of me and the heat streaking down my spine as his skilled tongue dances with mine for several long moments.

Reluctantly, he pulls away, and the illusion disappears, revealing the medical bay and the rest of my family.

"Now we just need to get her back," Dad is saying as he strides over to Mom's bed.

My breath catches, and I forget all about the kiss.

This is it.

Valerian squeezes my hand reassuringly as Dad touches Mom's forehead with his fingertips and closes his eyes.

We all wait in tense silence.

The seconds tick on.

My eyes meet Asha's, and I can see the same worry on her face.

What if it fails?

What if the accident did some irreversible damage after all?

Even Chloe is still, a tiny V between her little brows. She can sense the somber mood of the adults.

Dad removes his hand from Mom's forehead.

I can't see his face, so I have no idea if he's triumphant or devastated.

Slowly, I start toward the bed—and as I'm reaching out to touch Mom's hand, she smiles and opens her eyes.

EPILOGUE

EVERYONE WHO PARTICIPATED in the battle against Phobetor is in the dream world with all of Soma, my new home.

Over the last few weeks, my sister and I have convinced both sides of Soma, the Escapists and the others, to reunite into one people, and now all of us have gathered to honor the ones who perished during The Attack —including Soma's fallen leader, my grandmother and namesake, Bailey.

Soma funerals have two parts, Body and Mind. The Body part happens in the real world, where the flesh of the departed is recycled by special machines that perpetuate the cycle of life in the colony. The Mind portion happens in the dream world, like many other Soman rites of passage. Here, a dream construct of the departed is created jointly by everyone their life had touched, and then the construct delivers a farewell speech—a kind of reverse eulogy.

"Dear citizens of Soma," Bebe's construct says from a large podium. "During this somber occasion, I beg you to be joyful." Smiling beatifically, she looks at where our family is sitting. "The goal that our people have been toiling toward for countless generations has now been achieved. Nightmares are back to being mere dreams and no longer threaten to tear families apart. You get to return to normal—whatever will pass for normal in the future, be it parking this colony ship on a planet, or taking it on an interstellar voyage, or something I can't even imagine, being gone and all." She locks eyes with me. "Be at ease. I would gladly give up my life many times over for what we have accomplished. For the new world we created." She turns her gaze to my niece. "A world where my great-granddaughter can thrive. A world where..."

I miss the rest as Mom, who's standing next to me, begins crying—only to be embraced by Dad. She's been crying a lot since she woke up, tears both of pain and joy. Pain for all the years our family's been torn apart, for all the guilt and shame she'd carried in her subconscious for so long... for the desperation that drove her to throw herself under that car, and for everything that followed. Today, though, her tears are for her mother, and all the other people she's just recently remembered, only to discover they'd died during The Attack.

My own throat feels thick and swollen, my face wet. But underneath the pain of loss is hope. Hope that the future will be brighter than the past, that everything my family has been through has only made us stronger. And sure enough, as Bebe's eulogy proceeds, Mom lifts her face from Dad's shoulder and gives me a smile so full of tenderness and joy that I can't help but smile back and reach for her.

My twin, her thoughts mirroring mine, as they often do, steps up at the same time, and we all hug—Mom, Dad, and the two of us—treasuring this moment.

When I finally draw back, it's into the supportive arms of Valerian, who lends me his strength as the eulogy concludes.

I look up at him, and as our eyes meet, I know that with him and my family by my side, I can get through anything... even defeat another god.

As the Mind ceremony comes to an end, the fireworks begin—pyrotechnics that involve big bangs that birth baby universes like colorful bubbles in the sky above us.

It's the most majestic display the dreamwalkers of Soma could conjure up to honor the ones we lost—and a fitting farewell.

SNEAK PEEKS

Thank you for reading! I hope you enjoyed Bailey's story.

To be notified about my future books, sign up for my newsletter at
www.dimazales.com.

Ready for more action-packed sci-fi/fantasy? Check out:

- *Sasha Urban* - the fantastical urban fantasy series set in the same universe as Bailey Spade, where Felix and Ariel first appear
- *Mind Dimensions* - the exciting urban fantasy adventures of Darren, who can stop time and read minds
- *Human++* - the thrilling sci-fi tale of Mike Cohen, whose new technology will transform our brains *and* the world
- *The Last Humans* - the futuristic sci-fi/dystopian story of Theo, who lives in a world where nothing is as it seems
- *The Sorcery Code* - the epic fantasy adventures of sorcerer Blaise and his creation, the beautiful and powerful Gala

Do you enjoy laugh-out-loud romantic comedy? My wife and I co-write raunchy, geeky romcoms under the pen name Misha Bell. Visit www.mishabell.com to sign up for our newsletter and check out *The Love Deal*, an enemies-to-lovers workplace romance featuring a coupon-obsessed sextuplet and her high school nemesis/crush.

Now, please turn the page to read excerpts from *The Sorcery Code* and *The Love Deal*.

EXCERPT FROM THE SORCERY CODE
BY DIMA ZALES

Once a respected member of the Sorcerer Council and now an outcast, Blaise has spent the last year of his life working on a special magical object. The goal is to allow anyone to do magic, not just the sorcerer elite. The outcome of his quest is unlike anything he could've ever imagined—because, instead of an object, he creates Her.

She is Gala, and she is anything but inanimate. Born in the Spell Realm, she is beautiful and highly intelligent—and nobody knows what she's capable of. She will do anything to experience the world... even leave the man she is beginning to fall for.

Augusta, a powerful sorceress and Blaise's former fiancée, sees Blaise's deed as the ultimate hubris and Gala as an abomination that must be destroyed. In her quest to save the human race, Augusta will forge new alliances, becoming tangled in a web of intrigue that stretches further than any of them suspect. She may even have to turn to her new lover Barson, a ruthless warrior who might have an agenda of his own...

———

There was a naked woman on the floor of Blaise's study.

A beautiful naked woman.

Stunned, Blaise stared at the gorgeous creature who just appeared out of thin air. She was looking around with a bewildered expression on her face, apparently as shocked to be there as he was to be seeing her. Her wavy blond hair streamed down her back, partially covering a body that appeared to be perfection itself. Blaise tried not to think about that body and to focus on the situation instead.

A woman. A *She*, not an *It*. Blaise could hardly believe it. Could it be? Could this girl be the object?

She was sitting with her legs folded underneath her, propping herself up with one slim arm. There was something awkward about that pose, as though she didn't know what to do with her own limbs. In general, despite the curves that marked her a fully grown woman, there was a child-like innocence in the way she sat there, completely unselfconscious and totally unaware of her own appeal.

Clearing his throat, Blaise tried to think of what to say. In his wildest dreams, he couldn't have imagined this kind of outcome to the project that had consumed his entire life for the past several months.

Hearing the sound, she turned her head to look at him, and Blaise found himself staring into a pair of unusually clear blue eyes.

She blinked, then cocked her head to the side, studying him with visible curiosity. Blaise wondered what she was seeing. He hadn't seen the light of day in weeks, and he wouldn't be surprised if he looked like a mad sorcerer at this point. There was probably a week's worth of stubble covering his face, and he knew his dark hair was unbrushed and sticking out in every direction. If he'd known he would be facing a beautiful woman today, he would've done a grooming spell in the morning.

"Who am I?" she asked, startling Blaise. Her voice was soft and feminine, as alluring as the rest of her. "What is this place?"

"You don't know?" Blaise was glad he finally managed to string together a semi-coherent sentence. "You don't know who you are or where you are?"

She shook her head. "No."

Blaise swallowed. "I see."

"What am I?" she asked again, staring at him with those incredible eyes.

"Well," Blaise said slowly, "if you're not some cruel prankster or a figment of my imagination, then it's somewhat difficult to explain..."

She was watching his mouth as he spoke, and when he stopped, she looked up again, meeting his gaze. "It's strange," she said, "hearing words this way. These are the first real words I've heard."

Blaise felt a chill go down his spine. Getting up from his chair, he began to pace, trying to keep his eyes off her nude body. He had been expecting something to appear. A magical object, a thing. He just hadn't known what form that thing would take. A mirror, perhaps, or a lamp. Maybe even something as unusual as the Life Capture Sphere that sat on his desk like a large round diamond.

But a person? A female person at that?

To be fair, he had been trying to make the object intelligent, to ensure it would have the ability to comprehend human language and convert it into the code. Maybe he shouldn't be so surprised that the intelligence he invoked took on a human shape.

A beautiful, feminine, sensual shape.

Focus, Blaise, focus.

"Why are you walking like that?" She slowly got to her feet, her movements uncertain and strangely clumsy. "Should I be walking too? Is that how people talk to each other?"

Blaise stopped in front of her, doing his best to keep his eyes above her neck. "I'm sorry. I'm not accustomed to naked women in my study."

She ran her hands down her body, as though trying to feel it for the first time. Whatever her intent, Blaise found the gesture extremely erotic.

"Is something wrong with the way I look?" she asked. It was such a typical feminine concern that Blaise had to stifle a smile.

"Quite the opposite," he assured her. "You look unimaginably good." So good, in fact, that he was having trouble concentrating on anything but her delicate curves. She was of medium height, and so perfectly proportioned that she could've been used as a sculptor's template.

"Why do I look this way?" A small frown creased her smooth forehead. "What am I?" That last part seemed to be puzzling her the most.

Blaise took a deep breath, trying to calm his racing pulse. "I think I can try to venture a guess, but before I do, I want to give you some clothing. Please wait here—I'll be right back."

And without waiting for her answer, he hurried out of the room.

———

Order your copy of *The Sorcery Code* today at <u>www.dimazales.com</u>!

EXCERPT FROM THE LOVE DEAL BY MISHA BELL

Honey Hyman (do NOT call her "hon") is all leather, piercings, and tattoos. And yes, she may be just a tad deal-obsessed, but who isn't? It's not like her using coupons is stealing from anyone... unless, of course, those coupons are the fakes she created to help her elderly neighbors afford groceries from the Munch & Crunch, the uber-expensive supermarket that's replaced their local grocery store.

It really isn't fair for her to go to jail. Or to be blackmailed into working for the Munch & Crunch CEO whom she's supposedly defrauded—a CEO who turns out to be none other than Gunther Ferguson, her high school crush who once ruined both her school record and her life.

Let the war begin.

———————

The police? What the hell?

Heart thumping, I check the peephole.

Yep. They're dressed like cops.

Did a neighbor call them because of the caterwauling? It did sound like bloody murder. But how did they get here so fast? Unless…

Fuck. It can't be about the coupons again, can it?

"Open the door, or we'll be forced to open it," a hard-faced cop says.

Well, shit. I can't afford to repair this door.

There's no choice.

I open the door.

The cop looks from me to Pearl. "Honey Hyman?"

"That's me." And yes, I know my name sounds like a virginal membrane that people with diabetes should avoid.

"You're under arrest," he informs me. "For fraud."

My stomach drops. I turn to Pearl, who is as pale as the ghost of a toilet. My voice is strained as I say, "Let Blue know, okay?"

Blue is our clutch mate who used to work for the government, so if anyone can help with this, it would be her.

The rest is like a nightmare. I'm led out of the building, put in a police car, brought unceremoniously into the station, and shepherded into a room—all the while fielding a surge of adrenaline so strong I barely register any of it.

Did someone read me my Miranda Rights? If not, do I get a refund?

They didn't take my butterfly knife, which is weird because I always thought going to jail was like flying on a plane—weapons aren't allowed.

Maybe I'm not going to jail? Dare I hope?

I think back on the last two times I was in trouble. Both were actually interrelated situations.

First, there was Tiffany, a cheerleader who bullied me for ogling her uber-hot boyfriend, Gunther—something I *was* guilty of. Eventually, I stood up to her with a knife—only as a threat, though, since the last thing I wanted was to draw any blood. Unfortunately, the dumdum didn't notice said knife and got up in my face anyway, accidentally slicing her arm open. To this day, I don't know how bad the cut was, as I couldn't look at the wound on account of the blood. Since Tiffany didn't end up with a scar, I imagine the cut wasn't so bad—not that it helped me escape the resulting suspension and mark on my permanent record. On the bright side, that incident is what started my "don't mess with me" reputation, which I don't mind at all, as it has kept the other Tiffanies of the world away.

The second incident took place a year later, still in high school. It involved Gunther again—who was no longer with Tiffany at the time. Not that I kept track. Much. That time, not only did I get suspended and *really* tarnish my permanent record, but I also barely dodged the juvenile justice system.

It all started when I was little. For whatever reason, I became obsessed with all things saving money, including deals and coupons. After taking an art class my junior year, I realized that tweaking percentages on coupons with a white pen was just as profitable as counterfeiting money —so I did it, first for myself and then for the other kids at my school. As it turned out, one of the stores that lost money because of my creative initiative was owned by Gunther's family, so when Gunther learned of my activities, he tattled to the principal. Shit hit the fan, and I'm paying for it to this day.

My phone rings.

Huh. Another thing they didn't take.

I check it.

It's Blue. Good. Pearl must've told her to get in touch.

"Hi," I say, switching to a form of Pig Latin Blue developed when we were kids. "Let's talk quick. They might come back and take my phone."

"The quick version is, whatever they have against you is physical, not digital, so there's not much I can do here," Blue says.

Blue hasn't had any trouble with the law, but she doesn't seem to have much respect for certain legalities after working for—as she calls it—"No Such Agency." Case in point: she's just admitted to hacking into the police department's computers as casually as I'd admit to watching cat videos on TikTok.

"Can your former colleagues help?" I ask.

"Sorry, no," she says. "I know some feds, but that doesn't help your case. If you want, I can text you the name of an excellent lawyer."

"Sure." Except I have no idea how I'd pay said lawyer. Thanks to my high school mishaps, no college wanted me, and I never achieved my dream of becoming a wealthy business owner. Currently, I work part-time sweeping floors at a tattoo parlor and cutting hair at a barbershop.

"I can lend you some money," Blue says, clearly reading my mind.

"No." I hate charity. "I'll take the public attorney."

"It's coupons again, isn't it?" she whispers.

"I'm not sure I should talk about it," I whisper back. "Even in code."

I hear her type a few keystrokes. Then she whispers, "You don't need to say anything. I just checked, and the answer is yes."

Fuck. I want to smack myself. After years of walking the straight and narrow, I got tempted to play Robin Hood, and this is the result. My neighborhood family-owned grocery store was recently replaced by the uber-expensive Munch & Crunch supermarket, and my elderly neighbors told me that they're struggling to afford food. So I fudged a few coupons for them. Why is that even a crime?

"Someone is coming your way," Blue says, startling me out of my reverie. "Talk later."

Before I can wonder how she knows that, she hangs up and the door opens.

I gape at the man who walks in. The epitome of tall, dark, and handsome, he has neatly cut, smoothed-back brown hair that makes me think of corporate boardrooms and OCD. His strong chin and muscular jaw are clean-shaven to the point of shine, and his eyes, a vivid emerald-green two shades brighter than mine, are narrowed with disapproval, his full lips pursed tight.

Who is he, and why does he look familiar?

In that perfectly tailored suit, he's unlikely to be a cop. Perhaps a lawyer that I can't afford? It's possible, but there's something annoyingly honest and noble in his features that I associate more with Boy Scouts than with ambulance chasers.

"Honey Hyman," he says with distaste—and shock rolls through me as I recognize his deliciously deep baritone, one he's had since his teenage years.

"Gunther Ferguson?" I blurt incredulously.

Is it possible that I conjured him up by thinking of him on the way here, kind of like invoking a demon? Or maybe I fell asleep in the police car and I'm dreaming?

If not, then this man is what happened to the boy I hate, the one who got me into trouble in high school, thus proving that karma is a fucking myth. If there were any justice in the world, he would've grown warped and deformed with time, like an evil lord of the Sith, but the opposite has happened.

Like an Anne Rice vampire, the evil transformation has made him hotter.

"Is playing dumb your latest game?" Gunther pulls out a stack of coupons and tosses them on the table. "Are you going to pretend you didn't know that it's my store you've been stealing from?"

Stunned, I glance down.

Yep. Those expertly faked coupons are for that small-business-crushing Munch & Crunch. And indeed, they are my handywork—but that store is part of a multinational chain of supermarkets, so how can it be his? Unless...

"You own that Munch & Crunch, like a franchise?" I ask stupidly.

He scoffs. "I own the whole company. Like you didn't know that."

I blink. "How would I know that?"

He gestures at the coupons. "The same way you know how to make those look indistinguishable from the real thing."

Hold on. Is he just a clever cop? "I'm not about to incriminate myself. Assuming those are actually fake, I'm sure whoever created them did it to help out their elderly neighbors who used to shop at the place that your Munch & Crunch ruthlessly drove out of business. Those folks can't afford your regular prices. In any case, how could that mystery person know that you had anything to do with the store? I know the likes of you think you're the center of the universe, but that's just not true."

He sighs. "First, you did this same thing to my dad. Now me. If this isn't targeted, I have to assume you make so many fraudulent coupons that this has inexorably happened again."

I push the coupons away. "Not admitting anything—but what about bad luck?"

His full lips curl in a sneer. "I don't believe in luck."

"Oh, luck exists." Bad luck is the only thing that can explain how tempting his mouth looks—despite what it's saying.

"You can prevaricate as much as you want, but the case against you is airtight. In fact, I've been led to believe you'll face jail this time. Unless..."

Wait. Is this blackmail? "Unless what?"

A dozen naughty scenarios of what he might demand of me play out in my mind—some involving handcuffs (because police station), others candle wax (no idea why), and a bunch more featuring a bed covered in BOGO coupons.

His green eyes gleam triumphantly. "Unless you work for me. Then I'll drop the charges."

———

Order your copy of *The Love Deal* today at <u>www.mishabell.com</u>!

ABOUT THE AUTHOR

Dima Zales is a *New York Times* and *USA Today* bestselling author of science fiction and fantasy. Prior to becoming a writer, he worked in the software development industry in New York as both a programmer and an executive. From high-frequency trading software for big banks to mobile apps for popular magazines, Dima has done it all. In 2013, he left the software industry in order to concentrate on his writing career and moved to Palm Coast, Florida, where he currently resides.

Please visit www.dimazales.com to learn more.

9 781631 428425